Knights of Passion: The Complete Series

Knights of Passion

Ash Gray

Published by Ash Gray, 2023.

KNIGHTS OF PASSION: THE COMPLETE SERIES

First edition. May 30, 2023.

ISBN: 979-8223126973

Written by Ash Gray.

Knights of Passion
The Complete Series

Table of Contents

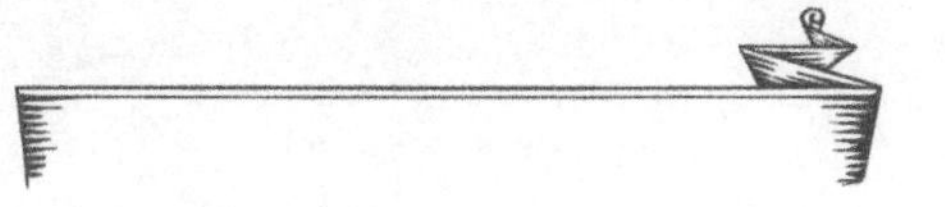

The Queen's Lust

Book 1

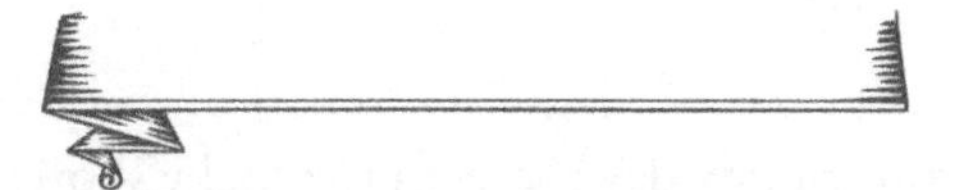

Chapter 1

It was a gray, cloudy day there on the rocky shore, as the wind swept over the ocean and the occasional sunlight broke through the wall of cloud. Zelda loved rainy days but not this one. Today, on the island of Vira'Toss, a man was being executed for trespassing, and executions were grim by nature.

Men weren't allowed on the island. The place was a women's sanctuary, protected by a veil of magick that froze them in place should they attempt to cross it. The veil was cast by the Order of Vira, a coven of sorceresses, where young women came to learn the ancient craft.

Zelda, who was twenty-two, had been living on the island since she was six, constantly surrounded by other women, young and old. She had nearly forgotten what a man looked like. The last man she'd seen had been her uncle, who sold her to the order for a sack of gold to pay his debts. She had been glad to be free of his beatings, but he was also her only living relative. She would like to have learned from him what her parents had been like. Now that she knew a few spells, she could have easily extracted the information from him. She often wondered if he was even still alive.

The trespasser was a tattered older man, gray hair and gray beard, though his body was hard and strong. His were the beginnings of old age. He was handsome and gray-eyed, and many of the younger sorceresses giggled and whispered about his good looks. Some of the older women eyed him as well.

Zelda looked at the man and felt nothing but a mixture of indifference and disgust. She had never understood what other women desired in men. To her they were unappealing in every conceivable way, while the women around her were absolutely exquisite.

There was Myriah, a beautiful olive-skinned woman with long, curly dark hair and bewitching green eyes. Zelda had seen her plump breasts and dark nipples once when they had sunbathed on the rocks one summer day, and how she had burned with desire.

Myriah stood nearby even now, draped in a green gown and velvet cloak, the gold clasp holding her cloak shut against the wind. She was eying the trespasser with interest and giggling with her friend, Iris of Low River.

Iris looked like most of the people of the river lands: her hair was white and her eyes violet. She wasn't particularly pretty, but the lips of her sex were wonderfully fat. Zelda had seen them bulge between her thighs when she was bending over naked in the shallows of the rocky beach, and she had not been able to forget it.

Zelda couldn't help her attraction to the other women and went out of her way to respect them: she never deliberately stared at them, touched them, or made comments. But the women of Vira'Toss kept her at arm's length just the same, so that her only friend was Wick, a small and shy elven woman who was also ostracized because everyone feared her extremely wealthy, extremely powerful parents.

Wick was standing beside Zelda even now. She must have been four feet tall and was draped in a simple dark green gown with a black cloak. Her long, raven-black hair fell silky and straight to the small of her back and was parted evenly in the front, falling around a small, child-like face.

Zelda always felt like a giant beside Wick, even though she was barely five feet tall herself. Many told her she looked like a sorceress from the fairytales: wild curly blonde hair that fell to the small of her back, startlingly blue, almond-shaped eyes, a curvy, graceful body, and a heart-shaped face that was gave her an almost innocent, angelic demeanor.

Zelda was wearing a blue gown the color of a robin's egg, and a gray cloak was wrapped around her against the wind. Her hair was a tousled mess and her cheeks were pink from the cold.

"We shall be awarded our staves at the feast tonight," Wick was whispering quickly. "And then our knights shall be bound to us!"

"So?" said Zelda distractedly. The trespasser was being made to stand on a large rock, his back to the sea.

"So?!" repeated Wick in amazement. "We shall be on our own soon! I am most terrified!"

"Can we speak of it later?" Zelda snapped and felt guilty when Wick sadly fell silent.

Wick was always going on about her anxieties, but now was not the time! Though they had been studying at Vira'Toss for years, the grand sorceresses had never demonstrated Dark Magick for them, instead forcing them to simply read about it in books. Dark Magick was any spell that could kill, maim, or torture. There were spells that could split someone's skull, turn them inside-out, break every bone in their body. What spell would be used to end the life of this man?

"You are obsessed with Dark Magick," said Wick bitterly. "You grow worse than my parents, even. You shall be a witch one day, I promise it."

"I—I am not obsessed!" Zelda insisted awkwardly.

Sorceresses who used Dark Magick illegally were either executed or became fugitives known as "witches." Dark Magick was only to be used in self-defense, and the man being made to stand on the rock could not have had any innocent reason for coming to Vira'Toss.

"Why do you think he dared venture here?" whispered Wick, as if she had read Zelda's mind.

"Because he's a fool," answered Zelda darkly. "He likely came to rape and steal our gold, but nothing except death awaits him here."

Wick was going to answer when the high sorceress apparated, appearing out of nowhere on the windy beach. The grand sorceresses were the older women who taught magick in the coven, while the high sorceress was the oldest and wisest of them all. Many thought High Sorceress Vizzora was at least two hundred years old, for a sorceress lived longer than the average human. She was tall and slender, with long gray hair that fell nearly to her feet and pale skin withered with age. In her youth, she had belonged to a river folk, and like Iris, had white hair and purple eyes.

High Sorceress Vizzora's purple eyes somberly scanned the crowd, and a silence fell over the gathered women. She stood very still near the bitter man on the rock, looking straight ahead, beyond the heads of the waiting crowd. She was draped in a long white gown and a white cloak was about her shoulders, shielding her from the wind. Her hands were folded calmly over the front of her gown as she said solemnly to the sea and sky,

"Trespasser, you are hereby executed for setting foot on Vira'Toss Isle. May the goddess have mercy on your soul."

High Sorceress Vizzora blinked, and the man standing on the rock shattered into pieces as if he were glass. There was no blood, no scream of pain. One minute the man was there . . . and then he was fragments swept gently into the ocean.

A soft scream rose from the watching crowd. Wick gasped in horror and covered her mouth with both hands. Only the grand aorceresses, the high sorceresses, and Zelda remained unfazed. Zelda stood watching with narrowed eyes as the remaining flesh-shards of the man were gently carried out to sea. The shattering spell. She remembered studying that incantation. She wondered if she would ever have to use it.

"Let us make haste!" cried Wick, still utterly horrified.

Zelda glanced up. The grand sorceresses were ushering the students back into the tower. The young women were all whispering frantically, "Did you see how calmly she did it?" "It's supposed to be a really difficult spell!" "Such a shame they killed such a handsome man!" "He was probably a rapist!" Still so handsome!" "Ugh!"

Zelda and Wick followed the others inside the tower, walking side-by-side amidst the chatter. Zelda was lost in thought and didn't come out of her reverie until she was back in the dorm room she shared with Wick, Myriah, and Iris. Myriah and Iris were already there, cloaks off, brushing each other's hair, still going on about the handsome trespasser.

Zelda untied her gray cloak and tossed it on her four-poster bed. They were supposed to be preparing for the games, which would take place that afternoon when the knights arrived. And later, they would prepare for the feast. Their year had been instructed to bathe, dress their hair, and don their best gowns. Queen Ellanara was coming to honor the four graduates, and four Falcon Knights would arrive from Falcon Isle, each one for the four graduates.

The knights who trained on Falcon Isle trained specifically from the time they were five years of age to eventually become the lifelong guardian of a sorceress of Vira'Toss. They were all women, of course, since a male knight would never be permitted to set foot on Vira'Toss. The Knights of Falcon were assigned to a sorceress long before they even met her. The knight that arrived for Zelda tonight would be a woman who had been destined for her since she was six years old, as that was the age Zelda had come to Vira'Toss.

"Are you not nervous about all of this?" demanded Wick. "You never fret about anything!"

Zelda glanced up. Wick had also thrown off her cloak and was standing over the trunk at the edge of her bed, rifling through it for her best dress. She held a deep red dress aloft to appraise it but paused to stare incredulously at Zelda, who was sitting calm and indifferent on the edge of her bed.

Zelda knew that Wick was nervous because she was a sheltered, spoiled little coward from a rich family with six older sisters who'd always protected her and were sorceresses to boot. No matter how much magick power was at her fingertips, she remained terrified because she had never been out in the world. But life as a sorceress would require daily interaction with the common folk, an interaction that mortified her.

Zelda, meanwhile, had spent her early years barefoot in the muddy streets, tricking rich idiots into focusing on her so that her uncle could pick their pockets. She was used to seeing men slit each other's throats, harass and rape women, beat children. She wasn't afraid to go out into the world and said so.

"All right, Little Miss Fearless," said Wick, rolling her eyes. She pulled out a deep blue gown and appraised it. It was very long. She tossed it aside and pulled out a black one. "So you are not worried about leaving the tower. Some of us are, though!" She shook her head. "I should have married the duke of Little Wing."

Zelda tried not to laugh. Wick had been sent to Vira'Toss when she was fourteen years old because she refused to marry a duke, who she'd described as "a fat little wart of a creature twice her age" who liked wagging his tongue suggestively at her in public. Wick's refusal to marry the duke had nearly ruined her life, but Zelda found it difficult not to laugh anytime the man was mentioned. The image of him being slapped at supper by Wick highly amused her.

"You would have been miserable," Zelda told her. "At least here you won't have to worry about your parents selling you off at market like a pig."

"I also won't have to worry about having gold or fine things," Wick retorted. She gave Zelda a sideways glance. "What are you wearing tonight, anyway?"

Zelda shrugged unhappily. Unlike Wick, she had not come to Vira'Toss with a trunk full of expensive gowns. When her uncle dropped her off at six years old at the ferry, she'd had nothing but the tatters on her back. Since then, the tower seamstress had made her gowns, which were all very simple and practical. She owned nothing fancy or elaborate like Wick.

Glancing at Zelda in sympathy, Wick picked up the dark blue gown from the bed. "This one is too long for me," she said.

"No, no, I couldn't," Zelda said hastily as Wick came to her. She staggered to her feet and stepped out of her slipper in her attempt to get away. She heard a giggle and hated that Myriah and Iris were pretending not to watch while whispering and laughing at her. Both women were from wealthy families as well.

"Come," said Wick. "Let us have a look!" So saying, she took Zelda by the hand and led her to the tall mirror that stood in the corner. She held the dark velvety blue gown over Zelda's front and experimentally draped a cascade of her golden hair over it.

"It brings out your eyes and the color of your hair," said Iris with sweet admiration. "It's a little low-cut, but you have lovely breasts. It won't go to waste on you. Your knight will love it."

Zelda's cheeks burned a little. "What do you mean? The Knights of Falcon are all women!"

"Exactly," said Wick with a laugh. "I hear they like what's between a lady's thighs. Half of them get sent to Falcon Isle because they tried to kiss another girl. Not *all* of them, mind you." Wick smirked. "But most."

Wick didn't elaborate. She left Zelda in front of the mirror and returned to her trunk.

Zelda held the dark blue dress against her body and tried not to blush, wondering what her knight would be like. A small, thirsty part of her was hoping her knight was beautiful and strong and craved women as hungrily as she.

Chapter 2

The milkmaid was a lively one and had to be shushed regularly, but Calain thought the long process of seducing her out of her panties had been worth the trouble. Down in the hay, in the shadows of the barn, she had buried mouth and fingers between the girl's trembling thighs, delighting in her moans and squeals and the hot moisture that rushed against her tongue.

Calain took her time. The barn was cool and shadowy, and it was still early in the morning. The horses had already been watered, groomed, and fed at the crack of dawn. They weren't going to set out for Vira'Toss for an hour, at least. She had time . . . She had time, she lied to herself.

"W-Won't . . . won't they miss you at b-breakfast, my lady?" gasped the milkmaid breathlessly.

"This is my breakfast," Calain moaned and sucked long and slow on the soft lips of the girl's sex.

The milkmaid giggled at Calain's words and moaned in pleasure. "Oh, my lady," she said huskily. "You are quite good at that . . . The other girls didn't lie!"

Just then, the barn doors banged open, flooding in sunlight. Calain lifted her face and squinted irritably in the sudden light. The milkmaid squealed and scrambled for her dress, pulling it on haphazardly with trembling breasts.

"Wait, wait . . . Have mercy . . ." Calain moaned, fumbling to squeeze one of the girl's large breasts as it swung wildly.

The milkmaid slapped Calain's groping hand off with a giggle and fled from the barn as Selene's voice rang through the room,

"Calain! For the sake of the *gods*! You can't keep your hands to yourself ten minutes before we set out?"

Selene's boots could be heard stamping through the barn. Then a heavy gauntlet grabbed the back of Calain's tunic in a fistful and pulled her up from the hay. Calain angrily shrugged Selene off and glared.

Selene glared back. She was a black-haired knight in Calain's year and was to set out that morning for Vira'Toss with Calain and to others: Cassandra and Gweneth.

Selene was already buckled into her silver armor, the falcon emblem polished on the breastplate. Her slanted, hawke-like eyes stared with disapproval from her ever-unsmiling face, and her black hair was, as always, neat and tamed into the usual long braid that fell down her back.

By contrast, Calain was a mess. Her bright red hair fell long and loose, an untamed mane about her shoulders, and she was not in her armor, instead clad in her rumpled tunic, boots, and leather trousers. Her tunic belt was loose, and she tightened it crossly as Selene watched in exasperation.

Their instructor, Knight Octava, had nicknamed them Chaos and Order and had often delighted in pairing them during training, not only to teach them to get along, but also to see their opposing personalities clash. They had even been paired today for the journey to Vira'Toss, a fact which Calain deeply resented.

"If you're finished being irresponsible and self-centered," said Selene coolly, "get your armor on and be at the gate in the ten minutes." With that, she turned and stalked off.

Calain glared after Selene, but truth be told, she was glad to have one of the page girls buckle her up. She always felt powerful and confident when in her armor, and she hated being away from her sword for any length of time.

When Calain arrived at the gate, the others were indeed waiting for her. Knight Octava, regal and dark-haired, sat high upon her black horse. Cassandra, with her pale blonde hair, and Gweneth, her light brown hair shaved in an undercut and tied a topknot, were also mounted and waiting. Gweneth and Cassandra had been paired the same as Calain and Selene. They were instructed to guard each other while on the road, for Falcon Isle wasn't protected by magick as Vira'Toss was.

Of course, Selene was also waiting, every inch of impatience and disapproval etched upon her face. Calain glared at her and silently hoped her sorceress was an ugly hag.

The journey to the ferry wasn't far from the fortress keep where they had spent their entire lives training. Calain knew they would only have to camp one night while riding during the day. And just like that, her life at Falcon Isle would be over, the only life she had ever known, and for what? So she could spend the rest of it protecting some delicate little sorceress flower from danger? And why? If the sorceresses were so powerful, why did they need knights to protect them? Calain ranted all of this at Selene on the second morning as they were riding for the ferry. Selene rode alongside her, listening in weary silence, as Gweneth and Cassandra rode side-by-side ahead of them, and Knight Octava rode solemnly at the forefront.

It was a bright, sunny day, which was a relief after last night's storm, which they had to dismally make their camp in. The storm had given Cassandra an uneasy feeling, and Knight Octava had agreed that something had probably happened at Vira'Toss: storms of great violence only occurred when there was foul magick on the air.

"The sorceresses have weaknesses even magick cannot overcome," Selene said when Calain had finished ranting.

Calain, who had not been expecting an answer, looked around in surprise. She was eating a rosy peach-colored apple and said around a mouthful, "Truly?"

Selene made yet another expression of disapproval Calain was long familiar with. "We learned about this in class!" she scolded. "You only graduated to full Falcon because of your swordplay, I swear. I feel sorry for your sorceress if she ever has to rely on your brain."

Calain scowled. "And I feel sorry for *your* sorceress if she ever wants to get bedded!" She was pleased when Selene the Saintly Virgin colored up in anger. "Or laugh or have fun! And another thing—!"

A laugh sounded from Gweneth, who was riding lazily on her white speckled stallion. "Let Selene be, Calain," she said, very amused. "She's right about you. I bet you don't remember your basic runes, either."

"Well, no, I do not," Calain admitted, but only because she liked Gweneth best.

"Maybe Selene's sorceress will fancy her," said Cassandra quietly.

"Haven't seen it in your dreams, have you?" Gweneth teased.

"No. But most elves like women with dark hair," said Cassandra in the same serene voice.

"That's right!" said Gweneth, as if she had remembered something hilarious. "Isn't Selene's woman an elfling? She's probably so little, Selene could put her in a pocket."

"She's from that family, that famous one with old elven blood," said Cassandra thoughtfully.

"The Blackwoods," said Selene indifferently. "Her name is Wick . . . Wick Blackwood. I feel sorry for her."

Calain laughed. With anyone else, it would have been a joke, but with Selene it was with sincere sympathy that she regarded her sorceress' name.

"Mine is Iris," said Gweneth. "One of the river folk, so no last name. Bet she's a good lay, though. Those river girls are wet and wild."

Calain agreed with a laugh, but Selene was not amused.

Though Calain had been training at the island since she was five, she and the other trainees had sometimes been taken on trips around the realms. The point was help them become familiar with the land, that they would be able to guide their sorceress through it later.

When Calain was sixteen, her year had taken a journey through the river lands with Knight Octava, and there, Calain had been kissed by the prettiest girl during the River Moon festival.

"Who was yours again, Cass?" asked Gweneth, breaking through Calain's reverie.

"Myriah Ornagon," said Cassandra.

Gweneth gave a low whistle. "From *the* Ornagons?"

Cassandra nodded indifferently.

Calain felt a little envious. The Ornagons were quite rich, and Myriah was still in good standing with her family, so Cassandra would be quite rich as well. She would have the best armor, the best weapons, and the best wine. And rumor had it, Myriah Ornagon was quite a beauty, with suitors coming from far and wide.

"What about you, Calain?" Gweneth prompted.

"Zelda," said Calain shortly. "No last name because she's a dirt-poor peasant, and knowing my luck, she'll probably be the ugliest of the lot as well."

Gweneth chuckled. "Assuming she even fancies women," she pointed out, still laughing.

"And assuming she'd even want you, Calain," added Selene quietly, "which is a rather large assumption."

More laughter from Gweneth, very loud and hearty this time. Even Cassandra's mouth twitched in a smile, which Calain couldn't stand.

Calain had been chewing on her apple but paused to glare at Selene before angrily chucking away the apple core. "One day, Sel," she said, pointing a finger, "I shall put my boot so far up—!"

Selene yawned and seemed unconcerned. Gweneth was laughing loudly. Cassandra was still trying not to smile.

"All right, all right, that's enough, you lot," said Knight Octava from the front. "We're here now. Shape up. Look smart."

Calain looked around. They had indeed come to the dock, where a large ferry waited to take them and their horses across. In the distance stood the Isle of Vira'Toss, its white tower reflected on the smooth sea like glass. The tower could be seen from the fortress on Falcon Isle, and how often had Calain stared at it, wondering what her sorceress did there? If she was sweet? If she was beautiful? If she fancied women? Now she felt bitter and did not care as much.

"You will all mind your manners and show proper etiquette with the queen," said an exasperated Knight Octava, "or gods be good . . ."

"Why are you looking at *me*?" Calain roughly demanded, and Gweneth snorted with laughter.

"Settle down, both of you," said Selene tiredly. "You are like little babes, I swear."

When they reached the island, Calain thought it seemed the opposite of Falcon Isle. Falcon Isle was a grim place of stone, mud, and steel, but this island was tall grass, flowers, and seashells. They led their horses up a dirt path that was lit by fairy lights, and when they reached the front steps of the tower, a young girl bowed and took their horses. There was already a number of horses being fed and watered in the stables, meaning the queen and her entourage had arrived already.

A fence led around the side of the tower to a field, where the knights would play their games after they had rested. Calain looked eagerly in the direction of the field. There was nothing she liked better than to display her strength, agility, and speed. She had spent years honing her muscular body, building her skill with sword and saddle. Knight Octava had once told Calain she was the best fighter and rider Falcon Isle had seen in decades, then expressed her regret that she may have inflated Calain's already big ego.

But why shouldn't Calain have a big ego? She was beautiful and she was strong and it wasn't going to last forever. Once she was magickally bound to her sorceress, she would live as long as the sorceresses did. Even still: two hundred years wasn't forever.

"Let us have something to eat before the games," said Knight Octava, pulling rations from her saddle bag and passing them around. "Sit down here and eat. The sorceresses will be out soon, and you may catch a glimpse of them before the games. We may even see Queen Ellanara!"

Calain's heart leapt. She moved close to the fence, peering at the wooden stands where the sorceresses would sit during the games. Perhaps she would get a glimpse of Zelda and determine at last if she was homely or fair.

"Calain," Cassandra said quietly and drew near. She looked very somber, which gave Calain a bad feeling. Whenever Cassandra looked like that, she had Seen something.

Cassandra glanced around to make sure the others could not hear. Knight Octava, Selene, and Gweneth were talking animatedly as they ate their meal beneath the tree.

"Be wary of the queen," said Cassandra gravely.

Calain lifted her brows. "Another one of your visions, Cassandra?" she said dismissively. She had nearly turned away when Cassandra grabbed her arm and peered hard into her eyes.

"This is no jest, Calain," Cassandra scolded, "so for once in your life, *listen* to me! The queen . . . A darkness hangs about her, and it reaches in your direction, it claws for you. Be *careful.* And do not drink too much wine, as you are wont to do."

"All right, Cass," Calain said soothingly, "I hear you."

Cassandra stared in Calain's eyes another beat, her serious gray eyes boring into Calain's face as if she were trying to read her mind. Then she turned away and rejoined the others under the tree as if she was satisfied, but Calain had only been humoring Cassandra. She did not put much stock in premonitions. Cassandra hadn't even been able to tell her the danger in detail! Vague warnings of the queen were meaningless!

As they sat beneath a tree near the fence, they could see the wooden stands begin to fill with the sorceresses and their knights. Many of the sorceresses attending were young and underage with no knights of their own, but all of the grand sorceresses had knights that were bound to them, women who would were known as legends on Falcon Isle. They, too, would be watching the games.

There was Knight Teresa, a blond and hard-faced woman who had slain the mighty bridge troll, Esotorc. And Knight Cecilia, whose portrait hung in the Falcon fortress after she defended it singlehandedly from an attack. And Knight Adelaide, who had killed a giant alone in close combat. Calain would be working to impress them as much as this Zelda woman she'd been given to.

At noon, when the sun had risen high in the sky, the sorceresses and their knights had finally filled the stands, emerging from the back door of the tower. Calain had had her breastplate removed for readjustment and was standing in the sunlight in naught but her linen undergarments and woolen hose, muscular shoulders and arms bare, skin glossy with oils as she flexed and rolled her arm experimentally. Her voluminous red hair was back in a messy ponytail and her eyes were narrowed on the distant stands.

Calain could see the queen sitting tall and regal, surrounded by the Rose Guard, her personal bodyguard of knights. Of course, she had only been permitted to bring the women in her guard, as males wouldn't have been able to move past the magick barrier.

The rest of the stands were filled by sorceresses, all of them young and old, gray and blond, some children, some elderly. They were surprisingly small in number. Along the back row, in the highest seats, sat the eldest sorceresses and their grim Falcon Knights.

"Want to know which one is yours?" said Knight Octava, amused by Calain's almost desperate staring.

"Yes," Calain admitted grudgingly.

Knight Octava smiled, which was a rare thing for her to do, and pointed to a small, busty blonde in the front row, who was draped in a pale blue gown and wreathed by a great deal of curly golden hair.

Mouth open, Calain drew closer to the fence and felt something inside her thump. It wasn't the thump she felt whenever she saw a fair maiden. This was something else, something in her heart, not her nether regions. Something had gripped her and would not let go. She wasn't entirely certain she wanted it to.

NORMALLY, ZELDA HATED attending the games. In the past, she had always found them boring. Having been at the tower for so many years, she had already seen the games played any number of times. But this time was different. This time the games were being played in her honor, and one of the knights belonged to her. Each woman in Zelda's class had been told the color of their knight's hair. Iris had the brown, Myriah the blonde, and Wick the black. Zelda had been told to watch for the red knight.

Zelda caught a glimpse of the red knight before the games began. She was standing outside the fence, startlingly tall, muscular, and *beautiful,* her mass of wild red hair tied back in a ponytail, and she hadn't been wearing armor! Instead, she stood openly in her linen bra, breastplate off, breasts high behind the fabric. She was massaging her shoulder and rolling her arm when an older knight said something to her. Her eyes traveled over the crowds and landed on Zelda, who felt her body thump when their eyes connected. The red knight didn't look away. In fact, she appeared completely smitten. Panicking, Zelda slapped open her fan and hid behind it, ignoring Wick's amused stare.

Then the games began. The high sorceress conjured ogres and giants and trolls and wolves, and the knights took turns battling them. Then the high sorceress conjured a tall knight in black armor whose visor was down. Zelda had seen this knight during the games before and wondered if he wasn't just an empty suit of armor. But empty suit or no, he was fierce and strong, and stood at the great height of ten feet, towering over the Falcon Knights, who were each a little above six feet at best.

The red knight was simply phenomenal. She tore through every foe, fierce and beautiful and strong, helm off, so that her red mane constantly flew about her in its ponytail. Her fighting style was brutal. She kicked, she punched, she roughly ripped her sword free after sinking its blade through the opponent's middle. Zelda was in awe of her. Before that moment, she had never thought much of swordplay, but now she found it amazing that anyone could fight so powerfully without magick.

The crowd loved the red knight as much as Zelda. The older Falcon Knights cheered and the sorceresses applauded her every win enthusiastically. The youngest sorceresses squealed in amazement and some fell into giggles each time she drew near the fence.

"I wish she was my knight!" cried a sorceress who must've been eight years old.

"So do I," said Wick. "Mine is the black hair, and she has skill, but she hasn't the passion of the red one." She waited for Zelda to agree and seemed very amused by her reluctance to do so.

"She has fought . . . well enough," said Zelda, trying to sound casual.

Wick grinned. "Just confess you want her. You want her to lick your honeypot! Is it dripping yet? It is, isn't it? I can tell!"

Zelda laughed before she could stop herself. "Wick!" she cried, aghast. "Do not speak in that filthy way!"

"Confess! Confess!"

"All right," sighed Zelda, whose fond eyes were on the red knight. "I confess: I have never felt this way before! I don't just want her, I want her to want me desperately! I shall wear your dress to the feast tonight after all. I shall lace it so tight, I shall be bursting out of it!"

Zelda and Wick giggled like schoolgirls.

"I shall help you!" Wick squealed.

"WHO IS THAT *stunning* creature?" said Queen Ellanara. "You don't know? Run and find out, you fool!" The queen had been in the act of boredly fanning herself with a golden fan but had stopped, her eyes fixed on the curly blonde head several rows beneath hers.

Queen Ellanara was a beautiful woman, middle-aged, with long dark hair gathered sleek over one shoulder. Her green eyes were hungry as they peered down into the lower row. The blond was wearing a light blue gown that hugged her naked shoulders so that her bare cleavage swelled. Her breasts were flushed as she giggled with her friend, and when she turned her head, the queen could see her cheeks were flushed as well. She was blushing with excitement from watching the red knight. Blushing with arousal? And she was *beautiful*. Those delicate little hands, the long lashes . . . The queen felt the lust in her stirring.

"That is Zelda, my queen," answered the meek handmaiden the queen had questioned. She had run off as told to find the answer as commanded and had returned breathless, clutching a stitch in her side. "She is bound to the red knight," the handmaiden added. "Or she will be tonight."

As the handmaiden was speaking, the red knight was galloping circles around the yard, displaying her riding skill on a beautiful chestnut stallion. She thundered by the stands another time, snatching a fistful of wild flowers that were growing in a web over the fence and dropping them in Zelda's lap as she galloped on. The women in the stands cheered and applauded while Zelda blushed more than ever, keeping her long lashes down as she brought a flower to her nose.

The queen glared with hatred at the red knight, who had swung out of the saddle mid-gallop and was bowing to the cheering crowds. She leaned over to Captain Gyda, the captain of the Rose Guard, who was sitting beside her. "Once the binding ceremony is done, remove the red knight."

Captain Gyda smiled sinisterly. "It will be done, my queen."

THE BINDING CEREMONY was a quick spellcasting that only took five minutes, but Calain thought it one of the most significant moments of her life. When night had fallen, they gathered on the field where the games had taken place. It was a clear, beautiful night, the velvety dark sky winking with stars above them.

The sorceresses had changed into their gowns for the feast, and Calain couldn't take her eyes from Zelda, who looked breathtaking in a dark blue gown, above the laces of which her great breasts were sitting like two loaves of baking bread. Gweneth had remarked under her breath that Zelda was "ripe" as the sorceresses were approaching, and Calain had elbowed her to silence, but she couldn't pretend as if Gweneth was wrong either: Zelda's breasts were like two pale melons, so plump, swollen, and full. Calain felt herself stirring and swallowed the hunger down. Zelda seemed pleased with her silent struggle and smiled sweetly at her, which only made Calain want her more.

Calain, Gweneth, Cassandra, and Selene stood in a line facing their sorceresses, and as everyone watched, they reached out and took the hand of their sorceresses, as if they might bend to kiss it. But they didn't. Instead, knight and sorceress stood holding hands and staring into each other's eyes.

Calain held Zelda's little hand as gently as possible, not wishing to hurt her, and peered very intently down into the large blue eyes across from her. She could tell Zelda was nervous and that she was trying very defiantly to shake her nerves and stare into Calain's eyes, but she kept glancing shyly down, the sweep of her long, pale lashes nearly brushing her cheeks. Calain gave Zelda's hand a playful squeeze and puckered her lips in a silent kiss. She had to hold back a laugh when Zelda's mouth opened in a silent gasp and her cheeks colored up. She looked up at Calain in amazement, as if she couldn't believe she was daring to flirt with her here, in front of everyone, during such a serious occasion.

Knight Octava stepped forward, hands behind her back, gleaming in her silver armor, and ordered, "Knights, make your vows!"

Calain, Gweneth, Cassandra, and Selene all began to recite at once,

"I am your Falcon Knight. I vow to protect, honor, and obey thee to the end of my days and with my very life, now and forever. I am yours."

Calain realized for the first time that the Binding Vow sounded almost like wedding vows. A small part of her panicked as she wondered if that wasn't what they secretly were, but then she looked down into Zelda's sweet, heart-shaped face, something in her melted, and she didn't care.

High Sorceress Vizzora was standing solemnly in her white gown and cloak, hands folded, as she calmly commanded, "Sorceresses . . . Bind."

Immediately, the four sorceresses' eyes began to glow with power. Zelda's blue eyes were now yellow spheres of light burning in her face. It was otherworldly, as if Zelda had been possessed by a spirit, for her curly golden hair was now hovering like snakes around her in an ethereal wind.

Calain couldn't have moved, couldn't have released Zelda's hand had she wanted to. Zelda had suddenly gained a startling grip. Her hand seemed to be made of steel as it held fast to Calain's. Then a light appeared, a gossamer strand of gold lacing and winding around their clasped hands. Calain's eyes stared, unseeing. She could feel the light spreading warm over her heart. A heartbeat filled her ears, growing louder and louder, accompanied by a second, and she realized the second heartbeat was Zelda's.

Then it was over. Calain looked at Zelda, feeling a little giddy and light-headed. Zelda's eyes had stopped glowing, her hair was hanging limply behind her shoulders again, and she was watching Calain with a hopeful expression, likely wondering if the spell had worked.

Calain knew she was Bound. She could still feel Zelda's heartbeat as if it were her own. If they were separated, she knew she would be able to follow Zelda's heartbeat and find her way back to her.

"Are you well, my knight?" Zelda asked nervously.

They were still holding hands, and Calain brought Zelda's small hand to her lips. She smiled when she felt Zelda's heart skip a startled beat at the gesture.

"Never better," Calain said. She glanced over at the others and saw Gweneth and Cassandra also talking to their sorceresses and shaking off the dizzying effects of the Binding. To her surprise, Selene and her sorceress, Wick Blackwood, were both looking right at them. Wick was looking at Calain with a sort of wistful longing, while Selene was looking at Calain with a startling amount of hatred.

Calain went still in surprise. She and Selene had always had a rivalry, but they had never truly *hated* each other. Calain was so shocked that she stared at Selene in disbelief for several seconds, while Selene stared back with bald hatred.

Chapter 3

The high sorceress announced that it was time for the feast. Everyone started moving for the tower steps, but Selene only tore her angry eyes away from Calain when Wick feebly begged her to come along. Blinking back to reality, she took Wick's arm and went with her toward the tower.

Calain turned to Zelda. She could tell Zelda wanted to ask what the incident with Selene had been about, but since Calain herself didn't know, she didn't bother explaining. Instead, she smiled, offered Zelda her arm, and led her to the tower.

The feast was one of the best Calain had ever been to. A band played a cheerful tune, and everyone danced merrily, even the dour and grim Knights of Falcon, who had exchanged their proud armor for tunic and trousers.

Calain wasn't wearing her armor either. That night for the feast, she was wearing a pale green tunic and brown leather trousers. Zelda, meanwhile, was still in her tantalizing dark blue velvet. When they looked at each other now, Calain could feel both their hearts racing: Zelda wanted Calain as greatly as Calain wanted her.

Calain offered to find a corner where they could kiss and grope in the shadows, but an appalled Zelda blushed to her hairline and said she didn't want her first time to be while Calain was drunk in the middle of a loud and noisy feast. It hadn't even crossed Calain's mind that Zelda was a virgin, but she respected

Zelda's wishes and fell to holding her in her lap and occasionally kissing her on the cheek instead, which made her blush and giggle girlishly.

There were three long tables in the feast hall. Two stood parallel to each other and were where the sorceresses and their knights dined, while a third table stood perpendicular to the other two. This was the high table, where the high sorceress, her Falcon knight, Queen Ellanara, and her Rose Guard all sat, watching the festivities and sipping from gold goblets.

Calain could feel the eyes of the queen upon her as she danced with Zelda (lifting Zelda in the air and swinging her easily about in one bulging arm as she giggled), though she wasn't entirely certain she wasn't imagining it. Every time she looked at the high table, the queen had looked away, but Calain was certain she'd felt the woman's sharp eyes upon her.

"You are drinking entirely too much!" Zelda scolded when Calain had downed her fifth goblet of wine and was slumped over at one of the tables.

Calain knew Zelda was right, but she was having fun and didn't want to stop. She banged her goblet on the table and called for the serving girl to bring more wine. The girl hurried over with a pitcher, which Zelda immediately confiscated.

"My lady . . ." Calain protested, voice slurred.

Zelda pointed to the open archway beyond the hall, which led to the courtyard. "Go and get some air, my knight!" she commanded, and because Calain had vowed to obey Zelda not one hour before, she grumbled as she slouched up from the bench.

Out in the courtyard, Calain stumbled into a tree, managed to grab a hold of it, and was sick in the flowers. As she was retching, she thought she heard boots quietly approaching up the cobbled garden path. She had barely straightened up when she heard the smooth ching of a blade being drawn, and the pommel of a sword connected with the back of her head in a burst of pain.

CALAIN HAD BEEN GONE a long time. There was a moment when Zelda thought Calain was hurt: she had felt Calain's heartbeat speed up in agony! But the moment was so fleeting, she told herself Calain merely had a headache from drinking so much wine. She was about to go looking for Calain when a servant came to her where she was sitting at one of the tables, bowed, and told her the queen had summoned her to her chambers.

Zelda glanced around: the queen had indeed left the high table, along with her Rose Guard. The high sorceress and her Falcon Knight were sitting alone there, talking quietly.

What was more, the little servant had not come alone. She was backed by two very grim-looking Rose Guard knights. Zelda recognized both of them from the rumors and gossip. The one on the left was Bodil, a fierce and gray-haired woman whose past was as legendary as any Falcon Knight. The one on the right was blonde Helen, a six-foot giantess with eyebrows so thick, they looked like caterpillars. The way both knights were standing, it looked as if they would grab Zelda and march her off if she didn't obey. So, wondering what in the world the queen could possibly want with her, Zelda got to her feet and went with the knights.

The queen had been given a bedchamber three floors up the tower. The higher they climbed, the more of a foreboding crept over Zelda. Calain had disappeared and was somewhere in pain. Zelda could feel the steady throb of what was indeed a headache, though not a natural one as she had supposed. Meanwhile, the queen had mysteriously summoned her? She started to wonder what excuses she could make to go and find Calain, but glancing at the somber knights either side of her, she knew they would accept no excuses.

Bodil knocked on the heavy oaken door of the queen's bedchamber. "My queen," she called, "we have the woman you requested."

Zelda scowled. The knight spoke of her like a slice of cake that had been fetched from the kitchens!

"Bring her to me and stand guard outside," called the queen.

Bodil pushed the door open, and large Helen grabbed Zelda by the neck and steered her in. Zelda indignantly wiggled free, hating the cold touch of the gauntlet on her skin. She glared up at big Helen, who glared down in shock, her eyes wide as if to say, "The gall!"

There was a tinkling laugh. "That's quite enough, Helen. See yourself out."

Helen looked as if it wasn't "enough" at all, but muttered, "Yes, my queen . . ." and marched out, quietly closing the door behind her.

"Come to me, my dear," called the queen.

Zelda looked around through the jungle of luggage and trunks and saw at last that the queen was sitting on the edge of her four-poster bed, her black hair a long veil around her. To Zelda's surprise, the queen was wearing a transparent housecoat draped silkily over black lingerie. Her hourglass shape and full breasts were apparent as she sat innocently brushing her long hair.

Zelda stood transfixed on the spot and felt rather like a trapped mouse. The queen's long nails and bright eyes were very catlike.

Queen Ellanara gave another tinkling laugh. "Don't be afraid, my dear," she said, setting aside the hairbrush. "Come, sit on my lap!"

Zelda knew she had no choice but to obey. Very reluctantly, she moved to the queen and perched stiffly on her knee. She didn't like the way the woman's eyes raked her cleavage.

"You're like a pretty package, aren't you?" the queen said huskily. Her eyes were still on Zelda's breasts, bright with hunger. With long nails, she pinched the lace on the front of Zelda's gown and slowly pulled. Zelda watched helplessly as her breasts were exposed, the fabric sagging away.

The queen gave a moan of longing.

Zelda recoiled. "My . . . my queen," she stammered and hugged her breasts to hide them.

"Come now," the queen softly scolded. "I know you desire women. You blushed like a bitch in heat for your knight."

Zelda colored up at once, horrified to realize the queen had been watching her during the games. "But I do not desire you!" she cried defiantly.

The queen's dark eyes filled with a glittering anger that frightened Zelda. But Zelda reminded herself she was a powerful sorceress now. No longer was she that frightened little girl who took beatings from her uncle! She drew herself up, looking the queen level in the eye. The queen did not like that.

"You shall do as you are told," Queen Ellanara growled in a dangerous voice, "or you shall be very sorry!" So saying, she snatched Zelda's hands away from her breasts. Zelda twisted to get away, but the queen held on to her wrists, kissing her neck, telling her to be still, that she would enjoy it, that she was a stupid girl.

Zelda was still twisting to get away when the bedroom door burst open. She and the queen both looked around: Calain was standing tall in the door, freshly buckled into her armor, sword in hand. Her face twisted into a sneer and she launched into the room.

"You dare!" gasped the queen. She threw Zelda from her lap and sprang to her feet, shouting, "Guards! Guards!"

Zelda watched from the floor, her mouth open, as Calain ran her sword through the queen's middle, cutting her off mid-word as she gurgled with a baffled expression on her own blood. Calain's face was twisted as the blood spattered her. "The guards aren't coming," she rasped and ripped the blade free. Eyes blank, the queen fell to her knees and collapsed forward on her face. She didn't move.

Breathless, Calain sheathed her sword on her back and looked down at Zelda, who suddenly felt so small and in awe of Calain, who seemed mighty and powerful above her, consuming all the room with her girth and height. Apparently, Calain had slaughtered her way there to save Zelda, for her armor was stained with blood, and she was bleeding from a cut on her chin and another on her temple.

Calain's green eyes were furious when she noticed Zelda's breasts were hanging loose from her gown. Zelda hastily laced herself up.

Calain knelt down to face Zelda. "Did she hurt you?" she asked with soft eyes. But before Zelda could answer, Calain gently gathered Zelda in her arms and lifted her. They looked in each other's eyes. Calain's heart had been pounding wild during her battle up the stairs, wild with exertion and wild with fear that Zelda had come to harm. Zelda had mistaken it for her own heartbeat, which she knew Calain had likely felt as the queen attempted her assault.

Zelda could separate their heartbeats now. Both hearts were slowing as they stared into each other's eyes, lost in infatuation. Then Zelda looked at Calain's lips and suddenly kissed her.

It was her first kiss. Calain seemed to sense this and was gentle as she responded, sliding her warm tongue against Zelda's with a soft hunger that thrilled her.

Their lips slowly peeled apart, and Zelda shivered breathlessly as Calain's soft kisses pressed warm up and down her neck.

"I'd never let anyone hurt you," Calain whispered in her ear.

Zelda miserably dropped her forehead against Calain's. "But the queen is dead!" she moaned. "You've slain her! We'll have to spend the rest of our lives running! Why did you not simply grab me and flee the room?"

Calain closed her eyes. "I know. I am sorry, my lady. I saw her forcing herself upon you and I lost my senses."

Zelda was going to answer when a voice called from the hall, "No time for necking! We have to run, Kay!"

Calain grimly carried Zelda from the room and out into the hall. To Zelda's surprise, the bodies of several Rose Guard knights were lying there, all slain, including Bodil and big Helen, who both lay bloody on their backs, staring blankly at the ceiling.

Standing grimly over the bodies were the other knights who'd arrived with Calain: Gweneth, Cassandra, and Selene, whose dark eyes passed over Calain in concern.

"We must head immediately for the ferry," Selene said. "We shall head for the shore of Arion and go our separate ways from there—"

"You shall live in exile if you aid us!" Zelda protested at once. She couldn't understand it that the knights all looked so completely unbothered.

"Calain is our sister," said Gweneth. She waved a hand at Calain. "Our idiot sister, but our sister just the same. We would die for her."

Cassandra nodded seriously.

Selene continued speaking as calmly as if Zelda had not interrupted, and Zelda knew that if there was a leader among the four, it was her.

"We shall be able to leave unhindered," Selene continued. "The other Falcons would never turn against their own and the sorceresses consider us theirs. We shall leave for Arion, split up to confuse the Rose Guard, and meet again in Arinol."

"Arinol?" complained Calain incredulously. "That's across the forest!"

Selene's eyes snapped irritably. "Well, if you would *rather* the Rose Guard caught us—"

"I'd *rather* not take orders from the likes of you!" Calain snapped.

"You slay the bloody *queen,*" snarled Selene, "and now you whine about my plan to save you?!"

"I don't need saving!" Calain shouted.

"What you *need* is someone to smack some sense into you!" Selene heaved back.

Calain and Selene started moving toward each other as if they would fight, and it was clear Calain had completely forgotten she was carrying Zelda in both arms. Thankfully, Gweneth stepped in and said, "All right, you two! Settle down or I shall find a piss bucket and slosh the pair of you!"

Calain and Selene bitterly backed away from each other, still glaring daggers. Their obvious contempt for one another was so strong, Zelda had to wonder why Selene was even helping them.

Cassandra stepped forward, her pale, shoulder-length braid loose from the fighting, her eyes on Zelda. "Zelda is the sorceress here. She outranks all of us. It is her command we shall obey."

Zelda was suddenly uncomfortably aware of all four knights gazing at her expectantly. She looked at Selene. "But you can't leave Wick behind! You made a vow! All of you did!"

"Wick shall be assigned another knight," said Selene indifferently. Something about the way she looked at Zelda made her shiver a little . . . and Calain's arms tighten around her.

Zelda avoided everyone's eye. She could feel them staring as they waited for instructions.

"We shall do as Selene has suggested," Zelda said, because she was too tired and too frightened to think of anything else. She noticed that Calain wanted to protest but bitterly swallowed it down. Selene watched Calain, silently amused.

"As you say, sorceress," said Cassandra. She looked at the others. "What are we waiting for? Let us make haste!"

Chapter 4

They made certain to prepare well for the journey forth. Zelda packed a small bag of clothes, grabbed the stave she'd been awarded that night, and hugged a crying Wick farewell. She was surprised when High Sorceress Vizzora came to her and told her she could stay if she wanted to, that they would get her a new knight, that she needn't throw her life away, but Zelda had already made up her mind. She went to Calain and quietly took her hand, then looked pointedly at the high sorceress, her chin lifted, unaware of how Calain smiled down at her. The high sorceress understood. She nodded, and her eyes were twinkling fondly as she said, "My knight and I are much the same. We have been together for three hundred years and couldn't bear to separate even now." Zelda was shocked to hear that. Three hundred years!

Once Zelda had packed her things, they went to the kitchens, where the servants gave them plenty of bread, wine, dried meat, and cheese. Some of the older Knights of Falcon gave the younger four encouragement and advice. Then the four knights took their horses from the stables, and they were off, sailing on the ferry for the opposite shore.

They traveled in silence, for which Zelda was grateful. She wasn't certain she could take anymore bickering between Calain and Selene, who were avoiding each other's eye. Calain was still bitter that Zelda had chosen to follow Selene's advice, but she didn't complain, instead holding Zelda tightly from behind as they stood on the ferry, sailing against the wind. Calain's arms were almost possessive in how tight they were, and she kept shooting glares at Selene, who ignored them both completely.

On the shore, they mounted their horses. Zelda did not have a horse and would have to share with Calain. She blushed prettily when Calain picked her up by her tiny waist and set her on the chestnut as if she weighted absolutely nothing. Then Calain mounted behind Zelda, took up the reins, and the group was riding in silence for Arion, a small village just off the coast.

Zelda was painfully aware of her breasts bouncing as they rode at a brisk trot. The others were hard-bodied warriors clad in silver armor, hair streaming in messy ponytails and braids, but Zelda was soft-bodied and sore from already from the saddle. She wasn't wearing armor or even trousers that would have protected her. She was draped in the same dark blue gown she'd worn to the feast. Her cleavage was exposed and her skirts flying up to reveal her shapely legs, and her golden curls were ever-tossing long around her. She felt almost naked and kept worrying her laces would come undone, exposing her breasts again.

But at the same time, she . . . *enjoyed* it. The four knights were watching her while struggling almost desperately not to. All of them were watching her, wanting her, and Calain was in a quiet state of panic about it. She kept tightening Zelda's laces over her breasts, smoothing down her skirts when they flared up. Zelda could feel Calain's heart thumping anxiously: she did not want the others to see any part of Zelda.

Amused, Zelda twisted around as they were riding and kissed Calain tenderly on the lips to soothe her. She could feel the others watching from the corners of their eyes and could feel Calain's heartbeat slowing to a drowsy content and smug triumph.

At Arion, they dismounted near the village outskirts, as the distant mountain curled its finger against the stars. Calian shared a one-armed hug with each of the other knights, even Selene, though she looked as if she was trying to break Selene's arm.

"We will meet again," said Cassandra, nodding seriously at Calain.

"And if we don't, we've bought it," added Gweneth with a smile.

"Guard your lady well," said Selene, though her intense brown eyes were on Zelda.

Zelda's heart skipped a beat when she saw the longing in Selene's eyes.

Calian noticed it as well and bristled. "Yes, I shall guard *my* lady," she growled pointedly.

Selene's lips curled in a small, amused smile. She turned, mounted her black horse, and galloped away, moving east along the coast. Zelda thought she looked magnificent, her black hair streaming in a silky plait behind her.

Cassandra bowed to Zelda and murmured, "My lady . . ." Then she and Gweneth likewise mounted and took off, heading in separate directions around the outskirts of Arion on their snorting horses.

Calain turned to Zelda, and without a word, lifted her onto her horse again. Zelda shivered as she was placed in the saddle, wondering how Calain's strong hands would feel on her body without the gauntlets.

Calain mounted behind Zelda, and as if she'd read Zelda's mind, she took off her gauntlets and let them hang from the saddle. With bare hands, she took up the reins and said quietly, "You wanted to head for Arinol, so we shall take a path northwest, away from the others, and proceed around through Corriol Forest. Does that please my lady?" she asked playfully.

"Everything about you pleases," Zelda answered, glancing at Calain's strong hands as they jerked the reins.

Cailan clicked her tongue and the chestnut took off, snorting in response. They rode hard and fast, as if Calain was trying to reach the cover of the trees as quickly as possible. Zelda understood why: the queen's court sorceress used birds as spies, and her spies were everywhere. She could possess any bird, anywhere, and see through its eyes. At least in the forest, there were caves and ancient passages to hide in.

They were riding so hard, Zelda knew they would reach the forest before nightfall. And indeed, the trees were mere feet away in the distance one hour before dusk. Calain raced them across the green field, her armor gently bumping against Zelda's stave, which was on her back.

As the trees drew ever nearer, they were riding so fast that Zelda's breasts were practically flapping and her laces were sliding loose. She wanted to draw them tight again but was afraid of releasing the horse, whose mane she clung to as she bounced painfully in the saddle. To her surprise, Calain handed her the reins, and without warning, she grabbed the front of Zelda's gown and ripped it open, forcing her high breasts to shiver free as she screamed softly in shock.

With a strength that made Zelda's sex throb in delight, Calain grabbed one of her heavily bouncing breasts in a fistful and groped it until Zelda blushed, her hungry mouth burying a kiss in a Zelda's neck as she impatiently ripped back the skirt of Zelda's gown and crammed a hand down the front of her panties.

As the horse carried them into the forest, Zelda's shrill cries of pleasure startled the birds to flight. The court sorceress definitely hadn't seen them.

CALAIN PACED BACK AND forth at the mouth of the cavern. They had been hiding in the cave for days, waiting for the five Rose Guard knights who searched for them to leave the forest. Queen Ellanara's sister would know she had been murdered almost immediately, as the high sorceress would have been obligated to have told her, even if she hadn't been obligated to stop the murderer.

Calain wanted to simply kill the Rose Guard knights and be done with it, but Zelda had been firmly against it. She insisted that if they started killing people, the bodies would leave a trail, making it easier to find them, but Calain knew the real reason was her gentle heart.

Zelda had grown up poor on the streets and had witnessed many atrocities, but instead of letting it harden her or change her, she had stayed soft and sweet instead. Calain had secretly witnessed her weeping over an injured bird and healing it with her magick. Zelda was so ashamed of her gentle heart, however, that she would have been mortified if she knew Calain had seen her.

At the same time, there was a darkness to Zelda that Calain could not deny. She had the feeling that, if push came to shove, Zelda wouldn't hesitate to use Dark Magick. It was somehow both comforting and disturbing.

Calain was determined to keep Zelda out of a situation where she would need to resort to Dark Magick in the first place. If she saw the Rose Guard knights as Zelda slept, she would slay them and dump them secretly in the lake. She could overpower five of them easily. Falcon Knights were not some of the most elite knights in Realm Eriallon for nothing.

Calain had taken off her armor to bathe and rest hours before but had not put it back on since. Deep in the cavern, there was a waterfall and a pool of sweet, cool mountain water that trickled down from the nearby mountain. Calain had meant to hide Zelda away in the mountain, but if the Rose Guard knights who currently lurked the forest saw them traveling to the path, they would pursue, and Calain wasn't exactly certain how many there were. So far, she had only marked five.

She wondered how many of the queen's guard had pursued Gweneth and Cassandra and hoped they were well. Selene could be lying face-down in a ditch for all Calain cared . . . No. That wasn't true. While Selene was indeed annoying to her, Calain didn't wish the woman any real harm. But she also secretly hoped they would not cross paths with Selene again any time soon. It had dawned on her that Selene wanted Zelda, and she suspected that Zelda wanted Selene as well. It felt almost like a betrayal that Zelda desired another, even if she hadn't acted on it.

Calain comforted herself that at least Zelda seemed to prefer her to Selene. The way she had looked at Calain as they made love beside the waterfall, the way she had clung to her and shivered in her arms . . . Zelda was so sweet and delicate and beautiful, and her blue eyes were always full of such innocent adoration whenever she looked up at Calain. Calian had kissed every inch of her skin, even the places that tickled and made her giggle helplessly, and she hadn't wanted to stop.

As the days went by, Calain planned out their journey in her mind. A few days in the mountains, perhaps, down the other side, and across the field to Ternia, a city so vast they could easily become lost in its crowds.

"Calain?" called Zelda's sleepy voice from the back of the cave.

Calain was standing at the mouth of the cave in her linen smallclothes and woolen hose, arms folded, lost in her reverie as she gazed out at the shadowy forest. It was midday, a relatively safe time to ponder in the mouth of the cave, as the Rose Guard knights slept during the day and searched for them at night. There were birds nearby but not many, and Calain wondered how long it would be before the court sorceress started searching the forest with her bird spies instead of relying on the Rose Guard—

"Calain?" Zelda called again.

Sword on her back, Calain reluctantly turned from the mouth of the cave and walked back to the waterfall, where Zelda was lying on her side, half dozing on Calain's spread cloak. After Calain had torn the dark blue gown, she had returned to the light blue one, which Calain preferred anyway, since it brought out her eyes and golden hair.

Zelda looked beautiful lying there, her little feet bare, her dress rumpled up to reveal one slender leg, her hair a golden mess of curls about her. Her hair was gold as a coin, not pale or platinum. She yawned through pink lips, and her heavy breasts lifted behind the fabric of her gown.

Calain felt herself stirring, remembering what those full, high breasts had felt like in her hands, so soft and yielding, and so large they had spilled between her fingers. She knelt down and gently pulled the laces on the front of Zelda's gown, revealing one of her breasts. The pink nipple was rigid. Calain leaned down and suckled tenderly. She felt Zelda's heartbeat quickening in response.

"Oh . . . Oh, Calain, not right now!" Zelda begged with a sort of helplessness that told Calain she was aroused.

"I wanted to talk to you!" Zelda protested.

Thinking she would initiate sex later anyway, Calain took off her sword and laid it aside with the belt. She lay down beside Zelda, putting a muscular arm behind her head. Her chestnut horse was nearby, grazing lazily on what little grass had sprouted in the cave, and she watched it fondly. She had always called the horse Arthur after her father. She wished her father could meet Zelda. He would approve of her.

"I think we should leave for the mountain," Zelda said. "We can't hide here forever, and your horse is getting restless. He told me."

Calain paused. "He . . . told you?" She had forgotten sorceresses could speak with beasts.

"He also said he didn't like you . . . touching me on his back," Zelda added awkwardly.

Calain glanced guiltily at the horse.

"He says he's been with you for two years?" Zelda prompted.

Calain wrapped an absent arm around Zelda, who snuggled close.

"Aye," Calain said. "Every Falcon gets a horse after they complete training. I named him Arthur for my pa."

"Your pa?" Zelda asked with interest.

Calain stared at the smooth ceiling of the cave, remembering. "He had to give me to Falcon Isle when I was little because he realized he couldn't feed me anymore." She smiled. "But they let him come to visit sometimes. Men are allowed on Falcon Isle, mostly because the women there are too strong for them to pose any real danger. Most are afraid of Falcon Knights and wouldn't come to the island anyway."

Zelda looked up at Calain in wonder with her round blue eyes, and Calain suddenly realized that Zelda probably didn't understand just how strong Falcon Knights actually were. Did they tell her nothing on Vira'Toss?

"The last time I saw my pa, I was about twelve," went on Calain. "He was so proud that his little girl was a knight! I haven't seen him since, which means he must've gone on to the gods." She paused and said softly, "I miss him."

Zelda rubbed a sympathetic hand over Calain's stomach. Calain took her hand and kissed it.

They lay in silence for a while, and then Calain asked, "What about your father, my lady?"

"I don't remember him," Zelda answered in a small voice. "I think he was fair, like me, and Mother had red hair . . . Both of them are dead. That's all I know. I was raised by my uncle, and he sold me to Vira'Toss to pay his debts."

"What a bastard," said Calain incredulously, and Zelda laughed. "He's my only living family, unfortunately," she said.

"You have me now," said Calain, tightening a protective arm around Zelda.

Zelda's lashes fluttered in delight, and she snuggled closer. They had fallen into a content silence when a sarcastic voice said, dripping with disdain, "How *sweet.*"

Calain's eyes sprang open. Several women were standing over them, draped in black robes and hoods. Upon each forehead was the same mark: a black bird, wings spread in the shape of a cross. Calain immediately recognized them as Raven's Cross, a coven of dark witches. She felt a fool for not recognizing the rune marking on the cave wall, which would have marked the cave as theirs.

Calain scowled and reached for her sword, which was on the ground nearby. To her frustration, the sorceress who had spoken blinked, and her sword slid out of reach of its own accord.

Calain sat seething. Beside her, Zelda was clutching Calain's arm and glaring up at the women. Zelda wasn't powerful enough to fight seven sorceresses on her own. She knew it and looked very angry about the fact, while the sorceresses looked very amused, their eyes alight with silent laughter.

"Poor thing," said the witch who had spoken before, "to have such a dunderhead for a guardian."

The other witches laughed.

Calain's chest heaved. She started to spring up, not knowing what she would do, and the lead witch lifted her hand, fingers spread. Calain was blown back, and darkness fell over her as she lost consciousness.

Chapter 5

Zelda watched in helpless horror as Calain flew away like a ragdoll, hit the ground, and didn't move. Outraged, she shot to her feet, the bare soles slapping the smooth cavern floor, and with furious blue eyes, she conjured the first Dark spell she could think of. One of the witches, one on the far right, had an expression of wide-eyed panic, as if she knew what was happening seconds before it happened: she burst into fragments like shattered glass, and the wind swept her away.

Contrary to being angry, the remaining six witches looked at Zelda with interest. Many looked at her with new eyes, as if they hadn't quite seen her before. The lead witch had a calculating look Zelda didn't like.

"Well, well, well," said the lead witch in her smooth, purring voice. She sounded impressed. "I didn't realize they taught Dark Magick at that little *school* of yours."

"They—They don't really," Zelda stammered, suddenly embarrassed and ashamed. She had practiced Dark spells on her own, "killing" and "maiming" rocks and twigs. She hated that her skill made the witches suspect she was anything like them. But if she was honest . . . she had enjoyed blowing that witch away in Calain's defense. Her eyes scanned the women, and she wondered how many more she could pick off before they overpowered her.

"Not many, I'm afraid," said the lead witch, emerging from Zelda's thoughts, and Zelda looked at her in surprise: she was a Reader! Zelda immediately threw up a defensive mental wall, but she knew it was a feeble, if not useless, attempt to shield herself and hated it when the women laughed softly in dark amusement.

"Though not a bad attempt to shield me out, I'll give her that," said the leader, whose eyes were bright with interest as they bore into Zelda's face. She took a step forward, and Zelda stiffened, but she only said in earnest, "You show real promise. Join my coven, child, and I shall teach you *real* magick, not that horse shite they taught you at Vira'Toss."

Zelda didn't know what to say. She couldn't decide if the witch was serious or toying with her. "And if I say no?" she said, lifting her chin.

"The we shall chop you up," answered the lead witch, "and cook you in a stew."

More dark laughter. They all looked so sinister standing there in their black robes, joking or not. Zelda glanced over at Calain, who was still out cold on the ground.

"She shant be harmed," said the lead witch calmly. "Not unless she is foolhardy enough to follow."

And she will be, Zelda thought unhappily. She looked at the witches, who were waiting in silence, their hungry, amused eyes upon her. "All right," Zelda said, swallowing. "I'll come with you."

To Zelda's surprise, the lead witch smiled, showing tiny fangs at the corners of her mouth. She was an elf! Hungry eyes still on Zelda, she lifted her hand toward the waterfall, and the water split like a curtain, revealing a dark tunnel lit by torches of green flame.

"After you," said the lead witch in a voice that was not unfriendly.

Glancing a last miserable time at Calain's still body, Zelda lifted her skirts and waded with bare feet through the pool, toward the dark tunnel, wondering what horrors waited for her on the other side.

WHEN CALAIN AWOKE, someone was gently dabbing the blood from her face. She was lying on her back and could feel the cold stone floor of the cavern beneath her. Nearby, the waterfall rushed gently to fill the pool, sending up a chill mist. Night had fallen, for the cavern was dark but for the unearthly glow of the water and the gentle flicker of the torchlight. Green flames . . . there were green flames nearby.

Calain turned her head toward the light and saw that the waterfall had parted, revealing a long, dark tunnel that was lit by green torchlight. The torches stood in brackets along the walls, their dancing flames gently beckoning. Calain gritted her teeth, knowing Zelda had been taken down that tunnel and the way had been left open, deliberately taunting her.

"Do not rise too quickly," warned Selene, who was kneeling on one knee over Calain.

Calain looked up in surprise. Selene had a damp cloth in her gauntlet-covered hand, and her usually neat black braid had come half undone, so that licks of hair fell in her dark eyes. She had obviously come there in great haste. Behind her, her black horse, Apple, was grazing beside Arthur. Both beasts looked unconcerned.

"*Selene,*" Calain sneered, leaning with difficulty on her elbow. She snatched the damp cloth and pressed it with a wince to her throbbing temple. "The devil are you doing here?"

Selene's brown eyes became cool at the less-than-friendly welcome. "Saving your sorry hide, apparently," she said. "I was in a tavern when I heard Raven's Cross had seen you and intended to take Zelda. I circled back to aid you and followed them to their lair. You are most welcome, by the way."

Feeling guilty for her attitude, Calain staggered to her feet. After all, it wasn't Selene's fault that she fancied Zelda. Who wouldn't fancy her? And at least she'd kept her hands off of Zelda . . . so far.

Calain clumsily started donning her armor and felt another rush of guilt when Selene helped her without a word. As they buckled in silence, Calain waited to be lectured and scolded. After all, Zelda being taken was her fault. If she had recognized the rune on the cave wall, she never would have taken refuge here, and Zelda would still be safe. But the lecture never came. Selene was calm and quiet as she helped Calain into her silver armor, and her eyes glanced with occasional worry at the throbbing cut on Calain's temple.

"Did you come for Zelda or for me?" Calain asked, no contempt in her voice.

"You are my sister in arms," Selene said at once, as if it should have been obvious. "My foolish, annoying sister," she added, rolling her eyes, "but my sister all the same. If you are in danger, I shall come."

"And Zelda?" Calain prompted. Her voice was still devoid of contempt, instead filled with sincere curiosity.

Selene swallowed hard, as she always did when difficult feelings arose. Her eyes were determinately on a buckle as she tightened Calain's vambrace. Eventually, she confessed somewhat bitterly, "We both know I want her desperately. Since the moment I saw her, something stirred inside me, and I knew I must devote my life to her protection." Her eyes darkened.

"But as it turned out, she was not Wick Blackwood, she was Zelda, the woman you had scorned only hours before, and as with everything, the gods gave you what I craved most." Finished helping Calain, Selene abruptly turned toward the tunnel.

Calain awkwardly took her sword up from the floor and harnessed it to her back. Selene always wore her sword on her hip, but Calain liked reaching up for hers, not across.

As they sloshed through the pool together, Calain said, "I have bedded her already. If your heart is set on it, you may finger my lady. I suspect she fancies you as well. Just . . . do not put your mouth upon her. That is mine."

Selene scowled. "Do not speak of Zelda as if she were your leftover supper!"

"I did not mean it in that sense!" Calain snapped. "But if you crave her, and she craves you, I do not see the harm."

There was a pause as they stepped up from the water and onto the smooth stone floor of the tunnel mouth. They stood side-by-side, and Selene gave Calain a sidelong glance. "Truly?" she said. "I could touch Zelda, and you would not throttle me?"

"So long as you don't put your mouth upon her sex," Calain confirmed.

Selene seemed amused by that, and Calain hated it. But rather than tease Calain, Selene returned her attention to the task at hand, her expression becoming grim as she gazed down the dark tunnel.

"There were seven of them that took her," said Calain darkly. "We could overcome seven if we were to sneak upon them, but they shall know we're coming now." She shook her head. "If only Gwen and Cass were here, we would stand a better chance."

"Well, they are not here," said Selene calmly, as if she were merely stating an unfortunately truth. "We shall sneak upon the witches as best we can, and remember: the only certain way to kill a Dark witch is to behead her."

"Let us go already and cease lecturing!" Calain snapped.

They moved down the tunnel together, which was just wide enough that they could walk shoulder-to-shoulder. They tried to tread softly, minding the jingle of their armor, their swords drawn and ready. They advanced so slowly that their footsteps were barely a whisper in the silence.

The tunnel wasn't very long. It ended at a misty room hewn of rock and lit by many melting candles, their wax dripping gooey over rocks, open books, and the lips of large lack cauldrons. The cauldrons were steaming and their fires roaring, as if they had only just been abandoned, for there were no signs of any witches about.

The next room was much the same, and the next: empty but for melting candles and open books, bubbling cauldrons and bones. Eventually, they could hear chanting coming from the next room, the voices echoing, so that the room sounded cavernous.

Selene stopped, holding out her arm to stop Calain. "It sounds as though there are many of them down there," she said, "but I have brought something that will make slaying them easier." So saying, she pulled a stone from her satchel. It was a small pebble about the size of a chicken egg with a glowing white rune carved upon it.

Calain knew what the stone was. When activated, it prevented spells and cleared the effects of those that had been cast. It was a Bane Stone.

"Why did you not mention this before?" Calain demanded irritably.

"I didn't think we would need it," Selene answered, "but there must be twenty witches down there!" She jerked her head. "Come."

They moved together through the next misshapen, rocky opening and found themselves standing on a ledge above a large cavern. A sloping path led down the ledge either side to a room that was full of witches draped in black robes. Selene was right: there must have been twenty-odd witches in the room, which was large for a witch coven. Most illegal covens tended to keep small to avoid the law, but apparently, Raven's Cross had grown bold in their power.

The witches were chanting as they crowded in a circle around a pillar. The words were a strange language Calain didn't understand, perhaps a demon's tongue. The voices were rising almost feverishly to the ceiling. Calain wondered what they were so excited about. And then the crowd of witches parted and Calain saw her: Zelda was standing naked against the pillar, bound by rope, her curly golden hair tumbling long around her. She was trembling as she watched a witch approach with a long dagger.

"Now!" Selene hissed, throwing the Bane Stone into the crowd below.

The witches whirled, indignant that they had been interrupted in their ritual, while Zelda lifted her head, and her eyes glowed with admiration as Calain came storming down the slope.

Just as the day she'd fought in the games, Calain could feel Zelda's hungry eyes on her as she tore through the shrieking witches, beheading them left and right, her red hair tossing, her eyes glinting. It was like lopping heads off daisies: unable to channel their powers, the witches were simply fleeing in terror.

When Calain had beheaded her last witch, she cleaned her blade on the dead woman's robes and sheathed it on her back. When she glanced up, she was furious to see Selene had reached Zelda before her. Selene cut the ropes away, and as they tumbled to the floor, she reached up and gently took Zelda by her narrow waist. Blushing, Zelda braced her small hands on Selene's strong arms, and her breasts shivered as she was lifted down from the platform. She stared into Selene's eyes for a moment, Selene stared down at her with a serious fire, and for one torturous second, Calain thought they would kiss. But the moment passed. As if she had remembered herself, Zelda's eyes turned on Calain. She brightened and ran to her.

Heart leaping, Calain opened her arms and laughed as she caught Zelda to her breastplate. Zelda's sweet smell and softness was, as always, overwhelming as she crushed against Calain, showering her face with doting kisses.

"You were amazing, my knight!" Zelda cried between frantic kisses. "Did they hurt you?" She pulled back to glance anxiously over Calain.

Calain looked down at Zelda, soft affection in her eyes, and kissed her on the forehead. Zelda gazed up at her, eyes glowing fondly.

"Come," said Selene, who had turned her back, as if she couldn't stand observing them much longer. "Zelda can dress back at the waterfall, then we set out for City Ternia."

Calain was so happy to have Zelda back, she didn't question Selene's orders. Instead, she gently swept Zelda into her arms, and her heart skipped a beat when Zelda gave her another doting look and nuzzled her head under her chin.

I love you, my lady, Calain thought, tightening her arms protectively around Zelda.

Chapter 6

Zelda dressed again at the waterfall, choosing a pale green gown from the satchel she had been forced to leave behind there. Calain helped her dress, pulling her panties up until they were tight against her swollen sex, fastening the back of her gown for her. And though Selene kept her back to them, Zelda knew she was trying very hard not to watch. When Zelda was fully dressed and ready to depart, Selene turned to them, and her cheeks were flaming the tiniest bit. Calain seemed amused by this, though Selene, if anything, seemed irritated.

Selene wanted them to leave the forest immediately and set out for Ternia, the city she'd been hiding in when she came across the witches of Raven's Cross and their plans.

Zelda was worried. The leader of Raven's Cross and a few of her witches had escaped the massacre of their coven and would not be pleased that Calain and Selene had unwittingly stolen their new recruit. For Zelda, seeing no other option, had agreed to undergo the initiation in the hope that perhaps Calain would save her before it was complete. For once she was magickally bound to Raven's Cross, she would lose her tie to Calain and instead become bound to the lead witch, Melvalda.

Melvalda bound all her witches to her, that she might track their whereabouts and summon them by magick. And though the binding was merely practical, Zelda had observed a keen lust in Melvalda's eyes and suspected that many of the women in Raven's Cross were actually her lovers.

As they camped in the forest, Zelda related her fears to the knights but was careful to conceal her suspicions that Melvalda desired her. To her great frustration, Selene dismissed her concerns, stating that she carried many Bane Stones and would secure even more once they had reached Ternia.

Since Zelda's rescue from Raven's Cross, Selene had become distant and cold. She did not meet Zelda's eye and often said the words "my lady" with a stiffness that stung.

On the third morning, they made camp yet again. They always traveled during the night and slept during the day, mimicking the pattern of the Rose Guard so as to avoid them. Selene had gone to gather firewood, leaving Zelda alone with Calain.

"Selene is in a dour mood. What is the matter with her?" Zelda asked when Selene was out of earshot. She was surprised when Calain, who was eating an apple, suddenly grinned at her across the barren firepit.

"She fancies you," Calain said in much amusement and took another bite of her apple, watching Zelda for a reaction.

Zelda didn't know what to think. She had suspected. There were a few times when Selene had given her a look, but she never really thought . . .

"Do you fancy her?" Calain asked.

Zelda looked over and could tell Calain was trying to keep her face straight and devoid of emotion. She took a sloppy drink from her wineskin and uncouthly wiped her mouth with the back of her gauntlet. She looked at Zelda with a neutral expression, waiting.

"Well, I'd be lying if I said she wasn't attractive," said Zelda, thinking of Selene's tall, powerful body and her fierce, slanted eyes. She often thought Selene looked like a dark goddess of battle, especially when she was fighting. She looked at Calain suspiciously. "Why?"

"Why not have a go with her?" Calain suggested, and it was obvious she was trying to sound casual and not at all jealous.

Zelda laughed in disbelief. "You would never be able to contain yourself! I saw how you slew the queen. You can't stand anyone touching me – or looking at me, even," she added, thinking of the way Calain had frantically covered her as they were riding only days before for Arion.

"I can control myself!" Calain protested indignantly, her pretty green eyes firing.

Zelda looked at her fondly and wanted to kiss her. Instead, she took a chunk of bread from her satchel and bit into it. "And why should I sleep with Selene? Why do you want this?"

Zelda could tell Calain was pleased by her hesitation. She needed to be the one Zelda wanted above all else and seemed to fear she was not. Zelda shook her head: if only she could make Calain understand how much she adored her.

"Tis not about what I want," Calain said, shrugging moodily. "Selene and I haven't always seen eye to eye, but she is like a sister to me, and I regret seeing her so unhappy. She's a virgin, can you believe that?"

Zelda raised her brows in surprise, but given Selene's serious and dutiful nature, it wasn't *that* surprising.

"Never touched a maiden in her life," Calain went on, "because she was saving herself for the woman of her dreams. Turns out the woman of her dreams is you—"

Zelda's heart fluttered.

"—and she can't have you because . . . because it would wound me," Calain finished lamely. She looked up quickly, "But that's just what she thinks! It wouldn't wound me at all!"

Of course not, Zelda thought, amused. "And what about what I want?" she said. "Do I have a choice, or will you and Selene just pass me around like a goblet of wine?"

Calain looked at her indignantly again. "Of course, you have a choice! My lady jests, but this is a grave matter."

"Sex always is with you," said Zelda, still amused.

Calain smiled. "So long as the lady is pleased," she said and took another swing of wine from the wineskin. But she swallowed and became somber. "If you were to agree to the matter, I should give Selene instruction. She has never pleased a lady before."

Zelda held down a blush, imagining Calain instructing Selene on how to make her climax. "*And remember, our lady craves two fingers, not three. Her sex is most sensitive and tight . . .*"

"Don't give Selene instructions," Zelda begged. "You will humiliate her! Wait until we are in her room in Ternia. She said she would get us a room at an inn there. Make some excuse to leave us alone together, and I will take care of the rest."

Calain did not look very happy about that. Zelda beckoned her, and Calain came around the firepit and sat beside her. Finished with her bread, Zelda sat on Calain's lap and smiled when the knight closed her strong arms about her. Calain's eyes were still sad.

Zelda laughed in disbelief. "You asked me to do this!"

"I know," Calain said glumly, "but I wanted to be there. Now I feel you shall steal away with her when I am not present, and perhaps she will put her mouth upon you."

Zelda blinked in amazement. "What is so wrong with that?"

Calain looked at Zelda incredulously, the green eyes wide. "I cannot bear the thought of another's mouth tasting what I have tasted, giving you pleasure I alone have given! What if she is a better lover than I? The very thought makes me want to run a blade through her, I confess."

Zelda laughed. She touched Calain's face and gazed warmly into her eyes as she said, "You know you shall always be my champion. My champion in every conceivable way."

Zelda was glad when her words seemed to sooth Calain, who gave her a soft, doting look. They kissed with slow affection, and their lips had barely peeled apart when Selene returned with an armful of firewood.

Seeing Zelda being held so tightly in Calain's lap, Selene's face hardened as she dropped the firewood in the pit and set about stroking up a fire.

"All right, Selene," sighed Calain, "let us put an end to your longing."

Flames sprang to life and danced in the firepit. Her work done, Selene rose to her feet, dusted off her bare hands, and frowned in confusion at Calain. Without another word, Calain took Zelda by the waist and easily turned her about. Zelda felt like a small child as she was maneuvered around by Calain, who then placed Zelda's thighs atop her own and spread them with her knees. She took off her gauntlets, and Zelda blushed as she realized what was happening.

Selene seemed to realize as well. She had been in the act of putting her gauntlets on but angrily threw them down and blushed crimson to her hairline: Calain had roughly yanked Zelda's front laces loose, exposing her shivering breasts to the chilly morning air. Her pink nipples stood rigid against the cold, then grew even harder when Calain's strong, warm hands cupped her breasts and massaged.

"What is the meaning of this?!" Selene demanded, outraged. "Cease fondling the lady, Calain! You will not humiliate her in this base way!"

"I agreed to th-this," Zelda admitted breathlessly. She was flushed with arousal as Calain aggressively stroked her breasts and buried kisses in her neck, moaning all the while. Very slowly, Zelda reached down and drew up the skirt of her gown, exposing her panties. Her thighs were spread, forced wide as they were by Calain's knees, and she could feel how tight her panties were becoming as her lips swelled with arousal. She liked that Calain was pawing her with abandon, that Selene was standing there, watching as if she wanted to devour her.

"Come here, Selene," Zelda said huskily.

"My lady . . ." began Selene uncertainly.

"I command it," Zelda said over her.

Swallowing hard, Selene came around the firepit and practically dropped to her knees before Zelda, as if she had suddenly gone weak. She looked at Zelda's breasts with a startling hunger, and shocking Zelda and Calain both, she ripped Zelda's panties away, exposing her soft pin sex. Her gaze zeroed on it with narrow-eyed thirst.

Calain reached down, splitting the lips of Zelda's sex with two fingers, and sitting in Calain's lap, legs spread, Zelda shivered as Selene slowly slid two fingers deep inside her. Then Calain cupped one of her breasts, offering it to Selene, who buried her face in its softness, the plump flesh rising against her closed and frowning eyes as she gently suckled.

Zelda couldn't contain her soft screams of pleasure as the two strong knights carefully worked multiple orgasm from her trembling body. Calain's hands and mouth were firm and aggressive, while Selene's hands and mouth were gentle and caressing. Both combined thrilled her to shocking heights of ecstasy.

THEY WERE SILENT THE rest of the way to Ternia. Calain's mind kept going back to Zelda squirming breathlessly in her lap, screaming softly as she was fingered, sucked, and groped to a climax again and again. They had pleased her six times in succession, and Calain had wiped her moisture away with a kerchief before a lust-addled Selene could lick it away herself.

Selene seemed embarrassed by her own hunger. Calain knew she had never given in to her desires before that morning at the camp and was mortified about it now, no doubt praying to her gods for forgiveness.

Zelda was also quiet, resting her head against Calain as they rode together in the saddle. Calain could not guess what she was thinking and it frustrated her, but Zelda also didn't seem to regret what they'd done, which was good. If anything, Calain sometimes caught her staring off with a dreamy expression. Was she lusting for Selene? Calain was afraid to ask, afraid to wonder. Her only comfort was Zelda's doting kiss each morning before they slept and Selene took her turn keeping watch.

One morning, Calain found she could not sleep and sat with Selene on first watch. A low fire burned in the pit against the cold as Zelda slept nearby, curled up in her gray cloak. Calain thought once again that she looked like an innocent beauty from a fairytale with her golden curls and pink cheeks. When she glanced up, it was to find Selene staring at Zelda as well, her eyes soft with affection.

"Is your lust sated?" Calain asked playfully. She supposed enough time had passed that it was safe to tease Selene.

Selene helplessly shook her head. "I only want her more. But she will never want me as she craves you, and her heart is not Bound to mine."

"What about Wick Blackwood? She *is* Bound to you, and she was a cute little elf—"

"Who also doted on *you* and wanted *you,*" said Selene through her teeth. "All she could talk about at the feast was how skillfully you fought, how well you rode. All the fair maidens have always preferred you, and you know it." So saying, she glared at the fire.

Calain didn't know what to say. She couldn't even pretend Selene's words weren't true, and Selene wasn't one for comforting lies.

"Perchance there will be another woman that stills you so," said Calain soothingly. "Zelda is a great beauty and a sweet spirit, but she is not the only maiden with such qualities."

Selene smiled sadly at Calain's attempt to comfort her. "Perhaps," she agreed, though Calian could tell she was humoring her. After a pause, Selene said weakly, "There *are* no women like Zelda. I shall be on one knee before her the rest of my days. She makes me weak."

"She makes me strong," said Calain quietly.

THEY CAME TO THE EDGE of the forest on the fifth day. It was dark, the stars twinkling in the sky, and Calain and Selene traveled on foot, guiding their horses forward by the reins, while Zelda sat tiredly on Calain's horse, Arthur. In silence and darkness, they moved across the field to the distant silhouette of Ternia. Zelda couldn't wait to reach the inn, to sleep in a warm bed and eat hot food. Her thighs and backside were also aching from the saddle, and there was a deeply imbedded line of dirt under her nails that could only be removed after a soak in a warm bath.

:It isn't much farther,: soothed Arthur, the horse's mind linking into Zelda's.

:Good,: Zelda linked back. She had been able to speak to animals since she was seven. All sorceresses could eventually as a side effect of expanding their consciousness to learn magick.

:But You should warn your knights,: linked the horse, *:that there are goblins up ahead, waiting to ambush us.:*

:Goblins!: gasped Zelda.

:Yes,: said Arthur in disgust, *:I can smell the horrid little things. Do hurry and warn them.:*

Zelda did as Arthur suggested and warned the knights of the goblins waiting ahead. There was a ruin of giant old stones in the middle of the field, a crumbling structure once used by the ancients to worship the gods. Selene predicted the goblins were camped there, as there was no other structure for miles, and she was correct: they ventured into the ruin only to find themselves under fire.

Arrows rained down on them from one side of the ruin, and scowling, Zelda extended her hand, throwing up a shield of gossamer white light, off which the arrows harmlessly bounced. The goblin archers shrieked in outrage. Zelda reached out with her mind, and in seconds, they were shattered. More screams of rage when the other goblins saw their comrades obliterated.

More goblins leapt out of hiding with crude, nicked swords and daggers, green men and women with saggy breasts, with pointy ears and hooked noses, long yellow nails and sharp teeth, all about three feet high. There must have been a round two-dozen of them, but Calain and Selene tore through them with ease, while Zelda aided them with her spells.

Ten minutes later, Calain waded through the staring dead, taking what treasures she could from the goblin corpses. Anything she found could be traded for gold in Ternia, and the more gold they had, the better.

"A pack of playing cards!" Calain cried in delight and kissed the cards enthusiastically.

Zelda and Selene were sitting on a large stone brick together. Calain had come out of the battle cheerfully unscathed, but Selene had taken a deep slash on her hand that had nearly severed her gauntlet.

Zelda carefully pried the gauntlet off and tisked. "The wound looks deep!" she scolded, as if Selene had deliberately slashed her own hand.

"I am fine, my lady," Selene insisted, breathless with pain. "Save your magick."

"Hush," said Zelda, who was cradling Selene's bloody hand in both her own. The gash smelled foul: poison. Goblins were known for coating their weapons with it. Zelda summoned the strongest healing spell she knew. A second later, her eyes were glowing, and Selene's hand was growing stronger. Zelda could see the green poison leaving her veins, until the throbbing web of them had disappeared from her palm. Color returned to Selene's hand, and she flexed the fingers firmly. Zelda held down a blush, remembering how those strong fingers had flexed so deep inside her only days before.

Zelda looked up. "How is the pain?"

"Terrible," Selene answered, and Zelda knew she meant her heart, not her hand. Selene cupped Zelda's cheek. Zelda felt her heart thudding quicker as the strong, beautiful knight gazed at her with that serious fire again. Then all at once, Selene had leaned down and was kissing her. It was a tender kiss, though full of yearning. Selene's gentle tongue slid warm against hers, and Zelda found herself moaning as her heart sped up in excitement. Calain must've felt her heart, too, for the next thing she knew, Selene's mouth had been ripped from hers, a string of saliva all that linked their lips.

Zelda opened her eyes and watched in horror as Calain, who had grabbed a fistful of Selene's black hair, threw Selene bodily on the ground and proceeded to beat her in a kind of mad trance.

"Calain—have you gone mad?" Selene snarled, shoving Calain away by the face.

Calain was not to be deterred. She came right back, fully prepared to swing again, but Selene caught her off-guard with an uppercut to the face, and she tumbled over on her back in a spurt of blood.

Both knights were getting to their feet to continue the fight when Zelda jumped up and shouted, "Stop it! Stop it, both of you!"

For the first time since they'd been together, Calain looked as if she was going to disobey. Instead, she got to her feet and glared at Zelda so hard, it stung.

"You . . . let her . . ." Calain panted. "You let her kiss you!" She waved an angry gauntlet at Selene.

Selene was bitterly nursing her busted lip. She glared at Calain as she shook out a kerchief to clean away the blood. "The lady may kiss who she pleases," she said quietly. "She does not belong to you, Calain."

"No, I belong to her!" Calian snapped back. She looked at Zelda again, and it was clear she was waiting for an explanation.

But Zelda didn't have one. The truth would hurt Calain, and the truth was, she hadn't stopped Selene from kissing her because she hadn't wanted her to stop.

Calain seemed to realize the truth anyway. Zelda couldn't stand the hurt in her eyes.

Calain looked at Selene. "It you kiss her again," she said in a low dangerous voice, "I shall cut you in half!"

Selene didn't look impressed, instead turning wearily away.

They mounted their horses and rode the rest of the way to Ternia in silence. Zelda shared a saddle with Calain as before, and there was something stiff about the way Calain rode, always careful to avoid actually touching Zelda if she could. Calain was hurt and angry and cold and everything Zelda (and likely Selene) had feared she would be.

And as they rode on in grim silence, Zelda realized why Calain was so angry: kissing was affection – even kissing *down there* —and Calain was afraid Zelda would fall in love with Selene. She was terrified.

Zelda smiled to herself and only loved the foolish woman more. If Calain was so frightened that they would love each other, she shouldn't have suggested they have sex! But Zelda was starting to realize Calain wasn't the brightest candle.

And what would be so terrible if Zelda *did* love Selene? Why couldn't she love them both? Why couldn't they share her as they had that morning in the camp? That *wonderful* morning in the camp . . .

As dawn was approaching, they drew at last near the gates of Ternia, at which two men from the city guard stood watch as a steady stream of wagons, horses, and travelers filed in from the road. Selene pulled the hood of her cloak up, and Zelda and Calain followed suit as they smoothly fell in with the crowd.

No one paid attention to them. The gaggle around them was singing, laughing, and talking over the cluck of caged chickens and the baa of sheep. Selene was riding very close beside them, so close that her knee nearly knocked Calain's. Without warning, Calain reached over and squeezed Selene's knee, a silent apology. At the same time, her strong arm closed around Zelda's waist in a trembling hug. Zelda reached back and touched Calain's face, and Calain buried an apologetic kiss in her neck, brushing the fabric of the hood briefly aside with her nose.

They rode through the gates, the city spreading away before them. Zelda was in awe. Ternia was a vast city, reaching as far as the eye could see to the distant horizon. Crowds pressed in from all sides: babies wailing, children running and giggling, merchants peddling their wares, drunks shouting, women giggling as young men offered them flowers. The buildings were made of clay bricks and flowers were bursting from every vacant space, white and red and pink and orange.

"It's *beautiful*," Zelda breathed, and smiled when she felt Calain's hand on her thigh in acknowledgement.

Zelda could understand why Selene had hidden here. It would be easy to disappear into the crowd, never to be seen again! The city was vast and the crowds so thick, they were a wash of color. Calain seemed to be thinking along the same lines, for she whispered in Zelda's ear, "Stay close to me until we have reached the inn, my lady."

"And then stay closer?" Zelda teased.

"Careful," Calain whispered back, "or I shall put on a show before these good folk."

Zelda laughed.

"If you two are done whispering and giggling," said Selene irritably, "we have arrived."

Zelda looked up to find they had indeed arrived at the inn. A stable boy ran up to take Selene's horse, and when Zelda and Calain had dismounted, another appeared to take Arthur.

A haggard man with foul breath jiggled a can in their faces, demanding coins. Another man leaning against a nearby building leered at Zelda's breasts in a way that made her physically ill, and an old man hobbled by, whistling at Zelda as he went, so that Calain flushed angrily.

"Nice tits," said yet another man as he passed Zelda.

Calain tensed and reached for her sword, but Selene grabbed her arm and hissed, "Stay your temper! Shall we brawl in the streets with common scoundrels and bring the Rose Guard running?"

Calain irritably snatched her arm free but did not pull her sword. She looked anxiously at Zelda, and Zelda arranged her face to look unbothered. In truth, however, Zelda felt unsettled. She had spent years sequestered away among women, and after only a few days of having left that sanctuary, she was already being preyed upon and harassed. She had always counted herself lucky that her uncle hadn't sold her to be raped for coin in a whorehouse, that she had avoided sexual assault and exploitation. Now she was in the world of men again, and she was beginning to wonder how long her luck would last.

"We shall not allow a man to lay a hand upon you!" Calain said fiercely, and Zelda felt yet again as if Calain had read her thoughts. They had warned her at Vira'Toss that the connection would allow her knight to Read her on a very basic level.

Selene nodded in agreement with Calain. "Also, you are a fully trained sorceress of Vira'Toss and an enemy of the crown. Nothing and no one can stop your use of Dark Magick now."

"Except Bane Stones," Zelda said. A man with a Bane Stone: her worst nightmare.

"Trust us to protect you, my lady," said Calain.

Zelda had been gazing off anxiously. When she looked up, Calain and Selene were looking at her with narrow eyes as licks of hair slapped across their determined faces in the wind. They seemed so confident in their abilities and looked so fierce and strong, that she felt herself relaxing. She nodded and said a little breathlessly, "I . . . I trust you."

Calain smoothed a gentle hand over Zelda's back and smiled at her, and Zelda felt something inside her melt. How could Calain think she didn't love her best?

Inside the inn, Zelda was alarmed to notice wanted posters of their faces on the wall behind the bar. Heart thudding in silent panic, she blinked, and the faces on the posters changed to resemble pug-faced mountain trolls.

The man behind the bar was suspicious, even after realizing the wanted posters looked nothing like them. After all, they were two Falcon Knights traveling with an unknown sorceress and were easily identifiable as such: Calain and Selene still had the Falcon emblems on their armor, while Zelda was carrying a silver stave with a large pink crystal on the top.

Zelda needed her stave for the more powerful spells. Casting without focusing the power could cause innocents to be harmed or else just cause the spell to backfire and split her in halves. But Calain and Selene should have had their emblems removed days ago. The second they were alone in their room, Zelda held out her hand, casting a spell that made the Falcon symbols on their breastplates invisible.

Calain and Selene spoke of taking turns on watch. Selene always took first watch, so Calain and Zelda stripped to their smallclothes and climbed into bed.

Zelda had never been so happy to feel a mattress beneath her body. She sank gladly into the pillows and turned on her side. Calain spooned against her, hugging her almost possessively from behind, her breath tickling Zelda as it breezed through her hair. Two minutes, five, and Zelda had fallen asleep.

Zelda awoke again when someone touched her face. She went still: Selene had removed her armor and slipped into bed with them. She was in her linen underclothes, the coverlet pulled over her muscular shoulder, her black hair loose and beautiful in its silky curtains. She was lying on her side, facing Zelda. When her pretty dark eyes went to Zelda's lips, Zelda knew she wanted to continue what they had begun out in the field.

Calain was still asleep and still hugging Zelda. Zelda could tell by the pace of her heart that the red knight was dreaming deeply, but she was still afraid of waking her. She looked at Selene with longing, torn by her desire and her fear. She did not want to hurt Calain, but she wanted the thrill of Selene's tongue against hers again.

Selene cupped Zelda's cheek and peered with yearning into her eyes. She leaned close, and very slowly, she slid her tongue against Zelda's in a deep, hungry kiss. Zelda blushed to her hairline when she felt Selene's hand close on her sex over the fabric of her panties. The knight gently pinched Zelda's clitoris and thumbed it carefully through the fabric as she kissed her.

Zelda felt her clitoris swelling and throbbing with arousal in response, and she couldn't help it: she started to moan softly. Alarmed, Selene kissed her more deeply to muffle her cries, but this only gave her more pleasure and made her moan louder. She tried to stifle her voice, but Selene's fingers felt so good touching her. Her trembling thighs clenched in delight on the woman's fingers, and Selene grunted and blushed a little, becoming breathless with arousal.

And then it finally happened: Calain stirred with a moan and opened her eyes. She stared at them in surprise – at Selene with her hand cupped over Zelda's sex as they kissed. Selene calmly pulled her hand away from Zelda and stopped kissing her. She and Zelda stared at Calain, waiting for her outburst. To their great surprise, Calain gently tugged Zelda's panties down, then placed Selene's hand over her sex. She didn't do anything else. She merely lay there, holding Zelda and looking at Selene expectantly.

Selene hesitated, then slowly slid her fingers inside Zelda's warm sex. Zelda frowned, closed her eyes, and sighed as she was fingered deeply and slowly, her sex becoming more moist by the minute. Selene was breathing rapidly and Calain's muscular arms were trembling around her, and she realized they were both becoming aroused just from witnessing her helpless pleasure.

"By the gods, she's dripping wet . . ." Calain panted. "Zelda, you're so beautiful . . ." She whispered huskily in Zelda's ear, "I shall lick your pussy until you squirt against my tongue."

Zelda shivered and blushed to hear Calain's words. She lay trapped in Calain's strong arms, trembling and gasping, as Selene caressed her into a deliciously overwhelming climax. She screamed softly as her moisture released over Selene's gently coaxing fingers. In the wake of her passion, she sagged breathlessly and felt a thrill of happiness when Calain and Selene both showered her mouth and neck with slowly, lazy kisses.

Calain hadn't seemed jealous or angry the entire time Selene was fingering Zelda. It was when Selene placed her mouth between Zelda's thighs that Calain finally lost control. Face tight with rage, she roughly nudged Selene away from Zelda's sex and lowered herself over it instead. She was sucking passionately when, not to be hindered, Selene grabbed a fistful of Calain's red hair and snatched her off. They went tumbling to the floor and then it was happening all over again – they were fighting over her!

Zelda sat up, her legs folded to the side as she leaned on one hand and watched, appalled, as Calain and Selene rolled across the floor, grunting and hitting and yelling in a rage. Zelda blinked, and the two women were lifted apart and into the air, where she held them suspended with her mind. She was relieved when both women seemed to calm down. She could feel Calain's heartbeat slowing, and Selene, who was always so calm and controlled, seemed deeply ashamed that she had lost her senses. She cast her eyes down. So did Cailan.

"If we cannot play nicely, we shall not play at all," Zelda scolded them.

Calain and Selene glared at each other. "Yes, my lady," they chorused like abashed children.

Zelda gently set both women on their feet again and released them from her magick. She laid back on the bed again and spread her thighs and was pleased when both tall, muscular women looked at her sex with sharp hunger.

"Come, Calain, and lie here next to me," Zelda called.

Calain moved around the bed and laid at Zelda's side, taking her once more into her arms from behind. Zelda took Calain's hand and guided it into spreading the lips of her sex with two fingers. Calain trembled, longing to sink her face between Zelda's thighs. She compensated instead by grabbing a fistful of Zelda's heavy breast with her free hand, and as she groped hungrily, she brushed aside Zelda's golden curls with her nose and kissed her neck and shoulder up and down.

Selene watched from where she stood, swallowing hard, struggling to control the urge to move before she had been commanded.

"Here, Selene," Zelda called, squirming breathlessly as Calain's passionate groping and kissing continued.

Selene obeyed at once, lowering herself once more between Zelda's thighs with eyes that glittered hunger. She started licking and sucking gently, closing her hands around Zelda's thighs to hold her near.

Calain, who was still holding the lips of Zelda's sex open with two fingers, paused in her groping and kissing to stare with narrow-eyed envy at Selene, who was licking away with slow hunger.

Oh, Calain, will I ever tame you? Zelda thought. She guided Calain's face to hers and kissed her to calm her. Calain fell to eagerly kissing her neck again, her strong hand hard and firm as it milked Zelda's blushing breast until the pink nipple stood rigid.

Locked between the two muscular knights as they licked, kissed, sucked, and caressed, Zelda's head fell back and her perky breasts heaved as a climax trembled through her body, drawing a soft scream from her lips.

THEY HID FOR THREE days in Ternia thus, making love morning and night, taking turns on watch. . . .taking turns on Zelda. Calain and Selene learned to get along, though only just. Calain still occasionally became angry and bitter should Selene place her face between Zelda's thighs. Eventually, the two knights tasted Zelda's sex together, though how it had happened, Zelda wasn't sure. One thing led to another, and before she knew it, they were both between her legs, kissing her thighs, sucking the lips of her sex, fingering her slowly as they sucked on her clitoris, bringing her to a trembling climax.

Zelda awoke one morning snuggled between the two knights, their muscular bodies like a hard wall around her. They were tousled and undone from the night's exertions and talking quietly about their next move, the best places they could hide in the city, how they were going to earn coin. When they noticed Zelda was awake, they playfully kissed her cheeks either side, over and over, and she squealed with laughter until they had stopped. Breathless, she rose from the bed and washed herself at the washbasin.

Selene rose as well and began plucking her scattered armor pieces from the floor. Calain slouched into a chair beside the low-dwindling fire.

According to Selene, they were running out of gold. To hide in a city like Ternia was expensive, unless one had no issue sleeping in the gutter. They had six crowns and three coppers between them.

Zelda thought about beginning a practice as a healer or perhaps selling potions and tonics. But she had to remind herself that they couldn't make moves to settle in a place permanently yet: they still had yet to find Gweneth and Cassandra in Arinol.

What Zelda needed to do was a lesser skill, like laundry or dishwashing. The coin from such work could tide them over until they were ready to leave Ternia. But when she brought it up with Calain and Selene, they were both adamantly against it.

"Why?" Zelda demanded impatiently. "We need gold, and I can find work in a lady's house easily."

"You risk exposing yourself, my lady," said Selene grimly. "There are eyes throughout the city. It is safer for you to stay here, hidden in the inn, until Calain and I can move you."

Move her, as if she were a piece of furniture! Zelda thought irritably. She folded her arms. "All right, what will we do for gold, then?"

"I've been winning a lot of card games," Calain said, shrugging.

Selene's lips tightened. "I told you to stop gambling our coin! You're so incredibly irresponsible! That you ever became a Falcon—"

Calain tensed and kicked herself up from the chair. "And what have *you* been doing to get any gold? So far we have been surviving on *my* coin!"

Selene stood calmly, armor pieces in her bulging arms, but Zelda could tell by the tightness of her mouth that she was losing patience.

Zelda tiredly pinched the flesh between her eyes, her golden curls tumbling forward. "Fine. You two stay here and bicker. I'm going to look for work—"

Calain and Selene both started protesting at once.

"My lady, you can't go out there alone!"

"You will make yourself a target of the Rose Guard!"

"Let one of us accompany you!"

"Enough!" Zelda snapped. When she looked up, the women were mouthing silently like fish: her burst of frustration had stolen their voices. Perplexed, they kept mouthing for a moment before they'd realized what she'd done.

Zelda pulled her slip and gown on, then stepped into her slippers. She silently summoned her gray cloak to fall around her shoulders, her tired eyes on the two knights, who made a move to try and stop her, but another silent spell had rooted them to the spot. They watched—half helpless, half indignant – as Zelda swept from the room.

Chapter 7

As they were riding into town, Zelda had noticed a bakery on the right side of the road. She would go there and offer to wash dishes. She had turned down an alley seeking a shortcut when a man spoke behind her,

"Well, well, well," said a man's deep voice. "Look what we have here: the queen-slayer's whore."

Zelda turned. Two men were blocking the alley. She could hear another pair moving up behind her. She glanced coldly at them all. They were peasants, mud-stained and wearing rags, teeth missing, scruffy beards. They were looking at her with greedy eyes.

"There's a bounty on your head," said the man who'd spoken. " 'Wanted Dead or Alive, Six Thousand Crowns,'" he recited and gave a low whistle. "Six thousand. That's what they pay for queen-slayers these days? I could feed a small orphanage with that."

Zelda summoned a spell and gasped when nothing happened. She looked at her stave: the crystal was dim and without a hint of light. It had not answered her. And a heavy feeling of having been drained was pulling her down, falling over her like cold water.

The man who had spoken chuckled and pulled something from his pocket. It was a small, smooth stone with a glowing rune on it. A Bane Stone.

Zelda felt her heart freeze with anger and fear. She took an uncertain step back. The man with the Bane Stone nodded, and the men behind Zelda grabbed her. One grabbed her arm and the other grabbed her neck. Their fingers were so hard, they hurt, and Zelda resented the sob that escaped her when the men forced her to her knees. Her knees banged the ground, smacking over in a web of pain.

The man with the Bane Stone drew close to Zelda, chuckling darkly as he yanked open his pants. A penis stood in Zelda' face. She recoiled in disgust, thinking it looked like a hideous worm.

"Come on, girl," said the man, and his friends laughed. "Give us a little suck before we hand you in to the city guard. But don't tire yourself out. I'll expect they'll want their t-turn—"

The last word gurgled in the man's mouth as a sword blossomed in his chest. He and his friends stared in shock at the bloody blade as he teetered there, coughing blood. Then the sword was ripped free with a spatter, and the man dropped away to reveal Calain, who was standing there in her armor, chest heaving, red hair falling wild in her eyes.

The men fled at once. The nearest tried to flee past her, but she brought the sword around and his head came off, rolling away down the alley. As Zelda knelt there, watching and shivering, Calain quickly dispatched the last two. Then she took the Bane Stone from the dead man's pocket and brought her sword down on it in a shower of sparks.

Zelda breathed: the feeling of having been drained was lifting, but she was still transfixed with horror at what had nearly happened. She was realizing for the first time how lucky she was to have Calain to protect her in a world where such atrocities happened to women every day unchecked.

"My . . . My lady . . ." Calain panted. "Selene is coming with our steeds. We must flee the city. These dogs have alerted the city guard . . . my lady?" Calain knelt down, coming into Zelda's vision. The green eyes were soft with concern. She touched Zelda's face. "Zelda. Are you well? Did they harm you?"

Zelda looked at Calain and suddenly thought she was the most beautiful thing she'd ever seen. She threw herself at Calain's neck and hugged her tight, sobbing and sobbing and trembling all over. Calain's strong arms closed around Zelda. She stroked Zelda's hair and kissed her head and whispered, "It is all right, my lady. I came for you . . . I will always come for you . . ."

Zelda cried all the harder. Why did Calain have to be so sweet? So strong and so beautiful? She pulled back and kissed her wetly, frantically, over and over on the mouth and all over her face. Calain let the frantic kisses happen, blinking in complete bafflement.

The sound of hooves proceeded Selene, who ran to them, leading Apple and Arthur forward by their reins. She tossed Arthur's reins to Calain and swung into the saddle of her own horse, though her eyes danced over Zelda's tearstained face in concern.

Calain set Zelda on her horse, then climbed up behind her, and they were off, galloping through the city at a breakneck pace. The city guard tried to stop them at every turn, but Zelda took her staff in hand, and reaching out her other hand, fingers spread, she glowed with power as she sent the guards tumbling away like leaves.

Only the guards were hit by her magick, such was the power of Zelda's focus. Calain helped her keep balance by wrapping a strong arm around her waist as she steered, and when they reached the city gate, Zelda glowed all the brighter as she forced it open with her mind, and they charged through. She heard the guards shouting "Gods be good!" as they scrambled out of the way, and the three of them thundered away down the road, leaving City Ternia behind.

THEY HAD ESCAPED TERNIA through the western gate, which opened upon a road leading through trees and wild country. There wasn't a city or even a village for miles, which meant they were back to sleeping on the ground. They would also have to hunt, for they would soon run out of rations. And to make matters worse, their escape from the western gate had sent them off-course. They were supposed to head toward snowy Arinol, which was to the northeast, and they had fled west.

All of this Selene noted grimly and with much frustration, but Calain said she was only glad to be alive and took a long swig of wine to celebrate.

Zelda agreed with Calain. If they had been captured and turned over to the city guard, it would have been awful. All of them would have been executed, but not Zelda, not immediately. As the would-be rapist in the alley had hinted, the city guard would have violated Zelda first.

Zelda couldn't stop thinking of it, and she could tell Calain couldn't either. Sometimes She caught the red knight staring at her anxiously and knew her mind was back in the alley, that a dozen scenarios were running through her head: what if Calain hadn't gotten there in time? What if the men had overpowered her as well? What if . . .?

Noting the others' silent horror, Selene gently but firmly reminded them that there was no point dwelling on the past or torturing themselves with events that could have but had not even happened. She then wrapped herself in her cloak and slept, leaving Calain to take first watch.

They had camped off-road, at the edge of the forest that spread onward to the west. The trees here were not like Corriol. They were black, gnarled, and twisted, and their leaves were dark.

It was said that the further west one traveled, the more Dark Magick one would find. They were heading into the lawless lands of hags, trolls, and goblins. Even as they turned north toward Arinol, they would still have to venture through the dark forest.

While Selene sat sleeping against a rock, Zelda curled on her cloak beside Calain, where the red knight sat, poking the fire with a stick. After five minutes of trying, however, Zelda realized she could not sleep and sat up with a sigh, resting her head on Calain's shoulder.

"Are your thoughts still with the alley, sorceress?" Calain asked unhappily.

"Yes," Zelda admitted in a voice that trembled. "The horror of even seeing that man's . . . genitals. How could I recover had he forced it upon me?"

Calain put her arm around Zelda's shoulders and stroked her golden hair. "Then the next time," she said, "I will punch the man in his phallus."

Zelda laughed softly. So did Calain.

"Punch his erection," Calain added, "until his pelvis splinters and he cannot stand. Does that please my lady?"

"Tis no more than a rapist deserves," said Zelda darkly. "I am most certain the scoundrel has harmed many others."

"He will harm no one now, rest assured," said Calain. "Only the worms will suffer as they digest his rot."

"Poor worms," said Zelda.

They laughed again.

Then Calain said with soft admiration, "My lady was a goddess today."

"Was I?" said Zelda in surprise.

"Do you jest? You shone like the shun as we rode from Ternia, and men trembled before you . . . *I* trembled."

"You're trembling now," Zelda whispered.

The strong arm that curled tight around Zelda's shoulder was indeed shaking. When Zelda looked up, Calian's eyes were bright with desire but distant with a memory.

"As we rode, I held tightly to your waist. I held so tightly, but it was like holding to a volcano on the verge of erupting. So much power inside your little body . . . It was frightening . . . and exciting." She looked down at Zelda. "I am in awe of you, my lady. Would that you felt the same."

Zelda frowned. "How can you say that?"

"I have seen the way you look upon Selene, how your body quivers when she touches you. You cannot contain yourself—"

"As if I didn't melt every time you looked at me," Zelda said over her. She gave Calain a trembling kiss on the mouth and whispered in breathless frustration, "I love you, you foolish woman!"

Calain smiled. She gently gathered Zelda into her arms, lifting her onto her lap as if she weighed nothing. Then she rested her forehead against Zelda's and whispered, "Truly? Does thou love me?"

Zelda touched Calain's face. "Of *course,* I do." She trembled when Calain snatched her close in her embrace and kissed her with an aggressive passion that left her blushing and gasping when their lips came apart.

"Would that I could tear every bit of fabric from your flesh and give you my passion until the sun had risen," Calian said, a glint in her eye Zelda had never quite seen before.

It was a ravenous look, as if Zelda were a succulent meat dripping with moisture, tempting her to divide and taste it.

"But this is a dark and dangerous land," said Calain, glancing past Zelda at the black trees. "We would do well to keep our wits about us."

"I wonder when we will have the chance to lose our wits again," Zelda said unhappily.

Calain kissed Zelda's head to comfort her, though she seemed amused nonetheless by her disappointment. "Rest, my lady," she said. "Tomorrow we follow the river north, and tis a long trek."

THE NEXT MORNING, AS they continued north, they followed the *Wilde River* and thankfully, they would not have to cross it. For the river had taken its name from the fact that many had perished in its rapids. At the moment, however, they journeyed alongside the calmer portion, where the waters were smooth and placid.

Dark and dangerous as the western forest was, the day was bright and beautiful, with birds singing and creatures chirruping. It was such a lovely day that Selene wondered if some enchantment hadn't been placed on the forest to make them lower their guard. She was annoyed when the other two laughed at her theory. Neither of them had the sense to be cynical, Selene bitterly noted. No, they were too busy falling in love.

Around midday, Zelda insisted on stopping to bathe in the river, for she could not abide being dirty. Before the knights could protest, she had grabbed the soap from her satchel and unlaced her gown. Selene's lecture caught in her throat the moment Zelda's gown and slip dropped away, revealing her curvy body and the soft blond fuzz on her sex and underarms. Her long golden hair swept forward in a curtain and her shivering breasts swung down as she leaned forward to scoop water to her dirt-stained face.

As Zelda was leaning down again, the fat lips of her pink sex bulged between her thighs, and Selene felt her cheeks flame as arousal swept over her. Selene heard a moan and realized Calain was standing beside her, also staring at Zelda, the green eyes soft with longing. She had removed her armor and was in her in linens and woolen hose. Without even looking at Selene, Calian passed Arthur's reins to her and crept up behind Zelda. She playfully pounced, hugging Zelda from behind, and Zelda squealed with laughter as she was swept off her feet. Calain was laughing as well as she spun with Zelda in her arms, and the sunlight played upon them in beams as the sparkling water of the river splashed.

Selene stood there, holding the reins of the horses, and feeling so far away as she watched the other two. She was an intruder, a voyeur, watching moments that were meant to be private and intimate. They were so engaged in each other that they seemed to have forgotten she was even there.

Was this the way it would always be? Selene minding the horses while Zelda and Calain startled the birds?

Feeling she might as well rest while she had the chance, Selene tied the horses to a nearby tree, sat, and removed her armor piece by piece. She was patting her sweaty forehead with a kerchief when Zelda called her name and beckoned to her.

Selene looked up. Calain was wading ashore, looking happy and content. She clapped Selene's shoulder with a strong hand as she passed and went to the horses, where she took out cheese and bread and began to eat.

Zelda was still bathing in the water, smoothing the soap down her body. She looked up at Selene and smiled, beckoning to her again.

Puzzled yet curious, Selene rose and stepped into the shallows of the river, the muscles of her bare arms glistening when the water splashed her. Like Calain, she was now in her linen bra and woolen hose. As she drew nearer, the flowery smell of Zelda's soap wafted toward her on the breeze. She stopped when she was facing Zelda and looked down at her.

"My lady summoned me?"

Zelda frowned and laughed. "Always so serious, Selene. Here." She offered Selene the soap, and when Selene had clumsily taken it, she turned her back, pushing her long hair over her shoulder and waiting. Selene just stood there, feeling like a fool, too afraid of violating Zelda because she had misunderstood. Zelda laughed again and took Selene's hand, guiding the soap along the undercurve of her high breast.

Selene swallowed hard and gently squeezed. Zelda's skin was slippery, and her fingers slid right over her breast to the nipple, smoothing it in a brief cone-shape before she let go . . . and massaged again.

Zelda rested her head back against Selene and sighed. She took Selene's other hand and guided it over her other breast, so that Selene was now slowly massaging both in careful fingers.

Zelda's breasts were plump and so full, they filled Selene's hands in fistfuls. She squeezed gently, and they heaved in her grasp when Zelda, eyes closed, shivered in pleasure.

Selene's nostrils flared as arousal throbbed afresh between her legs. Her hands were shaking. She looked over to see what Calain was making of this. The red knight was sitting with her knees partially drawn up. One elbow was on her knee, and she was holding her wineskin as she watched them with narrowed eyes. Her cheeks were slightly pink with desire.

"It's like you're afraid to touch me," Zelda said in amusement. She turned to face Selene.

"I am," Selene said at once. "You are not my lady."

Zelda smiled up at Selene, her pretty blue eyes crinkling. She took Selene's arms and placed them around her, then placed her arms around Selene's neck as she said, "I am both your lady."

"Calain doesn't seem to think so," Selene answered.

Zelda lifted her pale brows. "Truly? You are touching me now. Does she seem angry?"

Selene glanced over at Calain again. No, Calain did not seem angry. She had stopped watching them completely and was grooming the horses. Selene didn't totally trust Calain's lack of anger, though. She knew her too well.

"Forgive me, my lady," Selene said with a flat laugh, "but I have known Calain far longer than you. I know her temper and her moods. If she is not angry now, she will be later. I could ride her horse, don her armor, even borrow her sword, and she would be content to share it all, but she would sooner slit my throat than allow me to touch her woman."

Zelda frowned, and Selene knew she had offended her, but notably, Zelda did not remove her arms from Selene's neck.

"I am not Calain's property," she said. "I am not a horse or a sword. I do not belong to her. Indeed, it is quite the opposite: she belongs to me. She has said so herself." Zelda's pink lips turned in a little smile and she glanced with soft affection at Calalin.

"And what am I?" Selene asked in much amusement. "Another horse in your stable?"

"If you choose to be," answered Zelda at once, her blue eyes bright with a fondness for Selene that surprised her.

Selene smoothed her hand down Zelda's golden curls, thinking how wonderfully soft they were, how sweet-smelling from the soap. She wanted to kiss Zelda but resisted and said instead, "And will you tame me as you have tamed Calain?"

"You are already quite docile," Zelda said warmly and stroked Selene's dark hair. "You seem so cold and hard, but you are really very gentle behind all that, aren't you?"

Zelda's eyes were so sweet and doting, Selene surprised herself when she suddenly lifted Zelda, hefting her gently, so that her soft backside rested on Selene's arms. Zelda's lashes fluttered, and she blushed with delight at Selene's display of strength. She looked down at Selene with admiring blue eyes, bracing her small hands against Selene's shoulders. Her heavy, full breasts were nearly in Selene's face, but Selene was looking into Zelda's eyes. Those beautiful, bewitching eyes.

Very slowly, Selene loosened the grip of her arms, and as Zelda slowly slid down, Selene kissed her belly . . . slowly sucked her pink nipple . . . kissed her neck . . . Zelda's small feet found the muddy earth beneath the water, and Selene closed her in her arms and kissed her mouth. She felt Zelda melting in her grasp and was pleased when she felt the woman's small hand pushing through her hair, silently urging Selene's gentle tongue deeper and harder. Selene obliged with delight, smoothing her hands over Zelda's soft, warm body as if she could not touch enough.

THEIR JOURNEY THROUGH the dark forest continued and was mostly uneventful. They did not come across any Dark witches, though they were attacked once by pixies in the night, whose sharp little teeth nicked them until they were forced to flee on horseback as Zelda summoned a spell to repel them.

They also came across two large trolls, who rose hairy and green from their hiding place in the mossy mud. Each troll had two beady black eyes and ears like bats. They were also as blind as bats. They sniffed and snuffled with their small noses as Zelda and her knights crept by them, leading the horses along on foot.

And then, at last, real danger found them when they met a black spirit as they passed through a hollow. The spirit had the shape of a slender man with pointed ears: the angry ghost of a slain elf.

This was not a foe the knights could engage with their blades, though Calain, determined to protect Zelda, tried to anyway. The angry spirit howled, stretching to ten feet in height as it grabbed Calain by the throat and lifted her bodily from the ground. Calian's legs dangled as she clawed at the hands that choked her, and she spit salvia and blood.

"Calain!" shouted Selene, who stood there feeling helpless, sword in hand.

Zelda swept forward with her stave, the pink crystal glowing, her eyes like beacons, and cast a banishing spell. The black spirit howled as it realized what was happening, howled in fury and shock, the flames of its eyes growing wide. A roaring portal opened behind it, sucking and spinning, so that their hair slapped their faces. The spirit was pulled through the portal like a cloud of vapor, leaving Calain hovering in midair momentarily before she dropped.

Nearly panicking, Selene tossed aside her sword and ran forward, arms out. Calain's limp body fell heavily in her arms.

Zelda was still focused on the portal, face creased with anger and determination. She snapped her spread fingers into a fist, and the portal closed, causing their hair to fall limp again.

Heart in her throat, Zelda shouldered her stave and ran to Selene, praying that Calain had survived. To her relief, Calain was alive but very weak, breathing gently in Selene's arms. Her throat was covered in purple bruises from the spirit's angry hands. She was barely conscious. If Zelda pushed past her fear and horror, she could feel Calain's heartbeat just barely pulsing.

"It nearly sucked the life from her," Zelda said miserably as she realized what had happened.

"H-Heal her, my lady," Selene said, and her voice was shaking. Zelda had never seen her so afraid.

Zelda sadly shook her head. "This will take more than a healing spell. She will need to rest. We must set up camp."

And so, they made a pallet of moss and leaves for Calain, right there in the gloomy hollow, and laid her limp body atop it to rest. Selene dug a firepit and gathered firewood, which Zelda set aflame with her stave. And then the waiting began. They sat either side of Calain, watching her still body for changes, trying to keep her warm beneath her cloak, as the fire crackled and the birds sang.

Selene seemed beside herself with worry, and like Zelda, she almost never left Calain's side. Her eyes remained fixed on Calain's still face, as if willing life and light back to it.

"She was always such a mighty battle maiden," Selene said hoarsely, "I'd forgotten for a while that she could be hurt."

"What about at Vira'Toss when the Rose Guard attacked her?" Zelda reminded her.

Selene snorted. "A trifle. Captain Gyda did not fight fair, and even then, she was no match for Calain. Calian was knocked over the head but awoke as they were dragging her away and gave them hell. Gwen and I happened upon the commotion, and we joined in. Cassandra came along last, and those Rose Guards knew they were finished. The queen's guards are no match for the Knights of Falcon."

Zelda glowered as she thought of the queen. It was because of the queen's lust that they were here now, watching Calain suffer.

Zelda was kneeling on the opposite side of Calain from Selene. She noticed Selene was silently weeping, tears streaming from her eyes, and reached over and took her hand.

"Calain will recover," Zelda said firmly and peered into Selene's wet brown eyes.

Selene dismally nodded and wiped away her tears with the heel of her hand. "No doubt you think me silly and weak, crying here like a babe."

"Not at all," Zelda said soothingly. "But sometimes it's easy to forget you're people, too, that you hurt and feel frightened and sad, just like me. You're all so big and strong and brave, you Knights of Falcon."

"Is that how you see us?" asked Selene with a weak laugh.

"Yes," Zelda admitted. She cupped Selene's cheek and caught a tear with her thumb. "I never thought I'd see someone like you weep."

"S-Someone like me?" Selene repeated unhappily.

"You always seem so fearless and certain," Zelda answered. "You always know what to do."

"And now I haven't a clue," Selene said weakly, her eyes on Calain, who slept solemnly between them.

Still cupping Selene's cheek, Zelda leaned closed and kissed her softly on the lips. They touched foreheads, mourning in silence a moment over Calain.

"Tell me about the others," Zelda said, drawing back. She looked down at Calain, smoothed her red hair, and took her limp hand in her own. She sniffed to hold back tears. If she didn't keep them talking, they would both fall to pieces crying.

"Tell me about Gweneth and Cassandra."

Selene blinked thoughtfully. "Gweneth is as immature as Calain, though in a different way."

"Oh?"

"Yes. Calain is irresponsible, reckless. Gweneth jests constantly. She takes nothing seriously, or pretends not to. It gets tiresome. But she is as loyal a friend as you will ever find."

"Gweneth is the brown-haired one, isn't she?"

Zelda recalled Gweneth's undercut brown hair and smirking lips. She'd been a cute, boyish woman, quite small for a knight, yet taller than most women all the same, with laughing blue eyes and small hands and feet. She had been assigned to Iris, and Zelda held back a laugh, imagining how furious Iris and Myriah must've been, having lost their knights to her, for Gweneth and Cassandra both would soon be in her company.

Zelda felt bad for Wick, though. While Wick could easily take another knight, she would not find one as beautiful and strong as Selene. It was almost as if Zelda had stolen the best knights from the batch and fled with them.

"Yes," Selene answered. "Gweneth had the brown hair. Cassandra was the blonde."

"Tell me about her. Cassandra."

Selene smiled sadly. "Many believed she should have been a sorceress, not a knight."

"Truly?"

"Mmhmm. She has the Sight. Her visions and sudden strong intuition have saved many lives. She was always closer to me than Gweneth and Calain, though I suppose it's because we are more alike."

Zelda remembered Cassandra. She had worn her pale blonde hair in a messy, shoulder-length braid, and her serious gray eyes had been wreathed in pale lashes. She had come across quite solemn and silent, speaking very little at the feast, which had driven talkative Myriah mad. Perhaps it was a good thing Myriah would have another knight now.

IT WAS WHEN DUSK CAME and darkness began to fall that Calain finally awoke. The purple bruises had gone from her throat and she seemed stronger, though she trembled as she sat up. Selene hastened to drape Calain's cloak about her, and Zelda frantically kissed Calain's cheeks again and again.

Calain laughed. "All this fuss over one spirit?"

"You could have died! Do not jest!" Selene scolded. She glanced at the horses, which were grazing nearby. "Can you ride? It would not be wise to linger in this place after dark."

Calain started to get up, frowned, and sat hard again. "No, no . . ." She dismally admitted.

Selene clicked her teeth impatiently. "Then you will ride with me and Zelda will take your horse." She looked at Zelda. "Do you agree, my lady?"

Zelda was looking anxiously at Calain. She had never ridden without her before, and with Calain so weak, she did not want her far away. It was with great difficulty that she agreed, knowing that she would not be strong enough to hold Calain up in the saddle.

When Zelda gave a miserable nod, Selene readily swept Calain into her arms, and with effortless ease, sat her on Apple's back. She climbed up in the saddle behind Calain, taking the reins in one hand and wrapping her free arm about Calain, who was dazed and teetering.

Zelda climbed up on Arthur's back, and then they were off, putting as much space between themselves and the haunted hollow as possible.

Zelda couldn't stop watching Calain and Selene. She had never seen them so close together. Now their muscular bodies were moving against each other in the saddle, powerful and flexing, even in their armor, and she couldn't stop thinking of how they would look holding each other while naked, their wild hair tangled around them in the sheets.

They traveled the night through, encountering nothing but the occasional pack of black wolves, who fled before Zelda's magick. At the crest of a hill, they came to a cave that had been laid over with decorative stone at the entrance. The passage was just large enough for them to walk the horses down, even while mounted. A cold wind whistled from it, faint and mysterious.

Zelda and Selene dismounted, leaving Calain in the saddle as they led the horses toward the cave with slow apprehension.

"It looks elven," said Selene.

Zelda lifted her brows but tried not to look too impressed: Calain seemed annoyed by the fact that Selene could identify elven writing.

And truth be told, Zelda *was* impressed. Not many beyond sorceresses could interpret elvish. Even Wick, who was elven herself, had struggled with it in school. It was likely that the Knights of Falcon had been taught to read it, but as with everything that wasn't swordplay or riding, Calain had likely neglected those studies.

"It says it is a passage north," said Zelda after a moment of reading the curly letters upon the stone.

"It could be safer than the forest," said Selene. "It might even bring us to Arinol faster."

"Tell me we aren't going in there," moaned Calain from Apple's saddle. "There could be traps or trolls. Old elven ruins are dangerous."

Selene looked at Zelda. "What say you, my lady?"

Zelda knew Calain would be resent her for agreeing with Selene – yet again – but she answered, "We shall take the ancient passage."

Calain groaned but made no other protest as they passed inside the tunnel.

When they had stepped into the darkness, Zelda conjured light to her stave. They waited as a gust of startled bats swept by them, and then they started forward.

The tunnel angled down, taking them deeper and deeper underground. Zelda could almost feel the weight of the earth above them, pressing down on the ancient stones that lined the ceiling above their heads. The horses were unsettled by it as well. Zelda heard Arthur grumble in complaint that Calain was right (they should have stayed on the surface), while Apple occasionally said she didn't like it, it was too dark and cold.

Eventually, the ground evened out again, and they were passing through not a dark tunnel but a series of rooms connected by open archways. Zelda's stave was the only light, and so the group remained close to her as her crystal's sphere penetrated the pitch black, illuminating stone chairs gilded in gold, tables, statues, fountains crested in rubies.

"How has this place not been picked clean by thieves?" Calain said in awe.

"Because even the greediest thief wouldn't come down here," said Selene with a snort. "The passages are dark and go very deep. Torches, rations, camping gear . . . A thief would be too poor to afford the amount of supplies it would take to live long enough to steal something."

"What about thieves who were hired by rich lords?" Calain pointed out. "Elven merchants and the like."

Selene pointed to a place on the floor where the light of Zelda's stave was shining: bones. A skeleton was sitting there alongside a sack of jewels, flesh picked clean by rats. The skeleton's leg was broken.

"Even with the right amount of gold, a thief's got to be clever," Selene said.

"And in good health," said Calain with a snort. "I've taken many falls. Never broken a bone."

Zelda found herself intrigued by the rooms they passed through. So much beautiful old furniture, treasure, vases bursting with glowing flowers that had been enchanted to last forever.

A plaque on the wall had deemed the place Cariel's Cross, a rest stop for weary travelers as they passed through the forest. There were even rooms with beds, stone slabs that had been gilded with gold, their pillows and sheets long since having rotted away.

They passed through the ancient rest stop for days, following the signs on the walls that led them north, as apparently, the rest stop had passages that also led south, east, and west. They encountered no dangers aside from a goblin that had made it deep within and ran, screaming and gibbering, at the sight of them. After the goblin, they found the remains of a very large troll, and Calain theorized that the troll had broken the thief's leg.

Sometimes they stopped to sleep in the rooms, on the hard stone beds. Selene would feed the horses grain from her bag while insisting Calain not take watch at all, instead taking turns with Zelda as Calain rested.

Once as Calain slept nearby on a stone bed, Zelda and Selene sat opposite each other in stone chairs. It was Selene's turn to keep watch, but Zelda couldn't sleep. She had leaned her glowing stave against the wall, and it was by the stave's light that she could see Selene's worried face. Selene was staring sadly at Calain and slightly frowning.

"I let her come to harm," Selene explained when Zelda gave her a questioning look.

"Don't be absurd," said Zelda at once, amazed.

Selene only shook her head. "I knew she was reckless, that she would leap past me, but I was too slow to stop her."

"Calain is responsible for her own actions, foolish as they are," said Zelda, looking fondly at Calain's sleeping face.

"And yet I feel responsible for her," Selene said with a sigh. She shook her head and smiled sadly. "I have known her since I was but five years old, a babe at the island like all the others. I had come from a noble family who had been disgraced. Treason against the queen."

Zelda gasped. She had never heard that, though it wasn't uncommon for Falcon Knights to come from questionable backgrounds.

"Aye," said Selene, acknowledging Zelda's shock. "My father and mother disagreed with the queen's politics. They disagreed so greatly, in fact, they were executed."

Zelda put a hand to her mouth. "Oh, Selene, I'm so sorry."

Selene smiled wryly. "I think they'd approve of my siding with the one who killed her. Queen Ellanara was a foul person *and* a foul ruler. A nasty combination." Her eyes went to Calain's sleeping form again and softened. "So there I was, dumped at Falcon Isle by a grandmother who didn't want me, and all the other girls wanted me even less. No one was interested in my friendship . . . except Calain." Selene laughed softly. "I don't think she had the sense to shun me, the fool."

Zelda had been staring fondly at Selene as she listened. Now she looked over at Calain, trying to imagine her at five years old, perhaps with her wild red hair in braids, running about covered in mud.

"You seem close," Zelda agreed. She laughed. "Even if you *do* constantly bicker."

"We are like two small children fighting over a wooden horse," Selene apologized.

Zelda laughed. "So I'm the horse this time, am I?"

"You are many things another would desire," Selene said. She was looking at Zelda with the serious fire in her eye again, and Zelda quivered under her gown.

Without warning, Selene reached over, grabbed Zelda's chair, and dragged her close, as if she and the heavy stone chair weighed less than a feather! Zelda's heart was pumping fast as she was brought close to the knight, who took Zelda by the hips and lifted her onto her lap, so that Zelda straddled her.

Selene took off her gauntlets, and looking with soft admiration at Zelda's face, she touched her cheek. Zelda hugged Selene with her thighs, slipped her arms around Selene's neck, and felt small and delicate, as if the bigger woman's armored body devoured her with its strength and girth. She was still thinking of the ease with which Selene had pulled her near in the chair and was looking in Selene's face in an almost childlike wonder when Selene spoke again.

"You are the fairest maiden I have ever laid eyes on," she said. "If only I were Bound to you."

"I wonder if I could have two knights Bound to me," Zelda said, thinking of Melvalda, who Bound all the witches of Raven's Cross to her.

Selene laughed softly, a deep and pleasant sound. "Calain would never forgive us. The Binding is like a marriage, and Calain holds you very dear."

Zelda's heart fluttered to hear those words. She wondered what Calain was saying of her to Selene when she could not hear.

"Ignore my griping," Selene apologized. "It is enough that you permit me to follow where you go. I will always protect you, my lady." Selene stared hard at Zelda, a promise in her eye, and Zelda quivered again, wishing for Selene's hands upon her. She tightened her arms around Selene's neck and kissed her sweetly on the lips.

Selene trembled with desire. Her sudden kisses trailed down Zelda's neck, and then she was bending Zelda slowly backward. Perplexed, Zelda allowed Selene to lay her head and shoulders on the chair she had vacated only moments before. Then Selene's hands pushed up Zelda's skirts, smoothed hot up Zelda's thighs, and slipped off her panties. She stared all the while at Zelda with a hard sort of thirst in her eye, and Zelda's heart skipped a beat when she realized what was about to happen.

Selene took Zelda's hips in her strong hands and lifted them, drawing Zelda's sex to her hungry mouth. Zelda gasped when she felt Selene's hot tongue glide gently inside her. As she was pleasured with slow, loving licks and sucks, she melted into the chair, but her heart was beating faster and faster, and she was afraid Calain would feel it and awake.

Zelda looked over, and to her horror, Calain was indeed awake. But she was merely lying there, eyes devoid of anger, watching with quiet hunger as Selene's head moved slowly between Zelda's thighs.

Zelda had the odd feeling that, because they were Bound, Calain could feel Zelda's pleasure as her own. Still looking Calain in the eye, Zelda unlaced the front of her dress, allowing her high breasts to push free of the fabric. Selene immediately massaged her breasts and thumbed the pink nipples. Zelda's body flushed with pleasure, and she saw Calain's eyes hood, as if she were feeling it, too.

Always one to take her time, Selene slowly massaged Zelda's breasts and sucked gently on the throbbing clitoris just above the lips of her sex, until she shuddered and gasped to a climax. She looked in Calain's eye as the pleasure thrilled through her and saw Calain was silently gasping and shuddering as well.

Chapter 8

As they continued through Cariel's Cross, Calain grew stronger and eventually recovered enough that she could walk on her own and no longer needed to ride one of the horses. Zelda was glad to see her in good health again but a little irritated that Calain had tried to conceal what was happening to her each time Selene pleasured Zelda. She could probably feel echoes of Zelda's pleasure, however faint, and knowing just how good Selene could make Zelda feel was probably driving her mad.

Zelda was starting to warm to the idea of Binding Selene to her more and more. If she did, then both knights would feel echoes of her pleasure and perhaps Calain would feel less bitter and jealous if she knew Selene was feeling *her* skill in bed. But Zelda knew Calain would never agree to it, and not wanting to upset Calain in her fragile condition as she recovered, Zelda did not bring it up.

Their last night in Cariel's Cross, Calain sat watch as Selene slept on one of the stone beds, and Zelda sat up with her. They sat in silence for a long time, side by side, in stone chairs. Zelda kept thinking of how easily Selene had pulled her near in such a heavy chair and asked Calain how it was possible.

"Well," said Calain, "we are no ordinary knights, my lady. As we train, we are infused with a magick elixir that makes us three times stronger than the average man."

"And twice as large as the average woman," said Zelda, glancing in appreciation at Calain's muscular frame. The red knight must have been six feet tall.

Calain smiled at Zelda's lusting. "Aye," she said, playfully flexing her big arm.

Zelda giggled, feeling like a silly schoolgirl all over again. She suddenly wished Calain wasn't always in her armor. She missed running her hands over the woman's hard muscles, seeing them flex when she moved, as she had seen back at the inn, when Calain was in her smallclothes.

They fell into a content silence. Zelda's eyes fell on Selene, who was dozing gently on her back, and Calain looked at Selene as well.

"I know you saw me the other night, my lady," Calain said with shame.

"But you liked it, didn't you?" Zelda said. "At least you haven't attacked Selene over it. Unless you were saving that for whenever we return to the surface."

Calain laughed. "Tis you I should vent my rage upon – here, you naughty woman!" she cried playfully, and Zelda squealed when, without warning, Calain flipped her over her lap and pulled up her skirt.

Zelda's panties were roughly yanked down, and Calain's hand smacked her backside. The slap was playful and didn't hurt at all, but it was just hard enough to make Zelda's buttocks jiggle. She squealed with laughter and bucked. Calain was laughing as well. She reached under, and after groping blindly, she yanked Zelda's laces loose, so that her breasts hung free, jiggling wildly every time a series of slaps came.

Calain groped one of Zelda's swinging breasts, and then the spanking because less playful and more erotic. Calain's knee impatiently knocked Zelda's thighs wider apart, further exposing her sex, and then her sex was spanked until it was hotter and wetter, until it was swollen with arousal and splashing with moisture from each soft slap.

Zelda could not contain her moans. She froze when she saw Selene stir and open her eyes. Selene looked right at Zelda, and Zelda blushed to her hairline, knowing how she must have looked to her: slung over Calain's lap with her breasts hanging and her exposed backside red and punished, her panties hanging off one dainty ankle.

Selene slowly sat up. "What the devil?" she said, though she seemed amused.

Calain's hand rubbed soothingly over Zelda's cheek, which was still red and raw from the spanking. "Join me, sister, in punishing this naughty wench!"

Zelda laughed. "How dare you!" she said in mock indignation.

Without hesitating, Selene sat in a chair beside Calain, so that Zelda's cheek was gently placed on her thigh as she lay across both their laps. Then without warning, Calain flipped Zelda onto her back, and she squealed in soft surprise, now laying on her back across their laps, looking up at them, her breasts standing, heaving with her breathless laughter. But the laughter quieted in her throat: they were both looking down at her as if they would devour her.

Selene cupped one of Zelda's breasts and massaged it, slowly smoothing her fingers to the nipple and down again, caressing the softness in her hand. With each stroke, Zelda flushed brighter from the pleasure. And then she felt Calain's strong fingers slide in her sex and curl, and she frowned, her pink lips parting in a gasp.

As the knights fondled her to a slow climax in their laps, their narrowed eyes never left her face, taking in every gasp, frown, blush, and sigh and becoming more aroused themselves. They were as breathless as she was by the time she had blushed and shuddered, her moisture spilling over Calain's fingers in delicious release.

THE NORTHERN EXIT FROM Cariel's Cross brought them to the edge of the dark forest. The earth sloped down away from the trees to a field, beyond which was the road leading to Arinol.

"At last," breathed Calain, who was sitting on Arthur behind Zelda.

Selene was beside them, sitting on Apple. They were at the edge of the trees, looking down at the road, and it was morning, though cloudy and cold. Zelda shivered in her gray cloak, and when Calain wrapped it tighter about her, she smiled.

"Come," said Selene, whose dark eyes were scanning the field below for foes. One hand was on her sword hilt, but seeing the way was clear, she spurred Apple down the hill.

Calain clucked her tongue and bid Arthur follow with a slap of the reins.

"But why Arinol?" Calain asked as the horses carried them side by side up the road.

Selene gave Calain a side glance as if she should have known. "Arinol is on the coast," she said. "We will book passage on a ship and leave the realm. Eriallon is no longer safe for you and Zelda."

"And you," Zelda said sadly.

"Yes," said Selene quietly. "And I."

Zelda looked at Selene in sympathy as she realized all the woman had given up to help them. She could never return to Eriallon. The quiet, easy life she could have had with Wick would never come to pass, and instead, she would spend her life running, fighting, and sleeping on the ground. Zelda felt in some way as if she had destroyed Selene's life, despite the fact that she hadn't exactly asked for her help.

Calain must've been feeling guilty as well, for she was quiet for some time as they rode. Then she said unhappily, "I hope Gwen and Cass made it here."

"I'm sure they have," said Selene by way of comfort.

Arinol was a small, snowy fishing village on the east coast. Many ships came and went at its port, which meant the inn was often crowded and they knew they would find no vacancies there. Instead, Selene announced that they would find Gweneth and Cassandra and leave immediately.

As it turned out, however, they did not need to go looking. Zelda, Calain, and Selene rode into snowy little Arinol to find Gweneth and Cassandra fighting in the streets. They were outnumbered three-to-one by knights of the Rose Guard and were fighting desperately.

"Stay clear, my lady," said Calain. "They will have a Bane Stone!" And without waiting for Zelda to respond, Calain sprang from her horse and into the fray.

Now it was four against ten. Calain and Selene were as amazing as ever, but Zelda had to admit Cassandra and Gweneth were impressive in their own right. Brown-haired Cassandra was small and fast, often too fast for the lumbering Rose Guard knights, who swung at her in frustration and often missed – while Cassandra was graceful and patient. She moved as if she were in a dance and fought with none of Calain's wild passion or Selene's precision.

When the fighting had stopped, the bodies of the Rose Guard knights littered the streets in their golden armor. Villagers crept into the sunlight, wrapped in cloaks against the cold, staring with open mouths.

Gweneth alone had lost her feet. She lay on her back in the snow, moaning in pain but mostly unharmed. Selene clapped a hand on her forearm and pulled her roughly up.

"What took you so long?" Gweneth complained, but she pulled both Selene and Calain into a rough, one-armed hug each.

Zelda slid off Arthur's back and drew near. When Gweneth and Cassandra both saw her, they bowed and murmured, "My lady . . ." Cassandra was quite solemn, but Gweneth gave Zelda a playful wink as she straightened up.

Cassandra drew near, leading two horses. One was white with brown splotches and the other was a tawny gold. She gave the reins of both to Gweneth.

"What are you doing?" said Gweneth suspiciously.

Sensing something amiss, Calain and Selene also looked intently at Cassandra.

"More of the Rose Guard will be here soon," Cassandra said grimly. "If you are to have any chance of escape, one of us must stay behind. They will overwhelm you before you reach the boat otherwise."

"Don't be absurd," said Calain. "You're coming with us—" She fell silent and angrily bit her lip when Selene grabbed her arm.

"You will meet us in Priine," Selene said, looking Cassandra hard in the eye.

Cassandra solemnly nodded.

Gweneth, like Calain, was looking as if she wanted to protest. But she heaved an angry breath instead and turned her eyes with effort from Cassandra to Selene.

"I'll take you to the ship we booked passage on," Gweneth said.

Selene nodded. "Hurry."

Zelda didn't like the idea of leaving Cassandra behind either, but she also knew that if they all died there in Arinol, everything would have been for naught: the slaying of the queen, surviving Raven's Cross, even Calain's near miss with the spirit in the hollow.

They boarded a sturdy little vessel called the *Atross,* and as it pulled away into the sea, they could see Cassandra alone, fighting against a fresh tide of Rose Guard knights. They had come storming into the village, just as she'd said, and if she hadn't been there to block them, they would have board the ship, for the ship was still near enough for them to hop from the pier and onto the deck.

Cassandra was one against many but held her own. Eventually, she was fighting so hard that her pale blonde hair had come loose of its braid and was tossing about her in streams as she dodged and spun.

They watched Cassandra fight until she and her enemies were a blur of color on the wharf, and they could watch no more.

Selene turned her back. "She is a skilled fighter and a Knight of the Falcon," she said to Calain and Gweneth, who were looking anxious. "She will survive and return to us."

"I'd feel better if you had the Sight," returned Gweneth. It was meant to be a joke, but she looked angry enough to pounce Selene. "How could you leave her behind?"

Selene's dark eyes were sad. She kept walking, guiding the four horses away.

"Well?!" Gweneth shouted at her back. "Oh, mighty leader?!"

Selene's back stiffened with hurt but she did not answer and continued walking.

Gweneth looked as if she would lunge after Selene, but Calain put a heavy hand on her shoulder and murmured something. Gweneth calmed herself but snatched her shoulder free and stalked away below deck.

"Will she be all right?" Zelda asked anxiously.

"Gwen or Cass?" said Calain unhappily. She turned away with a sigh. "I shall help Selene with the steeds. Get some rest, my lady." She gave Zelda's cheek an affectionate touch, and then she was gone after Selene.

Zelda glanced around, remembering for the first time that she was on a ship. All around her, men were stomping back and forth, eying her up and down lustily, smiling in ways she did not like. Sailors who had probably not seen a woman naked in weeks. Zelda wanted to be away from them, for their staring and smiling made her skin crawl.

Turning to the stairs, Zelda went below deck and moved up the gloomy hall, looking for an empty cabin. She passed a few rooms where the sailors were playing cards around a barrel, rooms where they were smoking or lying in hammocks strumming lutes.

At last, Zelda came to a room that appeared empty. The door was ajar to reveal two bunk beds and in-between them on a nightstand was a washbasin.

Suddenly keenly aware of the filth on her body after the long trek through Cariel's Cross, Zelda hurried into the room, closing the door behind her. She dropped her satchel on the floor and immediately began to undress, letting her panties, then her slip, then her gown fall to the floor. She scooped water from the basin into her small hands and began washing herself: her breasts, her arms, her buttocks. She leaned down with swinging breasts to clean her small feet, then smoothed more water over her pubic hair. She was fondling her sex clean when she heard a moan and looked up, freezing where she stood.

Gweneth was sitting on a stool in the corner, frozen in the act of lighting a pipe. She and the stool had been behind the door when it was open, but Zelda had closed it and had unwittingly proceeded to undress before her.

Zelda colored up to her hairline and quickly covered her breasts.

Gweneth shot up from the stool. "My lady . . . My sincerest apologies . . ."

"Why didn't you tell me you were there?" Zelda moaned.

"So stricken was I by your beauty . . ." Gweneth said, unabashed, and winked. She started to go, but Zelda said with resignation, "No, don't go. I'd rather not be alone on a ship full of men anyway."

And Gweneth was her knight now, Zelda thought. They would be traveling together. It was only a matter of time before she had seen Zelda naked.

Gweneth picked up her pipe from the floor and instead of lighting it, she shoved it in her satchel and sat on one of the lower bunks. She continued to watch Zelda with a sort of absent fascination as she went back to bathing.

"Calain and Sel are fucking you, aren't they?" Gweneth said, so that Zelda paused in shock and stared at her.

Zelda's large blue eyes blinked. She held down a blush and went back to bathing. "W-Why do you say that?" she asked, trying to sound nonchalant.

Gweneth smirked. "Well, it wasn't a secret Calain was, but Selene was a virgin last I saw her. Now she looks as if she knows what's under your gown. Am I wrong?"

Gweneth was sitting with her knees spread boyishly, her elbows on them, leaning forward as she smirked at Zelda. She looked mischievous, as if she had found a delicious bit of entertainment. She liked seeing Zelda stammering and awkward. She thought it was funny!

Zelda took a breath and calmed herself down, determined not to be provoked. She didn't know why, but Gweneth made her feel like a tongue-tied little girl.

"Why do you want to know?" Zelda asked coolly. "Do you fancy yourself as lucky?"

Gweneth lifted her brows. "Hmm. More woman than shy little girl, then. So Calian has made a woman out of you." She still looked amused, and Zelda hated it.

"What do you mean?" Zelda demanded.

Gweneth smirked again. "I remember how you were at the feast. You were blushing and coy, always giggling like mad whenever Calain vaguely breathed in your direction. It was rather cute, if not annoying."

Zelda glared. Who did this Gweneth think she was, speaking to a sorceress like this?! She curtly lifted her chin and turned her back – and squealed when Gweneth grabbed her by the hips and snatched her onto her lap.

Blushing, Zelda caught her breasts to stop them jiggling. "What are you doing?" she demanded.

Gweneth had taken off her gauntlets and tossed them aside. Now she stroked Zelda's long golden hair. The laughter was gone from her blue eyes, which were instead now doting and soft. Zelda felt her angry heart slowing as she looked into Gweneth's eyes.

"Do Calain and Sel toy with the lady?" Gweneth asked.

Zelda blinked. "Toy with me?"

Gweneth seemed amused by her ignorance. "You are innocent yet, then. *Toys.* A leather phallus. A strap."

Zelda's eyes grew round in bafflement.

Gweneth reached over, unbuckling her satchel and drawing out a belt, which she let hang from the bag. "Take my belt," she calmly ordered.

Zelda hesitated in annoyance. It was she who ordered the knights around and saying so was on the tip of her tongue. But she was curious what Gweneth would do. When she looked up, it was to find Gweneth watching her silent struggle in amusement. Suddenly defiant, Zelda's lips tightened, and she ripped the belt from the satchel.

Gweneth chuckled, taking the belt from Zelda. "Very good, my lady. Now stand with your shoulder toward me . . . Doesn't matter which one . . . That's right . . ."

Still curious, Zelda followed Gweneth's instructions. She watched in utter confusion as Gweneth ran the length of the leather belt between her thighs, then she started rubbing the smooth leather against her sex. Slowly . . . forward and back . . . forward and back . . . Zelda gasped as her sex was caressed toward slow arousal with the belt.

Gweneth picked up speed, feeding the belt faster and faster between Zelda's thighs, until her hips were following it. She found herself thrusting her hips forward with the belt, so desperate was she to keep feeling its caress, as Gweneth watched her curvy body twisting with narrowed eyes.

Gweneth didn't slow down. She brought the belt higher and higher with every stroke, until Zelda could feel it lightly brushing her throbbing clitoris.

"No, no, too intense!" Zelda begged. She thought she would faint.

Gweneth immediately took the belt away and drew Zelda down on the bed. Zelda lay on her back, her sex pulsing with pleasure, her breasts heaving as she sought to catch her breath. She could hear Gweneth moving around the room, and a second later, she was hovering over Zelda on her elbow, showing Zelda something long and phallic-shaped.

"What is that?" cried Zelda, for it looked like a black banana.

"Tis a leather phallus," said Gweneth. "It won't break your maiden head . . ." She drifted off, and Zelda blushed when she felt Gweneth's fingers briefly glide inside her. "Hmm. You still have it. So Calain and Sel were gentle lovers after all," she teased.

"S-Shut up," said Zelda, blushing to her hairline. "Put it . . . Put it inside me."

"You may not like penetration," Gweneth warned her. "Not every woman likes the sensation."

"Do it," Zelda said, "but remove your armor."

Gweneth smirked but obeyed, allowing her armor to fall away one piece at a time. "Shall I use the harness, my lady?"

"Harness?"

Gweneth pulled a leather harness from her satchel, and Zelda watched as she strapped it around her pelvis, then she screwed the leather phallus in place, so that it looked as if she had a leather erection. Zelda blushed prettily as she realized what the contraption was for.

"You bed many a lady with this, I take it?" Zelda teased.

Zelda did not like it when Gweneth seemed unfazed by the question. It seemed impossible to truly embarrass or shame her, and Zelda still felt bitter about her earlier taunting.

Without acknowledging Zelda's teasing, Gweneth gently guided Zelda into facing away from her on hands and knees. Zelda waited, feeling foolish as she pointed her bare backside at Gweneth. For several seconds, nothing happened, and she realized Gweneth was simply looking at her. She blushed, imagining the knight's lusty eyes upon her – and then her blue eyes fluttered wide in a gasp as she felt the leather phallus slowly plunge between the lips of her sex.

Gweneth knocked Zelda's thighs wider apart with her knee and guided her into pointing her backside by placing a firm hand on the small of her back. Then she began to thrust, deep and slow, every plunge of the leather phallus careful not to harm her as it sank through her moisture.

Zelda rocked slowly on her knees, her breasts swinging gently, as Gweneth moved against her. She closed her eyes and frowned, gasping with pleasure.

Gweneth leaned down and hugged Zelda from behind, consuming her in the hard, muscly wall of her strong arms. Trapped in the bigger woman's grasp, Zelda felt overwhelmed by Gweneth's powerful body, and it thrilled her, feeling the woman's muscles heaving as they rocked together on the bed.

To Zelda's surprise, Gweneth kissed her cheek, then her neck, and grunted, "Tis hard to get it in . . . Your sex is wet but still so tight, my lady . . . Does it hurt?"

"No! Don't stop!" Zelda begged. "By the gods, don't stop . . ."

Gweneth hunched her back and plunged the leather phallus deeper, so that it curled inside Zelda and she gasped in delight.

Zelda noticed Gweneth was breathless and grunting more, her thrusts becoming almost frantic: she was close to climaxing. So was Zelda. Her body pulsed with pleasure when Gweneth grabbed one of her heavy breasts in a frantic fistful and fingered her throbbing clitoris. As soon as her clitoris was touched, Zelda shuddered and felt her sex gushing over the leather phallus in sudden release. She almost screamed out, but Gweneth covered her mouth, and her desperate cries of delight were muffled behind Gweneth's hand as her cheeks flamed red.

BY SOME MIRACLE, CALAIN and Selene never suspected Zelda and Gweneth of having slept together. Zelda wondered how that was possible: if Calain could feel echoes of her pleasure, then she should have known what Zelda had done. Instead, she seemed to believe Zelda was pleasuring herself at night, while Selene was worried about Cassandra and suspected nothing at all.

And so, a week passed aboard the *Atross,* and Zelda, guilty as she felt, continued sleeping with all three women while struggling to keep Calain and Selene oblivious. She intended to tell them eventually, but if they found out and started fighting on the ship, it could end badly. She could just see one of them falling overboard in a fistfight, and she did not want to make a spectacle of herself in front of the sailors, who made enough mocking, nasty comments as it was.

As the days went by, Zelda started to fancy herself quite clever and in complete control of her knights. Then the night came when she overheard them at a game of cards. They were in the cabin the four of them shared, and Zelda had been about to enter when she heard them talking and lingered outside the door instead.

"You used a strap, you say?" Calain was saying. "And she liked it?"

"Sighed and wiggled her little hips like mad," answered Gweneth.

Zelda stifled a gasp behind her hand.

"I would have liked to see that," said Selene with interest.

"And the leather phallus," prompted Calain. "You say she likes it as well?"

"Mmm," answered Gweneth. "The first time she clenched up. I think she was worried it would hurt. The last few times I thrust pretty deeply. She was gushing."

Zelda blushed furiously.

"I wish to make her wet like that," said Calain with longing.

"Tis not so much the penetration," Gweneth explained. "What the lady enjoyed was being held, feeling my strength. She became so wet when I held her in my arms. Screamed so loud I had to cover her mouth."

"That makes sense," said Calain thoughtfully. "Selene and I have mostly worn our armor."

"We did not at the inn," said Selene. "She liked that."

"I bet she did," teased Gweneth. There was a papery slap as she laid down a card. "I win."

A groan from Calain and Selene. More papery shuffling as new cards were dealt.

"I want to use the leather phallus on her," said Calain. "You must teach me how, Gwen. Since you told me of how hard she gushed in your arms, I have thought of little else. I want to grope her tits, and feeling her shuddering under me as she releases her passion."

Zelda blushed to her hairline. At first, she wanted to be angry that they had known about her tryst with Gweneth and had pretended not to, but after hearing them talk so seriously about trying to please her, she didn't know how to be angry anymore. Calain seemed very eager to learn to make Zelda feel good, and Selene sounded like she just wanted to watch. And the way Calain was drilling Gweneth, it sounded as if Gweneth was every bit as experienced as she had guessed.

"I can give you instruction," said Gweneth, "so that you do not do her any unintentional harm. Penetration can be tricky to master."

"Make certain she is moist before I put it inside," said Calain. "You have told me that much."

"Three fives," said Selene.

"Impossible," challenged Gweneth.

Papery slapping as cards were laid down.

"Fine," muttered Gweneth bitterly. "So what shall we do in Priine?"

"Wait for Cass," said Calain at once, almost indignantly.

"I was talking to our fearless leader," Gweneth sneered.

"Don't start," begged Calain in a low voice. "Cease your anger. Selene is doing her best."

"Since when do *you* of all people take Selene's side in a quarrel?" Gweneth demanded in amazement, but she laughed. "I suppose the two of you have bonded while sucking Zelda's tits together."

Embarrassed silence from Calain.

"We will do in Priine whatever our lady commands us," said Selene firmly.

Gweneth snorted. "By the gods, has she got you whipped."

"And she shall whip you as well, if it pleases her," said Calain. "We are her knights, Gwen."

"Maybe you are," Gweneth said, "but I am not in love with her. I am not her devoted slave. I just want to fuck her until she does that cute little squeal."

Listening outside the door, Zelda scowled and folded her arms. It wasn't so much that she wanted to dominate and control the knights. It was the fact that Gweneth didn't seem to care for her and insisted on speaking of her as an emotionless lay. And yet, the last time they were together, Gweneth had rubbed her back and kissed her head as they cuddled in bed.

"I want her to sit on my face," said Selene, starling Zelda from her reverie.

Zelda's mouth fell open. Selene had said the words quite casually, as if she had remarked about liking garlic bread.

"I saw a woman do that once," Selene went on. "It was that time our year took a trip through Anderoc."

"Ah yeah," said Gweneth, fondly remembering. "That flower girl with the big tits. What was her name?"

"Sherry," Selene supplied.

"Right. Big tits, little waist like that," went on Gweneth fondly. "Squealed when you squeezed her. She liked a good squeeze."

"Tell me you didn't," growled Selene. "I *fancied* her and you—!"

"Sel!" laughed Gweneth incredulously. "*Everyone* fucked Sherry! Girl would spread her legs if you glanced at her twice—"

The scrape of a chair.

"Sel, sit down!" Calain begged.

"You shut your filth mouth about Sherry!" Selene yelled.

"Let go of me!" Gweneth snarled. "Let go, or I swear by the gods—!"

Chairs scraping again. Clothes rustling as they sat down. Gweneth sounded out of breath.

"You're mad, the pair of you," said Gweneth in amazement. "You almost gave me a black eye over Zelda, even though you let Sel here fuck her seven times, and now Sel nearly kills me over a girl she saw riding a woman's face in the bloody street!"

Calain and Selene were guiltily silent.

"Mad, the pair of you!" Gweneth went on. "This is why I shall never fall in love."

Selene laughed flatly. "You won't have a choice. Tis a feeling, not an act."

"Tis both," said Calain quietly. "That's what neither of you understand."

"All I know is, you grab my throat like that again, and I'll thrash you, Sel," said Gweneth bitterly. "I don't care if you've got a hundred pounds on me."

"Do you never stop to consider that perchance you are wrong?" said Selene wearily. "That it was *wrong* to seduce Zelda? That it was *wrong* to – *touch* – Sherry?"

"Look who's talking," said Gweneth. "Did Calain not put a boot up your ass when she caught you kissing Zelda? As if Zelda was just a chair who stood there and was acted upon! That's what's wrong with you two. You don't hold your women responsible. Sherry fucked me because she wanted to! Zelda sat on my leather phallus because she wanted to—!"

Zelda blushed miserably.

"—and she let Selene eat her for supper because she wanted her to!"

Silence. Angry breathing from Gweneth. The rustle of cards shuffling.

After a while, Calain cleared her throat and asked tentatively, "How was it? When she sat upon your phallus?"

"Mmm. I loved watching her little sex clenching on it," Gweneth answered. "And the way her tits bounced when she rode."

Silence as the three of them fantasized, and Zelda blushed hotly.

"Shite. Now I'm beside myself," Calain said.

Selene laughed. And it was so rare to hear Selene laughing heartily like that, that Zelda couldn't believe it. She realized in that moment how much Selene had missed being with her friends.

"Then let us speak of something else," said Gweneth. "Like what we shall do in Priine, for instance. After Cassandra returns to us. We need to have a plan. We cannot leave it up to the sorceress. She has never been away from Vira'Toss before only recently, while we have been beyond Eriallon."

"True enough," agreed Calain.

"There is a place to the west of Priine where we can hide," said Selene thoughtfully.

"Surely you don't mean Veracru," said Calain dismissively. "Tis but a small farming community. If we draw the Rose Guard there, many innocents will perish."

"No," said Selene irritably. "I mean the old knight academy."

"Ah. Wolf Fortress," said Gweneth. "The place would still have enchantments upon it."

"And if Cass misses us at Priine," Selene added, "she will know to venture there."

"But so will the Rose Guard," Gweneth said grimly.

"That is a chance we will have to take," said Selene. "Better a fight at the old fortress than in a city. No civilians would be harmed. And the old fortress still has protection enchantments, which Zelda could strengthen. She is very powerful."

"I know. She's got you both under her spell," muttered Gweneth.

"And she hasn't enchanted you?" said Calain, amused.

"She will *never* enchant me," vowed Gweneth, laughing.

FOR SOME REASON, ZELDA took Gweneth's refusal to submit as a challenge. As far as she was concerned, the three women *were* her knights, and Gweneth needed to get in line or get left behind.

The first step was to simply stop having sex with Gweneth. When Gweneth came to her at night and rubbed her back, she ignored it. When Gweneth hinted of using her leather phallus or pleasuring Zelda with the strap, she ignored it. Instead, Zelda would sit in Calain's lap and kiss her passionately as Gweneth bitterly pretended not to watch, or she would sit in Selene's lap as Selene fingered her while Gweneth was in the room, pretending not to notice.

Calain and Selene were rewarded for obedience, while Gweneth was driven to madness and irritation with the hell of unsated lust. As far as Zelda was concerned, she was an unruly steed who, like Calain, needed to be brought under control.

But Gweneth refused to be broken in. She stopped propositioning Zelda for sex, and stopped allowing herself to become a captive witness should Zelda initiate sex with one of the other two. So Zelda upped the stakes: she rode Gweneth's leather phallus while Calain was wearing it.

Gweneth walked in the cabin one day to find Calain lying on her back on one of the lower bunk beds as Zelda sat facing her on the leather phallus. Zelda was leaning back on her hands and sliding herself up and down on the phallus with her hips, while Calain watched with narrowed eyes, thumbing and caressing Zelda's throbbing clitoris. Zelda's cheeks were flaming and her brows frowning as she gasped softly in ecstasy, her breasts flapping as she brought herself up and down. Calain, suddenly beside herself, took Zelda by the waist and lifted her easily, bringing her up and down, muscular arms flexing, so that Zelda frowned all the harder, her head fell back, and she released her passion.

Calain moaned as well, and with their passion spent, Calain sat up and gathered Zelda in her arms, showering her with lazy kisses. Zelda rested her head against Calain and happily closed her eyes under the affection. But they both looked up when they heard a thump.

Gweneth had fallen to her knees. She was trembling. She bowed her head and knelt there, shaking.

Selene had come in and closed the door behind her. Her face was flushed from having watched Zelda and Calain make love, but now her eyes were on Gweneth, who was still shuddering on the floor.

"Well, Gweneth?" said Zelda softly. "Shall you submit? How long can you outlast your own craving?"

Calain held Zelda in her arms, quietly looking down at Gweneth. Zelda thought her green eyes were pitying.

Selene also seemed to pity Gweneth. She knelt beside her and touched her hair.

Gweneth lifted her head. Her face was flushed, her eyes aching when they looked at Zelda.

"I . . . I submit," Gweneth gasped. "Sorceress . . . I am yours."

Zelda turned in Calain's lap, leaned her back against Calain's chest, and slowly spread her thighs. She saw the eyes of Gweneth and Selene both light with hunger when they fell on her sex.

"Come to me, then," Zelda whispered, "my knights."

Eyes fixed on Zelda's sex, Gweneth and Selene crawled across the floor to her, and both knights buried their faces between her thighs, sliding their tongues in turn deep inside her sex. Zelda sighed and blindly stroked their heads, as she turned her face to Calain and kissed her, sliding her tongue warm in her mouth. Calain kissed her hungrily back, caressing her heavy breasts in fistfuls, and as the three knights closed in, caressing and kissing her skin, sucking her nipples and her sex, she wondered how delicious it would be when there were four of them.

Handfasting the Warrior Queen

Book 2

Chapter 1

Priine was just a day away. Zelda could see its silhouette in the distance. She thought it pretty already, the round glowing paper lanterns, the streamers. The captain of the ship had let her look through his spyglass, and she had seen the colorful buildings, had listened to him tell her of the great mosaic in the square that formed a ring of color around the fountain.

Now it was night, and she couldn't have seen much, not even with a spyglass. She stood on the dock of the *Atross* beside Calain, her gray cloak and hood draped over her against the cold. Calain was also wrapped in a cloak and hood, and her sword had been buckled at the hip as a result, a fact which she hated.

Together they stood facing Priine, each lost in her own thoughts. Zelda knew her knights meant to venture to Wolf Fortress, but she wondered what would happen to them afterward. Would they always be fugitives living on the run? She didn't look forward to sleeping on the ground the rest of her life, and missed Eriallon. They hadn't even set foot in Realm Koradara yet and already, she missed Eriallon.

"What would you have done, my lady," asked Calain quietly, "if I had not made ill your life?"

"You did nothing of the sort!" Zelda said at once. "You did your duty, Calain. You protected me! Queen Ellanara would have forced herself upon me."

"Would that I had cut her head off," said Calain darkly. "Her kind are used to having whatever they desire on a whim, even people."

There was so much loathing in Calain's voice, Zelda asked a little fearfully, "Is that how you see me?"

"What? Of course not, my lady!"

Zelda cast her eyes down. Was she as bad as Queen Ellanara, controlling the knights with their lust, using them to sate her own? She looked up when Calain gently took her hand. Calain was looking down at her with earnest green eyes, locks of wild red hair reaching from under her hood.

"We knights please you because we *wish* to," said Calain soothingly. "You have forced this enslavement upon none of us," she added with a little smile, "Not even Gweneth, who sought to use you for her base desires without pledging herself to you first."

"I don't understand her," Zelda admitted. "Most knights seek a maiden to devote themselves to, as champion and lover. Why does Gweneth oppose it so?"

"Gweneth was hurt before," Calain answered, frowning sadly. "Since then, she believes love and duty and honor to be foolish, romantic notions. She wants none of it out of fear, not because she doesn't care for you."

"Gweneth cares for me? She has known me so little."

"As have I and Selene. Like us, she is beginning to care, and it frightens her. She does not wish to lose control. But there *is* no control when it comes to love. Only devotion."

Zelda was silent as she meditated on Calain's words. So Gweneth was afraid because she had been hurt. Selene had been afraid of hurting Calain. Was there nothing Calain feared? Zelda looked up at her knight and thought with admiring blue eyes of all the times Calain had charged into battle and decided that, no, there was nothing Calain feared.

"Why that warm look in your eye?" Calain asked playfully. "I sense I shall be kissed. I shall keep still and hope."

Zelda laughed. She rocked up on tiptoe and kissed Calain slowly on the lips. She was pulling away when Calain grabbed her about the waist and kissed her back, hungrily sliding her eager tongue deep in Zelda's mouth. She closed two hard gauntlets over Zelda's backside, and Zelda's moan was smothered by the kiss.

Zelda pulled her mouth away. "Oh, Calain, not here!" she begged as Calain showered her face and neck with kisses. She did not want the sailors to watch them.

Calain let go, giving Zelda one last kiss on the cheek that made her smile. Then she stood behind Zelda and wrapped her in her arms. Zelda let her head fall back against Calain, feeling safe and content in the wall of her strong arms.

"But my lady did not answer my question," said Calain.

"Hmm?" said Zelda, who was too busy feeling drowsy and content in Calain's arms to think. The kisses were still lingering on her skin.

"What would you have done," Calain said, "if not for Queen Ellanara?"

"Most sorceresses go back to their village and become the Wise Woman there. The ones from the city like me would open a shop and sell a trade, like healing or talismans. I'm quite good with potions."

"So you would have opened a potions shop, and I would have lived with you there and guarded you . . ." Calain's voice trailed off as she thought dreamily of that life.

Zelda thought wistfully of it, too. A cozy little shop, and she and Calain would have lived in it together, content and carefree. Now any chance of that life was gone.

Calain kissed Zelda's head and said, "You shall have your potions shop one day, I swear it. Perhaps not in your home city of Perth, but it shall be yours, and Selene and Gweneth and I will guard it with our lives. Cassandra as well, when she returns."

Zelda frowned sadly, her blue eyes staring anxiously at the distant silhouette of Priine. "Tell me truly, Calain," she said, "do you regret the way things shall be? Instead of having me to yourself, you must share me with the others. Does it not bother you?"

"In truth, my lady? I was sad to part from Selene, Gweneth, and Cassandra. They are my sisters in arms, and apart from my father, they are the only family I have ever known. Now because of our devotion to you, we shall stay together always, laughing together, fighting together..." Her gauntlets wandered to Zelda's breasts and squeezed. Zelda closed her eyes and her lips parted in a soft gasp as pleasure flushed through her. "Making love to you together," Calain whispered huskily in her ear. She released Zelda's breasts and hugged her close again. "What more could I ask for?" Calain whispered happily.

Content enough with that answer, Zelda closed her eyes and smiled.

SINCE GWENETH HAD YIELDED and come into the fold, the knights of Falcon Isle were well-behaved for the rest of their voyage to Priine. No one lost their temper and attacked anyone else, and Gweneth, now humbled and a little embarrassed, had stopped teasing and mocking Zelda, though Zelda suspected the change was only temporary.

Gweneth just couldn't seem to help herself when it came to hurting Zelda's feelings. Why she took such amusement from it, Zelda could not understand. Perhaps Gweneth was just mean.

Or perhaps she was jealous of Zelda and Calain. The latter seemed most likely.

Whatever the case, Zelda decided to confront Gweneth about her behavior later, when they had left the ship and its leering crew behind. She hated bickering in front of the sailors, who treated the four of them as a supreme joke and enjoyed gossiping about them over card games and observing them scathingly from afar.

That three women were in the thrall of one was quite obvious to the men, no matter how Zelda struggled to hide it, and they enjoyed watching the knights fighting over her. As a result, Zelda had begged the knights to stop fighting. She hated more than anything that their drama was on display for the same men who leered and lusted after her as she passed. Such men, who hated women who loved women, viewed such bickering as proof that male and female pairings were superior – rather than full of occasional conflict and disagreements like most relationships everywhere.

Zelda and the knights shared a cabin with two bunk beds standing either side a nightstand with a washbasin. Selene and Gweneth typically slept alone, unless Zelda chose to crawl into their bed with them. Selene was always quite pleased should Zelda choose to join her, and Gweneth was surprisingly gentle and sweet, taking Zelda in her arms and going back to sleep without missing a beat. But most of the time, Zelda slept in Calain's arms, smiling in her sleep, heart fluttering should a sleepy Calain suddenly kiss her golden hair or grope her breasts as she was dreaming.

The knights didn't need to wear their armor aboard the ship, and in fact, the captain had cautioned them against it in the event that one of them might fall overboard. And so, Calain, Selene, and Gweneth spent weeks in tunics, trousers, and boots, the sleeves of their tunics rolled back to reveal their muscular arms. Zelda loved seeing them out of their armor, because she could clearly see their fine, hard bodies, the way their muscles flexed, the way their breasts moved behind the cloth of their linen bras.

It was also easier to access their bodies. Once when Selene was sitting up on her bed, lacing up her boot, Zelda sat up behind her, slid her little hand down the front of Selene's pants, and fingered her. She had never fingered a woman before, though she had thought of it often since knowing Calain's hungry touch. She slid her hands down the front of Selene's smallclothes and could feel her soft, warm sex, how the lips yielded to her touch, soft as petals. She thought it curious that a woman as hard and strong as Selene could have a part of her that was so soft and delicate and vulnerable.

Selene seemed shocked at first, then happily resigned to Zelda's touching, if not pleasantly surprised. She stopped trying to lace her boot and simply sat, her knees apart, biting her lips as Zelda's clumsy hand touched her. Zelda's exploring fingers found Selene's fat little clitoris, and Selene's entire body tightened when Zelda caressed it gently.

Zelda stopped in alarm. "Oh! Did I hurt you?"

"No," said Selene hoarsely. "Quite the opposite. My lady . . . Touch me again . . ."

Zelda's heart leapt. She sat up on her knees, looked over Selene's shoulder, and undid her belt and pants. Once Selene's trousers were sagging open, Zelda held her smallclothes away from her belly and could see her sex more clearly. It was wreathed in a swath of dark, curly hair. The smell of Selene's pubic hair was sweet, a mixture of flowery-scented soap, salty sweat, and leather. But the knights always smelled like sweat and leather. The scent was something that had begun to arouse Zelda.

Biting her lip, cheeks flaming as arousal swept through her, Zelda split Selene's soft pubic hair with two fingers, revealing the fat lips of her dark sex. Selene's nipples were dark as well. Zelda often thought of the woman as her "raven beauty," so dark and powerful and yet stunning.

Zelda gently turned Selene's face to hers and kissed her, and as she did, she found Selene's little clitoris again and gently caressed it, until Selene's cheeks were flushed and her clitoris was throbbing in Zelda's grasp, gently rolled back and forth between two fingers. Selene moaned something unintelligible behind their kiss, but Zelda was hardly listening, for her own sex was swelling with arousal in her panties. She slid her fingers inside the hot sheath of Selene's sex and began to stroke, and Selene gasped, her lips trembling against Zelda's.

"Oh . . . Oh, my l-lady . . ." Selene whispered, blushing more brightly as Zelda's careful fingers sank deeper through her moisture. Selene's muscular arms were tight and trembling as she wrestled with the intensity of her pleasure, and it occurred to Zelda for the first time that Selene had never been touched by a woman before. Zelda was the first.

"My lady . . ." Selene whispered helplessly. She cupped Zelda's cheek. "Oh, *Zelda* . . ." And she kissed Zelda hard, thrusting her tongue in her mouth.

Zelda kissed Selene back almost desperately, her mind feverish now with the thought of going down on her. With sudden hunger, Zelda's fingers became rougher, harder, curling so that Selene's hips were moving with them. Selene pulled her mouth free and panted as her hips jerked in little spurts, licks of black hair tumbling in her hooded eyes, sweet lips gasping, brows frowning in baffled ecstasy. Zelda looked at her with narrowed-eyed lust, enjoying how helplessly aroused she was, how deliciously wet her sex, and because of Zelda! Zelda's touch had done this, had rendered this strong, powerful woman to shivering, gasping, and begging.

Zelda fingered Selene until the knight was so moist, she was gushing over Zelda's fingers. Then her muscular body tightened as she climaxed. Baffled, trembling with pleasure, Selene reached blindly for Zelda's face, cupped her cheek, and kissed her again as the moisture of her sex gushed hot over Zelda's fingers.

AFTER SUCCESSFULLY bringing Selene to a climax, Zelda made it up in her mind that she was going to do the same to the others: pounce them one by one when they were least expecting it and make wild and desperate love to them, until they had gushed over her fingers! Unfortunately for her, the knights were on to her before she could surprise the other two. Calain, Selene, and Gweneth shared everything, even their sex lives, and so, it was only natural that Selene would have told the others what Zelda had done to her so aggressively and hungrily.

So, when Zelda tried to surprise Gweneth in her bed one evening, she was pinned to the bed instead. She squealed with laughter when Gweneth, blue eyes twinkling, pinned her wrists above her head and kissed her neck again and again, slowly.

"How . . . How did you know?" pouted Zelda, breathless with giggles.

"Did you think Selene wouldn't tell us?" said Gweneth, amused. "She said you fucked her like a mad woman, fingered her so hard, you tore her smallclothes."

Zelda blushed.

"She was quite beside herself about it," Calain added. She paused to unlace the front of Zelda's gown very carefully with her teeth. As the gown sagged down, Zelda's large breasts were exposed, standing plump and rigid with small pink nipples.

Gweneth slowly sucked one, letting go gently, so that Zelda's large breast wobbled as it was released. Zelda melted from the pleasure.

"What did you think to do to me?" Gweneth whispered huskily and swirled her tongue over Zelda's ever-hardening nipple.

"F-Finger you," Zelda admitted, breathless with arousal and blushing with the confession.

Gweneth laughed softly. "You're so cute. You little vixen." She rubbed her nose against Zelda's and smiled into her eyes with twinkling eyes.

Zelda surprised them both when she suddenly kissed Gweneth on the mouth. "Why can't you be sweet like this all the time?" she whispered, letting her head drop again into the mass of her long golden curls.

"Sweetness isn't my nature," answered Gweneth with a laugh. "You may as well ask a viper to stop biting."

"You can be sweet when you want to be," Zelda insisted.

"Maybe I don't want to be," said Gweneth, who wasn't really listening to Zelda anymore but staring at her large breasts. She sucked slowly on the other one, and Zelda trembled. Then Gweneth's kisses traveled down. She released one of Zelda's wrists to reach down for her panties, and Zelda took her chance: she wiggled free, rolling on top of Gweneth and pinning her to the bed in her place.

Gweneth laughed lightly as she lay under Zelda, who was now sitting astride her lap, looking down at her mischievously. Her small hands were pinning Gweneth's wrists above her head, a position which caused her big breasts to hang near Gweneth's face. Gweneth lifted her head and gave one of Zelda's swinging breasts another slow, delicious suck. Zelda trembled and blushed.

"G-Gweneth. . . ."

Gweneth laughed softly. "Even when you have dominated me, you yield as soon as my mouth touches you."

Zelda scowled.

"Do not be angry, my lady," laughed Gweneth. "I surrender. I am yours to toy with." She gave her hips a playful little thrust, making Zelda bounce suddenly on top of her and her heavy breasts jiggle.

"Oh!" Zelda cried as she was bounced and blushed again. "You're impossible!"

"You're beautiful," Gweneth whispered seriously.

Zelda's heart thumped at the look in Gweneth's eyes: she looked as if she wanted to devour Zelda. It was a look Calain and Selene had given her when they were aroused and wanting her, but coming from Gweneth, it always made her squirm – squirm in a way she both loved and hated. Even sitting on top of Gweneth, she was not truly in control and she knew it. Gweneth hadn't really yielded to her. Perhaps she never would.

Feeling annoyed and defeated, Zelda released Gweneth and turned away, leaning forward on her knees and preparing to rise from the bed. She squealed in surprise when Gweneth grabbed her by the hips and drew her backside to her face. She thought for one moment that Gweneth would kiss her backside, but instead, she pushed Zelda's skirts up, yanked down her panties, and buried her face in Zelda's soft sex.

Kneeling with her back her to Gweneth, her legs trapped in the hook of Gweneth's strong arms, Zelda gasped as the big woman's tongue slid deep in her sex, plunging between her lips and pausing to caress and suck them, then sliding deep inside her again. Her cheeks flushed from the pleasure and she could not stifle her cries of delight.

Gweneth smoothed a hungry hand up Zelda's narrow waist, and as she was licking and sucking her sex, she groped one of Zelda's breasts until her back was spasming, trying to hold still against the pleasure. Zelda's thighs trembled. Gweneth was tasting her with a slow skill that was driving her mad. She would scream. She would scream and scream and the sailors would hear! Goddess, no, that would be terrible! So she bit her lip and trembled all over as Gweneth's careful tongue worked her to an orgasm, and when she finally climaxed, it was with a violent shudder and a muffled cry.

ZELDA DIDN'T BOTHER trying to surprise Calain. Like Gweneth, Selene had already told her what Zelda had done, and now there was no doubt Gweneth had told the others how Zelda had sat on her face, biting her lip to stifle her screams as Gweneth tormented her with lips and tongue.

And indeed, one night, as the others were sleeping in their bunks and Zelda and Calain were lying together in bed, Calain teased Zelda about her playful pouncing of the others and asked why she had not been pounced.

"Because the surprise is ruined!" whispered Zelda, who was lying in Calain's arm, her cheek on Calain's shoulder. She had to admit she felt cheated. Calain was the one she wanted to surprise most of all.

"What would you have done to me," Calain whispered, "if you had surprised me first?"

Zelda blushed a little as she thought of it. "I would have thrown you on the bed, peeled you out of your tunic . . ."

"Yes . . .?"

"Suckled your breasts . . ."

"My lady!" gasped Calain in mock horror and laughed. "My, but you are naughty!"

Zelda laughed as well. "I wasn't finished! I would have fingered you and gone down on you . . . Tasted the sweet lips of your sex . . ."

"What if you did those things," said Calain, "and I pretended to be surprised?"

"It's not the same," Zelda insisted, pouting.

Calain laughed again. "I'm sorry we ruined your fun. My lady may have her way with me any time she pleases."

Zelda smiled.

"My lady wanted to . . . taste me?"

"Y-Yes," Zelda admitted, blushing. "I've seen the way your sex looks when you are bathing. It's all wreathed in red hair, and the lips are so pink and plump . . . I want to suck them."

"My lady watches me bathe?" said Calain, amused. She smoothed a big hand up Zelda's slender back and down her long golden hair, listening.

"Y-Yes," Zelda admitted. "Why wouldn't I watch? You're so beautiful and strong. Sometimes I can't believe you're my knight." She climbed up on top of Calain and looked down in her face. "I love you, Calain. You know that, don't you?"

Calian's green eyes softened. She reached up and touched Zelda's face with a tender hand. "And I love you, Zelda. I have loved you since I first laid eyes on you."

"Truly?"

Calain smiled, remembering. "You were sitting in the stands in that blue gown. You were so nervous, but you were the fairest maiden there. No wonder the queen wanted you. I sometimes think that if I had the power, I'd have taken you for myself as well."

"No, you wouldn't!" Zelda said at once. "You're kind and good and brave. You're nothing like the queen!"

"I don't know how good I am," Calain said, frowning, "but I will be kind and good and brave and anything you ask of me, so much as I am able. I will always be true."

Calain looked so earnest that something in Zelda melted and she leaned down and kissed her.

"Your breasts," Calain whispered, lips brushing Zelda's, "feel so good against me, my lady. They're so soft and warm and heavy . . ." She reached between them and pulled Zelda's laces free, so that her breasts poured out and rested with swelling cleavage on top of Calain's. Calain stared at them hungrily a moment, then kissed Zelda suddenly on the mouth, thrusting her tongue deep inside, so that Zelda's lashes fluttered as her backside was squeezed.

PRIINE WAS AS WONDERFUL in person as it had seemed through the captain's spyglass. The city was so colorful and bursting with flowers, it seemed an eternal festival was happening. Jesters juggled in the streets, men walked on stilts, people wore colorful animal masks, women shook tambourines (and their breasts), and children ran, tossing confetti and blowing soap bubbles.

It was a lively place full of color and laughter. But it was a little too lively for a prolonged stay, Zelda thought. Already, she missed the quiet of Vira'Toss Tower and would be happy when they had moved on.

At least the threat of the Rose Guard was less likely here. Priine was in Realm Koradara, a land across the sea from Eriallon, and belonged to the good queen, Queen Carys. The Rose Guard would have to spend weeks on a ship to reach them, and even then, Queen Carys would not take kindly to their presence in her realm. They were all but safe outside of Eriallon. All but Cassandra.

They rented a room at an inn, and then the waiting began. Naturally, none of the knights were in the mood to make love, worried as they were for Cassandra, and Zelda respected their feelings, giving then space to worry and grieve, and comforting them when they needed it.

On the eighth day, Selene went down in the morning to check the horses, and Gweneth, who was so bored she was starting to go mad, went with her, leaving Calain alone in the room they shared with Zelda.

It was a large enough room, with a double bed against the wall, three arched windows, a nightstand with a washbasin, a fire, and a few sitting chairs with a small table. They had left their traveling satchels in a pile on the floor in the corner, and their cloaks had been tossed in another pile across a chair.

Zelda washed her face at the washbasin, as behind her, Calain slouched wretchedly in one of the chairs, knees wide, her red hair a mess. Zelda had never seen her so distraught. She came up behind Calain and massaged her shoulders. Calain briefly put a grateful hand over Zelda's hand, then Zelda continued massaging. Before long, Calain had dozed off.

It had only been eight days, but the three knights seemed to be falling apart at the seams. Calain, for instance, hadn't slept in three days, while Gweneth had become somber and moody, and Selene was hardly eating. Zelda kept reminding them that a ship from Arinol to Priine could take up to three weeks, but far from comforting them, this seemed to only upset them more.

As Calain was dozing, Zelda donned her cloak and left the bedroom, quietly closing the door behind her. It was morning, but already, the people of Priine were singing in the streets and playing instruments. She could hear a flute downstairs in the tavern.

Zelda thought she would sit outside on the step and observe the crowds and their antics. To her surprise, Gweneth was already sitting there. The inn steps had been painted a bright, festive red, while the door was a warm green, and orange flowers were bursting from the clay pots that stood near the bottom step.

Zelda thought the riot of color in the city made Gweneth seem plainer than she really was, with her brown hair and blue eyes that were almost dark as the evening sea. Gweneth also wasn't wearing her armor, and her tunic and trousers were of plain, neutral colors: a gray tunic and brown trousers with boots of a darker brown. The sleeves of her tunic were rolled back to reveal her bulging arms, and she was carving a chunk of wood with a knife.

Fascinated by Gweneth's skill, Zelda sat on the step beside her and watched for a while. She loved the way Gweneth's strong hands and arms and even the flesh of her collarbone flexed as she carved. The misshapen chunk of wood was slowly taking the shape of a beautiful woman with long hair. The woman was standing straight and proud with one hand out to cast a spell. Zelda realized with a slight blush that the wooden woman was her likeness.

"Where is Selene?" Zelda asked, hugging her knees. "Is she in the stable still?"

"No," answered Gweneth, eyes on her work. "She went to market for something in other."

"A potion to test if I've impregnated her?" Zelda joked.

Gweneth's once somber mouth curled in a half-smile at the joke, but the smile went away in another second, and she said with a frown, "We are sterile, my lady."

Zelda looked at her in surprise. "Truly? All the Falcon Knights?"

"Aye," said Gweneth. "Makes sense, does it not? They'd want to control how many of us there are. Can't have supernaturally strong women roaming the countryside, spawning. That sort of thing terrifies the men, you see."

And so it should, thought Zelda in amusement.

"There's a tribe of Wilde Women to the west of here," went on Gweneth. "They scare the shite out of the local men. Very big, very strong women. Naturally born like that, no magick potions. They steal men and use them to make their children."

"Truly? Or are you having me on?" said Zelda suspiciously.

"I speak truly. The Wilde Women aren't as strong as we Knights of Falcon, but they are strong enough to strike terror in the hearts of men. And no one could ever close the womb of one." Gweneth glanced curiously at Zelda. "Are sorceresses not sterile, my lady?"

Zelda lifted her brows. "Why would we be? Magick isn't handed down by blood. Tis learned. Natural mages are very rare."

"Makes sense," said Gweneth thoughtfully. She went on carving, her eyes on her work. "So if you let some other knight get you with child, I shall know it isn't mine."

Zelda laughed. "No man shall touch me. I do not fancy men."

"Didn't say it had to be a man," said Gweneth. "I have been all over the realms, seen some outlandish things: mystical pregnancies between two women . . . Talking beasts . . . A well that granted wishes . . ."

"Did you make a wish?"

"Aye."

"What did you wish for?" Zelda asked almost eagerly.

"If I tell you, it won't come true," Gweneth said with a wink. But her jovial mood dropped away yet again and she said quietly, "Selene thinks we should head to Wolf Fortress if Cassandra has not arrived in another day."

Zelda frowned. "But how could she arrive here so quickly? It took us nearly three weeks!"

"There are other ways to travel aside from ships, faster ways. Cariel's Cross, the elven ruin that brought you to Arinol so quickly, is one."

"I have read of portals," said Zelda thoughtfully, "but tis strange to think of anyone but a sorceress using one."

Gweneth scoffed. "Of course, tis strange to you if you believe mages alone have power in this world."

"Why did we not take a portal then?" demanded Zelda irritably.

"The steeds, for one," answered Gweneth. "They do not sit well with magick and would not cross through without much coaxing. Cassandra is alone without her steed. It should be easy for her to arrive here quickly."

"We should have left you behind and brought Cassandra," said Zelda, feeling cross. Gweneth was always teasing and mocking her, as if she were a silly little girl who knew nothing of the world. She hated it because Gweneth was probably right.

"Do you truly wish it so?" asked Gweneth, amused.

"Truly!" Zelda snapped. "I bet Cassandra is nicer! And a better lover as well –" The word was cut off in her throat when Gweneth kissed her. She went still. The knight had never kissed her like this before, with a gentle sweetness that made her heart flutter.

As their lips caressed, Zelda felt Gweneth press the little carving in her hand. Then she pulled back, smiling. "That shut you up quick," she teased, and Zelda blushed furiously: she couldn't deny that Gweneth was a good kisser.

Gweneth winked and went back inside the inn.

Zelda looked at the carving in her hand. Gweneth had given her likeness a sweet, heart-shaped face and long hair that was blowing back. Her waist was tiny and her hips round and her breasts high, and she stood in a pose of dignity, strength, and power . . . The carving was how Gweneth saw Zelda.

LATER THAT NIGHT, ZELDA found herself in bed with the three knights as they slept around her. All of them were so miserable, she had offered to take the first watch. And so, they slept around her in their smallclothes while she sat upright among them, fully dressed.

Calain slept on Zelda's right. She was on her side, breathing gently, one muscular arm draped almost possessively over Zelda's leg. Selene was on Zelda's left, using her thigh for a pillow. The two of them looked almost as innocent as children as they slept, big and powerful as they were. Zelda smiled and touched their hair. Then her eyes went to Gweneth, who was sleeping on the other side of Calain. She was on her back, and her undercut brown hair was loose of its usual bun, so that the curls fell in her eyes as she dreamt.

Zelda was tempted to pull Gweneth closer with her mind. She wanted all three knights within her reach, the better to observe their powerful bodies as they dreamt. She also thought disturbing Gweneth would be a fun way to get back at her for the morning's teasing. She was just thinking of lifting the woman with her mind when a disturbance outside drew her attention.

Prying herself carefully from the sleepy grasp of Calain and Selene, Zelda rose from the bed and went to the window. She looked out and gasped:

Cassandra was down in the dark street, fighting off three Rose Guard knights in their golden armor. The sound of blades clashing was growing almost desperate as they backed Cassandra against the wall. She was tired and making mistakes, while the Rose Guard knights were fast and strong.

There was no time to wake the others. Zelda grabbed her stave and ran down to help. Outside, moonlight pooled over the scene, glowing upon Cassandra's pale hair. Zelda ran forward to cast a spell and felt the draining sensation plunge over her like ice water: the Rose Guards had a Bane Stone.

Trembling, Zelda staggered to her knees. It was a powerful Bane Stone, more powerful than the trifling one the bandits had used.

"Ha! I knew her sorceress *bitch* would come running," laughed one of the Rose Guard knights, a giant bull of a man with mean little eyes.

There were only two Rose Guard knights left, for Cassandra had slain the third as Zelda was coming down the stairs.

"Get the mage bitch," said the giant knight. "I'll take care of the bird knight."

The second knight, a stout man, moved toward Zelda where she knelt gasping in the street. That seemed to set Cassandra into furious action. Without warning, she brought her sword around and sliced the bigger man's neck open. He went staggering back, screaming and spurting blood, before falling over on his back, where he lay gurgling as he choked on his own blood.

Seeing that both his companions were now dead, the last knight made a wild swing with his blade at Zelda, as if desperate to slay her before Cassandra could stop him. He failed.

Cassandra lunged between them, parried with her blade, then roughly shoved him back. Before he had regained his footing, Cassandra had cut off his head. More blood spattered.

Glancing around in an almost paranoid fashion, Cassandra grabbed Zelda by the arm, pulled her to her feet, and backed her into the wall, so that they were standing face to face and hidden in shadow. Then they just stood there, facing each other, waiting.

They were so close, they could have kissed, and Zelda looked up into Cassandra's tense face and realized for the first time how startlingly pretty her gray eyes were, how the moonlight caught them and made them glow with flecks of light. She was also painfully aware of the knight's tight, muscular body heaving breathlessly beneath her armor. Some wild, mad part of her wanted Cassandra to pin her to the wall and kiss her. But Casandra wasn't paying attention to Zelda. The knight's serious gray eyes were narrowed. She was listening, her hand on the sword at her hip.

Zelda looked up at Cassandra's tense face and wondered what they were waiting for. She had almost asked when Cassandra mouthed, "Hush!" and she closed her mouth again.

Another minute passed, and then the answer to Zelda's unspoken question appeared: two Rose Guard knights rode into the moonlight. One was a man, the other a woman. They halted and dismounted when they saw their dead comrades in the street and looked around, their eyes scanning. For some strange reason, their eyes did not seem to register Zelda and Cassandra as they stood against the wall in the shadows. Instead, their eyes passed right over them, and they turned, mounted their horses, and rode sway.

Cassandra took a shaking breath when they had gone, and Zelda suddenly realized the knight's gauntlet was holding tightly to her hip. Cassandra's hand relaxed. She released Zelda and backed away. As Zelda watched, she went to the Bane Stone, which was glowing on the ground, and smashed it with her sword. Immediately, Zelda felt the heavy feeling of being drained lift away.

"You cast a cloaking spell!" Zelda realized. She went to Cassandra, who was standing there panting as if she would fall over.

"Yes," Cassandra managed hoarsely.

"But how?" Zelda asked in amazement. "And why didn't you just finish them off with your sword...?" The words died on her lips when she noticed the blood dripping from Cassandra's gauntlet.

"Oh, no," said Zelda. "Let me see."

"Tis the arm, my lady, not the hand," panted Cassandra when Zelda went for her gauntlet.

Zelda reached for the buckle of the arm plate and saw the plate fall away to reveal Cassandra's slashed arm and torn linen bra, which was just torn enough to reveal the side of her breast. Ignoring the bare curve of the woman's breast with difficulty, Zelda placed her hand over the arm wound. Her eyes glowed briefly, and the bleeding wound sealed itself.

"Thank . . . Thank you, my lady," Cassandra panted. "Now . . . Let us rouse the others and leave this place."

Chapter 2

Zelda had so many questions to ask Cassandra. Where had she learned magick and why hadn't the Bane Stone any power over her? Zelda hadn't been able to cast, but Casandra had cast very effectively and without a stave or wand.

When they returned to the inn, the others were both angry that Zelda had ventured out alone and relieved that Cassandra was alive and had defended Zelda. The knights scolded Zelda, and Calain grabbed her arms, peering into her face to see if she was hurt. Then they gathered around Cassandra, gave her one-armed hugs and pats on the back, and asked if she was well.

A breathless Cassandra explained apologetically that the Rose Guard knights had followed her through the portal, as she had been unable to close it, and though Zelda had healed her arm, she was too exhausted to continue fighting.

"Can you ride?" Selene asked, clutching Cassandra's shoulder.

Cassandra managed a breathless nod.

"Good. We have Sunny down in the stable," said Selene. She looked at Calain and Gweneth. "Let us don armor and make for Wolf Fortress immediately."

And so, the knights donned their armor, grabbed their satchels, and all of them set out for the stables. Outside, the three Rose Guard knights were still lying in dark pools of blood as moonlight played upon their staring eyes. The one without a head was still spurting from his neck.

The knights guided their horses from the stables. Zelda went to Calain's horse, Arthur, as usual, but Selene held out her arm to block her.

"What are you doing?" demanded Calain.

"Zelda must ride with Gweneth," said Selene.

"What?!" said Zelda and Calain together in borderline outrage.

Gweneth was nearby, avoiding everyone's eye as she adjusted the saddle on her white speckled stallion, Bron.

"We are going to part ways to confuse the Rose Guard," said Selene.

"Don't be stupid," said Calain at once.

Selene's nostrils flared and her lips grew tight. She was losing patience. "Be still and listen to me, Calain, you insufferable—!" She broke off, trying to calm herself.

Cassandra put a soothing hand on Selene's shoulder and said quietly, "Go on, sister."

Selene took a breath. "Cass can barely stand. She may not be able to sit her saddle. I will send her with you, Calain. You will tie your horses together, that you may steady her. You are the only one strong enough to support her."

Calain looked anxiously at Cassandra, who did indeed look ready to collapse. "Of course, I will aid her," Calain said.

"When we leave here," went in Selene, calmer now that Calain was listening, "we will head our separate ways into the forest and hide there for one day and one night. Then we each shall head to Wolf Fortress." She looked around at everyone. "Is that understood?"

"Let us go forth already," Gweneth complained.

Calain pulled Zelda into a kiss that made her tremble. When they broke apart, Calain touched her forehead to Zelda's and said, "We shall meet again."

Behind Calain, Gweneth rolled her eyes. "Always so dramatic," she mocked and laughed softly when Calain lightly punched her.

Everyone mounted. Gweneth took Zelda by the waist and lifted her easily onto Bron's saddle. Then she climbed up behind Zelda and snapped the reins. The horse took off.

As they were thundering away up the quiet street, Zelda looked back a last time at Calain, and it occurred to her that she and the red knight had never been apart since they had met. Calain must've been thinking the same thing, for she lifted her gauntlet in sad farewell. Then the horse turned the corner, and Zelda could see Calain no longer.

"You most really love her," said Gweneth in amusement. "She must be a worthy lover. Nothing else makes sense." She laughed.

"There are *many* reasons to love Calain," Zelda said irritably.

"As there are many reasons to love you," answered Gweneth, giving one of Zelda's heavily bouncing breasts a brief squeeze.

Zelda flushed to her hairline and hated that she had enjoyed the brief groping. Though Gweneth could be sweet, she was still always flippant and mocking. Zelda could not decide the woman's true feelings, and it frustrated her. She still had the carving Gweneth had given her in her satchel. Was that the real Gweneth or was it the one always poking fun of her? Perhaps the jesting was how she showed affection. Zelda was realizing she did it to everyone.

They continued on in silence, flying through the gates of Priine and into the green countryside. Zelda could see hills and farmhouses in the distance. An endless stream of trees lined the dark horizon, the forest Selene had spoken of.

Gweneth turned off the road and galloped them toward an abandoned farmhouse, where she dismounted and led the horse inside with Zelda still seated in the saddle. When she reached up and took Zelda by the waist, her eyes were soft. Startled, Zelda's lashes fluttered in pleasant surprise, and she braced her small hands on Gweneth's arms as she was lifted down from the saddle. Her breasts jiggled heavily when Gweneth set her on her feet. For several seconds, Gweneth merely stared down at Zelda and seemed to be meditating on something. Zelda stared back, secretly hoping the beautiful knight would kiss her, but Gweneth blinked and moved past Zelda, instead pacing at the open barn door.

Disappointed, Zelda didn't know what to do with herself, so she sat on an old milk stool and watched as Bron idly picked hay from the floor and chewed it.

"What you did tonight was foolhardy," Gweneth said, startling Zelda when she spoke into the silence.

Zelda straightened indignantly. "Excuse me?"

"Going down to help Cassandra," Gweneth elaborated, shaking her head, "when you should have woken us. There was no reason not to have woken us."

"There was no time!" Zelda snapped. "While the three of you were donning your armor, she would have been slain!"

"We needn't have fought in our armor," Gweneth answered calmly. "We would have rushed to her defense in the nude if the situation had warranted it."

"My presence caused a distraction," Zelda insisted, "and Cassandra defeated them."

Gweneth still didn't seem to approve. "You're as hotheaded and stubborn as Calain. No wonder you yearn for each other so. We should never have let you take watch. We should have tied you to the bedpost."

Zelda's chest heaved angrily, and she shot to her feet, her cloak coming loose and falling off. "You just try it!"

"There's a post right there," Gweneth said, nodding at the wooden barn post that stood near Zelda. Now she was smiling and looking amused.

Zelda trembled. She took an angry step forward. "You try tying me to that post and I'll . . . I'll—!"

Smirking, Gweneth quickly advanced, backing Zelda against the barn post. She towered over her. "You'll. . . .? What? Turn me into a frog?"

Zelda blushed. "Perhaps!" she said defiantly.

Gweneth liked that. She laughed and her eyes were bright with desire when she said, "Or maybe you'll just stammer and grow moist."

Zelda's blush brightened. Gweneth was the only one who spoke to her so suggestively, and as angry as she was at the moment, deep down, she liked it. She *hated* that she liked it! She was tired of being treated like a delicate thing that needed to be protected! She realized in that moment that was all she was to Gweneth. Calain saw her as powerful, and Selene wanted to protect her because she loved her, not because she saw her as weak. But Gweneth saw her as a silly little girl, who ran recklessly into danger, who couldn't defend herself. To Gweneth, Zelda was a pretty, dumb plaything that needed to be babysat.

Zelda looked into Gweneth's eyes and hated how they twinkled with laughter. She blinked, and Gweneth's face spread in shock when she was frozen on the spot, unable to move a muscle. She could only move her eyes, which she turned down at Zelda in a heated glare.

Zelda smiled up at Gweneth, relishing in her helplessness. "I don't need you!" she said haughtily. "I don't need *any* of you, and I'll prove it." So saying, she took her gray cloak up from the hay, whirled it around her shoulders, and marched out, leaving Gweneth helpless as a statue behind her.

ZELDA DIDN'T TAKE GWENETH'S horse. She was tempted to, but furious as she was, she didn't want to leave Gweneth stranded in the middle of the countryside, while she could have easily to used magick to get anywhere she pleased. Apparating was very difficult and even dangerous (lesser mages had lost limbs trying), but Zelda could do it if she focused. Right now, she wanted to be as far from Gweneth as possible. Selene said they should all meet at Wolf Fortress, but Zelda didn't feel like explaining why she had arrived there alone.

As she marched (in a quick, angry stride) across the open green fields outside the barn where she'd left Gweneth, Zelda realized that she needed to be alone for a while, that she hadn't been alone since she'd lived with her uncle as a child (he had often neglected her). She wanted to gather her thoughts, calm her angry feelings toward Gweneth, and try to come up with some sort of plan for her future. For Calain's earnest questions aboard the *Atross* had set her thoughts in motion: what was she going to do with her life now? She could not, she *would* not spend the rest of her (very long) life sleeping on the ground! Oh, no. And her gowns were fast becoming rags! She needed coin, she needed a home, she needed proper clothes, she needed stability. And she did not want to live in Wolf Fortress, a cold old building in the middle of nowhere!

Zelda stopped and turned, gazing at the line of trees on the distant horizon. It was a forest, dark green and mysterious. Selene had mentioned hiding there, so how dangerous could it be? But it was quite far away without a horse. Zelda closed her eyes and focused her entire being on appearing in the unknown forest. She felt her ears pop as she disappeared, and a second later, she opened her eyes to find herself standing in the dark forest.

Zelda gasped: the forest was *beautiful.* It wasn't as dark and scary as it had seemed from a distance. Instead, it was bursting with flowers. Vines loaded with blossoms hung from the trees, and the treetops were a dark, rich green. The abundance of flowers made the forest smell heavenly as Zelda walked through it, listening to the hoot of owls and the happy song of night birds.

Zelda traveled for three days in blissful solitude, drinking at the little streams, eating apples from the trees, humming to herself, happy and content and suddenly glad to be alone, even for a little while. She never found trouble. No goblins. No trolls. No evil spirits. The forest had a light, clean aura to it, as if no wicked creatures could even have entered had they tried. So far, Zelda had only come across butterflies, little rabbits fleeing in the undergrowth, startled deer that fled at once when they saw her, and the occasional raven or sparrow, watching her silently from the trees.

The birds unnerved Zelda. They did not behave like normal birds, though she couldn't see how the court sorceress of Eriallon could have been using them to spy. Magick had its limits and could only reach so far. Depending on the strength of the sorceress, magick couldn't even cross water, and Zelda was on a different continent entirely, assuming the court mage hadn't followed her to Koradara.

If the birds weren't being controlled by the court mage of Eriallon, then it was possible they were being controlled by a sorceress who was local to the area and was using them to watch Zelda. Zelda didn't like that. While the forest had a clean feeling and she could not detect any Dark Magick, she did not like being spied upon. She decided she would leave the strange forest as soon as possible and head for Wolf Fortress after all . . . If only she could find her way out.

It was on the fourth day that Zelda came across the crystals. They were massive, rising out of the earth and pushing their great way up between the trees like gargantuan teeth. They were white and pink, purple and pale blue, all glowing and humming softly with power. And there were so many of them, it was becoming hard to continue on, for soon, they were blocking the path and forming a wall.

What was worse, the presence of the crystals seemed to have the same effect on Zelda as a Bane Stone, and she realized they must've been what Bane Stones were carved from. The symptoms were barely noticeable at first. She felt a little drowsy the first hour, and as she kept walking, she started to feel more fatigued, then too sluggish to lift her feet, until by the fifth hour, she knew she would not be able to cast a spell.

Zelda felt foolish for storming off and leaving Gweneth's side. If the woman weren't so insufferable! But she knew deep down that no one else was to blame her for actions. She had acted on impulse, allowing her emotions to control her rather than the other way around, and now she was lost in a strange forest, too tired to use her magick to escape it. If some creature were to come along, she wouldn't even be able to defend herself physically. She tried lifting a stick as a makeshift weapon and her tired arms shook before she suddenly dropped it. The crystals seemed to be sucking the life out of her.

On the fifth day, as Zelda was sitting on the ground and miserably willing herself to go on, wolves appeared between the crystals. There must have been seven of them, and they were no ordinary wolves. They were black and scruffy, and twice the size of a normal wolf, their eyes red spheres that seemed to hover as they peeled out of the darkness, their long fangs dripping with yellow saliva. Heart pounding, Zelda scooted back on her seat and felt the solid cold side of one of the giant crystals against her back. She pressed herself to the crystal, as if it could save her, and the wolves seemed amused by her desperation. She saw the laughter in their red eyes. It reminded her of Gweneth and she glowered.

:Are you lost, little lamb?: mocked the wolf in the lead, its mind linking with hers. It was bigger than the others, a female with wild black fur flying in every direction, and thick fur around her ears that formed a shaggy mane.

:She smells like other meats,: said a smaller male at the back of the group. He snapped his jaws hungrily. *:What's in the bag, little lamb?:*

Zelda was indeed carrying dried meat she'd purchased in Priine. She thought of offering it to the wolves in exchange for her life, but she knew they preferred fresh meat. They were going to eat her, here, in the darkness, beneath the moon, and Calain, Selene, and the others would track her down to find her bloody bones.

The wolves were hissing with laughter as they closed in. One leapt forward and ripped Zelda's dress with its teeth. She screamed softly and her body tensed, though the wolf's teeth had only grazed her skin. Her dress had been torn in the front, exposing her slender belly and breasts. Another wolf leapt forward, and she cringed when it grabbed her sleeve, tearing it off. Would they undress her first? She supposed they didn't want to eat her clothing as well.

Trembling, Zelda closed her eyes, miserably resigned to her fate. And then . . . a whimper and a shriek. Zelda opened her eyes and gasped: one of the wolves had lost its head. The severed head rolled away as the other wolves watched in horror. Then their leader howled, and all of them scattered, still whimpering, as the giant figure of a woman swung a great blade threateningly after them and managed to kick one in the backside with her boot. A yelp from the assaulted wolf, and then the sound of paws frantically tearing through the undergrowth.

When the wolves had gone, the giant woman turned around, breathless, and stabbed her great two-handed blade in the earth. She leaned against the blade and eyed Zelda curiously.

Zelda sat in shock, fumbling to cover her breasts as she leaned back against the giant crystal behind her. The woman before her was as big as a Knight of Falcon and just as muscular, but she wasn't wearing silver armor. Instead, she wore black leather armor that exposed her muscular arms, her bulging legs, and her rippling midriff. She was also draped in animal furs and hides, and upon her head was a horned circlet made of bone. Her long, auburn hair fell in curtains either side a face that was surprisingly young and sweet and not hard or scarred by battle at all.

When the big woman spoke, it was in a language Zelda did not understand. Seeing Zelda's confusion, the big woman cleared her throat and said in broken common tongue, "Woman lost?"

Zelda hesitated and nodded, feeling too tense to speak. Who was this wild barbaric woman? And was she a danger to Zelda? She couldn't decide. The woman didn't seem threatening, though she was certainly dangerous. With all her bulging muscles, she probably could have broken Zelda's neck with a headlock alone.

"Woman sorceress?" asked the big woman, pointing to Zelda's stave, which she had dropped to the ground. The woman didn't seem to approve. Her face darkened.

Zelda knew it would probably be a bad idea to let on that she was a sorceress, so she shook her head and said, "Walking s-stick."

The barbarian woman didn't seem to believe Zelda, and she cursed, realizing the woman was far smarter than she appeared.

The barbarian fixed Zelda with a hard stare, but after her eyes had traveled over Zelda's body (lingering momentarily on her exposed breasts), they softened, and she said with grudging curiosity, "Woman travel alone through Dark Bloom? No defense? No companion?"

The way the barbarian spoke, she sounded as if she was scolding Zelda. Zelda wanted to be angry, but she was realizing that perhaps Gweneth – and the barbarian stranger – were right about her. She was foolish and impulsive. She was a child who needed to be babysat.

"Yes," Zelda said with much shame. "I am alone." She thought it best not to mention Gweneth or any of the knights. If the barbarian wasn't dangerous, perhaps she had friends who were.

"Woman come with me?" offered the big woman. "Yrsa keep woman safe."

Zelda hesitated. When she looked into the woman's dark green eyes, they were gentle. They reminded her of Calain, so she slowly nodded and said, "I'll . . . come with you."

The apparent Yrsa nodded and rose to her feet, towering over Zelda again from her great height, so that Zelda gulped and felt her body quiver. The barbarian sheathed her great two-handed blade in the harness on her back, then she leaned down, grabbed Zelda gently by the arm, and pulled her to her feet. Zelda barely had time to gain her bearings before she had been flipped over the woman's shoulder, and she blushed when Yrsa clapped a meaty hand on her backside to hold her in place as she turned and stomped away through the trees.

Chapter 3

Zelda felt the alarm bells ringing through her mind when she realized the giant barbarian had left her stave behind in the grass. But she couldn't cast spells with the giant crystals around anyway, and she wanted the barbarian to believe her a helpless ordinary woman. Somehow, she knew her survival depended on it.

The barbarian woman carried Zelda for what seemed only twenty minutes, moving in silence, occasionally grunting as she stepped her great legs over fallen trunks or squeezed between the crystals. The giant crystals never disappeared, instead growing more numerous and thus causing Zelda to feel even weaker.

Sensing Zelda's growing fatigue, Yrsa gave Zelda what she probably thought was a comforting squeeze on her backside, but instead, Zelda only felt sudden arousal and blushed to her hairline. Yrsa's hand never left Zelda's backside and was firm and strong as it griped her cheek. Its relentless touch was making Zelda more and more excited, though she knew the barbarian woman was groping her absentmindedly, as if she were carrying home a slain deer and trying not to drop it.

Only twenty minutes, and the silhouettes of huts appeared in the dark. A great bonfire was blazing at the center of them, and Zelda could see more of the giant warrior women standing around smaller fires, giant swords on their backs, bows in their hands, knives strapped to muscular thighs. As they entered the village, the warrior women turned and stared with popping eyes at Zelda, and Zelda (blushing furiously) remembered her dress was torn and her breasts were bare. She struggled to cover them as the warrior women pointed and whispered and muttered excitedly.

One woman cupped her hands on imaginary breasts and licked her lips at Zelda as she was carried past, so that Zelda blushed brightly and the crowd of warrior women laughed good-naturedly at her. Zelda looked every which way and could see the lust in the women's eyes, but she did not feel threatened or disgusted by them. They were teasing her and meant her no offence. She was probably a funny enough sight, hanging over Yrsa's shoulder with her big breasts hanging out and her hair flying.

The entire village seemed to be made up women, for there were no men in sight. There were little girls in dresses made of bear hide, running back and forth, their braids flying as they skipped stones and fought each other with sticks. There were old women with long gray hair sitting beside the many fires as they sewed clothes and sharpened skinning knives.

There were also young women who didn't appear to be warriors. Instead, they wore dresses and were short and slender and devoid of muscle. Many of these young women were weaving baskets late into the night, breastfeeding (female) infants, preparing food, or sitting in the laps of big warrior women, who kissed their lips or stroked their long hair and even publicly groped their naked breasts, which no one seemed to find unusual.

Zelda thought she could guess how the women reproduced. Gweneth had told her stories of the women who lived in the wild, capturing men and having their way with them, before releasing them again at knife-point into the forest. If these were the Wilde Women Gweneth had spoken of, the women who were feared and reviled by men due to their astounding strength, then it was likely the stories were true.

Ysra appeared to be taking Zelda to a specific hut, for she followed a path without stopping or wavering, until at last, she came to hut with bones hanging over the doorway. She passed through the curtain of bones without pause and deposited Zelda on the earthen floor inside, speaking in her language as she did so.

Zelda's hair fell in her face as she was placed on the floor, sitting upright. She pushed it back and looked around. Yrsa had sat her on a fur mat beside a barren firepit. The hut was one room, with bones, dried vegetables, and cooking tools hanging from the ceiling. Toward the back was a fur pallet very low to the floor, where the occupant slept.

Yrsa was still speaking in her language when an old woman stepped forward from the shadows and interrupted her. The old woman had long gray hair that fell to her knees and hung loose around her round face, and she was draped in black bear hides. "Yrsa!" she scolded. "Speak the common tongue in the poor thing's presence. She must be scared to death."

Yrsa respectfully took a knee when the old woman appeared, and it suddenly occurred to Zelda that the old woman had apparated: she was a witch. She was draped in green robes and furs, on the hood of which a a crown of antlers rested. She was leaning on a stave, which was little more than a wooden stick with black raven feathers tied to the end alongside a long piece of crystal. The draining sensation had not let up, for the giant crystals grew throughout the village, but the presence of the raw Bane Stone on the old woman's staff made Zelda feel even weaker.

"I am known as Revna," said the old woman, speaking careful common tongue. "I am the elder of the village, meaning the young ones come to me for advice. I saw you wandering our forests through the eye of one of our ravens. When the wolves came for you, I sent Yrsa to protect your life."

A pause. Zelda didn't know what to say as she sat there, clutching her dress shut over her naked breasts. Eventually, she stammered, "Th-Thank you."

The old woman nodded. "You may stay here, child, if it pleases you. But you will become Yrsa's responsibility if you do."

"Her responsibility?" repeated Zelda in surprise.

The old woman nodded seriously again. "Yrsa will share her bed with you. Yrsa will share her food with you. Yrsa will teach you our ways. For it was Yrsa who insisted we protect your life. I thought you a danger to us, and I meant to leave you to the wolves."

Zelda looked quickly at Yrsa. She wanted to thank the warrior woman, but Yrsa kept her eyes trained steadily on the floor. She was still kneeling reverently before the old woman, her head down.

"You should understand," went on Revna, "that to share Yrsa's bed is a great honor. Yrsa is queen of this forest. It is she who leads the warriors here in our expansion as we claim more territory in Dark Bloom Forest. The women here respect her and will view your status as her woman as unearned. You will have to earn your place here by being a good wife."

Zelda hesitated. "A good wife?"

The old woman lifted her brows in surprise. She seemed sincerely taken aback. "Yes, of course. You shall marry Yrsa and become her woman. Why shouldn't you? You said you had no place to go. You were lost and alone in our forest and clearly running from something if you dared set foot here on your own.

What else will you do? Where else will you go in your condition? And Yrsa is one of the most beautiful women in our village. Not only that, she is the strongest and the best hunter. She will provide for you, keep you safe, give you a home." The old woman snorted. "You should be kissing our feet in gratitude. All of these riches handed to you on a silver platter, and because Yrsa looked in the water's mirror and loved you."

Zelda sat in amazement for a moment. Her eyes slowly turned to Yrsa, whose head was still down, and she was surprised to realize the woman was blushing! But Yrsa did not lift her face nor did she speak. She knelt and remained completely still.

"Perhaps you have a lover elsewhere," said Revna shrewdly. "Perhaps you would return to this other."

Zelda hesitated. She was on the verge of lying, of denying the existence of Calain and the other Knights of Falcon, but she could see it in the old woman's face that she already knew the truth.

Her eyes still fixed on Zelda, Revna summoned a bowl of water from the shelf. Zelda knew she was doing it telekinetically. The bowl floated past Revna and set itself on the floor before Zelda, where she sat clutching her gown shut over her breasts.

"Go ahead, child," said Revna softly. "Look into the water's mirror."

Zelda hesitated and leaned forward. The vision that met her eyes froze her on the spot: Calain lying dead on her back, staring into the sky, blood trickling from her lips and her eyes. "No!" Zelda shrieked. More images. Selene lying dead beside Calain, bleeding from the throat. Cassandra taking a blade to the belly. Gweneth gurgling as her throat was slashed—"No, no, no, no!" Zelda screamed. She backed away from the bowl of water, accidentally kicking it as she scrambled, so that it tipped over and spilled in the barren firepit. Tears rose to blind her, and she buried her face in her hands and wept hard.

Zelda didn't know how long she cried, but her heart fluttered when she felt Yrsa's big hand close uncertainly on her shoulder. When she didn't flinch from the woman's touch, Yrsa moved her hand to the top of Zelda's golden head and smoothed it down Zelda's long hair, again and again, stroking her, until her sobbing slowed and she lifted her face. She stared with dead eyes into the distance, unseeing. Her Calain, dead. No, it couldn't be so! And yet, the visions had been so real! And it was her fault! Her fault! If she hadn't run from Gweneth, they would have met at Wolf Fortress, and everything would have been fine!

Shaking all over, Zelda dropped her head forward and cried helplessly again. She didn't protest when Yrsa carefully gathered her in her arms and lifted her, carrying her from the hut. As she was carried away, Zelda didn't see the look of satisfaction on old Revna's wrinkled face.

Chapter 4

Calain worried for Zelda but tried to keep her mind on the task at hand. As she and Cassandra rode out of Priine together, their horses were tied, and Selene had been right: Cassandra could barely stay her saddle. She rocked and swayed dangerously, looking as exhausted as if she would simply tumble over from Sunny's back.

Calain kept a steady hand on Cassandra's arm as they rode into the trees, and when they had found a suitable place to make camp, she helped Cassandra down from the saddle, made a pallet of leaves for her, and bid her to rest. Cassandra dropped off immediately, and Calain set about building up a fire.

By the time Calain's work was done, it was nearly dawn. She sat at the fire, tired from the long ride, took off her gauntlets, and warmed her hands. The first streams of sunlight were reaching through the trees and birds were singing. It was a quiet enough forest, full of flowers growing in veils from the trees. There were few dangers here, and the Rose Guard knights were not familiar with the land, which was their greatest advantage.

Calain had spied giant crystals growing between the trees, the source of the Bane Stones which robbed sorceresses of their power. She worried for Zelda even more, knowing her lady must cross through the crystals, but she comforted herself that Zelda was safe with Gweneth . . . if the two had not killed each other yet.

An hour after dawn, Cassandra stirred when she smelled Calain heating rabbit stew. She sat up, and they broke their fast together.

After eating in silence for some time, Cassandra said, "Tell me truly, Calain. Are the three of you fucking the sorceress?"

Calain nearly choked on her stew. Cassandra had asked the question quite casually, as if she had merely asked about the weather.

"Saw that in your crystal ball, did you?" Calain managed after washing the stew down with wine.

"You sound like Gwen," said Cassandra, amused. "But take heed, Calain. You must control your feelings of jealousy and anger."

"Why?" Calain asked sharply. Cassandra only gave unsolicited advice when there was danger.

Cassandra didn't answer. And Calain, knowing she would get nothing more from Cassandra, did not press her for an answer.

Calain and Cassandra had never spoken much while growing up together on Falcon Isle. The core of their friendship was based around the many times they had sat in content silence together, after a sparring lesson or after a riding lesson in the training yard. Cassandra didn't speak much to anyone aside from Selene, and even then, she was quiet, mysterious, often gazing off thoughtfully, in a world she shared with no one. But Calain knew one thing: Cassandra was loyal. If one of her sisters needed her, she would come running, and Cassandra had sacrificed herself more than once to protect the others.

Cassandra's insistence that she stay behind in Arinol was not the first time she had ever pulled such a feat. The others had learned not to bother arguing with her, for when Cassandra was determined to protect someone, there was no stopping her. She was also somewhat skilled with magick, which made her one of the deadliest, if not the most difficult to defeat in their year.

And so, it wasn't odd at all that Calain and Cassandra spent most of their journey traveling in silence through the forest. As the days went by, Cassandra's strength returned to her, and before long, she no longer needed to keep her horse tied to Calain's, nor did she need Calain's strong hand to hold her up.

On the fifth day, as morning light streamed down, the knights rode out of the trees and across of a field toward Wolf Fortress, the gray stone stronghold that stood abandoned in the heart of the Dark Bloom Forest. It was not abandoned now, however. Calain was relieved to see smoke rising from one of the chimneys and knew some of the others had arrived ahead of them. Perhaps everyone was there. Her heart leapt when she thought of seeing Zelda again, whose eyes and lips and hair she had ached for during her trek through the forest with Cassandra.

"Remember," said Cassandra as they rode side by side, "stay your temper, Calain. We cannot afford to fight each other just now."

Calain glanced irritably at Cassandra. If something was wrong, why couldn't Cassandra just tell her?! "You did the same thing when Queen Ellanara was going to have me slain," said Calain, annoyed. "You gave vague warnings that did nothing to prevent what eventually happened!"

Cassandra answered, calm and serene, "Because my visions are often vague. I told you what I could. You did not heed."

Calain glanced away guiltily. That was true. Cassandra had warned her not to drink too much, and she had anyway, which had led to Zelda sending her outside for air . . . which had led to the Rose Guard knights cornering her.

"I'm sorry," said Calain heavily. "You gave up your life to aid me, and all I can do is yell at you."

"Stay your temper," Cassandra repeated calmly and spurred her horse on.

The front gates of the fortress were open, as if whoever dwelled inside was waiting for them. Calain followed Cassandra through the gates and under the stone archway, into the barren yard. They both pulled their horses to a stop and glanced around. The place seemed desolate. Wooden training equipment had been abandoned in the yard and had broken and deteriorated over time. There were still practice targets with arrows in them, as if the Knights of the Wolf had packed up and left in the middle of training.

The stable wasn't far, and Calain was happy to see Apple, Selene's dark horse, was standing in a stall and dozing there. So was Gweneth's speckled stallion, Bron. Relief flooded Calain: everyone was here! She dismounted and led Arthur to the stables. Cassandra dismounted Sunny and did likewise, but she seemed grim.

"What is it?" said Calain, patting Arthur and unsaddling him. "Why do you look so dour?"

"Stay your temper," Cassandra warned again.

Calain sighed. "Why can't you be normal?" To her relief, Cassandra gave a little smile.

They climbed the steps and entered the front hall together. Someone had lit the torches in the brackets along the walls. They could hear voices and followed them to the old kitchen, where Selene was poking the fire in the brick oven and adding logs to it, while Gweneth sat at a small table behind her, hair messy as she nursed an old bottle of wine. Both women were out of their armor and wearing tunics and trousers instead, though their swords were still buckled to their hips.

"About time," Selene said without looking up from the oven. She added another log and poked the fire to life with a hot poker.

The flames leapt, lining her sweaty face in gold light. "We're having venison tonight. Wash your hands in the bucket over there."

"You knew we were soon coming?" asked Calain in surprise.

Selene nodded. "I spied you earlier when I went out to hunt. A few Rose Guard knights were following you. I took care of them." She spoke very casually without looking at Calain and Cassandra as she turned to the skinned deer that hung nearby.

Gweneth didn't speak. Her eyes were miserable and bleary from drinking. She was sitting with her forehead in her hand, the wine bottle in her other hand, staring at the table. Her undercut brown hair was loose of its topknot and falling in her face in pale, curly tendrils.

Calain looked between the two women. "Where is Zelda?" she blurted.

Selene stood upright, glanced reprovingly at Gweneth, and wiped her hands clean of deer blood on a nearby cloth. She took a breath and said, "Zelda was provoked into leaving by Gweneth."

Calain felt her chest constrict, felt her heart suddenly pounding in her ears. She looked quickly at Gweneth for an explanation, but it was hard to see Gweneth's face. She was seeing red.

"Calain . . ." Cassandra warned in a low voice.

"And you haven't searched for her?" Calain demanded incredulously.

"We thought about it," said Selene unhappily. "The pair of us have only been here two days, and we figured you would arrive soon. Then I saw you in the forest and thought it would be best if we all knew what had happened and planned our next move from there. So we waited for you."

"You provoked her into leaving?" Calain said, glaring at Gweneth.

"Zelda cast a spell on her that made her stand still for a day," said Selene, who glanced darkly at Gweneth again.

Calain also glared at Gweneth again. "Serves you right. You can never stay your buffoonery. You must provoke and tease!"

"I know," said Gweneth with a flat laugh. "I've made things ill. Shocking, isn't it, Calain? Usually it's you who steps in it—" The last word was barely out of her mouth when Calain lunged and had tackled Gweneth out of her chair and to the floor. Calain's hands seemed to take on a mind of their own. They flew out from her, grabbed Gweneth about the throat, and proceeded to slam her head on the hard stone floor over and over . . . and over. Panting and grunting through her teeth, she was vaguely aware of Cassandra shouting her name, of Selene trying in vain to pry her off. Gweneth gasped and sputtered in her grasp, and it was satisfying. She kept slamming her by the neck until her eyes were rolling back in her head. Cassandra knelt down to help Selene, and Calain shouted angrily as she was finally dragged from Gweneth.

"Stop this madness!" Selene yelled.

Calain snatched herself free of Selene and Cassandra, who stood staring at her, waiting for her to lunge on Gweneth again. Gweneth lay sprawled on the floor in a daze, the wine bottle shattered nearby.

"Zelda could be out there, in danger!" Calain yelled. "And because of her!" She waved a disgusted hand at Gweneth. "And you," she shouted at Selene, "just sitting here, roasting venison, as if it were nothing!"

Selene's chest heaved angrily. "I just *told* you—!" she snarled, stepping forward, but Cassandra grabbed her arm.

"I shall find Zelda myself," said Calain, "because I love her. I'd never let anything happen to her! You three sit here and drink your wine and roast your venison!" And with that, Calain turned on her heel and stormed from the kitchen. She could hear Cassandra and Selene exchanging words behind her but didn't care to try and catch what was being said. Her heart was pounding too loudly in her ears.

Calain ran down the steps to the stable. She would follow the beat of Zelda's heart and find her that way. The Binding linked them for that specific purpose. She quickly saddled Arthur, who looked at her irritably, having believed he was free to sleep for the evening.

"Sorry, old boy," Calain said, leading Arthur out of the stable by his reins, "but Zelda needs us. She's in danger!" Calain swung up into the saddle and had almost charged off when she saw Selene running fast down the front steps, her black hair streaming in its braid.

Selene ran to Calain, where she sat astride her horse, and grabbed the reins. "Wait, Calain! Do not do anything reckless! Come back inside! Rest, have something to eat, and then we shall all go looking for her together—!" But Selene's words were lost to the wind when Calain smacked her hand away and spurred her horse, charging off through the gate and back into the Dark Bloom Forest.

CASSANDRA GENTLY GATHERED Gweneth's limp body in her arms and carried her up the stairs to the old barracks, where she deposited her in one of the beds that stood in neat uniform rows. There, she bandaged her bleeding head and left her to rest.

Wolf Fortress had been abandoned for fifty years. The tattered remains of the bedsheets smelled of stale age and the feather-stuffed mattresses smelled of decay. When Cassandra returned to Selene in the kitchen, she remarked on the stronghold's sad state and lamented that it had been abandoned.

"Aye," agreed Selene, who was presiding over the venison as it roasted in the oven. "But it had to be abandoned."

"Yes," agreed Cassandra unhappily.

Fifty years ago, the knights of Wolf Fortress had rebelled against the queen of the land. All of them, down to the smallest page girl, spoke out against Realm Koradara's war on Realm Eriallon. The knights refused to lend the queen their blades, and so she exiled them to the far north. The knights were forced to abandon Wolf Fortress, though many believed some had lingered in Koradara and were in hiding.

"So Calain has taken off alone into the forest," Cassandra said heavily and took Gweneth's vacated seat at the small table. It wasn't really a question, more a statement.

"Yes," answered Selene tiredly. "And you knew she would, didn't you?"

"It doesn't take the Sight to predict Calain's moods," said Cassandra, and Selene laughed in agreement.

But the laughter faded from Selene's face and she stared thoughtfully at the flames in the oven. "What shall we do?" she said unhappily. "We both of us need to stay here. Someone must watch over Gweneth, and hunt, and watch the road for enemies. That is not a job for one." Her lips tightened. "I could *strangle* Calain for injuring Gweneth and then abandoning us here alone! I can understand her fear, but she must one day realize that Zelda is no helpless weakling who needs us to come running each and every time. She is a sorceress! She has had her training, same as we."

"And she grew up on the streets of Perth," agreed Cassandra. "That is no small feat."

"We will wait until Gweneth is well, and then I suppose we must go after them both. I want to be angry with Calain, but truly, Gweneth is as much to blame. She loves to torment Zelda, and this time she has taken it too far. When shall she learn respect for our lady?"

"Do not worry so for Gweneth," said Cassandra, who looked very amused. "I examined her head wound. Calain has given her a nice souvenir to take heed from."

CALAIN RODE IN SILENCE through the forest, the green canopy above casting shadows over her grim face, Arthur's reins in hand, listening for any sign that Zelda was near. She followed Zelda's heartbeat for three days, and the closer she came, the stronger she could feel it. She knew that very soon she would be holding Zelda in her arms or perhaps fending off her captors. She was ready. Her hand kept going to her sword hilt in tense anticipation.

Selene and Cassandra had behaved as though Calain were overreacting and should not worry so greatly for Zelda, but had the pair of them failed to notice the giant crystals all over the forest? It was from those crystals that Bane Stones were carved! If Zelda was wandering through the Dark Bloom Forest alone, she was unable to cast magick. She was defenseless!

On the fifth day, Calain came across two knights of the Rose Guard. She had been riding loudly and confidently through the trees, while they were so careful and quiet, she hadn't heard them sneak upon her. One grabbed her leg and dragged her sideways from the saddle, and the second struck the pommel of his blade across her lowered head. Her ears rang as the helm vibrated against her hair. She saw spots and felt a rush of fury as her body was dragged helplessly down from the saddle. Grunting in pain and anger, she fell hard on her face in the dirt. Behind her, she could hear Arthur bucking and neighing in outrage.

One of the Rose Guard knights yelled as he dodged Arthur's kicking hooves. Calain heard fast footsteps as the other came to her. She turned over, hand on her sword hilt, prepared to draw and parry. . . and froze when she saw an arrow blossom on the knight's eye. He had been standing over Calain with his sword raised, ready to strike her. Now his rage-filled expression smoothed to shock. He collapsed forward, and Calain scrambled out of his way just in time.

The second knight watched in horror as his friend was felled. He put a hand to his sword hilt and whirled – just in time to receive an arrow in the face.

Calain sat very still, her gauntlet still on her sword hilt, wondering if she, too, would be riddled with arrows. When no arrows came, she slowly got to her feet.

"Stay your weapon, knight," called a woman, "and we shall stay ours!"

Calain followed the sound of the voice and saw three women standing in the shadows of the trees, hoods drawn up over their wild black hair. They were very big, as tall as Calain, at least six feet in height, though they were also slender and light on their feet, with only tight, lean muscle. They were not at all bulky, and seemed to favor leather armor, black wolfskins, and bows. They were Wilde Women.

Elven Wilde Women. Calain caught the hint of a pointed ear in their tangled hair, and their lean builds also spoke to their ancestry.

Calain knew the Wilde Women had always had an unspoken respect for women knights. Perhaps because they were so similar.

She nodded to the women and took her hand away from her sword hilt. "My thanks, friends," she said.

"And we thank you," said the woman in the lead. "We shall melt their armor down and make arrowheads of it." Beside her, the other archers nodded, looking very pleased. She stepped forward into the sunlight, and though her face was still half in shadow, Calain could see that it was lined with slight wrinkles and her black hair was graying. On her head she wore a helm and cloak made from the skull and hide of a great black wolf. "I am Ulga the Greater," she said and jerked her head at one of the smaller women behind her. "She is Ulga the Lesser, my daughter." (Ulga the Lesser nodded, a mere adolescent by the look of her.) "The other is Trova, my sister." (Trova nodded.) "We are women of the Black Wolf Clan and this is our forest."

"I am Calain, a knight of Falcon Isle."

The three women lifted their brows in surprise. The two behind Ulga the Greater murmured together in their language while giving Calain curious stares.

"You are far from home, Calain, Knight of Falcon Isle," Ulga the Greater said in sympathy and surprise. "But I know why you have come. You are tracking your woman through these lands."

"Yes," said Calain eagerly. "Have you seen her?" She did not like it when the women exchanged dark glances.

"We have seen her," spoke up Ulga the Lesser. She looked very grim and even angry. "The bear queen, Yrsa of the Black Bear Clan, she came along when your woman was cornered by wolves and she took her."

Calain tensed in outrage. "Who is this Yrsa and where can I find her – that I may rip off her head!"

"Take heed, young knight," said Trova quietly, but in a voice that was nonetheless hard and strong. "Yrsa is no game. If you approach her, your life will be forfeit. She will not give up your woman without a blood challenge."

Ulga the Greater nodded in agreement. "For years, my clan has sought to drive that demon out! She is a dangerous and deadly foe, even for you." Before Calain could protest, she added, "But I will tell you, Calain Falcon Knight. I will tell you where to find her, and do you know why?"

"Why?"Calain asked.

Ulga the Greater stepped closer. This time her face was in full sunlight, and Calain could see that she was missing an ear and one eye. Her lips tightened in cold fury. "Because Yrsa is a *beast* that should be put down! And in all my years, you are the first woman I have ever met who could perchance slay her."

Chapter 5

Zelda didn't know how long she slept, only that she wished she could sleep forever, stay in a dreamless, death-like state and never wake up. The pain of living, of being awake and thinking and moving, was too great. She cried and cried. And it seemed it went on for days without end.

She knew she had been placed in Yrsa's bed, a large pallet that had been draped in black bear fur across a mattress of bird feathers. The bedroom was separated from the rest of the hut by a curtain, and every now and then, Yrsa came through the curtain with food or water or clothes or simply to sit beside her and dry her tears. Then she left through the curtain again, always sleeping outside the room, as if to give Zelda privacy.

Zelda didn't know what she did to deserve such care and devotion, but Yrsa was fast becoming a source of both curiosity and comfort to her. On the fifth day, when she was feeling well enough to stand, she rose from the bed and went to the curtain, where she peered out and spied on Yrsa.

Yrsa was in the front room, standing over the firepit and poking the flames within to life. It was after supper and she had just finished eating (as had Zelda), but it was a cold night, and she was warming herself over the flames. Zelda realized she was getting ready for bed, for the big woman took off her giant two-handed blade and placed it in its holder on the wall, then stretched, thrusting her breasts to the ceiling, and knelt down, adjusting the pile of furs she had been sleeping on since bringing Zelda to her home.

Zelda felt guilty. Yrsa had fed her and comforted her and cared for her for five days now – this after saving her life!—and Zelda hadn't even spoken so much as two words to her!

Zelda pushed aside the curtain of beads and entered the front room, where Yrsa was preparing to sleep. Yrsa was already lying on her side on the furs but paused and looked up at Zelda in surprise. She sat up on her elbow and said, "Is Zelda hurt? Does Zelda need anything?"

Zelda smiled, touched by the woman's concern, and shook her head. "You have already given me the world," she said sadly. She was wearing a deerskin dress, like the other slender, non-warrior women in the village, and around her shoulders was wrapped a thick shawl of very warm black bearskin. Yrsa had also left her gifts of jewelry: earrings made of bear fangs, necklaces made of bear claws. She was wearing it all to show her gratitude.

Yrsa went still when she noticed. Her eyes glanced over Zelda in surprise, at the jewelry and the dress she had donned, drinking in how she looked in them, lingering over her shapely legs. Then her green eyes softened as she said, "Zelda look . . . beautiful." She sat up, folded her legs, and patted her thigh. "Zelda sit on Yrsa lap."

Zelda blushed a little, imagining herself in the big woman's arms. She came to the fire and sat on one of Yrsa's hard thighs, blushing a little more to feel how muscular and strong it was beneath her. Yrsa closed one big arm around Zelda and pinched her chin with a large finger and thumb, looking into her eyes. Her gaze was soft and admiring. Zelda trembled beneath the hunger in her green eyes and shyly cast her eyes down. Yrsa was so big, she seemed to consume the world, and Zelda felt dwarfed in her grasp. And yet, the hard wall of the woman's body around her made her feel safe. She had felt this way with Calain once. She nearly cried but held it down.

"Zelda speak to Yrsa?" Yrsa requested, taking her hand from Zelda's chin and letting it fall on her thigh. "Zelda voice pretty. Make Yrsa happy."

Yrsa wanted to talk? Zelda didn't mind. There was so much she wanted to understand! "Revna is a witch," Zelda said, frowning, "but she can cast magick around the crystals?"

Yrsa grunted. "Revna natural witch. Crystals have no power over natural witches."

Zelda stared off thoughtfully. Now she understood why Cassandra had been able to cast that cloaking spell: she was a natural witch! Natural witches were rare, but they existed and they were greatly feared. It was likely Cassandra had been sent off to become a knight in the hope that she would lose her power, but she never had.

"Only natural witches can be trusted," Yrsa said darkly. "Other kind, not so much." She looked down at Zelda. "Yrsa suppose Zelda is safe, though."

Zelda froze guiltily. "You know I'm a . . . witch?"

"Yes," said Yrsa darkly. "Yrsa was afraid you would attack her in the forest when she came, but the crystals had drained you, and Yrsa knew then you weren't natural. Yrsa still worry you might attack her and leave this place. Zelda have no reason to stay."

"Yes, I do," said Zelda, smoothing her hand over Yrsa's thigh and looking her in the eye. She gave Yrsa what she hoped was a look warm with lust. It must have been, for Yrsa went still and looked down at her in surprise.

"So Zelda will stay with Yrsa?" Yrsa asked, sounding both sad and suspicious.

"I won't pretend I'm not attracted to you," said Zelda helplessly. "And Revna was right . . . I . . . I have nothing." Her lip trembled as she thought of Calain and Selene staring with empty eyes, of Cassandra and Gweneth being cut down so viciously . . . And she couldn't go back to Eriallon, she couldn't survive on her own without her knights in the city. Just like that, life had exiled her to the wild, to her newest protector. She felt like a weak little bird, passed from cage to cage, never able to defend and care for herself. Her own helplessness infuriated her.

"Then Yrsa take care of Zelda," Yrsa said soothingly, and Zelda's heart fluttered in happiness and gratitude.

"And you," Zelda said, looking up at Yrsa thoughtfully. "Revna spoke very highly of you. So why aren't you married already?" She was amazed when Yrsa's cheeks flamed the tiniest bit.

"Yrsa was betrothed," the big warrior woman admitted. "Was going to marry Signe, though Ysra cared little for her."

"Then why marry her?"

Yrsa shrugged her muscular shoulders. "No women in the village interest Yrsa. Many beautiful, yes, and many ask for Yrsa to handfast. But Yrsa not in love with any of them. Only agreed to handfast Signe because she wanted Yrsa badly, chase Yrsa for years, try to entice Yrsa at the festivals by dancing naked before her." Yrsa made a face, and Zelda laughed.

"Is Signe not a fair maiden?" Zelda asked, highly amused by Yrsa's disgust.

"No, Signe is fair. Has tits big as melons and fine, strong legs. Wide hips. She will bear many strong daughters, and there are many warriors who desire her."

"Then why don't you desire her?"

"Yrsa does not love Signe," Yrsa said simply. "Yrsa has only ever loved . . ." She trailed off as she looked at Zelda, then she looked away again, embarrassed. "Zelda should be wary of Signe. She will be angry that Zelda has taken her place."

"I can handle Signe," said Zelda dismissively, "and anyone else who comes along!"

Yrsa seemed very amused by that but did not comment.

UNFORTUNATELY FOR ZELDA, she could *not* handle Signe, nor any of the other non-warrior women in the village, who were known ubiquitously as "the hearth wives" because they stayed home and did not hunt. All the hearth wives seemed to have taken Signe's side and were cruel to Zelda as a result. When the women gathered to weave baskets or prepare meals, they mocked Zelda in their language, Signe the leader among them, her eyes scathing each and every time she looked at Zelda.

The mockery escalated to physical violence. The women would walk by as Zelda was sitting outside Yrsa's hut, clumsily weaving a basket, and as they mocked her lack of skill, they would yank her hair and keep walking. Such meanness continued, with Signe tossing food in Zelda's face at village meals and then laughing at her when she didn't retaliate before insulting her in a string of nasty words in her language. The other women often joined in, pointing and laughing at Zelda.

The bullying went on for one week. Zelda didn't think there was anything she could do to defend herself without becoming exiled from the village. She was a newcomer and an outsider who had yet to earn her place. Revna had told her she must prove herself a good wife, and so, after her first conversation with Yrsa around the fire, she had taken to cooking Yrsa's meals and cleaning Yrsa's hut and rubbing Yrsa's shoulders when she came home, tired from the hunt. She knew she was on trial, that her place in the clan was precarious, and so she was afraid to cause trouble by fighting back against Signe and the other hearth wives.

But Zelda was tired of being bullied, too! One night over supper, as she sat with Yrsa around the fire in their hut, she complained about Signe and the other women. "They despise me!" she moaned, rubbing her head where her scalp was sore from all the hair pulling. To her surprise, Yrsa looked at her across the fire with a mixture of pity and amusement.

"It's not funny!" Zelda said at once.

Yrsa shook her head. "If Zelda is to survive in Black Bear Clan, then Zelda must become a bear."

Zelda blinked at Yrsa, not understanding. There were many tribes of Wilde Women, and Yrsa's was that of the black bear. The Black Bear Clan had rival clans of Wilde Women nearby. Another clan, known as the Black Wolf Clan, had been trying to take over Dark Bloom Forest for years, but the Black Bear Clan was steadily pushing them out. The people of the Black Bear Clan often referred to themselves as bears, which Zelda found silly and confusing, and now Yrsa was doing it again.

"Bears do not let other bears mark their territory," Yrsa elaborated. "If other wives wish to push Zelda out, Zelda must stand firm. Like bear."

Zelda went still when she finally understood what Yrsa was saying to her: Yrsa was giving Zelda permission to crack some skulls.

Yrsa smiled when she saw the look of realization in Zelda's eyes and went back to her meal, lifting the giant roasted stag leg from her wooden plate and taking a great bite.

THE NEXT MORNING, ZELDA cooked Yrsa breakfast as usual, then kissed her goodbye when she set out to hunt. Then, after cleaning up the dishes, she sat on a mat in front of Yrsa's great hut, as usual, and practiced weaving baskets. When Signe came by with her friends and attempted to bully Zelda and pull her hair, Zelda launched to her feet and gave Signe the back of her fist. Signe fell hard on her seat. Blood actually flew, and when Signe looked up, she was missing a tooth. She touched an indignant hand to her jaw and stared up at Zelda, her eyes wide in shock.

Everyone had gone still, staring at Zelda. The other hearth wives and a few warriors in the village stood outside their huts, clutching infants and hunting bows, watching with interest. Children had also stopped mid-play to stare. Everyone had seen what Zelda had done.

Zelda towered breathlessly over Signe, her blue eyes blazing. She had grown up on the streets of Perth, fighting in the mud with other children, and sometimes against grown men who wanted to steal her. It was the first time since she was a child that she had drawn blood from a bully. She had to admit....it felt good.

The flustered hearth wives pulled Signe to her feet, and all of them backed away, still staring.

"Signe ever touch Zelda again," said Zelda, speaking brokenly in the language of the Black Bear Clan, "Zelda will rip off Signe head! I am Zelda, woman of Yrsa, woman of queen bear!"

Signe stared at Zelda in disbelief. She was as beautiful as Yrsa had said, with long, flowing black hair and a round, pretty face. Her breasts and hips were quite big and round, her thighs full. She was wonderfully curvy and pretty. Zelda thought it was a shame they couldn't get along, perhaps share Yrsa between them.

To Zelda's surprise, Signe lowered herself to her knees, staining them with dirt as she folded forward in a bow. Her friends did likewise, and when Zelda looked up....the whole village was bowing.

AFTER SHE STOOD UP to Signe, Zelda became known as First Hearth Wife to the clan. The other hearth wives respected her, bowing their heads as she passed, and the warrior women looked at her with longing, as if they wished her for their own. Completely baffled, Zelda asked Yrsa about the sudden change in the clan one night as they sat together beside the fire in Yrsa's hut. Zelda was sitting in Yrsa's lap. Yrsa's muscly legs were folded and her big arms were around Zelda.

"It because aggression desirable trait in woman, while submission is weakness," Yrsa explained, sounding very proud of Zelda. "Yrsa wish she had been there to see Zelda punch Signe."

Zelda blushed when Yrsa, without warning, cupped her heavy breasts in fistfuls and whispered huskily in her ear, "Did Zelda's big tits jiggle when she swung?"

Zelda shivered. Yrsa had never touched her like this before. Zelda had kissed Yrsa on the cheek every morning, and at night they had cuddled in bed, but it had never gone beyond that. Now her heart raced with excitement. But to her disappointment, Yrsa only kissed her cheek and announced that it was time for bed.

Frustrated that Yrsa would not make love to her, Zelda sought the advice of the other hearth wives, who were all so eager, kind, and sincere now that she had shown strength and dominance. Signe in particular was vying among the others to befriend her. It was she who led Zelda by the arm to the great flower fields beyond the village, where purple flowers veiled the grass in a sweet-smelling carpet.

Many hearth wives were already in the flower field, chatting in little circles as they weaved baskets, braiding each other's hair with flowers, exchanging jokes and complaining good-naturedly about their warrior wives. Little girls ran back and forth in the sunlight, giggling as they played hide-and-seek in the tall grass.

The Black Bear Clan women seemed so happy and at peace. Zelda realized with a skip of her heart that she was now one of them. She would live out her days here, laughing and cared for, perhaps raising children of her own. Yrsa would protect her. No more running and hiding and sleeping on the ground. Now she shared the bed of a warrior queen!

Signe chose a free spot in the grass and beckoned Zelda to kneel there with her. She knelt behind Zelda, and after stroking her long golden curls in wonder for a time, she gently started to plait it, weaving in purple flowers as she worked.

"Yrsa has not touched Zelda," Signe gently explained, "because she does not believe Zelda heart is true."

"But I love being with Yrsa!" Zelda protested and was surprised by her own words. It had only been a few weeks, but it was true she had grown fond of the warrior queen.

"Then you must show it," said Signe, who sounded very pleased by Zelda's eagerness.

Zelda hesitated. "Why are you helping me, Signe? I thought you wanted Yrsa for yourself."

Signe hesitated, her hands slowing in Zelda's hair, and said a little sadly, "Signe loves Yrsa, yes. Has loved Yrsa since she was a child and has long wanted her. Signe want Yrsa to be happy. Could not say she loved her if she did not want her happiness."

Zelda stared at her knees and was silent for a moment as Signe continued braiding her hair. She felt guilty. Signe was in love with Yrsa and was set to marry her, but along came Zelda and took her dreams away. How would Zelda feel if some other sorceress had come along and turned Calain's head? She would have been furious, too, though she would not have taken it out on anyone as Signe had. She supposed the aggressiveness was part of being a Wilde Woman. Perhaps it ran in their blood.

"How can I prove to Yrsa that my heart is true?" Zelda asked.

"Zelda will not like the answer."

"Tell me, Signe, *please.*"

Signe sighed. "Zelda must handfast Yrsa—"

"Handfasting is marriage, isn't it? I don't mind that. I wish it!"

"—and Zelda must have Yrsa child."

Zelda paused. She spun around and faced Signe, who seemed confused by her shock.

"First Hearth Wife –?"

"Have her *child*?" Zelda repeated. "How is that even possible?"

"So Yrsa has not told Zelda? Revna will make potion with your blood and blood of Yrsa. You must drink potion to become with her child."

Zelda paused again. "So you don't kidnap men and rape them to make children?"

Signe looked at her in amazement for a beat and then burst out laughing. "Kidnap men? First Hearth Wife is so funny!" She laughed again, shaking her head.

Zelda turned back around, feeling foolish. She thought of what Gweneth had said about mystical pregnancies and thought she understood: the Wilde Women reproduced through magick. Perhaps it was the reason they were so big and strong.

Chapter 6

The last great black wolf fell with a whimper as Calain brought her blade down, severing its head from its shaggy neck. The wolves' black bodies were scattered around her, staring, bleeding from long fangs, twice the size of normal wolves. There were nine of them. An entire pack had attacked her! Gweneth had told Calain that the black wolves found across the realms were not like their small grey brethren, who shied from humans and chased only deer and rabbits. No, the black wolves were vicious and went brazenly after a lone human the moment they spotted one. They were known as Skoll Wolves. Gweneth had told Calain that, though she didn't want to think of Gweneth right now.

Panting, Calain wiped her blade clean in the grass and sheathed it on her back, for she had left her cloak back at Wolf Fortress. She wondered what the others were doing, if they had set out after her yet. Probably not. She had likely cracked Gweneth's skull, a fact she wasn't proud of, and the others would have their hands full nursing her back to health.

Calain turned and glanced around irritably. Her satchel had been spilled during the fight, and the contents were scattered, some sliding into the water, for she had camped beside a stream. Muttering crossly to herself, she stuffed everything back in her satchel and stood again when she heard the sound of approaching hooves.

When the wolves had attacked Calain's camp, Arthur had taken off a little way into the trees. Now the horse came back, slowly and apprehensively. Shaking her head, Calain went to him and patted his long face.

"Thou art craven at the best of times," Calain teased the horse.

Arthur snorted indignantly.

"Really?" said a woman. "I thought he was quite brave – for a horse. He kicked one of the wolves in the face for you. Or didn't you see?"

Calain whirled, her hand going at once to her sword hilt. But her eyes fell on the owner of the voice and she went still, her lip curling.

It was the dark witch who had abducted Zelda back at the forest outside Ternia. The leader of Raven's Cross. The symbol – a black raven with wings spread to form a cross – was still upon her forehead. She was alone, draped in a long, tight-fitting black gown, her long, dark hair covered by a black cloak and hood. The gown bared her generous cleavage to the sunlight, milky white and swollen breasts large enough to rival Zelda's. She looked at Calain in calm amusement with her dark, glittering eyes, her pretty face framed by curtains of black hair.

"*You*," said Calain darkly. "Foul witch."

The woman smiled under her hood. "A pleasure to see you as well, Calain, Knight of Falcon. I don't believe we've ever been properly introduced. I am Melvalda, high priestess of Raven's Cross."

"And kidnapper of women," said Calain roughly.

Melvalda pursed her lips in mock hurt. "I never kidnapped Zelda. She came with me willingly. She's like a bitch in heat, that one. You're running off all valiant to save her, but she's fucking the bear queen as we speak."

Calain tensed. "Cease your lies, snake!"

Melvalda only continued to smile. "Oh, lying, am I? You poor fool. She's really got you around her finger. You really think she's this innocent little dove, don't you?" She waved her hand, conjuring a great bubble that hovered between them. Inside the bubble, scenes appeared: Zelda standing in a field of wildflowers, facing a giant barbarian woman, flowers in her golden hair; Zelda tying her hand to the barbarian woman's big hand with white cord and smiling; Zelda drinking a potion with a shaking hand . . . Zelda in the barbarian woman's lap, head falling back as the big woman suckled one of her breasts and fingered her beneath her dress of furs. . . Calain was shaking. She could feel it, the big woman's fingers gliding hungry in her sex, the thrill of the woman's lips on her nipple, the quickening of Zelda's heart. It was real. She could feel it. It was real!

Melvalda waved a pale hand, and the bubble and its imagery vanished. "Did you see the potion Zelda drank?" she asked. "It will make her with child. *Yrsa's* child."

Still shaking, Calain turned her back. "You lie."

"No. Zelda has married Ysra and is carrying her child."

Calain stood with her back to the witch, suddenly blinded by tears. "She . . . She had no choice. She was forced to wed!"

"Are you crying, sweet knight?" said Melvalda softly, but there was no mockery in her voice.

Calain bowed her head, trembling all over. "Why have you shown me this?" she demanded through her teeth.

"Have you forgotten, sweet knight," answered Melvalda, and now her voice took on a sarcastic sweetness, "that only two full moons ago, you *massacred* my coven and stole my newest recruit to boot? Did you think I would not seek compensation?"

"Compensation?" Calain repeated dully. She was suddenly too miserable to care about anything Melvalda was saying. She only knew that her heart was broken, and that the pain of it was unbearable. Just nights ago, Zelda had looked Calain in the eye and told her she loved her. Now she was married to another and having her child! Had it all been a lie?

"Zelda will have a child," Melvalda said. "I have seen it, and it shall be mine. You will take Zelda from the barbarian queen, and you will bring her to me, here, beside this stream. I will never get my hands on the child inside her otherwise."

"I will not help you!" Calain roared.

Melvalda was silent a long moment. Then she said quietly, "Very well. You will take Zelda from Yrsa—I know you will because she's trained you quite aptly, her devote little dog – (Calain tensed) and I shall take Zelda from you. The child *shall* be mine."

Calain whirled, intent on slicing Melvalda's head off, but the witch had gone, having left Zelda's stave in her place.

Chapter 7

Though she was now married and pregnant with her warrior wife's child, Zelda still thought of Calain every day. Sometimes she thought she could still feel Calain's heartbeat, but how was that possible if Calain were dead? Perhaps it was the madness of grief. The images Revna had shown her had seemed so real, too real to be a lie, and Revna was a kind old woman who looked after her always. She did not believe the old woman capable of such deceit.

But Zelda still missed Calain regardless. Sometimes she fell to sitting and staring for long hours, dreaming of those nights when Calain had held her so close and made love to her. She missed Calain's laugh and the way her green eyes had fired with lust anytime they caught a hint of Zelda's cleavage, the shape of her backside through her gown as she was bending... She missed the way Calain had always smelled like grass, leather, steel, and wine. She missed the way Calain used to hold her so tightly as they were sleeping. She missed Calain's sloppy, sleepy kisses in her hair.

And she missed the others, too. Selene's gentle hand on her back as they slept . . . The way Cassandra's pale eyes had looked upon her the night she rode before Calain in the saddle, so serious and yet burning with lust . . . She even missed Gweneth's teasing and felt silly for becoming so angry. But she had to admit, at least here, with the Black Bear Clan, she was not treated like a delicate little flower who could not defend herself. No one here scrambled to protect her. She was expected to protect herself!

Once they were wed, Yrsa had set about teaching Zelda to shoot a bow and to fight with a blade, things she would have learned as a child had she grown up with the Black Bear Clan. Zelda was clumsy and hopeless with a blade, especially since she had no muscles and the blade was too heavy, but she was pleased to discover she was very good with a bow! Unable to use her magick because of the giant crystals throughout the village, she was glad to have some way to defend herself and went about with a quiver of arrows always upon her back and a bow in her hand.

One day, Zelda looked at her reflection in the washbasin and didn't recognize herself. She had fully transitioned into a barbarian, swathed in fur garments, covered in mud, her golden curls wild and uncombed and slowly becoming matted. She had spent so much time with the hearth wives, braiding hair and chatting happily, that her hair was now loaded down with beads and feathers and flower petals. She looked truly wild. And the wilder she looked, the more Yrsa seemed to want her.

One night after supper, Zelda bent to toss another log on the fire and screamed softly in surprise when Yrsa pushed her fur dress up over her backside and proceeded to lick and taste her sex until she was gushing and her thighs trembling. Yrsa buried her face in Zelda's sex and grunted, eating away at her like a ravenous hog, until Zelda could not hold back her screams of helpless ecstasy.

And Yrsa wanted it all the time. Her lust was insatiable. In the morning. In the afternoon. In the middle of the night. She never hesitated. Whatever Zelda was doing, Yrsa simply barged up to her, threw her over her shoulder, and stomped off with her, as the hearth wives and the warriors laughed and cheered.

Zelda blushed whenever Yrsa publicly grabbed her and carried her away, but she liked it. She liked how big and strong and aggressive Yrsa was, grabbing her by the waist and the hips and flipping her easily around in bed, kissing and licking and tasting and groping with an abandon that often left Zelda panting and blushing, breasts heaving as she lay in the tousled mess of her hair and the tattered remains of her clothes.

And Yrsa's muscly hands were so hard and strong, Zelda could always feel the woman's touch long after she had gone. The press of her fingers on Zelda's breasts was ever-lingering from her groping.

Hunting wasn't all Yrsa did during the day. Because she was queen of the Black Bear Clan, she often held court in the great hut at the center of the village. There, her throne sat on a dais, covered in black bear fur and guarded by two dour-faced warrior women. And she would sit there all day, settling disputes and complaints, granting requests, listening to grievances.

Once she had married Yrsa, Zelda took to joining her wife in the throne room. There was only one throne, and so, she often wound up sitting on Yrsa's knee or kneeling at her boot as Yrsa absently stroked her hair. The supplicants were always speaking in the quick, grunting language of the Black Bear Clan, but Zelda had learned a few words over the weeks and soon found herself interrupting to make suggestions. She begged for mercy for a pair of Black Wolf women who had been captured and who Yrsa had planned to execute; she helped settle a dispute between two wives who wanted a divorce; and she helped an old woman get retribution who had been robbed by one of the younger women. Before long, the people of the village looked to Zelda for guidance as much as they looked to Yrsa. It had been three weeks now.

By the end of the third week, Zelda's pregnancy was showing. She couldn't believe it! She lifted up her shirt and showed Yrsa, who seemed very proud of the fact.

Yrsa placed a large hand on Zelda's round belly, fingers spread, and said with pride and joy, "My daughter kicks inside you! Feel how strong her tiny fists? The claws of a bear! She is the reason you have become so Wilde, wife of my heart!"

Yrsa was sitting on the bed as she spoke, rubbing Zelda's belly. Zelda was standing over her at the side of the bed. She smiled down at Yrsa as the warrior woman leaned closed and kissed her big belly.

"But how is it possible?" Zelda asked helplessly. "We were only married less than two weeks ago!"

"The pregnancy magick," said Yrsa. "Faster than normal pregnancies. Zelda will be bear me many strong daughters, and my brood will swarm this forest, and we take it at last from those black *dogs*."

Zelda knew Yrsa was speaking of the Black Wolf Clan. She did not pretend to understand why Yrsa and her clan hated them so, though she wished all the Wilde Women would at least compromise and try to be friendly. What was the point fighting each other? The violence seemed so senseless.

Yrsa would not allow Zelda to sit on the floor while large with child, and so, the next day as she sat on her throne, Yrsa had Zelda perch on her knee. She absently stroked Zelda's long golden hair as one of the warrior women came in and announced that they had a visitor.

Many warriors and hearth wives stood and knelt along the walls in the great room and began to murmurer and whisper amongst themselves. As the murmuring rose, Revna, who was standing with calm dignity at the foot of the dais, went still and glanced quickly up at Zelda. Zelda went still as well, staring down into the old woman's frightened eyes. *What have you done, old woman?* she thought. Revna lifted her chin and looked away.

"A visitor?" said Yrsa roughly when the messenger had finished speaking. "We do not allow visitors! Why have you not bring her in chains?" She was speaking (broken) common tongue for Zelda's benefit.

The messenger shook her head and said helplessly in the tongue of the Black Bear Clan, "We could not tame this one to chain her! She should have been a Wilde Woman! She nearly killed us all when we approached! Many have already fallen to her blade—!"

Yrsa was outraged. "What?! You could not overpower a single woman?" she bellowed in her tongue.

"She is not like other women! She is stronger than us, faster! She has called a truce," said the messenger desperately. "We give her your woman, and she doesn't . . . slay us all." She lowered her voice and added, "I believe she could, bear queen. Save face and let this one go." She glanced at Zelda.

Yrsa's lips tightened and she placed a resolute arm around Zelda that felt like an iron wall when it enclosed her. "Never! Send this trespasser in, and I will slay her, here, in my throne room, and drink wine from her skull!"

Yrsa spoke in her own tongue again, but Zelda had understood most of what had been said and gasped in horror. "You can't fight this stranger for me!" Zelda begged, placing a small hand on Yrsa's big arm, but her pleas went ignored. Yrsa simply stroked Zelda's hair and did not answer her. Her dark green eyes were fixed with determination on the distant curtain of the hut.

A moment later, and the stranger entered the throne room to a fresh round of murmuring and whispering. Revna tightened at the sight of her.

Zelda felt her heart stop: it was Calain! Calain approached the throne at a hard march, covered in the blood of her foes, jingling in her silver Falcon armor, fury and determination etched upon her face, her red hair wild as she carried her helm under her arm. In her hand was Zelda's stave, which she threw down at the foot of the throne. Her eyes blazed an accusation when she glanced at Zelda, who felt her heart skip in anguish and shame. What must she look like to Calain, sitting there *pregnant* on the knee of another woman? But suddenly, Zelda didn't care. *Calain was alive!* Before Yrsa could stop her, she pushed herself up from her lap and ran as fast as she could to Calain, who caught her in her arms as she crushed against her.

"Calain! Oh, Calain! They told me you were dead!" Zelda sobbed, showering Calain's startled face in frantic kisses. "But you're alive! Oh, Calain!"

Zelda's heart leapt happily when Calain let out a hearty chuckle and hugged her tight. "My lady!" she whispered into Zelda's hair. She pulled back and looked down at Zelda with soft eyes. "But what have they done to you? You're pregnant!" Her angry eyes went past Zelda to Yrsa. "And with the child of this . . . *creature*."

Yrsa's dark green eyes narrowed in a glare.

Zelda guiltily turned and looked up at Yrsa, who looked both furious and hurt by Zelda's open display of affection for Calain. The bear queen sat on her throne, very still, the hilt of her great two-handed sword held fast in one hand as she stabbed it with a meaty fist into the wooden dais.

"Yrsa didn't do anything to me," Zelda confessed. "I wanted to marry her." She placed a hand on her big belly and said, "I chose this."

Yrsa seemed pleased by that. She smiled into Zelda's eyes, and heart fluttering, Zelda smiled back. Then Yrsa looked at Calain in triumph.

"Did you hear her, bird knight?" called Yrsa from her throne, her deep voice booming around the silent room as everyone tensely watched. "Zelda wanted me. Zelda chose me. Zelda mine."

"No," Zelda said, startling Yrsa, who looked down at her sadly. Tears starting to her eyes, Zelda went on with a deep breath, "I only ch-chose you because – because Revna lied to me! She told me my love was dead!" She took Calain's arm and stepped close to her. "And in despair, I wed you, Yrsa."

More murmuring and soft cries of disapproval from the crowd in the throne room.

Zelda glared at Revna. "You lying old witch!"

Revna was holding her wooden staff with the crystal and feathers on the end. She was a tiny woman but stood very straight and proud, draped in black bear furs, with raven feathers in her mass of gray hair. She regarded Zelda coolly, turning her head so that her bear fang earrings swung as she said in common tongue, "I only did what I thought best. Yrsa is like a daughter to me. She loved you desperately. I wanted her to be happy, so I told you whatever you needed to hear so you would stay here, and I was right: I have never seen her so happy, so fierce and so strong, as she has been since you have taken to her bed. Your love gave her strength! And you were very happy as well, do not deny it!"

Calain didn't like that. Zelda felt her tense furiously.

"Enough," said Yrsa, waving a hand to silence the old woman. She looked down at Zelda and her eyes were still hurt, though she was trying very hard to look cold and indifferent, Zelda could tell. "Will you stay with Yrsa or no?"

Feeling wretched, Zelda squeezed her hold on Calain's arm and said, "I wish to leave with Calain. She is Bound to me, and I love her."

More murmuring and the crowd in the throne room shook their heads darkly at Zelda in anger and disgust. Many of them seemed to feel betrayed that she had chosen Calain, but Yrsa did not look angry at all. Instead, she said with a deep breath and a wave of her hand, "Then so be it. Zelda leave with . . . (her lip curled) Calain, the bird knight."

Zelda's heart leapt happily and she looked up at Calain, who was still staring bitterly at Yrsa, as if she wished nothing more than to slice her head off. But after glancing around the room, Calain looked down at Zelda and said softly, "Are you certain you would come with me, my lady?"

Zelda looked up at Calain in amazement. "What do you mean?"

Calain glanced around the throne room sadly, at the happy mothers carrying infants, at the wild and strong warrior women who watched them. "You look happy and well here," she admitted grudgingly. "I came here knowing the bear queen had you and ready to slay her to defend your honor! But now that I look upon her, now that I see she cares for your happiness . . . Zelda, maybe you were safer and happier staying here. The bear queen is strong and can protect you. She can . . ." Calain glanced down at Zelda's big belly, "give you children . . . She can give you a life that I cannot."

"I can't believe what I'm hearing!" Zelda cried, wide-eyed.

Calain touched Zelda's face. "With me, you would always be running, always in danger, always hungry and tired and aching from the saddle. That is no life for you. You deserve to have a home. You deserve to be happy. I want that for you!"

Zelda's heart melted to see the earnest in Calain's eyes. Then she looked at Yrsa, who was watching her in sympathy, and loved her as well. She stood there, torn between the two of them, and wondering what she had done to be loved so tenderly and so greatly by these strong, warrior women.

Zelda looked up at Calain and touched her face. "Calain," she said, shaking her head, "tis *you* I love."

Calain's eyes softened again, and she took Zelda's hand and kissed it.

"Then leave here," boomed Yrsa, trying not to look hurt. She stared past them instead. "Leave immediately and never return."

Zelda miserably dropped her eyes. She had not wanted to end things with Yrsa so coldly.

The messenger, the warrior woman who had announced Calain's coming, stepped near the throne, frowning as she said in the language of the Black Bear Clan, "My queen, you cannot allow your woman to simply leave from here. And with your child? Outrageous!"

Yrsa looked down at the messenger. "What is the meaning of this, Hilgard?" she boomed.

The messenger, the apparent Hilgard, shook her dirty-blonde head, the wild hair cascading with beads and bones. "Your woman has dishonored you by running to a stranger's arms and kissing her before all your subjects! You would look weak if you let her simply walk from here!"

More murmuring from the crowds and several women nodded sternly in agreement.

Zelda felt the fear swelling inside her. The messenger was right, of course: if Yrsa allowed Zelda to leave without a fight, she would forfeit her place as queen, she would lose the respect of her people. But if Yrsa fought, she might lose to Calain . . . She might die.

Zelda stepped forward. "Yrsa," she said sadly and peered up at the throne, "I . . . I never meant to cause you trouble."

Yrsa looked down at her with soft eyes echoing sadness. "Yrsa know," she said quietly. "It not Zelda fault. Zelda didn't make Yrsa love her." She lifted her face and looked past Zelda, cold and stern once more. "Yrsa challenges the bird night in a fight to death. The winner shall have Zelda. Does the bird knight accept?"

"Calain, no!" Zelda begged desperately.

"And what else shall I do? Leave here without you?" said Calain in amazement. "Tis madness that you ever married her!" She looked up at Yrsa and said loudly enough that her voice rang around the room, "I accept your challenge, bear queen! May the best warrior win!"

Chapter 8

It was only a few days before Gweneth was well enough that she could ride. Calain, thankfully, had not cracked her skull and had only left her with a few bruises. Selene quietly hoped that Gweneth's bruises would give her some pause and force her to reflect on her sharp tongue, but she knew she was hoping in vain.

Once Gweneth was well, the three knights mounted their steeds and took off into the forest on Calain's heels. Calain wasn't difficult to track. The red knight had left a very obvious path, so great was her haste, and had not even bothered to hide her old camp fires by filling the firepits. It was obvious to Selene that she had moved at a breakneck pace, so desperate was she to reach Zelda.

Selene secretly wondered if Calain hadn't been right to fear for Zelda's safety so greatly. She was the only one with a link to Zelda's heart, so she was the only one who could truly feel if she was in danger. There could have been something happening to the sorceress, something dire, and Calain had known on an instinctive level but no one had listened to her. Selene felt guilty for that, but she also felt a little bitter, knowing she did not share a connection with Zelda and thus, could not know if she was ill or well.

It took a little more than a week to catch up with Calain. During that time, they were attacked by giant black wolves and came across a few Wilde Women lurking in the shadows, wearing black wolf helms above their piercing, slanted eyes. The women never spoke to them and never approached them, instead watching them with narrowed eyes from a distance, their hunting bows lowered.

"The clan of the Black Wolf," said Cassandra quietly when they had passed yet another pair of tall women watching them solemnly from the trees.

"What do they know that we don't?" said Gweneth, bobbing astride Bron. "They remind me of you, Cassandra. They seem to know something serious is going on, but they keep it to themselves. If we were to ask, they'd probably give us vague limericks about the moon."

Cassandra smiled as she bobbed astride Sunny. "I don't know any limericks."

"More's the pity," sighed Gweneth, "I like limericks."

"Be still!" snapped Selene. She held up her arm, a silent command for the others to a stop. They did, and all three of them peered at the village ahead.

It was a very large village, stretching away as far as the eye could see, a small city of thatched huts made of wood and mud, smoking gently in the evening sunlight. Torches had been lit along the streets and stone braziers had been filled with fire. Everywhere, tall Wilde Women in black bear furs were moving toward the center of the village. A soft roar of enthusiastic chattering was coming from the crowd, and a great deal of smoke was rising from a bonfire at the center of the village.

Selene dismounted, staring at the village. Beside her, Gweneth and Cassandra dismounted as well.

"What say you, Selene?" said Gweneth cheerfully. "Shall we burst into a village full of giant, cannibalistic warrior women?"

"The Wilde Women are not cannibals," said Cassandra absently. She was staring into the village with her intense, serious gray eyes as she clutched Sunny's reins.

Gweneth rolled her eyes. "I was jesting."

"Well, stop," Selene snapped. "Be serious for once, Gweneth, and be still!"

"I *am* serious," Gweneth returned crossly. "Are we really going in there? Tis madness! There are only three of us and more than eight hundred strong of them! Probably more by the looks of them. You see all those crystals? Zelda could not cast in there. If Calain went in there alone, she is a fool."

"If Calain went in there," said Selene, "that's where we're going. Come." And she marched forward without looking back. She heard the others following.

They had nearly reached the village when two Wilde Women came out to meet them. To Selene's surprise, they kept their weapons sheathed and were smiling and seemed very amused by the sight of them.

"You friends of the bird knight?" said one in broken common tongue.

"She means Calain," muttered Gweneth, amused.

"We are," said Selene with a solemn nod.

The women exchanged amused glances. Then one muttered, "How many bird knights was First Hearth Wife fucking?" The other laughed loudly.

Selene's eyes narrowed irritably. "May we enter?"

"You may," said one of the women, surprising Selene.

"Head to center of village. You will find your bird friend there," said the other.

The two Wilde Women stepped aside. Selene hesitated and walked past them uncertainly, leading Cassandra and Gweneth forward and leaving their horses on the edge of the forest.

As they walked in a close group, many Wilde Women stopped to stare at them. Small girls, who were running and laughing, hopped to a halt and pointed as they squealed, "Look, Mommy! More bird women!" in their language. The children flapped their arms and squawked like birds, dancing in mocking circles around them as they walked on.

"Falcons do not *squawk*," muttered Gweneth bitterly.

The crowds of Wilde Women grew thicker the further in they walked. Many were simply ignoring Selene and the others now, only giving them a glance before turning their eager attention back to what was happening near the huge bonfire in the village square.

Selene pushed her way to the front of the crowd at last, and Cassandra and Gweneth emerged either side of her. The three of them stared grimly at the fight happening beside the blazing bonfire:

Calain was struggling in close combat against the biggest Wilde Woman Selene had ever seen. The Wilde Woman must've been over six feet tall, and her body, covered in leathers and bear furs, was bulging with muscles. Her neck alone looked thick enough to be a tree trunk. She had long, wild auburn hair and was wearing a horned circlet made of bone. In her meaty hands was a two-handed sword, huge and made of a gleaming black metal. She was lifting it above Calain and not for the first time: Calain was bloody and exhausted, though fighting valiantly.

"No!" screamed Zelda's voice.

Selene's head snapped around, following the sound of Zelda's voice until she spied her at last. Zelda was standing on the edge of the crowd, opposite Selene, Gweneth, and Cassandra, and . . . she was large with child! She was trying to run in and stop the fighting, and two Wilde Women, slender and small, were holding her back with solemn faces, griping her arms to stop her escape. As Zelda struggled to get free, an elderly witch stood beside her, chin lifted, watching the fight through narrowed eyes as she clutched a wooden stave bound with feathers.

Selene hardly recognized Zelda. In place of her long traveling gown and gray cloak, she was wearing leathers and animal hides, while her mass of curly blonde hair was braided, matted, and dangling with beads and feathers. She was also streaked with mud. It stained her bare knees and her hands.

"Gods alive!" muttered Gweneth, who was also observing Zelda's large belly and wild appearance.

The giant Wilde Woman lifted her sword further back with a grunt, as all around, the villagers chanted, "Crush her! Crush her! Crush her! Yrsa Bear Queen!"

Calain was on her knees, mouth dripping blood, waiting for the final killing blow.

"No! Don't kill her, *please*!" Zelda screamed and finally managed to break free of her captors. She ran into the fight, golden curls streaming, and threw herself on Calain, who had been about to take a blow from Yrsa's great sword. Instead, Yrsa staggered to stop herself, halted in surprise, and looked down at Zelda, sadness in her eyes. Zelda was hugging Calain's neck and weeping as she shouted, "Stop fighting! Please! Stop fighting! I don't wish either of you to be slain!"

The crowds booed and hissed.

"Crush her! Crush her!" the chant continued, but Yrsa did not lift her blade.

Panting, blood running in a line from her temple, Calain gently pushed Zelda aside and suddenly launched to her feet, bringing her sword down on Yrsa. Yrsa parried but too late and took a nasty cut to the face. She scowled and struck in retaliation, and Calain breathlessly parried, barely missing the blow. Their blades *chinged* above the continuous chant, "Crush her! Crush her! CRUSH HER!"

"No! Stop!" Zelda begged.

Calain, with sudden fever, was fighting hard and fast now. She was fighting so fast, Yrsa could barely keep up, and it was all she could do to block her blows. Before long, Yrsa had been disarmed and found herself on one knee, bleeding and panting, her head bowed as she waited for Calain's killing blow.

The chanting stopped. The entire village had fallen silent as they watched, as they waited for their queen to be felled. Selene waited tensely for Calain to lift her blade and finally end it. Beside her, Cassandra and Gweneth were also waiting with bated breath.

Calain stood over Yrsa for a long time, blade in hand, just staring down at the Wilde Woman as she panted to catch her breath, strings of red hair wild in her eyes. Then she said very calmly, "Thank you for taking care of Zelda." And with that, she took Zelda's hand and turned away from Yrsa with her, sheathing her blade on her back as she walked away. She stopped again in surprise when she saw Selene, Gweneth, and Cassandra standing there.

"Took you long enough," Calain said breathlessly. She nodded at the exit. "Let us make haste."

"Carry Zelda," said Selene. "We will move faster."

Zelda protested feebly, but Calain ignored her, instead gathering her gently into her arms. Then they marched through the silent village and back to their horses as the Wilde Women stood there, lining the streets, mutely staring at them.

Chapter 9

Back at Wolf Fortress, Calain tucked Zelda into one of the old beds in the upstairs barracks and begged her to rest. It was obvious that Zelda was very close to giving birth, and after recent strenuous events, she would need all the rest she could get. Selene added that Zelda probably needed to eat and went immediately to the kitchen to heat up the stove.

Down in the kitchen, as Zelda slept on the floor above, the four knights gathered, and Calain told them about her meeting with Melvalda in the forest.

"Melvalda seemed determined to take the child," said Calain unhappily. "Or else take Zelda while she was still large with it. She confessed she could not get past the Wilde Women to take Zelda. I tried to make Zelda stay with them, to no avail. She would have been safer there."

"I doubt you tried very hard," said Gweneth with a snort. "It didn't cross your mind to *tell* Zelda about Melvalda? Perhaps she would have stayed with the big bear woman then."

"No," said Cassandra, looking fondly at Calain where she sat across the table from her. "Zelda loves Calain. Nothing could have made her stay with the Wilde Women. Not even a witch of Raven's Cross. You fought well, by the way," she told Calain with a nod.

Calain nodded back.

Gweneth rolled her eyes and kept pacing, pausing occasionally to drink from a wine bottle, yet another one she'd taken from the old larder.

Selene was presiding over the oven fire and her back was to the others as she said, "The problem of Melvalda remains. She is susceptible to the stronger Bane Stones, and I still have a few . . . but Bane Stones do not work here at Wolf Fortress."

Calain looked up. "Why?"

"Because they would negate the enchantments put on the stronghold," Selene explained. "The enchantments here are powerful, for the Wolf Knights placed great faith in magick."

"And look what good it did them," said Gweneth, pausing in her pacing to darkly shake her head. "They were still forced out as all of Koradara stood by and watched."

"Stop drinking," said Cassandra. "It is souring thy mood."

"My mood is always sour," said Gweneth with a smile and took another drink.

"It was magick that made us Falcon Knights, Gweneth, in case you have forgotten," said Selene sternly. "Do not dismiss it so readily." She sighed, shaking her head as she went back to adding logs to the oven fire.

"Focus, you three. Zelda needs us! The enchantments couldn't keep Raven's Cross out," said Calain unhappily. "Is that what you're saying, Selene?"

"The enchantments could keep out most witches and all knights," said Selene, "but a woman of Melvalda's power? No. And a Bane Stone would only do so much if she was truly determined. Wolf Fortress cannot protect us from her, and I wish I could have foreseen it. When we decided to come here, it was to flee the Rose Guard. We had no idea we would be contending with Raven's Cross."

"When *you* decided we come here," corrected Gweneth, pointing with the hand that held the wine bottle and taking another bitter swig. She licked her lips as wine dribbled down them, watching Selene darkly. "Do not forget, Selene. This was your plan!"

Selene tensed and spun around. "Would you like to lead us, then, Gweneth? I have yet to hear any bright ideas from you!"

Selene and Gweneth glared heatedly at each other, and Calain thought they would come to blows. She had half a mind to thrash them both herself. Zelda needed their protection, and they were too busy bickering to figure out how to protect her! Her jaw tightened as she watched them.

"Calm yourselves, my sisters," said Cassandra soothingly, but her voice was just deep and stern enough to make Selene turn back to the oven with an angry breath and Gweneth return to her tipsy pacing. "We are all very tense and very tired with recent events," said Cassandra. "Whatever happens, one thing is certain: we cannot stay here. It isn't safe for Zelda and the child."

Calain glanced across the table at Cassandra, suddenly very glad she was there. Whenever there was an argument, she was usually the one to stop it. Calain had never seen her lose her temper.

"We need a place with protections Melvalda cannot pass," went on Cassandra thoughtfully. "Or else a hidden place she cannot find."

"She probably knows all the hidden places," said Selene. "If I had to guess, she is a very old witch to be so powerful. We were better off searching for enchantments she could not pass."

"Ironically, Vira'Toss would have been the perfect place to hide Zelda," pointed out Gweneth with a flat laugh. "No one could set foot there without permission, mortal or immortal. Even the gods scratch their heads on the shore."

"Hmm," said Calain thoughtfully. "Are there any schools of magick nearby? Perchance we could take Zelda there."

Selene shook her head. "There is one," she said regrettably, "and it is far north of here. The elven island, Menosea. By the time we had reached it, Melvalda would have been upon us. There is also little certainty they would allow us entrance. We are human. And we are fugitives from another land, with enemies on our heels. We are queen-slayers."

"Then it falls to us to protect her," said Calain firmly.

"*Or,*" said a voice, and they all looked up to find Zelda standing in the doorway, "I could ask someone for help."

Chapter 10

Horrified to see Zelda out of bed, the knights moved as one toward her, Calain and Cassandra scrambling up from their seats, all talking at once, all coaxing her back to bed or scolding her for being up and about. They all crowded close, towering above Zelda, and Gweneth even set aside her wine to take Zelda's arm, intent on carrying her back upstairs.

Zelda impatiently held up a hand, silencing them all. "Would it kill the four of you," she said, "to take direction from me for once, rather than treating me like some prized cow you must guard?"

Gweneth gave a half-smile. "You're a damn pretty cow," she said.

Zelda glanced up at Gweneth and smiled grudgingly. It was the first time they'd spoken since the argument in the barn, and some small part of her wanted to hold to her anger. But she looked in Gweneth's worried blue eyes and could see the knight regretted her earlier taunting.

The four knights still looked as if they wanted to protest, but instead, they obediently returned to what they'd been doing. Selene returned to the oven, and Calain and Cassandra sat at the table again. But Gweneth, instead of returning to her drinking and pacing, sat at the table with Calain and Cassandra, and when Zelda sat on Calain's knee, Gweneth silently reached across and took Zelda's hand, which Zelda acknowledged with a little smile.

The other knights seemed amused by Gweneth's humble devotion. They were all holding back smiles and pretending not to notice. Perhaps they thought Gweneth had finally learned her lesson. Zelda highly doubted that, though.

"You said something about seeking aid, my lady?" prompted Calain curiously.

"I don't know many powerful sorceresses who would cross the sea to protect me," Zelda admitted, "but there is my friend from the Order of Vira, Wick Blackwood."

Zelda thought she saw Selene fumble and nearly drop the hot poker. Gweneth also noticed Selene's reaction and smirked.

Deciding not to put Selene on the spot, Zelda pretended not to notice her sudden clumsiness and went on, "Wick comes from an entire family of sorceresses! She has six sisters who are of magick skill. They would apparate here in a heartbeat if I but asked Wick."

"And they would be powerful enough to stand against Melvalda?" asked Calain anxiously.

"They are elven," said Zelda at once. "Elves have always been the most powerful sorceresses!"

But even after assuring the knights that Wick and her sisters would come, Zelda still wasn't entirely certain they would. Wick had six sisters who were mages, it was true, but these six sisters also had lives of their own, and there was no guarantee they would drop everything and come running just because Wick had asked them.

Of all the sorceresses at Vira'Toss, Wick was the only one who would care enough about Zelda to come to her aid. The only problem was, Wick wasn't very powerful without her sisters, and most lesser mages could not make their spells cross water without the assistance of another. It was the reason witches and sorceresses lived in covens, for their numbers gave them strength. The fact that Melvalda had followed them across the sea to Koradara, very likely by apparating, spoke to the greatness of her power. But Melvalda probably wasn't alone, for Calain and Selene had not slain her entire coven.

Zelda didn't know what else she could do. She could barely defend herself in her condition, and even if she weren't pregnant, Melvalda still outmatched her in power. And so, she apparated to the floor above, and waddling to the mirror in the barracks, one hand upon her great belly, she swirled the dust from the glass with her other hand and spoke a spell into it, awaking it so that it glowed.

"Wick?" Zelda called as the glass swirled with purple light. "Wick, are you there? Can you hear me?"

If she was lucky, Wick would be standing near a mirror or other reflective surface and would respond. If there was no response, Zelda would have to try again later.

Zelda stood there, clutching her big belly, waiting for an answer, feeling helpless. Wick was her only hope. Without her help, she would lose the child growing inside her. Perhaps she would lose Calain and the other knights as well, for they would fight in her defense and they would lose. She didn't want to think of it.

Zelda was shaking when Wick's face finally appeared in the swirl of purple light. It was the same small, plain face, curtained either side by sheets of long, straight black hair, from which her pointed ears reached. To her surprise, Wick was glaring at her.

Zelda hesitated. "W-Wick? It's me! It's Zelda!"

Wick was very slow to respond. She just stood there, glaring at Zelda for a time, her face twisted in the utmost dislike and disgust. When she finally spoke, her voice was dripping disdain, "Yes, *Zelda,* I can see that tis you."

Zelda hesitated again. "Are you well? You sound strange?"

"No," disagreed Wick, "I sound very normal." She glanced Zelda up and down, her lips spreading in a nasty smile. "But you seem to be in a bit of trouble. As usual."

"Y-Yes," Zelda responded, the dread filling her. Wick seemed very angry with her, though she could not fathom why.

"You won't help me, will you?" Zelda realized, crestfallen.

Wick's nostrils flared. "No, Zelda, I will not."

Zelda shook her head, utterly baffled. "Why?"

Wick's eyes grew round in disbelief. "*Why*?" Her lip curled. "But of course, you're so vain and self-centered, you wouldn't even realize!" She took a deep, angry breath and accused, "You were a *terrible* friend! Always snapping at me and ignoring me, only speaking to me to unload your petty problems on me! Even now I am little more than a tool you would use for your own benefit! You've been gone *two months,* and the first time you contact me is when you're in trouble!"

Zelda stood in stunned silence as Wick glared hatred at her. She couldn't even find the words to argue. Wick was absolutely right about her: she *was* a terrible friend.

"I never meant you any harm," Zelda managed at last, and her words were true. To her surprise, tears filled Wick's eyes.

"I know," said Wick quietly. "Do not contact me again." With that, Wick's face vanished and the mirror darkened, leaving Zelda alone in the shadowy silence.

Chapter 11

After Wick's refusal to help, Zelda quickly realized that it was up to her to make a decision. Her selfishness and her tendency to use other people had not only harmed Wick but also Queen Yrsa, the other parent of the child she carried. Because Zelda had married Queen Yrsa, who she did not love, in order to secure an ideal life, Yrsa had likely lost her throne. Losing to Calain before her entire clan would have made her appear weak in their eyes and unworthy of their devotion. Yrsa had likely been exiled, a horrifying thought.

Zelda was beginning to suspect she was more like her uncle than she'd formerly cared to admit. For once in her life, she did not want to use another for her own survival, pleasures, and plans. This time, she would protect the ones she loved, not hide behind them as if they were human shields. She would not allow Melvalda to harm the Knights of Falcon! And so, Zelda made it up in her mind: she would turn herself over to Melvalda.

Zelda murmured a cloaking spell that would make her invisible and apparated in the door of the kitchen. Then she stood and looked wistfully at her knights, saying a silent farewell to each one of them.

Zelda thought the Knights of Falcon seemed very happy, despite the cloud of doom hanging over them. They rejoiced that Zelda was with them again, teased each other, laughed, and occasionally frowned with worry as they discussed Melvalda and Raven's Cross.

Zelda's sad blue eyes went to each one of them.

Dark and beautiful Selene was sitting at the table with the other three, presiding with them over wine, roast pheasant wings, and bread, and exchanging words with Gweneth, who had her boots on the table and was tilting back her chair as she spoke with a grin, curling her hands on invisible breasts. Selene slapped Gweneth's legs and told her to take her boots off the table. Gweneth obeyed, still talking and making suggestive gestures with both hands, at which Selene laughed.

Zelda would miss Selene's gentle kisses on her skin, the dark eyes that were always so soft and concerned for her. And she knew she would even miss Gweneth's teasing, as well as those rare moments of sweetness from Gweneth that sometimes seemed to slip through seemingly by accident.

Beautiful red-haired Calain was laughing loudly and banging her fist on the table at something Gweneth had said. She had removed her armor (all the knights had) and was in her linen bra and woolen hose. Her muscular arms and shoulders were bare, and they flexed wonderfully when she moved, the orange light of the oven fire lining them in a bright glow. Her red hair was wild and flying loose as ever as it tumbled long behind her shoulders. Zelda looked at Calain with tearful longing, knowing she would miss her the most.

Cassandra was the only one who wasn't laughing or speaking. Instead, she was sitting quietly and listening to the others, a small smile on her lips. But she went still as if she had sensed something, and very slowly, she turned her head and her eyes locked with Zelda's.

Zelda froze, her breath caught in her throat, waiting for Cassandra to reveal her to the others. She had nearly forgotten

Cassandra was a sorceress and might have seen through a cloaking spell. A lesser mage would have been fooled, but Cassandra was a natural witch and more sensitive to magick.

For a long moment, Zelda and Cassandra stared in silence at each other. Zelda did not bother pleading with her eyes and instead stood resigned to the fact that her cover was blown. To her surprise, Cassandra's serious gray eyes blinked sadly as she realized what Zelda meant to do, and she gave one solemn nod. She did not intend to stop Zelda.

Relieved, Zelda nodded in return, then turned and walked outside to the edge of the trees, where she closed her eyes and apparated.

When Zelda appeared again, she was outside Wolf Fortress, far from its enchantments, on the edge of the trees, as the Dark Bloom Forest pressed in around the stronghold. Clutching her big belly and suddenly determined not to be afraid, she lifted her chin and said with confidence,

"Melvalda! I am here! I am yours!"

"Are you?" Melvalda's silky voice preceded her. She appeared suddenly before Zelda, and she looked as beautiful and yet intimidating as Zelda remembered her. Her mischievous eyes glittered, black and slanted, as they bore into Zelda's calm face from the depths of her hood.

Zelda swallowed hard. "Y-Yes," she said. "I am yours."

Melvalda smiled like a cat, and lifting her cloak, she whirled it around Zelda and herself, so that they both disappeared on the spot.

The Revenge of Raven's Cross

Book 3

Chapter 1

Zelda blinked and was surprised to find herself not in a dank and dark cavern, but in the stone room of an old castle. The curtains were drawn shut against the day and the room was shadowy and dark. It was a bedchamber, with an old four-poster bed, the curtains around which had been drawn back to reveal a dark red coverlet. On the nightstand was a washbasin, and under the bed, Zelda could see a chamber pot.

It was a moderately sized room, with not much furniture aside from a fireplace and a sitting chair. There was also a great bathing basin on the stone floor near the hearth, devoid of water, and beside it, a bow of soap and washcloths. Zelda was surprised to see the bassinet that stood on a circular rug of black fur near the bed. The crib had been draped in black curtains and inside, blankets and pillows waited for a child . . . Her child.

Zelda put a sad hand to her big belly and stood there, staring at the bassinet. How would she get out of this predicament? She couldn't think to give up her baby! At night, she had sat in happy silence, smiling as it kicked and squirmed inside her, as Yrsa hugged her from behind and rubbed her belly. Two happy parents they had been. But Zelda had left Yrsa and had ruined her life to boot, only to turn around and abandon Calain, who had given up her life as a knight to protect her honor. So many women, destroyed because they had loved her. Zelda stared at the crib and started to wonder if her baby wouldn't be better off without her. But in the hands of Melvalda? The Witch of the Dark?

For that was how Melvalda was known. Gweneth, who was worldly and seemed to know a great deal about many things, had told Zelda and Calain of Melvalda's reputation in Eriallon. According to Gweneth, she was a very old, very powerful witch, and Gweneth had told them they were lucky to have escaped her the first time they crossed her path, especially given that they had massacred half her coven!

Melvalda had appeared in the room with Zelda, and when Zelda moved forward toward the bassinet, she hung back, watching Zelda quietly from her black hood, her long dark hair trailing over the front of her gown in dark rivers. Without a word, Melvalda waved her hand at the barren fireplace, and fire sprang to life there, heating the once-chilly room. Zelda was grateful, for she was still wearing her bear skins and furs, and the dress was quite short, exposing her legs and arms. She went to the fire and warmed her hands over it, and she could feel her belly warming as well as it protruding near the flames.

Zelda was aware of Melvalda standing behind her, still watching her with those intense black eyes. It gave her a chill, but surprisingly, not a chill of fear. It was a chill of . . . *delight.* Melvalda didn't just want her baby. Melvalda wanted *Zelda*. And Zelda had quickly realized that the first time they met back in Eriallon. The way Melvalda had looked at her, spoken to her in that hushed, purring voice, touched her with a groping hand. And she had liked it. To her great shame, she had blushed and felt her sex swell with hunger, and she hadn't wanted it to stop. She still felt the same way.

"This is your chamber," Melvalda said quietly. "None of my women will disturb you. I have forbidden it."

"Where are we?" Zelda wandered, turning her face to the window. She could see a gray sky and beneath it, a line of dark pine trees. A dark lake glittered in the pale sunlight, its surface dancing beneath a light sprinkle of rain.

"My castle, Ravenhold," answered Melvalda quietly. "It is in the Ghostly Mountains, far north . . . in Eriallon."

Zelda gasped, looking quickly at Melvalda. They had crossed the sea, traveling thousands of miles in an instant, leaving Realm Koradara far behind, and were once again in the realm where Zelda had spent her entire life. She felt a little hopeless: even if the Knights of Falcon were to rescue her, they were quite far away. Perhaps they would use a portal to find her.

"You will be safe here until the child is born," Melvalda assured Zelda.

"And after it is born?" said Zelda, still warming her hands over the flames, her back to Melvalda.

"That is up to you," answered Melvalda, surprising Zelda enough that she looked over her shoulder, brows raised. Melvalda smiled. "Did you think I would keep you a prisoner here? I only desire the child—"

"Why?" Zelda asked abruptly and straightened up. It had never occurred to her wonder why Melvalda wanted her baby. That she wanted it had been frightening enough. There were so many stories of witches snatching children for dark rituals and sacrifices or sometimes just to take on as an apprentice, to pass on knowledge. Zelda prayed it was the latter.

Melvalda didn't hesitate and answered truthfully, "I sense great power in you. It is untapped, but it is there. You will not join Raven's Cross, I know this now. You are too tightly Bound to that knight of yours."

Zelda blushed a little.

"But," said Melvalda, "your child will be a natural witch. She was conceived through a magick potion, by a Wilde Woman of all things. She will be a sorceress such as the world has never *seen.* Why shouldn't I bring her into my fold? Before you sell her off to Vira'Toss and continue tramping about the countryside as you do."

Zelda blushed furiously and scowled: by "tramping," Melvalda did not mean "traveling."

"I would never give her to Vira'Toss!" Zelda retorted.

Melvalda lifted her brows, unconvinced. "Somehow, I doubt that, Zelda. I doubt that very much. You see, you are a great deal like your uncle—"

Zelda tensed.

"—selfish, self-centered, only concerned with your own survival. You aren't ready to be a mother. You would give the child up in a heartbeat to regain your freedom—"

"You shut your mouth about things you don't understand!" Zelda burst, turning and taking a halting step toward Melvalda.

Melvalda surveyed Zelda calmly from beneath her hood. Her dark eyes were amused, for Zelda was standing with her small hands balled into fists and she was glowing with power. But Zelda did not have her stave, and she knew that casting unfocused magick could endanger her baby, so very slowly, she swallowed her anger and stopped glowing. She hated that Melvalda was so amused by her reaction, as if it had proved something.

"You're as wild and temperamental as your knight," said Melvalda, shaking her head as if it were a shame. "Do you know I asked her to make things easier for you both? To simply bring you to me? But she would rather risk her life for you, guarding you at the old Wolf Fortress in a hopeless situation, the fool."

Zelda's breasts were heaving, and she realized she was breathless with anger. "Shut up about Calain," she warned. She was surprised when Melvalda said benevolently, "As you wish, Zelda."

Zelda stared.

"It is not my intention to upset you," explained Melvalda. "You are carrying my child, after all." She smiled like a cat.

Zelda glowered and put quick, protective hands over her belly. But she looked down at it, and she wondered if Melvalda wasn't right. Was she too selfish to make a good mother? Perhaps giving the child up was for the best, even if it wasn't Melvalda she gave it to.

"You never really answered my question," Zelda said, still looking glumly at her belly. "You want my baby because it's powerful? Not to eat it or . . ."

Melvalda laughed darkly. "Eat it? Don't be absurd! The child will be a great asset to my coven . . . Or what's left of it," she said bitterly. "I am still rebuilding after the antics of your pet knights."

Zelda didn't know why she felt the urge to apologize, but the words came tumbling out of her mouth, "I'm so sorry!" She snapped her mouth shut and cast her eyes down, blushing and shocked by her own words. But she *did* feel sorry. The witches of Raven's Cross had never harmed Zelda. Even the initiation ritual, where they tied her naked to the post, would not have harmed her. Melvalda had been approaching Zelda with a dagger in order to cut off a lock of her hair, but no doubt Calain and Selene had interrupted it otherwise, and they were ruthless as they slaughtered every witch that they could.

When Zelda looked up, it was to find Melvalda watching her in surprise. After a pause, she said, "Truly? You are sorry for the senseless slaughter of my women?"

"Yes," Zelda repeated. She stiffened when she felt a hot light scanning over her mind, and she knew Melvalda was Reading her. She stood very still, waiting.

Finding no lie, Melvalda blinked in more surprise, and reaching up, she pulled off her cloak and hood, tossing it over the back of the armchair that stood near the hearth. Her long black hair shifted from the gesture, and Zelda caught a glimpse of Melvalda's pointed elven ears. She had nearly forgotten the woman was elven, though she was quite tall for an elf. Zelda thought it more likely Melvalda was elven-blooded and not fully elven.

"They were good women," said Melvalda, smoothing her hair to the side to reveal her long neck as she went to the armchair near the fire and sat. "They weren't particularly powerful and they weren't natural witches, but they were useful."

Zelda made a face as she waddled near Melvalda's chair, one hand on her belly and one hand on her aching back. "Useful?" she repeated reprovingly. "Is that all people are to you?"

"Yes," Melvalda answered, unabashed as she looked up at Zelda. "You see, I was not judging you before. I think it admirable that you use others to survive in a world that would seek every day to destroy you. And what other choice do you have? It is what many women have had to do."

Zelda couldn't deny that. Without magick, a woman was completely at the mercy of men, with nothing to protect her from their cruelty and violence. She knew that, deep town, terrible as her uncle had been, he had felt guilty for all the beatings, for cheating her of a happy childhood. And so, to repay her, he took her to a place where she could learn to become powerful rather than remain helpless. He helped her find a way to survive other men like him.

But how useful had magick been to Zelda, really? She thought of the Bane Stones, of the giant crystals they came from, of the men in the alley who had nearly raped her back in Ternia. She was a powerful sorceress, it was true, but she could be robbed of that power so easily!

"If you stay here with me," said Melvalda, emerging from Zelda's thoughts, "I can teach you how to defy the effects of a Bane Stone, and no man shall ever be able to lay a finger on you. You will need no besotted *knights* to defend you, either. I can teach you so many things they wouldn't dare to teach you at Vira'Toss."

Zelda frowned, her curiosity aroused. "But why? Why don't they teach us more spells at Vira'Toss?" She had always wondered . . . and resented the fact.

"Because," said Melvalda, lip curling, "the mages of Vira'Toss are bound to men. Oh, it may *seem* as if they hold the males out with their enchantments and veils and such," she went on before Zelda could protest, "but in truth? They are beholden to them. They are allowed their little women's paradise on the condition that they don't actually exercise their power. A woman in full power is what men fear the most. They do not want sorceresses learning how to properly use their magick. And so, the women of Vira'Toss are taught silly spells, trifling things that will serve the realm – healing spells and light shields and the like." She made a face. "*Light Magick*. Because they know men fear the Dark."

Melvalda fell silent, and the orange firelight reflected in her thoughtful eyes as she placed an absent black nail to her chin. Zelda looked down at her, at her pale cleavage and tiny waist, at the tight black dress that smoothed over her curves, and thought her a beautiful and regal woman.

About Melvalda's long throat was a black choker with a red jewel. Without understanding why, Zelda found herself transfixed as she stared at it. She could feel the magick humming from it, a gentle thrum on her heart. She had almost reached out, spellbound, to touch it, when Melvalda gently grabbed her hand.

Zelda blinked, coming to her senses, and looked down to see Melvalda looking up at her in calm amusement. "Look, little Zelda, but do not touch," she said.

"I am sorry," said Zelda hoarsely. "I do not know what came over me!"

"Tis quite all right," Melvalda answered and released Zelda's hand. She went back to staring into the flames, but Zelda wanted her to continue talking. She suddenly realized she liked the sound of Melvalda's purring voice, and the way Melvalda spoke of Zelda's selfish survival instinct without judgement was admittedly soothing after the self-flagellation she had done just the day before.

Zelda looked at the tall woman's lap and wanted to sit in it, wanted to be held, listen to her voice . . . perhaps be touched as well.

Melvalda's lips twisted in an amused smile as she emerged from Zelda's mind. "Sit," she said. "But remember: do not touch my necklace. The jewel may react and burn your skin."

"Yes, I'll remember," Zelda said breathlessly. She braced her small hand on the armrest and lowered herself carefully onto Melvalda's lap. Her belly was so big now that sitting down was becoming something of a feat, but she managed it.

Melvalda slipped her slender arms around Zelda and held her gently. Zelda's heart skipped a beat when the woman stroked her golden curls, her dark eyes dancing fondly over Zelda's face, down her neck, and to her breasts, the cleavage visible behind the low neck of her deerskin dress. Zelda's breasts were as large as Melvalda's, if not larger, and with her pregnancy, they had swollen ripe as melons. And they were sore. Suddenly self-conscious, she clutched her dress shut over them.

"Your beauty is perfection," said Melvalda in soft wonder. "As if some lusty god had carved you with great care and then sent you forth into my arms. These rags won't do for such delicate curves." She tugged gently at the fur shawl around Zelda's shoulders and let it fall away, then brushed aside Zelda's hands and tugged at her deerskin dress until it ripped slightly, revealing one of her milk-heavy breasts and the hard pink nipple.

Zelda screamed softly and blushed, but she did not move to stop Melvalda. Instead, she rested her head back and stared eagerly into the woman's face, her cheeks flaming with desire. She thought of Calain so far away, likely frantic wondering where she was, and felt terrible, she felt low . . . but she wanted this woman, this powerful, beautiful, wise woman, in a way she had never wanted any of the knights or even Yrsa. And besides, she had given herself to Melvalda to keep Calain safe.

Melvalda . . . who was older, more mature . . . more experienced. It excited Zelda.

"You lusty little thing," Melvalda said, looking down at Zelda's eager face in amusement. She tugged again at the deerskin dress, until it tore all the way down and sagged around Zelda's lap, exposing her plump breasts and protruding belly.

Zelda let her hands rest at her sides, her heart thudding fast, as she watched Melvalda's careful hands cup her heavy breasts from under. Melvalda was wearing many pretty rings, but they were on odd fingers . . . One was on her thumb . . . Another was on her pinky, another was on her third finger, though Zelda knew she was not married. Only Melvalda's index and middle fingers were free of rings, and her black nails were quite short. Zelda slowly blushed as she realized the reason.

Zelda bit her lip as Melvalda carefully massaged her breasts.

"They hurt, don't they?" Melvalda whispered in her ear.

Zelda breathlessly nodded.

Melvalda kept massaging, and without looking back at the woman, Zelda knew her eyes were glowing as she cast a spell. She could feel the pain tingling away and sighed, resting back against Melvalda and closing her eyes as the taller woman continued gently massaging.

Melvalda was careful not to accidentally milk Zelda, instead touching her lightly and nonetheless firmly. Her hands were not muscly and strong but slender and delicate. With her back against Melvalda, Zelda could feel the woman's heartbeat quickening: she was becoming aroused. With sudden aggression, she turned Zelda's face to hers and roughly thrust her tongue in her mouth, kissing her with a passion that made their heads twist back and forth.

As Zelda shivered and moaned under Melvalda's hungry groping and kissing, the older woman smoothed her hand over Zelda's belly and touched her sex. Her slender fingers gently caressed the lips, pushed through the golden pubic hair, and massaged her tiny, throbbing clitoris, until it pulsed harder with pleasure, and Zelda gasped as she felt her sex moisten.

Melvalda's fingers slipped inside, pushing slowly and carefully through the tight sheath of Zelda's sex, until Zelda was squirming in her lap. The woman's touch was exquisite. It was unlike anything Zelda had ever known. It was the expertise of an older woman, a woman who had touched many a moist sex.

Melvalda fingered Zelda deep and slow, occasionally sliding her fingers back to fondle her clitoris. Her other hand had not stopped massaging Zelda's heavy breast, until the pink nipple was rolling in her fingers, and her mouth on Zelda's mouth was hungry and commanding, her tongue sliding deep to taste as much as it could, her lips caressing with a strength that was startling.

Small and aroused and helpless, Zelda quivered in Melvalda's relentless grasp, feeling like a fly that had willingly flown into the arms of a spider. She trembled but could not hold back: with a choked gasp, she suddenly climaxed, her sex tightening and gushing moisture over Melvalda's careful fingers, and Melvalda laughed softly and whispered in her ear, "Why, you've soiled my gown. I suppose I'll have to . . . take it off."

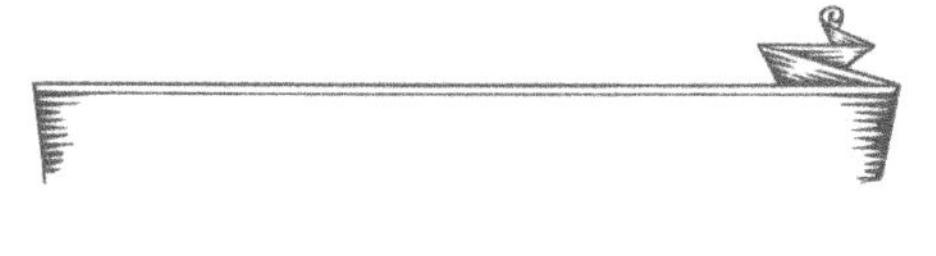

Chapter 2

Cassandra rode her horse in silence, listening calmly as the others ranted and raved about Zelda and how she had been kidnapped by Melvalda. They bickered, they raged, they worried, they blamed each other for not watching Zelda more closely, they blamed themselves for being negligent. Cassandra was the only one who knew Zelda had left willingly, likely to protect them from the wrath of the Witch of the Dark, but she had said nothing for fear of causing the other knights more anger and anxiety. If they knew Zelda had left them on purpose, they would be furious and beside themselves with grief.

It was the same way the knights always reacted whenever Cassandra sacrificed herself to help the others escape. She had given herself over to the enemy many times to protect her sisters in arms, so she knew better than anyone how Zelda had felt in that moment, standing there made invisible by her cloaking spell, watching them wistfully in the kitchen, and of course Cassandra had not attempted to stop her.

Cassandra also knew more about the Witch of the Dark than the others. Gweneth only knew the exaggerated wives' tales of the locals. She did not know the truth. Cassandra knew that Melvalda was not evil, that she would not force Zelda to give up her child if she did not want to. It was why Cassandra had been the least worried about defending Wolf Fortress, though the others never ceased scolding her for her everlasting calm.

After realizing Zelda was gone, the others had decided to pack up and head immediately for a portal back to Realm Eriallon. For Melvalda's stronghold was there, in the Ghostly Mountains to the north, upon a precipice no mortal could reach on foot. They would have to seek aid from the Adar, giant birds that were large enough to carry a woman upon their back. The creatures lived in the forests outside Ternia. How ironic, Cassandra thought, considering they had just come from there months ago. It seemed their adventure had led them in circles.

Cassandra led the others on horseback to the portal she had used to reach Priine, given that it was nearest and would only take a few days to reach. She cautioned them that Rose Guard knights would still be coming through the portal, but the others did not seem to care, so long as they were able to return to Eriallon and save Zelda.

Save Zelda. It seemed to Cassandra that they were always saving Zelda when she rarely needed saving. If Cassandra had to guess, Zelda was, at that very moment, making love to Melvalda or sleeping naked with her in her bed after having done so. She knew Zelda was in passion, for Calain—who could feel it when Zelda was experiencing pleasure – was occasionally red-cheeked and breathless for no reason at all.

Sensing that Zelda was orgasming miles away had put Calain in a sour mood. Yet again, Zelda had given herself to another, while leaving Calain behind in worry and fear. Calain was growing tired of it, Cassandra could tell, and Cassandra worried for her. She tried to assure Calain that there was a reason for what she was feeling, but she could not properly explain without confessing that she had allowed Zelda to turn herself over, and not wanting an argument, she kept the truth to herself.

If the others knew, they would blame Cassandra. They would yell and demand to know why she hadn't stopped Zelda.

Calain would thrash Cassandra, perhaps Gweneth as well, and what good would that do, fighting amongst themselves?

The portal they approached was an old archway in one of the ancient elven temples, which had been erected to some unknown goddess thousands of years before. The temple was made of ancient stone and towered above them in the moonlight, walls crumbling open like the mouth of a dragon.

Cassandra could see the archway on the dais. It was chipped and made of stone and swirling with light: it was still active. She glanced around and was glad to see there were no signs of recent activity in the room. Moonlight shone through the crumbling ceiling upon footprints that were days old in the dust.

They guided their horses through the broken wall of the temple, and the steeds, seeing the archway on the dais, began to stir, snorting and stamping in protest. Calain's horse, the chestnut, Arthur, bucked up on hind legs and had to be soothed by Calain, who sang softly to him as she stroked his long face.

"What shall we do with the steeds?" said Gweneth unhappily. "They will never pass through the portal."

"And we shall have to leave them again when we come to the Ghostly Mountains anyway," said Calain.

"Leave them here," said Cassandra calmly. "They will find their way back to Wolf Fortress and rest in the stables there until we return." So saying, she took the reins and saddle from her horse and dropped them to the floor in a small cloud of dust before giving Sunny a sound clap on the backside to send him off. The tawny horse snorted gratefully and turned, trotting from the broken temple at a quick pace, as if the thrum of the magick in the place were on his heels.

The other knights did likewise, unsaddling their horses and sending them on after Sunny, until the four Knights of Falcon stood alone in the temple, facing the dais and the portal upon it.

Selene took a breath as if to steel herself. "Let us go," she said. "Zelda will give birth soon. There is little time."

They all looked at Cassandra, waiting for her to pass through first. Cassandra wasn't surprised. They viewed her as the mystical, magickal one, the one who understood strange things like portals and ancient elven ruins. And perhaps they weren't wrong. Without protest, she mounted the steps of the dais and passed through the portal's light, unafraid.

A whooshing sound filled Cassandra's ears, she was blinded by light, and then she stepped forward and found herself in the ancient elven temple deep in the dark forest outside Ternia. The forest was known as Blood Horn, and it was a huge forest, with black trees and dark thorny flowers, full of evil spirits and trolls and goblins. It made up the western wild country of Eriallon and was home to the worst creatures and outlaws in the realm. It only made sense that Melvalda, Witch of the Dark, would make her roost in the mountain over it.

Cassandra knew that Melvalda herself wasn't evil any more than the forest was, just ruthless and pragmatic, which made her evil in the eyes of others given her methods. As a result, she had become an outlaw, going from sorceress (a legal mage) to witch (an illegal mage). Blood Horn was the safest place in Eriallon for an outlaw to hide, for not only did it lie beyond civilization, but it was full of so many dangers that even the Rose Guard was afraid to set foot within.

While it had been night across the sea in Dark Bloom Forest, in Blood Horn, it was early morning, the sun having already reached Eriallon with its fingertips to begin the day. Streams of pale sunlight broke through the dark canopy of green above, and already, sparrows were singing as owls tucked their beaks in their wings to rest.

Cassandra stepped away from the portal to make way, and almost immediately, Selene came through the light after her, blinking and disoriented, but only a little. Shaking her head and rubbing her eyes, Selene moved aside for the others: Gweneth came next and then Calain, both blinking furiously and coughing. Gweneth was coughing so badly, she leaned forward and heaved.

"Ugh," Gweneth moaned, straightening up as Calain clapped her soothingly on the back. "I hate traveling through portals! Tis dizzying and confusing and makes my stomach ill."

"Wine does the same, and yet you drink it still," Selene said.

"I wish I had your stomach, Cass. You are never bothered by the portals," said Calain, looking with fond admiration at Cassandra.

Cassandra knew it was her ancestry. Natural mages were usually the descendants of elves, and magickal things had little impact on those with elven blood. The more elven blood one had, the smaller the impact.

Cassandra had long suspected that Selene was of elven descent. Magick had little effect on her, and she was calm and level-headed like the elves of old, the ancient Tula-Dan bloodline, tall and serious elves, with slender frames and long hair.

Calain and Gweneth, however, were very human. They could not withstand the smallest spell, and were emotional and given to sudden rage to boot. They had not the serenity of those with elven blood.

Cassandra's mother had been an elf, so she was not bothered by portals and Bane Stones, and she could detect most spells. It was how she'd seen Zelda earlier that day in the kitchen, despite the strength of her (very impressive) cloaking spell.

Selene glanced around, and Cassandra knew she was looking for recent signs of Rose Guard knights, but there were none. The footprints in the temple's dust were several days old. Perhaps the queen's sister had given up sending her knights, for now.

"Should we approach the Adar in the night?" Calain wondered anxiously. "I wish to find Zelda quickly, but I do not wish to anger the Adar while doing so. The stories say they are dangerous and easily roused to fury."

"Like you," teased Gweneth.

"I fear the same rage," said Selene. "I have heard their talons can cut a woman in halves. Best we make camp and approach them in the morning. They will be able to see us more clearly by daylight and won't assume we are stealing upon them with ill intent."

Calain glanced around. "Should we make camp here in the temple? It seems safe enough."

"But if the Rose Guard comes through the portal, would we want to be sleeping here, waiting for them?" said Gweneth pointedly.

Calain snorted. "As if we wouldn't make short work of them. The queen's knights are piteous compared to Knights of Falcon."

"Even still," said Gweneth, "I would rather enjoy a good night's rest and not keep stirring to slay piteous knights. And imagine if a great number of them poured through and we were overwhelmed? Even you could not withstand more than a dozen of them, Kay."

"I am of a mind with Gweneth," said Selene, "and yes, tis scary."

Gweneth laughed.

"Let us make camp in the forest," Selene went on. She paused and eyed Calain anxiously. "But take care to avoid gravestones and dark hollows."

Gweneth was perplexed by Selene's last comment, but Cassandra knew the meaning behind it. While traveling with Zelda weeks before, Calain and Selene had stumbled across a hollow, where elven spirits were at unrest, and Calain was nearly slain. None of them had told Cassandra about it. She had seen it in a dream, and until that moment, she hadn't known if the dream was true or the fabrication of her worried mind.

They journeyed into the forest, their silver armor jingling softly, satchels on their shoulders, and traveled long into the darkness, making certain to put a great deal of distance between themselves and the temple. Cassandra led the way through the pitch dark, guiding them with the bobbing orb of light she'd conjured, its gentle glow lining the side of her face and pale hair in white fire.

When Selene was satisfied that they were far enough from the temple, they made camp. Selene dug out a firepit, while Calain and Gweneth ventured a little way into the trees for firewood, squinting by moonlight to find it. Cassandra remained near Selene, casting her orb of wisp-light over her, so that she could see to dig the firepit.

"We really shouldn't light a fire," Selene panted as she worked, "but tis cold tonight, and I am tired of living in fear. Let the creatures of the forest know we are here and fear us instead! For lo, we have a mighty witch-knight in our midst!"

Cassandra smiled. "All will be fine, Selene. You worry too greatly."

"Oh? Do you know this from a vision or are you merely comforting me?"

"I was merely comforting you."

Selene laughed breathlessly. "Oh."

"And there are no gravestones or haunted hollows nearby," Cassandra added soothingly. "Calain is safe." She smiled. "From all but herself."

Selene paused in surprise, then went back to digging as she said, "I won't bother asking how you know of Calain's injury. I shall just assume you are some sort of goddess and leave it at that. Pondering it is too much strain."

Cassandra laughed softly. "A fair strategy."

The others returned, and they stroked up a fire. Cassandra could have lit it with magick, but Selene cautioned her that she had used too much magick already by conjuring the wisp-light. Magick had a way of sending out vibrations, and there were many creatures that could feel them. Each time Cassandra cast a spell, she was drawing attention to them.

They sat around the fire, heated up the leftover stew, and discussed who was going to take first watch. Now that there were four of them, they would take watch in pairs. Calain volunteered to take first watch, and Gweneth volunteered to sit up with her, leaving Cassandra and Selene to wrap themselves in their cloaks and sleep on pallets of leaves.

Casting magick, even the smallest spells, had a way of exhausting Cassandra. She wrapped herself in her cloak, and as the heat of the fire spread deliciously over her, she fell asleep almost immediately.

CASSANDRA LOOKED OUT an arched window framed in stone bricks. It was warm here. A crackling fire was roaring on the hearth and spreading its heat over the side of her face. But outside it was cold. And gray. She could see trees in the distance. Pine trees. And a dark lake.

Her feet were bare, and there was a stone floor beneath them, piercing in its coldness. Where were her shoes? She must have been dreaming. In her dreams, she almost never had shoes.

"Cassandra?" said a sleepy voice. "Is that you? How did you get here?"

Cassandra turned. There was a great four-poster bed against the wall, its black curtains pulled back to reveal a dark red coverlet. Zelda was lying naked on the bed. She wasn't pregnant. Her belly was flat, her waist narrow, her breasts big and heavy and sharp with pink nipples. Golden hair curled between her legs, and Cassandra would still see it poking from between the back of her thighs when she turned on her side and sat up on her elbow. Her incredibly long, golden hair was a mass around her, spreading over the pillows and the coverlet and across one cheek. She pushed it back to regard Cassandra in surprise, her lashes fluttering.

Zelda's cheeks flamed the deepest red. "Cassandra," she said, "you are naked!"

Cassandra glanced down. She was indeed naked. She saw her own belly, rippling with muscles, and the calves and thighs that were bulging with muscles as well. And she saw her own sex, cloaked in curly, pale blonde hair that was almost white. She reached up and touched her head to find her hair had come loose of its messy plait and was brushing her shoulders.

"So I am," said Cassandra, looking up again.

Zelda giggled. "But why?"

"I don't know," answered Cassandra simply. "This is your dream, is it not?"

Zelda sat up, breasts jiggling, and stared thoughtfully. "I suppose it is! How would you know what the inside of this chamber looked like otherwise?"

Cassandra nodded as if to confirm her words. She had never been in this room before a day in her life, though she had been to Ravenhold.

"I feel . . . so alone." Zelda rubbed a small hand over her flat belly, as if she missed her child. She looked up. "Is Calain well?"

Cassandra's pale gray eyes had filled with hunger and she was barely listening to Zelda. The fat lips of Zelda's pink sex were poking from the back of her thighs, wreathed in innocent golden curls, beckoning.

"Tell Calain I did not wish her harm," Zelda was all but begging. "I gave myself to Melvalda to protect her – to protect all of you!"

Cassandra's eyes were still on Zelda's body, now drinking in the swell of her large breasts. "Let us not speak of Calain," she said and moved with a determined step to the bed. She saw Zelda go still and her breath catch in her chest when Cassandra crawled across the sheets to her, eyes blazing hunger. Without pause, Cassandra loomed over Zelda, who lay back, blue eyes round with shock and anticipation. Perhaps she had never realized before now how deeply Cassandra longed for her. But oh, she had longed.

Cassandra looked at Zelda's ripe pink lips with soft eyes, then leaned down and gently tasted them, sliding in her tongue. Zelda submissively followed her lead, kissing back gently, her body trembling.

Cassandra's gentle kiss deepened, and she closed a hard, strong hand over one of Zelda's heavy breasts. Zelda moaned through the kiss, and her lashes fluttered. She liked that, the strength of Cassandra's touch. It thrilled her. She closed her eyes and bit her lip as Cassandra's gentle kisses traveled down, over her soft breasts, to her pink nipple, which she sucked with slow hunger into her lips.

Zelda moaned again in deepest pleasure, curling her little fingers in Cassandra's hair as she gently suckled, the plump mound of Zelda's breast rising warm against her face. Her nipple was growing stiffer and harder, and as Cassandra caressed the other heavy breast, the nipple of it jutted as well.

Zelda's belly trembled almost violently with anticipation when Cassandra's kisses traveled slowly down and down to her sex. She kissed Zelda's trembling little thigh from the knee, all the way to her public hair.

Then finally, at last, she plunged her mouth into the hot, golden nest between Zelda's thighs and felt its sweet softness against her face as Zelda squirmed breathlessly. Very gently and slowly, Cassandra began to lick and taste, sucking the fat lips of Zelda's sex against her tongue.

Zelda melted into the wreath of her golden hair, and when Cassandra sucked gently on her clitoris, she gasped, thrusting her big breasts to the ceiling.

As she watched Zelda's breasts jiggling and heaving from her squirming, Cassandra could feel her own sex swelling with arousal and dripping with moisture. She plunged her hungry tongue between the lips of Zelda's sex, but it was only there a second before fingers curled roughly in her hair and her head was ripped away.

Pain spread over Cassandra's scalp like a burn as she staggered back from the bed. She fell hard on the floor and heard Zelda miserably cry her name.

"Mel – don't hurt her!" Zelda begged.

Heart pounding, Cassandra slowly looked up and went still to find Melvalda standing over her. The Witch of the Dark was wearing a tight black dress, from which her pale cleavage was fairly bursting, and a heavy black cloak and hood. She glared from beneath the hood at Cassandra, her eyes red flames, and hissed, "You dare!"

"Don't hurt her!" Zelda repeated, who was kneeling now on the bed and looking horrified.

Melvalda ignored Zelda completely. Her furious red eyes were fixed on Cassandra, as intently as if they might set her aflame with a spell. But Melvalda only waved her hand, fingers spread, and Cassandra felt her body scatter, as if she had been broken into pieces by the wind.

CASSANDRA AWOKE WITH a gasp, still wrapped in her cloak as she lay beside the fire. She blinked, sat up on her elbow, and looked around, wisps of pale blonde hair tumbling in her eyes. She was back. Back in Blood Horn, beneath its black trees, as creatures howled in the distance. Calain and Gweneth were sleeping soundly, wrapped in their cloaks near the fire, while Selene sat up on watch, staring into the flames.

"It is our turn to take watch," said Cassandra hoarsely. "Why did you not wake me?" She sat up and joined Selene around the fire.

"You were so tired from casting spells, I thought you should rest," Selene answered. She smiled. "Besides, your dream sounded interesting. I would not wish to be roused from such bliss."

Cassandra felt her cheeks grow a little hot. "Selene," she whispered, glancing at the others to make certain they were sleeping soundly, "if I tell you something in confidence, will you hold the secret to your heart?"

"I would never betray your confidence, you know that," said Selene at once.

Cassandra smiled gratefully, for it was true. She and Selene had always kept each other's secrets. She took a breath and said,

"My mother belonged to the Raven's Cross coven. I lived in Ravenhold for a time when I was a child."

Selene frowned. "But you have told me this before. Or have you forgotten?"

Cassandra shook her head. "There is more. Melvalda's witches are her *lovers.* Every last one of them. They are Bound to her as we are Bound to Zelda. And they are pledged to her, to stay true to her until death. They are not permitted other lovers.

"My mother betrayed Melvalda with a man and became pregnant with me. Melvalda was furious, but she allowed us to live in Ravenhold for a time. For my sake. Though she never forgave my mother."

Selene looked at Cassandra in sympathy. "Cass, I did not know. So that means Melvalda will know you upon our arrival. Does she hold you in contempt as much as she does your mother?"

"She has always resented me. I was the reminder of my mother's betrayal. My mother was her favorite, you see. The closest to her heart. But now I fear she shall slay me for what I've done."

Selene stared intently, her body completely still. "You are looking rather grave. What hast thou done, Cassandra?"

Cassandra glanced guiltily at Selene and confessed, "I met Zelda in her dreams. I made love to her."

Selene smiled, amused by that. "And Melvalda caught you," she guessed.

"Yes," said Cassandra unhappily. "I think she would have slain me on the spot if not for sweet Zelda's pleas for mercy."

Selene only laughed. "Is this what troubles you? Cassandra, it is not as if we were going to Ravenhold to have tea and cakes with Melvalda. We are going there to slay her and take Zelda back. Who the devil cares if the old witch is enraged?"

Cassandra shook her head. "It may sound odd to you, but I do not truly wish to harm Melvalda. She raised me. She taught me what little magick I know, gave me the tools to survive, and I have repaid her by violating her bed."

"Ah. So you are fond of the old witch," Selene realized.

"Yes," Cassandra confessed. "And I know that, deep down, she is fond of me. She really quite likes children."

"Which explains the predicament we are in." Selene glanced at Cassandra curiously. "What did you intend to do when the Adar took us to Ravenhold? Attempt to reason with Melvalda and the others? Gweneth believes her an evil hag, and Calain will not surrender Zelda without a fight, you know this. Melvalda also sounds determined to have her way. She wants Zelda's child. Perhaps Zelda as well."

"I could cast a spell and make her think the child is male," said Cassandra thoughtfully. "She would dismiss Zelda then in disgust. She has no use for males."

"Hmm."

"But I would have to get close to the castle, close to Zelda. Or perhaps enter her dreams again."

"And that would pose a risk," Selene realized, "for Melvalda will be guarding her dreams jealously now."

"Yes, but it is worth the effort, is it not? There is no denying she wants Zelda and the child both. Selene . . . In the dream, Zelda was naked in Melvalda's bed. She was lying there as if she had just made love to the woman. I would not be surprised if they weren't making love at this very moment, enraged as Melvalda was. She enjoys angry sex."

Selene sighed and poked the fire with a stick, shaking her head. "What a mess we are in. First Calain slays the queen, then she allows Zelda to be taken by Melvalda . . . That's how we came to this, you realize? Calain did not heed the warning letters on the wall and walked Zelda right into one of Melvalda's lairs."

"Gods alive."

"I know. But I cannot hold Calain completely at fault, buffoon though she is. If I were to see the queen forcing herself on Zelda, I might lose my senses as well."

Cassandra nodded quietly in agreement. Like the others, she had known Zelda only a small amount of time, and yet she felt very protective of her. She could not explain it. Even traveling with Zelda for the short while that she had, Cassandra had wanted with great desperation to shield her from harm. That night in the streets of Priine, she had been terrified, *terrified* that the knights of the Rose Guard would harm Zelda. She had fought with every ounce of strength remaining to keep their blades from her. The way Zelda had looked up at her as they were hiding in the shadows, with such innocent admiration, with such longing . . . It had touched something within her and a gentle flame had ignited.

"I believe we have all gone mad," said Cassandra with a soft laugh. "Craving Zelda as we do."

Selene laughed as well. "Aye. But tis a harmless madness. We will take her from Melvalda or we will die trying."

Cassandra hesitated and said, "Selene . . . What if I approached Ravenhold on my own—"

"Don't be foolhardy!"

"—and tried to reason with Melvalda? She knows me, Selene. Perhaps she will listen to what I have to say, allow Zelda and the child to go free. And if she doesn't listen, I could cast a spell, trick her into thinking Zelda's child is male. There's a chance we could end this feud without bloodshed."

Selene stared at Cassandra with her quiet, dark eyes, and Cassandra knew she was searching for an argument. But like

Cassandra, she would rather avoid bloodshed if possible. It was the elven in her, that serenity, that willingness to set aside emotion and listen to logic. Calain and Gweneth were too human, too emotional, too rash. They would never agree to Cassandra's proposal, and Cassandra was suddenly very glad they were sleeping.

"If I leave for the Adar now," went on Cassandra, speaking calmly and factually, "I can reach Ravenhold in only a few hours and approach Melvalda with peaceful intent."

"And give her another hostage," said Selene wearily.

"No," said Cassandra at once. "I may not be as powerful as Melvalda, but I know the castle. I know how to escape Ravenhold. I could even slip out with Zelda, if she would consent to come."

Selene paused. "What do you mean?"

"I mean that Zelda seems quite taken with Melvalda," answered Cassandra. "Already, she's speaks to her with affection, calling her 'Mel' as she begged and pleaded for me. It may be that she has chosen to join Raven's Cross."

Selene swallowed hard at that news and cast her eyes on the fire. Their dark depths echoed sadness . . . and anger. "My love for Zelda is so deep, devoted, and pure," she said, "and yet she spreads her sweet thighs for another so easily. And Calain . . . Calain is all she cares for." Selene lifted her eyes. "She asked for Calain when you saw her, did she not?" she predicted.

Cassandra nodded regretfully. "Tis not because she doesn't care for you," she said at once. "Zelda cares for all of us. But she is young and beautiful and surrounded by women who are constantly tempting and seducing her. There was always going to be competition for such a fair maiden as she."

"Aye," agreed Selene heavily. She smiled, and Cassandra thought her dark eyes looked determined. "When you bring

Zelda back from Ravenhold, I shall have to fight more aggressively for her attention. I shall have to woo her in order to win a prominent place in her gentle heart."

Cassandra smiled as well. "When I bring her back? Does that mean you agree to my plan?"

"Yes," said Selene, though she didn't seem happy about it. "I confess, the idea of you martyring yourself yet again does not sit well with me, but you have spoken truly: out of all of us, Melvalda may yet listen to what you have to say. If there is a chance we can end this quarrel without bloodshed, we should take it. Go now. I will tell the others later what has transpired."

"They will not be happy," said Cassandra, glancing at the sleeping forms of Calain and Gweneth, who lay curled still beside the fire in their cloaks.

"No," agreed Selene with a smile, "but when are they ever happy?"

Laughing at Selene's words, Cassandra rose and came to Selene. Selene rose as well, and they shared a rough, one-armed hug. Selene held on for a moment longer, and her arms were trembling. She smoothed down Cassandra's hair with a shaking hand.

"I almost lost Calain," Selene whispered hoarsely in Cassandra's ear. "I could not bear to nearly lose another sister. Come back to us! Promise me you shall try! Do not sacrifice yourself!" She pulled back, looking earnestly into Cassandra's face. "If you have not returned in five days, we shall come for you. And I pray the gods grant Melvalda mercy then!"

Cassandra smiled to reassure her. "I shall return, sister. If I have to crawl naked on my belly through hot coals." She was glad when Selene laughed. They pulled apart, and Cassandra lifted her hand in farewell before turning and walking off into the dark trees.

Chapter 3

Zelda awoke with a gasp when she felt Melvalda's hand on her throat. Melvalda's hands had always been gentle. Now her grasp was so tight, it frightened Zelda. Her eyes sprang open upon awaking to find Melvalda's accusatory dark eyes filling her vision. The woman was lying naked beside Zelda in the four-poster bed, leaning on her elbow, and Zelda could see the swell of her great breasts as they crushed together, the dip of her narrow waist, the rise of her pale hip. And though naked, she was still wearing the black choker with the red jewel. The jewel gleamed, reflecting the firelight like liquid.

"You *dare,*" Melvalda hissed, "bring one of your pet knights into my bed!"

"I . . . I didn't!" Zelda gasped. She was lying very still on her back, terrified, her breasts heaving. Melvalda's grip on her throat didn't hurt at all, but it frightened her nonetheless. She dare not move, but after Melvalda had stared at her in fury for a moment, she began to shake and weep.

Melvalda's dark eyes softened, and she relaxed her hold on Zelda's throat, but she did not let go. "Hush now, you frightened little doe-eyed . . ." She looked at Zelda's lips and kissed her roughly on the mouth, massaging her throat lovingly as she did so.

Zelda gulped on Melvalda's hungry tongue, then shivered and melted beneath the passion of the rough kiss. She felt her sex throbbing. Cassandra's hard, calloused warrior's touch had stirred something in her, a hunger for aggression and strength she had always craved when with her knights. She was thinking of Cassandra now as Melvalda kissed her, and her sex swelled with blood. Melvalda seemed to sense what Zelda was thinking and pulled back, looking down at Zelda irritably. Zelda blinked up at her apologetically.

"I suppose you didn't do it on purpose," sighed Melvalda, eying Zelda. "You wouldn't know how. I doubt you've ever dream walked before now."

"N-No, I haven't," Zelda said breathlessly.

Melvalda's hand smoothed from Zelda's throat to her cheek. She cupped Zelda's face, smoothing her thumb under Zelda's eye as she looked down at her thoughtfully. Zelda lay very still on her back, blinking innocently up at the woman and feeling a mixture of fear and arousal as little trembles went through her body. Melvalda was terrifying . . . in an utterly exciting way! She was so *angry* that Cassandra had touched Zelda . . . had made love to her . . . So angry and so possessive. And when she looked at Zelda, it was always with a hunger and with an ache.

"I am not one of your witches," Zelda quietly reminded Melvalda.

Melvalda sighed again. "I know. I . . . keep forgetting that." She leaned down and kissed Zelda on the lips again, hungrily.

Zelda's body stirred from the forcefulness of the kiss, from the brush of Melvalda's heavy breasts against her own. Slowly, she reached up and cupped the back of Melvalda's hair as their heads twisted through the kiss. She slid her knees up, spreading her thighs suggestively, and Melvalda did not hesitate to gently fondle her clitoris until it was throbbing hard between her careful fingers.

Zelda shivered. "Oh, Mel . . ." she whispered, her eyes hooding.

"If only you were not pregnant still," Melvalda whispered huskily back. "I would bend you in so many ways in order to eat your golden little pussy." So saying, she smoothed her fingers through Zelda's curly pubic hair.

Zelda blushed to her hairline.

Melvalda turned onto her back and took Zelda into her arm, drawing the coverlet up over them. Zelda smiled and snuggled close, and they lay there, cuddling in the silence, as the fire roared on the hearth, filling the room with almost sweltering heat.

Zelda felt drowsy from the day's events. She had made love so many times with Melvalda and again in her dreams with Cassandra. Between the two women, she was exhausted. She yawned, feeling content. Cassandra was almost as good with her tongue as Melvalda and Calain. Melvalda had more skill with her fingers, however. It was Calain who had the best tongue. Her strong, gentle Calain.

"Zelda," said Melvalda, stroking Zelda's long golden hair, "why is it that you will not stay here with me? I could hone you into a powerful sorceress. No man would ever harm you. No woman, either. Had you possessed the knowledge I can give you, you could have turned Queen Ellanara into a rat. No one would have known. And you would still have your life, here, in Eriallon."

"We have spoken of this," said Zelda tiredly. "I cannot stay with you. I cannot."

"Is it the red knight? That fool. What do you see in her?"

"I love her!" Zelda said indignantly at once. "She is beautiful and strong! Noble and good . . ."

Melvalda made a scoffing noise. "You are a child still if you think being noble and good are things to aspire to in this world.

People who are *noble and good* do not survive very long. And your knight isn't as noble as you think she is. She slew the queen without hesitation, didn't she? Stabbed her without blinking."

"She was defending me!"

"So that made it just? What did the queen do to you? Kiss your neck against your will? And that warranted death?"

Zelda was silent, trying to understand how Melvalda could guess so accurately what had happened at Vira'Toss. Perhaps she had taken it from Zelda's mind. It was the only explanation.

"You condone Calain's actions because there's a darkness in you," went on Melvalda with approval. "A darkness you barely begin to understand, but it is there. If you stayed here with me, I would make you blossom, my night flower. No one could stand in your way!"

Zelda frowned as she lay with her cheek against Melvalda's shoulder. "Why do you want me so badly?" she asked. "I am not unique in my beauty. I have seen some of your witches. They are just as beautiful, if not more beautiful than I."

Melvalda hesitated, and Zelda – who had expected dismissal and not an answer – was surprised when she confessed, "You look like a woman I loved once. She had yellow hair as well, though it was quite pale, and her eyes were innocent and round like yours . . . And so blue. Blue as the waters that run through the Old Forest. And yet, she massacred men and crushed all who stood in her way. She was no innocent dove, she. She was ruthless and wild. No one could tame her . . . Not even I."

"Where is she now?"

"I do not know. What does it matter? If she loved me, she would still be here."

Zelda sat up on her elbow, looking down at Melvalda, her golden hair tumbling in a curtain over her shoulder. "But I'm not your love! I'm Zelda! I'm someone else entirely!"

"I know," said Melvalda quietly.

"You think of her when you touch me," said Zelda, amused, "yet you rage at me for knowing Cassandra's touch."

Melvalda stared dully at the fire and suddenly looked very tired as she said, "I suppose I'm just a foolish old woman living in the past. If you wish to leave, leave. I shall not stop you. You know this."

"And if I wish to keep my child?"

"The child is mine!" Melvalda snarled at once, startling Zelda with her sudden anger. "I will let you leave with it, Zelda, but I will take it at a later date. Mark my words, I shall always come."

Zelda stared at her. "But you said before . . . This is because of Cassandra, isn't it?"

"You're just like Talaedra," said Melvalda, looking at Zelda bitterly. "You spread your legs as soon as you lay eyes upon another. But at least you didn't bring a man into my bed. At least . . ." She sighed.

Zelda miserably rubbed her big belly. She was still torn between giving up her child and fleeing with it. On the one hand, she had grown to love the life growing inside her. Each time it moved, she smiled and dreamt of cradling it to her breasts, of feeling its warm little body and hearing it squeal with laughter.

But on the other hand, would she truly be a suitable parent? She had been raised by a drunk who beat her daily – or whenever he found her new hiding place—and while she was confident she would never lose her temper and physically harm her child, she wasn't entirely certain she knew how to show affection or provide guidance. Her relationship with Wick had been evidence enough. She had never been a good friend to her, had never listened to her or supported her. No, she had been too self-centered for that.

"And at least it was Cassandra and not that insufferable red-haired knight," went on Melvalda, who rose from the bed and whirled her silky black housecoat around her shoulders. The housecoat was translucent, and Zelda could still see Melvalda's hourglass shape through it.

Zelda looked up in surprise to hear Melvalda's words. "What does that matter?"

Melvalda's back was to Zelda, and she did not answer. "Get some rest, Zelda," she said quietly. "And try not to bring any more knights into my *bed*," she growled. And with that, she disappeared on the spot.

CASSANDRA MOVED AS silently as her armor would allow through the black trees of Blood Horn. She did not conjure a wisp-light, for she was alone now, and the danger of being discovered was greater. But even in the dark, she knew her way to the great roosts of the Adar. The great birds always nested near elven ruins and any place there was magick.

Unlike horses and other creatures, the Adar were drawn to magick, loved the thrum of it. It was said they were magick themselves, once created to be the messengers of the gods, but when mortals fell out of favor with the heavenly realm, the gods ceased all communication, and the Adar were left to their own devices.

Cassandra knew she was close. She had just come upon the Stones of Hironna when Melvalda appeared suddenly in the moonlight. She stood tall between two of the ancient pillars, as behind her, the rest formed an avenue of pillars leading nowhere, for the great library that had once stood at the end had been devoured by the earth thousands of years before, leaving only the columns behind.

Cassandra simply stood, staring at Melvalda warily. She was afraid to approach her and felt justified in that fear. Sorceress though she was, Cassandra had never trained to full power and could never hope to match Melvalda in skill. She also knew her sword would be about as useful against Melvalda as a fifth wheel on a wagon unless she moved fast enough. Her only edge was the Bane Stone Selene had given her. It wasn't very powerful, but it was having an effect on Melvalda, however small, for Melvalda stayed where she was as well, surveying Cassandra bitterly across the space between them.

"You knights," Melvalda said darkly, "you can never make your own lives, choose your own paths. You swear oaths and follow after your masters like dogs."

"What do you want, Melvalda?" said Cassandra calmly.

Melvalda snorted and her dark eyes glittered derisively beneath her hood. "As if you were not on your way to persuade me to spare you and your friends, to hand over Zelda like your long-lost, prized possession." She shook her head. "You are not worthy of her. But she was raised in the mud. She has a poor habit of clinging to that which is beneath her."

"Has Zelda joined Raven's Cross then?"

"No," said Melvalda, and she sounded very bitter about the fact.

"There is no need for bloodshed," said Cassandra. "Let Zelda and the child go. You can find pregnant maidens anywhere. Why is Zelda unique?" She paused. "Unless you seek to soothe your ache for my mother."

Melvalda's dark eyes narrowed dangerously. "Do not speak to me of that whore."

Cassandra stiffened angrily, but her hand did not go to her sword hilt and instead shook a little before remaining still. She hated when Melvalda's dark eyes lit with silent laughter, mocking her struggle to remain calm. It was rare that anyone could stir Cassandra to anger, but she was feeling the fury thrumming in her chest.

"Do not speak ill of my mother," Cassandra quietly warned.

Melvalda's eyes laughed again. "Your '*mother*' deserves worse than mere words. You were a child when she and I were together. You know nothing of the cruelty she inflicted upon me. As if my heart were some trifle, she ripped it from my chest. When she left, she took you, half the coven, and half my soul. I was never the same."

Cassandra felt her angry heart soften to realize Melvalda regretted losing her. She knew Melvalda resented her for choosing her mother over staying at Ravenhold. She thought it a silly resentment. Why shouldn't Cassandra choose her own mother? Melvalda was elven. An elven giving over to such irrational emotion was rare enough that it could only mean Melvalda felt deeply hurt and rejected.

"I was a better mother!" snapped Melvalda, emerging from Cassandra's thoughts. She waved a disgusted hand. "Look what Talaedra has done to you! Grew tired of motherhood and dumped you on Falcon Isle, let them turn you into a mannish brute!"

"I do not regret my training as a knight," Cassandra said calmly, "and you would do well not to diminish it."

Melvalda reared her head back. "Well!" she said indignantly, though she was impressed, if not amused by Cassandra's calm command.

"I do regret that we parted ways so coldly," Cassandra said. "You were like a mother to me, and I loved you dearly, as much as I love Talaedra. Or is that so difficult to believe?"

Melvalda waved a dismissive hand. "And yet you disappeared from my life, never to contact me again. Surely the Knights of Falcon would have allowed you to write a letter. You did not. Enough of this! You may have your precious Zelda, but the child is mine."

"Why?"

Melvalda's eyes grew wide to hear the question asked so simply, as if she were being unreasonable in her demands. "Why?! Your friends slew half my coven! Blood can only be repaid in blood."

"Then take me and let the child go."

Melvalda scoffed. "Perhaps if you were a little girl again, unsullied by whatever toxic potions they fed you to make you so brutely. You will never be a worthy sorceress now. Now you are the pale imitation of a man."

Cassandra tensed. "No. I am a woman. A strong woman. A powerful woman. That my power is different from yours does not make it inferior. Or why dost thou not draw nearer and find out?" So saying, Cassandra drew the Bane Stone from her satchel and threw it far away, so that it would no longer have an effect on Melvalda. Then she waited. To her surprise, Melvalda smiled.

"Perhaps I was hasty in my judgement. You are a woman after all to face me with no shield from my magick, not at all like the cowardly males who have knelt before me in terror."

"Shall you let Zelda's child go, then? Take me in its place?"

"And what would I do with you?" Melvalda demanded irritably. "The Falcon Knights have turned you. You have followed their path. It is too late."

Cassandra took a step toward Melvalda. "If my mother were to learn you had me in your possession, she would come running to Ravenhold. She would come faster than you could blink."

Melvalda went still and stared into the distance as if she had been stricken with cold water. Cassandra watched her quietly, knowing that seeing Talaedra again was what Melvalda wished more than anything, even more than her thirst for revenge.

"I . . ." began Melvalda and stopped again, biting her lip. She was embarrassed. Agreeing to lure Talaedra to Ravenhold would mean admitting she was wrong, that Talaedra *did* care about Cassandra, that Melvalda *did* care about Talaedra and longed to hold her again.

"You will come with me without a struggle, without resistance, and in return, I must let the child go free?" asked Melvalda. Her hungry eyes bore into Cassandra's face, and Cassandra knew she had already decided.

"Yes," said Cassandra simply.

Melvalda took a shuddering breath, and her great cleavage trembled. She swept toward Cassandra faster than her eye could follow and swung her cloak about them both. They disappeared on the spot.

Chapter 4

When Zelda awoke that morning, it was to find that Melvalda had left her a maternity gown on the edge of the bed. The gown was pale blue and quite long, draping over her big belly and covering her feet entirely from view when two Raven's Cross witches helped her lace it on. The witches also brought her a tray of food to break her fast, and then they departed. The entire time they were there, they said not a word, but their eyes said a great deal. Their eyes smirked, glittered with laughter, softened with admiration as they brushed Zelda's long hair. By the time they had gone, Zelda had the feeling she was going to wind up living trapped in Ravenhold forever. The witches were too smugly pleased about her presence for her to expect otherwise.

Zelda had finished her meal and was sitting on a chair at the window, looking out at the lake and rubbing her large belly, when Melvalda and Cassandra suddenly appeared in the room, standing beside the blazing fire. Zelda looked up in shock. To her relief, Cassandra seemed unharmed. She was wearing her silver Falcon Knight armor and even had her sword still. But her face was tense.

"Now I shall summon your mother," Melvalda said to Cassandra, but her eyes were on Zelda, "and we shall see. We shall see."

Cassandra swallowed hard.

Zelda wanted to ask what was happening but decided to keep silent and watch. It was clear to her that Cassandra had struck some sort of deal to be there, likely martyring herself again given the fact that she was alone. Zelda looked at Cassandra for any hint or clue, but Cassandra only looked back at her with the same calm, pretty gray eyes Zelda remembered so fondly from her dreams. Cassandra's eyes, as ever, yielded nothing of her secrets, but she smiled reassuringly at Zelda. Zelda smiled back and did indeed feel a little better, comforted to have Cassandra there.

Melvalda scowled when she noticed the silent exchange between Zelda and Cassandra, but she said nothing of it, instead going to the fire and tossing her hand at it. Brilliant sparks showered in the flames. Then they waited and waited, Melvalda staring at Zelda, Cassandra staring out the window, Zelda staring at her belly and wondering how this madness had become her life.

After about five minutes of awkward silence, there was a whoosh in the fire and a woman in a long gray gown and cloak stepped out of the flames. She had to duck to leave the hearth, she was so tall, and when she had straightened up, her long, pale blonde hair tumbled back, revealing a lovely face, with pink lips and pink cheeks and round, startlingly blue eyes. Long, pointed ears protruded from her smooth, straight hair either side her face: she was an elf.

Melvalda stood very still, staring at the elven stranger who had emerged from the fire. Cassandra was also looking at the woman, and Zelda was startled to see how desperately she was trying to control the emotion in her face. Occasionally, her lip would tremble, her eyes would veil with wet tears, but she was struggling hard to remain solemn and did for the most part.

The elven woman looked around in wonder – from Melvalda to Cassandra to Zelda and her pregnant belly—and gave a laugh that tinkled in the silence. "What the devil is happening here?" she asked in amazement.

"Hello, *Imalla*," said Cassandra hoarsely.

Zelda knew that "*imalla*" was the elven word for "mother" and looked at Cassandra in quick surprise. Cassandra didn't look at her, instead staring at the tall, blonde elven woman.

The elven woman smiled. "Cassandra," she said warmly. She laughed her tinkling laugh again. "What strange and bizarre predicament do you find yourself in this time, Daughter?" She glanced around. "At least there are no giants this time."

"Very rarely have I sought your aid," said Cassandra, "but I need your power tonight. So does Melvalda."

To Zelda's surprise, Melvalda blushed to her hairline at Cassandra's playfully insinuating words. Zelda almost laughed to see it. She had never imagined Melvalda of all people could look so embarrassed.

"Do not make light," said Melvalda reprovingly. She looked at the elven woman. "Well, Talaedra? Shall you greet me after all these years or shall you stand in my castle and continue to ignore my presence?"

Talaedra shook her head, looking quite amused. "Haven't changed a bit, I see. Still so dramatic. It is quite unbecoming of an elven, Melvalda."

"As if I had no reason to be dramatic—!" Melvalda snapped but caught her breath and controlled herself. She said in a more level voice, "You betrayed me with another and then abandoned me and took Cassandra with you! Took her after you let me grow fond of her! There is plenty enough reason for my anger!"

Zelda raised her brows. She was starting to understand more and more what Melvalda's obsession was with her and her unborn child. Melvalda's pursuit of Zelda had nothing to do with Zelda at all and everything to do with Cassandra and her mother.

"And so you seek to replace Cassandra by stealing another's child?" said Talaedra, who also seemed to quickly guess what was happening. She gestured at Zelda as she spoke, then turned her head and looked at Zelda. "And you would replace me as well, it seems. This one bears some resemblance to me on top of everything else. Most disturbing."

Melvalda's face darkened. "Must you jest about everything?"

"I must," returned Talaedra, unabashed. She took a breath and said in a more serious tone, "If you must know, I didn't take Cassandra from you. She wanted to go with me because she knew I would allow her to become a knight and you would not. Tis that simple."

Melvalda looked quickly at Cassandra. "Does your mother speak truly, child?"

Cassandra hesitated and said, "Yes, Melvalda. I know you think little of the Knights of Wolf, but I have long wished to join their ranks. If they hadn't been exiled years before, I would have gone to them. The Knights of the Raven would not have me because I am too human. The Knights of Falcon were the next best academy. Not elven but still . . ."

"I wish you had told me this, child," said Melvalda, who was listening with calm concern to Cassandra's confession. "Tis true I think little of the knight academies, but at least under the tutelage of an elven Knight of the Wolf, you would have learned both magick and the blade. Now you have fallen behind in your magick studies. You are only half of what you could have been." She tisked. "I could have found a Wolf Knight to mentor you easily. Why did you conceal this desire from me?"

"You know why," said Cassandra unhappily. "You hate knights and everything they stand for, even elven knights. You think they are too masculine. You despise masculine women."

"And you did not write to me because you were ashamed?" said Melvalda apologetically. "Because you feared my disapproval?"

Cassandra cast her eyes down.

Melvalda looked helplessly at Talaedra. "Well," she said heavily, "perchance you were a better mother than I after all. If she was this afraid to come to me . . ."

"That is the past," said Talaedra. "Can you let it go, Melvalda? Or will you punish this young woman for my sins?" She gestured again at Zelda.

Melvalda stared at Zelda, her eyes unseeing as she thought with much regret of what she had done. Then very slowly, she said, "I . . . But I must have . . . something. Compensation. Something! Her knights slew my women! Blood must be repaid in blood."

Cassandra stepped forward. "I will stay in Zelda's place."

Melvalda stared. "We have been through this, child. What good does that do me?"

"No doubt there is some spell that could make me a child again," said Cassandra. "You could train me, raise me however you liked, bring me to my full power as a sorceress. I would yield."

Melvalda stared at Zelda again, struggling to decide.

Talaedra stepped forward and placed a soothing hand on Melvalda's arm. "I, too, will stay with you . . . After I have returned Zelda to her knights."

Melvalda looked quickly at Talaedra. "You will?"

"Yes, my love," Talaedra said. "And I shall explain to you where I have been all these years. And we shall fall in love all over again and raise Cassandra together."

Melvalda didn't seem to believe what was being said. She stared at Talaedra for a long time, but Talaedra simply stared back, smiling and sweet. There seemed to be nothing but sincerity in Talaedra's eyes. If she was lying, Zelda thought her an excellent liar.

Eventually, Melvalda said with a sigh, "Fine. Return the girl to her bumbling knights. No doubt they are beside themselves with lust and grief. And you . . ." She looked at Cassandra and placed a hand on the silver vambrace that covered her arm. "You will stay here with me. I shall make you a child again, and you shall be my apprentice, as you were always meant to be!"

Cassandra serenely nodded.

Zelda caught Cassandra's eye and did everything in her power to make her eyes scream, "No!" but Cassandra only smiled sadly at her.

Smiling, Talaedra came to Zelda and offered her small hand. The nails were perfect and white, trimmed down and clean, and her gold rings were on the same odd fingers as Melvalda's. "Come," she said kindly, "I shall take you back to your knights."

But how did she know where they were? Zelda wondered. She took Talaedra's hand, and the second she did, they had vanished.

Chapter 5

Calain was a little furious to learn that Cassandra had run off to sacrifice herself yet again, but for the sake of the peace, she swallowed her anger. It seemed to her she had been swallowing her anger for days and days. For she could feel it whenever Zelda experienced pleasure. She could feel that evil witch making love to her!

And Zelda was enjoying Melvalda's touch. That hurt probably more than anything else. And the more she had to endure Zelda's ecstasy at the hands of another, the more she began to wonder if she should even bother going to rescue her. Maybe Zelda had joined Raven's Cross. Maybe she liked being with Melvalda more than Calain.

Because Cassandra had left the party, the knights had taken to keeping watch one at a time again. That night when they made camp, Gweneth immediately went to sleep, and it was Selene's turn to keep watch.

Calain did not prepare a pallet of leaves. Instead, after helping to set up camp, she strapped on her traveling satchel and stood pointedly over Selene, who was sitting beside the fire.

Selene looked up, and realizing what Calain meant to do, she shot to her feet. "Calain! What—!"

"I am leaving, Selene," said Calain, "and there is nothing you can say that will change my mind."

Selene shook her head. "But why? What changed?"

"Nothing," said Calain. "Things have always been so, only I was too foolish to see it."

"Calain, wait. Talk to me," Selene said. "The forest is too dangerous for you to—"

"So is loving Zelda," said Calain with a sneer. "Do yourself a favor and leave her service. She cares for none of us. Only her own base pleasure—"

"That is not so!" said Selene adamantly.

Calain looked at Selene in sympathy. "Look at you, still under her thrall. Perhaps Melvalda was right about all of us." She glanced at Gweneth, who was sleeping soundly. "Perhaps Gwen was right as well. Loving Zelda is a fool's errand."

Selene's lips tightened. "Do you have any *idea* how much Zelda dotes upon you? What the rest of us would give to have her look at us the way she looks at you? She adores you!"

"She uses me," said Calain.

Selene's eyes were still impatient, though Calain could see she had resigned herself to the fact that she could not change Calain's mind. Instead, she said in a weary voice, "Where will you go?"

"Back to Koradara, for I am a free woman there. Perhaps I shall return to Wolf Fortress. Or find a new woman and pledge myself to her. A woman who is true."

Selene smiled sadly. "You will never find a woman like Zelda, and you know it."

Calain scowled. "Spare me your attempts at conversion. I no longer worship at Zelda's altar. Fare thee well, Selene." And with that, she turned and took off into the darkness. She did not look back.

SELENE WANTED TO BE angry with Calain, but she really didn't have the time. Almost immediately after Calain had gone, they were set upon by Rose Guard knights. A crowd of them suddenly stormed the camp, screaming, "For the queen!" at the top of their voices, blades raised. Selene snapped to her feet at once and engaged them coldly.

Gweneth roused to action the second she heard the fighting, and together, she and Selene fought desperately, but they were losing. There were simply too many of the queen's knights. They kept pouring out of the darkness like a swarm of locusts. Selene and Gweneth were soon fighting back-to-back.

"They are too numerous!" shouted Selene, parrying a blow. "We may have to retreat!"

"Where the devil is Calain?" snarled Gweneth, furious as she parried and viciously kicked a knight back with her boot.

"What's wrong?" mocked the knight Gweneth had kicked, a woman with messy black hair. "Can't stand a real punch? I didn't take a foul potion like you. I earned my strength!"

"What strength?" Gweneth retorted and took off the woman's head.

Another Rose Guard, enraged by what Gweneth had done, fell upon her roaring. Gweneth dodged the attack but just barely, taking a slash across the face.

"This is going badly," Gweneth said, spitting blood. "Shall we run screaming on the count of three?"

But as it turned out, there was no need to retreat. There was a sudden bang and a flash of light, followed by another, and another. The musky lavender smell of magick fire lingered in the air. Panicking, Selene grabbed Gweneth and dove to the ground with her. They lay there facedown, listening to the bangs and the screams, coughing on the smoke, watching as Rose Guard knights collapsed around them, hair and faces singed, smoke furling from their golden armor.

When the smoke had cleared, Selene and Gweneth looked up, coughing and sputtering, to see Zelda standing there beside a tall, beautiful elven woman.

"So here we are," said the elven woman, smiling serenely between the curtains of her pale blonde hair. Selene thought there was something vaguely familiar about her.

"I have delivered you to your knights and saved their lives to boot. Truly, I am on a roll. Be well, Zelda," said the woman, and with that, she disappeared on the spot.

Selene and Gweneth got to their feet, and both stared at Zelda, who was standing there in a pale blue gown and looking at them in relief. She was still large with child.

"What is going *on*?" moaned Gweneth, taking off her gauntlet and pushing a weary hand back through her hair.

"Where is Calain?" Zelda asked breathlessly.

Selene held down the urge to reply that Calain was busy off being a fool. How could Calain think Zelda did not love her? She appeared in their camp out of no where, and the first words out of her mouth were of Calain. Typical.

"Where is Cassandra?" Selene returned.

"Where is my wine?" said Gweneth tiredly.

NOT WANTING TO SLEEP in a camp full of dead knights, they packed up and moved on. But because it was too dark and too dangerous for Zelda to travel in her condition, they didn't go very far. Selene led the others in the direction of the portal she and the other knights had come from, intent on using it to follow Calain back to Koradara in the morning.

They made camp again and built up a fire, and then Selene and Zelda exchanged their news regarding Cassandra and Calain. By the time silence had fallen over them, everyone was very tired and unhappy. The only sound was the swish of Gweneth's wineskin.

"So that was Cassandra's mother," said Gweneth into the silence. "She never told me she was half elfling. Now everything makes sense."

Selene glanced up irritably. " 'Elfling!' Tis a foul word. A Falcon Knight is above such base language."

Gweneth rolled her eyes. "Tis late and I am very tired. Spare me your lectures, Selene."

"Don't start bickering, *please*!" said Zelda tensely, and the other two women fell silent. Sitting there clutching her belly, she looked as weary and miserable as Selene had ever seen her. Tears were in her eyes. If only Calain could see how her abandonment had hurt Zelda.

Selene thought of the time Calain had nearly been slain by the spirit in this very forest. Zelda hadn't left Calain's side, had sat up fretting over her all night. And yet, because Calain was unconscious at the time, she hadn't been witness to it. That was the tragedy of the situation: Calain had never seen for herself how dearly Zelda cared for her. And Selene, who strived almost desperately for Zelda's affection, was always a front row spectator to her great love for Calain. Sometimes Selene thought the gods did love a good jest.

"Are you well, my lady?" Selene asked with soft concern. "Maybe you should rest."

"Not until we figure out how to save Cassandra," Zelda insisted.

"My lady," Gweneth said gently, "there is no saving her. Melvalda is powerful, and you are heavy with child, unable to cast without your stave, and we knights could not stand alone against her entire coven. There are many of them at Ravenhold."

"So what did you intend to do to rescue me?" Zelda said pointedly.

"We intended to die for you," said Selene simply. Gweneth nodded in solemn agreement, and Zelda looked at them both, aghast.

"You can't mean that!" Zelda cried.

Gweneth frowned at Zelda. "Of course, we do. We swore ourselves in service to you."

"Anyway, we needn't worry so for Cassandra," said Selene. "Melvalda shall not harm her. Especially not if her mother is involved in matters. We must focus on getting you to safety. In the morning, we shall head back to Koradara, and perhaps Calain will be waiting for us at Wolf Fortress."

Zelda didn't seem comforted by Selene's words. She miserably dropped her head on Selene's shoulder, then trembled and turned her face, weeping into Selene's neck. Heart heavy, Selene closed Zelda in her arms and kissed her head. She glanced across the fire and saw Gweneth watching Zelda with a mixture of sadness and anger, as if she, too, were fed up with Calain.

Chapter 6

As she was marching hard through the dark trees, Calain could hear a fight breaking out back at the camp. The sound of blades meeting made her stop in her tracks and listen with a pounding heart. She had almost turned about and gone back to help, but at the last minute, she shook her head and kept marching on.

Why should she involve herself anymore in the antics of the other knights? Let them fight the Rose Guard, let them bleed defending Zelda – Zelda, who didn't even care for them! Calain was done.

Calain headed all night in the direction of the portal, trying to put as much distance between herself and the camp as possible. When the sun came up, she was still marching on, though becoming sluggish and tired. She did not stop for several more hours.

Moving at such a quick pace as she was, it only took Calain three days and one night to reach the ancient elven temple where the portal stood. During that time, she only came across a few Skoll Wolves (which she easily slayed), a small tribe of goblins (which she quickly dispatched), and – of all things – a Wolf Knight.

It was night, and moonlight was reaching in pale fingers between the trees when a troll rumbled up out of the earth, covered in moss and grass, and blocking Calain's path. Before

Calain could dodge, it had lifted a big paw and swatted her away from its lair like an annoying fly.

Calain flew ten feet through the air before her back slammed a tree. She had not been wearing her helm, hot from walking as she was, and the back of her head spread in a web of throbbing pain. Spots exploded before her eyes, and she slid to the ground, on the verge of passing out.

Sitting there in a daze, Calain could feel the ground shaking as the mighty troll lurched up from the mud with a roar. Calain could smell its foul breath already. It was coming to finish her off, she the intruder, who had so obliviously stomped across its home.

The troll's shadow loomed over Calain. It looked down at her with its angry, beady little eyes and roared as it reared back, preparing to strike. Calain sat there, too blinded by pain to move, resigned to her fate. And just when it seemed the troll was going to strike, a blade blossomed in its chest, and its furious roar abruptly turned to a gurgle.

Calain looked up, and the troll looked down, just as baffled. The blade was of magick make, for it was glowing a bright, ethereal blue. The light was so radiant and strong, it cast the troll's face in a ghostly glow.

Another second, and the glowing blade was ripped free in a splash of black troll blood. The troll's tiny eyes rolled back in its head as it was pulled from the snatch of the blade, and it tumbled backward in a toss of leaves, shaking the earth as it fell.

Red hair streaming in her eyes, Calain looked up and saw what was unmistakably a Wolf Knight standing over her, for the knight was elven and wearing the silver, leaf-engraved armor of a Knight of the Wolf, with the magick sigil of a wolf upon the breastplate.

Fifty years ago, the queen of Koradara had begun a war against Eriallon and had attempted to conscript the Knights of the Wolf. The Wolf Knights had opposed her and were exiled from the realm, leaving their magick stronghold, Wolf Fortress, abandoned.

The Wolf Knights were an elven order, and all of them were women, which was why their knights fought with enchanted swords and spells (for only women could wield magick). Now living in exile, they were somewhat mockingly known as "witch-knights," a term that did not begin to do justice to their power.

The elven woman standing over Calain was slender and short, like most of the modern day elven bloodlines, for only the ancient elves were tall. She was barely five feet tall, though Calain knew there was great power contained in her little frame, not unlike Zelda. Her pointed ears poked from long, messy, jet-black hair, which fell around a deceptively young face. Calain knew the woman had to be much older than she appeared, for the Wolf Knights were an ancient order who had stopped recruiting fifty years before.

The Wolf Knight's eyes were a startlingly bright violet, and they practically glowed in her pale face when the moonlight shone upon them. She was watching Calain intently, and at last, she sheathed her sword on her back and said, "A Knight of Falcon. What are you doing out here alone, Little Bird?"

The words weren't intended to be insulting, Calain knew, but they reminded her of the bear queen, who had mocked her as "the bird knight," who had nearly defeated her and taken Zelda, and she snarled as she staggered to her feet, "None of your business, dog knight!"

"My name is Arryn," said the knight calmly, turning to watch as Calain stormed past. "And you would do well to remember that. Perhaps I won't step in to slay the next troll . . . Calain, Knight of Falcon."

Calain stopped in her tracks. "How dost thou know me?"

"The earth has ears," answered the elven knight calmly.

Calain sighed. "Whatever that means," she muttered, and to her surprise, the Wolf Knight laughed good-naturedly.

Calain couldn't help but smile. She turned to the Wolf Knight and said apologetically, "Much thanks, friend, for saving my life. Please forgive my foul mood. I am not myself tonight. Or perhaps I am more myself than ever."

"No offense taken, Knight of Falcon. What brings you out here alone? Hast thou not pledged thyself in service to a maiden?"

Calain had the feeling the Wolf Knight already knew the answer to her own question. But she said defiantly anyway, "I served a maiden once, aye, and that devotion was spat upon. Honor and duty are for naïve, romantic fools. Who should know that better than a Knight of the Wolf? Your entire order turned their back on duty and defied the queen when she beckoned you."

"Knights belong to their mages, not the crown. You know this. When the Knights of the Wolf turned away from the queen, it was on the orders of our ladies, the sorceresses of Menosea."

"So you were just doing what you were told," Calain realized in disgust.

"Yes," said Arryn quietly.

Calain waved a gauntlet. "And your lady? Where is the woman whose command was worth surrendering your life for? She made you a fugitive and a rebel without even seeking your council, and then she abandoned you! No doubt for the arms of another."

"In a manner of speaking," said Arryn in the same quiet voice. "She is dead."

Calain went still, stung with guilt and surprise.

"And I suppose the goddess does hold her to her breasts now."

"I am sorry."

"Are you not always?" returned Arryn. She paused, staring at Calain with her calm, catlike eyes, and Calain absorbed the soft reprimand in shame: it was true that she had been nothing but rude since meeting Arryn, and the woman had just saved her life.

"And so you wonder the forests alone?" asked Calain in sympathy. She looked at Arryn and wondered if she wasn't about to become her, a rogue knight with no lady to serve, no duty, and no purpose.

"In search of a lady worthy of my service," answered Arryn. "I should only be so lucky as you, to have a woman like the sorceress Zelda in my thrall, doting upon me, hanging upon my every word, sacrificing herself to protect my life, when it is supposed to be quite the other way around."

Calain scowled. She knew not to even bother asking how Arryn knew of Zelda. "Zelda is not in my thrall!" she protested hotly. "She has used me. She has always used me."

"If you would like to believe that, then it will become so. In your mind, at least. And you shall always be unworthy of her love."

Calain's scowl deepened. "I thank you again, Knight of the Wolf, and I bid thee farewell." She turned abruptly and stamped off, snatching her silver helm from the mud as she went.

"Tred carefully, Knight of Falcon!" called Arryn after her. "On the earth and on fair Zelda's heart!"

Calain had met the Wolf Knight one day ago, but the woman's words had haunted her ever since. How had she known about Zelda and her involvement with Calain? How had she known Calain was a Falcon Knight? For Zelda had enchanted Calain's armor to hide its emblem ages ago.

Arryn reminded Calain of Cassandra. Always mysterious, always calm and serene, always knowing things she should not know. She wondered if it wasn't simply the way of elves. Many elves she had met had been the same, rarely stirred to anger, always serene, far too magickal for their own good, far too knowledgeable without explanation of the secrets of others.

The elves were such a powerful, all-knowing people, and yet their mighty empire had crumbled thousands of years ago, and it was humans who ruled the land now. Koradara had once been an elven realm, which was why vestiges of its elven past were so prominent there. In that time, the land had been known as Ionmiris, and the old Wolf Fortress had been known as Ellondhold. Calain remembered that from her studies as a child at Falcon Isle, even if she never remembered the damned runes.

Calain marched faster and faster, her heart pounding. She was very close to reaching the elven temple and the portal that waited inside. It was day, though Blood Horn was murky-dark and shadowy as ever, bugs chirping and beasts growling in the distance. The crumbling temple was directly before her, beams of sunlight streaming through its open roof. She stepped inside, her eyes fixed on the portal and its swirling light . . . .and halted when two laughing Rose Guard knights stepped from behind it.

Calain's face darkened and her hand went to her sword hilt, but she paused again when she heard more of the knights behind her. Calain's head turned every which way. The knights were coming from every direction, smiling darkly as they lifted shields and slowly pulled blades.

Calain's scanning eyes quickly counted a round dozen, but even more appeared before she had finished counting. She might have been able to pick off a few of them, but there were simply too many, even for a Falcon Knight. They would overwhelm and slay her. She had walked directly into a trap.

Calain decided to die fighting. She roughly drew her blade as the Rose Guard knights closed in.

"Good," said a Rose Guard knight with solemn approval. She was not mocking or unkind but sincere. She was a tall older woman with a scarred face and graying brown hair that had been cropped short, so that she resembled a spiky-feathered bird of prey. "Die on your feet, fearlessly, like a woman," she said with the same approval. "Women do not fear pain. We know it all of our lives."

"True enough," agreed Calain and gave the older warrior a serious, respectful nod – then lunged at her and brought down her sword.

Chapter 7

Cassandra had forgotten what it was like to be a child, for the world to be much bigger, for furniture, trees, and adults to tower away eternally to the sky. But Melvalda's spell had brought it all rushing back. And now she was small again, barely seven, a skinny little girl wearing a knee-length tunic dress and stockings. Melvalda had tried to make her wear shoes, but she insisted on running through the castle in bare feet.

The witches of Raven's Cross were kind to Cassandra. They patted her on the head, pinched her cheek, and gave her sweets from the kitchen. Sometimes she sat on their laps in the evening, and they told her stories of trolls and giants while she made her face sticky with chocolate.

At night, Melvalda lovingly brushed Cassandra's long hair and told her of all the great things she was going to do. She was going to be a mighty sorceress, Melvalda said, and she was going to lead an army that would conquer all of Vallinwir and bring the seven queens to their knees in submission. And then Cassandra would make herself queen of all the land and rule for all eternity. Or at least a thousand years. Cassandra had enough elven blood that she could have lived for thousands of years, Melvalda suspected, for Cassandra's mother was of the ancient bloodline of the Tula-Dan.

Cassandra listened to Melvalda's dreaming and scheming with the blissful indifference of any ignorant child, swinging her legs as she sat in the chair, impatiently waiting for the hair brushing to end. Sometimes her mother came and scolded Melvalda for filling Cassandra's head with dreams of conquest. The two would begin to argue, but always, they would fall to kissing, and then Cassandra was sent off to bed as they continued, sitting on the edge of the bed in each other's arms.

Cassandra loved being in Ravenhold. There were so many places to climb and explore, so many secret chambers and forgotten rooms. There was even a forgotten garden with a swing on the other side of the castle, locked behind a gate, which Cassandra had unlocked with a spell and entered, walking through the broken statues and fountains in awe.

Every day, when she wasn't taking magick lessons from Melvalda, Cassandra was exploring the castle, chasing the ravens from the parapets, and climbing to the rooftops to stare in curiosity at the dark lake and the pine trees beyond. She had no memory of her life as Cassandra the Knight of Falcon. She did not remember Calain or Selene or Gweneth or even Zelda. She did not remember the spell of age reversal being cast upon her or that it had been done to sate Melvalda's rage that her family – Cassandra and Talaedra – had abandoned her.

Cassandra only knew that she was a seven-year-old girl, whose mother was elven, and whose father was an unknown human man, who Talaedra and Melvalda never spoke of unless they were angry and bickering.

And Cassandra, oblivious to who she truly was, lived as a child for one week in Ravenhold. For some reason, as the days went by, Melvalda became increasingly sad and guilty. Cassandra would often catch the woman staring at her apologetically, and more than once, she took Cassandra into her arms and wept ceaselessly.

Cassandra didn't understand why Melvalda's mood had changed from happy and hopeful to reflective and sad, but it happened again one night when Melvalda was brushing Cassandra's hair as usual beside the fire. She suddenly sat hard in the armchair and stared into the flames. Her eyes were wet with tears.

Cassandra, baffled by the woman's tears, climbed up into Melvalda's lap and let her skinny legs swing as she stared sadly into Melvalda's face. "Raven Mother," she said with frowning concern, "why dost thou weep?"

Melvalda laughed through her tears and looked down at Cassandra fondly. "I had forgotten you used to call me that. Raven Mother. I have missed you so, Little Dove."

Cassandra frowned, not understanding. Then her eyes fell on the red jewel that Melvalda always wore bound to a black choker about her throat. The octagonal jewel reflected the firelight in its liquidly surface. The effect was mesmerizing.

Cassandra had been warned many times not to touch the jewel and had tried to touch it many times regardless. With her curious, round child's eyes, she stared at it now, then glanced furtively at Melvalda, who seemed too distracted with her grief to notice what Cassandra was doing.

Cassandra's hungry eyes went back to the jewel. It was like a succulent fruit or a bit of candy, tempting and teasing her. She reached up and – before Melvalda could stop her – snatched the jewel from the witch's throat, choker and all.

Melvalda gasped feebly. "Cassandra—no!"

But it was too late. The jewel had been ripped clean away in Cassandra's small hand. As Melvalda had warned, the jewel shone with light and burned viciously, as if in protest that it had been taken from its owner. Cassandra squealed in pain and dropped it, but luckily, she had dropped the jewel fast enough that it did not burn her flesh. She was merely stung and her skin blistered. She sucked her fingers, pouting, but when she looked up, she went still in shock.

Young and beautiful Melvalda was now an old woman, humpbacked and sagging with wrinkles so thick, her face was nearly obscured. Her once-black hair was now white, a long cloak of silky strands cascading long around her slouching shoulders. Her breasts, once large and swollen, were shriveled and empty, and skin drooped around her sad eyes as she looked down at Cassandra in miserable resignation.

Cassandra's mouth fell open. "I . . . I'm sorry, Raven Mother. I did not mean to . . ."

Melvalda smiled, her wrinkles pulling, and Cassandra saw she was missing teeth: even her teeth had been an enchantment!

"Of course, you meant to," Melvalda said. "The gods have goaded a child's curiosity to teach me this hard lesson."

Cassandra frowned, not understanding.

"I sought to take your life from you," Melvalda explained, "and fashion you to my liking. Such a completely selfish action, when I have lived as I have pleased for thousands of years, with no one telling me who to be and which path to follow." She smiled again. "Any who tried to were scattered to the wind."

"I do not understand. Are you displeased, Raven Mother?" Cassandra asked, innocently blinking.

"No. I am *very* pleased that I have been shown the foolishness of my ways. Go forth, child. Be a masculine woman. Be a Knight of Falcon if you wish it. You do not need my blessing. You have never needed my blessing." So saying, she waved her hand, and light glowed over Cassandra in a flash.

Cassandra grew so big so suddenly that she staggered down from Melvalda's lap, nearly fell, and caught her balance. When she had straightened up again, she was a tall, muscular woman, towering beside the firelight, and the child's tunic she had been wearing was now a tight bit of cloth around her rippling belly, while the stockings had ripped and fallen away in shreds.

All of Cassandra's memories suddenly came rushing back to her: Falcon Isle, Selene and Calain and Gweneth, the events at Vira'Toss . . . making love to Zelda. She stared blankly into space and her pupils shrank as the memories were returned to her in an abrupt flood, and she was suddenly so overcome with emotion, she shivered and wept, hugging herself.

"There, there, child," said Melvalda, who was young again after fastening her choker back on. She rose from her armchair and took up her housecoat, draping it around Cassandra's bare shoulders. "Hush," she said soothingly, and she lovingly stroked Cassandra's pale hair, tears in her eyes. "Your armor is downstairs, on a stand, waiting for you. Your sword as well. Go forth and return to your Zelda. None here shall stop you."

Still shaking from the reversal of the spell, Cassandra's head turned, and she looked down at Melvalda, who was now shorter than her. The witch was smiling up at her kindly. Cassandra kissed her on the forehead and didn't see it when fresh tears sprang to Melvalda's eyes.

"Fare thee well, Raven Mother," Cassandra said. She turned and went to the door but paused again and added with a smile, "I shall write this time."

Chapter 8

Calain was not waiting at Wolf Fortress when Zelda, Selene, and Gweneth returned, but Cassandra was and so were the horses: Arthur, Sunny, Bron, and Apple. Relieved to see Cassandra alive and in one piece, Zelda ran to her and hugged her tight, bouncing up and kissing her on the cheek twice, so that Cassandra blushed a little and actually became flustered, which was rare for her.

They went to the kitchen to prepare a meal, and as Gweneth stroked up a fire in the oven, Selene skinned a brace of brown hare, while Zelda and Gweneth sat at the table and explained to Cassandra where Calain had gone. Cassandra had listened grimly but had not seemed surprised, which did nothing to comfort Zelda. Zelda had some small hope that Cassandra would predict Calain's safe return, but the sorceress-knight never had a vision and apologized when she saw the crestfallen tears fill Zelda's eyes.

During their stay at Wolf Fortress, Zelda spent a great deal of her time in one of the beds in the old barracks, crying herself to sleep or else weeping as she gazed hopefully out the window. How could Calain do this to her? How could Calain just leave her when she was heavy with child, frightened, and needed her the most? But Zelda reminded herself that Calain had every right to feel betrayed. No doubt she had felt it as Zelda and Melvalda were making love, and not understanding why Zelda had gone to Melvalda in the first place, she would have been furious.

And while Zelda had given herself to Melvalda to protect Calain, she could not pretend as if she hadn't hoped to be taken in the woman's arms. She and Melvalda had shared a mutual lust since first they'd met. There was no reason that Zelda had needed to be naked for the initiation ritual, Zelda knew that now. Melvalda had simply wanted to gaze upon her body, her great breasts and her tiny waist, to see how desirable she was before Binding them together.

And Zelda had wanted it. Deep down, somewhere in her soul, she had wanted to be Bound of Melvalda. Perhaps she missed the company of other sorceresses. As bored and lonely as she had been on Vira'Toss Isle, at least she had been surrounded by people who were like her and who understood her. The Knights of Falcon did not understand her and barely respected her power or her ability to defend herself. It was how the entire mess had started, with Gweneth mocking her!

Zelda had to admit, it had been nice to be among her own kind again. Even for a little while. But her lust for Melvalda and her longing for the company of mages did not mean she felt nothing for Calain or that she didn't love her knight! She had never loved anyone more! Indeed, she had never loved anyone at all! Calain was the first . . . *everything.* The first woman to stir her heart to wild beating, the first woman to kiss her, the first woman to make love to her. And for that reason alone, she would always have a special place in Zelda's heart.

Zelda was beginning to realize that she needed to do something to make Calain understand how greatly she loved her. Simply saying the words was not enough. Calain was a woman of action. She needed action as proof of Zelda's love. She needed Zelda to do something, take some risk, make some sacrifice, much in the same way Calain had given up life and reputation to slay the queen in Zelda's defense.

Zelda thought in frustration that she *had* made a sacrifice, only she hadn't told Calain about it. She remembered the casual way in which Melvalda had thrown Calain through the air when they were hiding in the cavern with the waterfall. She could have killed Calain so easily! And desperate to protect Calain, Zelda had given herself over to Melvalda. That was the truth, even if she *had* lusted for the woman, and she had risked the life of her child as well! For Calain!

Did Calain think so little of Zelda that she had simply assumed Zelda wasn't true? That her love wasn't real and pure? Zelda supposed that after everything with Yrsa, she could not blame Calain. Zelda had married another and become with her child! Calain knew that Zelda had been tricked by Revna, but the knowledge of what Zelda had done had to sting nonetheless. The thought of Zelda in Yrsa's arms, knowing Yrsa's touch, and being able to feel it – for certainly Calain had felt – would have driven her mad.

They had been living in Wolf Fortress undisturbed for one week when Zelda went into labor and her birth pains began. The knights scurried around the fortress in a blind panic, their armor off, their tunic sleeves rolled up as they ran back and forth with pails of water and clean cloths for the blood.

Selene stayed at Zelda's side the entire time, holding her hand and kissing her head, whispering gentle words of comfort, while Gweneth and Cassandra ran in and out of the room, looking for a proper knife for the cord cutting and constantly running to the well in the yard for fresh water.

It took two hours, but the baby finally arrived, pink and screaming as it slid into Cassandra's waiting arms. Cassandra lovingly wrapped it in a cloth and wiped it clean, as Gweneth took a knife she had sterilized in vodka and cut the cord. With the baby warm and clean, Cassandra gently placed it in Zelda's eager arms, and Zelda happily held it to her breasts. The knights gathered around, sitting on the bed and leaning in, and all of them looked down at the infant, who had stopped screaming to blink at them in silent wonder.

"She's beautiful," Zelda whispered.

"As beautiful as her mother," said Selene.

The baby was pink and perfect, Zelda thought, with a tuft of Yrsa's dark, auburn hair cloaking her little head. Her eyes were also Yrsa's eyes, dark green and round with innocent awe. She hiccoughed quietly as her eyes moved from face to face, but always, her eyes returned to Zelda, who she stared at with her mouth open. Then she wiggled close to Zelda's breast, smacking her pink lips sleepily to get at the nipple. Zelda lifted the baby a little and saw her nipple ease in her mouth. The infant began to suckle, and Zelda felt relief spread over her as her milk-heavy breast became lighter.

Zelda looked down at her tiny daughter and thought guiltily that Yrsa should be there, seeing her firstborn child. She wondered sadly for a moment where Yrsa was and if she was safe, but instead, she said miserably, "Calain should be here."

"Aye, we all miss her," agreed Selene.

"And I'll give her a good thrashing for you whenever we find her," said Gweneth angrily. She had left the bedside and was standing near the window, the sunlight playing upon her loose brown hair, her hands in the pockets of her trousers. Her undercut was growing out. Zelda thought it made her look softer . . . and more beautiful. But she knew a woman like Gweneth had probably never cared to look beautiful.

"Don't be cruel to Calain," Zelda begged. "She doesn't understand."

"She *never* understands," snorted Gweneth. "And I can't *believe* you defend her so earnestly after she broke her holy vow to guard and defend you always. She was always going on about her father, but he would turn her over his knee if he knew what she'd done. I may provoke and tease you, my lady, but I would never leave your side." Gweneth looked at Zelda with such a serious fire, Zelda's heart skipped a happy beat.

"You are being too hard on Calain," said Selene tiredly. "Let us not ruin this happy moment with bickering. Calain made her choice. She acted impulsively and on emotion, as she always does. Give her time to cool down, and when she chooses to return, we shall welcome her with open arms."

Gweneth made a scoffing noise, as if she was still intent on thrashing Calain. "Of course, we shall. But I still have a debt to repay her. I have not forgotten what she did to my head in one of her mad tantrums."

Zelda was on the verge of asking what Gweneth meant – for no one had told her about Calain's assault on Gweneth weeks before – when a bird appeared, standing on the sill of the open window. It was an arched window, framed in stone bricks, and the bird was a sleek black messenger raven. It tilted its head and clacked its dark beak, waiting, a roll of parchment attached to its thin leg.

Selene was sitting on one side of Zelda and had her arm around her as she leaned in, looking at the child. Now she glanced up at the raven in surprise. "What the devil?" she muttered.

Cassandra, who was sitting on other side of Zelda and cooing over the baby, also looked up. Zelda watched her, but there was no sign in Cassandra's expression that she knew what was in the letter. She seemed as surprised as everyone else.

Gweneth, who was the only one already standing, turned and went to the messenger raven. She took the parchment from the bird, which took off immediately with a loud "Kraa!"

"It has the seal of the queen of Eriallon!" Gweneth said and hastily broke the seal, unrolling the letter. They all watched on tenterhooks as she silently read. Eventually, she looked up at them and said, "Shite of the gods. The queen has Calain."

Zelda stiffened. "What!"

Gweneth crossed the room and gave the letter to Cassandra, who sat up and read the following aloud:

To the sorceress Zelda,

I have in my possession one of your rebel knights, the one by the name of Calain, the Queen-slayer herself. Calain shall not be harmed if you journey to my castle immediately and present yourself before me.

I have a proposition for you, a small task I shall ask you to perform, and in return, you shall have your knight back, and I shall drop all charges against you. You shall be able to return to Eriallon and live here without fear.

If you do not come within a fortnight, I shall execute the Queen-slayer and place her head on a pike outside my keep, to show all what happens to those who threaten the life of a queen.

Consider carefully, Sorceress.

Your sovereign,

Queen Cilia.

Finished reading, Cassandra lowered the letter and looked unhappily at Zelda.

"So Cilia is queen of Eriallon now," said Selene, who sounded relieved.

Zelda looked quickly at Selene. "Is that a good thing? Does she mean what she says in the letter?"

"Cilia is Ellanara's younger sister. She is more honorable than Ellanara was," answered Selene. "Even still, that isn't saying much. We should rescue Calain from her clutches, but I am not certain we should do her bidding."

"How shall we rescue Calain?" Gweneth snorted. "Storm the Gold Keep on our own?"

"There must be someone who would help us, Gweneth," Selene returned patiently. "You act as if we were always on our own in the world—"

"Because we *are*," said Gweneth.

"—but Cassandra's mother was willing to aid us," went on Selene. "There must be others like her that would as well. Perhaps we could seek out the knights from other orders. The Knights of the Wolf would be near impossible to find, and I don't know how willing they would be to aid humans, but the Knights of the Stag or the Knights of the Dragon . . ."

"The Knights of the Dragon?" Gweneth sneered. "Those arrogant . . . I'd rather have my teeth pulled."

Selene sighed. "Once again, Gweneth, you whinge without offering an alternative."

"I am not *whinging*," Gweneth said irritably.

"I shall tell you what we shall do," said Zelda, and they all looked at her. "I shall make the journey to the Gold Keep—"

"No, my lady!"

"You can't!"

"Tis a trap!"

"—and I shall see what the queen wishes of me," went on Zelda. She looked at all of them resolutely, and she suddenly realized she was tired of how they coddled her and never listened to her suggestions, let alone her commands. So she lifted her chin and said firmly and loudly, her voice ringing in the silence, "And the three of you will stay here and care for . . . the baby." She looked down at the infant, which was still suckling, and realized she didn't have a name for the child.

When Zelda looked up again, the three knights were watching her quietly. She could tell they were stifling the urge to protest and held back a smile as she looked at them.

"If you are going to leave us," said Cassandra after a pause, "we shall need milk. A nursing cow or a goat. Or perhaps we shall find a woman in Priine, if one of us dares to return there. In other words, we need time to make arrangements, my lady."

"Unless you cast a spell and fill one of us with milk," said Gweneth with a smile.

Zelda smiled at the joke but it was a weak smile. She felt heavy in her heart: her Calain had been captured, and all because of her! If she hadn't given herself to Melvalda and upset Calain by sleeping with her, Calain wouldn't have stormed off her own. She sadly cast her eyes down.

Almost as if she had read Zelda's mind, Selene reached over and touched her shoulder. "My lady," she said gently, "the fault lies with no one. Calain cannot help her nature, I fear—"

Gweneth nodded, laughing softly, and Cassandra smiled, both of them thinking fondly of Calain.

"—and you did as you thought best," went on Selene. "When you return from Eriallon, we shall be waiting for you here, with the child."

The baby had stopped suckling. Zelda looked down at her and smiled, smoothing a hand over the child's auburn hair.

"Have you thought of a name yet, my lady?" asked Selene in a hushed voice, her eyes on the infant.

Zelda paused thoughtfully, then smiled as she said, "I like the name . . . Aereth."

The Light of Lythara

Book 4

Chapter 1

As Cassandra had suggested, Zelda did not set out immediately for the Gold Keep in Eriallon. She knew the knights would need time to find a milk substitute or a wet nurse to feed Aereth. Cassandra volunteered to head into Veracru, the farmland countryside, and find a nursing goat she could purchase or – if it came to that – steal. Not wanting to leave Calain to her fate any longer than they had to, she donned her armor and set out immediately on Sunny with a tether rope for the prospective goat.

Gweneth decided to patrol the battlements and watch for enemies, having realized they had left the fortress unguarded while Zelda was giving birth. And so, Selene was left alone with Zelda and the baby. They sat upright in the bed together, looking down at the child as it rested on Selene's breasts. The tiny girl's fat cheek pushed plump in her eye as she dreamt, sucking absently on her little finger, her wispy auburn hair tumbling in her eyes.

"Aereth," whispered Selene, her arm around Zelda, who snuggled happily against her. "I shall guard her with my life until the end of my days, my lady. This I swear to you."

Zelda smiled. Selene's hand was stroking her long golden hair, and it felt so soothing, she almost wanted to sleep. But she kept her eyes open. There was no time to rest. Calain was in danger! The thought of leaving her child behind to return to

Eriallon frightened and saddened her, but she could not leave Calain to her fate.

Calain should have been there with them, in Wolf Fortress, smiling on the baby, sharing meals, sparring in the yard. It felt wrong that she wasn't there. Zelda had felt Calain's heart quickening to alarming heights a few times, and she knew the queen of Eriallon had spoken true in her letter. Even if she didn't actually have Calain hostage, Calain was most certainly in danger, and Zelda needed to follow the beat of her heart to find her. As soon as Cassandra returned, Zelda would set out.

Selene twitched aside the fabric of Zelda's unlaced gown-front, exposing one of her breasts. Though Aereth had fed recently, Zelda's breasts were still heavy with milk. They were swollen and plump and the pink nipples rigid. Selene looked at the exposed one with hooded eyes and gently cupped it, massaging it carefully. Zelda lifted her chin at this touching and closed her eyes.

"Do they ache, my lady?" Selene asked anxiously.

"Only a little. I know a spell to make them better—" Zelda halted and blushed. Melvalda had taught her how to ease away the ache in her breasts with a healing spell, and she was embarrassed, knowing Selene had probably realized the lesson had been *hands-on*. Melvalda had carefully caressed Zelda's swollen breasts until they were both aroused, all the while working out the soreness. She hated that Selene had realized what she'd almost admitted, but Selene didn't say a word about it, instead sighing and muttering, "By the *gods*, do I miss sucking your tits."

Zelda laughed, her breasts wobbling. Selene cupped the exposed one gently as it jiggled against her fingers. Her dark eyes were full of hunger and longing as she looked at it.

"Here . . ." Zelda whispered. "Help make them lighter . . ." So saying, she rose up on her knees, offering her heavy breast to Selene. Selene, with Aereth sleeping obliviously on her chest, turned her head with eyes that burned hunger and slowly sucked Zelda's small nipple into her lips. She suckled deeply, cupping Zelda's heavy breast so that it spilled over her gentle fingers.

Zelda sighed in relief and blushed a little as the milk lifted away, dripping down Selene's lips as she suckled. Selene pressed her face deeper, until Zelda's pale breast had risen in a mound against her face. She reached up as she was suckling and pushed Zelda's hair back over her shoulder, tugged at her laces, until her gown had suddenly fallen away, then her slip, and she slid her hand in Zelda's panties and gently fondled her clitoris.

Zelda bit her lip as her clitoris throbbed to life, pulsing with hunger under the gentle stroke of Selene's careful fingers. Selene's touch was tender as always as she slowly worked Zelda to gasping and sighing. Zelda could barely hold herself up on her knees, for her thighs were trembling. She reached out blindly and cupped Selene's face as she suckled, stroked her dark hair, and whispered her name. Then Selene's fingers slid deep inside her sex, plunging slowly and deliberately through her sudden moisture, and Zelda's head fell back and she called out Selene's name. Selene moaned as she suckled deeper, and Zelda's hungry sex clenched tight over her fingers.

Later, as the sun was setting in the window, Zelda lay snuggled in Selene's bulging arm, sleepy-eyed and content after a round of five orgasms. Selene seemed drowsy and content as well. Little Aereth was still sleeping on her chest, unaware that anything had taken place, and Selene was stroking her hair.

"I should not have touched you so soon after giving birth," apologized Selene.

"This was a mystical pregnancy," Zelda reminded her. "I am healed already."

"That is good to know."

Zelda looked up at Selene, then suddenly kissed her on the cheek. Selene blushed a little.

"I don't know what I would do without you," Zelda confessed, resting her head again on Selene's shoulder.

Selene looked down at her in surprise. "You mean that, my lady?"

"Yes," said Zelda. "You're always there when I need you, even when I don't deserve it."

There was a pause, and then Selene said soothingly, "I know you feel guilty for Calain's behavior, but you should not. You did the best you could with the knowledge you had at the time. Any of us might have done the same in your place. Calain will understand. Eventually. She was always a bit slow."

Zelda laughed softly. "I hope you're right."

Selene hesitated, then said, "My lady, I have something for you. A gift."

Zelda glanced up in surprise. "Oh?"

"Yes. I was going to give it to you back in Priine, but th-then . . . e-everything with Cassandra a-and . . ."

Zelda tried not to laugh: Selene was flustered and nervous and her cheeks were flaming! How cute! What could this present be? Zelda sat up and smiled, looking at Selene eagerly, ignoring the fact that one of her heavy breasts was still hanging from her gown-front and beading creamy white milk.

Selene carefully sat up as well, allowing baby Aereth to slide gently onto a pillow, where she lay on her belly, still sucking her stubby finger. Selene then tucked Zelda's large breast back into the fold of her gown and laced it up for her. Zelda watched curiously.

"This present requires that I am properly robed, I see," Zelda teased.

"It does, my lady," said Selene, smiling. When she had finished lacing Zelda up, she took a small box from her trouser pocket and opened the lid, presenting the contents to Zelda.

Zelda gasped, her blue eyes fluttering wide. A necklace with a gold chain was inside, and fastened to the chain was a beautiful blue jewel that almost perfectly matched Zelda's eyes. "Oh, Selene!" Zelda cried, tears rising in her eyes.

"I s-saw it in the window and thought of you," Selene stammered nervously and blushed more brightly than ever. "Do you like it?"

"I love it!" Zelda cried, carefully sliding the necklace from the box. She held it aloft, staring at it with large eyes. "No one has ever given me a present like this! This is something a highborn lady would wear!"

"I thought you could enchant it," said Selene, "to protect you from the Bane Stones. Then my lady would be safe."

"Yes," said Zelda thoughtfully. "Melvalda taught me a charm that I could use to make their effect on me lessen."

"I imagine she taught you a great many things," said Selene.

When Zelda looked up, Selene was smiling at her. The words had been playful and teasing, but Zelda blushed prettily. "Yes," she admitted. "I can't pretend she did not. She is an older woman. She knows much in the way of pleasing a lady."

"Perhaps I should have asked her for instruction," joked Selene. "Here . . ." She took the necklace and gently fastened it about Zelda's throat, so that the great blue jewel rested just above her cleavage.

Zelda looked down and pinched the jewel in her slender fingers. It gleamed innocently in the dusk-light that reached, pink and purple, through the window. Zelda closed her eyes and cast the spell, and when she opened them again, she could feel the jewel humming now with her charm. She looked up at Selene fondly and leaned forward, kissing her on the lips.

Selene blushed a little brighter. "It suits you," she said. "I knew it would bring out your eyes. And now it has a charm to protect you when I cannot."

Zelda touched Selene's cheek. "I promise, I shall return and I shall return with Calain. You needn't fear."

Selene smiled sadly. "I am always afeared for the ones I love, even when I needn't be. Tis my nature."

Zelda laughed. "I suppose it is."

Without warning, Selene took Zelda in her strong arms and kissed her passionately. Zelda moaned and slid her arms around Selene's neck as their heads turned and they frowned through the kiss.

CASSANDRA RETURNED that evening with a mother goat and her kid, both on tethers tied to her horse. She led them into the training yard, and since there was no barn, she allowed them to roam the stables and eat the hay there. And now that there were goats roaming the fortress, and now that Cassandra had safely returned, the knights decided to close the gates of Wolf Fortress against the press of Dark Bloom Forest. For Zelda had not been able to verify the strength of the stronghold's enchantments. She confessed that elven magick baffled her.

With Cassandra's return, Zelda had one last meal with the knights. Then she packed her satchel and went upstairs to say farewell to her baby.

Little Aereth cooed happily when she was awoken by her mother. Her green eyes, so like Yrsa's, opened and brightened with joy, and she giggled shrilly when Zelda tickled her ear.

Smiling, Zelda lifted the baby into her arms and cradled her, swaying back and forth and humming. The baby looked up at her in happy content.

"I promise," Zelda said soothingly, "I'll come back to you. And my knights shall watch over you. And I shall bring Calain. You'll like her. She has green eyes like you. And she's brave and strong and sweet and gentle. And one day when you're older, I shall take you to see your other mother, Yrsa, the bear queen! And she will love you."

Not understanding a word that was being said, Aereth blinked, then suddenly smiled, showing her toothless mouth, as she reached up with pudgy hands and snatched clumsily at Zelda's long, golden hair.

Zelda smiled and hugged the baby close. She heard footsteps, and when she looked up, Gweneth and Cassandra had come. Gweneth was walking slowly with her hands in her pockets, while Cassandra was walking serenely with her hands behind her back. Both women watched Zelda and her baby with soft affection in their eyes. They drew near, and Gweneth stroked Aereth's hair as she watched the child fondly. Cassandra put a massaging hand on Zelda's shoulder.

"We shall guard her with our lives," said Gweneth, still looking down at the baby, who cooed at her touch. Her dark blue eyes flicked up to Zelda. "Just focus on bringing Calain back, hmm?" She leaned over and kissed Zelda slowly on the lips. Zelda felt something in her hiccup, as it always did whenever Gweneth kissed her so sweetly.

Then Cassandra turned Zelda's face to hers with a gentle hand. The gray eyes were alight with such serious fire that Zelda felt her heart thump. And then Cassandra was kissing her fervently and so hungrily, she moaned before she could stop herself.

When Cassandra had pulled away, she and Gweneth drew near and huddled close, their arms around Zelda, their foreheads touching hers. Zelda shivered between them as the baby continued to reach up, snatching at her hair. She knew they were praying for her safe return – not to any particular gods. They were simply frightened.

"I *shall* return," Zelda promised.

Gweneth's hands were shaking. To hide the fact, she kissed Zelda on the head, then gathered Aereth from Zelda's arms and into her own, turning away. "Selene is downstairs milking the goat," she said with a laugh. "I'm going to find a cloth or a horn or something, so we can feed this little goblin."

Zelda knew Gweneth was trying very hard to stay nonchalant and not become emotional. Meanwhile, Cassandra was simply standing, her hands in her pockets, staring at Zelda with a sort of ache that startled her.

"Fare thee well," Cassandra said quietly, her voice very soft and very sad.

Zelda managed a trembling smile. Then she turned and left the fortress.

Chapter 2

As Zelda moved through Dark Bloom Forest, she half-expected Calain to appear, stomping toward her through the trees, her messy red hair streaming, her eyes apologetic that she had been so foolhardy and so rash. Zelda hoped, wished, and prayed, but it never happened. She came across nothing but the odd goblin, a sleeping troll pup down in the mud (which she calmly stepped over), and a fox that fled with its tail streaming at the sight of her.

Calain, no matter how Zelda didn't wish it to be so, was in danger. Zelda found it odd, as if some god had reached down and reversed their reality, for it was always she who needed rescuing. There was always someone who had captured Zelda, some woman who wanted Zelda for herself or else coveted Zelda's power. Queen Ellanara . . . Melvalda . . . Even the Black Bear Clan had unwittingly "captured" Zelda through Revna's manipulations. But now Calain was the one in danger. Zelda prayed she hadn't been seriously harmed.

Queen Cilia had given Zelda a fortnight to reach the Gold Keep in Eriallon before Calain was executed. And so, Zelda had decided to apparate directly into Artas, a small wood on the outskirts of Alleren, the city capital where the Gold Keep resided. Apparating across water would be risky, but Melvalda had convinced Zelda that she was strong enough to do it. If she wasn't, Melvalda wouldn't have been so keen to have her join Raven's Cross.

Zelda had learned a great deal about herself while with Melvalda. She had learned to recognize the strength of her own power and had walked away from Ravenhold with a slew of new spells. Now she knew how to fight pixies and fairies, not just repel them. Now she could apparate great distances, create her own staves from scratch, and she had even learned to Read minds a little.

Zelda would always value her time with Melvalda, mad as it had been, and wondered what the ancient Witch of the Dark was doing at that very moment. Cassandra had said she seemed very happy with Talaedra when she had left.

As Zelda traveled through Dark Bloom, she was happy to realize the charm she had placed on Selene's necklace was working: the giant crystals had little effect on her, making her only vaguely drowsy. She had to travel far enough from Wolf Fortress that apparating would work, but she also had to stay far enough from the crystals that they would not hinder her magick. The necklace made things easier.

While walking, she found a long white tree branch that had broken off and fallen on the ground. She took it up, intent on using it as a stave and thinking the slender, twisted twigs on its tip pretty. Then, realizing she had walked far enough, Zelda apparated.

Chapter 3

Calain hung limp in her chains, strings of red hair falling in her face. They had stripped her of her sword and her armor, leaving her in naught but her linen bra and woolen hose. Her arms had been chained to the wall behind her and were spread wide, her legs as well, so that she hung forward in the shape of an X, her head down.

Calain wasn't certain how long she had been there or if it mattered. There was no leaving. Her fellow knights couldn't possibly save her. The Gold Keep was one of the most impregnable fortresses in all the realms. And no mage could apparate within its walls, not even Melvalda, one of the oldest witches alive.

Calain was going to be executed for her murder of the queen, and no one was coming to save her. She hung in her chains for days with nothing but that thought tormenting her sluggish mind. No food, no water, and only one merciful stream of sunlight from a barred window in the cell opposite.

Unfortunately, there was also a woman in the opposite cell who kept staring at Calain. Calain hated it. The woman was small and blonde and reminded her of Zelda, which drove her mad given how angry she was with the sorceress. Part of her wondered if she wasn't hallucinating due to hunger and thirst. Except the woman was an elf and Zelda was human.

The woman was filthy and wearing nothing but what looked like a torn potato sack. Her bare arms and legs were covered in smears of dirt, and her yellow hair was frizzy and wild and filthy and so long, it fell to the back of her knees. When Calain was first brought to the dungeon, bloody and exhausted after her battle with the Rose Guard, the woman had scrambled like a frightened rat to the far back of her cell and had watched Calain from the shadows.

And that was how it had been for days: Calain hanging in her chains, pulsing with bruises and cuts, hungry and exhausted, while an elf's slanted eyes glowed at her from the shadows of the opposite cell. Sometimes Calain dozed in her chains, only to wake and find the elf still watching from the shadows. She started to wonder if the woman ever slept. Then she started to feel angry, and she started to shout for the woman to stop staring at her. Still, the eyes persisted.

And so, Calain gave up and accepted her circumstances. She tried to make peace with it as best she could. What was she living for anyway? She was a knight with no cause to serve, no maiden to protect, no duty, and nothing to fight for. Everything she had trained for her entire life had amounted to this. She wanted to fight and win her life back, but with no reason to continue living, she sank in her chains and surrendered to her fate.

"You're the one!" said a small, amazed voice.

It had been silent in the dungeon for so long, Calain nearly started at the sound of someone's voice. She looked up and was surprised to see the elven woman had come to the bars of her cell and was gripping them as she looked out at Calain. Her body was pressed to the cell, so that her heavy breasts swelled against them. By the gods, Calain thought irritably, the woman even had big breasts like Zelda.

"I'm the one?" Calain repeated hoarsely.

The woman nodded. "You're the queen-slayer!"

"Took you all this time to figure that out, did it?" Calain croaked.

"Well, all you humans look the same," answered the woman crossly. She lifted her brows and asked, "How did it feel?"

"How did what feel?"

"Running your blade through her!" said the woman with such feverish delight that Calain looked up at her in amazement.

The woman was staring at Calain between the bars with bright, hungry eyes.

"I felt . . . nothing," Calain realized. "Rage. Anger. And then . . . nothing. I took no pleasure in slaying Ellanara."

"Pity," said the woman, whose mouth turned down in a pout. "You're a Falcon Knight, though. You're strong. Why don't you break your chains?"

"And go where?" said Calain with a flat laugh.

"Anywhere you want," said the woman indignantly. "Why, you could break your chains and snap your bars and stroll right out of here, easy! And yet you just sit there in your chains! Like a kicked puppy!"

Calain stared at the woman witheringly, trying to decide if she were foolhardy or crazy. "Even if I wanted to escape," she said, "—and I don't—I would never fight my way out of here. This is the stronghold of the Rose Guard army! I'd be overwhelmed. Tis how I came to be here."

The woman rolled her eyes as if Calain were the slow one. "You don't have to fight your way out, don't be silly. There are secret passages all over the castle. I could show you."

Calain hesitated. The thought of walking out, of escaping this place, was suddenly sounding more and more possible. But then she thought of Zelda and the misery washed over her again.

She dropped her eyes. "No. Even if I escaped from here, where would I go? What would I do? I have nothing to live for."

The woman tisked impatiently. "Then find something to live for!"

Calain slowly looked up. The woman was looking at her eagerly, her eyes bright.

"Come on," the woman coaxed. "If you help me escape . . ." She slowly lifted her potato sack, revealing her round hips, her flat belly, and the swell of her great breasts. They were pale and swollen and the pink nipples were hard.

Calain ignored the hunger that stirred in her and quickly dropped her eyes again. "No," she said firmly. "I don't exchange women's bodies for services, as if they were coin or chattel."

The woman looked at Calain in surprise, and her mouth was open, as if no one had ever said "no" to sex with her before. "Well, what if I lay with you because I wanted to?" she said, glancing up and down Calain's muscular frame. "Thou art the handsomest woman I've ever yet seen. I would make it good for you." She puckered her lips in a kiss.

Calain was surprised when her own lips parted and she laughed softly. She couldn't remember the last time she'd laughed. And suddenly, she remembered what it felt like to have women flirting with her, chasing her, propositioning her. Women had ceased their pursuit of her since Zelda. She hadn't realized how greatly she'd missed it until that moment.

"We would have such fun together," said the woman, laughing as well.

"I don't even know your name," Calain realized.

The woman coyly glanced down, her pale lashes sweeping her cheeks. She blushed a little as she said, "My name is Imodel, but you may call me whatever you wish, sweeting." She fell silent and waited, her eyes fixed on Calain.

Calain looked into the woman's round blue eyes – eyes that were so like Zelda's—and felt an ache in her chest. The woman had challenged her to live for herself, not for her duty, and in that moment, she made a decision. Still looking in Imodel's eyes, Calain's lips tightened, she grunted, and her muscular arms tensed before ripping free of the wall, one chain after the other.

Imodel gasped in delight, bounced on her little feet, and fanned herself with her hand. "My, but you're strong!" she shrilled.

Calain pulled her feet free next, then ripped the cuffs and their chains away with her hands. She went to the bars of her cell, and as Imodel watched with her mouth open, she gripped two of the bars and pulled them apart, until there was enough space to step out.

"Oh my!" Imodel gasped when Calain had done the same to her cell bars. She stepped through the space in her bars and stood before Calain, staring up at her, transfixed. "As if it were nothing!" she cried.

"Show me the way out and make haste!" Calain said.

Imodel's lips twisted in a smirk. She grabbed Calain's hand and pulled her off down the corridor.

Chapter 4

Zelda stood in the great throne room of the Gold Keep, staring up at the white throne, on which Queen Cilia was sitting. The new Rose of Eriallon looked almost exactly as her sister had: long dark hair and dark green eyes. Only she was so young, she came across as more of a kitten than a full-grown cat. She couldn't have been more than eighteen years old and sat stiffly on the throne, a skinny adolescent, with small breasts and narrow hips, surrounded by her advisors and courtiers.

And yet, girl though she was, the gold crown of a woman sat upon Cilia's dark hair. She looked down at Zelda from between curtains of black hair that had been swept behind her shoulders in a low braid. She was wearing a long red gown, and in her small hand was a gold scepter.

"What do you mean Calain escaped?" Zelda said as she stood there, feeling numb. She had demanded to see Calain as proof that she was still alive, that she had actually been captured, but the queen had admitted – rather angrily – that Calain had escaped.

"I *mean*," said Queen Cilia through her teeth, "that your precious *Calain* ripped herself free of her chains, ripped open her bars, and escaped the castle through one of the secret passages, injuring a great number of my knights in the process. She took with her a very valuable prisoner, but because I wish your aid, I shall not send my knights in her pursuit. Instead, you will fulfill a task for me, and then Calain can drown in the sea for all I care. The damage she has done to my castle!"

Angry murmurs of agreement rose from the court.

"How do I know you haven't executed her?" said Zelda at once.

The queen lifted a slender brow. "I thought you were Bound to her with some spell or other," she said, gesturing an impatient hand. "Can you not feel that she lives?"

It was true that Zelda could feel that Calain was alive, she just didn't want to believe what she was feeling. A few minutes after arriving in City Alleren, she had felt . . . pleasure. As if someone were kissing her! And then her sex had swelled to arousal, her clitoris had begun throbbing, so that she dropped the goblet of wine she'd been enjoying at the tavern and it spilled on the furious woman beside her at the bar.

If what Zelda had felt was real, then Calain was most certainly alive . . . and she was having sex! Very intense, passionate, on-going sex! While standing in the noisy tavern, Zelda had blushed with anger to realize it, and standing there in the throne room, thinking of it again, she blushed with anger once more.

"Trouble in paradise?" mocked Queen Cilia, who had been silently watching Zelda's angry expression. "Why, I'd almost suppose you *wanted* Calain dead."

Laughter from the court: twittering from the women fanning themselves with paper fans, and hearty bellows from the men sipping goblets. Even the royal advisors – a bearded man in a long robe and a woman with spectacles – smiled derisively at Zelda as they stood either side the throne.

Zelda swallowed hard, pushing down her anger and hating everyone in the room. But she mustn't lose her composure. Even if Calain were dead, Queen Cilia still knew exactly where the other Falcon Knights were and where her baby was. She could send the Rose Guard to surround the fortress, forcing the Knights of Falcon to hole up inside until they had slowly starved. Whatever the queen's task was, Zelda was obligated to do it or watch everyone she cared about perish.

"Yes, Calain is alive," said Zelda, waving a dismissive hand. "But tell me, your highness, what is this task you have summoned me for?"

"'Your highness' now, is it?" said Queen Cilia in amusement.

Zelda tried not to show a reaction. In truth, she had been rather rude since her arrival, demanding to see Calain and completely ignoring etiquette. She knew that if she weren't a powerful sorceress, the queen would have had her arrested for disrespect alone by now. But she was useful and there to be used.

"You are my queen," said Zelda calmly. "Or will be soon."

Queen Cilia smirked at Zelda's humble words, knowing they were mere appeasement, and said, "Look around, sorceress. It would seem there is no court mage present."

Zelda glanced around and noticed that there indeed wasn't a sorceress present in the court. Aside from herself. The court sorceress of Eriallon had been a woman named Alarien, an elf from Menosea who had served the queens of Eriallon for five generations. There had always been some discontent that she was a foreigner and an elf at that, but the royal family had ignored the suspicious complaints of their advisors and Alarien had stayed on for many years . . . until now.

"Do you mean me to find her?" asked Zelda after glancing around and seeing the sorceress absent.

Sinister laughter rose from the court that Zelda didn't understand, didn't want to understand.

Queen Cilia's cherry-red lips twitched in a dark little smile. "Not unless you fancy a trip to the nearest dung cart, where her headless body now lies."

Zelda stood stunned. More laughter rose from the court at her reaction.

"Alarien was a traitor, and she was executed," Queen Cilia elaborated, her lip curling. "She attempted to escape, and my knights went through a great deal of trouble to bring her in, powerful as she was, but it was done. Now I find myself in need of a new sorceress." She paused, her eyes fixed on Zelda.

Zelda stood there, white stave in hand, and felt the dread creeping up her spine. "Does her highness mean for me to . . .?"

More laughter from the court, this time mocking. Zelda glared around at them, wishing she could get away with shouting furiously for silence.

"No," laughed Queen Cilia. "Employ the woman whose rabid knight slew my sister? Don't be absurd. You would never be trusted here – Not that it were wise to trust anyone at court. Just the same . . ." Cilia straightened up and lifted her chin. "I have already chosen a new court mage, and perhaps I have chosen poorly, for she has wandered off. You will find her and bring her here to me."

It sounded like a simple enough task. Perhaps too simple. Zelda stood there, waiting for the catch.

"Her name is Lythara," said Queen Cilia, "and I fear she may have perished. She hath ventured to a place I cannot send my knights. Only a sorceress may linger there and live."

Zelda knew what place the queen was referring to but was hoping deep down that she was wrong. When the queen paused and looked down at her, Zelda said unhappily, "And where would that place be, your highness?"

“I think you know it very well,” said Queen Cilia. “Eido Loth, the realm of demons and dreams.”

Chapter 5

Imodel squatted naked over Calain's face, slowly twisting her hips around and around, so that her soft sex caressed Calain's lips as Calain tasted and sucked, pulling the fat pink lips of the elven woman's sex into her mouth. Imodel sighed, her hands on her knees as she arched her back and twisted her hips around again. Calain was in heaven beneath her, plunging her mouth as best she could into the heat and moisture of the woman's sex. But Imodel kept giggling and bouncing up in a teasing way. Calain thought it cute, but suddenly impatient, she grabbed Imodel by the hips and held her firmly in place. Imodel squealed at this aggression, and it wasn't long before she had shivered, trapped in Calain's strong grasp, and released her passion against Calain's eager mouth in a helpless climax.

Breathless and deliciously tired, Imodel wiggled her hips, playfully asking for release. Calain let her go, sitting up on her elbow and watching with narrowed eyes as Imodel sashayed down to the stream, hips swinging beneath her tiny waist, and squatted to bathe herself, her plump backside lifting as she spread her thighs.

They were in the mountains north of Alleren, in the rocky pastures beneath an open blue sky. The air was crisp and clear here and the waters pure. They had seen no one aside from the occasional goats grazing and nosy birds that drew near, tilting their tiny heads and looking with beady eyes for scraps food.

Calain thought it strange that the Rose Guard hadn't pursued them and said so several times, but Imodel told her to focus on the good, focus on her new life, and stop worrying.

The longer they hid in the mountains, the more Calain began to like the idea of a life there with Imodel. With a makeshift bow and arrows, Imodel hunted for game while Calain gathered wood and thatch to build a shelter. And there they lived beside the stream, making love under the open sky, cuddling warm beside the fire at night.

Calain was still worried that, eventually, someone would find them there and was glad she had taken a sword from one of the Rose Guard knights she'd felled, even if she hadn't managed to take any armor. At least she could properly defend them. But she knew they could not hide in the mountains forever, as much as she wanted to. They needed real shelter—and wine. Calain missed a good skin of wine.

"That time was good," said Imodel breathlessly as she scooped water in her hands. She tossed her yellow hair back and splashed the water over herself. It trickled over her breasts and dripped off her nipples, which Calain watched and felt herself stir.

"And the other times were not?" said Calain, pushing herself up. She was teasing, but Imodel answered seriously, "You were thinking of *her* that time, so it was better. More intense."

Calain froze. "What do you mean? I only e-ever think of you . . ." she lied. But she was a bad liar, and Imodel saw right through her.

Imodel gave Calain a withering look over her shoulder. "You called her name," she said. "I heard you. 'Oh, Zelda!'"

Calain blushed and didn't meet the elven woman's eye.

Imodel didn't seem angry. She went back to bathing as she said, "Whoever Zelda is, I envy her, that she can wring such passion from you. She's your lady, isn't she? The one you slew the queen for."

"Let us not speak of Zelda—"

"Why?" said Imodel at once. She paused in her bathing, staring at Calain. "You called me by her name. I think I have a right to speak of her."

Calain sighed irritably. "There is nothing to speak of! She was my lady, and now she is not." Calain got to her feet and grumpily started pacing, not knowing what she was doing. She just went back and forth, back and forth, the sunlight beaming on her naked shoulders and arms. She was still in her bra and woolen hose and was thankful the Rose Guard had left her her boots as well.

Imodel laughed. "That one will *always* be your lady. I can tell. And there's no escaping it."

Calain glared at Imodel but didn't stop pacing, her jaw standing out hard in her irritation. "You speak of things you do not understand. Perhaps if I knew more about you, I would call your name instead." She tossed a hand. "But I don't even know who you are!"

Imodel cast her eyes down. She was still squatting, and very slowly, she lowered herself to the grass and sat on her backside, hugging her legs. She had become very sad and was staring at her knees. Her shaggy blonde hair swept forward to hide her face, and Calain could see a long ear poking from it.

Feeling guilty, Calain came and sat beside Imodel. "Why art thou so secretive?" she asked gently. "Art thou a criminal? A murderer? I would not harm thee if I knew the truth."

Imodel laughed sadly, still staring at her knees. "You? You wouldn't harm any fair maiden who'd sat on your face. Tis your one weakness."

Calain laughed sadly as well, thinking of Zelda. How true that was. It was because of her fury at Zelda that Calain had stormed off alone and was captured by the Rose Guard. It was because of her love for Zelda that Calain had slain the queen and become a fugitive of Eriallon. Every low point in her life, Calain could trace back to Zelda. She wondered why she hadn't seen it before. Perhaps Gweneth was right: love made one an oblivious fool and it was dangerous to exist in such a state.

When Calain glanced up, it was to find Imodel watching her.

"You really love Zelda, don't you?" she said in amusement.

"I love no one," said Calain indignantly. "I am cold. And empty!"

Imodel laughed softly. "No. You love her. You wouldn't be so angry if you did not."

Calain looked away. She had no argument and she really wanted one. Finding no words to defend herself, she said irritably, "Don't change the subject, Imodel. Why were you imprisoned at the Gold Keep? What hast thou done?"

"Well, I didn't slay the queen," said Imodel with a laugh and looked away. "I only wish I had."

"What did you do then?"

Imodel took a shuddering breath and looked down. "I'm . . . Dost thou knowst anything of elven politics, I wonder?"

"I confess I do not," said Calain apologetically.

Imodel wasn't surprised. "Thousands of years ago," she said, "my people, the elven, ruled this land. All the realms were ours, and humans lived on the outskirts of civilization, in little villages and hamlets. Then the elven empire fell, my people scattered and diminished in number, and humans took control of the land."

"Yes. This is known to me, to everyone."

"What is *not* widely known is the fact that my people have been trying to take back the realms. We have formed a resistance known as Hidden Dragon and have been making moves to overthrow the human queens for decades now. The court mage, Alarien, she was one of ours. She spent years manipulating the queens and was found out and executed. I . . . was a servant in the castle. I was helping her. When they captured Alarien, they captured me. They were going to execute me, but they hadn't finished interrogating me first."

Imodel fell silent, staring at her knees, waiting for Calain's condemnation.

Calain found herself not caring either way. Human or elf, it didn't matter to her who ruled the land so long as she was free. She told Imodel as much, and Imodel smirked.

"And how do you expect to win your freedom, then?" said Imodel.

Calain hesitated. "What do you mean? I am no longer chained, am I?"

"But you are still a rebel and an enemy of the queen," said Imodel. "You cannot stay in Eriallon. Neither of us can."

Calain glanced down unhappily, knowing that Imodel was right. She picked up a pebble and idly chucked it at the stream, lightly splashing them both. "I wish I had never met Zelda," she said, squinting off at the distant pine trees on the lower pass.

"You don't mean that," said Imodel.

Calain scowled. "How can you know?" she asked sarcastically.

Imodel was smirking. "The way you sucked your mouth upon my sex? That passion and yearning was not for me."

Chapter 6

Zelda knew there were many dimensions, alternate realities ruled by creatures that weren't human or elven. There was Elwenhal, a dimension where the fae dwelled, holding an endless feast at the court of their fairy queen. There was a dimension where it was said the unicorns had disappeared to, having grown weary of hunters pursuing them for the medicinal use of their horns. There was a dimension to which the sorceress Anidrith had banished a tribe of giants after their attempted overthrow of Eriallon and all the realms. There was a dimension where it was said the dragons had retreated to sleep. And then there was Eido Loth.

Eido Loth was one of the darker dimensions, ruled by demons and cannibalistic creatures, that drank blood and sucked the flesh from bones while waiting for fresh prey. Sunlight was weak there and the sky always gray, the trees black, the earth barren and colorless and devoid of green life.

Why anyone would want to go there was beyond Zelda, who hadn't even set out yet and was dreading it already. At Queen Cilia's direction, she went to the study that had belonged to the old court mage, knowing she would find a portal there that would take her to Eido Loth.

And indeed, after wandering through a seemingly endless maze of curving bookshelves, Zelda had come to a dead-end, where the bookshelves curved around, encircling an ancient stone archway that swirled with light.

The light of the portal was moving so fast, it sent the hair whipping back from Zelda's face. "Absolute madness!" she said in amazement, for no one in their right mind would have a portal to Eido Loth in their study. If some demon or monster came through from the other side, it could wreak havoc on the castle, massacring all within. That it had been brought inside the castle, let alone left activated, was insanity.

Queen Cilia had explained that Alarien had hoped to use the portal as an escape route in the event that she was exposed as a spy. She'd been working for an elven resistance and wished to use the portal to reach one of the old dimensions. Unfortunately, the only dimension she could attune the portal to had been Eido Loth.

Queen Cilia had further explained that her new court mage, Lythara, had entered the portal to explore Eido Loth and hadn't returned in three weeks. Zelda thought it likely the woman was dead. She wondered what the queen would say if she returned with Lythara's body in little pieces in a satchel. For it was likely Lythara had been torn apart, given the monsters that lurked in Eido Loth.

Zelda took a breath, tightened her grip on her white stave, and stepped through the light of the portal. Almost immediately, she was beset upon by a giant monster. The creature was shaped like a gorilla, moving down on its knuckles, with great yellow tusks growing from its bottom lip, and a tiny tuft of hair upon its head. It was shaggy and gray, as if to blend with the colorless world around it. Zelda knew it was called a morgath.

The morgath bellowed when it saw Zelda exit the portal, reared on its tiny hind legs to thump its broad chest, and charged the twenty feet between them, scattering bones and rocks as it came. Heart pounding, Zelda held out her hand, fingers spread, and her eyes glowed with power, until they were white spheres blazing in her face. The tip of her white stave also glowed with a sphere of white light.

The morgath halted in place, completely frozen and only able to move its beady eyes in shock. It was the same spell Zelda had used on Gweneth, only its power was magnified and required a great deal of concentration given how large the morgath was.

The creature was the size of a young dragon, perhaps thirty feet in length. Zelda calmly strolled past it as it stood there, frozen in the act of running, its beady eyes following her for as long as they could.

Zelda halted and glanced around, stave in hand, her golden curls spilling long behind her shoulders, and she seemed to be the only thing of color in that desolate world. Dry, cracked, gray earth spread as far as the eye could see in all directions, the monotony broken only by the occasional spiny black tree, pile of bones, or flock of horned black birds.

As she walked on, Zelda noticed the lights that trailed away ahead of her in a line. They were wisp-lights, slightly larger than average and quite bright, so bright that they were difficult to stare directly upon in the gray gloom of Eido Loth. Zelda recognized their function immediately: the lights had been left by a sorceress as breadcrumbs marking her path in case she lost her way.

The lights had obviously been left by Lythara, which meant Lythara wasn't lost at all. She was either dead or – for some bizarre reason – had elected to vacation in Eido Loth for three weeks.

Perhaps Lythara was insane, Zelda told herself. For she could see no other reason to stay any length of time in such a horrible place. In just twenty minutes of walking, Zelda was attacked by bloodsucking bats, a two-headed snake, and three withered men, creatures that looked like human men but were draped in wrinkled gray skin, and in place of eyes, had black holes in their faces.

Withered men, like all the creatures of Eido Loth, ate flesh and craved blood. They shuffled toward Zelda, moaning and dragging their feet, reaching for her with long, mud-smeared fingers. But then something happened that made them halt. Zelda, without thinking, backed away from the withered men, passing through Lythara's trail of light. When she did, the light sparked brighter, and the withered men cringed in horror, shielded their faces, and scrambled back into their holes.

Zelda watched with interest as the withered men retreated. They were *terrified* of the light. *Lythara's* light in particular, for Zelda cast the same spell on the next dark creatures she encountered, to little avail.

Baffled, Zelda continued on, making certain to keep close to the trail of light Lythara had left in her wake. As a result, those dark creatures that sought to attack her quickly turned away, sometimes shrieking in terror as they fled.

What was it about Lythara's light that was so powerful, the most horrible creatures in Eido Loth were loath to approach it? It was beginning to seem more and more likely that Lythara had survived after all.

But Zelda didn't have time to wonder at Lythara's power, for she soon came upon a square black building that loomed large in the middle of the gray wasteland. The building had no door, instead standing open with a very large, rectangular doorway that led into a black hall.

The light of Lythara was flowing inside the building, so Zelda followed it inside. Torches stood in brackets on the walls and were lit with green flame. The flames reminded Zelda of the secret passage to Melvalda's lair. She knew the green fire was known as Wyre Light, for it shone eternally without end and had been created from the magick of the fae.

The hall flowed smoothly into an alley of bookshelves. It was just like the maze back in the court mage's study, for the bookshelves soon began to twist and wind, leading Zelda deeper and deeper along a narrow path, through the smell of musty old paper and stale leather. Sometimes the path widened enough that a crowd of people could have filled it. Other times, the path was so narrow, Zelda could barely squeeze through. But she kept following the light of Lythara regardless, moving deeper and deeper into the endless library.

Zelda came to yet another fork in the path and continued following Lythara's light by taking the path on the right. The path led her down a flight of stairs, on either side of which the walls were still lined in tattered old tomes.

Zelda was nearly at the bottom of the stair when one of the book titles caught her eye and she halted. She turned to face the book and couldn't believe it. The title read: *Zelda's Memory Vol. LIII: Sian.*

Zelda stood in shock and didn't think she could move. How was it possible? How could someone have written a book about her and Sian?

She knew it was dangerous to interact with the strange things in other dimensions, but now that she had seen the book, Zelda couldn't take her eyes from it. She reached out like one hypnotized and pulled the book off the shelf.

The book was so heavy, she leaned back and had to cradle it with both arms. The second it fell open, a white light spread from its pages, blinding her as she was pulled inside.

Chapter 7

Imodel had insisted on returning to Hidden Dragon, and unfortunately, Calain could not go with her because she was human, though she secretly wanted to. The idea of fighting for a cause again appealed to her. She wanted to pledge herself in Imodel's service and follow her throughout the world.

But Calain knew better than to ask. Imodel seemed far older than she appeared and very much an independent woman, the sort of woman who needed no Knight of Falcon to defend her. Back when they were escaping the Gold Keep, she had helped Calain fight and had lain out a few Rose Guard knights on her own. She was proficient in acrobatics, flipping through the air and kicking her enemies in the face, and she was deadly with a bow.

Calain was beginning to suspect that Imodel was in fact a trained assassin. The elves of Menosea had an underground order known as Venom Six (for there were only ever six assassins per cell), and during her years of training at Falcon Isle, Calain had come across a group of them while traveling with Knight Octava. Three of the assassins had been seated at the bar in a tavern – not even concealed in the corner! – wearing black clothing of a light, breezy material and shoes that were more akin to socks. Knight Octava had nodded grimly at them and whispered to Calain, "*Venom Six*."

Imodel was likely an assassin who had posed as a maid in the Gold Keep. Her joke about wishing she had slain the queen and her bloodthirsty eagerness to know what Calain had felt while doing it, on top of everything else, seemed to point to the obvious truth.

But Imodel refused to confirm Cailan's suspicions one way or the other. One morning, she simply kissed Calain on the nose, thanked her, and told her farewell.

"I do believe thou hast used me," said Calain, frowning down at Imodel.

Imodel stuck an indignant hand on her hip. "To escape certain death in the Gold Keep? Yes, I did. As if you didn't use me to forget about your lady. Except you cannot forget her, try as you might." She placed a sympathetic hand on Calain's heart and said, "Poor thing. Your heart is broken, but it will mend."

"No part of me is broken!" Calain protested.

Imodel laughed at the lie.

"Leave! I care not!" Calain said irritably and stepped back, so that Imodel could not reach her.

Imodel was still smiling. "Yes, you care so little that you scream at me and turn red."

Calain tensed and wanted to yell again, but she knew it would just confirm Imodel's words, so she stood there in silence, feeling foolish and helpless. She was beginning to wonder just how old Imodel was, for the woman had a way of making her feel like a silly child. It reminded her a little of Selene.

Imodel drew near and took Calain's hands. "Speak true, Calain. What do you feel?"

"I wish I could go with you," Calain confessed. "I feel you are abandoning me. As fair Zelda did . . . As my mother did."

Imodel frowned sadly and touched Calain's cheek. "What if I sat on your face one last time? Would that ease your sorrow?"

Calain sighed with longing and said, "*Yes.*"

And so, Imodel sat one last time upon Calain's face, and this time, she did not bounce away and tease. She bent forward so that Calain could reach her easily and allowed the knight to plunge her face between her thighs as deeply as she pleased, bringing her to a moist, breathless climax.

When Imodel had gone, Calain sat alone on the green slope beside the stream, her arms resting on her knees, her sword on her back, and watched the sunset as she meditated on Imodel's words.

Imodel had forced Calain to recognize who she was. She was a knight, whose very existence centered around service. If she was not living her life in service, she was not happy nor living true to her purpose.

Imodel had also made her realize there was no shame in loving Zelda. If only Zelda felt the same.

It was then, as the sun set over the mountains, that Calain made her choice. She would set forth to find a maiden to serve, a maiden who was true and who would love only she. But before leaving Eriallon, she would do what she had longed to do since she was thirteen: she would visit her father.

When she was small, Calain and her father had lived on a small farm on the outskirts of Alleren. The entire area was farmland as far as the eye could see, a community of common folk, whose crops and dairy filled the markets of Alleren. Calain's father had run a small chicken farm with only the help of Calain and a young girl named Siobhan, who hadn't been quite four years old when Calain left at five.

Calain remembered thinking Siobhan was her sister, until her father explained that he had taken her in when her parents (their neighbors) died during the winter of the plague. Siobhan had been with them since she and Calain were both in swaddling, and she had nursed at the breasts of Calain's own mother.

Calain wondered what had happened to Siobhan. When Calain was sent to train at Falcon Isle, the farm had been failing. Her father was frightened they would not survive the winter, so he sent Calain away. Had he sent Siobhan away as well?

Calain walked beside the road leading from Alleren, careful to keep off the road itself and close to the thin cluster of trees that grew alongside it, so that she might duck inside its shadow when travelers passed by. Fortunately, there were not many travelers on the road. A man driving a horse and cart to the city had stared suspiciously at her silhouette in the trees, but seeing how big and strong her figure was, thought better of approaching her and kept driving.

Eventually, Calain came to the dirt road that led to her father's farm. But she had barely walked up it when she was spied from the windows of her father's little house. As she drew near, she saw her elderly father come hobbling out on his cane, the sunlight falling upon his now-gray hair, and with him came a beautiful red-haired woman Calain didn't recognize.

The red-haired woman was fresh-faced and young, with small feet and hands and a tiny waist. Her great freckled breasts were practically bursting from the low collar of her peasant's dress, and her long, bright red hair fell in wild curls around a young, pretty face that was also freckled. She grinned when she saw Calain, her blue eyes crinkled up, and she screamed, "Calain?! Gods be good! I don't believe it!"

Calain's father laughed merrily as the red-haired woman came running down the steps—breasts bouncing, arms open, hair streaming – and smashed into Calain.

Calain choked as she was hugged tightly around the neck. The young woman kissed her face again and again while squealing, "Calain! Calain! Tis I!"

Calain awkwardly hugged the woman back, trying to ignore how wonderfully her giant breasts were crushing against her. "Uh . . . Hello . . ."

Sensing how stiff and awkward Calain was, the woman pulled back and said with an incredulous giggle, "Calain, don't you recognize me! Tis I! Siobhan!"

Calain stared in utter shock. But before she could reply, her father came hobbling up, laughing and grinning all the while. He had shriveled into a tiny man the size of a child. He dropped his cane and held open his arms, and grinning, Calain stooped down and hugged her little father.

Arthur laughed and hugged Calain back, patting her wild red hair as he said, "Calain! My big, strong girl! Ease up now, you'll break me right in half!"

Calain chuckled and couldn't resist: she lifted her little father clear off his feet in a hug. They laughed loudly together as Siobhan stood by, watching them fondly.

CALAIN WASN'T SURPRISED her father's farm hadn't been raided by bandits. No one was foolish enough to harm the father of a Falcon Knight, and the symbol of the falcon had been carved on her father's house as a warning. Because of that symbol, Arthur and Siobhan had lived here safe for eighteen years.

Calain's father invited her inside, and he bid Siobhan to bring some of his old clothes for Calain to wear, so that his daughter could stop traveling about in her smallclothes. Siobhan gladly obeyed, bringing Calain a tunic and trousers, which

Calain gladly put on. Then she and her father sat together beside the fire, while Siobhan went out to the barn to tend the one horse and cow on the property.

"My girl," said Arthur proudly as he watched Calain eagerly devour the stew Siobhan had brought her. "My girl is a Knight of Falcon. And so big and strong! No one could best you! Not even the Rose Guard!"

Calain looked up in surprise. "Art thou not ashamed of me? I slew the queen. I am a traitor to the realm."

"You acted in your lady's defense," said Arthur seriously. "You betrayed no one."

Calain stared darkly into the fire. "It wasn't worth giving up my life for her. The lady wasn't true."

Arthur frowned. "I hope you slew the one you caught her with," he scolded, as if he suspected she had not.

"I did not catch her in the act of betrayal," Calain admitted.

Arthur's frown deepened. "Then how dost thou know she hath betrayed you?"

"I felt it in my heart," Calain said, feeling foolish under her father's disbelieving gaze.

"So let me get this straight," said Arthur slowly. "You abandoned your lady because you *suspect* she hath betrayed you?" He scoffed. "Do the young people not believe in *talking* any longer? Have your brains rotted from wine?"

Calain stared at her stew. She didn't have to explain about the Binding. Her father knew about it. She had written to him about her training in many letters, and because her father could not read or write, Siobhan had read them to him. He had shown Calain the letters as soon as she'd entered the house, and tears had filled her eyes because she had spent years believing the old man dead. Her father had never answered because Siobhan could read but could not write.

"So a little magick spell made you suspect something," went on her father, speaking of the Binding, "and just like that, you betrayed your vows?"

Calain didn't want to admit it, but her father had a point. It didn't even occur to her to speak with Zelda first. She had simply jumped to conclusions and left Zelda's service. But perhaps Zelda hadn't lain with Melvalda without reason. Calain blinked as she considered it.

Seeing that he had reached Calain, Arthur wearily shook his head and muttered, "I suppose it could have been worse: the gods could have given me sons."

Calain smiled.

"Now finish your stew," went on her father, "and then you say your farewells to Siobhan, and you march back out there and find your lady."

"Yes, Pa," said Calain and tipped back her bowl to drink the rest of the stew off. She set the bowl aside on the nearby table and stood, leaning down to kiss her now -grumpy father's head.

"Hmph!" said Arthur, trying to appear stern and disapproving, though his lips twitched in a pleased smile nonetheless.

Out in the barn, Siobhan had just left the cow's stall and was fastening the door shut when Calain playfully snuck up and hugged her tightly from behind. Siobhan squealed in shock, then laughed when she recognized Calain's bulging arms about her and gave Calain's arm a playfully scolding slap.

"Siobhan," Calain said happily, her face beside Siobhan's face as she hunched down, hugging her from behind. She brushed aside Siobhan's red hair to look at her cleavage, and Siobhan took a shaking, nervous breath that made her breasts heave nicely.

"Thou hast grown quite large," Calain joked, squeezing Siobhan's big breasts in fistfuls. She felt her sex stir to arousal.

Siobhan giggled, her breasts trembling in Calain's grasp. But she went still again and took another nervous breath when Calain's hands gently massaged her breasts through her dress.

"You've grown big as well. I hardly recognized you! You're so s-strong," Siobhan whispered breathlessly, "but so g-gentle . . ." She sounded frightened.

Calain paused her massaging. "Shall I stop, my lady?"

"N-No," whispered Siobhan, who was shaking slightly. "Don't s-stop. . . I am only afeared your father shall find us."

Calain peeled the low collar of Siobhan's dress down over her breasts, exposing how plump and high they were. The little pink nipples were jutting with her arousal. Calain cupped her breasts and massaged again, loving how warm and soft they were, thumbing the nipples gently. Siobhan sighed and her head fell back against Calain, the movement thrusting her high breasts forward in Cailan's hands.

Calain set her boot on the nearby milking stool, and reaching down, she drew Siobhan's leg up, so that it draped across her own.

Siobhan blushed when Calain's hand drew up her skirts and slid without hesitation down the front of her panties. "W-What if your f-father . . ."

"He won't come," said Calain absently and buried a kiss in Siobhan's neck as she continued massaging her breast and fingering her. She caressed Siobhan's clitoris, which was fat with arousal, and heard Siobhan moan, saw her blue eyes stare, unseeing, in baffled shock, saw her lips part in a gasp. Perhaps she had never been touched before. Had she spent her entire life hidden away on the farm?

Siobhan shivered. "Oh, *Calain*. . . By the *gods* . . ."

Calain slid her fingers carefully in Siobhan's sex and felt her tight maidenhead, a ring of resistance. So no man had broken her. She felt relieved by the knowledge. She thumbed Siobhan's nipple gently and felt Siobhan's sex grow moist, felt Siobhan's maidenhead relax and admit her. Slowly, her fingers sank through the hot moisture of Siobhan's sex, sliding deeper and deeper the wetter she grew. Siobhan's head was still back on Calain's shoulder, and she was moaning.

"Thy are so moist," Calain whispered in Siobhan's ear. "Would that there was time to taste you."

Calain worked Siobhan slowly to a climax, and it was like the gradual blossoming of a flower. After much trembling and moaning, Siobhan eventually released, her little sex clenching over Calain's caressing fingers.

But once they had made love, Siobhan tucked her breasts away and seemed overcome with great shame. She did not meet Calain's eye, instead going to the horse with her head down as she said, "Arthur said you could t-take the horse. . . We shall find an-nother . . ." She suddenly broke down crying, her shoulders shaking.

"What's the matter?" said Calain in concern and drew near behind her. She hesitated and hugged Siobhan from behind, kissed her cheek.

"Oh!" cried Siobhan miserably. "Why did you have to be so sweet? Why did you have to turn up here when I had f-finally accepted my fate, reminding me of all the things I cannot have?"

Calain was baffled. "What do you mean, Siobhan?"

"I am to marry thy father!" Siobhan blurted through her tears.

Calain tensed, then grabbed Siobhan by the shoulders and spun her around. Siobhan bowed her head, weeping helplessly in Calain's grasp.

"Marry my *father*?" said Calain in disgust. "He is more than twice thy age!"

Siobhan looked up at Calain miserably. "He needs children to run the f-farm or we shall lose it. I have nowhere else to g-go, and I am f-fertile and . . ."

"No!" said Calain, who refused to believe it.

Siobhan sniffled unhappily, but she smiled through her tears, gazing fondly up at Calain as she said, "You're like some dream, so strong and powerful. I told myself you would take me away from here, but I know you already have a lady." She shook her head. "She is so lucky."

Calain thought guiltily of Zelda. She looked down at Siobhan again. "But I don't understand. Why must thou marry my father. . .?" But the words died on Calain's lips even as she was saying them. She knew very well that women had few choices in the world. The average woman's options were marriage or a whorehouse. Even if Siobhan's parents had lived, it would have been the same.

"We can't all be a Knight of Falcon," said Siobhan, smiling through her tears. She kissed Calain on the lips and ran sobbing from the barn.

Chapter 8

Zelda couldn't believe it, but she was standing in the city of her childhood. It was Perth, which was not far south of Alleren. She was standing outside the hovel she had shared with her uncle in the mud-stained slums, and she could see herself, a little girl of maybe four, sitting on the front steps and poking a stick in the mud. Her child-self wasn't alone either. Another little girl with wild brown hair was sitting beside her, also poking the mud with a stick.

"Sian," said Zelda happily, her blue eyes staring with soft affection at the little brown-haired girl.

Both little girls were wearing torn, filthy tunics with no hose and no shoes because they could not afford them. Instead, their feet were bare and stained with mud, as were their faces.

Zelda remembered Sian had always been rather boyish. She had a filthy rag tied back in her hair and sat beside Child Zelda on the step with her knees wide open. She freely scratched herself, so that Child Zelda giggled.

Zelda and Sian had always been inseparable. Zelda's uncle had often mocked them, asking sarcastically if they were betrothed when he caught them holding hands.

"One day I shall be a knight," said Sian confidently.

"But how?" said Child Zelda hopelessly. "Your parents have to take you. They don't take runaways, and your mother would never allow . . ."

"Then I shall slay my mother!" cried Sian, leaping to her feet and pointing her stick triumphantly at the sky.

Child Zelda giggled. "You wouldn't do that!"

"I would!" said Sian, lifting her chin. "I shall slay her, and then my father shall take me to Falcon Isle to be a knight." She glanced at Child Zelda apprehensively and asked almost coyly, "Would thou love me if I did?"

Child Zelda blushed a little. "But I dost love thee now!"

"Dost thou?" said Sian with round blue eyes. She sat on the step again, staring at Child Zelda eagerly. "And would you wear my favor?"

Child Zelda shyly fanned her lashes down and blushed as she said, "Of course, my knight!"

"Then you are my lady," said Sian, removing the filthy rag from her hair and draping it across Child Zelda's waiting hand.

Child Zelda was suddenly overcome with a burst of giggles, and she leaned over and pecked Sian on the lips. Sian seemed very pleased by this, but before she could speak, the door behind them burst open, and Zelda's drunken uncle staggered out, golden strings of greasy hair hanging in his face, cheeks flaming from wine.

Child Zelda and Sian froze in terror.

"So you fancy other girls, eh?" slurred Zelda's uncle with a leering smile. He grabbed a rough fistful of Child Zelda's hair, and the little girl screamed, tears springing to her eyes. "Perchance I'll sell you to a whorehouse, put you to work entertaining some men!"

Child Zelda twisted and shrieked as her uncle tried to pull her inside the hovel by her hair. A furious Sian leapt to her feet and launched herself at Zelda's uncle. Zelda's uncle lifted his boot – and adult Zelda turned away just in time to avoid reliving the sight of Sian being kicked in the face. Sian screamed from the blow and sobbed. Zelda could still hear her child-self screaming and crying as she closed her eyes. When she opened them again, she started to find herself face to face with a woman she didn't know.

The woman didn't belong in the memory any more than Zelda did. The memory was dull, almost colorless, while Zelda and the stranger stood out from it, full of color and life and wearing fine clothes compared to the people of the slums, who were draped in rags.

The stranger was a young elven woman with long, flowing, straight white hair, upon which she wore a crown with white feathers. She was quite short, reminding Zelda of Wick as she stood there in her long white gown, the sleeves of which hung over her hands.

The elven woman, arms folded, uttered a word in a strange language, and the memory vanished, so that they were standing on the dark stair again, surrounded by books. Zelda had the big tome *Zelda's Memory Vol. LIII: Sian* in her arms.

The stranger took the tome from Zelda and placed it back on the shelf. "I needn't tell you how reckless that was," she said. "If I hadn't been here, you may have become stuck in your own memory, watching it on an endless loop for all eternity."

Zelda swallowed hard, silently agreeing that being trapped in that memory would indeed have been horrific. "But what is this place?" she asked, glancing around.

The elven woman turned from the bookshelf and appraised Zelda in surprise. "If you braved the dangers of Eido Loth while knowing so little about it, one is left to assume you are one of the queen's lackeys?"

Zelda stiffened indignantly. "So you must be Lythara," she said coolly.

"I am. And you are Zelda the Queen-slayer? Or was that your knight?" Without waiting for an answer, Lythara turned and drifted down the stair. As she went, a trail of wisp-lights blossomed from her gracefully-lifted hand. Her long sleeve hung from her slender arm like a wing.

"You know me?" asked Zelda, following.

"All of *Alleren* knows you. The queen was furious when you slew her sister. Demanded the Order of Vira send a description of you and the knights who fled with you, and of course they had to obey."

"And she chose you to replace Alarien?"

"Obviously."

"But you're an elf," said Zelda. She didn't wish to be rude, but she was baffled.

"Should I be anything other? A dragon perchance? Or a unicorn?"

"No, it's just . . . The elven rebellion and . . ."

"Not all elves care to restore the days of former glory," said Lythara, who had paused to glance over the titles of a few books. She kept going, the wisp-lights trailing behind. "The queen knows she has my fealty."

"She sent me in here to rescue you."

"Ha. Does she have so little faith in me?"

"She wants you to return."

"Obviously, but I'm in the middle of something, as you can very well see."

"What if I aided you? Then you could return, the queen could pardon me, and everyone would be happy." Zelda smiled a little sardonically. She was surprised when Lythara halted on the stair, gave her a sideways glance, and smiled quite sincerely.

"All right," said the elven woman, turning to face Zelda. "It seems I've been a bit rude. I . . . apologize. It's just that I've been here for three weeks and I'm so close!"

Zelda frowned. "So close to what? What is this place?" she asked for the second time.

Lythara turned away again. "Come. If you are to aid me, then I suppose a history lesson is in order."

Zelda followed Lythara down the stairs, through the cold and eerie gloom. There were no Wyre torches here, and she realized that if not for Lythara's light, they would have been stumbling through pitch darkness.

Of course, Zelda could have conjured a wisp-light herself, but Lythara's light was different. It didn't just function to push back the darkness but also to repel dark creatures, which likely would have swarmed inside the building otherwise. Zelda knew it must've been because Lythara was an elf. Elven magick was stronger by far than human magick. That humans had ever taken the realms from the elves was a mystery for the ages, Zelda thought.

"There is a place where all thoughts, memories, and dreams gather," said Lythara, descending the stair, still trailing light from her hand. "This isn't it, of course. The dimension is called Edolel and is believed to be the mind of, well, a goddess. A long time ago, there was a sorceress named Ithrel who decided to steal the thoughts and dreams of Edolel. This library is her collection."

Zelda glanced at the books on the walls in wonder, and she might have been skeptical if she hadn't just tumbled accidentally into one of her own memories. Seeing Sian again had been wonderful . . . and terrible.

"Ithrel created a device that would *farm* – for lack of a better word—the thoughts and dreams and memories of Edolel," went on Lythara, quite businesslike. "The device is still here and still functioning after thousands of years. I wanted to bring it with me back to our world, but it would be too much fuss, dragging the thing back while constantly battling monsters."

"But the dark creatures fear your light," said Zelda. "I saw them flee."

"The lesser ones, yes. So you didn't encounter any demons? That was lucky."

They came to the bottom of the stair at last. Lythara lifted her hand, sending a stream of light toward the ceiling, where it split into spheres and hovered, illuminating the large room below.

Zelda took a step forward. It was a great circular room. The walls were covered in yet more old books, and tattered pages littered the floor like a mosaic. There were reading podiums with books open upon them, and torches with green flames of Wyre Light had been fastened to them. Archways opened in the bookshelves at intervals, leading to other rooms, the contents of which were dark, devoid as they were of Lythara's light. Only one of the side rooms had been lit by the sorceress, and it was full of piles of books that had been pulled from the shelves and left on the floor.

There were even more book piles in the room where they stood. Zelda accidentally tripped over one of the piles, sending books sliding every which way, and was scolded by Lythara, who complained she had just set her work back six hours.

At the center of the main room stood a machine, black and narrow. It looked like a birdbath with gears nailed to the sides. Attached to it was a lever, and on the floor beside the machine, more piles of discarded books.

"What I'm about to tell you is strictly confidential," said Lythara. "It cannot be repeated on pain of death."

"My life is already in the hands of the queen. What's one more danger?" said Zelda tiredly.

"I have spent three weeks here looking for information on dragons."

"Dragons?"

"Yes. Where have they gone? Why have they disappeared? Did they perchance leave nests behind? Etcetera."

"*That's* what you braved the perils of this land for?" said Zelda incredulously. "Who the devil cares if the dragons are gone so long as they're gone?"

Lythara scoffed impatiently. "Do humans know so little of their own history? The only reason your people were able to overthrow the elven empire was your taming of the dragons! Then the dragons grew weary of being used like mere beasts and they disappeared! The elven resistance is trying to find them—"

"But if the queen finds them first, she can curtail the resistance," finished Zelda.

"Exactly," said Lythara. "The only trouble is, there isn't a single book here about them, not a memory, not a thought! It is as if the dragons wiped themselves from the mind of the goddess and from existence itself."

"Or," suggested Zelda, "the elven resistance found this place first and took all the books on dragons."

"A possibility I was loath to consider," said Lythara. She looked at Zelda with sudden interest, as if she had never quite looked at her before. "But you are human. You carry the genetic memory of your ancestors. You could use the machine to try to recall the dragons."

"If it gets me forth from here and back to my baby," sighed Zelda unenthusiastically.

"Excellent. Step over here," said Lythara, stepping aside, "and think of the dragons, and pull the lever. Think *very hard* of the dragons."

Zelda tried "very hard" to think of the dragons, but when she pulled the lever, she was blinded by white light and suddenly found herself in a memory that had nothing to do with dragons whatsoever.

Zelda was standing in a training yard. Muscular adolescent girls with ponytails were standing in a row, firing arrows at targets, as an older woman instructed them with her hands behind her back.

Other girls were sparring with wooden training swords inside a fenced area. Zelda paused when she noticed two girls in particular: a red-head with a voluminous ponytail and a girl with dark black hair pulled back in a single plait. They must've been twelve years old at least. The redhead was going at it a little too enthusiastically with her wooden sword and was getting careless. The dark-haired girl got in a good strike that disarmed her.

"Ouch!" cried the redhead, sucking her hand. And then, to everyone's horror, she tackled the dark-haired girl to the dirt and started beating her. Everyone in the training yard stood transfixed to watch. The dark-haired girl fought back, and they went rolling through clouds of dirt, screaming and shouting.

Zelda stood staring. It *couldn't* be!

"Calain! Selene! Cease this insanity at once!" shouted the dark-haired woman who'd been instructing them. She lunged forward, reached into the fray, and yanked both girls out by their collars. She was about to scold the pouting girls further when the redhead shouted, "Pa!" and broke free, taking off at a mad dash across the yard.

Zelda watched fondly as Child Calain threw herself into the arms of a middle-aged man with shaggy brown hair. The man chuckled as he caught Calain in a hug and rested his cheek with a smile on her wild hair.

Smiling, Zelda drew near to listen with interest.

The man pulled back and looked down at Calain, who was tousled, sweaty, and smeared in dirt. He laughed. "Look at you! You're nearly as tall as your pa!"

"Where is Ma?" asked Calain, eagerly glancing around.

The smile on Arthur's face faltered. "Calain . . ." He cleared his throat. "Your ma is a good woman who loves you *very* much, but she left to seek her fortune elsewhere."

Calain looked crestfallen. "Is she coming back?"

"No, child," said Arthur gently.

Calain's lip trembled. "B-But I need her. She said she'd always be there!"

Before her father could answer, Calain tore free of his arms and ran from the fortress, out the gate and through the grass.

"Calain!" Arthur called miserably.

Looking concerned, Selene ran after her.

"You're doing this on purpose," said a peeved voice.

Zelda started to find Lythara beside her, arms folded, looking irritable, and what she was supposed to be doing – finding memories of dragons – came rushing back to her.

Lythara uttered a strange word, and they were pulled from the memory. Zelda looked around to find herself back in the bizarre library, standing beside the black machine, on the pedestal of which was a book that's title page named it: *Calain's Memory Vol. XXVI: Lowri.*

Zelda looked up from the book to find Lythara glowering at her from the other side of it. The elven woman snapped the book shut, her eyes still fixed rather angrily on Zelda.

Zelda frowned. "I haven't done anything."

Lythara lifted her white brows. "Oh? You have done *nothing* except distract and sabotage since you've been here! You are trying to stop me finding the dragons!"

Zelda stared in disbelief. At last, she said, "You're mad! You've been here too long."

"*Am I* mad? *Am I?*" went on Lythara, a crazed sort of light in her eyes. "You aren't the first spy to come here, trying to protect Hidden Dragon—"

"Hidden Dragon?"

"Though they must be desperate if they're recruiting humans now. Is your knight a part of this as well? Is that why she slew Ellanara? She left holes in half the castle and took one of those Hidden Dragon *lunatics* with her when she fled. I saw it when I scryed the castle! Is she waiting somewhere for you? Perhaps I'll send you back to your elven friends together!" Her crazed, paranoid eyes grew wider. "Yes, you are Bound, so it's possible! To Menosea!"

Before Zelda could protest, she was blasted full force in her face by Lythara's white light, which the elf cast from both her hands.

Chapter 9

Little Aereth was barely a week old and already crawling around the castle. The Knights of Falcon were shocked but made haste to sew the child a tunic and breeches so she wouldn't scrape her knees and a bonnet to protect her little head from the sun. Selene was the best seamstress of the group, so she made the clothes with Cassandra's aid, while Gweneth carried the child on her shoulders as she patrolled the battlements and told her stories about the realms.

The knights didn't seem to realize it, but Aereth was fully aware of most everything they said. She didn't understand the words at first, but the emotion helped convey the meaning, and before long, she could understand full sentences and even read a little.

Aereth was rapidly growing and evolving, and the poor knights could hardly keep up. She robbed them of their sleep all night, often waking up screaming and disturbing the knights who weren't on watch. She needed more nourishment than the average child and grew out of her clothes almost overnight, so that the knights were constantly sewing, feeding, and changing swaddling.

By week three, the knights had circles under their eyes. They sat in the old courtyard together as Aereth crawled happily through the wild flowers, which were overgrown with weeds. Cassandra was washing soiled swaddling in a basin, her sleeves rolled up as she scrubbed it against the washboard; Selene was sewing Aereth a new pair of breeches; and Gweneth was supposed to be keeping an eye on Aereth, but she kept getting distracted by the conversation. Gweneth and Selene were sharing a stone bench that looked ancient while Cassandra sat on a low stool beside the washbasin, scrubbing serenely away.

"But how is it possible?" Selene was saying as she frowned on her sewing. "At this rate, she'll be a child next month!"

"She was conceived through a magick potion, according to Zelda," said Gweneth pointedly. "I suppose it's possible in the same way it's possible we can punch holes through stone."

"Good way to bloody your hands," laughed Cassandra. But her gray eyes grew somber as she said, "Zelda has been gone far too long. The time may have come to act."

"And do what?" demanded Gweneth. "We cannot ride off into peril with the child – Get *back* here, Goblin!" Gweneth said with a laugh and dragged Aereth back by the seat of her breeches.

Aereth pouted. There was an old pond nearby and it was whispering, calling to her. She wanted to crawl to it, but Gweneth was watching, so she picked up the wooden horse she had discarded. Gweneth had carved it for her, but she was bored with it. She idly stuck it in her mouth.

"Two of us could stay here with the babe," said Cassandra, "and one of us could strike out for Alleren, try to discover what has become of Zelda. She could be imprisoned there for all we know!"

"If only we were Bound to her, we would know if she were ill or well," said Selene heavily.

"We can't let Cassandra keep martyring herself," Gweneth said. "I shall make the journey to Alleren, and you two shall stay. Zelda won't be too fussed if I am slain."

"This isn't the time to jest!" snapped Selene.

"Who is jesting?" Gweneth protested.

The knights continued their anxious conversation and didn't appear to be paying attention to Aereth. Now was her chance. She set off through the grass and weeds at a quick crawl.

"Yes, closer, child!" called the voice from the pond, whispering, hissing urgently.

Aereth finally reached the pond and knelt on the edge of the water to look in. It was cloudy, covered in a skin of twigs and dead leaves. But as Aereth watched, a space cleared in the center of the pond to reveal a woman's smiling face.

The woman in the water was beautiful. She reminded Aereth of her mother, for she had pink lips and long golden hair. But very long pointed ears reached from either side of her face, and her eyes were a vibrant green. They were hungry, calculating eyes and not like Zelda's gentle blue eyes at all.

Sensing she was frightening Aereth, the woman in the water smiled, her eyes softening as she reached up and offered Aereth a piece of fruit. Aereth didn't know what it was, but it was a soft piece of plum. Aereth only knew it was food and gazed at it hungrily as it rose from the water before her. She was tired of goat's milk and honey and bread . . .

"That's right," said the woman in the water. "Take it, child."

Aereth snatched the soft bit of plum and crammed it in her toothless mouth. The smirking face in the water disappeared. Aereth didn't even notice: the food was delicious! She could still taste its sweetness on her tongue. She sucked the juice from her fingers – and screamed when her stomach burned with pain, blood flying from her mouth. Behind her, the knights scrambled frantically to their feet.

Taming the Wolf Knight

Book 5

Chapter 1

For the first time in her life, Selene didn't have an immediate plan. Zelda's child was sick. She'd eaten something from the courtyard – no one could discern what – and had been coughing up blood for days since. Selene had to assume it was a rock or a stick. Children sometimes swallowed dangerous things. But there was no true way to know without the aid of a healer or a sorceress.

The knights were terrified. They blamed each other. They argued. They sat up with Aereth the night through, watching her sleep, waiting for more coughing and blood. Because they didn't know what the matter was, they had no clue how to treat the sickness. They debated riding the girl to a healer in the nearest town, but reentering Priine could put them at risk of capture, and they had little coin between them.

Then one night, after Aereth had screamed, cried, and coughed blood for hours, Selene realized the child's injury was not getting better and was, in fact, getting worse, and she knew what she must do.

"We have to do *something,*" Gweneth snarled.

The three knights were standing outside the door of the barracks where Aereth slept, in the dark and cool hall, as moonlight fed through the nearby window. Gweneth and Cassandra were facing each other while Selene sat on one of the wooden benches that lined the hall. Selene thought Cassandra looked as calm and serene as ever, even in the middle of their panic and fear. It was a little maddening, especially when Selene herself was ready to tear her hair.

"We cannot just sit here and watch her die!" Gweneth was saying angrily.

Selene thought it strange, but for once in her life, she was actually glad for Gweneth's emotional display of frustration. It made her feel better about her own misery. She felt so helpless, watching that sweet child suffer, knowing the hurt it would cause them all – cause Zelda – if she should perish.

Cassandra turned and faced the window, her hands in her trouser pockets. She looked almost angelic as moonlight streamed over her pale skin and hair. "I already suggested writing to Melvalda and my mother for aid. Both of you refused. What else do you wish of me?" There was a bitter, tired note in her voice, and Selene had to remind herself that Cassandra was as frantic and unhappy as they were, even if she did not show it.

Selene and Gweneth exchanged guilty glances, but Cassandra's words were true. When Cassandra suggested sending a raven to Melvalda for aid, they both declared that they would chop off Melvalda's head if she even set foot in the gate. As far as Selene and Gweneth were concerned, Melvalda was evil. She had coerced Zelda into laying with her, had nearly taken Aereth for her own, and had attempted to keep Cassandra trapped in the enchanted form of a child – all to soothe some old wound of hers from twenty-odd years before. She was a selfish, dangerous, evil old woman, whether Cassandra could see it or not.

"I . . . have an idea," said Selene heavily, and the others looked at her.

Selene dropped her forehead in her hand and couldn't believe she was even bringing it up, but they were out of options.

"It will require some travel," she said, "and we must abandon Wolf Fortress. Probably for quite some time."

Gweneth waved an impatient hand, gazing at Selene intently. "Tell us your idea."

Selene lifted her face. "We must travel north of Dark Bloom, to a small town near Menosea. My grandmother lives there."

"Can she help the child?" asked Cassandra sharply.

"My grandmother is an elven witch," said Selene quietly. "She is . . . quite powerful. She hates humans, but she will aid us. There will be a price, but she would never turn a sick child away."

"Then what are we waiting for?" said Gweneth impatiently. "Let us depart!"

They set out immediately. The knights donned their armor and repacked their satchels. Selene gently wrapped little Aereth in a blanket and tied the blanket around her chest as a makeshift carrier. Then she headed down to the stable, where the others were waking the horses. The Knights of Falcon mounted their steeds and galloped off into the night.

They kept mostly silent, riding as fast as they could. Selene knew there was no portal that could take them close to Eldaris, the village where her grandmother dwelt and where she had grown up, surrounded by elves. They would have to make the journey there on horseback and hope they reached the village soon enough.

As if the sickness in her sensed something, little Aereth was quiet for the duration of the journey. She did not scream, cry, or cough blood, instead sleeping deeply in the blanket that wrapped her, only opening her eyes to suck the milk-soaked rag that Selene occasionally offered.

As they traveled, they encountered no one. No Rose Guard knights, no monsters or wolves. Just cascades of flowers and crickets chirruping. They did not even see a sign of Wilde

Women in the trees, which would have been welcome, considering the circumstances.

"Do you think the Wilde Women would aid us?" Cassandra wondered one night as they sat around the fire at camp. "They have magick of their own, and Aereth is the child of one of their greatest warriors."

"*Was* the child of one of their greatest warriors," Gweneth corrected. "Yrsa was defeated by Calain, remember? And in front of her whole clan. If they didn't exile her, then they killed her. Either way, Aereth wouldn't be welcome among them."

"They would turn away a sick child even if it were one of their own?" Cassandra said in disbelief.

"Aye," said Gweneth heavily.

Selene thought that cruel but said nothing as she gently rubbed the milk-soaked rag against Aereth's lips, coaxing her to suckle. "If only Zelda were here, she could feed the girl for us," she muttered, for she had grown weary of trying to make stubborn Aereth suck the wet rag.

"If Zelda were here, this wouldn't be happening," said Gweneth. "I suspect whatever ails the babe is magick in nature. Some lurking creature saw an opportunity and took it." She glanced at Cassandra. "Are you sure you found nothing in the courtyard?"

Cassandra shook her head. "I searched it all over, but the vibrations there were normal. Nothing sinister whatsoever. I cannot fathom it."

"What was she doing right before she took ill?" Selene asked.

"She was looking in the pond," said Gweneth helplessly, as if it were the most innocent thing in the world. "She kept trying to get at it all day."

"Hmm. The pond," said Cassandra thoughtfully.

"Does it mean something?" Gweneth asked.

Cassandra sighed and leaned forward, resting her elbows on her knees. "There's probably nothing more magickal than water," she said heavily, "but that still doesn't tell us what sort of curse was put on the child."

"Grandmother will know," said Selene. "Just a little further, and we shall come to her village."

They arrived at Eldaris the next day, after having been set upon by Skoll Wolves on the edge of the forest. Gweneth and Cassandra took care of the wolves easily, while Selene stayed aloft on her horse, clutching Aereth tight with one arm as the child sobbed and wept in fear.

Like Arinol, Eldaris was a small fishing community. It was built right along the beach, on the shores of the *Arinath* sea, and while there was no snow, it was still quite cold. People wore coats and hats and gloves and staggered up and down the sand with capes flaring. Only in the summer was it warmer, and at the moment it was Fall.

And though Eldaris was small, with barely four hundred elves living in it, it was always full of hustle and bustle because of so many elves going to and from Menosea, the mysterious island to the north. Menosea housed a coven of elven sorceresses, the Order of Tirathell, as well as – supposedly—the underground training cell of Venom Six, an order of elven assassins, and also – again, supposedly – the headquarters of the elven resistance. Most of what went on at Menosea was based on hearsay. It was only known for a fact that the island housed a school of magick and that boats were always coming and going back and forth with supplies.

Selene stood on the edge of the village, having dismounted Apple, and stared at the place she used to call home. It looked exactly as it had when she'd left it. All the houses had the same strange elven shape to them, with roofs like sunken cones and front steps that were rounded off, not cornered, so that it looked as if the steps were made of bubbles or cascades of pebbles.

As ever, it was a dark and gloomy day in Eldaris and looked as if it was going to rain. Elves were heading out to fishing boats, or else returning at the dock with large nets weighed down by fish. Children were running and playing, pigtails flying, and Selene saw a little dog chasing two girls up the middle of the street, leaping playfully at their skinny legs.

As she stood there, Selene thought of her own childhood, how she'd run in bare feet through the sand during the summer, how her grandmother had scolded her for collecting seashells that still had creatures living inside. The other children hadn't liked her. She was a human and all the children in Eldaris were elves. She didn't belong there. And even now, standing there holding Aereth, she felt like an outsider looking in. It was as if she had never even lived there, for elves who had known her as a child and recognized her now as an adult simply turned their backs and ignored her.

"Are you well, Selene?" asked Cassandra with concern.

"Aereth isn't well. That's what matters," Gweneth firmly reminded them.

Selene shook herself and steeled her heart against the glares and cold-shoulders. "Come," she said and led the way down the street, pulling Apple's reigns.

Selene led the others through the winding streets, to a small hut with the same cone-shaped roof as the others. As they went, elves peered from windows or else stood in their sand-swept yards, whispering and staring. Selene and the knights drew near the hut, leading their horses behind them. They hadn't left behind Calain's horse, Arthur, for they had no idea when, if ever, they would return to Wolf Fortress. The horse followed cautiously behind them, his reins tied to Cassandra's horse, Sunny.

They stood outside the hut and gazed up at it, looking for smoke and signs of occupancy. Seashells and green algae and the nests of seagulls were all stuck to the roof as if someone had glued them there. Selene could see a thin wisp of smoke rising: her grandmother was home.

Selene took a deep breath, steeling herself again, and releasing Apple's reins, she climbed the step and knocked on the door, one arm cradling Aereth in her swaddling. Then Selene stood there waiting. She heard Gweneth and Cassandra dismount and draw near behind her, heard movement within the hut as her grandmother stirred. The old woman's face appeared in the window near the door, pinched and angry and small, as Selene remembered it. Then the door flew violently open, and Selene looked down at her tiny grandmother.

Neserie was a small old woman with a hunched back, barely four feet tall. She wasn't pretty by any means, with a wart on her chin and a toothless mouth that was sucking inward in folds of skin. Her wrinkles were so heavy, they nearly obscured her face, and her white hair was a long curtain falling either side her biting, pitiless black eyes. In her pointed ears were rings of gold. She was wearing a patched little dress and no shoes or socks and she smelled like garlic. Selene thought her grandmother looked exactly like a witch in a child's tale.

Neserie stood there in the doorway, looking up at Selene as if she had interrupted her nap. "What in blazes are you doing here?" she said angrily. No greeting, no concern, just immediate disapproval and annoyance.

Selene was so used to her grandmother's hatred that she didn't blink an eye, but she knew Gweneth and Cassandra were likely standing shocked behind her.

"I thought I told you never to come back," went on Neserie . "I know you're a fugitive. If you're looking for a place to hide, it's not here."

"Gods be good," muttered Gweneth in disbelief.

Neserie glared past Selene at Gweneth. "And you brought your raggedy knight friends with you. The nerve! Not that I blame them for slaying Ellanara, but I don't want any trouble."

Selene took a shuddering breath and said, "Grandmother, this child needs healing." So saying, Selene opened the bundle to reveal Aereth's small, pained face.

"A human brat," said Neserie indifferently. "It isn't yours. You're sterile, thank the gods! Why should you care?"

"It is my lady's child," answered Selene calmly. "I am sworn to protect them both."

"And now that you've failed them both, you've come to me. Hmph. Just like your damned father."

Selene's father, Emyr, had been a highborn human knight of a noble family. He was injured in a battle on the edge of Dark Bloom and was brought to Neserie for healing in Eldaris. It was how Selene's parents had met.

Selene's mother, Gilme, had been a simple fish-netter, heading out on her boat every morning to catch fish she could sell to the Order of Tirathell. Like Selene, she had never shown any aptitude with magick nor any desire to learn. When she saw Emyr sleeping in her mother's house, she loved him. And when Emyr awoke to her singing, he loved Gilme.

Emyr's parents had been as pleased as Neserie to learn that their son had eloped with a common elf, which was to say not pleased at all.

"Please," said Selene, offering the child again. She knew that if she kept Neserie focused on the child's pain that she would win her over.

Selene was right. Neserie looked at Aereth's miserable face again, and her pinched, angry face softened in sympathy. Grudgingly, she held the door open as she said, "Fine. Bring the babe inside."

Relief filled Selene and she led the others inside the cool, shadowy hut.

Neserie's hut was one floor, but there were several rooms all sectioned off by curtains of seashells. Neserie led them to the room where she often nursed back to health those sick and injured who came to her. It was a small, plain room with one low, wooden chair, a nightstand, and a single, narrow bed against the wall. The small square window that stood over the bed shed a pale beam of sunlight across the sheets.

Selene gently laid little Aereth on the sheets and hovered anxiously over her, loath to leave. She was unhappy but not surprised when Neserie shooed them all out, telling them to wait in the front room and not to touch anything.

"Your grandmother's a bit shite," said Gweneth when they were all sitting on grass mats in the front room.

A low fire was blazing in the firepit. Selene stared into the flames, straining to hear what her grandmother was doing to Aereth. She could just barely hear murmuring and chanting. The smell of incense grew strong.

"Why didn't you tell us you were half-elf?" Gweneth went on. She sounded a little hurt that the information had been kept from her.

Selene looked up. Gweneth was staring at her. So was Cassandra, though her eyes were full of pity with no hint of bafflement or surprise.

Selene looked back at the fire as she said, "Is it not obvious? I grew up in an elven village where I was shunned for being half-human. Then Grandmother sent me away to a human order to become a human knight. I didn't wish to be shunned for being half-elf."

"No, instead you were shunned for being bossy and obnoxious," teased Gweneth. She looked across at Cassandra. "Remember what she was like? Always telling us what to do!"

"I thought she was a rather short instructor myself," joked Cassandra.

Selene smiled, listening in content as they teased her and suddenly very glad they were there. All her life, all she had ever wanted was to belong, to be loved. She had only ever known the comfort and joy of acceptance with the Knights of Falcon.

The knights looked up when Neserie hobbled into the room. She folded her arms as she said bitterly, "Well, you've really done it. You let the child eat food not of this world."

Selene went still. "What does that mean?"

"It *means* she is being pulled into another dimension," answered Neserie impatiently. "Likely by the fae. They're the only ones mad enough to steal little brats. All that soiled swaddling and the constant screaming and whining." She looked with narrow-eyed dislike down her crooked nose at Selene. "Brings back so many memories."

It was Selene's turn to be impatient. "Is there nothing you can do?" she said, getting to her feet.

"I placed the child in deep slumber," Neserie answered. "It won't stop the transition, but it will slow down the process."

Selene held out her hands. "Is there no way to stop it?!"

Neserie lifted a brow, arms still folded calmly. "With your sword, girl? No. With magick? Yes. Unfortunately, I cannot venture into Elwenhal to bring the child back. She doesn't know me. She would not listen if I beckoned."

"Can none of us be sent?" Selene desperately implored, and behind her, Gweneth and Cassandra rose to their feet, nodding seriously.

Neserie snorted. "The human? No," she said, nodding at Gweneth. "You are also too human," she added disdainfully as she gazed at Selene. Her thoughtful eyes went to Cassandra. "But your other friend, she has the blood of the Tula-Dan. I can see it in her."

Selene shook her head. "But what does all that matter?"

"Humans aren't allowed in Elwenhal," said Neserie, "unless they are babes, *or* unless they force their way in with magick." Her thoughtful eyes went to Cassandra again, scanning her with interest. "Your friend has magick and the blood of the old elves. I could send her to Elwenhal, but there is no guarantee she could return. If her magick was stronger... but it isn't." She shook her head. "And I sense such *potential* in you, child. But you became a knight? Such a waste."

Cassandra barely reacted, remaining calm and serene as ever, though Selene noticed a slight line of irritation appear between her brows in the barest of frowns.

"Then send me," Cassandra said, seriously and dutifully. "My lady's child is in peril. We cannot afford to linger."

Gweneth stepped close to Cassandra and said in a low voice, "Do not martyr yourself, Cassie! If your magick isn't strong enough –"

"Calm yourself, Gweneth," said Cassandra soothingly. "I shall find Aereth in the other realm and keep her from the fae as long as I can. In the meantime, you must find Zelda! She is our only hope now."

Gweneth nodded, but Selene knew she felt as frustrated as she did: how were they supposed to find Zelda? Only one of them was Bound to her, and that one had abandoned them.

"This way then, child," said Neserie, leading Cassandra down the hall.

Gweneth watched Cassandra and Neserie leave the room and shook her head darkly as she said, "None of this would be happening if not for Calain."

"Gwen . . ." Selene said wearily.

"Tis true and you know it," snarled Gweneth. "She is reckless and irresponsible and a child! She turned her back on her duty, and it upset *everything.* We are lost without her!"

Selene tried to find the words to defend Calain, but she knew Gweneth was right. Calain had left the group, upsetting a balance they hadn't consciously been aware of, and now. . .they were lost.

Chapter 2

Calain was lost. She had been riding her father's horse down the road in a state of misery, and trying not to think of Siobhan, when she was blinded by a white light and suddenly found herself sitting astride the horse in a pearly fog.

The fog was so thick, Calain could see nothing, and her frightened horse kept bucking and rearing, so that she had to dismount and lead it by the reins.

The horse's name was Lucky, which Calain found ironic given the circumstances. Lucky was a sturdy brown stallion, very nervous and flighty, for he had never been into battle or braved strange lands. He was soft and sheltered, used to the quiet of the farm. It took a great deal of singing and soothing before Calain could get him to move forward through the mist.

The further in they went, the thinner the fog seemed to become. Calain could see dark shapes in the distance, buildings that were low, trees. She moved toward them, and noticed that – for some odd reason – the beat of Zelda's heart beside her own was growing stronger. It could only mean that Zelda was near, but why would she be here in this fog of all places?

Calain tried to ignore Zelda's heartbeat, instead moving toward the shapes in the distance. They were growing more distinct, and she could hear voices, the clash of blades, the soft bray of horses. The sounds were all too familiar. She was nearing a training yard.

Maybe she had come to a fortress belonging to other human knights. The Knights of the Stag, for instance. She prayed it was not the Knights of the Dragon.

The strange mist finally cleared, and as Calain stepped out of it, she halted to find herself face to face with a forest of arrows. Several elves stood in a row before her, clad in the black, silky garments of assassins, their eyes slits in the depths of their hoods.

One elf had their hood down, a male with a mass of long yellow hair pulled back in a thick tail and slanted eyes that were a bright, startling blue. His mouth was twisted in a sneer as he aimed an arrow straight at Calain's face. The elf seemed vaguely familiar.

Beyond the row of hostile elves, it was as Calain had assumed: a fortress of wood and stone rising sturdy to the blue sky, with red rooftops and delicate elven architecture. Cold statues of wolves guarded the gate either side, which was open on the training yard, and the elves training there had stopped to stare at the confrontation.

"You *dare,*" hissed the male elf, "set *foot* on this island, human? I don't know how you passed the wards, but you're going to be *very* sorry you—"

"Eiran!" shouted a familiar voice. "Don't hurt her!"

Calain looked up and couldn't believe it: Imodel was running toward them, though she was hardly recognizable now that she was wearing clothes. She was dressed in the same silky black garments as the other elves, but her hood was down and her bow on her back. She came running across the gravel yard, yellow hair streaming loose behind her, big breasts heaving, and halted in front of Calain, grinning up at her.

Calain had to admit she was glad to see Imodel as well. Her heart fluttered as she looked down into the familiar blue eyes.

"What is the *meaning* of this?" snarled the male elf with the bright blue eyes. "You know the penalty for humans who trespass on the island is death!"

Imodel rolled her eyes. "Be still, Eiran! This is my knight! The one who rescued me from the Gold Keep."

Upon hearing this, the elves lowered their bows, looking at Calain in a new light. They put their weapons away, and one, a woman with green eyes, said, "Then she is owed a blood debt. The human may rest here then be on her way."

With that, the elves turned away. All but the male with the blue eyes, who was staring at Calain with a startling amount of hatred. "This is the one," he said to Imodel, "who you bragged so shamelessly that she took you in the mountains?"

Calain held back a laugh, knowing that to do so would have only provoked the elf. But as it turned out, she might as well have had her laugh, for the male sheathed his bow on his back and suddenly lunged on her, screaming, "You fucked my sister! I'll kill you! I'll kill you!"

Calain went down hard, the wind knocked out of her. She barely had time to block with her arm when the male elf, in a snarling rage, began to punch at her face again and again. Calain shielded herself with her forearms and only made defensive maneuvers, not wishing to accidentally injure Imodel's brother, who – true to his bellows—seemed hell-bent on killing her.

Calain was vaguely aware of Imodel somewhere screaming, "Stop it! Stop it! Leave her alone!" and of elves gathering to watch the fight with interest.

Eiran, with his relentless punches, managed to get a few blows in, leaving a cut on Calain's temple and busting her lip. She retaliated with a knee-jerk reaction, giving the elf an uppercut to his face that snapped his head back.

The watching elves cheered, but Imodel screamed in horror.

"Stop it! Stop hurting each other!" Imodel shrieked, and grabbing a fistful of Eiran's yellow hair, she pried him off.

Eiran fell hard on his seat, watching darkly as Imodel leaned over Calain.

"Are you all right? Did he hurt you?" asked Imodel breathlessly and cupped Calain's face with one small hand.

Calain kissed Imodel on the lips, which made Eiran tense and lurch to his feet.

"Stay off my sister, human!" Eiran warned.

Imodel helped Calain to stand, but her reproving eyes were on her brother. "Leave her alone, Eiran! Or tis I you shall spar! And I shall not lie down and allow you to pummel me!"

With the fight over, the other elves lost interest and moved on.

Eiran's face twisted. "I can't *believe* you're defending her! She hath sullied you! She hath taken your innocence! You are spoiled now by her touch—!"

Imodel laughed. "As if I were a jug of milk!"

"No, you are my sweet, innocent sister, too naïve to understand she hath been defiled!"

Calain glanced in bafflement at Imodel and didn't see the sweet innocence Eiran did. It was clear to her that Imodel was a woman grown, a confident lover, and a murdering, bloodthirsty assassin to boot.

"You are being foolhardy, Eiran," dismissed Imodel. She was still protectively clutching Calain's arm, which seemed to infuriate her brother.

Eiran's chest heaved. "Are you yet too enamored of her to see it? She took you without even pledging herself to you as champion!"

"She did not take me, I took her!" Imodel announced.

Eiran stubbornly went on, pointing a finger all the while, "You are lucky she hath not made you ill with vile human diseases! She may stay here because she hath saved your life, but if she touches you again, I shall slay her in cold blood!" With that, he turned and marched away toward the fortress.

When Eiran had gone, Calain took Lucky's reins and looked down at Imodel, whose blue eyes were sparkling almost girlishly in excitement.

"Want to have sex in the wine larder?" Imodel asked brightly.

Chapter 3

Zelda stood in the mist, blinking in the aftermath of Lythara's blinding light. Lythara had mentioned sending Zelda to Menosea, but all Zelda could see was the mist, ever swirling around her. She tried penetrating it with a beam of light from her stave but to no avail. And so she wandered blind, hoping the mist would eventually have an end.

Zelda had hoped in vain. The mist went on and on in every direction, white as clouds and cold. And as she walked hopelessly on, Zelda began to feel Calain's heartbeat. It was racing faster and faster. Calain was excited. Calain was having sex...*again.*

Zelda took a shuddering, angry breath and marched on, trying to ignore what she was feeling. And then she heard it: the howling. The sound sent a shiver up her spine. Whatever the creatures were, they were not normal wolves, and sure enough, Zelda saw them peel out of the mist, glowing blue and translucent.

One. Then two. Twelve. Then twenty-six. The number of them was ever doubling, and Zelda knew she would not be able to banish them as she had the angry spirit that had attacked Calain in Blood Horn. These creatures were not the spirits of dead wolves but creations of magick designed to keep intruders out. They would never stop coming so long as Zelda wasn't welcome.

Zelda fought anyway, thinking of her baby and how she must get back to her, thinking of the Knights of Falcon and how much she missed them. She was consciously aware of Selene's necklace about her throat. It gave her a strength she couldn't explain as she glowed with power, shattering the ghostly wolves to vapor with a silent spell.

But there were just too many of them. Zelda was surrounded and growing weary when a glowing sword sliced through the mist and down through one of the ghostly wolves, scattering its essence.

Zelda looked up. The glowing blue blade was followed by a small elven woman in silver armor. The armor was engraved with curly leaves and flowers and appeared somewhat ancient in its make, as if the elven knight had taken it from an ancient elven tomb. The blade as well seemed archaic. Zelda had never before seen its like.

The stranger, though small in stature, had a menacing air about her that the ghostly wolves heeded as she advanced with her blade ready. They had been bold with their attacks on Zelda, but the wolves were cautious with the knight, who slew each one that lunged at her, quickly and quietly.

"Be gone," said the knight in a low, calm voice and lifted her blade in fight stance again. "Be gone! I speak for the lady! She is welcome here on my behalf!"

The ghostly wolves responded by howling and vanishing. When they had gone, the elven knight sheathed her blade on her back and regarded Zelda calmly with her glowing violet eyes.

Zelda, breathless and panting, was leaning tiredly against her stave and straightened up, regarding the woman curiously.

"Who...?" Zelda began and suddenly felt too tired to finish the sentence.

"I am Arryn, a Knight of the Wolf. And this is Menosea. At ten o' clock on a Monandaeg morning," answered the knight, and her pink lips curled in a small smile.

Zelda smiled back, feeling at ease. *You are beautiful,* she thought, looking at the knight. In the past, Zelda had typically been drawn to women who were big and strong and would take her with dominance and strength. And then there was Melvalda, whose feminine beauty, age, and expertise had been her draw. But this woman was unlike the others Zelda had craved. She was masculine, but she was so small, and there was an innocence about her. Zelda couldn't explain how she knew, but she knew that the knight was untouched, that she never lain with a woman. But why? The elf had to be quite old. Her armor was ancient and the maturity was apparent in her eyes.

Arryn turn awkwardly away, and Zelda realized with a blush that she had been staring for quite some time at the knight.

"You must stay with me," said the knight. "If you are found wandering the island alone, you will be slain. Humans are not permitted here." With that, she took off at a brisk pace, holding her hand out, so that the mist scrolled away before her.

Zelda hurried to catch up and watched in awe, wondering what sort of spell Arryn was using. She was a knight, but she was a sorceress as well. It was the way of elven knights; it was their tradition to use magick. Though the Wolf academy had been abandoned in Koradara, there was still the Raven Fortress in Eriallon, where the elven Knights of the Raven continued the tradition of enchanted blades and spells.

Looking at Arryn, now it suddenly made sense to Zelda why Wick had been sent to Vira'Toss, a school of magick that was primarily for humans. She could not imagine poor, clumsy little Wick with a sword. And perhaps the elven sorceresses of Tirathell simply hadn't wanted Wick because of her family. The

Blackwoods were notorious meddlers, always up to their necks in political schemes, and openly affiliated with human interests.

"Aren't you curious how I came to be here?" Zelda asked.

"No," answered Arryn. "You are the queen-slayer. Your case is quite famous among we elves. Many of us rejoiced when Ellanara was slain. I have been . . . following you for some time."

Zelda couldn't believe it when she saw the knight's cheeks flame a little.

"You've been following me?" Zelda repeated, baffled.

"I was curious to see the one who had slain the queen of Eriallon. I followed you to Blood Horn and saw you there with your knights. I . . . I didn't want you to come to harm, so I watched—"

"Why?" Zelda asked abruptly.

"Because I . . ." Arryn halted and licked her lips, not meeting Zelda's eye.

Zelda watched her curiously and felt a sudden affection for her. "Because you desired me."

"Yes," Arryn admitted hoarsely, turning her face away, so that her black hair fell forward to hide her expression. "Not since my lady have I felt. . . Not in a thousand years have I . . ." She trailed off breathlessly and suddenly said, "Come."

Zelda looked up and saw they had come to the end of the mist. The swirling fog opened upon a forest; the leaves of its white trees vivid green. It was a bright morning. Birds were singing and the sky was blue. And it was warm! Zelda was grateful to have the cold chill of the mist finally off of her and stepped gladly away from it.

"Anamora Forest," said Arryn, gazing thoughtfully at the trees ahead. "I will guide you through to the port on the other side, and then you must find your own way back to Ellondhold. You cannot apparate from the island. Even I cannot use my portal spells here, or I would take you directly back to Dark Bloom."

They passed into the forest together, coming under the shadows of the trees.

"Dark Bloom? So you really *have* been following me," said Zelda, amused. "Why not say hello? Are you shy?" she teased.

Arryn smiled. "As if you did not have enough loyal knights at your beck and call," she answered good-naturedly. "Are you building an army?" she teased back. "Shall I alert the new queen?"

Zelda smiled. She liked this teasing. It wasn't mean-spirited, like with Gweneth, and Calain had never been quick-witted enough to talk with her like this. Meanwhile, Selene and Cassandra did joke some of the time but not nearly as much as Zelda would have liked. Arryn seemed to strike the perfect balance in that regard.

"So you didn't approve of Ellanara?" asked Zelda with interest.

"No elf did," said Arryn with a snort. "And apparently, neither did your knight."

Zelda thought of Calain and wondered if Arryn, for all her spying, was aware that one of Zelda's knights had forsaken her. She could still feel Calain's excitement as she made love to some other woman and wanted to break something! But could she really be angry with Calain? How many times had Zelda forced Calain to endure the maddening sensation of her pleasure in the arms of another?

"How is Calain, by the way?" Arryn asked lightly, as if testing the water.

"Ah," said Zelda shrewdly, "so you *do* know."

Arryn smiled. "I came across your knight in Blood Horn. She was nearly slain by a very grumpy troll. I saved her."

Zelda hesitated. She wanted to ask about Calain, but she didn't want to appear too concerned. "Oh?" she said casually, though in secret, her heart was racing. If Calain had been harmed, she would have felt it, but she worried for her still.

Arryn smiled, as if she knew exactly what fears and worries were going through Zelda's mind. "Your knight was unharmed, though quite angry with you," she said apologetically.

Zelda hesitated again, wondering miserably if she really wanted to know what had been said. "What did she say?"

"She did rant at me about how false duty and honor were," answered Arryn wearily. "She seemed to believe you had betrayed her with another."

Zelda cast her eyes down as they walked. So it was as she had feared. Calain believed she had gone willingly to Melvalda. While it was true Zelda found Melvalda attractive and had secretly desired her, she wouldn't have gone to her nor lain with her if she didn't think it would protect Calain's life. If only she could tell Calain that! But instead of even bothering to speak with her, Calain had stormed off and had forsaken her duty!

"Calain is such a hot-headed fool," Zelda said bitterly.

Arryn smiled. "If Calain were anything other than what she is, you would not love her."

Zelda didn't answer because she had no retort. So instead, she changed the subject. "And you? Do you not have a lady you are sworn to? Why do you follow me?"

Arryn's violet eyes were down as she answered, "My lady . . . perished one thousand years ago. Suffice it to say I failed in my duty."

"I am sorry, Arryn. I did not realize."

"There is no need to be sorry. I failed my lady, not you."

"And now you wander the world alone?" Zelda said in sympathy. For the Wolf academy had been abandoned for fifty years, and the Knights of the Wolf scattered to the wind in exile. "Aren't there any other Knights of the Wolf you could travel with?"

"There are," said Arryn, "but I have always been . . ."

"A lone wolf?" Zelda teased.

Arryn smiled. "I suppose it is a fitting jest. But I am content enough on my own. I have made a home for myself in Edhen."

Zelda lifted her brows, feeling ashamed that she had no knowledge of the place. "Where is Edhen?" she asked tentatively. "I have never heard of it."

"And nor would you have," answered Arryn. "Tis ancient land, long forgotten by humans and elves, and shielded by magick, so that only those old enough to remember it shall find it. There are few alive today old enough to recall Edhen. They say it is the place where all life began in our world . . . In Vallinwir."

"What's it like?" Zelda asked with interest.

Arryn stared ahead, smiling. "Forgotten creatures do live there. Unicorns, dragons—"

"Dragons?" Zelda gasped.

"Aye," said Arryn. "But they are peaceful creatures, not the fiery beasts from the tales. They would have been discovered long before otherwise."

"And what more?"

"There are old buildings there, from the first cities. Statues. Fountains. But all of it has been overrun by the forest. And tis peaceful and still, no raging beasts, no wolves or trolls, no goblins. You could search all of Vallinwir and you wouldn't find a more tranquil forest."

"I would love to go there," said Zelda dreamily.

"Perhaps you shall one day. But right now, you must find your knight and then find your way from Menosea."

Zelda halted. So did Arryn.

"What do you mean?" Zelda said sharply.

"Your knight is near at hand," said Arryn simply. "Do you not feel her, my lady?"

Zelda tried to keep the anger from her face. She mostly certainly *could* feel Calain! Calain was *still* having sex! She knew she wouldn't be able to answer Arryn without yelling, so she tightened her lips against her anger and kept walking, taking breaths to calm down. Arryn moved forward as well, leading her once more through the trees.

"Calain is here?" Zelda said at last. "I mean, you did see her with your own eyes?"

"I learned that a human did suddenly appear at one of the training cells," confirmed Arryn. "It sounded like magick mischief was afoot, so I went into the mist to investigate, and there you were. It was Lythara who sent you here, was it not?"

"Yes," said Zelda, lifting her brows in surprise. "How did you know?"

"I did follow you to Alleren. I knew you were walking into a trap, but I could not reach you in time to warn you."

"So the queen never intended to pardon me?" Zelda said indignantly.

"Most unlikely, my lady," Arryn confirmed. "You did slay her sister. Or your knight did. The entire realm was calling for blood when you fled. When Lythara cast her teleportation spell, it effected Calain because she is Bound to you."

"If I were to die, would Calain die as well?" Zelda asked with sudden dread.

"It depends on the manner of death," said Arryn unhappily. "I was Bound to my lady, and as you can see, she has long since passed on to the gods, whilst I linger here."

Arryn sounded so unhappily that Zelda said with hesitation, "May I ask what happened to her?"

"She drowned at sea," said Arryn, looking away. "Such a simple way for such a powerful sorceress to die, it was almost cruel. I could not remove my armor in time to leap in and save her, and no one cared to aid us because it was a terrible storm. The ship was coming apart and the crew was scattered trying to save it."

"That is terrible," said Zelda wretchedly.

"Truer words have ne'er been spoken."

"And you have been alone all this time? One thousand years and you never found a lady?"

"No lady turned my head until . . ." Arryn drifted off and her cheeks turned a little pink. "Never mind, my lady. Let us focus on the task at hand."

"But this is important," said Zelda. "I want to know how you feel about me."

"Why? To soothe the ache of Calain's betrayal?" asked Arryn sharply.

Zelda felt a little stung. "No!" she said at once. "I admit, I *do* wish vengeance on Calain. Nothing would please me more than to lay with another woman and rouse in her a furious jealousy! But . . ." She looked with soft eyes at Arryn again. "I do honestly desire thee." She smiled. "And why shouldn't I have an army of knights?"

Arryn smiled as well. "At least you are honest in your hunger," she said, and they both laughed.

They came to a clearing, where a cluster of giant stone bricks stood. Some of the stones stood upright in pillars, while others had fallen over, long strings of bright green grass growing in a web over them. A spray of white flowers dotted the clearing, releasing a lovely scent that made Zelda smile.

Commenting that Zelda looked weary on her feet, Arryn led her to the stones and bid her sit. Zelda chose a stone brick that wasn't quite covered in grass and sat, smoothing her skirts against her backside.

Arryn sat beside Zelda (her legs dangling over the enormous stone brick) and reached into the traveling satchel that was strapped across her chest and rested at her hip. She pulled out a small stone that was round and smooth as a pebble and matched the shade of her violet eyes almost exactly. The stone glowed gently as she held it out to Zelda.

Before Zelda had even touched the stone, she could feel the magick humming from it. She took it in her slender fingers and turned it over. There was no rune upon it, so it was not a Bane Stone. She looked up at Arryn. "But what is it?"

"Tis a Summoning Stone," said Arryn. "It is bound to me. Turn it in your fingers, and I shall come."

Zelda smiled. "Are you saying . . . Are you my knight now?"

Arryn smiled. "I have been yours since I first did lay eyes upon you," she answered. "But I shall not travel always at your side. I value my solitude too greatly."

Zelda looked at the stone in her fingers. "And you will come to me? How?"

"I travel quickly around the realms by casting portal spells."

"So you can open a portal anywhere and move as you please," said Zelda, impressed.

"Yes," said Arryn quietly. "Tis how I followed you."

"Were you with me in Dark Bloom? Were you the reason I encountered so little trouble there?"

"Yes. I left your side too soon, it seems. For eventually, you were taken by the Wilde Women, were you not?"

"Tis . . . a long story," Zelda admitted sheepishly.

Arryn was sitting with her knees spread and had one hand on her thigh, the elbow poking out as she gazed thoughtfully into the trees. She was so beautiful sitting there, with her pretty pink lips and her slanted eyes and all that long, silky black hair falling around her pointed ears. And she smelled the heavenly way knights always smelled, of leather and salty sweat. It was a smell that had come to drive Zelda mad, for it reminded her of Calain and the first time they'd made love. But Arryn also smelled of *magick.* The sweet lavender scent of magick hung ever about her skin and hair.

Kiss her now! Zelda thought, gazing with longing at Arryn, who was lost in thought and not paying attention to Zelda at all. *Kiss her! Just do it!*

With a shaking breath, Zelda leaned over, turned Arryn's face gently to her own, and kissed her warm on the lips. Arryn stiffened in surprise, but only for a moment. She tentatively kissed back, her soft lips massaging Zelda's in a submissive way that made Zelda burn with lust and want her all the more.

And Arryn's skin was so incredibly soft for a knight! Zelda knew it was because she was an elf. Cassandra had been the same way, and now Zelda knew it was because of her elven blood.

Zelda's hand was still cupping Arryn's cheek, and she smoothed it to the back of Arryn's head, where she curled her fingers in the silky-soft hair and kissed her deeper, almost roughly, so that their heads turned through the kiss. Arryn was trembling a little, and when Zelda pulled back, she was blushing.

"What is it?" Zelda whispered, pushing Arryn's long hair over her shoulder with the back of her fingers.

"I . . . have never lain with a woman," Arryn admitted, embarrassed. "My lady perished before we could." She frowned anxiously. "I'm afraid I shall not be an adequate lover."

Zelda smiled. "Then just lie there and look pretty."

Arryn laughed, but she was still trembling.

Zelda reached out with her mind, unbuckling all of the buckles on Arryn's armor with one swift thought. Arryn gasped as her ancient armor and her harnessed sword tumbled suddenly away, falling harmlessly on the grass nearby. She shivered in her linen bra and woolen hose and awkwardly crossed her arms over small, high breasts.

Zelda leaned close and kissed Arryn again, smoothly unlacing her linen bra as she did. She leaned forward as she kissed the anxious knight, guiding her to lie back on the great stone brick, and she pulled the linen bra away, leaning back to look down at Arryn's breasts. They were small and perky and slightly curved, standing high from Arryn's chest and jiggling a little when she took a nervous breath.

Arryn didn't seem to know what to do with her arms. Zelda looked at them, thinking they weren't bulky like Calain's but the lean muscles were wonderful just the same. Zelda placed Arryn's arms above her head, loving when the toned muscles in her shoulders flexed and her little breasts were pulled up high from the motion. Then she leaned down and sucked slowly on Arryn's pink nipple. Arryn moaned, her pale cheeks flaming a little, as Zelda continued to suckle gently, closing her eyes and frowning as she did.

Zelda blindly reached for Arryn's woolen hose and started inching it down over her hips. Her hands explored, closing briefly on Arryn's hard, muscular backside and groping it fistfuls, so that Arryn shuddered in her grasp. She found Arryn's sex and could feel the soft, silky hair that cloaked it. She ran her fingers through the hair momentarily, thinking how nice it felt against her skin, and then fumbled blindly for the lips of Arryn's sex. They were small and soft, neatly tucked away inside the outer lips, so that they were hidden. Zelda fondled them, still suckling at Arryn's breast and feeling herself stirring to arousal.

Arryn was moaning and gasping, shocked and trembling with pleasure one moment, baffled and blushing the next. Her muscular belly was trembling, so were her thighs.

"Relax," Zelda whispered, trailing kisses over Arryn's skin to sooth her. "Relax, Arryn, my Knight of the Wolf. . ."

"Tis . . . so intense," Arryn whispered, blushing harder.

It should be after one thousand years, Zelda thought.

Zelda's kisses trailed down and down, until at last, her hungry mouth found the sweet little sex cloaked in black hair. She plunged her tongue slowly between the pink lips of Arryn's sex and watched, her cheeks flaming with desire, as Arryn writhed on her back, her small breasts pointing to the treetops and jiggling softly with her every move.

Zelda continued slowly thrusting her tongue as her hands wrestled off Arryn's boots and woolen hose. When the little knight's legs were finally free, she hooked her hands behind each knee and pushed them up, spreading Arryn's shapely thighs and further exposing her sex. Arryn looked down at Zelda between her breasts and blushed. Zelda smiled and buried her face in Arryn's sex again. She was pleased when Arryn's head fell back with a helpless cry, and she thrust her breasts to the treetops once more, gasping, violet eyes wide in astonishment, as Zelda's hungry tongue caressed her to her first climax.

Chapter 4

Calain woke with a start, sitting up breathlessly in the nest of her discarded clothes. Imodel had been sleeping in her arm but sat up as well when Calain released her. Calain couldn't breathe. Her chest was heaving rapidly, her cheeks were flaming, and she was wildly aroused. No . . . *Zelda* was wildly aroused!

Calain glanced desperately around, as if she would spy Zelda somewhere in the wine larder, making love to someone else. But all she saw were great barrels of wine spreading away in rows. What was happening? Was Zelda sleeping with Melvalda again? Or had she found yet another lover? Calain gritted her teeth and decided it did not matter – she would *kill* whoever it was! Her pa was right! She should have stormed Ravenhold and murdered Melvalda in her bed!

"Going to . . . cut off . . . someone's head!" Calain said through her teeth, struggling to pull her trousers on.

"But what's the matter?" said Imodel in amazement. Like Calain, she was naked and sitting upright in the pool of her black clothes, her great breasts trembling with her slightest moment. Her pink nipples were rigid in the cold of the larder, which had made them so deliciously wonderful to suck minutes before.

Calain stood and buttoned her trousers, then reached down and snatched up her linen bra. "*Nothing's* the matter," she snarled, "except Zelda! Always Zelda! She hath driven me mad for the last time!"

"You felt it again, didn't you?" said Imodel, amused. "Zelda off with someone else . . . tasting someone else. . . ."

"Do not jest," warned Calain, pausing to point a finger. She snatched her tunic up and pulled it on next, her bright red hair bursting through the collar.

Imodel folded her arms. "Oh, I'm sorry. I forgot how serious your knightly vows are to you. That's why you abandoned Zelda and fucked me for six hours in the wine cellar."

Calain scowled. "Do not mock my pain."

"Oh, poor sweeting," said Imodel, not unkindly. She got to her feet, picking up Calain's sword and sheath from the floor as she did. She offered them to the knight.

Calain took the sword and strapped it to her back once more. "I felt her *fucking* someone again," she said through her teeth.

"So *you* may fuck who you please but not fair Zelda?" pointed out Imodel, touching a finger to her lip in mock thought.

Calain paused and sputtered, "That's—That's not the point! I did stray *after* her betrayal! And this time I shall slay them – whoever they are!—and keep their head as a trophy!"

"*My*, aren't we bloodthirsty!" said Imodel gleefully. "If only I could go with you to see this bloodbath. Shall you kill Zelda as well?"

Calain frowned. The thought hadn't even crossed her mind. "What? No! Of course not!" she cried, horrified.

Imodel pouted. "Well, I suppose I'm not surprised. You do *love* her after all. . . ."

"I do *not* love her!" Calain shouted, pointing a warning finger at Imodel, who only giggled at her in great amusement.

"You're so cute when you're angry," Imodel said lustily, hunger in her blue eyes. Her big breasts jiggled slightly, and

Calain, feeling the arousal suddenly flush through her, groped one of Imodel's heavy breasts in a strong fist and kissed her roughly on the mouth.

Imodel shivered in Calain's grasp, and when Calain had turned away, she giggled and twirled a lock of yellow hair around her finger, staring after her in delight.

Calain mounted the stairs and had barely set foot on the landing when a sword came down on her. Her reflexes were immediate: she reached out and caught the wrist beneath the hand that held the sword, coming eye to eye with Eiran, who was sneering as he trembled in her grasp.

"This isn't a fight you shall win, Eiran," Calain calmly told him.

Eiran flushed angrily. "You dare!" he hissed. "You *dare* trespass on *our* land, fuck *my* sister—"

"Were you looking to fuck her yourself?" Calain mocked.

Eiran twisted free with a roar, startling Calain as he flipped away from her. Calain was staggered from the motion, and as she caught her balance, she saw Eiran land, crouched like a cat twenty feet away.

Calain slowly reached back for her sword, reminding herself that Eiran – though weaker than her – was still a trained assassin of Venom Six. He had been wearing the black uniform when first she met him, and it was likely he was proficient with a sword. His threats were not empty.

"I want no quarrel," Calain said.

"Then you should not have fucked my sister!" Eiran shouted and launched at Calain.

Their blades met, crossing hard. Calain gritted her teeth as she shoved Eiran off. He was not as strong as she, for she had the strength of three men, but he was light and fast. As Calain lumbered after him, he was quick to dodge and parry, always just out of her reach, leaving little cuts and slashes where he could, until Calain was dripping blood from her trousers and sleeves as she struggled, grunting and roaring, to catch him.

"Thought you would just stroll in here," snarled Eiran, "and take whatever you wanted! You humans took our land, and now you think you can take our women!"

"As if women were things to take!" Calain scoffed, bringing her sword down on Eiran so hard, he staggered as he parried. Calain roughly kicked him back before he had caught his footing and slashed him across the cheek. Blood tossed from the blow, and Calain came at Eiran again, punching him against the wall and dazing him, so that he dropped his sword. She pressed her forearm to his throat and held him in place, and he dangled there, gasping and sputtering and prying pointlessly at her muscly arm.

"I shall not slay thee," said Calain, "because it would hurt thy sister too greatly. But hear this: your sister is a woman grown, not a little girl and not a possession to defend. She lay with me because she chose to, and tis no business of yours." So saying, Calain sheathed her sword on her back and released Eiran, letting him drop to the floor. She could still hear him gasping and sputtering as she marched away.

Chapter 5

Zelda lay with Arryn on the giant stone brick, holding the smaller woman to her breasts, smoothing a loving hand again and again down Arryn's long black hair. All around them, white flowers swayed in the gentle breeze, birds were singing, and sunlight shed warm over their naked bodies. It was a beautiful day, and Arryn was the most beautiful part of it. So pale and shy and pretty, yielding to Zelda's hungry touch with a moan. Zelda couldn't stop thinking of how desperately Arryn had sobbed with arousal as Zelda's mouth had sucked upon her sex. How desperately she had twisted and blushed until suddenly, she had released her passion! Zelda wanted to taste her again, wanted to watch her curvy body heaving, wanted to see those violet eyes blinking yet again in bafflement and shock as the pleasure thrilled through her.

Arryn's eyes were closed now, and she was resting her head contently against Zelda's shoulder. Her cheeks flamed the tiniest bit when Zelda groped one of her small breasts.

"They are so small and soft . . . like the rest of you," Zelda whispered huskily as she massaged the little breast in her fingers, enjoying the supple give of it, the way the nipple hardened from her touch. She leaned closer and whispered in Arryn's pointed ear, "You surrendered to me so sweetly."

Zelda kissed Arryn hard on the mouth, and Arryn kissed her back with the same gentle submission, allowing Zelda to overpower her as she pleased. She was trembling in Zelda's arms when Zelda pulled away again.

"What's the matter?" Zelda whispered, kissing Arryn's forehead, her ear, her cheek.

Arryn shrugged, moaning when Zelda kissed the tender flesh between her neck and shoulder. "I love surrendering to you a little too greatly, my lady," she confessed. "It . . . frightens me."

Zelda kissed Arryn's lips again, nibbling the bottom lip as she pulled away. She smiled into Arryn's eyes, and Arryn smiled back.

"I suppose we had better get dressed," Zelda said with great regret. "I must find my way back to my baby. Will you come and see her?"

They sat up and began to dress. Arryn stepped into her woolen hose, and Zelda pulled up her panties.

"I have seen her already," Arryn confessed.

Zelda smiled. "I do not mean your spying. I mean I wish for you to properly meet her! And all the Falcon Knights! Selene and Gweneth and Cassandra would welcome you like a sister, I am certain of it." She let her gown fall over her head and adjusted it against her heavy breasts.

"And Calain?" said Arryn, smiling. She was struggling to buckle on her armor. Zelda drew near and helped her.

"Calain likely won't be at Wolf Fortress when I return, you know that," said Zelda quietly.

"And you've no intention of finding her?" said Arryn in amazement.

Zelda laughed mirthlessly. "Why? You told me already: Calain despises me! She thinks I abandoned her for Melvalda! She probably thinks I'm with Raven's Cross right now!"

"How does thou know what Calain thinks," said Arryn gently, "unless thou asketh her?"

Zelda dropped her eyes. Arryn was now fully armored, and Zelda turned heavily away, not wanting to think of Calain any longer. It was too painful. Behind her, Arryn buckled her scabbard across her chest, so that her sword was on her back. Her violet eyes were pitying as she watched Zelda's sadness.

"If you truly love Calain," said Arryn soothingly, "you will find some way to reconcile. Calain loves you. This I know."

"How do you know?" said Zelda to the ground.

"Because she's coming right now to slay me," answered Arryn.

Zelda looked up and went still in shock: Calain was marching at them through the trees, her face tight with rage, her red ponytail streaming. She was not wearing her silver Falcon armor and was instead clad in a tunic with the sleeves rolled up and plain trousers. She had been pulling a brown horse along by the reins, but she released it when she laid eyes on Arryn, she sneered, and her muscly arm bulged when she reached back for her blade.

"Gods be good," Arryn muttered weakly as Calain ran at her, big and strong and flexing with powerful muscles. Arryn pulled her blade just in time to parry a wild blow from Calain. Their blades sparked as they crossed.

"Calain, don't!" Zelda cried, aghast.

Calain ignored Zelda and pressed her blade down hard on shorter Arryn, who grimly held her at bay. "All that *lecturing* you did," Calain sneered, "about cherishing Zelda's heart and duty and honor – and you're fucking her behind my back!"

Arryn shoved Calain off. "Whose fault is that? If you hadn't abandoned your duty, I wouldn't have had to step in!"

Calain roared and ran at Arryn, who – being lighter and smaller – easily sidestepped her. Calain nearly lost her balance but caught herself and whirled, bringing her sword down on

Arryn again. They fell into a series of exchanged blows, blades clashing almost wildly. Arryn was merely parrying and deflecting, but Calain was trying almost desperately to draw blood. Her strikes were brutally hard, so that Arryn's blade trembled to repel her. She finally managed to disarm Arryn, who held out her hand and deflected a blow with a shield of light that sprang from her palm.

Calain shouted angrily as her blade harmlessly bounced off the light-shield. She ran at the shield, slashing at it madly, until Arryn's arm was trembling as it became difficult to sustain the spell. Lips tightening, Arryn held out her other hand, and Calain froze mid-swing, sword in hand. She was only able to move her eyes, and they darted back and forth in shock and fury.

"I shall take my leave," said Arryn breathlessly. She summoned her sword to her hand and sheathed it on her back, looking reprovingly at Calain through strings of black hair. "And you shall not follow, young knight. . .. If you know what is good for you. Fare thee well, fair Zelda." And with that, Arryn turned and marched into the trees. Calain remained frozen until she had gone.

When the spell had lifted, Calain dropped to her knees, clumsily losing her sword in the process. She reached for it in the leaves and closed her fingers on the hilt.

"Calain . . ." Zelda said apprehensively. She came to Calain and put a careful hand on her shoulder, but when Calain tensed against her touch, she drew her hand away, feeling stung.

Calain snatched her sword from the leaves and sheathed it on her back, her back to Zelda. "Do not touch me," she said in a low voice. "Only the gods do know where thy hand has been."

Zelda blushed angrily. "As if you had any room to talk! I felt you fucking other women, Calain!" she practically screeched.

Calain turned to face her in surprise, and Zelda was satisfied by the look of shame that passed through her green eyes. Those damned pretty green eyes. Zelda had to admit that, furious as she was, it was good to see Calain again. She had missed her eyes and her wild red hair, the sound of her voice, the way her muscles flexed when she moved . . . That puppy face she always made when she was guilty.

"That's right!" Zelda yelled at Calain, furious now, tousled hair falling in her blazing blue eyes. "The Binding goes both ways! Did you think I would not notice?!"

"I knew you would notice," said Calain darkly, "I just didn't think you would care." She marched past Zelda to the horse she'd abandoned, which was grazing nearby, indifferent to all that had happened.

"Why wouldn't I care?" demanded Zelda, turning to watch as Calain went to the horse.

"Because you were too busy riding Melvalda's fingers, perchance?" said Calain scathingly, not looking at Zelda. She was about to swing up into the saddle when Zelda rushed to her and grabbed her arm. She paused and looked down at Zelda angrily.

"Take thy hand from me," Calain complained. "There is nothing more to say—"

"There is *everything* to say, you *stubborn* . . .!" Zelda closed her eyes and took a breath to calm herself. They would get nowhere if they started name-calling. "I lay with Melvalda to protect you!"

"Horse shite," said Calain at once. "You lay with Melvalda because you wished to! I felt it when you did. You enjoyed what she did to you!" She glanced at Zelda's small hand again and said, "Release me."

"No!" Zelda said at once. "I shall never let you go!" She threw her arms around Calain's neck and hugged her tight. And then she went still, determined not to be pried away. To her surprise, Calain very slowly twisted around in Zelda's grasp and closed her strong arms around Zelda. She squeezed, hugging Zelda tightly to her, and neither of them knew why, but they suddenly began to cry.

"Thy shall send me to an early grave with thy madness," said Calain helplessly into Zelda's hair. "Why did thou lay with Melvalda! And Yrsa! And Arryn as well! I should kill them all for having touched you!"

"Oh! But that's how we got into this mess! You slew the queen!" Zelda said, pulling back to laugh through her tears.

Calain's eyes softened as she looked down at Zelda, and Zelda felt a thump in her. For a second, she was a virgin again, lying naked beside the waterfall, so breathless and nervous, as Calain came to her with hungry green eyes.

"I did miss thy laugh," Calain quietly confessed. "And thy eyes, the scent of thy hair . . ." She held Zelda close again and nuzzled her nose in her hair.

Zelda happily huddled in Calain's bulging arms and closed her eyes as all the old feelings of safety and happiness and content came rushing back to her. "Were you really going to abandon me?" she asked.

"You are rotten to the core and would have deserved it," Calain said, but she did not sound angry.

Zelda laughed weakly. "Yes," she admitted, "I would have . . . I wanted Melvalda. I . . . liked it when she touched me. But I wouldn't have gone to Ravenhold if she hadn't threatened you. I couldn't let all of you die for me defending Wolf Fortress!"

Calain pulled back and looked down at Zelda. "Then next time, speak to us, Zelda! We are not small children you must conceal. We are your knights! We should do things together, not alone!"

"I know that now," said Zelda, gazing lost in Calain's eyes.

Calain grudgingly smiled. "I did miss thy doting blue eyes," she confessed. She took Zelda by the waist and lifted her easily onto the horse, then climbed up behind her. "The port is just west of here. The elves of this island have told me. We could try to book passage and leave the island. You cannot apparate from here." So saying, Calain gently snapped the reins, and the horse started off at a trot.

As they rode along, Zelda could feel Calain's hard, muscular body against her own, and it suddenly felt as if everything in her world had finally been put right. For Calain was near her again, her hard body against Zelda's, her strong arms encircling her as she steered the horse, her warm breath upon Zelda's golden hair. The absence of it all was something Zelda never wanted to experience again! But then she reflected on Calain's words and found herself distracted.

"The elves of the island," Zelda repeated suspiciously. "Are these elves, perchance, the women you have lain with?"

"What does it matter?" said Calain evasively.

Zelda wasn't satisfied with that answer, but she supposed she had all the time in the world to drill and interrogate Calain until she learned the truth. It didn't seem fair that Calain knew who all her lovers had been. If Zelda wanted to confront one of Calain's lovers about staying away from Calain, she wouldn't know where to begin!

They rode for the port in silence, though Calain occasionally grabbed Zelda's bouncing breasts in playful fistfuls, making her giggle. She blushed a little, thinking of the first time Calain had touched her. It had been on horseback, and it had been the first time her sex was ever stroked, her clitoris massaged, her breasts groped. Her entire body had felt as if it was pulsing and throbbing and awake with desire, and then Calain had stripped her naked at the waterfall, and the rest was a blur of helpless orgasms as she was licked, sucked, and massaged for hours.

"What is my lady thinking of, I wonder?" said Calain when they had left the forest at last. "Thy cheeks are bright as any apple." She sounded a little suspicious. Perhaps she thought Zelda was thinking of Melvalda or one of her other lovers.

Zelda was embarrassed to admit it, but she answered, "The f-first time we made love."

Calain was silent a moment, then said quietly, "Oh." Zelda thought she seemed pleased by that and was in a good mood by the time they reached the port.

The port to Eldaris was packed with elves departing in cargo ships. Shipments of potions and herbs were being loaded in boxes onto the waiting ships as elves ran back and forth, preparing to depart.

The elves glared upon seeing them, and Zelda knew before they had even dismounted the horse that they would not find a ship willing to carry them across the sea. Once they overcame their shock and outrage that humans were on the island in the first place, the elven captains all sneered at them and turned them away, stating they would not give passage to humans. One captain mockingly gave them directions to the nearest Venom Six cell in the hope they would be riddled with arrows on approach.

"Why Arryn thought I would find a ship to take me across is beyond me," said Zelda tonelessly.

"She places greater faith in her people than they deserve," said Calain, putting a soothing arm around Zelda.

As they were standing there wondering what to do, a little elven girl came up to them. She had been carrying cargo boxes onto a boat, but having noticed their predicament, she dropped the box she'd been carrying, ducked beneath a long box that was being carried by two shirtless elven men ("Hey!" one of the men shouted), and ran up to Zelda and Calain, hair streaming.

Zelda looked down at the girl, whose auburn hair reminded her of Aereth. "Yes?" she said kindly.

"You won't get no ship out the port," said the little girl, speaking with the broken jargon of a peasant. "Cap'ns 'round here would sooner let you swim to Eldaris. But the mermaids hava ship under the water you can take. They might give it to you if you ask nicely, I reckon."

"Um . . . Thank you," said Calain awkwardly.

The child nodded seriously, then turned and ran off, back to the ship she'd come from. The men there were shouting for her to get back to work.

Calain looked down at Zelda. "Did any of that make sense to you?"

"Yes," said Zelda, feeling greatly relieved. "If the mermaids tell us where the ship is, I could raise it from the water and use it to carry us to Eldaris."

Calain stared off as it occurred to her. "Ah." She looked down at Zelda. "Then what are we waiting for? Let us make haste!"

Chapter 6

It had been years since Cassandra had been to Elwenhal. The first time she visited the realm of the fae, she was a child, having been lured there by the fairy queen. The queen of the fae took children for many reasons: boredom, hunger, to decorate her great tree-palace, to give as a reward to some minion who'd been promised payment. When Cassandra was stolen, it was because Queen Anindel was bored and sought a pretty child to entertain her court. She had chosen Cassandra because she'd heard her singing near the birdbath in one of the courtyards of Ravenhold.

Of course, Melvalda hadn't hesitated to enter Elwenhal and threaten the fairy queen to her face that if ever she touched Cassandra again, she would split her in halves with her mind. From that day onward, it was said that Melvalda was the only sorceress in all of Vallinwir who the queen of the fae had ever feared. It was Cassandra's only leverage now, as she walked through the great trees of Elwenhal, her hand on the sword at her hip.

The fae hated steel and metal. Cassandra could see them down in the undergrowth, watching with glowing eyes as she came. Some were tall as she and some were small, naked little men and women, wearing nutshells and bird beaks as hats, covered in moss and leaves and mud. They hissed when they saw the gleam of Cassandra's sword and the silver armor that encased her, hissed and retreated into the shadows.

Here in this world, it was always twilight. The orange and purple light of dusk reached long through the towering trees, stars winking on the dark edge of the sky, the distant moon hovering just above the ever-setting sun. Birds sang softly, trapped forever between day and night, and creatures growled and stirred, hunting in the dusk-light for prey that kept to the shadows.

Cassandra walked serenely forward, though her heart was racing in her chest. She called Aereth's name a few times and received no answer, though she was certain she was getting close. Aereth was a child born of magick, and as a result, she left a magick residue wherever she went that made it easy for a sorceress to follow her.

The third time Cassandra called Aereth's name, she heard a giggle. Cassandra turned her head, listening. Another giggle. "Aereth?" she called, and her voice seemed to echo through the still trees.

The giggling grew louder. A second later, and Aereth appeared, chasing a butterfly that kept landing on her nose. The child was happy and unhurt and wearing the same tunic, breeches, and bonnet that she wore back in the other world, where she was lying in pain in a bed, in Neserie's hut, in Eldaris.

Aereth rose up on her mud-stained knees and clapped her hands, attempting and failing yet another time to catch the butterfly. But she was having fun. She giggled and chased it again on all fours. The butterfly drifted on and landed on Cassandra's shoulder, opening and closing its orange wings slowly, and when Aereth laid eyes on Cassandra, she squealed in delight and clapped her hands.

Smiling, Cassandra leaned down and lifted the girl onto her hip. She was shocked by how big Aereth had grown. The girl was now roughly the size of a five-year-old but still could not walk.

"Sandra!" said Aereth, smiling through a gap in her teeth. She reached for Cassandra's face and giggled shrilly.

"Talking now, are we? And look at how big you are!" Cassandra said in wonder, holding the child in a tight arm. "Your mother will be amazed to see you . . . If we ever find our way out of here."

Cassandra glanced hopelessly around at the trees and curling vines and flowers. Neserie had warned her that she would have to find her own way out once she was in Elwenhal. At the time, Cassandra was confident that she would find her way back through a pool of water, since that was one certain way to enter the land of Elwenhal from Vallinwir, but looking around now, she realized she hadn't seen a pool of water since she'd been there. Not a pond, not a stream, not a lake.

The butterfly on Cassandra's shoulder lifted away suddenly, and Aereth let out a shriek of laughter and made a grab for it. As Cassandra watched, the butterfly hovered before them, and in a twinkle, took the shape of Queen Anindel, the fairy queen of Elwenhal.

Queen Anindel was just as Cassandra remembered her: quite tall and beautiful, with long pointed ears reaching from curtains of waist-length, blonde hair, and eyes that were as deeply green as her forests. Her eyes had always reminded Cassandra of Melvalda, for they were calculating and sometimes cruel. But she looked at Cassandra fondly now, her pink lips turning in a small smile.

"Cassandra," said Queen Anindel pleasantly, "you have returned to me."

"Not to you, my lady," Cassandra corrected. "I have come for the child."

"And shall you give yourself to me in her stead?" said the queen curiously.

"No, my lady," Cassandra answered. "I shall give you nothing."

Sudden giggling and twittering from the trees. The nearby fairies found that amusing. So did Queen Anindel, whose smile slowly widened.

"But you know the laws of this land," said Queen Anindel. "If you take something from Elwenhal, you must leave something in its place."

"Except the child is not truly here," Cassandra pointed out.

Anindel's eyes snapped irritably at this. "True," she admitted. "But the child *will* be here eventually, body and soul. Her mother will arrive for her too late. And you know what shall happen to you if you linger here. You, also, shall be trapped body and soul. Then you both shall be mine." She smiled. "As it should have been years ago."

Cassandra was once again reminded of Melvalda and hated to admit it, for she saw Anindel as an evil woman, stealing children from their cribs and giving them to her minions to toy with. She knew the only reason Aereth hadn't been tormented and harmed was because she wasn't truly present in the dimension yet. The fruit was still taking time to draw her over.

Cassandra closed a protective arm around Aereth, who had dropped her forehead against Cassandra and was watching Anindel quietly from behind wisps of auburn hair.

"Zelda will come in time," Cassandra said confidently. "And even if she doesn't, she would never allow you to keep her child! She will come here, and she is a sorceress mightier even than Melvalda."

More twittering from the trees. Cassandra's eyes moved back and forth, glaring at the unseen watchers.

Anindel had also laughed, her smile widening to reveal pin-point fangs at each corner. "Do you know why Melvalda is more powerful than I? Because she is half-fae and half-elf. A rare breed of halfling, for our kind do seldom lay with elven. But as a result, she is one of the most powerful mages in all of Vallinwir. It comes solely from her blood. She owes nothing to skill. This *Zelda* you speak of could not hope to match Melvalda's power. You are lying to unnerve me." She tilted her head. "Or perhaps to comfort yourself."

More giggling from the trees.

"Zelda will never let you keep her child," insisted Cassandra somberly. "*That* is the truth. Which you shall learn if you continue this foolhardy game."

Queen Anindel only smiled, her green eyes bright. "*We shall see.*"

The Mermaids of Menosea Book 6

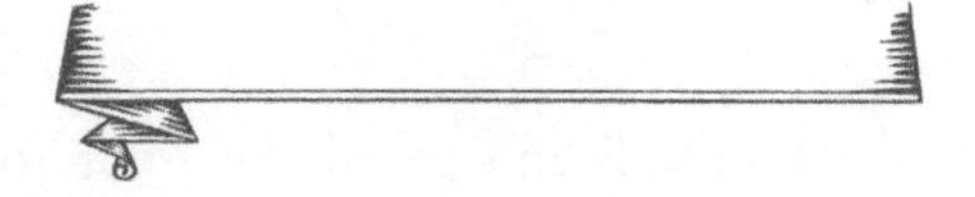

Chapter 1

Selene couldn't sit still and paced the front room of her grandmother's hut restlessly. Cassandra had been in Elwenhal with Aereth for days. Both were lying in a deep sleep in separate beds. Neserie had instructed Selene and Gweneth to take turns feeding Cassandra a mixture of honey and milk while she did the same for Aereth. Both still had a swallow response, because they were not truly in the realm of the fae, but rather sleeping as they passed through. The mixture was supposed to sustain them until Zelda came to Eldaris or until Cassandra found some way to return with the child, which Neserie didn't think she would.

And if Selene was honest with herself, she didn't believe Cassandra would return either. She and Gweneth had sent a letter by raven to Zelda, but the gods only knew if it had reached her. Aereth was slipping away into Elwenhal. They were running out of time.

"Stop pacing and sit down, for the sake of the gods," complained Neserie, who was mixing a potion over the firepit for a client. She tossed in a seagull's orange severed leg, and the cauldron expelled a floom of purple vapor, lining her grumpy, wrinkled face in shadows from under.

Selene stopped pacing and sat down. Obeying her grandmother was subconscious and automatic, since she had been conditioned to do so since she was a very small child with the slapping of a broom if she did not obey. Even now, as a big, strong knight capable of punching through stone, she remembered the broom coming down and mindlessly obeyed. In that moment, she was glad that Gweneth was in the other room with Cassandra and could not see her trauma on full display.

Sitting on a grass mat beside the fire, legs crossed, Selene felt like a little girl again as she watched her grandmother dramatically stirring the cauldron with a great ladle. She had always thought Neserie a true witch, so stereotypical was she, with her warty chin and her patched dress and her black, evil eyes.

That morning, Neserie's long gray hair had been plaited in two braids that trailed down her front and over her sagging breasts. Selene knew that, in her youth, her grandmother had been quite beautiful, and elven men had come from all over Vallinwir for her hand. But Neserie, like most sorceresses of old, did not care much for knights and never allowed one to pledge himself to her service nor did she take a man to her bed. Selene had always half-suspected her mother had been created with some potion or spell.

Looking at the stern woman now, Selene wondered what her life would have been like had she stayed in Eldaris and perhaps become a fish-netter.

"What . . . the devil are you . . . staring at, girl?" panted Neserie irritably, rocking forward and back as she stirred the cauldron. She was glossy with sweat from the heat of the fire and her efforts combined, and she paused to mop her brow with her apron.

"Why did thou send me to Falcon Isle?" Selene blurted. It was a question she'd been longing to ask all her life, since she was a little child too frightened to do so. "Was it because I'm too human?" Selene guessed unhappily.

Neserie continued mopping her brow with her apron, her face twisted in disdain as she stared bitterly at Selene. "No," she said, surprising Selene. "Though that was a part of it. So much of my strong elven blood was in you, yet you were born with the face of the filthy human who stole your mother from me." She paused to stare at Selene with great dislike.

"I am not my father," said Selene coldly.

"Oh, but you *are*," said Neserie unhappily. "Look at you! The same hair, the same eyes, the same blundering submission! And you became a knight because you *wanted* to—just like him! Before you even *knew* your father had been a knight, you were ranting on about it." She waved a dismissive hand. "But it's not the reason I left you there."

"Then why?" asked Selene in the same cold voice.

Neserie's eyes narrowed and she took an angry breath that flared her nostrils. "Because you were *common,*" she said through her yellow teeth. "Nothing remotely extraordinary about you. Cast spells weaker than farts, couldn't mix a potion worth a damn. Even your swordplay as you bounced around my yard was mediocre, but I knew the Falcon Knights would take you because they were low in numbers and desperate for recruits."

Selene sat stung and trying not to show it. She kept her face smooth and impassive as her grandmother went on.

"It's not your fault," Neserie said, taking up the ladle and stirring again, and her voice was not unkind. "Your mother was common as well, and she passed it to you." She paused, frowning in frustration. "I just don't understand it! I created her to be the most powerful sorceress in Vallinwir, to be the star of my legacy!" She bitterly shook her head. "But the girl had no magickal talent whatsoever! All she cared about was fishing! Fishing!" She bitterly shook her head another time and went back to stirring the cauldron.

"So," said Selene slowly, "you took me to Falcon Isle because tis what I wanted, and not because you despiseth me or despiseth children or humans?"

Neserie snorted. "I *despise* humans and I *despise* children, as you very well know! But . . . You are still my grandchild. You were my responsibility, and so was your happiness." She went back to stirring without another word.

Selene was very happy, for she knew Neserie had just come the closest she ever would to saying that she loved Selene. But Selene knew better than to show any emotion in the presence of her grandmother, who blanched at tears and touch, so she arranged her face into a cold mask and stared at the fire.

Just then, Gweneth came in, the jingle of her armor proceeding her, and sat on a grass mat beside Selene. "That our supper?" she teased, nodding at the cauldron. "I could go for some toad's eyes or whatever rubbish it is."

Neserie cackled, looking at Gweneth fondly. "You drink this half-concocted *mess*, and you'll turn into a duck, girl. And don't blame me!"

"'Twould be an improvement!" said Gweneth, opening her arms.

Gweneth and Neserie laughed, and Selene stared at them, caught somewhere between amazement and bitter jealousy. Gweneth and Neserie had been joking, laughing, and carrying on for days! Neserie seemed to like Gweneth more than she'd ever liked anyone, even Selene, her own grandchild! But Gweneth was a human, the very thing Neserie hated most!

Selene told herself it was because the two of them were so mean. Gweneth loved making jokes at the expense of others, even herself, and Neserie loved listening to her jokes, especially if they were aimed at Selene. Watching them now, Selene comforted herself with the fact that her grandmother had recently admitted to caring about her.

"Perhaps we both should drink it, Selene," said Gweneth, elbowing Selene. "Your grandmother seems fonder of ducks than we."

Selene wasn't feeling very quick-witted or jovial and did not readily have an answer. Thankfully, something happened that distracted everyone.

There was a sudden whooshing sound, not unlike the sound the ancient elven portals made when they were active, and Selene saw the air divided by a shimmering circle of light.

"You *dare* intrude here!" screeched Neserie, taking up her broom.

Selene and Gweneth scrambled to their feet and drew their blades. A shadow was coming through the light, a shadow in the shape of a knight! The knight was not wearing a helm. They could see the long black hair and the elven ears, the hint of a face. It was a woman.

Selene and Gweneth stood ready to fight as the knight stepped down into the room. The portal closed behind her and disappeared, causing everyone's hair – which had been beating about their faces – to fall limp.

Then the knight drew herself up and looked at them with her calm violet eyes. She was a small elven woman, clad in very ancient silver armor that had been engraved with delicate leaves and flowers. Her sword was an enchanted blade that glowed with blue light, but it was sheathed on her back, and her expression was serene: she did not wish to fight.

Seeing this, Selene and Gweneth lowered their blades, but to their shock – and to the shock of the strange knight – Neserie lunged forward and began beating the elven knight about her head with the broom.

"You *dare* – burst – in – here," Neserie shouted between whacks, "—and muddy my floor!"

And indeed, the elven knight had tracked mud across the wooden floorboards and all over the nearby throw rug, so that it was soiled.

The elven knight cringed from the blows. Then huffily, as if she'd had enough, she extended her hand and cast a light-shield, off which the broom harmlessly bounced, bits of straw flying.

Neserie stopped whacking and snorted, indignant that her righteous blows had been hindered.

"Grandmother, let us hear what this stranger doth have to say," Selene begged, and to her surprise, Neserie bitterly tossed the broom aside and went back to stirring her cauldron.

The stranger dissolved her light-shield by closing her open hand in a fist, and she straightened up, glancing around with hesitation. "Are there any more violent old women about? With forks, perhaps? I do not mind brooms so much, but sharper things might harm me."

Gweneth laughed, sheathing her sword on her back. "Who are you, stranger?"

Selene did not sheath her blade. "And why have you come?" she asked calmly.

"I am Arryn, a Knight of the Wolf," the stranger answered just as calmly, "and I have come with the news that fair Zelda is on her way to Eldaris, though she does not know you are here. She believes you at Ellondhold still. One of you should remain at the port and wait for her and Knight Calain to arrive."

"Calain?" said Selene sharply and exchanged a look with Gweneth.

"Are you one of Cilia's minions? What trick is this?" said Gweneth with a laugh.

"If it were a trick," answered Arryn, "'twere a poor one." With that, she turned away, extending her hand to open another portal. They watched as she passed through, and as the portal was shrinking from sight behind her, Neserie shouted after Arryn, "You knock next time! Or I'll use a fork!"

Chapter 2

As the elven girl had advised them, Zelda and Calain moved further along the beach, away from the port, traveling in the direction of the rocks that loomed in the shallows, wet from the waves and shining in the sun. It was where the mermaids usually sunbathed, according to the girl, but as they approached, Zelda's heart sank, for she could see none. The rocks were bare except for seashells and strings of seaweed.

Clinging to Calain's hand for balance, Zelda climbed out onto the rocks, found one that was leaning out like a precipice, and walked along it to the edge, beyond which the glittering *Arinath Sea* spread away to the opposite shore. Somewhere on that opposite shore, in the heart of Dark Bloom Forest, Zelda's daughter was waiting for her!

There was another rock growth at the precipice ledge that grew upright like a natural podium, and Zelda rested her hands upon it, looking out at the water. "My daughter is out there, Calain," Zelda said happily. "She will love you. I cannot wait until you have met."

Calain slid her strong arms around Zelda and hugged her sadly from behind. "I am sorry I was not there to help you birth her. You should never forgive me for abandoning my duty. Even if you had wronged me, you needed me. I should have been there."

Zelda rubbed Calain's arm. "It doesn't matter now. Let us put the matter behind us and think of all the happy days we shall spend together, watching Aereth grow to a woman."

"Is that what you named her? Pretty."

Zelda's eyes narrowed in thought as she gazed at the sea. "I wonder what she shall grow to be. A knight? A sorceress?" She smiled. "A basket weaver?"

"Melvalda wanted her for her power," Calain reminded Zelda. "That's what you said. She is to be a great sorceress."

"She'll have the natural ability, yes," said Zelda, "but she doesn't have to choose that. Look at Cassandra! She chose to be a knight. And you!"

Calain laughed softly. "Could you see me as anything other?"

"No," Zelda admitted, and they both laughed.

"I would never have fit into the world of motherhood and gowns," said Calain. "My father sent me away to Falcon Isle to give me a chance to be as I am and thrive. I know that now."

"And your mother?" said Zelda quietly. She had not forgotten what she had seen in Edolel's book, the memory of Calain learning that her mother had abandoned her, and now that they had reconciled, she couldn't help asking. She suddenly wanted to know everything about Calain there was to know.

Calain was still and silent for a time, then she said heavily, "I spent my entire life furious at my mother for abandoning us. Then I abandoned my family when they needed me most!" Calain smoothed a grieving hand over Zelda's flat belly, which once had been large with child. "Now I am no different from Lowri," she said in a low voice. "I cannot even hate her anymore."

"I am certain your mother had good reason for leaving," said Zelda soothingly.

"Yes, I know," said Calain. "Tis what angers me. I spent years thinking my mother an evil woman for turning her back. Now . .

. Now I wonder if there wasn't some grave reason for her absence, and I spent all the time pointlessly angry. Perhaps my pa wronged her. Perhaps her family forced her to come home. There could have been a million reasons, and my pa kept them from me, never told me the truth! I suppose he wanted me to love him and not her."

"Couldn't you find your father and ask him?" Zelda suggested gently.

Calain was quiet for so long, it made Zelda anxious. Finally, she said in a low, unhappy voice, "I cannot return there."

"But why?" Zelda wondered. "You may learn the truth! And you needn't beat yourself up over leaving me any longer. I may have done the same in your place. I confess, when I felt you with that other woman, I wanted to find you and *strangle* her."

Calain chuckled. "I did not think you capable of such fury, sweet Zelda. Not until I was standing there in the forest, and you screamed and screamed at me. In an odd way, I suppose I enjoyed it."

Zelda laughed as well. "You enjoyed it?"

"Well, I did not think you would care if I lay with another," Calain said. "Not when you were off with Melvalda and Raven's Cross. But then I saw how hurt and angry you were, and how you looked upon me as if you wished to burn me alive . . . and I knew you cared."

They laughed.

"Well, at least I finally got through to you. But you mustn't harm Arryn if we see her again," Zelda scolded. "She saved me from the wolves in the mist. She saved you as well! She has done nothing but watch over us and protect us."

"I suppose she hath nothing else to do," said Calain darkly.

"Calain," Zelda begged.

"All right!" Calain relented irritably. "If we see Arryn again, I shall try to be civil. I owe her my life, but that does not entitle her to my woman!"

Zelda smiled when Calain's arms closed tightly about her. She had to admit that she enjoyed how possessive Calain was. In all her life, no one had ever . . . *wanted* her. Her uncle had hated her and had dumped her at Vira'Toss, and most of the other mages at Vira'Toss had scorned and ignored her. She was a peasant and a lover of women, and so the women had avoided her. Zelda suspected that Wick alone hadn't feared befriending her because Wick, too, desired women. But Wick hated her as well. Before Calain, only Sian had ever cared about Zelda, cherished her, protected her, and now Sian was gone. She hadn't seen her since the day her uncle kicked the girl in the face, breaking her nose. Like Zelda, Sian had been dirt-poor and wouldn't have been able to afford a healer. It was likely the broken nose had become infected and she had died. In other words, her uncle had indirectly murdered Sian. Zelda decided to push the thought away.

"Who was the woman you laid with?" Zelda asked, startling Calain.

"Why the devil would thou wish to know that?" Calain asked in amazement.

"You know all of my lovers," said Zelda. "If you wanted, you could go forth and find Melvalda and chop her head off. But I have no idea who you've lain with! What if I wanted to slay them?"

Calain laughed in disbelief. "So I should give you their names, that you might slay them?"

"Yes!"

They laughed again.

"But I'm curious," Zelda said, serious now. "I keep wondering what they looked like, what you saw in them." What could have made Calain's heart stray, *s*he wondered.

"Well, why did thou want Melvalda? You share your secrets first."

Zelda smiled. "I suppose I wanted her because she's older and experienced. And she knows things. I enjoyed learning from her. Not that way!" she cried when Calain laughed quietly.

"I bet thou enjoyed it," Calain muttered, reminding Zelda of her conversation with Selene just days before. She wondered what Selene and Gweneth and Cassandra were doing. Were they playing with little Aereth? She tried to imagine them tossing Aereth in the air and tickling her and the thought made her smile.

"I lay with the woman who helped me escape the Gold Keep," Calain confessed. "You would not know her, so it isn't as if you could find her. She was an assassin, so I guarantee you could not."

"What did she look like?" asked Zelda, disappointed. She would have liked to scry the woman, at least. See her with her own eyes. But if the woman was an assassin, she probably wore a charm against such invasive spells.

"She looked like you," Calain softly admitted.

Zelda blushed a little. "So you have a type, then."

"Perhaps. . ." Calain said absently, and Zelda knew she was looking at her breasts. Zelda was wearing a pale blue gown, which was low around her bare shoulders, exposing her swollen cleavage to the cold sea air. It was a gown with nursing folds in the front, so that she could quickly free her breasts to feed Aereth. Cassandra had brought it to her along with the goats she'd purchased in town.

Zelda's suspicions were confirmed when Calain's strong hands closed on her breasts in fistfuls. "By the *gods* . . ." Calain muttered. "I have missed the feel of your massive tits in my hands." She tugged gently at Zelda's laces and watched the fabric fall away, exposing her high, plump breasts, which were still full of milk. The tiny pink nipples were rigid. "I suppose you missed my feeling them," teased Calain, referring to Zelda's hard nipples.

Zelda blushed to her hairline. She was indeed aroused from Calain's hungry touch, but she would not be distracted. She covered her breasts quickly with the loose fabric and said, "Who was your first love?"

Calain paused. "Why art thou asking me so many questions?" she said with a laugh.

It was because Edolel's book had made Zelda realize just how little she knew of Calain. The other Knights of Falcon knew more about Calain than she ever would! The way they had sat around the table with Calain at Wolf Fortress, laughing and teasing over food and wine. Zelda suddenly craved that intimacy, not just with Calain, but with all the knights.

"I want to know you," Zelda said.

Calain seemed pleased by that and closed her arms around Zelda's waist again. "As my lady commands," she said. "My first love? Don't believe I ever loved a woman before you. But my first kiss, that was Siobhan."

"Siobhan?" Zelda asked with interest. "Who was she?"

"Her parents died when she was little. She was our neighbor and had nowhere to go, and her father had been my father's friend, so Pa took her in," said Calain. "I was five when Pa sent me off to be a knight. Siobhan was four. She grabbed me and hugged me and then . . . kissed me on the mouth. Before that I'd thought she was my sister and asked Pa what was wrong with her, slobbering on me so."

Zelda laughed.

"She was my first kiss," Calain said a little wistfully. "Pa said she was always asking for me when I left. I used to dream of going back to the farm and stealing her away." For some reason, Calain grew quiet and sad, and Zelda wished she had not pried. It sounded like a painful memory, not unlike her memory of Sian. She was too afraid now to ask what had become of Siobhan.

Zelda turned to face Calain and kissed her on the mouth to sooth her. "Well," she said breathlessly, "I'm glad you chose to stay at Falcon Isle and become my knight. You're the best thing that's ever happened to me, Calain."

To Zelda's disappointment, Calain only looked down at her doubtfully.

"I place more faith in actions, fair Zelda," Calain said. "Not words. But I haven't forgotten how you screamed at me," she added with a smile, "so I shall believe thee for now."

Zelda smiled back but still felt a little sad. So she was right: Calain needed Zelda to *do* something to show that she cared. Words would never be enough.

Without warning, Calain took Zelda by the waist and lifted her easily, sitting her on the rock podium behind her. And then she roughly yanked Zelda's gown back open—which she had laced shut – so that one of her heavy breasts trembled free. Zelda blushed a little when Calain cupped it in a meaty hand and squeezed, watching with narrow eyes as the white milk beaded out. She leaned down and suckled deeply, and Zelda gasped when Calain's other hand yanked up her skirts and roughly plunged down the front of her panties, fingering her sex until her cheeks flushed, and she grew moist over Calain's roughly coaxing fingers.

Zelda fumbled blindly for the back of Calain's neck and cradled her head as she suckled. Her head fell back with a swing of her golden curls, and sitting there, legs wide, as she was fingered, sucked, and licked, she had to admit that she had missed Calain's rough aggression, her strength, and her relentless, unapologetic hunger. Calain was desperate to get at Zelda, pushing up her skirts, tugging at her laces, impatiently yanking at her panties, as if she longed to rip her clothes off right then and there. But it was the only gown Zelda had at the moment, and Calain was struggling so terribly to control herself that she was trembling.

In a daze of lust, Calain trailed hot, sloppy kisses up Zelda's neck to her mouth. Her tongue extended, so did Zelda's, and they closed mouths in an eager kiss. Calain was still fingering Zelda, her fingers gliding deeper and deeper through her moisture, curling so that Zelda's hips were almost thrusting with the motion. Zelda's lips gasped against Calain's, and Calain nibbled Zelda's pink bottom lip as she slid her fingers deeper, harder, until Zelda was rhythmically gasping and her cheeks blushing.

"Shall my lady scream for me?" Calain whispered huskily. She kissed Zelda's cheek and whispered in her ear, "No one is near . . ." She pulled back to glance over Zelda's body. She was looking at Zelda with green eyes that glittered hunger, and Zelda knew what she must've looked like to her: one breast hanging out, her golden hair tousled, her skirts hiked up, and her thighs spread. Calain had not removed her panties, and they were stretched over her muscly hand as she continued fingering, deeper, faster, Zelda's moisture washing over her again and again.

Calain showered Zelda's neck and shoulder with frantic kisses, and Zelda knew she was close to a climax. Her mouth found Zelda's nipple again, she sucked on it slowly as her fingers plunged deeper, her thumb gently massaging Zelda's clitoris. Zelda's lashes fluttered as her clitoris throbbed beneath Calain's firm touch, pulsing harder and harder, until she could not stifle her cries and indeed began to scream softly, breathlessly, again and again. With her head back as Calain suckled her large breast, she stared, unseeing, at the blue sky, her pink lips parted, and she screamed in shock and delight as she climaxed, her body trembling all over.

Calain suddenly closed her arms around Zelda and held her tightly, kissing her neck, her cheek, as Zelda trembled in the strong wall of her arms. In the wake of her climax, Zelda sagged in Calain's arms, panting to catch her breath and deliciously tired. Calain was still holding her so tightly.

"If only . . . I could rip off . . . thy gown," panted Calain, pulling back to look down at Zelda with the same hungry eyes. She kissed Zelda's lips and whispered, "You shall sit on my face one day, shant you?" She kissed Zelda's mouth again and again. "Shant you?" she whispered between breathless kisses.

"Y-Yes," Zelda panted, blushing bright at the thought, and caught Calain's lips to hers, sliding her tongue in her mouth in another passionate kiss.

"You sat on Gweneth's face but not mine," said Calain. "Tis not fair!" She dropped her forehead against Zelda's, and they laughed, staring warmly in each other's eyes.

"What *is* all the screaming and moaning about? And may I join?" asked a delighted voice.

Breathless, Zelda and Calain glanced around and noticed a woman's head and arms had appeared on the rock at their feet. She was leaning forward out of the water . . . and she was completely naked. No smallclothes, nothing. Her narrow, naked back disappeared into the water, and her big breasts sat on the rock, crushed together in great mounds of cleavage. Long red hair framed her heart-shaped face, falling smooth either side bright blue eyes with pupils that were narrowed like a beast's. Zelda would have thought her an elf if not for her startling eyes.

"What . . . Who are you?!" cried Zelda, hastily tucking her breasts away.

"You don't look very bright, bless your heart," answered the woman in the water, "so I shall tell you plainly: I am a mermaid." Behind her, her legs splashed up, and the toes were webbed. They could momentarily see her backside bobbing on the surface of the water before she dipped her hips down again.

"Oh," said Calain, happily relieved. "We've been looking for thee all morning!"

The mermaid glanced up and down Calain's muscular frame. "Have you now, my beauty?"

Calain smiled at that, but when Zelda looked at her indignantly, she sheepishly cast her eyes down.

Zelda snapped up from the rock podium, standing pointedly in front of Calain. "Yes," she said sternly, "we have. We are stranded here on Menosea. We need a way back, and a girl at the port told us you could help."

"The elves wouldn't help you, eh? Typical," said the mermaid, highly amused.

Zelda went on to explain about the ship the elven girl at the port had mentioned, and to her surprise, the mermaid listened to her politely, leaning her folded arms upon the rock and staring up at her intently, as if Zelda and Calain's unfortunate situation were of the utmost concern. Zelda wished the woman would cover her breasts or at least sink them beneath the water, but she seemed to enjoy Calain's discomfort and her silent struggle not to look at them.

When Zelda had finished speaking, the mermaid tisked. "Hmm. That *is* a predicament, isn't it? Yes, my fellow mermaids and I *do* know of a sunken ship nearby, and yes, I *could* point you toward it . . . But then," her eyes moved to Calain, "you would leave me!" she said, sticking out her bottom lip in a pout. "And I would miss you so terribly!" She smiled up at Calain and fluttered her lashes prettily. Behind her, her little foot came up again, playfully kicking the water, the webbed toes spread.

Calain smiled, amused by the mermaid's flirting, but Zelda was *not* amused. She said at once, brusquely and coldly, "No. You may *not* have Calain. She is my knight. She is Bound to me!"

"And yet, she doth lay with other women," pointed out the mermaid, smirking. "I heard you arguing up and down the beach. You were loud enough to wake the gods themselves, but mermaids have fantastic hearing regardless." Her pointed ear, which was webbed along the bottom edge, twitched as she spoke.

It was true that Zelda and Calain had argued. Zelda, who was anxious to return to Aereth and feared they were stranded, had lost her patience, blaming Calain for the situation they were in and yelling at her once more for having lain with other women. Calain had shouted back – like a stammering adolescent – that Zelda had started it by lying with Melvalda. They bickered until they were exhausted, and somehow, had wound up making love on the rock.

Zelda didn't think she could withstand it again so soon, feeling Calain's excitement as she lay with another. She was still furious about the last woman Calain had lain with – while Zelda was off weeping for her, giving birth, and being attacked by monsters in dark dimensions!

"You expect me to let you lay with Calain," said Zelda through her teeth, "or else we shall be stranded here?"

The mermaid smiled and blinked innocently.

Zelda started to glow with power. "Do you understand that I am a sorceress? That I could turn you inside-out by blinking?!" Her voice was rising.

"Whatever you can do," returned the mermaid in a bored voice, "it mustn't be much if your knight hath strayed."

"Oo!" Zelda screamed and raised her fist, prepared to dive down and punch the mermaid square in the face. Behind her, Calain gasped her name in shock and grabbed her slender wrist to stop her. Calain's big arm locked around Zelda's waist, holding her back as she squirmed, intent on attacking the mermaid. Realizing she could not break free of Calain without magick – and not wanting to harm Calain—Zelda took a breath to control herself. Calain hesitated and let go.

The mermaid didn't seem bothered by Zelda's anger. "I shall meet thee on the beach in one hour's time." Her eyes moved between them, silently laughing. "I shall let the two of you . . . mull it over." With that, she sank away beneath the water with a soft plop.

Chapter 3

Calain couldn't understand why Zelda was so angry about the mermaid's proposition, but if she was honest with herself, it pleased her greatly to see Zelda, red-faced and furious, attempting to punch someone in her defense! Before that moment, it hadn't occurred to her how possessive Zelda was of her, a fact which she enjoyed immensely. But because Zelda seemed truly upset with how things were going – and because most of it was Calain's own fault – Calain tried to conceal how pleased she was as they walked along the beach together against the gentle wind.

It was a fine day. The sun was bright, the sky was blue, and the sea was calm. In the distance, they could see ships streaming across the still water in the direction of Eldaris. That none of the ships had consented to carry them still infuriated Zelda, who was watching their sails angrily, her blue eyes narrowed. Calain wasn't bothered, though. She hadn't expected the elves to help them and thought they had every right to be suspicious of two humans who had mysteriously appeared on an elven island where they were specifically not allowed to linger.

"How did we come to be here anyway?" Calain asked. Between all the arguing, kissing, and random sex, it had only just occurred to her to ask. They stood side by side on the yellow sand as the brown horse, Lucky, lingered idly behind them, his mane and tail streaming in the wind.

Zelda explained about her journey to Alleren to free Calain and the queen's task that she should venture into Eido Loth to find Lythara, who had in turn banished them here under the suspicion that Zelda was working for Hidden Dragon.

"Me, a spy for the elven resistance!" Zelda cried and shook her head. "The utter absurdity!"

But Calain was smiling. "You did all of that for me?" she asked in soft amazement.

Zelda stammered and blushed a little, not meeting Calain's gaze. "Well, I thought you were in danger," she said, looking off at the sea, the wind dragging her golden hair in streams across her eyes. She was embarrassed!

Calain grasped Zelda's shoulders and gently turned the sorceress to face her. "Why dost thou try so hard to conceal thy heart's yearnings?" she asked. "If only you were more open, I would know that you cared."

Zelda looked up at Calain in disbelief. "I tell you all the *time* that I love you! I cannot control that you do not believe it!"

Calain shook her head. "Words are worth the wind," she said. "Who knows that better than I, a knight who turned her back on her vows?" she added guiltily. "But knowing thy did go through so much trouble to save me . . . I don't know what to think. I only know it makes me love thee all the more . . . Would that I could rip thy gown to shreds to show thee how much, but my lady would never forgive me."

Zelda laughed. "That's right, I would not!" she cried, clutching indignantly at the front of her gown.

"But I would love to see thee lying naked on the sand," Calain whispered.

Calain closed her arms around Zelda, hooked them under Zelda's backside, and lifted Zelda off her feet, leaning back to gaze up at her. Zelda's cheeks flushed pink from the sudden lifting, and she fumbled quickly to brace her small hands on Calain's strong shoulders as she gazed down at her. Her blue eyes were soft with affection as golden licks of hair streamed across them in the wind.

"You are so beautiful, Zelda," said Calain, gazing up at Zelda absently. "I suppose it isn't surprising that so many women have tried to lay claim to you. I shall have my hands full the rest of my life, trying to beat them away with my blade."

Zelda laughed, her golden brows pinching in a frown. "And I don't have competition? That infernal mermaid wants you, not I! And you want her!"

"I do n-not!" Calain said at once and hated the stammer in her voice that betrayed her.

Zelda lifted a skeptical brow.

Calain set Zelda on her feet again. "What if I lay with the mermaid—" (Zelda scowled) "—just the once! And then she will aid us, and we can return to Wolf Fortress! Your daughter is waiting for us, Zelda!"

"Our daughter," Zelda corrected, "for you shall aid me in raising her. And what if the mermaid doth try to steal thee? There are so many stories of them dragging people beneath the sea . . ." She looked up at Calain anxiously.

"You shall stay near and watch," said Calain, so that Zelda colored up.

"I shall not!" Zelda said hotly at once but bit her lip, and Calain knew she was thinking of all the times she had had sex with Selene in front of Calain, forcing Calain to watch. Now she was refusing to be subjected to the same – even if it meant finding their way home—and the unfairness of it had just occurred to her. She cast her eyes down.

It was then that Calain noticed the jewel around Zelda's throat. It was blue and matched her eyes almost perfectly. She pinched it in her thumb and index finger to examine it and saw Zelda's cheeks flame a little.

"One of your lovers did give this to you," Calain guessed and sounded a little suspicious, if not downright angry. She scowled. "Please tell me you weren't foolish enough to take anything Melvalda offered! What if she cursed it? Or used it to bind you together?"

Zelda colored up angrily and snatched the jewel from Calain.

"Or was it Yrsa?" said Calain darkly. "Did you flee back to your 'bear queen' in my absence?" She glanced down at Zelda's stomach. "Did you make another child?"

Zelda's breasts heaved. "It was a gift from Selene!" she said loudly. "She gave me it to me, and I charmed it to protect me from Bane Stones!"

Calain didn't know why, but she was amused by that. Selene was very obviously trying to woo Zelda, to make Zelda love her more. By giving Zelda an ornament to wear, she had ensured that Zelda would think of her from time to time. She had purchased space in Zelda's mind.

Calain knew she would have to give Zelda something now. Even though she knew Selene could never take her place in Zelda's heart – for Calain was the one who had touched Zelda first, who had given Zelda her first passion—she could feel the competition closing in. It thrilled her a little, as the prospect of besting Selene always thrilled her.

"What . . . are you *smiling* for?" asked Zelda in amazement. She sounded both confused and amused.

Calain looked up and realized she had gone off into a reverie, that she was smiling to herself. "Nothing," she said at once. "But I do believe I should lay with the mermaid."

Zelda's face darkened. "Because you want to or to leave this place?"

"To leave this place!" Calain insisted, though she knew she was lying. The mermaid's breasts were fantastic, and Calain had wanted to grope them the moment she had seen them, something she suspected the mermaid very well knew.

Zelda seemed to know it, too. She was glaring steadily at Calain, and Calain had never seen her so frustrated: Zelda wanted to leave the island, but she did not want to share Calain with the mermaid.

"It will be over quickly," Calain assured her. "Do you not wish to leave this place? The elves are likely to slay us in our sleep if we stay."

Zelda heaved a shuddering breath. "*Fine*," she said through her teeth. "But if she tries to take you, I shall slay her, and we shall find another way off the island."

"As my lady commands," answered Calain, who found Zelda's shuddering fury both amusing and arousing. She had to keep resisting the urge to kiss Zelda, for Zelda seemed likely to shove her off in that moment.

They heard sloshing in the shallows and looked up to see the mermaid rising slowly from the water. Seawater cascaded her over body, dragging down her long red hair, dripping off her pointed ears and her sharp nipples, and dragging down the red pubic hair that cloaked her sex. She was shaped like Zelda, which meant she was shaped just the way Calain liked: hourglass curves, with round hips and large breasts, her waist tiny, her smooth belly flat. Curiously enough, she had no belly button and there were little fins on her ankles.

Calain tried not to gaze upon the mermaid with lust, for Zelda caught her eye and glared hard at her. Calain still couldn't quite believe the rage and possessiveness Zelda was displaying and didn't know what to think. All she knew was, she wanted to make love to Zelda, fiercely and roughly, every time her angry blue eyes turned upon the mermaid. Zelda was like a dragon guarding her hoard the way she stared down the mermaid, and Calain was that precious hoard. It thrilled her.

"Do not worry, fair Zelda," Calain said quietly. "I belong to thee."

Zelda smiled.

As they watched, the mermaid waded serenely toward them, hips swaying, as the sea lapped at her dainty ankles. She came to a stop some ten feet away, calmly observing them. Her smirking cat-eyes went from Zelda's angry face to Calain, who was trying very hard not to look too pleased about the situation.

"So," said the mermaid, "have you decided?" She looked between them again.

"And you swear you shall tell us where the ship is?" pressed Calain.

The mermaid's eyes laughed. "Words are worth the wind, fair knight. Is that not what you have whispered to your lover?"

Zelda heaved an angry breath. "If you go back on your word, you will *be* the wind," she warned darkly.

The mermaid lifted her red brows. "Ooo! I like her!" she said to Calain.

So do I, thought Calain, who was looking at Zelda's flushed face and heaving breasts with quiet arousal. But she turned her eyes with difficulty back to the mermaid and said, "I shall lay with thee, and thou shall tell us where the ship lies."

"Agreed," said the mermaid, slowly smiling as she gazed with longing up at Calain.

Calain turned without a word to Zelda and yanked her laces free.

Zelda gasped as her gown, then her slip, then her panties tumbled around her ankles from the quick snatch of Calain's rough hands. She covered her heavy breasts in shock, which the mermaid was eying. "Calain, what—?!" was all Zelda managed before Calain had leaned forward and casually flipped both Zelda and mermaid over her shoulders and stomped off with them.

Chapter 4

After much debate, Selene and Gweneth decided that the strange knight who'd burst into Neserie's house through a portal had in fact been telling the truth. For while elven knights weren't exactly fond of humans, they also didn't go out of their way to deliver messages to them without serious cause, nor would one bother taking a portal across the realm just to set a trap. If anything, by walking up to Selene and Gweneth with her sword sheathed, Arryn had made herself vulnerable. She easily could have been slain! If Calain had been there, there was no doubt in Selene's mind that the red knight would have run Arryn through before she'd fully left the portal.

And if Arryn really was a Wolf Knight, then she had no allegiance to anyone, not even Queen Carys. Wolf Knights were exiles and rogues, having been commanded by the mages of Menosea to lay down arms. It was not the way of the elven to engage in open fighting. No, the mages of Menosea would rather take back the realms through stealth and sabotage, if the rumors in Eldaris were anything to go by. The elves treated their knights as relics of a bygone era, while their assassins were venerated.

Selene was relieved to know that Calain was safe and was on her way there with Zelda. Once the sorceress arrived, she would be able to enter Elwenhal and rescue both Cassandra and Aereth. The only thing that worried Selene was the fact that Zelda must go there alone. Zelda was a powerful sorceress, but could she slay the fairy queen?

Selene supposed there were ways Zelda might outwit the woman. Fairies were highly susceptible to Bane Stones, as well as iron. Zelda could waltz into Elwenhal with a sword while never casting a spell, and the creatures would scatter in horror. Knowing that was enough to comfort Selene that at least Cassandra, who was fully armored and armed as she dreamt, had not ventured into the land of the fae completely defenseless.

The sun was setting when Selene, needing a breath of fresh air, decided to sit on the step outside her grandmother's house. She watched a little sadly as the elven children ran up and down the street, chased once again by their little dog, who nipped playfully at their heels. Some small part of her almost wished she had stayed in Eldaris a little while longer, been a carefree child for a few more years. Knight training was demanding, often forcing young girls to grow into women overnight. When one was training to become a knight, there was very little time for play, and those early years of youth were spent studying history and learning swordplay. But it couldn't be helped, for little girls had no choice but to begin their training early: the potion that would make them big and strong had to take effect before they reached puberty.

As Selene sat on the step, lost in thought, she heard the front door of the hut open and shut behind her, and then Gweneth sat on the step beside her. She seemed pleased about something.

"Your grandmother is hilarious," said Gweneth to Selene's unspoken question. "I thought she'd be a right demon, but she doesn't take herself seriously. And she doth know how to trade blow for blow with that sharp tongue of hers." She elbowed Selene and wagged her brows. "Wonder what she was like when she was young, eh? She has *huge* tits. Bet they were fine as any goddess. If she were younger, I'd make a lay of her so fast—"

"*Gwen*, would you not wonder aloud about my grandmother's breasts? I would rather not lose my noon meal all over my nice shiny armor," said Selene tiredly, and Gweneth laughed.

"Then best learn to projectile vomit."

Selene couldn't help laughing at that.

"What are you moping out here for?" Gweneth asked. "Worried about everyone? Tis your way, I know."

"Everything used to be so simple," Selene said heavily. "Seems since the moment we left Falcon Isle, we have been in peril."

"Amen to that," agreed Gweneth. "But things will settle down. Zelda will return, she'll bring back Cassie and Aereth, and then we shall all go home to Wolf Fortress and get drunk and live happily ever after." So saying, she lifted a skin of wine she'd taken from the hut and squirted a red stream into her mouth.

Selene gave a toneless laugh. "I hope you are right. I shall need a week's sleep after all this stress and bother."

"Sleep? I shall need a week's worth of fucking! All this trouble we've gone through for Zelda, minding her babe and scrubbing the fortress floors! I expect many hours loving for this."

Selene made a face. "Sex is not a barter or an exchange. It is an act of love between—!"

"Yes, yes, I was *jesting*, Selene," said Gweneth tiredly. "By the *gods.*" She squirted more wine in her mouth.

Selene bit her lip. "I apologize. I'm in a foul mood. I haven't slept well since Aereth took ill."

"No, since Calain left us," Gweneth corrected. "I've been marking it." She sighed. "And one of us has to go down to the port and wait for Zelda, which means the other shall have to stay here and mind Cassandra. Seems neither us shall sleep tonight. And all this because of Calain!"

"Be fair, Gwen. It isn't *all* Calain's fault. Imagine things from her perspective. She is Bound to Zelda! Each time Zelda lays with another, she feels it! If it were me, it would have driven me howling."

"Aye. Calain was already crazy *before* she was Bound. Being driven to jealousy has just made her worse. The knot she left on my head! Love has made her absolutely mad."

"And what about you?" said Selene in amusement. "You care for Zelda. I see it every day."

"Yes, and I'm absolutely mad for it," said Gweneth with a nod, and Selene laughed. Gweneth waved a hand. "Look at me, sitting here, steeped in this insanity! It wasn't supposed to be this way. I was supposed to become the knight of a river girl and go back with her to Low River and guard her talisman shop or what have you. But instead, I am here, waiting for my friend to come back from the fairy realm, and my *other* friend to return with our lady from some *other* mad venture!" She shook her head and squirted more wine in her mouth.

"Do you regret it?" said Selene, who had watched Gweneth rant in quiet amusement.

"Not a bit," said Gweneth at once, with such a casual air that Selene laughed.

"But I do look forward to settling down," Gweneth went on. "I think we all shall need a long rest after this string of events."

"I wonder if we have been pardoned," said Selene. "The Knight of the Wolf didn't say. She just mentioned that Calain was with Zelda."

"I can't say I care much," Gweneth admitted. "I have no special place in my heart for Eriallon. Let Queen Cilia banish us!"

"That's right," said Selene, remembering. "You're not from Eriallon, are you?"

"No. I hail from Ellormest. Many elven ruins there, ancient things, old places the rest of the world has forgotten. It would be a good place to settle instead of returning to Wolf Fortress."

"Aye. If Queen Cilia hasn't pardoned us, then it would be foolhardy to return to Wolf Fortress with her knowing we were there," agreed Selene.

"We shall have to discuss it with Zelda," said Gweneth thoughtfully, "but Ellormest would be a good place to take the child. Tis mostly wilderness, a few villages, wandering nomads, no large cities like in Eriallon and Koradara."

"Mostly *wilderness*? And you want to raise Aereth there?"

"She would be hidden from the dangers of the city," said Gweneth almost defensively. "You wouldn't understand, Selene. You grew up in this little village, in a small community, where you were protected by your grandmother, a powerful, scary, old witch! The city is no place for a young girl."

Gweneth sounded very bitter as she was speaking, and Selene remembered that Gweneth hated the city specifically because she had grown up in the wild. Selene knew that if she were to tell Gweneth about Zelda's near-rape in Ternia, she would just see it as proof that cities were dangerous. And perhaps she wouldn't be wrong.

"So how came you all the way from Ellormest to Eriallon?" asked Selene. "You never told me as I recall."

"Well, Ellormest is all wilderness and roaming nomads, eh? If I wanted to be a knight, there was no academy nearby. I would have to leave my home. Eriallon and Falcon Isle were closest. So my mother and father put me on a wagon and kissed me goodbye."

"Just like that?" said Selene in surprise.

"Well—no," Gweneth admitted. "My mother didn't want me to run off and be a knight. She wanted me to stay with the caravan, learn the herbalist trade from her. And my father, he didn't want to let me out of his sight. Was afeared for me so far away in another realm. But my parents have six other girls, so I don't suppose they were too fussed."

Selene laughed flatly. "I bet they wept for you every night," she teased.

Gweneth smiled.

"So we all became knights because we wanted to," Selene realized. "Cassandra didn't want to be a sorceress, Calain wanted to be a knight, I wanted it, you wanted it. . ."

"Were you expecting a sob story?" Gweneth said, lightly teasing.

"Yes," Selene admitted. "I thought we all had them."

"No. You're the only one," said Gweneth, grinning, and she laughed when Selene gave her a playful shove.

"But come, Selene," said Gweneth seriously and nodded at the village. "You didn't have it that bad."

Selene glanced around at the quiet little village. There were people sitting on their steps, strumming lutes, brushing each other's hair, singing and happy in the drowsy content of twilight. Mothers called children home, fathers tossed their daughters in the air. Selene saw a brother and sister skipping home through a thin patch of grass, a bucket of seashells in ones hand. It was a cozy, content little village, with no crime and little violence, where nothing much ever really happened, and because of that, the elves of Eldaris enjoyed a freedom that the elves in the city did not – *Selene* had enjoyed a freedom the children in the city did not, even if she had been lonely, even if her grandmother hadn't been the most affectionate. She looked around and suddenly realized it could have been far worse.

"No," said Selene, watching wistfully as the sun set beyond the spread of the rooftops, "I suppose I didn't have it that bad at all."

Chapter 5

Calain found a lone palm tree standing along the beach, casting a cool shadow over the sand, and there, in a patch of wet grass, she laid Zelda and the mermaid down and proceeded to make love to them both. Zelda was shocked but could only gasp when Calain slid her large fingers, sudden and hard, between the fuzzy blonde lips of Zelda's sex, then buried her face between the mermaid's thighs, nuzzling her nose against the red hair there.

The mermaid was in ecstasy, thrusting her great jiggling breasts to the sky, gasping, crying out, her pale cheeks flaming, her cat-eyes hooded in a daze as Calain grunted and moaned, her redhead moving between the mermaid's trembling thighs almost ravenously. Zelda wanted to be angry, but she didn't even have time to watch or be furious and jealous, for Calain was fingering Zelda even as she was sucking upon the mermaid's sex, and it was so delicious, Zelda was melting in the grass and sand, her eyes closed, moaning as Calain's strong fingers roughly coaxed her to arousal. Her clitoris was throbbing so hard, it was maddening, and Calain's thumb stroked it, coaxing it to pump faster and faster, causing her sex to swell hungrily with blood.

Eventually, Calain's fingers were thrusting so hard that Zelda's hips were jerking with them. Her sex released, the moisture gliding hot over Calain's relentless fingers, until she was crying out, as beside her, the mermaid also screamed softly, at the mercy of Calain's hungry lips and tongue.

Then Calain switched and her mouth was between Zelda's thighs, hot and eager, as her hand went to both women's breasts. She caressed and massaged their breasts as she slid her tongue hard and deep inside Zelda, who blushed and twisted on her back, thrusting her big breasts to the sky. She glanced down and realized Calain was watching her and enjoying the sight of her curvy body gyrating against the pleasure. Calain's cheeks were the slightest red and her green eyes were narrowed with silent satisfaction. She looked at Zelda as if she would devour her and seemed intent on doing just that as her head moved fast between Zelda's trembling thighs.

Zelda was very pleased to see the mermaid watching Calain with longing, no doubt wishing she had tasted her with the same passion. But Calain's true passion was for Zelda.

Breathless, breasts heaving, Zelda reached down and caressed Calain's red hair. Calain closed her eyes and slid her tongue deeper, frowning with delight, her strong hand massaging Zelda's heavy breast until it flushed with pleasure and white milk beaded free.

Calain leaned up and suckled gently on Zelda's dripping nipple. Then her breathless mouth found Zelda's mouth in a messy, passionate kiss. She was still groping the mermaid's big breast, and she went to it next, sucking it slowly, pausing to drag her tongue around the nipple, so that it hardened yet more and the mermaid sighed.

But even as Calain was suckling at the mermaid's breasts, she never took her hand from Zelda. The hand that groped Zelda's breast so hard smoothed down her trembling belly to her sex, and the fingers slid in again, roughly curling, so that Zelda gasped as the pleasure flushed through her afresh. Before long, her hips were thrusting again as Calain aggressively coaxed her toward a climax.

Breathless and panting, Zelda frowned, closed her eyes, and arched her back against the sand, thrusting her breasts to the sky as Calain's fingers worked her hard. She was embarrassed by her own screams, but by the *gods*, Calain's touch was torturous, and she was vaguely aware of the mermaid screaming in soft shock beside her as she, too, was fingered hard toward a climax.

They screamed out together, Zelda and the mermaid, and in the silence that followed, Zelda could hear panting from them all, and the soft sound of lips touching skin. Zelda opened her eyes and saw Calain trailing slow kisses up the mermaid's belly, over her breasts. She paused to pull on the mermaid's pink nipple, sucking it into her lips and releasing it, so that the heavy breast wobbled. Then she kissed the mermaid's neck, her cheek, and finally, she plunged her tongue in the mermaid's mouth, and they kissed hungrily.

Zelda lay there, watching breathlessly, and felt her sex swelling with arousal again. Calain still hadn't taken her hand from Zelda, and now she hooked her hand on Zelda's waist and easily drew her near, as if she had picked up a pillow. She turned on her back, clutching small Zelda in one arm. The mermaid snuggled in Calain's other arm, and they all lay there, breathless beneath the palm tree, as sunlight streamed warm over their skin.

Huddled in Calain's tight, strong arm, Zelda breathlessly rested her cheek against Calain's shoulder and laid her hand on Calain's chest. Through the web of her tousled golden hair, she looked across and saw the mermaid doing the same. The narrow pupil of her cat-eye peeked at Zelda from behind strings of red hair and she smiled. She reached over with a webbed hand and stroked Zelda's cheek with the back of her fingers. Zelda blushed a little, surprised by this affection.

Still panting to catch her breath, the mermaid closed her eyes. Calain smoothed a hard hand over the mermaid's backside and squeezed. The mermaid giggled. Then Zelda felt Calain grope her backside as well and couldn't help also giggling. Calain always made her feel like a silly little girl, so flustered and embarrassed! But she liked it. The feel of Calain's strong hand so hungry on her backside made her clitoris throb gently.

Zelda glanced up. Calain was still looking at them with eyes that burned lust. She smiled and suddenly spanked their backsides. It was a playful wallop that made both of them giggle, their eyes flying wide in surprise. Calain spanked them again and again, so that they giggled harder and harder, their big breasts jiggling against her, which she seemed to enjoy watching.

Then, green eyes still narrow with hunger, Calain's hands smoothed over both their backsides, and her fingers slid in their sexes. Zelda and the mermaid both lay on Calain's chest, watching each other gasp and sigh in shock and delight as they were fingered from behind. They arched their backs, thrusting out their backsides, not to admit Calain's fingers further – which was what happened – but in automatic response to the startling pleasure.

Calain fingered them deep and slow, watching them sigh, gently plunging her fingers, as if to savor the sensation of their tight lips squeezing around them.

Zelda was becoming incredibly aroused, not just from Calain's touch, but also from watching the mermaid sighing and twisting helplessly opposite her. Calain was right: the mermaid *did* have fantastic breasts. They were perfect, so plump and full, and the nipples were rock-hard.

Even as she gasped helplessly from Calain's fingering, Zelda's eyes traveled to the mermaid's face and she realized the woman was watching her as well. The mermaid's cat-eyes were filled with lust. She leaned over, cupped Zelda's face, and kissed Zelda on the mouth with a hunger that startled her.

Surprised at her own desire, Zelda kissed the mermaid back, thrusting her tongue against hers in a kiss that turned their heads. And as Calain fingered them to yet another climax, they moaned through the kiss, their sexes gushing over Calain's relentless fingers.

THE SEX SEEMED TO GO on forever. Zelda never wanted it to end! The giggling, the kissing, the fingering. . . But eventually, they all grew very tired, and Calain fell asleep with Zelda and the mermaid locked in her bulging arms.

"Tis getting late," Zelda observed, her eyes on the twilight sky. "I didn't want us to linger after dark. Surely you could tell me where the ship is now?"

The mermaid pouted. "Leaving so soon?" she said, lifting a small foot behind her.

"I must return to my baby," Zelda said apologetically.

The mermaid glanced at Calain, who was still dozing between them, and said, "Then come. I shall show you where the ship is!" So saying, she took Zelda's hand and pulled her up.

"We can't leave Calain here alone!" Zelda protested.

"Tis not too far," the mermaid assured her, amused by her worry for Calain.

They walked together against the wind, side by side, as the sun set over the water. Zelda hugged herself, her golden hair streaming across her face in the wind, and appreciated for the first time just how beautiful Menosea was, with its palm trees and white flowers. If not for the hostile elves, she might have stayed forever.

"You really love her, don't you?" said the mermaid. She sounded wistful. She laughed girlishly. "You nearly took my head off when I said I wanted to lay with her."

Zelda tried to hide her embarrassment, but the mermaid was only teasing her good-naturedly. "Calain is my true love," she confessed, smiling as she thought of Calain's loving kisses on her skin just minutes before.

"I used to love someone like that," said the mermaid, still sounding wistful.

"What happened?"

"Her heart strayed. . . And she found another."

"Oh . . . I'm sorry."

"Don't be sorry. Just be careful of your knight's intentions. If she strayed once, she will stray again."

Zelda was silent as she struggled to find an argument, but she had no experience with love and relationships. Calain was her first . . .everything. She was beginning to feel cheated by the fact that she had spent most of her life in a tower and was beginning to wonder if sequestering her child away to some magickal land was what was best for her.

"How much of our argument did you hear?" Zelda asked apprehensively.

"Enough to know that neither of you are happy," was the somber answer, "and unless something changes, I suppose you shall stay that way."

Zelda hated that the mermaid was right, but they did indeed need to find a way to protect their family from the outside world, or there was always going to be a Melvalda or a Queen Cilia threatening their happiness.

After a few minutes, the mermaid stopped and faced the sea. "Out there," she pointed. "An old cargo ship that sunk ten years ago. So not too long. You may yet salvage it."

Zelda heard steps behind her and turned to see Calain coming their way across the sand, the wind beating back her red hair. She was leading Lucky by the reins and was carrying Zelda's clothes and her stave. She drew near, kissed Zelda on the cheek, and said teasingly, "Weren't leaving me behind, were you?"

Zelda smiled. "I said I'd never let you go, didn't I?" She turned back to the sea, looking in the direction the mermaid had pointed. She felt slightly distracted that Calain and the mermaid were watching her so intently. She took her stave from Calain and took a step forward so that the others were behind her. Then her face creased in determination. She extended her hand in a lifting gesture, and she as did, the ship slowly rose from the sea.

Zelda heard Calain and the mermaid gasp but did not allow their awe to break her concentration. The ship was quite heavy to lift, despite the fact that it was broken in half. She focused on lifting only the prow, for she could feel with her mind that the broken stern was far heavier. As she focused, the tip of her stave grew brighter and brighter, until the front half of the ship was hovering just above the sea, water softly roaring as it cascaded from the sides in all directions. Zelda closed her hand into a fist, hardening the cascading water into ice, and sculpting the ice into a gangway, so that they could use it for a stair.

"Gods be good," Calain whispered, staring at the hovering ship with wide eyes.

The mermaid also stood stunned at Zelda's display of power. Zelda was quite pleased to see that. "Thank you for your aid," Zelda said to her. She laughed and added, "And for the sex."

The mermaid giggled. "Wait until I tell the girls I had you *both*! Take care! And do visit!" She bounced up and kissed Calain on the cheek, then kissed Zelda's cheek as well. She was wading into the water when Zelda called to her.

"Wait!" Zelda called.

The mermaid stopped and looked over her shoulder, around the curtain of her red hair. Her long lashes fluttered in surprise.

"We don't even know your name!" Zelda laughed.

The mermaid smiled. "My name is Rhian," she said sweetly and turned, walking forward into the waves. They watched her sink lower and lower, her hips swaying. Then her head disappeared under, and a second later, they saw her burst from the water and turn a flip in the air as her legs joined to form a tail.

Chapter 6

Arryn, the elven knight, hadn't been lying. As Selene stood on the dock that evening, she was astonished to see the broken, jagged prow of a ship soaring fast over the water, as Zelda, Calain, and a sturdy brown horse stood upon it, their hair streaming back in the fading dusk.

The horse was horrified and had to be calmed several times by Calain, who was holding to its reins, while Zelda stood nearby, leaning upon the prow's side with both hands, smiling as her golden curls streamed back with the skirts of her blue gown.

The elves on the dock were as shocked as Selene to see such a display. Many had been loading boxes onto cargo vessels or hauling nets of fish onto the landing when they glanced up and froze to see the severed prow of a ship gliding toward them through the air.

The ship prow lowered itself at the dock, allowing Zelda, Calain, and the horse to step easily onto the landing (the horse neighing and struggling in horror). Then it sank quietly beneath the waves and disappeared.

Zelda brushed her gown off and glanced around, but it was Calain who noticed Selene first. She gave a bright laugh and yelled Selene's name, leading the horse toward her.

"Selene!" Zelda shouted, her face brightened, and to Selene's pleasant surprise, Zelda ran to her and crushed her in a hug, smashing her great breasts and the flowery scent of her golden hair against her. Baffled and laughing, Selene caught Zelda in her arms, and as Zelda showered her face with frantic kisses, she knew for the first time in her life what it was like to be Calain, on the receiving end of such wild and happy affection.

Zelda backed away, beaming at Selene, as Calain drew near.

"Selene! How came thou to be here?" laughed Calain, momentarily neglecting the horse to pull Selene in a rough hug that nearly choked her.

As Calain clung to her, Selene had to admit she was relieved to see Calain unharmed, happy, and glowing, despite how angry she was with her for leaving. Her lips gave away to a smile as she stroked Calain's wild red hair and patted her back. But then the reason she was there returned sharply to her mind, and her eyes moved grimly to Zelda as she dreaded the news she must convey.

Zelda and Calain stepped back to happily regard Selene, and Selene knew she must have looked grave, for the smiles fell from their faces.

"Aereth," Zelda said at once, her voice trembling. "Something has happened!"

"Yes," Selene said hoarsely.

Zelda stepped forward, staring at Selene intently. "Take me to her!"

Chapter 7

Cassandra, strong as she was, soon found it difficult to hold Aereth on her hip for long hours at a time. She knew it was because she was dreaming and not truly in the fairy realm. Being only half there made her weaker, a fact which Queen Anindel seemed to find very amusing as she surveyed Cassandra with her mischievous green eyes.

As they were standing there in the forest, waiting – for Zelda to arrive, for Aereth to cross over, for something to change – the fairy queen decided to conjure her entire court to the spot. As Cassandra watched, a giant tree burst from the forest floor in a spray of twinkling lights and split open to form a great alcove, inside which fairy lights bobbed against the twilight, and wooden tables loaded with meats and wine appeared. The fairies all began feasting, laughing and carrying on loudly, playing flutes and lutes, and Queen Anindel reclined at a great wooden table loaded with food that she had conjured near Cassandra and Aereth, watching them with a smirk as she sipped wine from a goblet.

Behind the fairy queen, fairies were giggling and diving through the air, fighting each other, drinking wine and sharing large roasted hog's legs. Cassandra knew that, back in the other world, her friends were sustaining her with drips of honey and milk, but it was the sort of sustenance that was given to an infant. Cassandra needed *food.* She could feel the rumbling in her belly as she watched the fairies biting with great exaggeration into glossy roasted goose and mutton. She thought she would snap.

Aereth also seemed famished. The girl had grown to the size of a seven-year-old and had figured out how to walk, which made it twice as difficult to restrain her. She kept trying to run to the tables, to the food, and would suddenly take off when Cassandra had relaxed her grip. But always, Cassandra would become alert and snatch the girl back by her tunic, tucking her under her arm again, so that she hung there, pouting and resigned, as she watched the fairies feasting.

Cassandra knew that eating anything in the fairy realm was a mistake, as it would bring them both over, body and soul, trapping them there in Elwenhal much faster than whatever small bit of food Aereth had been given. At least in their half-state, there was a better chance they could escape. And there was no certainty that Zelda would arrive . . . or that she was even still alive.

Cassandra didn't want to think of it, but she knew it was a very real possibility that Zelda, by venturing to Alleren, had walked directly into a trap. If not for Aereth, the Knights of Falcon would have gone with her to the Gold Keep and the queen's letter be damned. But instead, to save the life of Calain, Zelda had been forced to go forth alone.

And if Zelda *had* survived the Gold Keep, then Cassandra and Aereth's predicament was just another mess for her to clean up. Though she was hopelessly trapped, Cassandra suddenly felt as bad for Zelda as she did for herself. The last few months had been a series of ongoing madness: first Queen Ellanara, then Melvalda, then Queen Cilia, now this. Zelda would need a long rest if they survived it all, and Cassandra suddenly felt determined to make certain she had it. For she couldn't help blaming herself that Aereth had been taken by the fairy queen.

If she had been watching Aereth more closely, if she had been honest with Calain about *why* Zelda had given herself to Melvalda . . . but Cassandra's inaction had contributed to the madness of the last few months just as much as Calain's impulsiveness, Gweneth's sharp tongue, and Selene's worry and sorrow.

As Queen Anindel was sipping from her gold goblet, two tiny fairies fluttered down on dragonfly wings, bearing a spiny crown of twigs between them. The fairies dropped the crown carefully on the fairy queen's head. Queen Anindel smiled at Cassandra and took another sip from her goblet, rings glittering on her slender fingers. She had dressed herself in a long, deep grown gown and her cleavage was pouring from the top, a fact Cassandra was struggling to ignore.

"Join me, Cassandra," said Queen Anindel, voice oily as a snake. She picked up a fork, speared a small tomato on it, and plunged the tomato in her mouth, very slowly, smiling as she chewed. The sweet red juice slid down her chin and she licked it away with a startlingly long tongue.

Cassandra ignored her rumbling belly and turned her eyes away with great difficulty. She was still clutching Aereth under her arm, who was feeling heavier and heavier as the drowsing effect of crossing over became stronger.

"Want food!" Aereth complained with a scowl and suddenly kicked her legs and swung her arms in a mad tantrum. She bucked until she had tumbled free of Cassandra's arm and fell in the grass with a happy cry. Feeling dizzy, Cassandra made a lazy snatch at her but missed, and the girl squealed with giggles, racing away as fast as her skinny legs could carry her.

Cassandra felt too weak to run after Aereth and stood there, watching in tight-lipped frustration as the child ran to Queen Anindel, jumped in the woman's lap (Queen Anindel laughed in delight), and started ravenously cramming food in her mouth, until juice and grease was staining her little face.

Queen Anindel smiled as she stroked Aereth's auburn hair, which had grown out past her shoulders and was a wild mess of curls about her. But the fairy queen's eyes were fixed with quiet hunger on Cassandra. "Come to me, Cassandra, dear. What is the point resisting now? Either you are trapped – in which case you might as well enjoy yourself – or darling Zelda is coming to save you, in case . . . you might as well enjoy yourself." She smiled, showing pinpoint fangs.

Cassandra sighed, slowly walked to the table, pulled out a chair, and sat beside Queen Anindel, who regarded her calmly.

"Why don't you take off that armor?" Queen Anindel asked quietly.

Cassandra tensed. She knew she was safe in her armor, that its metal protected her from the magick of the fae. She opened her mouth to refuse, but something happened . . . She saw her own hand lift to the other, and then she started to remove her gauntlet. It fell away to the grass as the fairies hovering nearby twittered with giggles. Aereth kept stuffing food in her face and gulping from wine goblets and didn't even look up as Cassandra mechanically stripped off her armor piece by piece.

As the armor fell away, a small voice in the back of Cassandra's mind was screaming for her to stop, but her hands kept going, and when she looked at the fairy queen – who was smiling at her so widely – she knew she was in the woman's thrall. It had finally happened: she had been in Elwenhal long enough for the fairy queen to take control of her.

When Cassandra's hands stopped moving, her sword and armor were in the grass beside her chair, and she was sitting at the table in nothing but her linen bra and woolen hose. Fairies twittered and zoomed back and forth over her head, laughing at her but staying clear of her piled sword and armor.

Cassandra felt her head turn toward the fairy queen, though she knew she was not turning it herself. She was forced to look at the woman – her face tense with anger – and saw Queen Anindel was sitting with her fingers thoughtfully touching her chin, as Aereth kept eating away at the glossy meats and fruits on the table, ignoring them both.

Queen Anindel tilted her head, studying Cassandra with soft eyes, as if she were some fascinating art piece on display. "Yes . . . You grew to be quite beautiful, Cassandra, as I always suspected you would. Those eyes . . . Those piercing gray eyes. . . And the hair. . ." She made a gentle gesture with her hand, and Cassandra felt her pale blonde hair tumble free of its braid, so that it fell to her shoulders, brushing the bare skin softly.

"Now, I think you would be more comfortable without the smallclothes, don't you?" said Queen Anindel.

Cassandra mechanically reached for her linen bra and was about to strip it off when a voice rang out through the forest, "What in *blue blazes* have you done to them?!"

Queen Anindel looked around, and Aereth even paused her ravenous eating to glance up. The fairies stopped laughing and playing and paused in their merriment to stare, the music abruptly ceased, and the silence drew out.

Desperate to see what was happening, Cassandra tried to move. She was pleased to realize she could move her own head and followed the gazes of the others: Zelda was standing at the edge of the feast, stave glowing with power.

The Fairy Queen of Elwenhal

Book 7

Chapter 1

Frantic to rescue Cassandra and Aereth, Zelda cast a portal spell and went immediately to Elwenhal. Because she had gone there body and soul – rather than through dreams as Cassandra had – Gweneth knew Zelda would be in full power and did not envy the fairy queen the fight to come.

She didn't envy Calain, either. The second Zelda had gone, Gweneth lunged on her. They went rolling across the floor, scattering grass mats and upsetting pots and pans as they yelled and punched each other. As Calain rolled on top of Gweneth and punched her in the face, Gweneth was vaguely aware of Selene and Neserie yelling. Neserie was angrily waving her broom and shouting something unintelligible, while Selene kept reaching in, trying to grab them apart, only for them to roll suddenly out of reach.

Gweneth lay on her back and spit blood, glaring up at Calain, whose face was twisted as she pulled back, preparing to punch again. Gweneth blocked the blow with her forearm and gave Calain a sharp uppercut to the face. She was satisfied to see Calain go tumbling back and lunged on her, grabbing her in a headlock.

Calain grunted angrily and pried at Gweneth's bulging arm with her fingers, but Gweneth held on. Calain's nonsense had caused all of it – Cassandra's capture at the hands of Melvalda, Aereth being kidnapped, Cassandra's capture *again* at the hands of the fae—and Gweneth wanted to make her suffer for once. Calain was always doing stupid things and facing no consequences with all the rewards! Predictably, she had won back Zelda's love, which Gweneth did not believe she deserved at all.

"You are like small babes!" Selene bellowed in much frustration, but it was Neserie who finally stopped the fight.

Standing cold and calm, Neserie glowed with power, licks of loose gray hair beating about her wrinkled face in an ethereal wind. Her eyes glowed, and they saw the door fly open of its own accord, and Gweneth and Calain were lifted bodily and hurled out. As they landed sprawled in the yard, the door slammed again behind them.

Gweneth had landed hard on her face. She sat up on her elbow, spitting sand and blood, and glared at Calain, who had landed beside her.

"Have you gone mad, Gwen?" said Calain in amazement. She stared at Gweneth with wide green eyes.

Gweneth rolled her eyes and lurched to her feet, dusting herself off. "And of course you would play the doe-eyed innocent after all you hath done," she snarled, going to the step and sitting down. She watched as Calain dusted herself off and sat beside her, then she laughed. "Or perhaps you are truly so dense that you cannot see how your actions have shaped events. Sometimes I forget thy art a featherhead."

Calain rested one elbow on her knee and stared at Gweneth in disbelief. "You would blame *me* for everything that has transpired, when your sharp tongue sent Zelda alone into Dark Bloom? I should have given thee more than one lump back at Wolf Fortress."

Gweneth cast her eyes down. She had almost forgotten the argument with Zelda in the barn. She had mocked Zelda, dismissed her power as a sorceress, and treated her as a child. She was ashamed for having done so and suddenly realized the anger she was directing at Calain was more truthfully anger toward herself.

"Why dost thou hurt her so?" Calain demanded, but her voice was softer now. She was bleeding from her busted lip but ignoring it to focus completely on Gweneth.

"Zelda is not Annora," Calain said soothingly.

"I know," said Gweneth hoarsely.

When Gweneth was a child, she had loved a girl named Annora. She and Annora had grown up in the same caravan and had fallen in love. When she was seven years old, Gweneth set out to become a knight, and Annora had promised to be her lady and to wait for her return.

Though knights were typically assigned to a sorceress, they could choose another lady to champion if they found their own. So when Gweneth returned to Ellormest at fourteen to visit her young love, it was with the expectation that Annora was still there, waiting for her. Instead, she discovered that Annora was betrothed to a boy of fifteen from another caravan. The boy's name was Dylan, and he came to blows with Gweneth, who horrified Annora with her new super strength when she broke the boy's jaw.

"He can give me a life, children, a f-family," Annora had explained when the fighting had been stopped (by the frantic caravanners), tears in her eyes, "while with you I would just be..."

"Happy?" Gweneth had supplied, and Annora had run away weeping.

"You're always so distraught," present-day Gweneth said to Calain, "that Zelda hath lain with some other woman, but be glad it was never with a man."

Calain snorted. "What the devil difference does that make?"

Gweneth gave her a withering look. "We are not attracted to men. Tis a state in other women we shall never understand, nor shall they ever understand us, and that lack of understanding can divide two women so easily."

Calain still looked perplexed, so Gweneth laughed, shook her head, and clapped her on the shoulder.

"Never thee mind," Gweneth said fondly. "Do not strain thy featherbrain."

"You must be kind to Zelda," Calain scolded, getting back to the point. "You jest often about her power, but only because you have not seen the full strength of it."

Gweneth thought she had certainly gotten a taste of Zelda's power. The sorceress had forced her to stand still for a night and a day, completely helpless and trapped with her own thoughts. It had forced a great deal of needed introspection on her.

"I have been as docile as a lamb since she fled us," protested Gweneth, her face twisting. "Do spare me these lectures."

"As you will. But only because I am too exhausted to continue. Tis been a long week."

"And a lot of women, if Zelda's scathing glares are anything to go by."

Calain awkwardly scratched the back of her red hair. "Noticed that, did you?"

"Aye," said Gweneth with a laugh. "When you were approaching up the lane, that elven woman across the way winked at you, I saw it, and Zelda looked as if she would flay thee alive if thou responded."

Calain laughed as well, though in a dispirited sort of way. "It was only three women—"

"*Only three?*" Gweneth's eyes popped. "As ever, the women do flock to thee, and thou acts as if twere nothing! I want details: positions, tit sizes, was she a good snatcher?"

Calain laughed, this time with genuine delight, and Gweneth suddenly felt as if everything were back to normal, as if they were in their bunks on Falcon Isle, sharing stories of the maidens they had lain with, as they always did.

Just then, the door opened behind them and Selene emerged. Like Gweneth and Calain, she was out of her armor, instead wearing a tunic and trousers. She came down the step, her hands in her pockets, and shook her head at them wearily.

"Grandmother hath said the two of you are not allowed back inside," Selene said, looking down at them sternly, "and I agree with her."

"Your grandmother's a hag," taunted Calain, and Gweneth laughed.

Selene's lips tightened. "Be that as it may," she said (Gweneth laughed again), "she is correct about your thuggish behavior. We are knights! Not small children quarreling over trifles! We are to behave with dignity at all times! What was the quarrel anyway?" She looked between them.

"Never you mind," said Gweneth.

Calain looked intently at Selene. "How is Zelda? And the others? Have they returned?"

"No," said Selene heavily, "and I expect it shall be a while. That is how these magick things tend to unfold."

"Don't worry, Selene. Perhaps Zelda's new necklace will guide her back to us," said Calain mockingly.

Selene colored up.

Gweneth looked curiously between them. "New necklace?"

"Aye," laughed Calain. "Selene gave Zelda a bauble to win her affection . . . or to get more lay time? Most likely both. She pretends to have no appetite but is the greediest of us all—"

"Shut your mouth, Calain," Selene said quietly, "or I shall shut it." Her dark eyes were fierce.

Calain looked up at Selene in amusement. "What shall you buy her next, Selene? Nipple clamps?"

Selene tensed, as if she would pounce on Calain and thrash her, and Gweneth, laughing, got to her feet and held out her arms. "I know tis tempting to punch Calain's face in," said Gweneth, "but you are right, Selene. We should not continue to fight amongst ourselves. Truly, it is adolescent."

Selene still stood tense with rage as she stared into Calain's mocking green eyes. Eventually, she abruptly turned away, and they saw her march off down the street, wandering blindly, her dark braid streaming. Gweneth started to go after her, but Calain said wearily behind her, "Let her go."

Gweneth turned back to the step and sat beside Calain again. For as long as she could remember, Calain and Selene had been at each other's throats. The day she arrived on Falcon Isle, she had walked into the training yard, and the two were going at it while Knight Octava struggled to pry them apart. And in the years that had followed, they had continued in the same vein, fighting over women and weapons, horses, and even the attention of those knights who mentored them at the academy. Yet at the same time, they loved each other like the closest sisters. It was madness.

Gweneth had never understood Calain and Selene's rivalry, try as she might. She had six sisters who all got on with her wonderfully. They didn't fight or hit each other but instead protected and cared for each other. She supposed it was a part of caravan culture, for there were few families among the caravans that bickered the way Calain and Selene did, and if they did, they were asked to leave. Caravan people were very strict about keeping the peace.

"Why dost thou constantly provoke her?" Gweneth asked, leaning forward and resting her elbows on her knees.

Calain's eyes were still on Selene's retreating back, and now, instead of glittering with mirth, they were dark and bitter. "She seeks to make Zelda love her more than I," she said grimly.

"*Or,*" said Gweneth in exasperation, "perhaps she seeks Zelda's attention. Zelda is always moaning on about you. The whole time you were gone, she was insufferable. Weeping and carrying on. 'Oh, where is my Calain!'"

Calain glanced away guiltily.

"Anyway, what does it matter if Selene gives Zelda a present? I have given her presents as well," said Gweneth. "So hath Cassandra."

Calain looked at Gweneth in surprise. "You've given Zelda presents?"

"Aye. A carving I did of her."

"That's not the same as a necklace!" Calain said at once. "Selene is clearly trying to woo her."

"What does it matter?" laughed Gweneth.

"Zelda is my lady! Or at least, she was mine first, which means she should love me the most! Selene is trying to replace me in her heart!"

Gweneth only laughed. "Love hath made muttonheads of the pair of you."

Calain looked at Gweneth irritably. "And what about Cassandra? What did she give?"

"A new gown," said Gweneth. "The one she was wearing when she came here, in fact. Zelda needed new clothes after the whole Black Bear madness, so Cassandra went shopping for her while she was in town."

"What was she in town for?" said Calain in amazement, for venturing into town was still dangerous, as they were still wanted by the Rose Guard, or had been at the time.

"To find a goat that was nursing. Zelda was all determined to run off to save you from the Gold Keep. We needed a way to feed the babe," said Gweneth pointedly, and she was glad when Calain dropped her eyes in much guilt and shame.

"I have caused all of you so much trouble," Calain admitted. "I slew the queen, and you became fugitives to aid me. Then I threw away your sacrifice by turning my back on my duty, by dismissing my vows. Truly, I apologize."

"I shant be happy until you wash all my linen and cook my supper seven nights in a row," Gweneth teased and was glad when Calain smiled. She didn't want her to suffer *too* greatly.

"I shall never leave again," Calain promised. "Not just because of Zelda, but for your sake as well. Zelda hath told me how the Rose Guard nearly overtook you and how Cassandra's mother had to step in to save your lives. That wouldn't have happened had I not forsaken you. Perhaps Arryn was right. I am just a child, unworthy of you all, unworthy of the oath I took."

"Arryn? The elven knight?" said Gweneth, amused. "So she *is* a friend of yours after all. She came here and warned us of your arrival."

Calain scoffed and now she looked a little angry. "I wouldn't call her a *friend.* I caught her fucking Zelda – Tis not funny!" she growled, for Gweneth had burst out laughing.

Gweneth finished laughing with a happy sigh. "And let me guess," she said, shaking her head, "you tried to chop her head off, but she handed your backside to you. She was small but seemed formidable." Sort of like Gweneth herself, she thought. She had always been a little small compared to the other knights, but she had rarely been felled in battle.

"She did *not* defeat me!" Calain said indignantly. "We were evenly matched! If she hadn't resorted to cowardly spells—!"

"All right, good Calain. Do not work yourself up into a hissy fit. Come." Gweneth stood. "Since we are no longer allowed inside the hut, let us find Selene and make certain she is well. It is foolhardy for any of us to wander alone knowing we are wanted by the law."

"Aye," agreed Calain wearily and got to her feet.

They started off down the road as darkness fell, ignoring the suspicious stares of the elves on their doorsteps. After a while, Calain said with hesitation, "Did Zelda really weep for me?"

Gweneth laughed. "Why? Would it make thee happy?"

"Yes," Calain admitted, and Gweneth laughed again.

"Aye, Calain. Zelda wept . . . She sobbed and her big tits heaved while she sat on my face."

Calain playfully elbowed Gweneth, who laughed again as they continued down the street.

Chapter 2

Zelda was draped in the blue gown Cassandra had bought for her, her golden hair a mess in her eyes, as if she had run. She was breathless and furious and glowing with power, as was the white stave in her hand, but the fairy queen didn't seem impressed.

Zelda stepped forward in a rage. "What are you playing at?" she shouted.

The fairy court turned their heads as one to look at Queen Anindel, who smiled as she said, "Welcome, Zelda. We have been waiting for you."

Hearing this, the fairies burst into giggles as they darted around Zelda on insect wings, and Zelda glared at them, her eyes moving back and forth as if she might burn them with her gaze. But she looked at the fairy queen again, and she suddenly realized she was in someone else's territory now, where magick and spells had different rules. She could not burst in and simply start casting. No, she would have to switch tactics to escape this place with Aereth and Cassandra intact.

"Where is my baby?" Zelda asked.

Queen Anindel smiled. "Right here. Or don't you recognize her?" she said, indicating the child on her lap with a wave of her hand.

Zelda's eyes went to the girl, and her lips parted in shock. It couldn't be! When Zelda had left for the Gold Keep, Aereth was a newborn baby in swaddling. Now she was a little girl, skinny arms and long legs, sitting on the fairy queen's lap, with grease and juice stains on her face. Her cheeks were bulging with food, and food was dribbling down the front of her clothes, which were torn and becoming rags from her quick growth spurt. The fairy queen had mended the rags with leaves and twigs, which made Aereth appear as wild as one of the twiggy fae lurking in the grass nearby.

Aereth was looking at Zelda and frowning, her green eyes straining, as if she was trying to remember Zelda. It was said that children often lost their memories in the realm of the fae if they lingered too long there.

Heart thumping dread, Zelda walked toward the table, fairies scattering out of her way in the leaves, and said desperately, "Aereth? You remember your mother, don't you?"

Aereth frowned. Then very suddenly, she shouted, "Go away!" and turned, hugging the fairy queen's long neck. The fairy queen closed loving arms around Aereth, who glared with such hatred at Zelda that Zelda halted again, stung.

"Aereth . . ." Zelda whispered sadly.

"Took you long enough to get here!" Aereth shot back, pouting. "You don't care about me! You're not my mother!"

Zelda scowled at the fairy queen, whose green eyes were silently laughing at her. "What nonsense has this – fairy-monster!—been filling your head with?"

Giggles rose from the fairies, and Queen Anindel gasped in mock horror at the insult.

"I am your mother and I love you!" cried Zelda, drawing closer to the table still. She reached for Aereth and grabbed her arm. "You are coming home with me now!"

"No! Let go!" Aereth sobbed, twisting to get away.

Zelda held on, thinking her daughter was like a feral beast. And indeed, Aereth gave an earsplitting screech that could have rivaled any monkey. The hair standing on her neck, Zelda let go of her daughter in horror, and Aereth leapt up and scrambled away, disappearing into the trees.

"No!" Zelda shouted, panicking. "Aereth!" She started to run after the girl, but she halted again when she remembered Cassandra. She couldn't leave Cassandra here alone, but Aereth . . . Zelda stared into the trees, feeling helpless. Eventually, she glared at the fairy queen. "What did you do to my daughter?"

"I did nothing. You have come too late," said Queen Anindel calmly. "Aereth is *my* daughter now."

Zelda's chest heaved. "And what have you done to Cassandra?" she demanded.

But Zelda could see that Cassandra was clearly under Queen Anindel's spell. She was sitting very straight at the table, as around her, the fairies bobbed on the air, laughing and eating and throwing wine on each other. Cassandra was in her smallclothes! Her bare, sculpted shoulders were lined with shadows in the dim glow of the fairy lights, and she was staring with empty gray eyes into the distance.

"No more than you have done to her," said Queen Anindel calmly. "How many times have you commanded her out of her armor and she hath mindlessly obeyed?"

Not enough times, Zelda thought. She had only lain with Cassandra while in her dreams. When they were living at Wolf Fortress, there hadn't been much time to lay together. She had spent those weeks weeping for Calain, then she gave birth, then she left for the Gold Keep. . .

"Don't you miss her touch?" asked the fairy queen slyly.

Feeling strangely lightheaded, Zelda stared at Cassandra as if she hadn't quite seen her before. Yes. Yes, she would like very much to see Cassandra without her smallclothes again. She took a step toward Cassandra. Then another. And another. She dropped her stave as she went, her blue eyes fixed on Cassandra's pretty face.

"Yes," whispered the fairy queen, her mischievous eyes turning to follow Zelda. "Yes . . . Undress her. Make love to her." She waved a hand. "Rise, fair knight, that your lady may unrobe you."

Mindlessly staring into the distance, Cassandra rose from her chair and turned to face Zelda. She did not look down at Zelda, she simply stared into the distance and waited.

Zelda's heart was pounding in her ears. She reached up and reached round and untied Cassandra's linen bra. It tumbled away, revealing Cassandra's breasts, which were small and high and rigid with pink nipples. Cassandra's rippling belly trembled a little at the exposure but she was otherwise still. Then Zelda reached out and slowly closed her hand over Cassandra's breast in a gentle massage, and she saw Cassandra's cheeks flame the tiniest bit. Zelda paused. Cassandra was still conscious on some level, helplessly forced to stand there and endure Zelda's groping.

But Zelda didn't think she could help herself. The strange lightheadedness continued. Her hand smoothed over Cassandra's soft breast another time, and she felt her sex swell with desire, she saw Cassandra's cheeks flame brighter, and suddenly, she couldn't remember Aereth or Calain or the even the fact that she was in the fairy realm. Suddenly, all she could think about was making love to Cassandra. *Desperate* love, the way she had always dreamed.

Cassandra was suddenly able to move. She looked down at Zelda, and her gray eyes were burning with the same serious fire that had always made Zelda's clitoris throb. She looked at Zelda with quiet longing and frowned in silent pleasure when Zelda massaged her breast another time.

"My lady . . ." Cassandra whispered breathlessly. "We must . . . fight this enchantment . . ."

Zelda shook herself against the spell and glanced around. She gasped. They were no longer in the forest, standing among the tables of the fairy court. They were in a field of flowers. The flowers were purple and spread to the horizon as far as the eye could see. And it was no longer dusk but day, bright and blue, not a cloud in the sky. A chill wind picked up, ruffling Zelda's golden hair and making her shiver, so that she pressed herself without thinking against Cassandra's hard body. When their skin touched, Zelda realized with a jolt that she was completely naked. So was Cassandra.

Cassandra's eyes softened, and she closed Zelda in her arms, trying to keep her warm against the wind. The moment she did this, the wind dropped, and Zelda knew they were being manipulated. But . . . it was hard to resist, to focus . . . She looked up at Cassandra and found herself lost once more in the serious gray eyes she loved so dearly. She closed her eyes, huddled happily in Cassandra's bulging arms, and dropped her head against the bigger woman, trying to remember why she was there.

"What are we doing here?" said Cassandra, who sounded as confused as Zelda felt.

"I am. . . unsure," Zelda admitted, frowning. She looked up at Cassandra and felt the blood rushing to her sex again. Cassandra's body was so firm and strong and toned with muscles, but her breasts were so supple, her skin so soft . . . Even her calloused warrior's hands were not as hard as Calain's or Selene's. Wait . . . who was Calain? Who was Selene?

"I think I came to make love to you," Zelda said thoughtfully. "My mind insists upon it."

Cassandra stared down at her in surprise. "Does it?"

"Nothing else makes sense." Zelda's eyes traced hungrily over Cassandra's breasts. Cassandra was so tall that her breasts were nearly in Zelda's face. Zelda rocked up on tiptoe and sucked one of the pink nipples slowly in her lips.

Cassandra gasped. "My . . . My lady . . ." she moaned in weak protest. She grabbed Zelda's shoulders and held her at bay. For a moment, it seemed her senses had returned to her. She looked down at Zelda and said firmly, "We did come here for grave reason!" She gasped, remembering. "Aereth! Your child!" Cassandra spun away, looking back and forth across the field, as if she would spot Aereth in the flowers. "Aereth!" she called. "Aereth!"

"Who is Aereth?" said Zelda, who was staring lustily at Cassandra's hard, muscular backside. She smoothed her hand over one of the cheeks and gave it a squeeze, to which Cassandra whipped around again, her cheeks blushing.

"Zelda! You must fight what is happening! The fairy queen, she hath placed a spell upon us to dist-tract . . ." Cassandra's voice broke when Zelda's slender fingers slid suddenly in her sex. Her eyes hooded as Zelda carefully worked her.

Zelda could feel her clitoris pumping harder in excitement. The little knot of pleasure was pulsing fast between her thighs as Cassandra's warm sex squeezed on her fingers, growing moist and deep. She reached for Cassandra breast with her other hand and massaged it, thumbing the little nipple at the end of each slow stroke.

Fingered and groped so lovingly, a tremble of helpless pleasure went through Cassandra. She dropped her forehead against Zelda's, grasped Zelda's shoulders in both hands, and whispered hoarsely, "Thy hath touched and caressed all reason and sense out of me! My hunger for you hath made me weak . . . Fair Zelda . . . Thy mustn't make love to me . . . Mmm . . ." She moaned when Zelda slowly fingered her deeper. "Z-Zelda . . . Zelda! Cease your fondling!"

Cassandra's hands tightened on Zelda's shoulders, and the knight lifted her bodily in the air, holding her at bay. But holding Zelda away did nothing to end Cassandra's lust. Zelda could see her suffering gray eyes pass over her body – her heavy breasts, her narrow waist, her wide hips, the swirl of golden hair between her legs – and the knight blushed all the brighter.

"I cannot . . . l-look upon you," Cassandra stammered, setting Zelda on her feet again. She turned away. "We mustn't gaze upon each other. It makes us weak to the spell!"

Zelda wasn't listening. Her eyes were on Cassandra's backside again, and now she was wondering what it would feel like to have the pale hair between Cassandra's thighs moving soft against her mouth. Soft and warm and moist . . . She had never gone down on any of the knights. The prospect thrilled her. Wait . . . What knights? Were there others? Zelda frowned into space, straining to remember.

Cassandra tentatively turned to face Zelda. "Zelda, we must focus. We must look for Aereth—" The words choked in Cassandra's mouth when Zelda tackled her without warning to the flowers.

They fell in the grass together, Cassandra scrambling to cradle Zelda in her arms and cushion her fall. Zelda caught her breath and lifted her head beneath the tangle of her golden hair to find her great breasts were crushed against Cassandra's and heaving as she panted. Cassandra was breathless as well and staring with burning gray eyes at Zelda's cleavage.

Hunger stirring between her legs afresh, Zelda leaned down and kissed Cassandra on the lips. Cassandra kissed back – with a strength and hunger that startled Zelda, her strong hands closing hard on Zelda's soft backside.

"Thy tits are utter perfection," said Cassandra, eyes narrowed on Zelda's breasts. She gripped Zelda by the waist and slid her forward easily, so that Zelda gasped in surprise as her breasts trembled, spilling over into Cassandra's face. Cassandra cupped one in her hand, lifted it so that the plump flesh spilled over her groping fingers, and sucked Zelda's nipple slow into her lips. She released, watching Zelda's moan with serious satisfaction.

"So soft," Cassandra whispered, sucking on the nipple again, releasing again. "So big and trembling with thy slightest breath. . ." She sucked again, and Zelda blushed and sighed, frowning from the pleasure.

Cassandra closed her arms around Zelda, pulling her close and allowing her breasts once more to fall in her face. She suckled one tenderly as it weighed down her, her arms tight around Zelda, who squirmed helplessly in her grasp, blushing and gasping as Cassandra's face moved against the swell of her heavy breast.

And then, as Cassandra's fingers were sliding in her sex, Zelda suddenly remembered why she was there. "Aereth!" Zelda cried, pushing herself up. She scrambled off Cassandra and sat up, glancing around, as if Aereth would be hiding in the grass nearby. "Aereth!" she called.

Cassandra, still in a daze of lust, sat up, gently turned Zelda's face to her own, and kissed her passionately, roughly thrusting her tongue in her mouth. Zelda gulped on Cassandra's tongue as she struggled to resist arousal. Her tongue slid against Cassandra's, pleasure trembled through her, and she moaned as the kiss deepened. *Who is Aereth?* she thought as Cassandra, still kissing her, backed her down on the grass, until she was lying on her back.

Cassandra's kisses traveled down to Zelda's breasts, and she pulled gently on her nipple a moment before the kisses continued, down her belly, to her thighs. Cassandra opened Zelda's thighs and looked at Zelda between them, her eyes bright with that serious fire again as she slid two careful fingers in her sex.

Zelda moaned and arched her back, thrusting her breasts to the sky as Cassandra's fingers slid deeper. She felt her sex squeeze hungrily on them, and then she was moist and her clitoris was pumping greedily, coaxing her to relax, to release, to give in to the pleasure. She could see her own great breasts rising and falling, heaving with her breathlessness, the massive mounds jutting with her tiny pink nipples. Cassandra was still kneeling between her thighs, still staring at her intently, her fingers slow and yet relentless as they plunged deeper through her moisture. Zelda heard herself helplessly whisper Cassandra's name.

"Thy sweet pussy," Cassandra was whispering, "so wet for me . . . Thy clitoris so fat . . ."

Zelda blushed. "But aren't we supposed to be . . . doing something? Looking for someone . . .?" The thought fluttered from Zelda's mind when Cassandra, still fingering her, sucked slowly on her clitoris.

Chapter 3

Aereth ran happily through the trees, pausing to take the strange fruits they offered and cramming them whole in her mouth. The more she ate, the stronger she felt, and the less she seemed to remember about the other world she had come from, the one with all the women in armor, and the sorceress . . . the sorceress with the warm blue eyes. The sorceress gave her the most pause, but she ignored the feeling and kept stuffing her face with food.

Eventually, Aereth came upon a group of fairies all sitting in a crowded circle, gazing down at something that was apparently very amusing. Her mother, the fairy queen, was among them, sitting on a tree root throne that was draped in a cloak of flowers. She looked very pleased by something. So did the rest of the fairies, who were hooting and laughing.

Aereth brightened and ran to Queen Anindel, flopping in her lap. The queen laughed girlishly at this and kissed Aereth on the cheek. "There you are, my little one!" she said, which made Aereth happy as she crammed more fruit in her mouth and swung her legs.

The fairy queen began to stroke Aereth's hair. "Did you have a pleasant time with Nimwe?"

Nimwe was a fairy woman who had been tasked with watching over Aereth when the fairy queen could not. She was of a greater size than most fae, as Anindel was, and not tiny like the winged fae who flitted about, giggling and making mischief. Nimwe stood at four feet tall, with pointed ears and a pretty smile. She was a beautiful woman, with tiny feet and hands, and long white hair and bright blue eyes, eyes that reminded Aereth of . . . someone. Nimwe's heavy breasts were full of the sweetest milk, and she fed Aereth from them whenever the child pleased, often stroking Aereth's hair as she gazed down upon her.

Aereth had been with Nimwe for hours before finding the fairy queen again. Sitting under a tree, Nimwe had told her strange stories of other realms, stories of unicorns and demons, of the gods and goddesses. Aereth had listened enrapt, but Nimwe had fallen asleep against the tree, and so Aereth had left her there.

"Nimwe tells good stories," said Aereth, "but she's always napping."

"Breastfeeding and chasing you about exhausts her, I suspect," answered Queen Anindel. "I placed a spell on her to fill her breasts with milk for you. The magick is draining her."

"You placed a spell on Nimwe for me?" Aereth asked in surprise.

The fairy queen laughed. "As if I would breastfeed you myself! No, let some other woman carry that sweet burden."

Aereth made a face. "But I don't *need* breastmilk!" she protested and crammed another plump fruit into her mouth.

"Tis a *special* breastmilk," said the fairy queen lovingly and continued to stroke Aereth's hair. "It shall bind you to this realm, so that you can never truly be taken from me!"

Aereth didn't know what to say to that. "What do you mean, Mother?"

"I mean you shall always return here!" said the fairy queen happily and hugged Aereth tight from behind.

Aereth frowned. "Shall I leave?"

"Oh, yes," said the fairy queen sadly. "You see, a powerful sorceress has come to take you away—"

"But I don't wanna go!" cried Aereth at once and turned in the woman's lap to face her.

The fairy queen seemed pleased by that. "Yes, child, I know. But you can always return here if you please. Nimwe's breastmilk will see to that. You shall never lose your tie to us!"

Aereth didn't feel comforted by the fairy queen's words, even if they did seem sincere. She turned back around and glumly stuck more fruit in her mouth.

There was a sudden cheer from the fairies gathered nearby, and Aereth realized they were looking through a window in the floor. Aereth slid off the fairy queen's lap and pushed her way to the front of the crown, where she knelt down and peered through the window.

There were people on the other side, and they were lying in a flower field far below. They were naked. Aereth thought she recognized the one lying her back. She had long golden curls and her breasts were large. They heaved as a second woman – quite muscular and tall – sucked hungrily upon the golden hair between her thighs.

The woman on her back seemed to be in a helpless daze of ecstasy. She was gasping and blushing and screaming louder and louder, the hair tumbling in her face. Eventually, she thrust her great breasts to the sky, her slender belly trembled, and she cried out, staring above with unseeing eyes. The fairies cheered greatly at this.

Aereth was puzzled. The blonde woman seemed so familiar . . . And she couldn't imagine what was so amusing about all the screaming and wiggling about.

"You shall do that one day with Nimwe," said the fairy queen, leaning down and gathering Aereth in her slender arms.

She carried Aereth away, and as they went, the trees began to form an avenue of pillars either side of them, leaning in to shield the fairy queen from the sudden light rain. Queen Anindel was carrying Aereth on her hip as the branches of a tree twisted around, forming a stair for her to climb. Fairy lights bobbed around them on the air as they rose higher and higher. They were heading for the queen's bedroom.

"I shall do that with Nimwe?" said Aereth, face twisting. "Why?"

"When you are a woman, yes," said the fairy queen. "I think you shall quite enjoy it. Did our guest not look happy?"

"No, she seemed . . ." Aereth couldn't find the word. "She seemed confused," she said at last. "She kept frowning and screaming and blushing. Why should I wish to do that?"

Queen Anindel seemed amused by that. "Oh, you shall wish it."

They came at last to the queen's bedroom, which was little more than a cluster of furniture standing in the cradle of the tree's branches. There was a four-poster bed with a green coverlet, a nightstand, a desk with books piled across it, and in the center of the "room," a throw rug that was green to match the coverlet. Here, fairy lights floated through the air like large fireflies, and Aereth wiggled down from Queen Anindel's grasp to chase them.

Looking sleepy and quite pleased with herself, Queen Anindel removed her crown of twigs and let it fall, so that several small winged fairies caught it mid-air for her and bore it away. She went to the bed and sat on the foot of it, summoned her brush from the nightstand (it flew into her hand), and began to brush her long blonde hair, humming as she did so.

Aereth eventually grew bored of chasing the fairy lights and turned, looking for something else to entertain her. The fairy queen's bedroom was full of pretty trinkets and baubles she had never been allowed to touch, all of them made of glowing crystals, wood, and gold.

There was a great crystal ball on a wooden pedestal. It sat there like a giant soap bubble, gleaming an innocent purple in the dim light of dusk. Aereth had been trying to get her hands on it since she'd been there, but the fairy queen had scolded her away the first time, and every time since, Anindel had been too fast and too sharp for Aereth to get at it.

Aereth was determined to have her curiosity sated, however, and was always looking for new opportunities to approach the giant orb. It glowed so gently, beckoning, humming with power, *calling* to her. She *had* to touch it, look at it, see what was in its crystal depths. But how? Perhaps she could create a distraction. She had a funny feeling she had played this game before, with another adult, in what seemed like another lifetime.

"Aereth," Queen Anindel called in a sing-song voice, drawing Aereth's attention away from the crystal ball. When Aereth looked up, the fairy queen was patting the bed beside her. "Bedtime, I think," she said.

Aereth moaned irritably but crawled up into the four-poster bed as she was bid.

"There, there," said the fairy queen, stroking Aereth's hair. "Dream, child. Dream of Falcon Knights and old elven witches . . ."

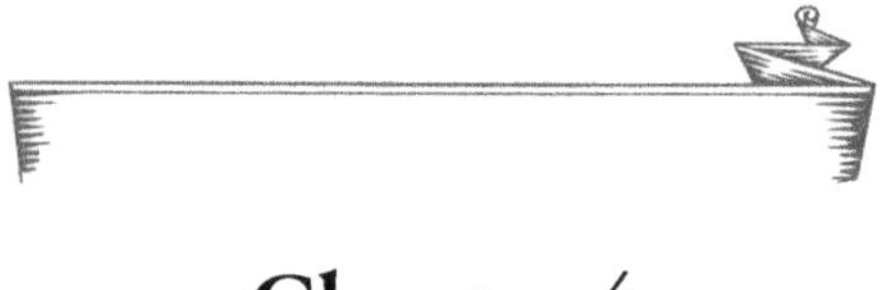

Chapter 4

Gweneth was relieved to find Selene hadn't ventured that far. When they finally caught up with her, she was standing alone at the end of the street, beside a brazier that flicked with orange flame. She was standing with her hands in her pockets, watching the sea, loose licks of black hair whipping in her eyes in the wind as her dark braid fell long down her back. When she saw Gweneth and Calain approaching, she did not seem pleased, but rather annoyed, and Gweneth held back a laugh, knowing she couldn't blame Selene.

Since they were small children, Gweneth and Calain had done nothing but torment and tease Selene. Sometimes it had been good-naturedly, and some of the time it had been deliberately to annoy her. She had always taken it in stride, only occasionally becoming angry enough to actually start a brawl with one of them. Tonight, however, Zelda, Cassandra, and Aereth were in danger, and Selene was on edge because of it.

Gweneth and Calain drew near Selene and stood with her in silence, also staring at the sea.

"Perhaps I can persuade Grandmother to allow you back inside," Selene said eventually. "Tis fast growing cold out here, and you should not suffer because of your short-tempered stupidity."

Calain laughed. "You have my thanks, Selene." She stared at the sea in silence a moment and then said, "What shall we do when Zelda returns, do you think? We cannot return to Wolf Fortress."

"You mean after the orgy in Neserie's living room?" joked Gweneth and was amused to see Calain and Selene both blush a little.

"Come, you were both thinking it, I'm just saying it," said Gweneth, folding her arms and gazing off at the sea as well. "Now that Cassie has returned to us, imagine the four of us having our way with Zelda." She saw the others stare off with glazed eyes as they thought of it, confirming her suspicions that they'd been fantasizing about the four of them laying with Zelda at once as much as she had.

"But not in my grandmother's living room!" said Selene, and the three of them laughed.

"Aye. Her skill with a broom is deadly," agreed Gweneth. "Best not."

"And not with the child near at hand," added Calain thoughtfully. "We shall have to be careful now that Zelda has a daughter. The gods forbid she should ever walk in on us."

"Aye," said Gweneth with a weak laugh. "I don't think I'm ready to have *that* talk just yet."

"You think she'll fancy men?" wondered Selene unhappily.

They all fell silent as they grimly considered it. If Aereth were to take a male lover, then it would mean raising a girl they could not provide romantic advice and guidance for. They couldn't even teach her about proper sex! None of them had lain with a man or really cared to know how it was done beyond the basics that everyone knew so far as reproduction went.

"If Aereth fancies men, we shall all be doomed," said Gweneth with another toneless laugh. "She and us both."

"Maybe she'd figure things out without us," said Calain, shrugging. "How hard could it be to fuck a man?"

Selene laughed. "Tis not the man's pleasure we worry about, tis Aereth's. We know what a woman should expect from a lover, but how do we tell her what to expect from a man? Just thinking of a man with a woman makes me ill, I confess."

They were silent again as they considered it.

Gweneth prayed the gods would be good and let Aereth fancy women as they did. Then they wouldn't have to worry about explaining a version of intimacy to her that they themselves did not grasp or even care about. Unless . . .

"Aereth was conceived of a Wilde Woman," Gweneth suddenly remembered with great relief. "All Wilde Women fancy other women. Perhaps Aereth will be the same."

"But Aereth is only half Wilde Woman," Calain reminded Gweneth. "She could just as easily be normal like Zelda . . . as 'normal' as Zelda is."

Selene laughed. "Aye. But I don't think anything about Aereth is going to be *normal.* She was born of a sorceress and a Wilde Woman through a magick potion! And now she's been captured by fairies, and the gods only know what horrors they are visiting upon her right now. She shall be changed forever."

The knights fell silent again, and this time they were angry.

"Would that we could enter Elwenhal," said Calain bitterly, "and lay the fairy court to waste."

"This time we must trust Zelda's strength," soothed Selene.

"And if she doesn't return?" said Calain quietly. She was looking at Selene like one lost, the green eyes strained.

Selene put a comforting hand on Calain's shoulder. "Then we shall stay together because we are sisters in arms."

"And stay celibate for a thousand years like Arryn?" snorted Calain. "I'd rather swallow my sword."

"*A thousand years*!" cried Gweneth, amazed. "How is Arryn still walking about sane?"

"More likely she's mad and good at concealing it," said Calain.

"Aye to that," laughed Gweneth.

Selene shrugged. "Perhaps we shall find another lady to serve . . . Or perhaps separate ladies, one for each of us."

"I dunno," said Gweneth, arms still folded. "I kind of liked all the group sex. If Zelda doesn't return, I shall find a woman who looks like her, and vent my sorrow in her bed."

Selene gave a soft, scoffing laugh. "Of course, you would."

They fell silent again, each lost in worry and fear. Then Selene said into the silence, "We should head back to the house in case Zelda returns. Grandmother doesn't like her. She called her a tart. We should not allow the two of them in a room alone."

"Aye," said Gweneth with a laugh, and the three knights turned and headed back up the street.

Chapter 5

Zelda squirmed and gasped on her back as Cassandra's feverish mouth sucked upon her sex, pulling wetly at the swollen lips, teasing her throbbing clitoris with light flicks and sucks. Zelda had only just climaxed and was struggling to catch her breath in the drowsy aftermath. She lay there, pink-cheeked, and not wanting it to end. Cassandra's mouth was relentless in its hunger for her, and each time Zelda looked down between her thighs to see the serious gray eyes blazing at her with desire, it sent a tremble through her.

"Sweet Zelda," whispered Cassandra, plunging her hungry tongue another time through the golden curls cloaking Zelda's pink sex. She closed her eyes and frowned, sliding her tongue deep inside.

Zelda also closed her eyes and frowned, her lips parting in bafflement as Cassandra's tongue plunged ever deeper. Her thighs trembled from the pleasure, and she almost closed them on reflex. Cassandra gently caught Zelda's thighs and held them apart with her strong hands, and held in place, legs helplessly splayed, Zelda moaned breathlessly as Cassandra's head moved slowly against her sex.

Zelda's mind felt sluggish, drowsy from the continuous pleasure. Her sex yielded easily to Cassandra's coaxing tongue, swelling and heaving and growing wet again and again against Cassandra's mouth.

"Your pussy is endlessly moist," whispered Cassandra huskily. "And tastes so sweet . . . So sweet I cannot stop . . . So soft. . ." She sucked on Zelda's throbbing clitoris. "So hot . . ." She sucked again. "And squirming against my tongue . . ."

By the gods, don't stop! Zelda thought, head rocking back and forth against the nest of her golden hair in a daze.

Face buried between Zelda's thighs, Cassandra reached up and caressed her great breasts in each hand. Zelda's lashes fluttered as her big breasts were squeezed in Cassandra's hard hands, coaxing the nipples to stand out harder as pleasure flushed through her. She gasped breathlessly and saw her breasts heave in Cassandra's hands.

In the same feverish daze, Cassandra trailed sloppy, hungry kisses over Zelda's belly, over her breasts and neck, to her mouth. Zelda eagerly extended her tongue, and they kissed deeply.

One of Cassandra's hands was still squeezing Zelda's heavy breast, and Zelda's cheeks flamed a little. She slid her tongue hungrily against Cassandra's, their heads turned, and they moaned through the kiss.

AERETH AWOKE WITH A start and sat up, listening. She was in the fairy queen's great four-poster bed, in her bedroom at the top of the tree, and Queen Anindel lay beside her, angelic face wreathed in cascades of her blonde hair, sleeping peacefully.

Aereth awoke because she'd heard a strange moaning. She could still hear it. She tilted her head, listening hard, and then she realized the moaning was coming from the purple crystal ball. It stood on its wooden pedestal still, winking innocently in the glow of the bobbing fairy lights, as the moaning continued to echo from it.

It suddenly occurred to Aereth that now was her chance. The fairy queen was sleeping, and the crystal ball was just sitting there on its pedestal, so mysterious, silently beckoning.

Glancing apprehensively at the sleeping fairy queen, Aereth hesitated and slid down from the bed. Her bare feet slapped the floor and she paused, staring at the fairy queen again. But Queen Anindel kept sleeping, a smile on her lips.

Realizing she wouldn't be stopped this time, Aereth brightened and ran to the crystal ball with her hair streaming. She barely stopped herself and slammed into the pedestal, so eager was she to get to it. As the pedestal swayed precariously, Aereth caught the large orb in both hands and gazed eagerly into it. To her surprise, the ball contained images of the same blonde women from the flower field. They were kissing and moaning. The muscular one kissed the other's neck, and the shorter one closed her eyes and gasped. Her cheeks were flaming, and Aereth noticed the muscular woman was doing something between the smaller woman's thighs with her hand. It was making the smaller woman moan loudly.

"No, child!" Queen Anindel shouted.

Aereth was so startled, she dropped the crystal ball, and it shattered on the floor in a floom of purple mist.

ZELDA PULLED HER LIPS free of Cassandra's and coughed as she and the knight were enveloped in purple smoke. When the smoke cleared again, they were standing side by side, fully clothed, in what appeared to be a bedroom at the top of a great tree.

To Zelda's surprise, Queen Anindel was sitting up in the four-poster bed and looking very sullen to see them there.

"Mother!" squealed a voice, and Zelda heard the patter of feet, then something had slammed into her waist and was hugging her.

Zelda looked down and smiled: little Aereth, now the size of a nine-year-old, was hugging Zelda so tightly, Zelda didn't think she would ever let go. She touched Aereth's auburn hair in relief, but the second the girl's hair touched Zelda's skin, she could feel something was wrong.

"What hast thou done?" Cassandra demanded of the fairy queen, for being a sorceress, she was able to see it as clear as Zelda, the change in Aereth's essence.

Zelda looked quickly, angrily at Queen Anindel, who slowly smiled, revealing her sharp fangs.

"The child is bound to Elwenhal now," said Queen Anindel quietly. "She must return here once a year –"

"Or?" Zelda snapped.

"*Or,*" finished Queen Anindel with a small, mocking smile, "she will perish." She looked between them, her green eyes laughing. "I told you it was too late."

Cassandra tensed and her hand went to her sword hilt, but Zelda was faster. Burning with sudden rage, Zelda's eyes blazed with power, and she extended her hand. The mocking smile was wiped from Queen Anindel's face when she was lifted bodily into the air. Her eyes widened and she gasped, clutching at her throat as if to pry off invisible hands.

Zelda—face twisted in fury, eyes glowing, hair beating back on an ethereal wind—was completely focused on choking Anindel with her mind and did not see the look of horror on Aereth's small face.

"Mother, no!" Aereth wailed, running toward Queen Anindel's hovering, gasping body. She turned and faced Zelda, tears in her eyes. "Mother, please don't hurt her! She's my friend!"

Zelda's rage was not sated. She wanted to keep squeezing and choking, wanted to punish Anindel and make her suffer, but she realized she was frightening her daughter, her small daughter, who—despite growing so fast—did not understand that Anindel was a villain.

Zelda glanced sideways at Cassandra and saw the Falcon Knight staring sadly at little Aereth, no doubt recalling her blind love for Melvalda, who Zelda had tried to persuade her was a villain, to no avail. Then she looked at Aereth again, whose face was pleading and pained. Very reluctantly, Zelda released Queen Anindel, the glow fading from her eyes, her golden hair tumbling limp again.

The fairy queen collapsed in a heap on the floor and knelt, hunched over and still gasping as she clutched her throat. She sheepishly lifted her eyes to Zelda, baffled by her power.

"Are you well, Anindel?" Aereth asked. She drew near the fairy queen, but Zelda said quickly, "No, Aereth! Come to me, and I shall send you back to your body!"

Aereth pouted, but she moved toward Zelda's outstretched hand and took it. Zelda's eyes closed, and the girl vanished. She did the same for Cassandra, taking her hand, casting a silent spell, and sending her back to Vallinwir. Cassandra smiled just before she vanished.

Still quivering a little with rage, Zelda turned her back to Queen Anindel, who was still kneeling breathlessly on the floor. She could feel the woman's eyes upon her back as she extended her hand, opening a portal back to Vallinwir.

"A part of her shall always be mine," said Anindel breathlessly, triumphantly, smiling a nasty smile. "She shall always be—" The word halted in her throat when a silent spell from Zelda snapped her mouth shut in a splash of blood.

Zelda smiled to herself and stepped through the portal.

Chapter 6

Back at Neserie's house, the knights greeted Zelda in much relief (and ignored it when Neserie yelled at Zelda for opening a portal in her sitting room). They gathered around and hugged and kissed Zelda, whose cheeks were kissed on all sides and were burning by the time they had stopped. And they took turns hugging Cassandra – Selene held on longest – and played with little Aereth, who squealed with joy to see them.

The knights were in shock, for Aereth had been an infant when she went to sleep and now she was a nine-year-old girl, with long arms and long auburn hair, the ragged tatters of her now-too-small clothing clinging to her long frame. Gweneth was the only one who didn't seem surprised and explained to the others that it was normal for the babes of Wilde Women to grow so fast.

Aereth leapt on Gweneth – who seemed to be her favorite – and Gweneth lifted the girl on her hip with a laugh and watched in amusement as she started talking very fast about her adventures in Elwenhal.

"And then, Nimwe and me climbed the tree all the way to the top," ranted Aereth, absently examining the boiled egg Neserie had given her to eat, "and I fell down from the branch, but the fairies caught me and lifted me away!"

"Who is Nimwe?" Selene asked, listening fondly, her hands in her pockets.

Aereth blushed a little. "My lady," she said, her lashes coyly fanning down.

Zelda noticed the knights exchange looks of relief and nearly laughed when she realized they had been afraid the child would fancy men.

"One day when I return to Elwenhal, I shall marry her!" Aereth went on. "Nimwe will be queen, and I shall be her love! Nimwe is the queen's daughter. She's a beautiful princess and—"

Zelda's face darkened. "So that was her plan all along! To wed Aereth to her daughter!"

"You mustn't be angry with Anindel, Mother," said Aereth sternly. "She loves me! I'm her daughter, too! You mustn't strangle her again!"

Gweneth grinned. "Did we miss something?" she asked Zelda.

Calain also seemed amused. She had been listening the entire time with her arms folded, but now she looked at Zelda, and her eyes were bright with silent laughter. Zelda suddenly remembered what Calain had said on Menosea about enjoying Zelda's anger, how beautiful she was when she was glowing with power. She had whispered it in Zelda's ear after they had made love.

"You lot had best pay me and be on your way," said Neserie, who was boiling a pot of seagull eggs over the fire. The flames lined her wrinkled face from beneath in shadows. "You've been here long enough. You'll led the Rose Guard right to my doorstep!"

Zelda was amazed that Selene's grandmother expected payment from her own grandchild. It was as if Talaedra had turned to Cassandra and asked her daughter for coin after rescuing her from Ravenhold. But Selene didn't argue. She took out her coin purse and tipped gold coins into Neserie's waiting hand, and as Neserie counted them, she told them again to leave. As they were filing out, she shouted something about them cleaning up the "horse shite" in her yard, but Zelda didn't catch it all because Selene wearily snapped the door shut, while Calain muttered, "*Hag*!"

Outside, the five horses were waiting in the yard as they grazed on the sparse grass there. Calain was happily reunited with Arthur, and Zelda decided to ride Lucky with Aereth. They all mounted, and then they were off, riding out of Eldaris and back to the flowery trees of Dark Bloom as the stars winked overhead in the sky.

They made camp after traveling a little way into the trees, and everyone was in a good mood, so happy were they to be together again. Cassandra and Aereth seemed famished after their time in Elwenhal, and so, they all ate, sharing what food they had left with the two as they sat around the fire.

Before long, Aereth fell asleep in Calain's lap while wrapped in the knight's cloak. Zelda was both happy and relieved to see how naturally her daughter took to Calain, who allowed Aereth to crawl into her lap and curl in her arms without any awkwardness or surprise, as if the child had done so a thousand times before.

When the knights asked Zelda where they were headed, Zelda told them without hesitation, "We must make our way to a city. Calain needs new armor, Aereth needs new clothes, and we all need fresh supplies."

"I have enough gold for an inn," Cassandra said. "Enough for one or two nights."

"Priine is out of the question," said Selene. "The queen has not pardoned us, and the Rose Guard may yet linger there."

"The Rose Guard is everywhere," Zelda reminded Selene. "But Priine is too noisy. I should like a good rest."

"Aye," agreed Gweneth. "And a good drink."

"There is Hawic to the east of Priine," said Calain thoughtfully. "We may have to scout ahead and slay a few goblins, however."

"And then what?" said Cassandra quietly. "We cannot return to Ellondhold. It has proven too dangerous." She glanced with regret at Aereth, who was sleeping in Calain's arm.

"I cast my vote for Ellormest," said Gweneth.

"Ellormest?" repeated Zelda curiously.

"Gwen's homeland," explained Calain.

"Tis quiet, beautiful," said Gweneth wistfully around a blade of grass in her teeth. She nodded at Aereth. "The babe would be safe there."

"I wanted to go to Edhen," Zelda admitted. She felt like a child admitting to some ridiculous dream, and she was surprised when, instead of teasing her, Gweneth said seriously, "Aye, my lady. Don't we all?"

Zelda blinked, puzzled. "What do you mean? How could you have heard of Edhen?" For according to Arryn, not many remembered it even existed.

"My people talk about Edhen as if it were some place you go to when you die," answered Gweneth with a laugh. "Tis a forest at the heart of Ellormest, but none can pass inside due to the enchantments. My people are simple folk, and none possess magick."

"Arryn spoke of Edhen as if it were hidden away somewhere," said Zelda, "but you say tis right in the middle of Ellormest?" she asked in wonder.

"Aye. The enchantments make it hard to spot, my lady," Gweneth explained. "People go in and come out confused, walking backwards, right back where they started. You are a worthy sorceress, but even you couldn't get us past the enchantments. Tis old elven magick."

Zelda took Arryn's Summoning Stone from her satchel. "But I know someone who can get us inside!"

"*Please*, don't say Arryn the dog knight," moaned Calain.

Zelda smiled, amused by Calain's irritation. "She is a Knight of the *Wolf*," she corrected (Calain rolled her eyes), "and she promised to come if I used this stone to summon her."

Calain glared at the small violet stone in Zelda's hand. And then, for some reason Zelda didn't understand, Calain glared at the necklace Zelda was wearing, which Selene had given to her. Zelda had the feeling Calain wanted to storm off but was held captive by her hesitation to wake Aereth. Zelda held back a smile.

"Then we all agree," said Gweneth excitedly. "We shall travel to Ellormest, and Zelda shall ask Arryn to let us pass inside Edhen."

"If the child shall be safe there," said Cassandra, though she seemed cautious.

"I shall do as my lady wishes—without complaint," said Selene pointedly, earning a glare from Calain.

Calain looked as though she would rather fall on her sword than accept help from Arryn, but she looked down at little Aereth again (who was sucking her fingers as she slept against her), and wishing for the child's safety, she said grudgingly, ". . .Aye."

THAT NIGHT AS EVERYONE slept around the fire, Selene and Cassandra sat on first watch together, and Zelda, unable to sleep for her anger against the fairy queen, sat up with them. Selene took the opportunity to steal away into the trees to relieve herself, leaving Zelda and Cassandra alone.

It was the first time they had been alone since Cassandra had joined them in Priine. Zelda wasn't sure all the dream meetings had truly counted.

"Are you well, my lady?" Cassandra asked. She was sitting on a fallen log beside Zelda, who was darkly poking the fire with a stick.

"I know the fairy queen's antics have rattled you," went on Cassandra in concern. "And then everything with Yrsa and Melvalda. . . And Calain."

Zelda glanced over at Calain, and her eyes softened with affection. Calain was sleeping on the ground with Aereth dozing on her chest, and it seemed right, as if it always should have been that way.

"If you need a listening ear," Cassandra said, "or perhaps a shoulder to weep on, I am always here."

Zelda looked up at Cassandra, whose serious gray eyes stared back at her dutifully, and she smiled.

"Yes, you *are* always there, aren't you?" Zelda said fondly. "But I have put what has happened behind me."

"Have you?" said Cassandra shrewdly. "Perhaps you have forgiven Calain and moved on from Melvalda, but you brood still on the fairy queen. You would like to slay her, which I would not advise, powerful as thou art."

"Yes," admitted Zelda, "I would have liked very much to have . . ." She trailed off, thinking angrily of Queen Anindel. "She stole my child!" Zelda burst angrily. "Now Aereth is enamored of her daughter, and one day she shall leave me!"

"I suppose you could visit," suggested Cassandra soothingly. "You are a sorceress and can enter Elwenhal as you please."

"But tis not just that!" cried Zelda. "What if Aereth grows up and decides she wants to be free of the contract, only now she is bound forever! Tis an evil thing to do to a child."

Cassandra cast her eyes down in silent agreement.

"And you!" scolded Zelda, making Cassandra look up. "You attempted to sacrifice yourself for me yet again! You would have been trapped forever in Elwenhal!"

Cassandra smiled. "Trapped forever while making sweet love to you? Twere no more horrifying a fate," she teased.

Zelda gave a relenting smile. "I mean it, Cassandra," she said heavily. "You cannot make such a sacrifice for me. The price was far too high. You would have been Anindel's plaything forever!"

"Tis my duty to protect your life and the life of your child," Cassandra answered gently. "I regret none if it." She was looking steadily at Zelda now, her eyes alight with hunger.

Zelda felt a thump in her and coyly glanced down, remembering how gently and yet hungrily Cassandra had tasted her sex. There was always something famished about the way Cassandra's mouth touched her, as if she had spent long days burning with unsated lust. Had she thought of Zelda all those times when she was traveling alone and Zelda was away with Calain and Selene? Had she hungered for her then?

"Do you think we shall ever make love outside our dreams?" Zelda said with a soft laugh.

"If I weren't afeared of waking the child, I'd chew my way through your panties right now," said Cassandra, startling Zelda.

Zelda blinked and looked up at Cassandra with her mouth open. The solemn knight had never spoken to her in such a suggestive manner, but then, they had never really been alone together.

Cassandra smiled at Zelda's shock. Her eyes went to Zelda's lips and she leaned close and kissed her.

It was the first time they had kissed in the real world, and so the pleasure was more vibrant, the strength of Cassandra's tongue more apparent as she gently touched the back of Zelda's neck, drawing her near with one hand. She was not wearing her gauntlets, and her hand was hard and strong. Zelda shivered with delight in her grasp.

Cassandra gently peeled her lips away and rested her forehead against Zelda's. "I swear by the gods, I shall have you alone soon," she said, breathless with arousal, and Zelda's heart leapt at the sharp look of hunger in her determined gray eye.

THE NEXT MORNING, THEY rode for Hawic, intent on fitting Calain in new armor and heading to a seamstress for Aereth. The trees grew so tightknit that they had to ride in a line. Calain and Selene rode side by side at the head of the procession, while Gweneth and Zelda rode side by side behind them – little Aereth in the saddle before Zelda – and quiet Cassandra brought up the rear.

It was a beautiful day in Dark Bloom, as ever. Birds sang, flowers cascaded in veils from the trees, and the sky beyond the green canopy above was a bright and cheerful blue.

The giant crystals pushed up from the earth, squeezing ten, eleven, twelve feet tall between the trees and humming softly with power. Zelda glanced happily at her necklace, glad for the fact that she now knew a charm that could protect her from their draining effect. Since Melvalda had explained to her why the sorceresses of Vira'Toss were restricted to Light Magick, she thought she understood why they were never permitted to learn the spells and charms that would protect them from Bane Stones. It was because the stones were men's way of controlling women with power.

"And there are unicorns," Gweneth was saying to Aereth as she rode Bron alongside them. She had been telling the child the legends of Edhen for some time while Aereth listened, enrapt.

Aereth loved Gweneth's stories, and Zelda thought with a smile that she was the only one who did. Having lived with Gweneth for years, the other knights were familiar with her tales to the point of irritation, while Zelda was more focused on getting Aereth to safety than anything else.

For Cassandra was right: the incident with Queen Anindel had left Zelda feeling paranoid. After listening to the knights explain how Aereth had been looking in the pond before she was taken, Zelda was fairly certain Queen Anindel had gotten past the fortress' enchantments by luring her child to the water. And suddenly, it seemed so easy that some lurking witch or fairy could swoop in and take her daughter yet again. Suddenly, she was terrified, when just a few weeks before, she had conceived the child while under the firm belief that she would always be protected by Yrsa, Revna, and the Black Bear Clan. Now it was just her and her knights again, against the world.

Zelda gazed sadly at the beautiful, flower-laden trees of Dark Bloom and wondered where Yrsa was and if she was well. This forest had been Yrsa's forest, and Aereth would have inherited its rulership had things been different.

But the child didn't know. Zelda still hadn't told Aereth about Yrsa and wondered if she ever would. Perhaps Aereth was better off not knowing.

"Bother the unicorns! Tell again about the Dragon Knight!" cried Aereth excitedly. She was eating an apple and took a big bite from it as she stared eagerly at Gweneth.

"Ah, the Dragon Knight," Gweneth obliged, clearly delighted to have someone so interested in her tales. "They say the ancient elven knights could shapeshift— That is, take on the form of beasts. Some, the most powerful, could take the shape of dragons. It was in this manner that the elven fought back during the human uprising. We humans had actual dragons, you see, so the elves invented a magick that could turn them into dragons and match our power."

"Is that why the elves are so angry?" Aereth asked. "Because we beat them in a war?"

"Elves live a long time and have long memories," said Cassandra quietly from the rear.

Gweneth nodded. "Cassie should know. Her mother is one of the last Tula-Dan, the ancient elves. That means she's thousands of years old."

"Whoa!" gasped Aereth.

"And the Dragon Knight would be much older seeing as the Dragon Wars were three thousand years ago," Gweneth went on thoughtfully.

"Why don't they just become dragons now?" wondered Aereth. "The elves in Eldaris seemed mad at humans. Why don't they just become dragons and eat us all?"

"Because shape-shifting is a lost art," answered Zelda before Gweneth could respond. "Humans have never mastered it, and only a rare few elven ever did."

"Aye," said Gweneth, pleased that Zelda had known the answer. "Your mother is right. The Dragon Knight is one of the last shape-shifters in existence – and she dwells in Edhen!"

Aereth's green eyes grew round. "Whoa! Shall we meet her?" She paused and asked with eager hesitation, "Shall we slay her?"

Zelda lifted her brows and exchanged an amazed glance with Gweneth. So Aereth had inherited Yrsa's bloodthirstiness. That was concerning.

"*Slay* her?" repeated Gweneth, affronted. "The Dragon of Edhen is a peaceful old creature. There have been many a tale of her swooping from the sky to protect the caravans. The nomad tribes of Ellormest have nothing but the greatest reverence for her."

"Oh," said Aereth, crestfallen.

"She is the reason so many seek to enter Edhen, that they might worship her," Gweneth went on. "A few suspect they have seen her in her elven form."

"What did she look like?" Aereth asked with interest.

"A small elven woman, not of the Tula-Dan but quite ancient just the same," answered Gweneth, "with long, black hair and violet eyes, and a sword that glows blue. . ." Gweneth trailed to silence as the realization hit her. Her eyes met Zelda's, and Zelda looked back at her, just as stung.

They fell into an awkward silence as Aereth looked between the adults in confusion. But Zelda knew what they were all thinking: was Arryn the Dragon of Edhen?

Map of Vallinwir

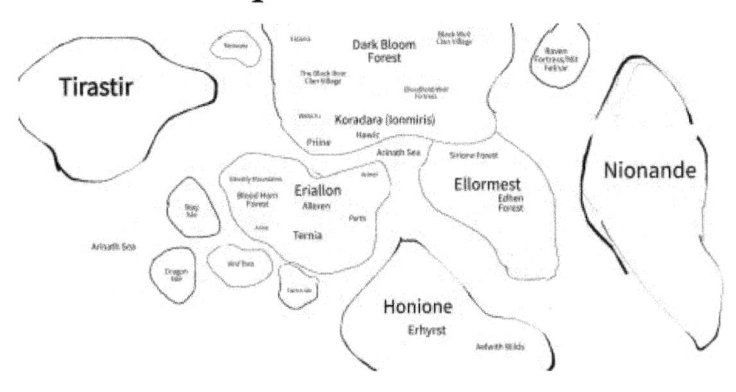

The Dragon of Edhen

Book 8

Chapter 1

Zelda, the four Knights of Falcon, and little Aereth continued on horseback to Hawic, moving in a tight procession through the trees of Dark Bloom Forest. Only now, the cheerful mood had been broken by an awkward silence that none could penetrate, not even Aereth with her squeaked demands to know what was the matter with the adults and why hadn't Gweneth finished telling about the Dragon Knight?

Zelda touched Aereth's hair and shushed her, and the child pouted and fell to snatching at the flower petals that kept drifting lazily from the trees. The knights were silent as Aereth played, sometimes casting Zelda the wary glance.

Zelda knew the knights were wondering if Arryn – a dragon shape-shifter! – could be trusted. All of them, that is, except for Gweneth, who seemed delighted by the prospect that Arryn was a legendary figure from the folktales of her people. She did not waste the opportunity to tease Calain that Zelda had lain with an epic being who had probably given her epic head, which had nearly brought the two to blows more than once. By the time they had left Dark Bloom Forest, Calain and Selene were both in a bad mood – Calain due to Gweneth's constant teasing and Selene due to continuously having to prevent their brawls over meals.

They had emerged from the forest just south of Priine and would have to continue traveling east to reach Hawic and avoid

Priine altogether. They made camp in the field as night was falling, as stars appeared in the purple edges of the endless sky and a gentle breeze bent the grass. Calain dug out a firepit, while Gweneth, Cassandra, and Selene hunted in the tall grass for twigs and broken branches that had blown over from the edge of the forest. The five horses grazed nearby, and Zelda heard Lucky complaining that he missed the hay from "the chicken farm."

In the distance, the ramshackle tents of goblins could be seen, rising lopsided above the grass. The goblins were not legally allowed to settle permanently so near the cities, but they were allowed to camp so long as they kept on the move. Zelda watched the smoke from their fires and dreaded having to battle them in the morning. The last thing she wanted in the entire world was to expose Aereth to bloodshed and violence.

Pushing her worries aside, Zelda telekinetically moved a few boulders around the firepit Calain was digging, so that she and the knights could sit on them. The rocks hovered momentarily over the dirt before she released them from her mind's hold, and they fell gently in a circle. She was vaguely aware of Aereth watching her in awe and she held back a smile. With the boulders in place, Zelda sat on one and watched as Aereth got on her knees and helped Calain dig the firepit. Calain was using a little spade, but Aereth was happily using her bare hands.

"Aereth!" Zelda cried, appalled, and Aereth sheepishly froze.

"I never get to do anything!" the girl wailed, flopping on the ground next to her mother. Zelda lovingly stroked her hair.

Calain glanced up at Aereth's pouting and smiled. "I have a feeling that one day you will do a great many things," she said, winking at the child.

Aereth brightened. "Shall I battle trolls and goblins? Like you and Auntie Gweneth?"

Calain glanced at Zelda, who looked horrified by the thought. "Calm yourself, Aereth. You'll give thy mother a heart attack. And since I am Bound to her, that wouldn't work out well for me." She caught Zelda's eye and smiled.

Zelda looked into Calain's pretty green eyes and couldn't help but smile back. Calain's smile always made her heart flutter. She had a feeling it was something that would never change.

Aereth watched the adults in bafflement. "You're Bound to my mother, Calain?" she said, her face twisting. "What does that mean?"

Gweneth had returned with a load of broken branches in her arms. "It means Calain can find your mother whenever she runs away and is naughty," she said playfully and dropped her load in the firepit.

Selene and Cassandra also returned with armloads of twigs. Selene stroked up a fire, and then they were eating supper around it as it flickered beneath the moonlight, sending smoke to the stars.

That night's supper was the last of the hare stew. Though Selene had hunted for them as they traveled through Dark Bloom, they were running low on rations. Zelda missed the bow she had used back when she was First Hearth Wife of the Black Bear Clan. She had been a good huntress, heading out with the other hearth wives to bag hares and pheasants. When she thought of those days now, it seemed as if that life had been lived in a dream. Aereth sitting beside her, messily gulping down stew, almost felt like the only evidence that it had been real.

The knights were happy again and fell to chatting and laughing easily. Aereth often joined in, making them laugh with her innocently squeaked questions about armor and horse riding. Zelda was silent and content as she listened to the happy banter. She focused mostly on Calain, who seemed to be in a jovial mood again, though occasionally, she caught Cassandra's eye across the fire.

Cassandra was looking at Zelda with a soft warmth in her eye that startled her. Cassandra had never quite looked at Zelda that way before. In the past, the witch-knight had always been serious . . . or burning with lust. But now, she was looking at Zelda with great affection. Zelda gazed back with a smile, wondering what she had done to earn such doting.

Eventually, the conversation fell to Arryn again – as Zelda knew it must—and the possibility that the elven knight was the Dragon of Edhen. Selene was cautious but still wanted to give Arryn a chance, while Gweneth was eager to meet Arryn again, so delighted was she by the notion that Arryn was a mythical figure that her people worshipped. Calain spoke of Arryn being the Dragon Knight as if it was proof that she had good reason to despise her all along, and Cassandra suggested more than once that Arryn could not be trusted (as Calain smugly nodded beside her, frustrating Gweneth).

Zelda couldn't believe it, but Cassandra was . . *.jealous*. She didn't like the fact that Arryn had lain with Zelda any more than Calain did, but she was less obvious in her jealousy, often dropping slight insinuations that made Calain nod in firm agreement.

Zelda almost laughed. Cassandra was so serene all the time, Zelda sometimes forgot that she could have negative feelings of envy or anger just like the other knights and couldn't believe it when she caught Cassandra glaring at the Summoning Stone Arryn had given Zelda.

The next morning, they continued across the open field to reach Hawic. Because goblins were scavengers, it wasn't uncommon for them to lurk in the fields outside of cities, and their little tent cities were dotted throughout the grass. A small band of them attacked as Zelda and her knights were crossing the field, running at them under the blue sky as they rode on the backs of tusked hogs. The knights made short work of them, while Zelda aided them with a few spells, but Zelda regretted that it had to happen in front of Aereth, who irritably pulled at Zelda's hand when it sought to cover her eyes and gleefully insisted on trying to watch the fighting.

The battle was thankfully over quickly, and the knights sustained few injuries. Zelda healed those who had been injured, Calain and Gweneth looted the bodies for things they could trade in town, and then the party had mounted and were moving toward Hawic again.

"Look, Goblin," said Gweneth to Aereth as they rode through the carnage. She pointed her blade at a dead goblin whose bloody mouth was open to reveal crooked yellow teeth. "That one's your pa!"

"It is not!" cried Aereth, who shrieked with giggles. But she blinked and looked up at Zelda, who was seated on Lucky's saddle behind her. "Mother...." She said slowly, "who *is* my pa?"

Zelda gave Gweneth a quick, scolding look (Gweneth shrugged apologetically), then said gently to the child, "I shall tell thee when you're older."

Aereth did not seem content with that answer, for she scowled impatiently. But then her eyes fell on the chipped blade of a dead goblin as they rode past, and she said, "Mother, why can't I have a sword?"

Zelda didn't feel that Aereth was ready for a weapon. But then she remembered that Wilde Women started training their babes the moment they started walking and talking, and most knights started as early as five years old. Aereth, meanwhile, had grown as big as a nine-year-old. It was time to pick a path and start her down it. At the rate she was growing, she would be a woman in two weeks with no skills if they did not.

Zelda glanced around at the knights, who were all riding their horses around her and trying to keep neutral expressions. None of them wanted to be thought of influencing Aereth one way or the other, and Zelda likewise wanted to allow Aereth to make her own choice.

"You would like a sword? Not a stave?" Zelda asked carefully.

"I want to chop off goblin heads! Like Calain! And Auntie Gwen!"

Gweneth chuckled. "Auntie Gwen now, am I?"

"Shall you teach me?" Aereth begged.

"If thy mother concedes," Gweneth answered, amused. "We do anything behind her back, she may just turn me into a frog." She winked at Zelda as she bobbed along on her horse and stuck a blade of grass in her teeth.

Zelda smiled, knowing that Gweneth was playfully referencing their argument in the barn. Given everything that had happened, the argument seemed so long ago.

Aereth twisted around to look up at Zelda, clasped her small hands together in prayer, and said, "Please, Mother? Shall I?" She stuck out her lip in a silly expression that made Zelda shriek out a laugh. Zelda didn't see it when the knights looked at her fondly, glad to hear her laughter.

"All right, little bear," said Zelda, touching Aereth's auburn hair with soft-eyed affection. "We shall buy you a sword in Hawic."

"Yay!" Aereth cried.

HAWIC WAS AS CALAIN had said. It was a mid-sized city, not loud and colorful like Priine. The people here weren't very friendly and kept to themselves, which suited Zelda and her knights just fine since they were fugitives on the run.

They made their way to the nearest inn, and when Cassandra had secured a room for them and they'd had a good hour's rest, they gathered outside in the sunlight. Aereth was clinging to Zelda's hand and talking excitedly about getting her first blade. She grabbed Gweneth's hand as well as she was talking and playfully hauled herself up in the air between both women.

Zelda gasped in shock to feel the strength in her daughter's arm, and Gweneth went completely still in surprise. They exchanged a look, but there was no time to speak, for Selene had started planning out their day in her commanding way.

"We shall all travel in pairs," said Selene. "I shall accompany Calain to the nearest smithy. Cassandra, you shall accompany Zelda and the babe to a seamstress. Gweneth, you shall stay at the inn and watch for signs of the Rose Guard."

"And if I see them what shall I do? Whistle very loudly?" said Gweneth sarcastically.

"You shall come and find Calain and I," answered Selene irritably. "Or fight them alone and be slain. Your choice."

"What about my sword?" cried Aereth, her hopeful eyes on Selene.

"Calain and I shall bring you one from the smithy. Worry not, little one," Selene answered, and Aereth grinned.

THE NEAREST SEAMSTRESS was a plump old woman who was appalled by Aereth's ragged tunic and breeches. "Tis as if she burst right out of them!" the old woman cried in much amusement, never dreaming that it was exactly what had happened.

The old woman had Aereth stand on a stool as she measured her, and then the snipping and cutting began as she refitted a tunic and trousers for the child.

While she waited for her clothing, little Aereth jumped on and off the low stool, pretending to fight imaginary foes with an imaginary sword. Zelda and Cassandra sat on a nearby bench and watched her.

"We shall have to buy boots for her as well," said Zelda, her eyes on her daughter's bare, filthy feet. She shook her head. "I'm sorry this is costing you so much gold, Cassandra."

"I am pledged to your service, my lady. My gold is your gold," answered Cassandra at once. "As soon as we are settled somewhere, we shant have to worry as much about paying gold for clothing. Serene is an excellent seamstress when she is well-rested, and I am not so bad at it myself."

"Truly?" said Zelda in surprise. "I always thought that sort of thing looked so complicated."

"Truly," answered Cassandra. "It is not so difficult a skill. They teach it to babes in the city."

The old seamstress, overhearing Cassandra, sniffed and irritably went, "Humph!" in her throat as she worked, pins sticking from her mouth.

"I confess," said Cassandra with a little smile, "we made Aereth's original clothes out of old bedsheets from the barracks."

Zelda smiled as well, but her eyes were sad and anxious. She was still watching as Aereth continued "slaying" an imaginary monster with her imaginary sword.

"Die, foul beast!" Aereth shouted.

"What troubles you, sorceress?" asked Cassandra. She was sitting with her knees wide apart, calmly watching Aereth as well, and Zelda thought she looked so big and strong, gleaming in her silver armor, a giant cased in metal.

"All she talks about is slaying things!" said Zelda in exasperation as she watched Aereth. "Tis appalling for a mother to hear that from the mouth of her innocent babe!"

Cassandra smiled. "Aereth is a Wilde Woman. Tis her nature. You were not so tame when you did nearly slay Anindel."

"But she would have deserved it!" Zelda protested at once. Her heart fluttered when Cassandra gently gave her knee a suggestive squeeze and said, "I was not scolding thee."

Zelda glanced up, and the intense look in Cassandra's eye made her a little breathless. She remembered what Cassandra had said about getting her alone soon and blushed a little.

But Zelda knew that getting her alone was going to prove challenging for Cassandra. Now that they were all together again, they hardly ever separated. If Zelda and Cassandra made love alone, without the involvement of the others, it would likely happen while everyone was sleeping. It was the only way she could see.

They went to the shoemaker next and had Aereth fitted for boots. By the time they returned to the inn, it was dusk. Calain and Selene were already there, waiting downstairs in the tavern with Gweneth. Selene had confiscated Gweneth's pint, which Gweneth protested against in a slurred voice, while Calain was wearing a new set of silver armor, which Selene had paid for and didn't seem ready to let her forget. With Calain and Selene bickering and Gweneth half-drunk, they all went upstairs to their room for the night.

Gweneth, tipsy as she was, was in no condition to keep watch. Selene helped her out of her armor and into bed, where she dozed off almost immediately on her back. Cassandra volunteered to take first watch, and so Selene and Calain also removed their armor and climbed into bed.

Zelda brought Aereth to the washbasin and struggled to clean the child's face, for Aereth kept squirming and sighing. Zelda managed to only get half the dirt off before she gave up, and Aereth dove with a giggle into the bed, where she fell asleep between Calain and Selene (Selene opened one eye, smiled, and pulled the coverlet over the child).

Cassandra, meanwhile, pulled a chair up near the window and sat on it, fully armored, her sword on her hip as she gazed out. Zelda removed her traveling cloak and watched Cassandra in frustration. She knew the tall, beautiful knight would never forsake her duty – keeping watch – to lay with Zelda, and there was no way Zelda could seduce her into it because she was fully armored.

Resigned to the fact that she would not be laying with Cassandra that night, Zelda walked over and sat in Cassandra's lap instead, deciding to keep her company for a while. Cassandra seemed pleased. She looked up with fluttering pale lashes and placed her arm around Zelda, but she still said in her soft, serious voice, "My lady should take her rest."

"I am happy here," Zelda said, resting her head against Cassandra.

Cassandra smiled. "You want to make love, I can tell. I have stirred it in you with my filthy talk of tasting your sweet sex."

Zelda blushed a little. "Perhaps."

Cassandra kissed Zelda on the head. "Go to sleep, my lady," she whispered, "and later, when Selene has taken watch, I shall meet thee in thy dreams."

Zelda smiled. She didn't know why, but she liked the idea of that. It was as if she and Cassandra shared a special, secret world that the others knew nothing of. But if she knew her knights well – and she thought she did – it was likely Cassandra had already told the others that she'd lain with Zelda in her dreams.

Zelda kissed Cassandra on the cheek and smiled when the knight's cheeks flamed a little. "Good night, Cassandra, my sweet knight," she said, rising.

"Good night," Cassandra whispered in a soft undertone, "my love."

Chapter 2

Though there had been no sign of the Rose Guard, they decided not to linger in Hawic just in case. Gweneth could tell it made Zelda nervous anytime they passed near a city. Now that Aereth had already been preyed upon twice – first by Melvalda and again by Queen Anindel—Zelda seemed adamant that it should not happen again and was almost beside herself with her anxiety.

In the morning, they departed from Hawic, and with the city at their backs, made their way south toward Ellormest. Gweneth was excited to see her homeland again, which she had not seen since she was a fourteen-year-old girl. She missed the rolling green pastures, and the ancient statues and pillars, which dotted the country all over. Such structures had been the scenery of every early childhood memory she possessed. Her first kiss had happened in an ancient elven ruin...with Annora.

Wishing to avoid bandits and highway men, they avoided the road, instead wading on horseback through wild country, which seemed to become wilder the further south they went.

Gweneth amused herself by telling Aereth the most horrible fairytales from Ellormest she could think of and laughing softly at Zelda's shock. Fearless little Aereth was eager for more bloody tales, but Zelda sternly forbade it, so Gweneth fell to watching the drama between her friends instead.

Calain and Selene were still bickering over the fact that Selene had dared to gift Zelda a necklace. Only, they knew Zelda would command they cease the arguing if she knew what it was *really* about, so they disguised their bickering by picking at each other over trivial things. The argument back at the inn, for instance, hadn't *really* been about Calain's new armor.

Gweneth had the feeling Zelda knew this as well but did not want things to escalate in front of Aereth, so she allowed the knights to vent their rage with low bickering.

Meanwhile, as Calain and Selene were distracted by their never-ending rivalry, Cassandra was falling in love with Zelda. And she was falling *hard.* Gweneth had known Cassandra for years and could tell.

And she felt bad for Cassandra as well. For out of all the knights, Cassandra had spent the least amount of time alone with Zelda. Now she was trying to make up for it, and the other knights – unbeknownst to Zelda – were trying to give the two space to know each other. Selene had assigned Cassandra first watch for a reason, knowing Zelda would stay up with her, and Calain had not barged in on them any time they were alone.

Zelda seemed to think her knights were always scrapping over her – and she wasn't wrong – but they did help each other secure their place at her side as well. Back on the *Atross,* it wasn't an accident that Zelda had found herself alone with Gweneth so often. The knights wanted Zelda to love and accept all of them, which meant they had to share her time and attention to allow her to know them all.

And as far as little Aereth went, the knights scrapped over her as much as they scrapped over Zelda. All of them wanted Aereth to love them the most but – for the first time possibly ever – Calain was not the favorite. Aereth loved Calain's playfulness and admired her battle skills; she loved Cassandra's quiet strength and often fell asleep in her arms; and she doted on Selene for being a calm, commanding presence that brought order and security to a world that no doubt baffled her – but Gweneth was undoubtedly Aereth's favorite and had been since she was a babe in swaddling.

If Aereth wasn't riding with Zelda, then she was riding with Gweneth on Bron, and everywhere Gweneth went, Aereth was two feet behind, squeaking questions at her and hopping to keep up, until the knights had nicknamed her Gwen's Shadow.

Gweneth loved Aereth like a daughter, and as she held the girl while she was sleeping, she thought with a laugh that she would never have pictured her life this way. She had watched the other women in her caravan wed and have children and spend their time feeding and changing swaddling, and she had looked upon their sweet femininity and had decided she could never be a proper mother because she was so masculine. But now here she was . . .a parent. And a damn good one, she thought.

The closer they drew to Ellormest, the more Gweneth thought of taking the group to meet her parents. She wanted to proudly present them and say, "Look what I've become! This is my life! Are you not proud?" and beam with pride. For she was a knight in service to a powerful sorceress, one of the highest callings a woman could achieve!

But Gweneth knew her father would not approve of her becoming a rebel. Sune had met Calain once during Gweneth's visit when she was fourteen, and he had despised Calain ever since, declaring her a bad influence on his daughter. He would not approve of Gweneth allowing herself to become involved in Calain's misdeeds.

And as for Gweneth's mother, Kare, she had never approved of Gweneth becoming a knight and would try – yet again – to coax her daughter into staying with the caravan and marrying one of the women there. She had tried several times during Gweneth's last visit, which had only further prompted her to leave after everything with Annora.

They made camp in a copse at midday and took their noon meal around a low fire. Afterwards, Zelda and the knights rested and the horses grazed nearby as Gweneth gave Aereth her first sparring lesson.

The girl was a quick study, Gweneth thought. She paid close attention to everything and learned very fast. It wasn't long before she had disarmed Gweneth, who lifted her brows in pleasant surprise as she snatched her blade from the grass. Her fingers were bleeding from the blow: the child had drawn her first blood! Gweneth was bursting with pride but concealed it with her usual casual air.

"Did you see what I did, Mother!" Aereth squealed, leaping up and down. "I smacked it right outta her hand!"

"Yes, I saw, little bear!" called Zelda lovingly, and Aereth beamed with pride, sticking out her chest. Though Gweneth thought Zelda looked a little worried.

"Gweneth is shite with a sword, not much of an achievement!" shouted Calain, whose hand was playfully smacked by Zelda for swearing in front of the child.

Aereth shrieked with giggles.

Gweneth smirked, twirling her sword with a loose wrist. "Put your blade behind those words!" she challenged.

Calain lurched up, grinning.

"Oh, for the love of . . ." muttered Selene, who was sitting between Zelda and Cassandra as she drank water from her skin.

Breathless and eager, Aereth tumbled into Zelda's lap and watched with her mouth open as Gweneth and Calain sparred.

Calain was the best of them and always had been, but she had her flaws like anyone else, and anyone who had trained alongside her for years would have marked them by now. Their blades crossed in the sunlight as Gweneth managed to parry every playfully vicious blow bigger, stronger Calain brought down on her. Any random enemy who didn't know Calain would have been defeated easily in that moment, but Gweneth predicted Cailan's next move and disarmed her.

Selene and Cassandra playfully cheered, and Aereth clapped her hands, delighted by the knights and their frolicsome mood.

"Tis easy to disarm Calain," dismissed Selene with a laugh. "I know from experience!"

More laughter, to which Calain massaged her wrist, looking a bit peeved.

"You shall always be the best, my knight!" Zelda called.

Calain smiled with soft eyes at Zelda and bowed.

"Now I shall spar with Calain!" shouted Aereth, springing up with her sword. "Come, Calain! Teach me that thing you did! Pleeeeease?"

"All right, little one," laughed Calain, going into fight stance. "No, place thy feet a little wider . . . That's it . . ."

Gweneth joined the others, taking Calain's vacated seat beside Zelda in the flattened grass. Her hand was still bleeding from Aereth's blow, and Zelda tisked as she took Gweneth's hand and healed it, her eyes glowing momentarily with power.

"My thanks, my lady," Gweneth said breathlessly. She flexed her newly healed hand, then slid her gauntlet on, which she had not been wearing while training Aereth.

"She cut you with the strength of a woman grown," said Zelda in an appalled undertone, so that Aereth could not hear. "Why is she so wildly strong? And why art thou not more disturbed?"

Gweneth laughed dismissively. "I keep telling thee: Aereth is a Wilde Woman! Tis normal that she should have great strength and wish to slay things! One day she shall be a mighty warrior, and woe to any fool that doth stand in her way!"

"You should be proud and worry not," added Selene. "Aereth shall never be the prey of men."

Gweneth laughed softly, thinking it ironic that Selene of all people should tell someone not to worry.

"I shall feel about this as I please!" cried Zelda. "Aereth is a Wilde Woman without a clan. She hath no place in the world."

"Her place is with us," said Cassandra.

"And when she is grown? What shall she do? Where shall she go?" said Zelda pointedly. "She doesn't even have other children to play with. I have brought a child into the world who is doomed to live on the outskirts of society!" She fell silent, staring at Aereth miserably, and she did not see the soft-eyed look Selene gave her.

Selene slid her arm around Zelda, kissed her on the cheek, and said soothingly, "We shall figure it out together. Aereth shall not be punished because we are enemies of Eriallon. This I promise you."

Zelda looked fondly at Selene and kissed the knight slowly on the lips, though when she looked up again, her sad eyes were still on Aereth, who was laughing as she sparred with Calain.

As it turned out, Aereth was paying more attention to Zelda and the knights than they had guessed, for she burst out over supper, "Is Selene my father?"

Everyone went still around the fire. Aereth was glaring at them all, daring them not to answer her. She had been after the subject since Dark Bloom, and Zelda had always responded vaguely, while the knights – wishing to respect Zelda's wishes – hadn't responded at all, often changing the subject should Aereth bring it up.

But now, instead of asking, Aereth was demanding an answer. Her shrill voice had cut through their merry banter like a knife.

"Why Selene?" asked Calain, making a face that – thankfully – made Aereth giggle.

"Because she was kissing Mother earlier," said Aereth, "and they looked happy." Her eyes danced thoughtfully over Calain. "I hoped it was you for a while," she said to Calain, "because Mother loves you best, and you're the strongest and a proper warrior!"

Calain liked that and gave Selene a mocking glance across the fire. Selene returned an annoyed glare.

"Is it Gweneth?" Aereth asked Zelda eagerly. "I hope it's Gweneth!"

Gweneth laughed softly.

Zelda frowned. "Why do you think your father's a woman? That's not how it works, my little."

"But that's how I was born!" Aereth insisted stubbornly. "I've heard you all speaking of a magick potion, and you've called my other parent a woman! I've heard you!"

The knights looked with concern at Zelda, who was frozen on the spot.

Aereth made a face. "I knew you wouldn't tell me!" she accused and sprang up, fleeing into the tall grass on skinny legs.

"Aereth!" Zelda called helplessly.

Gweneth sighed, setting aside her bread. "I shall go after her," she said wearily.

"Let Cassandra or I go," protested Zelda. "We can follow her essence."

Gweneth only laughed. "One doesn't need magick to predict the whims of a child. I shall find her, my lady," she promised and marched off into the dark.

BECAUSE THEIR PARTY typically followed a wisp-light cast by Zelda or Cassandra, it had been a long time since Gweneth had had to light her torch. But she also couldn't pretend it wasn't difficult to see in the dark without magick. Night had fallen as they were eating supper, and the fields scattered throughout the wild country would have been pitch dark if not for the large moon in the sky.

It wasn't hard to find Aereth regardless. Gweneth walked toward the nearest tree, held the torch aloft, and wasn't surprised when its light flickered over a small boot. Gweneth's heart softened when she heard crying.

"Why dost thou weep?" Gweneth asked gently.

"M-Mother won't tell me who my father is. I think she's ashamed of her!"

"No, not ashamed," answered Gweneth. "More like ashamed of the circumstances surrounding your birth. She was tricked into the marriage – not by thy father, but by someone who wished them to wed. Your father suffered the most as a result of the union, and your mother lives in guilt because of it."

Aereth's sobs quieted, and Gweneth knew the child was relieved that someone had finally spoken to her directly and honestly, rather than trying to coddle her and protect her.

"Now come down," said Gweneth. "Tis dangerous to run off alone. We draw near Sirione Forest. Tis the largest forest in my homeland, even larger than Edhen, and there are many trolls about, even on the outskirts."

Aereth scrambled down from the tree, still sniffling a little. But she was distracted by the talk of trolls. "Truly?" she said eagerly as she was hefted onto Gweneth's hip.

"Aye. Not that you'd need help slaying them," Gweneth returned with a laugh, "but tis best you don't wonder off." She hefted Aereth higher. "By the *gods.* How old are you today? Twelve?"

Aereth giggled, but it was true she had grown yet again.

They returned to camp, and a distraught Zelda scrambled to her feet and closed Aereth in a hug, scolding her for having run off.

"Can Gweneth be my father?" Aereth asked.

Zelda laughed, pulling back to look at the child. "The knights are all thy father," she said. "And now tis bedtime." She looked in Aereth's eyes, and her blue eyes crinkled up in a kind smile. Aereth smiled back, and Gweneth noticed in quiet amusement that she had Zelda's exact smile.

Chapter 3

As Gweneth had predicted, they arrived at the edge of Sirione Forest within a few days, but to Zelda's dismay, there were Wilde Women there waiting for them. It was only a small group, but Zelda knew enough about Wilde Women to be wary. These women were – like the other Wilde Women Zelda had seen – quite tall and muscular and draped in animal hides, with warpaint striped across their faces, and grim expressions. They were also wearing bones as breastplates and helms.

The woman who stood at the forefront of the group wore the skull of a young dragon upon her mess of black hair. She stared at them with serious, slanted eyes.

"Wilde Women of the Dragon Clan," said Gweneth in an undertone to the others. "They must've watched us cross the fields." She was staring steadily at the women, and she looked wary, though her hand had not gone to her sword hilt and remained instead on Bron's reins.

"Shall we slay them?" wondered Calain, who reminded Zelda painfully of Aereth in that moment. Like Aereth, Calain's solution was always to slay first, ask questions later. It was how they'd all come to be standing there in the first place, for Calain had slain the queen of Eriallon without pause. Had she learned nothing?

"No," said Gweneth at once. "The Wilde Women of Dragon do not pick pointless battles. They are powerful, but they are cautious. If they are here, it is to learn why we seek to enter their forest."

"We will speak with that one," called the lead Wilde Woman, pointing her meaty hand at Gweneth. "For she is one of the sheep people and understands our ways."

"The sheep people?" Calain echoed, puzzled.

Gweneth sighed. "My tribe . . . herded sheep," she explained.

"Don't let Gweneth go, Mother," begged Aereth. "They shall kill her!"

"Hush, little bear," soothed Zelda.

Her eyes on the lead Wilde Woman, Gweneth dismounted and moved forward.

"Tred carefully, Gweneth," said Cassandra as she passed.

The other knights dismounted as well, and so did Zelda, pulling Aereth down from the saddle. All of them watched as Gweneth moved forward through the grass, until she was facing the lead Wilde Woman, who also left the safety of her group to approach. Zelda realized it was a show of trust: both had made themselves vulnerable to the other group.

Aereth clung to Zelda's hand, and Zelda noticed that her fearless daughter was yet again intrigued by a situation she should have been terrified of. Instead, Aereth was goggling at the Wilde Women in silent admiration and wonder. Her little sword was harnessed to her back, and Zelda knew she was itching for an excuse to use it. But against a Wilde Woman? Zelda tightened her hold on Aereth, thinking she would cast a light-shield around them if there was any fighting.

"I am Eydis, queen of the Dragon Clan," said the Wild Woman with the dragon skull upon her head. "Why do you bring strangers to Ellormest, sheep woman?"

"I am Gweneth, a Falcon Knight and a sheep woman no longer," Gweneth answered. "I bring my fellow knights, our lady, and her child. We seek refuge. We shall cause you and the nomad tribes no trouble."

Eydis snorted. "Unless you draw the Rose Guard here," she said shrewdly. "If you bring the Queen-slayer and her sorceress, then you bring trouble. We cannot freely allow you entry. If you seek entry, we shall each choose a champion and let the gods decide." So saying, Eydis made a beckoning gesture, and a large woman with a two-handed sword on her back stepped forward. "I choose Olga."

Big Olga flexed, and little Aereth's green eyes grew round as she gazed up at her in awe. Zelda didn't blame her daughter for her amazement: Olga must've been seven feet tall and was bugling with so many muscles, Zelda wondered how it was possible that she could move at all. Her sandy hair was a wild tangle around her, and she was draped in skimpy animal hides and dragon bones.

"Well?" said Eydis, who was now looking directly at Zelda. "Choose your champion and let's have done with this. I have children to feed."

Zelda saw the Knights of Falcon all turn toward her as one, draw their swords, and plunge their blades into the earth, taking a knee before her. They bowed their heads and waited for her to choose one of them.

Zelda hesitated. She thought the entire thing was foolish, and she didn't understand why anyone needed to fight. Why couldn't the Wilde Women just stand aside and let them through? She thought for a moment of pulling the Summoning Stone and calling Arryn. If Arryn was truly the Dragon of Edhen, then she could grant them entry, couldn't she? But the Wilde Women might misinterpret it as Zelda casting an offensive spell and attack.

"Choose, Mother!" said Aereth excitedly. She was still clinging to Zelda's hand and looked up at her mother with eager green eyes, her little face framed by sheets of tangled auburn hair.

Zelda's eyes went from knight to knight. They were all still kneeling before her, heads down, eyes down, dutifully waiting. She didn't want any of them to fight against Olga, who looked fearsome enough to slay even a Knight of the Falcon, but Calain was the best fighter, the strongest and the most skilled, and Calain had defeated a Wilde Woman before . . .. Zelda had the most faith in her abilities.

"I choose Calain," Zelda said.

The other Knights of Falcon weren't surprised. They rose to their feet again and sheathed their swords (Gweneth was smirking), as Calain approached Olga, her sword drawn.

"May the best warrior win," said Eydis tonelessly, who looked as if she'd rather be elsewhere.

And then the fighting began. It was as if Calain were fighting Yrsa all over again. Olga was a head taller than Calain and her blows were so brutal, Calain staggered beneath her weight as she parried. Their blades crossed and clashed as they fought in desperate silence, grunting and struggling, panting and gasping. Calain wasn't as big as Olga, but she was wild, passionate, and skilled, often tripping up the bigger woman and giving as good as she got.

Aereth watched, mesmerized, as the two big warrior women struggled against each other. Zelda thought of covering the girl's eyes but it suddenly seemed useless. What was the point trying to hide the world's ugliness from the child? Especially when she would probably be a woman in a mere matter of days?

Calain's mouth was dripping blood and she looked weary but she never paused, never hesitated, never ceased fighting, no matter how Olga cut her, kicked her, or punched her. Zelda couldn't stand it and thought she would burst if she had to see Calain harmed again. And just when she was on the verge of protesting, Calain disarmed Olga and followed up with an elbow to Olga's face, dropping her to a knee.

As Calain stood panting over Olga (who bowed her head in defeat), the Wilde Women looked at her with quiet approval, and Eydis nodded sternly. "The gods have spoken," Eydis said, and she and the Wilde Women stepped aside.

Zelda and the Knights of Falcon led their horses past kneeling Olga and through the avenue of solemn Wilde Women. Aereth skipped smugly beside Zelda and kept beaming up at Calain. And as soon as they were within the trees of Sirione, the girl couldn't stop gushing about how amazing Calain was and was still ranting on as they made camp.

"And then she brought the sword down again and I thought she would kill her," Aereth ranted at Gweneth, who was listening in weary amusement, "but Calian got her at the last minute, sliced her arm and disarmed her just like that!"

Selene knelt to dig out a firepit as Cassandra went into the trees to look for firewood. Gweneth went to look for firewood as well, little Aereth hopping in her shadow and helpfully collecting twigs.

Calain pulled up a log and sat heavily on it. She was still bloody and injured from the fight. Zelda sat beside her and took her hand, sliding off the gauntlet and unbuckling the vambrace from which her blood dripped.

"My poor knight," said Zelda heavily. Her eyes glowed as she touched Calain's arm and healed her injuries.

"Worry not," said Calain, flexing her newly-healed arm so that the muscles bulged. She smiled at Zelda. "I was glad to fight for my lady again." Her eyes softened, she touched Zelda's face, and they kissed.

Selene glanced up at them as she dug out the firepit, and she had a strange sort of expression. Zelda couldn't decide if she was jealous she hadn't been chosen to fight Olga or glad for once that she wasn't Zelda's favorite. But before she could ponder it, she noticed Selene clutching momentarily at her heart. The dark knight was frowning and her eyes unseeing as she stared into space.

"What is ailing you, my knight?" Zelda asked Selene and was half-rising from her seat.

Selene smiled, but it was a weak, false smile, and Zelda could see the sadness in her dark eyes. "Nothing ails me, my lady. A little heartburn, tis all. Blame Calain's poor cooking."

Calain laughed and playfully threw a handful of grass at Selene, who laughed and blocked the spray with her arm.

Zelda wasn't convinced, but knowing she would never get the truth from Selene, she decided to play along and secretly observe her.

"Will I be as big as Calain one day?" Aereth asked Gweneth, hopping along in her wake as the knight returned with firewood.

"You'll be as big as a mountain," laughed Gweneth, who Zelda knew was thinking of Yrsa, the bear queen.

Like Olga, Yrsa had been more than six feet tall and covered with bulging muscles. Zelda found it hard to imagine her cute, skinny, squeaky-voiced daughter growing into a giant muscle-bound slayer of beasts. The very thought horrified her more and more, for Aereth kept growing and growing. The child was approaching adolescence in what seemed the blink of an eye.

For the first time, Zelda thought she understood what had made Melvalda want to turn Cassandra into a child. Zelda was tempted to cast a similar spell on Aereth, make her stop growing, or at least grow at the rate of a normal child. But growing rapidly was common in the babes of Wilde Women, and to interfere with what was natural in Aereth – even if it was different and strange – would be to violate her. And so, Zelda resigned herself to watching helplessly as her child quite literally grew overnight into a woman.

They continued on through Sirione, following the lead of Gweneth, who knew the way to Edhen by heart, having lived near it the first seven years of her life. They camped in the evenings, while Selene and Cassandra went out to hunt for them, while Calain sang songs and Gweneth told stories. No one spoke of the Dragon of Edhen again, though Zelda knew it had to be on everyone's minds, even Aereth, who she sometimes noticed gazing at the sky eagerly, as if she might spot the dragon flying overhead.

Zelda thought the forest of Sirione as beautiful and serene as Dark Bloom, though there weren't nearly as many flowers, and instead of a constant shadowy gloom – caused by the dark shade of the leaves in the trees – the trees here had leaves of a brighter green, which made the sunlight that filtered through even brighter. There were also no goblins or signs of Skoll Wolves, though Gweneth cautioned them against trolls, who slept in the shallow surface of the ground, often covered in moss and mud.

As Gweneth had described, there were ancient statues, towering stone pillars, and crumbling buildings throughout the forest, and they passed many of them as they walked in their tight procession, leading the nervous horses on. Some nights they even camped between the broken walls of the ancient buildings, taking shelter against the wind and rain and lying on their backs, gazing up at the stars through the shifting canopy of leaves overhead.

The statues were all of giant elves in flowing gowns and robes, clutching books and staves, long hair blowing back, the delicate tips of their pointed ears and noses always having broken off. They were massive, rising as high as the towering trees, so that their heads disappeared into the bright green canopy above.

Zelda remembered Gweneth saying that there used to be large elven cities in Ellormest and that Sirione Forest had grown over them, pulling the buildings and houses down into the earth. She tried to imagine what the area had looked like without trees blocking the heads of the statues. The trees themselves were so enormous, they broke the statues and pillars with their roots as they burst from the soil.

"My ancestors," Cassandra said, gazing with interest at the elven statues as they passed beneath an avenue of stone elven scholars clutching books and staring solemnly into space. "The ancient Tula-Dan."

"Aye," said Gweneth. "The Tula-Dan were the first elven race, weren't they? But then elves started breeding with humans, and they became . . ." She glanced sideways at Aereth, who was listening keenly, and Zelda knew she wanted to say "elflings" but did not, instead saying without skipping a beat, "Smaller elves."

Cassandra and Selene smiled, having noticed Gweneth's silent struggle as well.

"Elfling" wasn't exactly a slur, but it wasn't a nice word, either. One thing Zelda had dreaded about Aereth's doting on Gweneth was that the child would start speaking like Gweneth. But thankfully, Gweneth had decided to censor herself for the child's benefit.

On a particularly windy day, one of the statues suddenly toppled over. The knights shouted, and Zelda barely had time to recognize the shadow falling over her before the statue was barreling her way. With no time to react, she cringed, resigned to her fate – and slowly opened her eyes when nothing happened.

Zelda slowly looked up. She expected to see Calain or Selene, but it was Aereth who had caught the statue, preventing it from crushing Zelda alive. Aereth held the enormous statue above her head on skinny arms, grinning from beneath it at Zelda, her face smeared with dirt. With the lift of her arms, the fabric of her tunic was pulled back against her, and Zelda noticed with silent horror that her daughter was growing breasts.

"Tis all right, Mother!" Aereth squealed, seeing the anxiety on Zelda's face. "I have saved you!"

Zelda's eyes went to the giant statue Aereth was holding and her mouth fell open.

The knights were impressed by Aereth's display of supernatural strength, but Zelda was absolutely horrified. For her, it was just more evidence that her daughter was rapidly growing up, and there was nothing she could do about it. Aereth was growing breasts and was getting as tall as an adolescent. In a couple weeks, would she be a woman? Would she leave them and run off to join the Wilde Women? Perhaps the Dragon Clan would take her, and then they would never see her again. And what could Zelda say to stop her? She could not tell a grown woman what to do.

That night, Cassandra had first watch yet again, and because Sirione was such a peaceful, tranquil forest, the sorceress-knight took watch alone. The other knights slept around the low fire, wrapped in cloaks, gently breathing. Aereth had chosen Selene for a pillow and was dozing soundly with her head on the knight's breastplate. Zelda frowned at them, thinking that soon Aereth would be too big even for that.

Zelda sat around the fire with Cassandra, unable to rest for her troubles. She stared into flames, trying to understand what the point of a rapidly growing child was. Was it by design or just a side-effect of the potion, an accident? She supposed it made sense that the Wilde Women would want to rapidly breed, especially the Black Bear Clan, who seemed so determined to take Dark Bloom from the elven Wilde Women. Yrsa had indeed boasted about producing a horde of daughters and having them take over the forest.

"What troubles you, sorceress?" Cassandra asked. She was sitting beside Zelda with her knees apart, idly snapping twigs and tossing them in the flames. It was such a simple, casual thing to do, that for a moment, Cassandra seemed like a normal person – and not a sorceress-knight who could dream walk, predict the future, and lift a loaded wagon over her head.

"*Aereth*," said Zelda wretchedly. "She caught that enormous statue as if 'twere nothing!"

"You have seen us pull similar feats, for we are as strong. And you yourself have lifted heavy objects with your mind," Cassandra gently reminded her.

"Yes," said Zelda wretchedly, "but it's just proof that Aereth is growing up! Cassandra. . . she is growing breasts!" said Zelda, as if this were the most horrid thing in the world.

Cassandra laughed softly. "Fair Zelda, why is that such an awful thing?"

"Don't you understand?" said Zelda almost desperately. "Soon she shall start bleeding, and then she shall leave us! That damned *curse* Anindel put on her will pull her into Elwenhal. She shall wed the fairy queen's daughter, and we won't see her for long years at a time!"

Cassandra reached over and put a comforting arm around Zelda. "I am sorry I could not prevent what happened. I did my best to protect her."

"No, don't you go blaming yourself again!" Zelda scolded. "This was no one's fault but Anindel's. None of us could have predicted what happened . . ." Her voice trailed off as she realized who she was speaking to, and she looked at Cassandra awkwardly and said, "That is . . . I mean . . ."

Cassandra smiled.

"You still aren't to blame!" Zelda insisted. "It isn't as if you could control your visions."

"True enough. But Aereth growing up won't suddenly end your relationship with her, Zelda. She will still visit us, and if we ever get around to teaching her letters, I am sure she shall write."

"That's right," Zelda sighed. "We haven't educated her! I suppose she'd be fine without knowing her runes. I mean, most of the Wilde Women can't read or write, and they're . . . fine. Aren't they?" she said uncertainly and wrung her fingers, looking up at Cassandra with helpless blue eyes. "But suppose she can't find a clan? She'll need to know how to read and write to survive in the city, and we—"

"*Calm* yourself, fair Zelda," said Cassandra soothingly and rubbed Zelda's shoulder. "Aereth will be fine. We shall teach her everything we know—how to fight, how to cast spells, how to survive in this world – and when she is ready, she will go forth and she will thrive."

Zelda didn't know why, but the confidence in Cassandra's words comforted her. All the panic, worry, and fear drained slowly out of her, her heart slowed, and she dropped her head against Cassandra's shoulder. Cassandra was still rubbing Zelda's shoulder, and she was not wearing her gauntlets. Her hard, strong hand gripped tightly on Zelda's shoulder a moment, then moved to the front of Zelda's gown. It was the gown Cassandra had bought her weeks ago in Priine, the blue maternity gown that had pockets in the front that opened, allowing her to breastfeed. Cassandra slowly pulled the front laces, and Zelda watched as one of her heavy breasts spilled out.

Zelda's breasts had stopped producing milk, but they were still plump and full and large, and the pink nipple was hard, in rigid anticipation of Cassandra's touch. Gray eyes narrowed in hunger, Cassandra's eyes turned from Zelda's exposed breast to her lips. She gently turned Zelda's face to hers, and as she kissed her, her hard hand closed on Zelda's breast in a careful massage.

Zelda kissed Cassandra back breathlessly, her cheeks flaming as the pleasure flushed through her. Cassandra's kiss deepened as her hand massaged Zelda's heavy breast, and her tongue slid slow and hard in Zelda's mouth, thrusting against Zelda's tongue with an insistence that made her shiver. They turned their heads through the kiss, and Zelda could feel Cassandra's other hand reach for her. In seconds, she was in Cassandra's lap, her back against the knight's breastplate as she gently tugged the rest of the fabric down, exposing both of Zelda's breasts.

Zelda leaned back against Cassandra, her large breasts lifting, and as Cassandra cupped her breasts from under and massaged them, Zelda turned her head, their breathless mouths found each other, and they kissed hungrily again. Zelda moaned before she could stop herself, and Cassandra pulled back, whispering, "Hush!" so that her lips brushed Zelda's lips. They kissed desperately again.

Cassandra's touch was hard and fervent, as if she had longed for this moment for days. It wasn't the same as sex in a dream. In a dream, the sensations were dulled because it wasn't real. Here, every touch, caress, and kiss was magnified by a thousand, so intense that Zelda could feel Cassandra's hands long after they had stopped groping her.

As they continued kissing, one of Cassandra's hands released Zelda's breast and tugged up her skirt, revealing her panties. Her hand smoothed over Zelda's thigh, and she carefully placed both Zelda's thighs over her own, spreading her legs so that Zelda's legs were spread as well. And then her hand had plunged down the front of Zelda's panties and was hungrily touching.

Zelda moaned again as they kissed. Cassandra's careful fingers were massaging her clitoris, which had already been pumping, but now it throbbed harder and faster, helplessly exposed to Cassandra's insistent touch.

Still fingering Zelda's clitoris and groping hard at her breast, Cassandra's kisses traveled down Zelda's neck to her shoulder. Up and down Zelda's neck and shoulder her hungry mouth continued, back and forth, until Zelda was shivering and blushing and on the verge of a sudden climax. Her head fell back against Cassandra, and her pink lips parted to cry out, but Cassandra was quick. Her hand released Zelda's breast (which jiggled hard from the motion) and covered her mouth firmly, muffling her cry, as she continued to fondle Zelda's clitoris to a hard pulse.

Mouth covered, breasts exposed, Zelda squirmed in Cassandra's lap, lost in a helpless daze of ecstasy, and it wasn't until she was trembling and in the middle of climaxing that she noticed Aereth watching them in wide-eyed fascination from behind the tendrils of her auburn hair.

Chapter 4

Gweneth was so happy to be in her homeland that it took her quite a while to notice that something strange was going on. On their third day in Sirione, she was splashing her face with water from her skin when she noticed Zelda and Cassandra trying very awkwardly not to look at each other while Aereth observed them very intently across the firepit. These incidents continued – over meals, as they were walking or riding, at night as they prepared to sleep. Gweneth thought of poking the beehive, of dropping a few jokes and seeing how Zelda and Cassandra reacted, but not wishing to stir up any drama and sour everyone's light mood, she decided not to bother. It was a shame because she relished the thought of mocking and humiliating Zelda and Cassandra for whatever it was, but she had other things to focus on – like avoiding her family's caravan.

As it turned out, Gweneth didn't have to poke and prod to find out what was going on because Aereth told her directly. It was the end of another day and the sun was setting beyond the trees as Gweneth, Selene, and Cassandra hunted for firewood in the nearby underbrush, while Calain dug a firepit, and Zelda used telekinesis to move a few boulders and heavy logs into place for seats.

Aereth had, as always, decided to follow Gweneth and help her collect sticks. Gweneth was bending to pick up a nice dry stick when Aereth blurted out, “Auntie Gwen? Will you tell me about sex?”

Gweneth nearly dropped the sticks she was already carrying. She straightened up, adding the new stick to her bundle, and looking in surprise down at Aereth’s serious, unabashed face. But she had to ask herself why she was surprised: in just three more days, Aereth now looked like a fourteen-year-old girl. She was nearly as tall as Gweneth—who was just under six feet—and was now a head taller than Zelda, and she had small breasts and wider hips and was taking on a woman’s shape. Her body was also more defined with muscle from their daily training sessions, but she hadn’t started bleeding yet, something which seemed to relieve Zelda greatly. Aereth had grown so much that there was one night when Selene and Cassandra had sat up for hours altering the girl’s clothes because she was outgrowing them – *again.*

“Tell you about . . .” repeated Gweneth because she felt too awkward to speak. She was the main one constantly reminding Zelda that a Wilde Woman babe becoming a woman almost overnight was completely normal, but she was finding it harder and harder to digest. Just days before, Aereth had been a sweet little girl swinging from her biceps and giggling. Now she was a serious young woman, standing with her arms behind her back and regarding Gweneth intently. She had tamed her long auburn hair back into a single plait in imitation of Selene.

“Sex,” Aereth prompted when Gweneth’s voice nervously trailed off. She had asked the original question without shame, but her cheeks flamed a little as she said, “I saw Mother and Cassandra . . . having sex a few nights ago.”

Gweneth laughed. Ah. So *that’s* what all the squirming was about! She went back to looking for sticks, wading through the bushes and flowers. Aereth followed closely.

"You saw them going at it," said Gweneth in amusement, "and now you want to know what it's like?"

"I can find that out on my own," said Aereth with a laugh, and Gweneth laughed as well. "What I want to know is, can I make another woman with child?"

Not wanting to hurt Aereth's feelings, Gweneth kept her face neutral as she straightened up, adding another stick to her bundle. "Not without the help of a powerful sorceress," she said. "You were right before, you know. You *were* conceived with a magick potion, but it was brewed by someone with a lot of ancient wisdom. You cannot make a woman with child by fingering her, Aereth."

Aereth looked a little embarrassed but also relieved.

Gweneth bent for another stick, pretending not to notice. "Why not ask thy mother this?"

"Because she is too embarrassed after what I saw," said Aereth with a laugh.

"Aye. I suppose she would be."

"And you're the only adult who... who listens to me," Aereth went on. "The others think I'm a babe still. They don't answer my questions. They pat me on the head and send me on."

"Don't take it too personally. They're just afraid. Most children grow at such a slow pace. It was just what? A month ago? That you were a babe in swaddling!"

"But I'm *not* anymore, can't they see that?" cried Aereth impatiently.

Gweneth moved off, looking for more firewood, and Aereth quickly followed, tripping slightly over a bush as she hurried to catch up.

"Auntie Gwen," said Aereth breathlessly, "I want your help finding... I want to find a woman!"

Gweneth halted in surprise and faced Aereth, who blushed brightly as she confessed, "Queen Anindel told me I would want to touch a woman one day. I told her I would not, b-but now I'm realizing she was right. I want to kiss another girl!" She glanced down and added sheepishly, "I think of it all the t-time."

Gweneth didn't answer right away. This was more difficult than she had ever imagined, and if she was honest with herself, she had never imagined it! Despite how quickly Aereth was growing, she had told herself that Aereth would always be that giggling little girl who followed her about.

When Gweneth looked up again, it was to find Aereth looking at her hopefully. Gweneth turned and picked up another stick, sighing as she said, "I was trying to avoid the caravans. I didn't want to run into my family or anyone I know. . . But I can see this is important to you, so I shall lead us on their trail. I know the path they'd take this time of year."

Aereth brightened. "Oh, thank you, Auntie Gwen!" she cried, leaping on Gweneth and hugging her. Gweneth dropped her bundle of sticks as she fumbled to catch the girl, and as Aereth kissed her cheek, she laughed, suddenly reminded of Zelda.

And so, the next day, Gweneth took them along the trail that would eventually lead them to one of the caravans. She knew what path the caravans would take this time of year because their pattern of movement was dependent on the sheep and what food grew where.

Aereth, now tall and bulging with her first lean muscles, rode the sturdy brown horse, Lucky, on her own, while Zelda sat once more before Calain on Arthur's saddle. They had taught Aereth to ride and she had taken to it quickly and effortlessly – as she seemed to take to everything. Gweneth was starting to understand why Wilde Women had gotten away with taking over so many forests. They were just too strong and multiplied too quickly for the crown to bother trying to control them.

It was midday when they finally came across a caravan. The long line of covered wagons moved slowly through the giant, moss-covered trees, surrounded by herds of baaing white sheep and running children who laughed in the sunlight, four hundred people all moving at their leisure in a crowd. Gweneth could see dogs, robed shepherds with staffs, heads wrapped in scarves. On the back of one tall wagon, a woman sat on a chair, singing and strumming a lute. The people were wearing colorful, patched clothing, beaded shawls and sandals, and many of the women wore thick gold bracelets and gold loops in their ears.

The caravanners were also covered in tribal tattoos. The women had swirling tattoos on their cheeks and hands, as did the men, and almost everyone was sporting an undercut, either a full one or a half one, while the rest of her their long hair was tangled with beads. Gweneth was relieved, knowing she could ask one of them to trim the back of her undercut for her, as Calain was rather bad at it and it had been growing out from neglect.

"I thought we were avoiding the caravans, Gwen," said Calain, who was riding Arthur with Zelda just behind her. "But you have led us right to one."

"I thought Aereth should actually see other people before we shut ourselves away in Edhen," answered Gweneth with a shrug. "There is no one there, you understand? No one can get inside Edhen but for the dragon, and those who *do* make it inside are never seen again."

"Do you suppose she eats them?" wondered Aereth aloud. She was riding Lucky beside Gweneth and looked almost gleeful at the prospect of the dragon eating people.

Gweneth frowned. "No, child. The Dragon of Edhen is gentle and good – *so good.* Right, Zelda?" She glanced back and laughed when Zelda blushed a little and Calain glared past Zelda's hair at her.

But if Gweneth was honest with herself, as much as she hoped Arryn was the Dragon of Edhen, she was not happy about the fact that Arryn had slept with Zelda any more than Calain was, she was just less likely to be open in her displeasure about it. None of the knights were happy. Gweneth could tell that even Selene did not approve, though she pretended to be uncertain and willing to give Arryn a chance.

Arryn had trespassed by taking Zelda to her bed. She was not a part of their group, and Zelda was not her lady. She had not sworn herself in Zelda's service, and if she had, Zelda hadn't broken the news to any of them. Would they arrive in Edhen to discover Arryn would be joining them permanently? Gweneth had the feeling that if such a thing was announced, she and the other Knights of Falcon would draw blades, and the end result would not be pretty.

The caravanners were jovial and carefree and didn't seem disturbed by the appearance of strangers behind them on the road. They welcomed Gweneth and the others eagerly, offering food and water, and Gweneth knew why: the caravanners of Sirione Forest were, as a rule, under the protection of the Dragon Clan. Every now and then, they would send one of their young virgin maidens to become the hearth wife of some large warrior woman, and in return, the Dragon Clan protected them from strangers, intruders, and trolls.

Not that there were many strangers and intruders in Ellormest. No one ever came to Ellormest because many people were superstitious and believed the place cursed. Ellormest was – according to legend—the place where the Tula-Dan met their downfall and perished of a mysterious illness. Many believed they had caught a disease from having established trade with humans, and that was the end of the Tula-Dan and beginning of the Ellomir, the modern elves, who were smaller and shorter lived.

"Alva!" shouted a man, and Gweneth groaned, for she recognized the old man. His name was Tyr, and he was an old friend of her father's. He was sitting on the back of a covered wagon and waved at her as she passed on horseback. Gweneth awkwardly waved back, wishing he would stop drawing attention to her, but it was too late. The caravanners were starting to notice her. Heads were sticking out of wagon windows and voices were shouting her name.

"That man called you Alva," said Aereth when they had ridden on.

"Yes," sighed Gweneth, "because Alva was my name . . . When I lived in this caravan."

Aereth blinked. "But why change it?"

"Because it's a nomad's name," answered Gweneth. "A foreigner's name. I wanted to belong when I went to Eriallon, so I took an Erialloni name."

"But what's the matter?" asked Aereth, noting Gweneth's weariness.

"I said I'd bring you a caravan, but I didn't mean *mine,*" said Gweneth with a helpless laugh. "I had thought never to see my family again, and I was fine with that."

Aereth frowned. "But why? I thought you loved your family! You told me so many stories about them!"

Gweneth didn't answer. It had finally happened: her parents had heard she was here and were rushing to her. She saw them pushing through the sheep. Her mother had gray hair now, as did her father. Her mother's hair was long, thick, and loose, but her father had a silver undercut tied in a topknot atop his head. Both were covered in swirling tattoos and wearing colorful shawls.

Her father was moving very slowly on a cane while her mother impatiently hurried him along.

Gweneth pulled Bron to a stop and dismounted. The others followed suit, and they stood in a little group, watching Gweneth's parents approach through the cloud of white sheep.

Kare, Gweneth's mother, nearly pounced her. She shrieked with laughter and pulled Gweneth – who was much taller than her now – down in a tight hug. "Oh! Alva!" she cried. "My youngest baby – my babe has come home!"

"So you're the youngest," said Selene, lips curled in a little smile. "That makes so much sense."

Gweneth rolled her eyes at Selene's words, but she didn't have a chance to shoot off a retort because her father hugged her next, and soon, both were crowding her. When her parents were satisfied they had smothered her enough, they stood back and looked at her, beaming, and Gweneth saw her own dark blue eyes in her mother's kind face. Then their eyes traveled over the others. Kare looked happy to see everyone, but Gweneth's father, Sune, glowered when he saw Calain. Calain smiled sarcastically at the old man.

"I see you still keep the same company," said Sune, glowering so hard at Calain that loose wrinkly skin slid down in his eyes.

Calain seemed amused by the old man's hatred of her and kept smiling.

"Oh, *Father,*" said Gweneth dismissively. "Calain is a good woman and a true sister in arms. She was a child when you first did meet her. Do give her a chance."

"Humph!" was all Sune said in reply to that. But his eyes moved over Cassandra and Selene, and he nodded in approval. "These two were well-behaved, that I recall. But elven children usually are. They've got strong elf blood; I could always tell . . . And who is this?" He smiled warmly at Zelda.

Gweneth took Zelda's arm and gently guided her forward. "Father, tis my lady, the sorceress Zelda. And this is her babe, Aereth. I am pledged to both."

Zelda seemed pleased and surprised by Gweneth's polite introduction of her, and Gweneth wondered if she had expected her to make some harsh joke about her promiscuity or the slaying of the queen of Eriallon. She couldn't blame Zelda for thinking that after all the taunting she'd done in the past.

Zelda spread her skirts and politely lowered herself in a curtsy to Gweneth's parents. Gweneth thought her parents were in love. They stared at Zelda dotingly, and then they crowded Aereth, who – in their minds – was the closest thing to a grandchild they would ever get from Gweneth. They marveled at how strong and tall the girl was, but when Kare pinched Aereth's cheek and told her she was a pretty girl, Aereth squirmed free and said with confidence, "I do not wish to be pretty! I wish to be strong!"

Sune happily clicked his tongue. "Smart girl!"

"Where are my sisters?" asked Gweneth, glancing past her parents. She didn't expect many of them to still be there. It was common for people to move between caravans due to marriage or friendship, but *none* of her sisters were standing behind her parents. For some reason, there was a young red-haired girl hovering behind Kare and Sune and clutching a lamb under her arm. She looked very nervous, and Gweneth was annoyed by her – she wanted the girl to move so she could look for her sisters.

"Let's see," answered Kare happily. "You already know Gull, Runa, and Selby married into other caravans – Runa took up the herbalist trade from me, isn't that wonderful? I had hoped you would, Alva – *Not* that I want to start another argument, but—"

"Selby is making bizarre clay pots or some shite," said Sune, shaking his head. "She was so good with a bow! What a waste!"

Gweneth laughed. Her father had never approved of Selby's random, weird undertakings. The last time she'd visited, Selby had been doing something strange with beads.

"Gull married a nice boy," went on Kare happily, "though he does seem a bit slow. Walks into trees, puts his pants on backwards, but he loves her and is kind. You remember him? I think he was here when you visited."

"Gull's mad husband?" said Gweneth. "Who could forget?" She heard Zelda laugh and had nearly forgotten the others were there, listening attentively to their happy banter.

"What about Bren?" spoke up Calain. She grinned. "I *remember* Bren!"

Sune glared at Calain as if he would burn a hole through her with his stare, and Gweneth held back a laugh: Bren was Gweneth's big-breasted sister, very pretty, and had been caught kissing Calain by Sune, who had nearly taken Calain's head off over it. Calain was now deliberately provoking the old man, and though Gweneth thought it funny, she gave Calain a scolding look nonetheless: the last thing they needed was for Aereth to witness Gweneth yanking her elderly father off Calain as he tried feebly to strangle her.

"Bren became a hearth wife during one of the yearly tributes," said Kare quickly, before Sune could yell, "with the Dragon Clan."

Gweneth looked around at her mother in surprise. "Bren was a tribute virgin?"

"Aye," said Sune, "and don't look so glum. Be proud! Your sister is *well* taken care of. And she fancied women anyway. It was perfect for her."

"She's madly in love with her wife!" said Kare gleefully to Gweneth, and Sune nodded smugly at Calain, as if to rub it in.

"And it's nice to have her nearby," went on Kare. She paused and added, "*Not* that I'm saying I wish *you* had become a Wilde Woman and stayed nearby. I don't want to start an argument—"

"I know, Mother, I *know,*" sighed Gweneth. "Dagmar and Ase? What of them?"

"We had Dagmar's wedding when last you came," answered Sune. "You remember that boy she married? His eyes were a little too together close for my liking. I didn't care for him much. They moved to Alleren."

"What the devil for?" Gweneth asked in amazement.

Sune shrugged bitterly. "You know your sister always hated being a nomad. She wanted the city life and she found a boy who felt the same. She still writes . . . not that it does us any good."

Gweneth knew why her father sounded so bitter: he and Kare couldn't read.

"Ase went off to Realm Honione to be a smithy," said Kare a little sadly.

Gweneth thought Cassandra also looked uncomfortable at the mention of Honione and couldn't imagine why. Gweneth lifted her brows at the news but she couldn't say she was too surprised. Her sister had always been heavily interested in the craft. "But what about her husband?"

"Eian died when bandits attacked the caravan a few years ago," said Sune heavily.

"Bandits?" said Gweneth in disbelief. "In Sirione?"

"I know," said Sune darkly. "The gall that they came here!"

"But how did they get in?" Gweneth said pointedly. "The Dragon Clan guards this forest like, well . . . *dragons.*"

"The gods do only know," said Sune. "Sometimes I think the Wilde Women *let* them in. We didn't give them a tribute virgin that year, you see. But don't go repeating what I said. A Wilde Woman hears you, she'll chop your head off."

"Alva . . ." said Kare, beaming. She gestured at the young girl hovering nervously in the shadows behind her. "I want you meet your younger sister."

"My what?" Gweneth repeated.

Sune straightened up proudly. "Her name's Enid. Turns fifteen this summer. She's our . . ." he chuckled "happy accident."

"I didn't think I could bear forth more children!" said Kare mischievously. "But your father and I did get frantic one night, and well . . ."

"Mother!" Gweneth begged, pinching the flesh between her eyes, and she heard Calain, Cassandra, and Selene laughing. Zelda was also smiling, greatly amused. Aereth was peering eagerly at the girl in the shadows, and Gweneth remembered that Aereth hadn't even been around people her own age before.

"Your mother and I are jesting," said Sune, smiling. "Enid lost her parents during the bandit attack, and we took her in."

Kare gently took the meek girl in the shadows by her arm and brought her forward into the sunlight.

The girl was quite shy and pretty, with pale blue eyes, and a round face hidden behind curtains of long, curly, red hair. She was wearing a colorful patched skirt and tunic and a beaded shawl and kept her eyes shyly down. The little lamb under her arm baaed softly and she patted its small head.

"Well, go on," gently scolded Kare. "Say hello, child!"

Enid glanced up and stammered, "H-Hello!"

"Hello!" said Aereth, confidently stepping forward. "I'm Aereth! Want to ride my horse with me?" She patted the side of Lucky's long face, and the horse snorted.

Enid looked up at Aereth with round blue eyes, as if she had never quite seen anything like her before, and Gweneth chuckled, privately thinking that she hadn't.

"Yes!" whispered Enid. Fumbling and nervous, she put down the lamb (which bounced off into the herd of sheep), and as everyone watched, Aereth lifted Enid by the waist and set her easily in the saddle. Enid blushed to see how strong Aereth was, and Gweneth was reminded painfully of Zelda and Calain. Then Aereth climbed up behind Enid, snapped the reins, and took off. Lucky galloped away alongside the caravan. Gweneth could hear Enid actually shrieking with laughter, they were going so fast.

"And don't go too far!" Zelda shouted after them. She frowned indignantly. "She didn't even *ask* me for permission first!"

"Aereth is growing up, Zelda," said Calain soothingly. "They are rebellious at that age." She glanced at the others, grinning. "Remember how we were?"

"Yes!" said Sune darkly before anyone could answer, and Gweneth held back a laugh.

"Well, since you're here, you might as well come to our wagon for supper," said Kare, holding open her arms (her shawl spread like wings from the maneuver) and herding them all along the caravan toward their wagon. She took Zelda's arm as they went and started drilling her with questions, and Zelda answered pleasantly, surprised that Kare had such an interest in her. But Gweneth wasn't surprised. It only made sense that her mother would want to know everything about the woman her daughter would serve for the rest of her life.

But Zelda didn't have the greatest background. She was a peasant from the streets of Perth who had been raised by an abusive uncle, and after that, she hadn't had many friends at Vira'Toss. Even her one friend, Wick, had apparently declined to protect her from Melvalda. Gweneth could see Zelda struggling and hesitating to answer Kare's questions, for she didn't want to unload a sob story on the woman and dampen everyone's mood.

Kare was nonetheless waiting eagerly and didn't seem aware of Zelda's awkwardness.

"Zelda doth mix potions well," said Gweneth, coming up and putting her arm playfully around Kare to distract her.

Kare brightened. "Oh! Then you must know something about herbs!" she said happily to Zelda.

"Yes, I do," Zelda said in great relief and met eyes with Gweneth, silently thanking her.

Gweneth winked at Zelda.

"Well, then," Kare said happily, "if my daughter serves you, and you're going to open a potions shop, then my daughter will be working in a potions shop – with herbs! Which means I got what wanted after all!" cried Kare triumphantly and playfully poked Gweneth's silver breastplate.

AERETH LOVED SHOWING off. She was a great rider (Calain had called her a centaur!) and did not hesitate to leap Lucky over low logs and bushes. Each leap and bound made Enid shriek with laughter and her red hair toss. When they had slowed down to a walk, Enid breathlessly confessed that she had never ridden a horse before. She looked back at Aereth with admiring blue eyes, her cheeks flushed from laughter.

Aereth looked down at Enid and thought she was the prettiest thing she had ever seen. Enid's hands were small and delicate, her lips sweet, her eyes round. Aereth was overwhelmed with the urge to kiss her, but instead, she fumbled with the reins and focused on the forest ahead. Alongside them, the noisy caravan continued forward, though now people were staring at them curiously from the wagons. Some of the friendlier ones waved.

"Do you like living in the caravan?" Aereth asked Enid. It suddenly occurred to her that she had someone from the wide, unknown world who was willing to talk to her, someone she could drill for information aside from Gweneth.

"I suppose so," said Enid thoughtfully. "I don't know anything else. I've lived in Sirione all my life. What about you? Do you just travel about with your mother and those knights?"

"Yes," Aereth said in surprise, as if she was only just realizing. "We lived in some sort of old castle when I was small, but I suppose we don't really have a home. Tis why we came here – to live in Edhen."

Enid giggled in amazement. "But no one lives in Edhen! No one can get in!"

"We can!" said Aereth confidently. "And once we have, we shall live there happy together. Selene will teach me to hunt, and Mother will teach me magick, and Calain will spar with me . . . And Gweneth will tell me stories. And Cassandra, she shall teach me to dream walk. She promised. And I suppose I must learn my letters, too. And to control my strength. Calain can punch through walls, Gweneth told me. She was jesting, but all the Knights of Falcon can."

"Wow!" said Enid, who had been listening in wonder. "Your mother's knights sound amazing. And is your mother really a sorceress?"

"Yes!" said Aereth proudly and was very satisfied when Enid looked impressed by that.

"I always wanted to learn magick," Enid confessed.

"So why don't you?" said Aereth at once.

"Well . . . I'm afraid to leave Sune and Kare alone, for one. They're old and can't take care of themselves. I should like to stay and help them."

"But you're sacrificing your own life," said Aereth pointedly. "Don't you want to see the world?"

Enid was silent for a moment and then she said, "You sound as if you're trying to convince me to come with you!" She laughed softly. "I almost wish you were. I know that if I stay here, some boy shall ask me to wed him, and I am afeared what shall happen if I say no."

"Why are you afeared?"

"Because I. . . fancy girls," Enid admitted in a low, frightened voice, as if she was afraid Aereth wouldn't approve.

Aereth laughed lightly. "So do I, Enid. Tis why I asked you to ride with me."

Enid was silent to hear that information, though Aereth noticed her cheeks flame brightly.

Aereth frowned. "But Gweneth's parents take no issue with women marrying women. Two of their daughters did!"

"Two? I thought it was just Bren."

"Aye. The one called Bren became a Wilde Woman, and Auntie Gwen is married to my mother . . . Sort of. All the knights are."

"The tribe has been pushing for more children lately," Enid said unhappily. "Since the bandits attacked us, our numbers have been low. It's made us an easier target, especially if the Wilde Women can't be depended on for protection. They seem to protect us on a whim these days."

"What if you ran away?" Aereth suggested seriously.

Enid glanced back at her in disbelief. "And go where? I'd get eaten by a troll or captured by bandits the same day I left the caravan."

Aereth was silent as she struggled to understand. She wasn't aware of it before that moment, but she had lived a very sheltered life, one where she never had to worry about her safety or the dangers of men. No man could have harmed her with her mother and the four Knights of Falcon constantly at her side, and even if she had been on her own, she was still strong enough to lift a house. She was not small, vulnerable, and alone like Enid, whose parents were dead, who had no one to defend her, and looking down at the girl now, she was beginning to realize how vulnerable and helpless most women in the world were.

"I wish you could come with me," said Aereth softly. "I would protect you, and you would be my lady."

"You aren't a knight," Enid gently reminded her.

"No," Aereth agreed. "I suppose I'm not. But you could be my wife. Or just travel with me. Be my love."

Enid smiled sadly. "That's very sweet, but I shall have my markings when I turn fifteen, and then the boys will start asking. They will expect me to become betrothed."

Aereth knew that by "markings," Enid meant tattoos. "What if I stole you away," she said, "and took you to a magick school? Then you could be a sorceress, like you wanted. I'd help you get there."

"You would never leave your mother and her knights!" said Enid shrewdly. "They're your family, and you love them a great deal."

"I would! I would leave them!" said Aereth at once. "I'm almost a woman! I heard my mother's knights talking, and I think I'm a Wilde Woman."

"Truly?" said Enid with interest.

"Truly! And Wilde Women grow fast. When I am grown, I shall come back here and steal you away, and then you can go to magick school or learn a trade or do whatever you please. I shall always protect you."

As they rode on, Enid looked up at Aereth, and her blue eyes were warm with affection. Then without warning, she kissed

Aereth on the lips. Aereth nearly dropped Lucky's reins, which didn't matter because Enid took her hands and guided them under her shawl . . . and over her breasts. For the first time in her life, Aereth felt arousal flush through her, and she kissed Enid with frowning abandon as Lucky lazily carried them forward.

"WHERE *is* that girl?" said Zelda crossly, peering out the back of the covered wagon. "If she isn't back by nightfall—!"

"Let the girl have her fun, Zelda," laughed Gweneth.

It was dusk and the sky was awash in watery orange and purple hues as the sun set beyond the trees. The entire caravan had stopped and the tribe had set up camp, their little fires blazing in a maze in the darkness as sheep baaed and pressed close throughout. Gweneth's parents had cooked them a hot supper of roast mutton, and now that the meal was over, Calain was helping Kare wash the dishes in a basin (they were laughing and carrying on and seemed to be enjoying each other's company), while Selene and Cassandra helped Sune set up a large tent.

Gweneth and Zelda were supposed to be getting the sheepskins they would sleep on out of the covered wagon, but Zelda kept pausing to stare out at the tent city and complain that Aereth hadn't yet returned.

Gweneth looked past Zelda's long golden hair at the tent her father, Selene, and Cassandra were erecting. It was a very large tent and had once housed Gweneth's entire family. Now that family was scattered to the wind. She was disappointed. If she was honest with herself, she had wanted to see her sisters.

"You set this up," Zelda accused, looking skeptically at Gweneth.

Gweneth was gathering a pile of sheepskins from the corner into her arms and laughed in disbelief. "What? I did no such thing. How was I to know my parents had adopted a girl after a bandit raid?"

Zelda wasn't convinced. "I *know* my daughter! And I know you! She asked you to bring us to a caravan so she could – so she could—!"

"Meet other people? Experience life? Have fun?" Gweneth supplied. She looked at Zelda fondly. "Zelda," she said soothingly, "you can't hide Aereth away from the world. I know you wish to protect her, but she has to be a part of the world. She has to live."

"I just . . . worry for her," Zelda said, bowing her head.

Setting aside the sheepskins, Gweneth drew near and slid her arms around Zelda. She had taken off her armor and left it in the covered wagon. All the knights had, for Kare had insisted they stay with the caravan, at least for a couple days.

With her arms around Zelda, Gweneth nuzzled her face against Zelda's soft hair, inhaled its sweet scent, and realized how much she'd missed holding the small woman in her arms. Zelda's curvy body was soft and warm in her embrace and felt good against her.

The sorceress seemed comforted by Gweneth's show of affection. She relaxed against Gweneth, closing her eyes as Gweneth stroked her hair.

"My first kiss was with a girl when I was Aereth's age . . . her biological age," Gweneth said with a laugh.

"Truly? Where is she now?"

"Married to a man in another tribe by now, most likely."

"That soothes not my fear for Aereth, Gwen."

Gweneth laughed. "No, I guess it wouldn't. But if Enid breaks Aereth's heart, well, that's just a part of life, isn't it?

Should she miss a good experience because part of it might be bad? I still remember how Annora's lips felt against mine. It was night, and we weren't supposed to be out in the ruins, but we were headstrong . . . and in heat like dogs. We couldn't keep our hands off each other."

Zelda laughed. "Even as a young girl, you were terrible."

"Aye, I was," agreed Gweneth, laughing as well. "If I'd been a boy, I would've fathered sixty babes by now."

"The gods have mercy on us all!"

They laughed again.

"Come along, you two!" Kare called to them. She was standing outside the newly erected tent as the others ducked inside the flap. "It's bedtime! Bring those sheepskins along now!" she said cheerfully and ducked inside the tent.

Zelda moved to rise, but Gweneth tightened her arms, making Zelda go still as she whispered in her ear, "Shall you share my sheepskin tonight, sweet Zelda? I've been a good girl."

Zelda's lips twisted in smirk. "I suppose you have, my knight," she answered, "but I like it when you're naughty." She looked up at Gweneth with her teasing blue eyes and touched Gweneth's chin and kissed her slowly on the lips. Gweneth's heart fluttered, as it always did whenever Zelda kissed her, and something inside her softened. She wanted to be afraid of how good the feeling was, and thinking for one horrible moment of Annora, she wanted to insult Zelda and thus push the good feeling away. But Gweneth held on to the feeling and let it glow inside her, determined to be unafraid. They touched foreheads, and Gweneth stared into Zelda's eyes, wondering how it was that Calain could have ever left her.

Chapter 5

When Zelda entered the tent, the knights were all standing inside with Gweneth's parents, who looked miniscule beside them. Sune and Kare must've been four feet tall, while the Knights of Falcon were taller than six feet and towered over them, standing with arms folded or hands in the pockets of their trousers, as Gweneth carried a pile of sheepskins in her arms. There was a candle lantern on the floor, glowing with the gentle orange flames of three large melting candles. It brightened the gloom of the tent and illuminated the pots and pans and the basin of dishes Calain had helped Kare bring inside.

Zelda stepped further into the room. The inside of the tent was larger than she had anticipated. There was one main room with two others sectioned off by curtains, which Kare was taking care to hang, while rambling happy that the knights were safe and fed and should rest, and wasn't it exciting that they were all there?

As if to get in one last hug, Kare grabbed Gweneth another time, while squealing, "My babe has come home!" Then she grabbed Zelda in a tight hug and cried, "And she serves a mighty sorceress! Gods be praised!"

Zelda laughed girlishly as she was squeezed, unaware that the knights were looking at her fondly.

Sune, now grumpy and tired, scolded his wife on to bed, "Come on now, Kare, let the girls get some rest! My back is aching!" He banged his cane grumpily, but it made no noise on the canvas floor.

Gweneth handed her mother two sheepskins from the pile in her arms. Kare took them, and after kissing Gweneth on the cheek another time with a sort of frantic eagerness (Gweneth laughed), she and Sune ducked inside one of the curtained rooms together.

Gweneth ducked past the other curtain, and Zelda and the knights followed. Zelda was still worried about Aereth and hardly paying attention as Gweneth spread the sheepskins on the floor and the other knights turned to her with anticipation. Zelda wrung her hands, thinking of Aereth, and when she looked up, it was to find the knights staring at her hungrily.

They were tall in the dark, faceless giants, bulging with power as they loomed over Zelda. Without their armor, she could see the muscles of their shoulders and arms curving, the bugling of their shapely legs and backsides in their trousers.

Cassandra had silently conjured a wisp-light and was looking at Zelda with narrowed eyes by its glow. So was Calain, who moved forward and slid her hands over Zelda's waist, kissing her neck. Selene came up behind, smoothed her hands hungrily over the fabric of Zelda's gown, and started tugging gently at her front laces. Zelda's breasts trembled free, and as Calain was kissing her neck, Selene cupped her heavy breasts in fistfuls and massaged them, kissing Zelda's neck on the other side.

Zelda trembled, trapped between the two large knights, who were kissing, touching, and undressing her slowly but with determination and without pause. She felt a hand in her hair. The hand cupped the back of her head, and then she saw Cassandra's hungry gray eyes, so serious and hard with lust as they gazed upon her in the dark. Still cupping Zelda's head, Cassandra crushed her lips to Zelda's in a passionate kiss.

Zelda kissed Cassandra back, feebly, shivering as she surrendered. There was something about Cassandra's quiet strength that always made her yield, yearning to be dominated, to be taken hungrily. She bent her head back under Cassandra's hard kiss, and as their lips caressed, their heads turned, while Calain continued kissing Zelda's neck and shoulders, now gently tugging her gown down, until it had fallen away to the floor. Selene paused in groping Zelda's breasts to impatiently tug away her slip, and then she was standing there in her panties, breasts bare, as the knights closed around her.

Zelda was on the verge of turning away from Cassandra to look for Gweneth when she suddenly felt the smallest knight somewhere below. Gweneth was on her knees, her hands groping Zelda's backside in fistfuls. She tugged Zelda's panties down with her teeth and plunged her tongue between her thighs.

Zelda's lashes fluttered. She stopped kissing Cassandra as her head fell back, lips parted in a gasp. As ever, Gweneth's tongue was strong and insistent, coaxing her sex to immediate arousal.

"We should lay her down," said Calain breathlessly. She cupped the back of Zelda's head and trailed kisses down her neck to her breasts, where she suckled slowly, pulling gently on Zelda's pink nipple, until she shivered and blushed.

"Here," said Selene. Her strong hands stopped groping Zelda's breasts and smoothed instead down her waist, where they tightened. She buried a fervent kiss in Zelda's naked shoulder as she lifted her easily by the waist and into her arms.

Breathless with arousal, Zelda was glad Cassandra's wisp-light was so far away now that the knights couldn't see how shocked and trembling she was by their hunger. She wished she could be sexually confident and dominate them as she had before, but with all four of them there, she suddenly felt shy and overwhelmed by their unapologetic desire for her . . . and she enjoyed it. She enjoyed surrendering to their strength and somehow felt ashamed.

Zelda clung breathlessly to Selene's neck as the dark knight carried her to the sheepskins. Selene's dark eyes were burning with lust, and Zelda kissed her softly on the lips. She had pulled her mouth back when Selene – without warning – caught her mouth to her own again and kissed her hard. Zelda's cry of surprise and delight was muffled by Selene's strong kiss. Never had the knight kissed her like that before! She was trembling all over when Selene's mouth had pulled away. And her clitoris was pumping, throbbing from the brief touch of Gweneth's mouth.

Selene gently laid Zelda on the sheepskins, and then the knights closed in, pressing their hard bodies around her. It was dark, even with Cassandra's wisp-light, but she could tell who was who by the familiarity she had with their hands and mouths alone. Gweneth had spread her thighs and was fingering her – Gweneth always liked to start with one finger, so frightened was she of harming Zelda with penetration – and it was Selene – hungry-eyed, eager Selene – who sucked now on her clitoris, pulling it carefully in her lips so that Zelda moaned and Cassandra had to smother her cries with a kiss. And it was Calain's strong hands that closed on her heavy breasts and massaged them until the nipples were jutting from her fists.

Calain sucked on Zelda's nipple, slow and wet, then trailed hungry kisses up her neck and closed her mouth on Zelda's in a sloppy, eager kiss that thrilled her. Cassandra's mouth, meanwhile, left wet petals tingling on Zelda's skin as she kissed her neck down to her breasts and suckled them next.

Their hard, strong hands were everywhere, touching, caressing, groping, and their mouths never ceased kissing and sucking. Gweneth and Selene took turns sucking gently on her clitoris and sliding their tongues through the lips of her sex.

Gweneth kissed her thighs carefully, frowning in her passion, as Selene sucked the fat lips of Zelda's sex slowly in her mouth, until Zelda's thighs were shaking.

"She's reaching her passion," Calain whispered hoarsely, and Zelda blushed, realizing that Calain could tell she was close to climaxing because they were Bound.

The red knight leaned back on her elbow and watched with narrowed eyes as Zelda's curvy body twisted, legs spread, against Gweneth's coaxing tongue. Cassandra was also watching Zelda squirm, her gray eyes on Zelda's big breasts as they wobbled gently.

Zelda stared at the ceiling, eyes unseeing, as her sex heaved against Gweneth's mouth. Gweneth slowly nuzzled her nose in Zelda's curly golden pubic hair, driving her tongue deeper, and Zelda blushed brightly as she finally climaxed.

"You must teach me to do that, Gwen," said Selene when Zelda had melted in the nest of her long golden hair and was lying there in a contented daze.

Gweneth laughed softly, trailing kisses over Zelda's thighs. "Teach you?" she said between kisses. "Not a chance! Tis the one thing Zelda loves me for!"

The other knights laughed, and Zelda looked up at Gweneth and smiled. "That is not true!" she said, holding her arms out to Gweneth.

Gweneth lay down beside Zelda, allowing the sorceress to hold her to her breasts as she stroked her pale brown hair. Calain snuggled close on the other side, and Zelda kissed her on the mouth, thinking that Calain still had the best tongue, even if Gweneth was damned good at making her climax.

Selene rested her head on Zelda's thigh, curling absent fingers through the curly hair of her sex, and Cassandra did likewise, smoothing a hand up Zelda's other thigh as she watched

Selene's fingers plunging through the hair. Each time Selene's fingers pushed up, the pink little head of Zelda's clitoris was revealed, and Cassandra stared at it, likely thinking of the time she had sucked upon it in the dream version of Melvalda's bed.

Happily surrounded by her knights, Zelda stared at the ceiling and breathed gently to catch her breath. She smiled to herself and thought it had been a wonderful day. She had spent the morning traveling with her knights, with Aereth, and they had met Gweneth's parents, who were adorable, and supper had been delicious, and now they were sleeping on the softest sheepskins she'd ever known.

"The lady is pleased then," said Gweneth, noting Zelda's smile in amusement. She kissed Zelda's cheek, and Zelda blushed a little.

"Shall we please her five more times?" said Calain, and Zelda blushed even harder.

Yes. A wonderful day. What could possibly go wrong?

AFTER ENID HAD PROMISED to show Aereth around the area, the girls dismounted Lucky, sending the horse back to the Knights of Falcon. Then Enid – grinning brightly—took Aereth's hand and ran off with her, red hair streaming. They giggled as they ran through the maze of canvas tents, past fires and people cooking and playing the lute. The caravan was settling down for the night, and at the center of the small makeshift village, a great bonfire was blazing and music was playing. It was a swift, jolly tune, to which the people danced in their colorful clothing, hopping on the spot and turning about. Children ran laughing and shaking tambourines, women danced wildly with their husbands.

"Come! Let's dance!" squealed Enid. "I haven't had someone to dance with since Pa!" And taking both of Aereth's hands, she pulled her into the crowd, and they danced together.

Aereth hopped breathlessly on the spot and couldn't stop grinning. She suddenly realized she had never danced with anyone before, but it was exhilarating! And Enid looked beautiful in the light of the fire. She had left her shawl on Lucky's saddle, and now that she was without it, her little breasts were bouncing and trembling as she hopped in her skirt, kicking her sandals. She noticed Aereth looking and deliberately shook them hard, making Aereth laugh.

Aereth and Enid were laughing so much and carrying on that they stumbled into someone who was dancing nearby. Aereth winced as she felt her boot trod on the person's foot.

"Ouch! Hey!" cried an indignant voice.

Aereth looked up to find a young girl about their own age scowling at her as she rubbed her sore toe. Her face and hands were lined in spiraling tattoos. She was tall and toned with lean muscles, and she was dressed, like Aereth, in patched trousers and a tunic rather than a dress or skirt, but she was still wearing sandals like the rest of the caravan people, and her wild blonde hair was half loose and half plaited, while one side of her head had been shaved bald. She also had a gold loop through her nostril. It gleamed in the light of the bonfire.

Aereth was surprised to notice the sword on the blonde girl's back. Most of the caravan people didn't carry weapons, only bows for hunting and skinning knives. This was the first time Aereth had seen someone with an actual blade.

"Sorry," Enid said quickly on Aereth's behalf and grabbed Aereth's arm. She looked tentative, almost afraid the two would start fighting.

But the blonde girl didn't seem that angry. Her blue eyes were on the sword on Aereth's back, and they were impressed. "Whoa! Nice blade!" She frowned. "Who *are* you? You're not one of the tribe!"

"How do you know I'm not?" said Aereth slyly.

The blonde girl grinned. "You don't have our accent, for one. You speak like someone from the city, or someone well-read."

Aereth cast her eyes about awkwardly: that was true. The Knights of Falcon and her mother had all been educated at their schools, and it was they who had taught her to speak, so she mirrored their speech patterns. She hated that it gave her away. She had wanted to blend in with the nomads.

"Also, you've got no markings," the blonde girl added. "You're too old not to have them! We usually get 'em at fifteen in the least." She smiled. "I'm Tai. What's your name, stranger?"

"I'm Aereth."

Tai held out her tattooed hand. Aereth expected to see something in it, but seeing nothing, she stared at Tai, perplexed.

Tai made a face. "Ain't you ever shook a hand before?" she said in wonder.

"Shook a hand?" Aereth repeated, completely nonplussed.

Tai, face still screwed up in confusion, looked at Enid for help. Enid shrugged.

Tai rolled her eyes and withdrew her hand. "Hey," she said, brightening, "you wanna spar? Put that nice blade o' yours to the test?"

"Not here!" Enid cried, alarmed.

"Of course, not here!" cried Tai. She looked eagerly at Aereth. "Come on! No one else around here 'believes' in weapons. Can you believe it? It's why we keep getting our bits handed to us by the Wilde Women."

"Where shall we spar?" Aereth asked, excited.

Tai grinned and jerked her head. "Come on!" She glanced at Enid. "Bring your woman with you!"

Skinny little Enid colored up to be called Aereth's woman but did not hesitate to take Aereth's hand.

Aereth felt no shame. As far as she was concerned, Enid was indeed her woman and she was glad Tai had recognized it. She tugged Enid along as she raced after Tai, who was running very fast through the camp, leaping over trunks and barrels, pushing her way through people and making them shout or laugh at her rudeness.

When Tai had come to a breathless stop, they were on the outskirts of the camp, facing an old stone structure that loomed gray in the darkness. Aereth could see it was a gazebo. Some of its pillars were broken, but the stone benches around the edge were still intact.

Enid glanced back at the camp and seemed relieved that they hadn't strayed too far. The tents and the fires were still clearly visible in the dark. "Spar quickly and let's return," she said, shrill and nervous as she glanced over her shoulder.

"Be still, fair Enid," said Aereth soothingly. "I shall protect you if anyone should come here." She thought the words would comfort Enid, for it was the way the Knights of Falcon often spoke to Zelda, but Enid just continued to look frightened.

"Spar quickly," Enid repeated, looking now at Tai. "And don't hurt Aereth!"

Tai laughed.

"Enid!" Aereth cried indignantly. "Have faith in me! Tai couldn't hurt me if she tried!"

"Back those words with your blade," said Tai, backing into the empty space at the center of the gazebo and reaching back to draw her sword. She was grinning.

Aereth smirked and drew her own blade, advancing on Tai. As Enid watched anxiously, the young girls sparred, bringing their blades down on each other, parrying, pushing apart, and struggling to draw blood. But they were both quite young and had never been tested in a real battle, so it was more of a clumsy scuffle than anything.

Tai kept glancing hopefully at Enid, and Aereth realized she was trying to impress her! Determined not be shown up, Aereth employed the trick she had seen Gweneth use and disarmed Tai easily. She swelled with pride when Enid let out a squeal of amazement.

"All right, all right," laughed Tai, picking her blade up from the stone floor and sheathing it. She looked at Aereth with bright admiration as she panted to catch her breath. "You're good! Who taught you?"

"One of my fathers," said Aereth proudly.

Tai goggled. "One of your fathers! How many do you have?!" She gave an incredulous laugh.

Aereth grinned. "Four," she said, as if this were the most natural thing in the world.

Tai laughed again, staring at Aereth in disbelief. "Aereth, you are . . . so *strange*," she said in amusement. "But a good sort of strange, I suppose."

Aereth grinned again. "And you weren't so bad yourself. Who taught you?"

"No one," said Tai, grinning and shrugging. "I told you already, they don't believe in weapons here."

Aereth frowned. "So they don't defend themselves when bandits come? What do they do?"

Tai shrugged again, this time grimly. "Scream and run, mostly." She stuck out her chest. "But not me! I fight back!" So saying, she rolled up her sleeve and showed them a long scar on her forearm. She looked at Enid hopefully, but Enid – rather than being impressed – rolled her eyes and wandered apart from them, pausing to sit on the stone fence that surrounded the gazebo as she stared at the distant camp.

Now that Enid was out of earshot, Tai drew close to Aereth, grinning at the back of Enid's long red hair as she said, "So . . . You get in her panties, yet?"

Aereth's brows went up. "What? No! I just did meet her!"

"So?" said Tai in amazement. "You could die tomorrow! What does it matter? If it makes you feel better, marry her first!" She grinned at Aereth.

Aereth laughed heartily at that.

Tai drew closer, looking at Enid's back again. "What do you think of a threesome, eh?"

Aereth blushed. She knew her mother sometimes had group sex with the knights. When she was still a babe in swaddling, the knights had talked about it all the time, unaware that Aereth remotely understood. And now that she was nearing womanhood, she had thought about it constantly. It couldn't be all bad if her mother loved it so.

But staring at Enid's back, the reality that she would have to leave the caravan reoccurred to Aereth, and she suddenly felt too sad to talk about sex. One day soon, she would have to return to Elwenhal. To Nimwe. Or she would die.

"Listen, Tai," Aereth said seriously, though she was looking at Enid. "I won't be staying with your tribe. I expect my mother and the knights will want to move on soon, and I'll have to leave Enid behind."

"Dammit," said Tai sullenly. "Just when I'd found a sparring partner!"

"Perhaps I'll come back," said Aereth, pleased that Tai wanted her around. "But would you do me a favor? Would you .

. . look after Enid for me? She's afeared some boy shall ask for her hand, but she wants to be with a woman, and well . . ."

"You want me to wed her?" said Tai in amazement, her brows going up.

"If you asked, it would save her from having to marry a man," said Aereth. "She doesn't want a man."

"Aye," said Tai, "she wants you! Why should I bind myself in an unhappy marriage?!"

"Maybe she'll want you, too, some day," said Aereth, who felt helpless as she gazed at Enid. But she didn't want to leave Enid to her fate, forced to become wife to a man and birth his children because the caravan demanded it be so. And Tai seemed strong, as if she could protect Enid.

"Shall you?" Aereth pressed.

Tai hesitated. She was looking at Aereth skeptically, but slowly, she said, "Well . . . I *do* fancy her. Perhaps I'll ask her when you've gone." She offered her hand again.

This time, Aereth took Tai's hand and squeezed it, and they smiled at each other. Aereth was about to speak again when a distant scream turned her head.

"Aereth!" Enid gasped. "Look!"

Aereth and Tai turned back toward the camp and froze in horror: bandits were attacking. The nomads were running and screaming, infants were wailing, sheep were frantically baaing. Aereth could see men in dark, ragged leathers cutting through the crowds with swords and waving torches, setting tents aflame as the people scattered.

Aereth and Tai looked at each other and drew blades.

THE BANDITS HAD CHOSEN the wrong day to attack the caravan, Zelda thought. In an instant, she and her knights were in the fray, fighting the bandits back from the innocent caravanners. Zelda could see that the bandits were after women and sheep. They snatched lambs under their arms, or grabbed women by the hair and sought to drag them off.

Calain sent an entire throng of them fleeing with her fury and strength, fighting back-to-back with Selene, who was coldly and solemnly cutting them down. Smaller, faster Gweneth ducked beneath swinging arms and kicked the bandits off-balance, laughing merrily as she fought, while Cassandra silently and serenely pirouetted, taking off a bandit's head in one clean turn.

Zelda helped by reaching out with her mind and "grabbing" the bandits, forcing them to stand still on the spot, their eyes darting in terror, until they were run through by one of the knights. Some of them she simply killed, setting those aflame who had burned the tents, or spreading her fingers to cast a scattering spell that sent them floating away in pieces. As she floated through the camp, hair and gown billowing about her, glowing with power, the caravanners were in awe of her.

Zelda had to admit she relished in the screaming terror of the bandits as they fled before her, but it was her turn to be afraid when she noticed Aereth and another young girl fighting the bandits. She floated to an abrupt stop and her heart nearly dropped to her feet.

Aereth was fighting alongside a young blonde nomad who also wielded a sword. They cut easily through the snarling bandits, ducking and kicking and swinging their blades. The blonde girl was in awe of Aereth, often pausing to do a double-take should Aereth lift a large bandit by his throat and toss him away.

"Aereth!" Zelda gasped.

Hearing her name, Aereth whirled and froze guiltily when she saw her mother marching up. The blonde girl watched in amazement as Zelda, eyes twin flames in her face, caught the surrounding bandits with her mind and they exploded in bloodless shards around the girls.

"Gods alive!" cried the blonde shrilly and goggled – completely frozen—at Zelda. She leaned close to Aereth, her shocked eyes still on Zelda, and said, "Is *that* your mother?!"

"Yes . . ." Aereth moaned, as if she couldn't be more embarrassed if she were standing there naked.

Zelda pointed back at Kare and Sune's tent and shouted, "What do you think you're doing, Aereth? You go right to the tent and wait, young lady, so I may yell at you more thoroughly when this battle is done!"

Aereth pouted – reminding Zelda of the small child she had been mere days before – and bitterly sheathed her blade on her back. She was about to slouch off when a shadow fell over them and she froze.

There was a deep roar from the sky, a roar that shook the earth and made Zelda's blood run cold. Protectively grabbing Aereth in her arms ("Mother!" Aereth protested as she was smothered by Zelda's large breasts), Zelda turned and gazed at the sky. All around, she saw the nomads and the Knights of Falcon – and even the bandits – stopping to do the same.

A dragon. A dragon was soaring across the moon! Zelda stood still and couldn't believe it. No one had seen a dragon since the Dragon Wars three thousand years ago, but there was one soaring over the camp, roaring long and deep. It passed across the full moon again, much closer now, and Zelda could see that it was green, its scales matching the bright green trees of Sirione almost exactly.

"God alive!" gasped Enid, who had come running out of Sune and Kare's tent. She stood in front of the tent with her mouth open, staring at the dragon. Sune and Kare emerged behind her, also gaping at the sky.

The dragon wheeled about, its neck extended, and several people ran, anticipating the floom of fire that rocketed from its open jaws. The fireballs hit the earth so hard, the ground trembled, but only the bandits were caught in the flame. Their screams were terrible as they were disintegrated on the spot.

The dragon turned again for another attack, and the balls of fire kept coming – *Floom! Floom! Floom!*—shaking the ground on impact, so that Zelda staggered and nearly lost her grip on Aereth. As their sheep baaed and fled in terror, the people of the caravan cheered and leapt on the spot, their voices rising even louder than the agonized screams of the bandits.

Horrified, Zelda sought to cover Aereth's eyes and gasped indignantly when her daughter squirmed from her grasp. Aereth went to the blonde girl, and they stood side by side, staring openmouthed at the dragon as it wheeled across the sky.

With all the bandits dead and gone, the dragon turned a last time, roared again, and soared away across the treetops and out of sight.

Zelda stood there frozen, unable to believe it. But she asked herself what she had expected. Hadn't she come here searching for the Dragon of Edhen? Had she just witnessed Arryn saving the caravan? And if so . . . why hadn't Arryn dropped in to say hello?

The people of the caravan were still cheering and dancing. Zelda saw them grab each other and hop on the spot, chanting over and over, "Dragon! Dragon! Dragon!" until the chant was almost deafening.

The Knights of Falcon came to Zelda, tiredly sheathing their blades. Calain, Selene, and Cassandra looked as disturbed as Zelda felt, but Gweneth was grinning from ear to ear.

"Did you see, Zelda?" Gweneth said excitedly, grabbing Zelda's arms. "It was her! It was the Dragon of Edhen!"

Chapter 6

They stayed with the caravan for several more days, which made Aereth happy because it gave her more chances to wander off with Enid and Tai. Sometimes she and Enid snuck off alone and kissed, hidden in the back of someone's covered wagon, or she and Tai would go off to the nearby ruins to spar, or the three of them would just sit together and talk. Enid seemed to warm to Tai, which made Aereth happy, though she still liked Aereth best, which made Aereth even happier.

Aereth even taught Tai to ride Lucky, which Tai was eager to do because they didn't really have horses for riding in the caravan. Horses were only for pulling the wagons, and any horseback riding was unheard of. But now Tai could ride, and thanks to a few pointers from Aereth, she could fight a lot better as well.

"What do you dream of doing when you grow up?" Aereth asked Tai one day as she, Tai, and Enid were sitting on a hill, watching the nomad camp at the bottom of the green slope. Enid was sitting between them, her bright red hair loose around her shoulders as she hugged her knees.

"I don't know," Tai admitted, lifting her brows. "I sort of like being in the caravan, though I wouldn't mind going on mad adventures! There's so much in Vallinwir to see and do! Like slaying giants or fighting witches!"

"Yes, I want to explore as well," said Aereth excitedly. "What if we all ran away together and became explorers? We could dive into old elven ruins, find lost things from the ancient times, battle monsters!"

"What have you fought," Tai asked curiously, "besides me and those few bandits?"

"I've just sparred with my fathers," Aereth admitted, "but one day I shall slay great monsters! Gweneth said there are half-men in the southern realms. Minotaurs and centaurs and fauns. All of them bloodthirsty and looking for battle!"

"Whoa!" said Tai excitedly.

"And there are ogres," went on Aereth, "and goblins as well!"

"I've heard of goblins," said Tai with interest. "Scavengers, right? Stories say they've always got good loot on them."

"Stories are true," said Aereth. "We fought goblins on our way here. They're all over the countryside outside Sirione."

Enid suddenly yawned, arching her back so that her small breasts lifted behind her tunic, and Aereth and Tai halted in their rambling to stare at them. Seeing that the other girls were mesmerized, Enid giggled at them and hugged her knees to her breasts to cover them.

"Honestly!" Enid scolded. "All you two do is rant on about slaying things and having sex with me!"

"What else is there?" said Aereth, perplexed, and Tai laughed.

The two girls had not, of course, had sex with Enid. For one thing, there was no way they'd ever get away with it, for they were being watched all the time by Zelda, who had placed a scrying charm upon Aereth, that she might see her in a reflective surface wherever she was just by whispering her name.

"When we are all women grown," said Aereth, "we shall all go on adventures together. And at the end of each one, Tai and I shall get drunk and fuck you, Enid."

Enid blushed a little and her pale lashes fluttered. "Aereth!" she cried, appalled but nonetheless pleased.

"And you shall enjoy it immensely," said Aereth. She and Tai leaned close and kissed Enid hard on each cheek, so that she blushed to her hairline and giggled between them.

Aereth tried to keep her budding relationship with Enid a secret, but since they were all living in the same tent and eating at the same meals, it was nearly impossible to hide it from Zelda and the knights, and even Sune and Kare, who thought it was wonderfully cute that Aereth now considered Enid "her woman."

The Knights of Falcon also seemed very amused by Aereth and Enid and thought them sweet. Zelda alone didn't seem to approve, a fact which nettled Aereth constantly. It was as if Zelda were trying to keep Aereth a child forever. She did not actively try to stop Aereth from spending time with Enid, but she kept them separated whenever they were inside Sune and Kare's tent together, often not allowing them to sit close and insisting that Enid continue to sleep in the same room as Sune and Kare, rather than cuddling at night with Aereth, as she so wanted to.

Aereth was a little relieved that she had an excuse to avoid sharing her sheepskin with Enid. Every night for the last couple days, she'd been having dreams of Elwenhal, dreams of Nimwe that left her breathless and aroused. She often awoke in the middle of the night, whispering Nimwe's name and longing for the flowery scent of her hair.

The tug and pull of Elwenhal was growing stronger and the dreams more intense. Zelda and the knights didn't seem to suspect anything was the matter – except for Cassandra. The sorceress-knight sometimes gave Aereth a searching look, and Aereth suspected that she knew what was happening, knew and said nothing, both for Zelda's sake and for Aereth's. For what was the point upsetting Zelda about something she could not change? Aereth was bound to Elwenhal and her time to return, it seemed, had come.

One sunny morning, Zelda and Enid had gone into the forest with Kare to gather herbs. Cassandra had gone with them, and Sune had gone to visit a friend, while Calain went off in search of Selene, who hadn't been seen in hours.

Gweneth had decided to remain behind at the tent, caring for the horses and looking after her parents' covered wagon. Aereth, as was typical, had chosen to stay with Gweneth. They sat around the barren firepit together, watching the nomads talking and laughing and carrying on at other tents. Gweneth was carving a chunk of wood with her knife, while Aereth sadly examined her blade.

"You know, you're about as glum as Selene lately. But how can you be with Enid in your lap?" said Gweneth, her eyes on her work as she carved.

Aereth held down a blush.

"I thought Nimwe was your lady," said Gweneth, frowning.

"Why can't I have more than one lady? Mother does," said Aereth at once.

Gweneth laughed and shook her head. "Ha. Your mother's daughter indeed. Though you may want to take care that Enid is aware of Nimwe and consents to your tie to her, hmm? What if she doesn't want to share you with another woman? You may find yourself in a world of hurt. Enid is small, but I'll wager she can pack a good wallop."

Aereth blinked. It hadn't occurred to her that Enid would be jealous. She thought everyone had multiple partners. Zelda and the Knights of Falcon had set the standard of what was normal for her, but now she was realizing their circumstance actually wasn't normal at all. Tai had called her strange, and glancing around at the monogamous husbands and wives in the caravan, she was starting to understand why.

"Gweneth . . ." said Aereth slowly, "how many girls are like me? Are there many Wilde Women?"

"Wilde Women are everywhere," answered Gweneth. She paused and looked up at Aereth quickly, the girl's words finally sinking in. "And who told you that you were a Wilde Woman?"

"I heard you talking," Aereth admitted, unabashed. "When I was a babe, you called me a Wilde Woman."

Gweneth sighed. "Well, we never meant for you to know. Don't let your mother know that you know, eh?"

"But why? What is the shame in it? The Wilde Women are powerful and strong, and they live free from society. They are not at the mercy of men."

Gweneth paused, and Aereth could tell she was choosing her words carefully. "Your mother's not ashamed that your father was a Wilde Woman. She's ashamed of the circumstances of your birth. I told you before, Goblin. Don't bring it up around Zelda. You shall hurt your mother if you do, and tis my job to protect her heart."

Aereth wasn't satisfied with that answer. "But who is my father? Can't you tell me that, Gweneth?"

"No," Gweneth said calmly. She looked up, pausing in her carving. "I am a knight sworn in service to your mother. I have sworn to obey her, and Zelda hath asked me to keep your parentage a secret. I have already near disobeyed by telling you as much as I have, and what good is my word if I do not keep it? I am not Calain." She snorted and went back to carving.

Aereth cast her eyes down in disappointment. Now she understood: if she wanted to know about her other parent, she would have to coax the answer from Zelda, and she knew Zelda would never tell her.

Gweneth continued carving. "It doesn't matter, Goblin. You've got four fathers in us. Selene, Cassandra, and I bathed you, and fed you, and wiped your little arse. We are your fathers. And Calain, she came around late, but she has cared for you this long journey and loves you just the same as we."

"Calain didn't keep her word about something?" Aereth prompted.

Gweneth frowned and swore under her breath. "Damn that you catch every bloody thing I say," she said with a weak laugh. "Never you mind about Calain. She is as I told my father: a good woman and my sister in arms."

Aereth sheathed her sword on her back, took a breath, and asked the question she really wanted to ask, "Gweneth . . . What if I don't want to live in Edhen? What if I just . . . left one night as you were sleeping?"

Gweneth paused and slowly looked up. "What do you mean?"

"I mean that I've been thinking about my future lately," answered Aereth, "what I want to do and who I want to be. I shall be a woman soon. I do not wish for Enid to see me in that state while she is but a girl still! And I can feel the pull of Elwenhal growing stronger every day. Soon I shall cross over into that world, and I fear breaking my mother's heart." She glanced down and added sheepishly, "And I am afeared of breaking yours."

Gweneth smiled sadly. "If you want to leave quietly for the fairy realm, Goblin, Zelda will understand. So will I and the other knights. We won't be *happy* about it," she smiled again, "but we shall understand."

Aereth smiled in relief.

Gweneth went back to carving, though her hands were nearly shaking with emotion. She didn't want Aereth to leave them anymore than Zelda did, but they knew the girl had little choice.

"If only Enid and Tai would grow at the same rate as I," Aereth said somberly. "I would have to leave them behind even if I weren't cursed by the fae." She sadly cast her eyes down.

"But at least thou did meet some girls, made some friends, and had some fun," said Gweneth, smiling. "How many girls did you kiss? Be honest!"

Aereth giggled. "Only Enid!" she swore. But she grew somber again as she said, "Gweneth, you shall take care of Mother and the other knights, shant you? Tell my mother that I love her?"

"Of course," said Gweneth, a crack in her voice.

Aereth rose to her feet. "And know that I dost love thee as well," she said, smiling. Then as Gweneth watched, she lifted her hand, and a circle of light divided the air. Aereth stepped into the light and through the portal . . . into Elwenhal.

And she was gone.

Chapter 7

Aereth had been gone for three days, but so had Selene. Out of the three remaining knights, Gweneth was taking it the hardest. Zelda often spied her standing alone on the edge of the camp, drinking and staring somberly into the trees. On more than one occasion, Zelda had started to go to Gweneth to comfort her, but both Cassandra and Calain had cautioned her that letting Gweneth process her grief alone was best.

"And what of Selene?" Zelda said when Calain had coaxed her for the umpteenth time to let Gweneth be.

The caravan was packing up to set out again, and still, Selene had not returned. Zelda and the knights did not wish to leave the area without her, and so they, too, were packing up so that they could venture into the forest and search for her.

On top of losing Aereth so suddenly and without even a goodbye, Zelda was near frantic to find Selene. Her golden hair was a tousled mess from her worried hands constantly pushing through it, and her blue eyes were panicking. She stood beside Calain as Cassandra watered the horses behind them, as Gweneth stood alone, staring grimly into the trees. It was another beautiful blue day in Sirione, but Zelda and her knights couldn't have felt more miserable.

"I confess," said Calain, who was unhappily watching Gweneth's back, "I keep thinking that if you were Bound to

Selene, you could find her for us. But Selene is still Bound to your friend."

"That's right," said Cassandra, as if she had only just remembered. She drew near, standing on the other side of Zelda. "Wick could summon Selene with the Binding, and she would have to go."

Zelda looked quickly at Cassandra. "No! You don't think Wick took Selene? What for? And why now?"

"You did say the last you spoke with Wick, she was angry," said Calain thoughtfully. "And I admit, I wasn't surprised, my lady."

Zelda looked up at Calain unhappily. "What do you mean?" Had Calain noticed her mistreating Wick? The very thought horrified her. She tried to think if she had been rude to Wick at the feast, but she mostly remembered dancing with Calain . . . and how the red knight had drunkenly suggested they have sex in a dark corner.

"I mean that she seemed bitter," Calain answered hesitantly. She glanced anxiously at Zelda, as if afraid she might upset her, and went on, "I noticed more than once how she did look at us with envy and hatred. I thought she may have desired me, though my ego could have imagined it."

"No," said Cassandra, soothing Calain. Her voice was soft and thoughtful as she said, "I did notice it as well. She did try to make Selene kiss her, and Selene would not consent. All night, Selene only had eyes for Zelda."

Zelda stared miserably into the trees. Would Wick really have taken Selene out of such petty spite? There was only one way to find out.

"Then I must contact Wick," Zelda said with resolve.

"If Wick really has Selene," said Cassandra grimly, "then she will not answer an attempted contact. Not unless she is the boasting sort. I could dream walk Selene, my lady, and attempt to discover where she is."

"And failing that, I shall find Wick and *take* Selene back!" said Zelda darkly.

"And we shall venture out with you," said Calain at once.

Zelda didn't argue. After losing Aereth, and after nearly losing Calain, she didn't want any of them to separate ever again. And why should she force the knights to stay behind when their friend was in peril?

"Perhaps it is time," said Gweneth, drawing near, "to summon our friend with the glowing blade."

Zelda, Calain, and Cassandra looked up as Gweneth approached, and Zelda realized she had been standing there, listening to them, for quite some time.

"No!" said Calain at once, and she scowled. "We can do this on our own. We don't need Arryn!"

"Think on this, good Calain," said Cassandra gently. "It is likely Wick has taken Selene to a stronghold, surrounded by enchantments and armed guards. She will know we are with Zelda and will have taken precautions to prevent our entry."

"But she won't know about Arryn," said Zelda, realizing.

"And Wick is an elven sorceress," went on Cassandra. "From what you have told us, Zelda, she was not that impressive in her casting, but her elven blood will still have given her an advantage. And perhaps she hath grown in power as you have. Arryn is an ancient elf, not Tula-Dan, but still very old and powerful, if Gweneth's stories are true. She would make a useful ally."

Calain didn't look convinced.

Zelda looked irritably at Calain. "This is to save Selene, Calain!"

"You assume Selene needs saving," said Calain dismissively. She glanced around at them and shook her head. "Did none of you consider that perhaps Selene left because she did want to?"

"Calain! Cease your jealous banter!" snapped Gweneth impatiently. "Does it pain you so to see Zelda ache for Selene? Selene was happy with us!" She looked to Cassandra for support, but Cassandra's expression was sad.

"No," Cassandra said softly, unhappily. "Selene did long for Zelda's affection and felt she could not compete with Calain. She told me."

Zelda glanced down at the blue jewel that sat just above her breasts. Selene had given it to her, and Calain had been right: the necklace had been a plea for Zelda's love and affection. She clutched it now, thinking fondly of Selene and wishing she had realized before.

"Still, we can't afford to make assumptions," said Gweneth, raising her brows pointedly at Calain, who glared at her. "We should find Selene before we forsake her and ask her for the truth."

"And you would have us summon that elf for this?" said Calain in amazement. She was looking at all of them as if they'd gone mad.

"We need Arryn!" Zelda snapped, losing patience.

"We *don't*," said Calain doggedly, but she added in a softer voice, "But if my lady chooses to summon the Wolf Knight, I shall yield."

Zelda looked at Gweneth and Cassandra, who silently nodded.

"Then let us find a quiet place to summon her," said Zelda. "Some place away from the caravan. Arryn travels by portal and would frighten them."

Gweneth suddenly grinned, surprising them all. "And let us hope she arrives as the Dragon of Edhen."

Essential Selene

Book 9

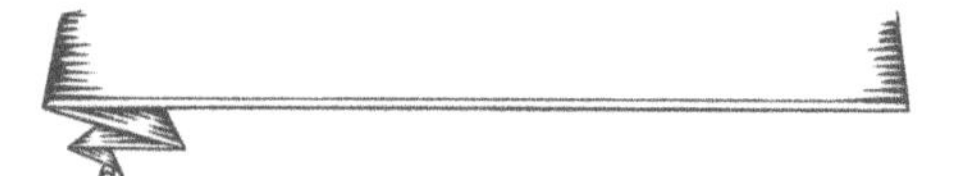

Chapter 1

Wick was sitting in an armchair beside the fire, the dark green cushions vibrant against her jet-black hair and gown. The gown's sleeves were slit up the sides, so that they fell like wings, leaving her white arms bare as she sat with her hands calmly in her lap, regarding Selene.

Arlonhold was the name of the castle to which Wick had whisked Selene away. It stood on an island in the middle of a great lake, in the heart of Dark Bloom Forest. The occasional small boat came to and from the island, bearing supplies for Wick's servants to keep life in Arlonhold running smoothly, but that was all. Aside from Wick's sisters, there were never any visitors here. Wick lived her life in solitude, seeing only her servants and receiving the occasional raven from one of her sisters.

Upon Selene's arrival, Wick had explained that the old castle had been given to her by her sister, Serian, who had taken pity on her that their parents had disowned her and left her threadbare. And so, instead of venturing into the city to open a shop or a healing clinic, Wick had settled here, living her life in luxury, wearing fancy gowns every day, eating succulent meats, and enjoying a lazy life of reading and soaking in her bathing basin.

Wick believed she now had everything. All she required, she told Selene with a lusty smile, was a lover to share it with for the next three hundred years. Wouldn't Selene be that lover?

Selene still hadn't answered, for she was . . . considering it. She was surprised with herself that she hadn't immediately said "yes," for she had come here in the first place because she believed she had no place at Zelda's side. It was she who wrote a letter to Wick, asking where she was and if she could not come and live with her. Wick had answered by appearing in a puddle near Selene's boot, smiling up at her from the water. And then a portal had opened, and Selene had stepped through to find herself here.

The last day she was with Zelda, Aereth, and the Knights of Falcon, Selene had sadly watched as everyone sat around the fire outside Sune and Kare's tent. They were all so engaged in one another, eating and laughing and chatting ceaselessly. Aereth had doted on Gweneth (ranting about Gweneth's prowess with a sword), Zelda had doted on Calain (lovingly feeding her spoonfuls of stew), and Sune and Kare could not stop praising Cassandra's magick abilities – such as her visions and the dream walking – which had aided Gweneth so many times, for the people of Ellormest had great respect for magick, even if they couldn't wield it themselves.

Selene had looked at the others and wondered what her place was. Did they really need her? And would Zelda ever truly love her? Zelda and Cassandra weren't aware, but Selene had seen them making love the very same night that Aereth had. And unlike young Aereth – who had been fascinated into a still state of open-mouthed shock – Selene had felt nothing but . . . bitter envy.

Zelda had never made love with Selene as she had with Cassandra! The way she had wiggled and squirmed in Cassandra's lap, the way she had so desperately and breathlessly crushed her mouth to Cassandra's . . . And she had climaxed her so *hard,* her belly trembling, her big breasts heaving . . .

And in that moment, Selene had asked herself if Zelda truly desired her, truly loved her, or was the sorceress just keeping her around as another blindly devoted protector? Had Calain, in fact, been right to leave Zelda's service? Was it silly to compete for her favor? Was Selene, as Calian had suggested, pathetic?

"Shall you give me an answer today, my knight?" asked Wick quietly, for it had been three days.

Three days of Selene saying she would consider, she would think on it, she would sleep on it. Wick had been extraordinarily patient, so confident was she that she would be granted what she wanted. And what she wanted was Selene.

Selene didn't quite know what to say or what to think. She had never been . . . *wanted* before! In the past, it was always Calain the maidens lusted for. And indeed, Selene still remembered how Wick had doted on Calain at the feast, going on and on about her! Did she think Selene had forgotten that?

Selene glanced over her shoulder and could tell that Wick had attempted to make herself appealing. While her breasts weren't very large, she had worn a gown that wrapped around her bare shoulders and boosted her cleavage, so that it was bursting from the front. And her usually straight hair she had attempted to curl like Zelda's. It tumbled long and silky behind her shoulders, and she was so small, her little slippers barely touched the hard stone floor.

Wick was watching Selene intently.

"This isn't even about me," Selene said dismissively.

Wick hesitated. "What do you mean?"

Selene turned around. "I *mean,* you care nothing for me! What has it been since Queen Ellanara was slain? Three months now? Almost four? And yet, it took you all this time to reclaim me from Zelda? And this after you gave me your blessing that I should go with her!"

Wick blushed guiltily, but she took a breath and said hotly, "*You* contacted *me,* lest you have forgotten!"

"And you did leap on the opportunity to hurt Zelda!" Selene shot back. She shook her head. "No, this isn't about me at all. Tis about Zelda and your bitter hatred of her. Not that I care. Not that any of it matters."

Selene turned and started pacing angrily. She was not wearing her sword and armor. Instead, her sword and armor were displayed on a nearby stand, and she was clad in trousers and a tunic. They were in the bedchamber Wick had given Selene. Selene was on the verge of telling her to leave but had to keep reminding herself that it was Wick's castle. Arlonhold would have been her home as well, had she gone with Wick instead of Zelda. It would have been her home. Such a beautiful old castle, and she had forfeited it for what? To aid Calain, who despised her? To protect Zelda, who cared not for her?

"Selene . . ." Wick said heavily. "I admit that I do despiseth Zelda," her nostrils flared in momentary anger, then her face softened and she said in earnest, "but my desire for thee is real."

Selene gave a scoffing laugh. "I saw the way you lusted for Calain! Do not lie to me!"

"What is wrong with wishing to be like Zelda and Selene?" said Wick quietly. "What is wrong with wishing to be loved?"

Selene moved across the room to Wick and stood over her. Wick looked up at her eagerly, her lips parted in anticipation. When Selene leaned down, Wick closed her eyes and leaned forward for a kiss, but Selene only touched her cheek and whispered hoarsely, "Leave me."

Wick sadly cast her eyes down, then rose to her feet and glided serenely out the door, her back stiff with hurt, letting the door close behind her.

LATER THAT NIGHT, SELENE found it difficult to sleep. Wick's calm insistence that she wanted to lay with her was driving her to distraction. Selene thought of simply going down to the pier and asking the ferryman to take her across the lake. Wick had told her she was allowed to leave any time she pleased, but was she truly? Wick had gone through a great deal of trouble to keep Selene there, posting guards outside her door, locking the door of her bedchamber at night, making her elven heart race with sudden passion . . . For Wick had touched herself, bringing herself to a climax, forcing Selene to feel her sweet pleasure as she lay sleeping . . .

But if Wick was telling the truth and Selene was allowed to depart. . . where would she go? Back to being another horse in Zelda's stable? Back to being the least valued, the least loved? She wondered bitterly if Zelda and the others had even noticed she was missing or if they even cared. Even Aereth hadn't seemed to care for her!

It took hours, but Selene finally fell asleep. She was lying on her back in the great four-poster bed and dozing gently when she felt sudden weight on the mattress. Her eyes fluttered open and she looked around to see Wick lying beside her, sitting up on her elbow under the coverlet . . . and she was naked!

Selene's lips parted in shock. "My lady!" she scolded, pulling the coverlet to her chin, for she was in her smallclothes.

Wick giggled softly, and when she tossed her hair, it changed with a ripple from jet-black to curly gold. She winked, and suddenly, she was no longer Wick Blackwood but Zelda, taller, curvier, with larger breasts that crushed together nicely, and a swath of curly golden hair cloaking her sex. The eyes that looked out of Wick's face now were Zelda's bewitching blue eyes, so round and innocent and sweet.

Wick slowly smiled in quiet triumph, twisting Zelda's pink, supple lips in a smirk. "I can feel your heart *racing*, my knight," she whispered.

Selene hated that it was true, but her heart was indeed pounding. She lay on her back, staring at Wick – who now looked completely and totally like Zelda—and could feel her clitoris throbbing to life. She barely managed to stammer, "M-My lady . . ." She didn't know what she was going to say. It was as if her mind had stopped functioning. Zelda had always had that effect on her any time she was naked.

Wick giggled again, shrugging up one shoulder coyly, so that her now-enormous breasts jiggled. She slid on top of Selene, and her heavy breasts swelled near Selene's face, the cleavage plump and swollen. Selene could see the tiny pink nipples standing rigid and hard. When she glanced at them with narrow-eyed lust, Wick's cheeks flushed.

"How I have longed," Wick whispered, "for you to look at me with such desire. But if I must look like Zelda to put that thirst in your eyes, then so be it." She looked at Selene's lips and gently kissed her.

Selene thought she had lost her senses, but she kissed Wick back, her hands smoothing over Wick's backside and squeezing at the soft cheeks in fistfuls. It was Zelda's backside, heart-shaped and soft, supple and giving in her hands. She squeezed and massaged again, watching Wick's cheeks grow brighter, and then her hands smoothed over the back of Wick's thighs and she spread them, baring Wick's sex to the air.

Wick blushed prettily and gasped when Selene's careful fingers slid between the lips of her sex, exploring. It was Zelda's sex as Selene remembered it: the lips were fat and swollen, and the tight maidenhead was still there – *still there*, even after Aereth's birth. Though Selene wondered if it wasn't, in fact, Wick's maidenhead she was fondling.

Watching Wick's blushing face for a reaction, Selene slid in one finger, then paused and slid in another. She felt the maidenhead yield soft around her fingers, stretching to admit her, and as her fingers traveled deeper, she saw Wick's eyes fluttering wide at the sudden pleasure. Her sex clenched and moisture washed over Selene's fingers.

"Oh . . . Oh, my!" Wick gasped, embarrassed. Her eyes hooded. "Oh . . . *Selene* . . . You're so good at that. . ." She closed her eyes. "By the gods, don't stop . . . So d-deep in my pussy . . ."

Selene slowly sank her fingers deeper and saw Wick gasp and arch her back, thrusting her backside out as she was fingered. Lying there, thighs spread, on Selene's belly, the arching of her back thrust her great breasts near Selene's mouth, and Selene caught one of the nipples in her lips and suckled deeply, until the plump mound of flesh was rising against her face.

Wick squirmed and blushed against the pleasure, whispering helplessly, "Oh, Selene . . . Touch me. . . You're so good . . . so good at that . . ." She frowned in ecstasy and trembled, and because their hearts were connected, Selene could *feel her pleasure.* She could feel how Wick's clitoris was throbbing, how her breast flushed with tingling pleasure with each suck on her nipple, how the lips of her sex filled with blood. . . Wick's throbbing clitoris was making her own clitoris pump hard, fast, strong with lust.

Selene pulled her lips from Wick's nipple and watched her absently as she fondled the lips of her sex. When Wick spoke, it was with Zelda's voice, with Zelda's sweet lips, with Zelda's blue eyes. She was saying everything Selene had ever wanted Zelda to say, and she was shocked by how aroused it was making her.

Wick cupped Selene's face in both hands, looking down at her with a sudden fierce hunger that startled her. "Fuck me!" she whispered breathlessly and crushed her lips to Selene's in a passionate kiss.

Selene obeyed, kissing Wick back with a fervent tongue as her fingers slid deeper, harder, faster, until Wick was rocking on top of her, until Wick's great breasts were jiggling, until the bed was shaking. She remembered how Zelda's sex had always reacted to her fingers, flexing and heaving and clenching on them as she grew moist, and Wick's sex – enchanted though it was – felt similar. *So* similar, Selene wondered how many times Wick had secretly studied Zelda's body.

Selene trembled helplessly as Wick's lips sucked at her own as if she would devour her. Zelda had never kissed her with such hunger, with such passion and desire! But Wick had dominated her completely, riding her fingers, demanding it harder, pinning her to the bed with her curvy body. Selene fingered Wick so hard, the elf was rocking almost violently when her head fell back and she choked out a cry. As she climaxed, her sex tightened, releasing its moisture over Selene's fingers, and pinned beneath her, Selene felt her belly tighten as she released as well.

Chapter 2

After agreeing that it was best to summon Arryn far from the caravan, they said their goodbyes to Kare, Sune, and Enid, and then Zelda and the Knights of Falcon led their horses into the trees of Sirione. Now that Aereth was gone, Zelda had taken custody of Lucky, and she led him by his reins into the shadows of the bright green canopy above as the others likewise led their horses forward.

Calain walked beside Zelda and had to admit she was a little sad that Zelda had her own horse now. She would miss holding Zelda in her arm as they rode together, feeling all that soft golden hair beneath her chin, tickling her nose with its sweet scent . . . watching over Zelda's shoulder as her breasts bounced.

Zelda caught Calain staring at her with longing, and seeming to guess what the knight was thinking, she smiled. "I could still ride with you, if you wanted, my knight," Zelda said warmly. "We could tie Lucky's reins to Arthur's, though I don't think they like each other much. I think Arthur is jealous of you and Lucky."

Calain laughed. "What? How could he be jealous? I only did ride Lucky for a little while."

Hearing Calain, Arthur snorted indignantly, and Calain laughed again and stroked the horse's long face. "Silly old horse," she said.

It was midday and birds were singing in the bright forest. Calain could still hear sheep baaing as the caravan took off behind them. The baaing slowly became more distant the further away the caravan drew and the deeper they walked into the forest. Kare had loaded them down with food and supplies before they'd departed, and Zelda's satchel was heavy with all the herbs the old woman had given her. Calain could see the wrapped bundles poking out in cascades of flowers and grass.

Calain thought Zelda looked like some beauty from another world as she walked slowly in her long blue gown, the sunlight playing upon her golden hair, her cleavage riding before her. It seemed to Calain a crime that Zelda should look so appealing, should so obliviously rouse her lust while such grave things were upon them: Aereth had been pulled into Elwenhal far sooner than any of them would have liked, and Selene had completely disappeared.

While Calain was sad about Aereth's departure and wished she could have said farewell to the girl, she had to admit she was furious about Selene's. At least Aereth was cursed and had no choice, but what was Selene's excuse for disappearing? For Calain was more than certain Selene had left as a result of their last argument. She wanted to rant and rave about it, but she knew the others – Gweneth in particular – would just remind her of the very recent time she herself had abandoned the group. And so, Calain bitterly held her tongue.

"Where are we going?" Cassandra asked no one in particular.

"There's an old dragon burial mound due east of here," Gweneth said as they walked. "We can summon Arryn there. Will be plenty of space for her to land . . . Assuming she comes as a dragon."

"She shall probably come as an elf," said Zelda, who sounded so fond of the elven knight that Calain resisted scowling. "She doesn't know that we know who she is . . . Or perhaps she does by now. She always knows things."

"Because she is always *stalking* us," muttered Calain darkly. "And why are there dragon burial mounds in Ellormest?"

"You sleep in class again?" said Gweneth, shaking her head. "Ellormest was the site of the last battle of the Dragon Wars! A lot of dragons died here. Most of them were elves who had shape-shifted, and no one could figure out how to turn them back once they were dead, so they just dug giant graves for them and put them in the ground. Other dragons – true, natural ones – came here to nest. They and their young were slaughtered during the wars."

"Ellormest is known as a dragon graveyard," Cassandra added, gazing thoughtfully at the great elven statue they passed. "The bones here do whisper their tales."

"Well," said Zelda, a little shaken by Cassandra's vague and mysterious words, "now I know where the local Wilde Women get their dragon skulls from."

"What shall we do," said Calain, "if Zelda uses the Summoning Stone and Arryn does not come? Has anyone considered that? And even if she does come, what then? We have no idea where Selene is or where Wick may have taken her. For all we know, we are wrong, and Selene just wandered into the forest and was eaten by a troll."

Though they wouldn't have gotten that lucky, Calain thought privately by way of a joke.

They fell silent. None of them had an answer because Calain knew she was correct: they *didn't* know for certain where Selene was or even if Wick had truly taken her. The notion had been Cassandra's theory, which she had based entirely on Selene's ever increasingly gloomy mood. But Selene was always in a somewhat gloomy mood, Calain thought.

After a while, Cassandra said with a helpless laugh, "Tis strangely ironic. Selene is the one who always knoweth what to do. Now that we need her guidance, she is the one we must rescue."

"Aye," agreed Gweneth. "I could use some of her bossiness about now."

"I could try scrying her to see where she is," said Zelda.

"No," said Cassandra. "If she is with Wick, then there will be a veil about her, preventing your ability to scry. Dream walking won't work, either. I already tried. She is most definitely charmed."

"Right . . ." Zelda said, remembering. She stared at the ground as she led Lucky along, and she looked so helpless and frustrated, Calain reached over and touched her shoulder to comfort her. Zelda smiled gratefully at Calain around the veil of her golden hair.

Calain looked away again. She knew all of it had to be hard on Zelda, losing both Aereth and Selene on the same day. Because whether Selene realized it or not, Zelda did care for her, Calain knew. If Zelda *didn't* care for Selene, Calain wouldn't have spent the last few weeks mocking Selene in a jealous fit about the necklace she had given Zelda. How could Selene not see that?

"If Selene is charmed," said Calain as a thought occurred to her, "does that mean she is with Wick? She could be with some other sorceress for all we know! Or lost in some elven ruin that is enchanted! She could be anywhere! Dammit all. I know she hath stormed off because I taunted her about the necklace she did give you, fair Zelda. I did not mean to make her so angry. It was in jest."

"Selene hath never taken your words lightly, Calain," Cassandra gently scolded. "Not even your jests."

"Yes," Calain admitted guiltily. "You are right. But why must she care so what I think?"

"Because she loves you, dullard," said Gweneth with a laugh. "If she didn't see you as a sister, your opinion wouldn't matter in the slightest."

"I did not ask to wield such power over her," Calain said unhappily.

"Thou did when thou didst befriend her," said Cassandra softly.

Calain was silent as she meditated on what had been said. She had violently attacked Gweneth for provoking Zelda into leaving the group, but here she had done the same to Selene. Perhaps Selene was right about her and Gweneth. Perhaps they were both immature children who needed to grow up, who did not deserve their knighthood.

They were coming upon the burial mound. Calain could see it in the clearing ahead, a great mound of earth, the top of which had been flattened smooth, and on the flattened surface, a stone altar. Stone steps had also been built in a uniform circle around the mound, making it easier to climb. Leaving the horses at the foot of the stair, Calain followed Zelda and the other knights to the top of the stair and approached the altar.

"Did people truly used to worship the dragons? Madness!" said Calain, looking with unease at the altar.

Gweneth shook her head. "People *still* worship them. Have you been listening to me at all?"

"No," Calain confessed, unabashed, and Cassandra smiled.

Gweneth made an impatient noise. "My people have worshipped the dragons for centuries and still do. They worship the Dragon of Edhen, the last dragon! And many still approach the old altars to pay their respects to the ones who are gone." So saying, she turned to face the altar, and Calain was surprised when she bowed her head in momentary prayer and tossed a handful of flower petals in the stone offering basin.

"Just in case," said Gweneth, raising her head again. "Sometimes the spirits of the dragons do linger and grow angry when their altars are approached without proper acknowledgement."

"So it wasn't safe to bring us here," Calain pointed out. The place made her nervous, and she knew it was because the ancient elven gravesite back in Blood Horn was still with her. How terrifying it had been to nearly die, to lie in the dark for so long, but she had told no one.

Calain realized she must've seemed afraid, for she looked up to find Zelda clutching her arm and smiling up at her. It was a false, brave smile for Calain's benefit, and Calain knew the haunted hollow in Blood Horn was still with Zelda as well.

"Fear not, Calain," said Gweneth with surprising gentleness. "I would never lead thee into danger." She looked at Zelda. "Shall we summon a dragon, my lady?"

Zelda reached with a shaking hand into her satchel and pulled out the Summoning Stone Arryn had given her back on Menosea. It was still glowing with soft violet light. As she held it, she looked inquiringly at Calain.

Calain glared at the stone and turned away. "*Yes*," she said to Zelda's unspoken question, "I shall stay my blade this time."

"This time?" said Cassandra, amused.

Gweneth was grinning. "I'll tell you later," she said to Cassandra, which made Calain glare at them.

Calain turned her glaring eyes away and tried not to look too bothered, but she could not stop thinking of the day in Anamora Forest when she had attacked Arryn and disarmed her. Arryn had maintained her calm and held her own, only to freeze Calain with a spell and coldly walk away. Calain had never forgotten or forgiven the humiliation, regardless of the fact that it was she who had started the quarrel. She hated losing, and knowing she had lost to one so small and thin as Arryn rankled her.

"Summon her, sorceress," said Cassandra quietly. "We are ready."

Zelda took a breath and turned the Summoning Stone in her fingers. It seemed like a such a simple thing to do that Calain almost didn't believe it would work, but the Summoning Stone reacted to Zelda's touch, vibrating softly and briefly in her hands. A second later, and a circle of light had split the air, growing wider as a shadow took form on the other side. The light spun so fast, Calain felt her red hair whipping back and saw the hair of Zelda and the other knights beating around their faces. As they watched, Arryn stepped through the portal and it sealed behind her, disintegrating in a splash of light, so that their dancing hair dropped again.

When the Wolf Knight appeared, Calain could feel Zelda's heart speed up in delight. Calain's chest heaved as she looked at Arryn, hating the sight of her. She could not pretend she hated Arryn purely because the smaller knight had beaten her. There was also the fact that Zelda seemed to like her so much. Arryn was calm, level-headed, mature, petite, knowledgeable, and skilled with magick . . . She was everything Calain was not, and it left Calain wondering if Zelda did not wish Calain were more like Arryn. Clearly, Zelda saw value in Arryn's traits or she wouldn't have lain with her.

"Fair Zelda," Arryn said pleasantly and bowed slightly to Zelda, so that Calain gritted her teeth.

Zelda smiled.

Arryn glanced around. "And the Knights of Falcon: Knight Cassandra, Knight Gweneth, and . . ." She smiled when her violet eyes alighted on Calain.

Calian's eyes narrowed in dislike, and she made no move to acknowledge Arryn.

Unbothered, Arryn turned her curious eyes back to Zelda. "But the dark one is missing, of course. Knight Selene."

"You know all our names," said Gweneth, amused. "What else has our lady whispered to you as she lay against your breasts?"

Calain tensed. Gweneth was deliberately but subtly mocking her and having great fun doing it, but before Calain could retort, Zelda stepped forward and suddenly impatient, waved Gweneth to silence.

"Arryn," said Zelda, looking unhappily into Arryn's patient, slanted eyes, "forgive me for summoning you here, but we need your help. Selene has gone missing and we don't know w-what to do."

Zelda's voice had cracked. Wanting to sooth her, Calain drew near behind her and rubbed her shoulder. Zelda reached back and touched Calain's hand.

Arryn's slender black brows turned in a sympathetic frown. "I supposed you had summoned me for that reason. Yes, Zelda. I did observe your dark knight passing through a portal. It was not quite four days before."

Calain's lips parted in shock. "And you did nothing to stop her?" she said indignantly.

Arryn, calm and patient as ever, answered in an even voice, "Why would I have?"

"Typical!" snarled Calain. She waved a hand at Gweneth. "The sheep people worship you as a goddess! And *like* a goddess, you do nothing as others suffer!"

Everyone waited on tenterhooks for Arryn to confirm that she was in fact the Dragon of Edhen, but Arryn's neutral face betrayed no emotion as she listened to Calain's accusation. Eventually, very slowly, the Wolf Knight said, "Knight Selene was not forced through the portal. She passed through of her own freewill, though it seemed with some regret."

Calain exchanged a grim look with Cassandra and Gweneth, and the three knights knew their suspicions had been confirmed: Selene had left them willingly, likely because – as Cassandra had speculated—she felt she had no place among them. And it was Calain's fault. Calain had caused this. She had to find some way to make it right.

"And do take care where you point a finger of blame, Knight Calain," Arryn added, sounding a little irritable now. She was looking at Calain with her intense violet eyes, and Calain stood still, feeling as if a hot light was slicing through her. "It was not I who goaded your Selene into leaving," Arryn finished.

Calain scowled but she had no retort: as ever, Arryn was correct about her behavior. She suddenly had the wild, furious urge to leap on Arryn and tackle her to the ground, but she knew she would need the knight's help to find Selene and swallowed her bitterness with difficulty. She felt Zelda squeeze her hand and knew the sorceress was silently thanking her for calming down. No doubt Zelda had felt Calain's heart speeding up.

"Then I suppose Selene must've gone to Wick after all," Zelda said. "I couldn't imagine who else would have cast a portal for her to pass through, and who else would Selene trust? Selene knew and trusted Wick, while a strange sorceress she would have fought against."

"It makes sense. Who else would want Selene?" Gweneth joked.

"She did awake in the night short of breath," Cassandra said thoughtfully. "It happened several times as we did approach Sirione. She seemed to think no one had noticed and wanted to keep it secret, so I did not question her on it. I suspect she hath been speaking with Wick in her dreams for some time."

"Speaking," said Gweneth, "or fucking?"

"This wouldn't have happened," Zelda said darkly, "if I had Bound Selene to me long ago." She shook her head, her eyes moving between the knights. "It was wrong that I should ask you all to pledge yourselves to me without Binding you! When we have Selene back, I shall Bind you all, and you shall truly be mine."

Cassandra and Gweneth looked at Zelda in surprise, though Calain thought they also seemed pleased.

"Let us focus on getting Selene back, fair Zelda," Calain said. "Any Binding you wish can be done later! Our next step is to find where Wick is," she said confidently, as if finding Selene were just a matter of time and planning now.

"And then what?" snorted Gweneth. "We burst in her hold and fight her army of guards on our own?"

"We probably could," Cassandra said with a shrug. Her eyes alighted on Zelda, and Calain knew she was thinking of how powerful Zelda had become since the incident with Melvalda. Only days before, Zelda had slain more bandits than the four Knights of Falcon combined.

"And how shall we get there?" Gweneth went on. "On the back of a dragon?" She looked at Arryn for a reaction, but Arryn (stubbornly, Calain thought) showed none.

Calain hesitated and said, "This will sound strange, but perhaps we shan't need our blades. If Selene hath willingly gone to Wick, then perhaps she could be persuaded to return to us."

"And you are the one to do it, are you?" said Gweneth skeptically.

"If I am the reason she hath left us, then yes," said Calain at once.

"I know where Wick Blackwood resides," said Arryn, and everyone looked at her.

Calain laughed in disbelief. "You doth know everything," she said contemptuously. "I suppose if I were to creep about spying on people, I would know everything as well!" she growled, but she fell silent when Zelda placed a coaxing hand on her arm.

"It is my business to know what is happening with my people," said Arryn coolly, and now her dislike of Calain was starting to show. Calain was glad she had gotten under the elf's skin and showed no remorse as she stared darkly at her.

"In fair Ionmiris," went on Arryn, "in my ancient homeland, Wick Blackwood hath been living in Arlonhold for the last three months."

"Ionmiris? You mean Koradara," corrected Calain triumphantly. She said it hoping to impress Zelda and prove that she knew as much history as Arryn, but Zelda only shook her head impatiently, as if she were scolding a child.

"Arlonhold," said Cassandra with recognition.

Gweneth looked at her quickly. "You know it?"

"Aye," Cassandra answered. "Tis a very old castle, surrounded by an enchanted lake. Tis no small wonder I could not dream walk Selene. She might as well reside in another dimension."

"But there must be a way for us to enter!" Zelda said stubbornly.

"The enchantments on the building are elven, my lady," said Cassandra gently.

Zelda looked defeated, and Calain knew why: elven magick was the strongest magick there was. Even Zelda could not slip past it undetected. The second they arrived at Arlonhold, Wick's guards would know before they'd even crossed the lake.

Zelda looked to Arryn. "Surely, you could get us inside? You are elven! And powerful as well!"

Calain glowered to hear Zelda praising Arryn, then glowered harder when Arryn smugly smiled.

The elven knight's amused eyes turned from Calain to Zelda, and they were gentle as she said, "I could sneak one of you past her enchantments. But only one. I shall not involve myself in your quarrel further."

"Tuh," said Calain darkly, a subtle implication that Arryn was a coward.

Arryn glanced irritably at Calain, then turned and lifted her hand. They watched as she opened a portal. A line of white light split the air, then spread to form a circle, swirling faster and faster, so that their hair beat about them. Through this magickal window, Calain could see a castle rising solemn above a lake, made of stone and wood, with little roofs that were cone-shaped in the elven design. Beyond the towering building, stars winked in the dark sky, and the moon was large, as opposed to southern Ellormest, where it was day.

"Choose quickly which one of you shall enter," said Arryn, who was standing calmly beside the portal, eyes narrowed against the rush of air, her long black hair beating about her face. "I shall allow it to close behind you, and then you must find your own way back."

Zelda and the Knights of Falcon all looked at each other.

"I am the one who should go," said Zelda at once. "It is I who Wick despiseth."

"No, my lady," said Calain, stepping forward. "It was I whose cruel words sent Selene forth, and so it is I who should fetch her."

Zelda hesitated, and Calain thought she looked as if she wanted to argue. But Zelda also knew that if anyone could get through to Selene, it was Calain. Calain and Selene had been friends longer than any of the Falcon Knights and knew each other very well.

"Then go, my knight," said Zelda, "and return quickly with Selene!"

Calain nodded dutifully and moved through the portal, but as she was passing through, she heard Zelda leap forward with a rustle of her skirts, and – before Arryn could stop her – she had grabbed Calain's hand and disappeared inside with her.

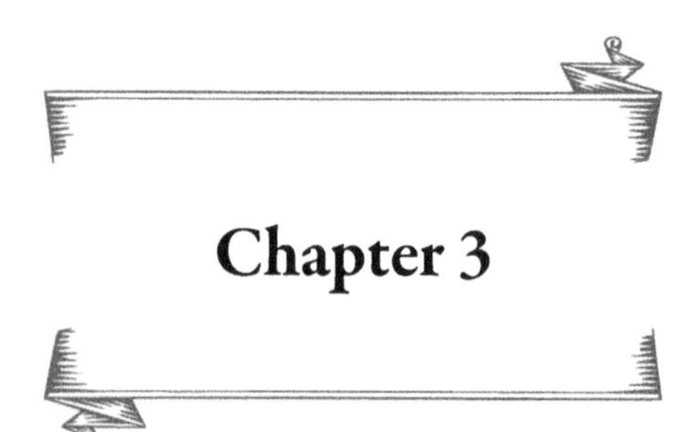

Chapter 3

The castle loomed above Calain and Zelda as they stood before it, side by side in the dark, and to Calain's surprise, it was not swarming in armed guards. Instead, it stood almost vacant in the moonlight, its torches lit with green Wyre flames that flickered gently in the cool breeze rolling off the lake. Perhaps Wick was overconfident in the strength of the castle's enchantments.

"She will have charmed suits of armor ready to defend her," said Zelda, as if she had read Calain's mind.

Calain was noticing more and more that Zelda was growing very apt at guessing her thoughts and feelings. She wondered bitterly if it wasn't yet something else Melvalda had taught her.

"Suits of armor are cheaper to employ," went on Zelda, amused, "also cheaper to replace, and Wick would be on quite the budget after having been disowned by her parents." She sounded darkly pleased by that.

"What is the quarrel between you?" Calain asked.

Zelda hesitated and answered guiltily, "I wasn't the best friend. The fault lies with me."

"Then your quarrel is the same as mine with Selene," said Calain, looking down at Zelda in sympathy. "I was a terrible friend, undeserving of her, and so she hath come here in despair. Quite a pair are we. What shall you say to Wick to sooth her?"

"Soothe her?!" growled Zelda, shocking Calain with her anger. "She hath taken my knight and likely seduced her to boot! She shall count herself fortunate if I do not slay her!"

Calain looked down at Zelda in amazement, but thinking of how she had slain Queen Ellanara without hesitation, she knew she would be a hypocrite if she should judge Zelda for her anger.

"Let us go forth," Zelda said. "Time is wasting." She started forward, but Calain grabbed her shoulders and turned her about.

"Calain? What—?"

"Speak truly, fair Zelda," said Calain somberly. "Did thou lay with Arryn to rouse my fury?"

Zelda blushed a little, and Calain knew she wanted to hide her face, but she was caught in Calain's grasp and helplessly exposed. Her swollen cleavage heaved as she took a guilty breath and confessed, "Yes! I lay with her to goad your jealousy and make you come running! I knew it would bring you to me, and I w-wanted you."

Calain blinked. "Then that pleases me, I suppose."

Zelda stared up at Calain in disbelief. "That *pleases* you?!"

Calain smiled. "It were better than you being madly in love with her. Now one other thing—"

"Calain!" Zelda protested.

Calain did not release Zelda's shoulders. "Dost thou love me more than Selene?"

Zelda laughed girlishly. "Calain! Thou art my true love!" She looked up at Calain with the round, innocently doting eyes Calain had come to love so well, and Calain felt something in her soften. She leaned down and kissed Zelda on the forehead, and she was pleased when she felt Zelda's heart beat faster.

Calain reached back for her sword. "Let us make haste, fair Zelda. There are suits of armor to slay!"

SELENE LAY ON HER BACK, staring up at Wick, who was sitting astride her lap, thighs apart, and still enchanted to look like Zelda. Zelda's large breasts were sharp with pink nipples as they jutted from Wick's chest, and Zelda's sweet blue eyes were smiling at her from Wick's face. Selene knew it should have made her happy, but because it was a lie, it only made her sad.

"What is the matter, my knight?" said Wick. She smiled and ran a small hand over one of her heavy breasts, causing it to wobble hard when it was dropped again.

Selene moaned with longing and felt her clitoris pumping hungrily between her thighs. She knew Wick could feel her arousal, for her cheeks colored up in response . . . Zelda's cheeks colored up.

"Nothing is the matter," lied Selene.

"It has been days," said Wick with Zelda's sweet voice, "and your friends have not come for you. . . *Zelda* has not come for you." She frowned in sympathy and touched Selene's face. "Do heed my counsel: *never* rely on Zelda to care for any that are not herself."

Selene tightened indignantly. "That is not true! Do not slander my lady!"

It was Wick's turn to look angry. "She is not your lady!" she snapped. "I am! You are Bound to me! Me!" She placed a tight hand on Selene's throat, holding her down with such a strength that Selene was shocked.

"You are *mine,*" Wick hissed, making Zelda's sweet face look as menacing as Selene had ever seen it. "I *lent* you to her that she might escape the *buffoonery* of her red knight. But as with everything I ever lent to Zelda, she did not care to return you."

"Do not call Calain a buffoon," Selene warned.

Wick lifted Zelda's golden brows in surprise. "You defend her? I thought you despised the red knight. All you did at the feast was glare hatred upon her! I assumed you fled with her to sate your lust for Zelda. I was not wrong in that regard, at least," she finished, looking sullen, and Selene remembered that Wick would have felt her making love to Zelda because they were Bound.

Selene closed a firm hand around Wick's wrist and pried the elf's fingers from her throat. She snatched Wick's other wrist, and Wick screamed softly and trembled in fear. But Selene only held Wick's arms apart and said calmly, "Enough of this. Take thy true form."

Wick was still shaking – so hard that her breasts jiggled – but she stubbornly did not obey. Selene shook her gently but firmly by the wrists (Wick screamed softly) and repeated sternly, "Take thy true form!"

Wick sobbed but obeyed. In the blink of an eye, she was her small self again – long black hair, pointed ears, dark eyes. Her body was narrow and small, and she was much shorter and lighter than Zelda.

Selene's eyes traced over Wick's body, and she thought her breasts and sex were fantastic. Wick's breasts were small and perky, and the pale pink nipples were standing erect from the plump little mounds. Wick's sex was the same pale pink color and was swathed in soft, curly black hair, from which the lips coyly peeped, swollen with arousal.

When Selene's eyes met Wick's, the elf was staring at her with a shy sort of shock and hesitation.

"Your eyes. . ." whispered Wick hoarsely. "You look as if you would devour me!"

"Thy tits and pussy are perfect," said Selene, making Wick blush scarlet. "So is thy ass. I can feel the sweet shape as you sit upon me—"

"S-Selene!" cried Wick, appalled.

"Why would thou hide behind the image of Zelda when thou hast such beauty of thine own?"

Wick laughed weakly and in disbelief. "Because tis *Zelda* that you love! I had to pretend to be her just to find myself naked on top of you! You didn't even notice my beauty until it was so!"

Selene looked up at Wick guiltily. "I cannot control who I love," she said apologetically.

"But you *can* control what you do!" Wick retorted, struggling in vain to wiggle free of Selene's grasp. "You did not have to come here and make love to me whilst knowing you only cared for Zelda!"

"I do not only care for Zelda," Selene said calmly, but her eyes were fixed with quiet hunger on Wick's breasts, which were jiggling wildly as Wick twisted to get away.

Noticing Selene's lust, Wick fell still in embarrassment.

Her dark eyes burning, Selene gently released one of Wick's wrists and stroked Wick's clitoris with her thumb, watching as the fat lips of her sex moved gently from the pressure. Wick's cheeks were growing brighter from each careful stroke, and Selene could feel Wick's heart beating harder, the pleasure that flushed hot through her, how breathless she was becoming. It was making Selene's clitoris swell and throb with hunger, and Selene in turn was becoming breathless. Was this how it was for Zelda and Calain? Double the pleasure, double the intensity?

Wick's eyes hooded, her pink lips parted in a sigh, and she twisted her narrow waist against the pleasure. Selene kept stroking her clitoris with narrow-eyed lust, until they both were breathless, panting the more intense their arousal.

Still gripping Wick's other wrist, Selene drew her down near and whispered in her ear, "Put thy sweet pussy on my face."

Wick blushed but she obeyed, crawling forward and kneeling over Selene's face, thighs spread. She gasped when Selene grabbed her by the hips and slowly guided her into gyrating, until her breasts were jiggling and her soft sex was brushing Selene's hungry mouth in slow, circular motions.

Watching the perky undersides of Wick's jiggling breasts, Selene plunged her tongue through the heat and moisture of Wick's sex and heard herself moan, heard Wick cry out in shock and delight from the pleasure, saw Wick's thighs begin to tremble as she struggled to hold herself up.

Wick's head fell back, she moaned helplessly, and just as she was climaxing, there was a bang as the door of the bedchamber burst open, and Zelda's voice rang out,

"Wick! Get thy pussy off my knight!"

OUT IN THE CORRIDOR, Calain had felled the last angry suit of armor when she saw Zelda tear a door open and float swiftly inside. They had been searching the castle from top to bottom, ripping open doors, shouting for Selene, and battling empty suits of armor as servants fled them, screaming in terror. Now it seemed Zelda had finally found Selene, for Calain could hear her yelling at Wick.

Calain hurried into the bedchamber just in time to see a naked Wick – who had been sitting on Selene's face a moment before—go flying across the room, sent by a silent spell from Zelda. The small elf hit the wall and fell over, frowning and in pain.

Selene was on the bed, and she was in her smallclothes. Her black hair was loose of its braid, and licks of it fell across her shocked eyes. She sat up on her elbow, amazed to see them there. But to Calain's confusion, she lifted her hand and shouted at them, "No! Do not harm Wick! My lady is blameless!"

Selene's sword and armor were on a nearby display, and she ran to them, snatching her sword with determination from the sheath. "Leave her be, I say!" she warned, standing protectively before Wick, sword drawn.

"She's enchanted!" said Calain in amazement.

Selene scowled. "No, Calain, you fool, I am not! And if you come nearer—"

"Capture her!" commanded Zelda. "I shall deal with Wick!"

Wick was getting to her feet, and she did not look pleased. Glowering hatred at Zelda, she summoned her dark green housecoat from the armchair near the fire, and it floated to her before settling around her shoulders as the sleeves slid neatly over her outstretched arms. Staring intently at Zelda, she lifted her hands to cast a spell.

"Calain, hurry!" Zelda snapped, though her furious eyes were fixed on Wick. The tip of her stave began to glow.

Calain obeyed, lunging at Selene with her sword. Selene parried and the two of them struggled, swords clashing, as Zelda and Wick sent spells back and forth across the room in several flashes of blinding light.

"Selene, can you hear me?" shouted Calain, as if she were speaking to a deaf person. "I have come to set you free!"

"Calain," said Selene through her teeth, parrying a downward swing from Calain's blade, "cease this insanity! I am neither enchanted nor a prisoner!"

"Exactly what an enchanted woman would say," panted Calain. "Don't worry, Selene! I shall save thee!"

Selene groaned in exasperation.

Calain knew she was stronger and more skilled a warrior. It wasn't long before she had disarmed Selene. Selene protested, but to Calain it just sounded like the ramblings of an enchanted person. Without pausing to listen – and frantic to get Selene to safety – Calain brought the hilt of her sword down.

"Calain!" Selene begged. "Wait, you—!" Selene's words halted in her mouth when Calain's sword hilt connected with her head and she tumbled to the floor. Sheathing her sword on her back, Calain gently gathered Selene's limp body and threw her over her shoulder.

With a last vicious wave of her hand, Zelda sent a spell at Wick that smacked her into the wall again, this time knocking her unconscious. Wick slid down the wall like a broken doll and sat slumped over. She didn't move, and Zelda stood over her looking guilty for a moment. Then she turned to Calain.

Calain stood in amazement. Zelda was now as powerful as an elf. Either that, or Wick was a piss-poor mage.

Zelda's blue eyes filled with relief. "You were able to take Selene alive! Thank the gods!"

"Let us take her armor," Calain said breathlessly. She laughed. "I haven't the coin to buy her a new set."

Using telekinesis, Zelda pulled Selene's armor from the nearby stand and charmed it to float alongside them. "I have it," she said, still breathless, tousled, and pink-cheeked from the fighting. "Come! Let us cross the lake on the ferry and take Selene to Wolf Fortress. It is the nearest place we can take her ."

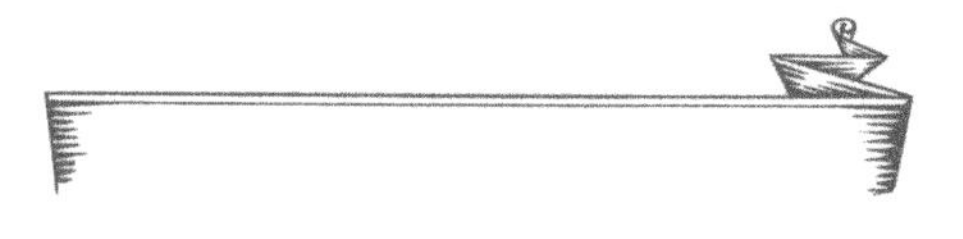

Chapter 4

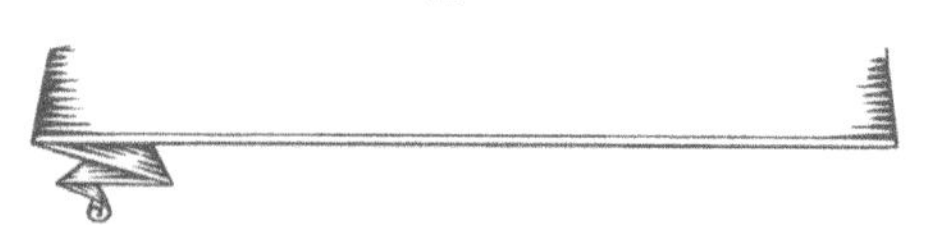

When they arrived at Wolf Fortress, Calain was surprised to find Gweneth and Cassandra already there with the horses. They explained that Arryn had sent them there with a portal, knowing that Calain and Zelda would bring Selene to the old fortress because it was nearby.

Calain would normally feel a sudden burst of anger any time the Wolf Knight was mentioned, but now that Zelda had confessed with a blush that she had only lain with Arryn to make Calain jealous, Calain felt a little smug to hear Arryn's name.

They tied Selene to a wooden chair in one of the solars, afraid that she was enchanted and would awake and attack them (the rope would not restrain her, they knew, but would hopefully slow her down). Then they stroked up a fire in the solar's hearth, allowing its warmth to flood the chilly room. Gweneth and Calain decided to sit with Selene for a while in case she awoke, while Zelda went upstairs to rest after the fighting. Cassandra went with her, and Calain and Gweneth grinned at each other, fully aware of what the other two were up to.

Calain and Gweneth removed their armor and set it on the display stands they'd brought to the solar. Then, still wearing their swords, they pulled up chairs and sat either side Selene, who was slouched forward in her ropes, head down beneath her long, tangled black hair. Selene was in nothing but her linen bra and braies – loose drawers – for she had been in her smallclothes when they'd come.

"So Wick had her completely seduced?" said Gweneth, who was sharpening her carving knife with a stone. "On her back, in her smallclothes and everything?"

"Aye," Calain answered. She leaned forward, resting her elbows on her spread knees, and watching as Gweneth sharpened the knife. "When we burst in, the little wench was riding Selene's face, fully naked."

Gweneth laughed heartily. "Doesn't sound too bad. Maybe you and Zelda should have left her at it for a while. What were her tits like?"

Calain shrugged. "I've seen better, though Selene was staring at her like she'd suck her tits right off."

Gweneth laughed again. "Well, Selene hath only slept with one woman before Wick. Zelda's massive tits are perfect. She *must've* been enchanted to think that little elf attractive after Zelda. I remember Wick at the feast. She was like a talking plank."

Calain laughed. "Gweneth! Don't be cruel."

"Why shouldn't I be?" said Gweneth, unabashed. "She seduced Selene away from us, enchanted her, and tried to keep her a sex slave! Making a mockery of her wee body behind her back is the least she deserves."

"I think Zelda wanted to slay her but restrained herself because they were friends once."

"Then she hath more restraint than you," said Gweneth. She nodded at Selene as she said, "Look at the lump you did give her!"

"Zelda will heal it," said Calain guiltily. "It would have been a smaller lump if she hadn't struggled so."

Gweneth snorted. "Or you just like hitting her."

Calain smiled. “Perhaps. But how could she be so stupid as to think she had no place with us? That somehow life would be better with Wick Blackwood, living shut up in that old, ugly castle?”

“Maybe because you kept telling her ‘twas so?”

“She never listened to me before. Why start now?”

“Ask her when she wakes,” said Gweneth, pocketing the stone and knife. “I’m going up to make a round on the battlements. Then perhaps I’ll surprise Zelda and Cassandra.” She winked and rose to her feet.

Calain laughed as she watched Gweneth leave the room. Then she folded her arms, slouched down in her chair, and decided to nap.

Chapter 5

When Zelda opened her eyes, Cassandra and Gweneth were sleeping either side her in the bed. The bed was a large four-poster and had belonged to the knight captain who had resided over the academy fifty years ago. They were in the woman's old bedchamber, and a fire was roaring on the hearth.

Gweneth and Cassandra were both naked, having laughed softly in shock when a feverish Zelda ripped off their clothes, and in the heat of her passion, had pulled them both down on top of her. Zelda pushed the coverlet back to appraise their strong, toned bodies. Cassandra was sleeping on her belly with her cheek on one of pillows, while Gweneth was sleeping as ever on her back, her undercut hair loose of its topknot and falling curly in her eyes. Zelda bit her lip and ran her small hand over the deep line of Cassandra's back, then touched the back of her fingers to Gweneth's cheek. But she was careful not to wake them. They were both exhausted and needed rest.

Lying there, Zelda suddenly remembered that Selene still needed healing. She had been so drained after the battle at Arlonhold, that she hadn't been able to heal her immediately. Now she rose from the bed, clumsily climbing past Gweneth with swinging breasts. She sat on the edge of the bed, and after summoning her housecoat, she closed it around her shoulders and went downstairs to the solar where they had left Selene.

Calain was there, sitting in a chair and dozing heavily, arms folded, her head bowed. Selene sat beside her, bound to a chair near the fire. She was slumped in her ropes, her head down. Zelda could see the bruise on her head. She knelt before Selene, and reaching up, touched the bruise. She saw it heal before her eyes, and as it disappeared, Selene's eyes fluttered open and she moaned, but she did not lift her head.

"Where am I?" Selene asked hoarsely.

Zelda didn't answer. She was too busy looking at Selene, whose powerful, muscular body was tight against the ropes. She was beautiful and she was strong and she was helplessly exposed, sitting there in her smallclothes, all that black hair loose around her.

Her eyes warm with lust, Zelda smoothed her hands up Selene's hard thighs and gently tugged her drawers down, exposing her pink sex. Zelda could see the small lips poking from the curly black hair and felt her own sex stir with desire. She realized in that moment that she had never gone down on any of the knights before. So determined were they in their lust, they always overpowered her, and she had always let them, thrilled by their strength and hunger.

But now, Zelda felt excited by the prospect of dominating one of her powerful knights and giving her the sweetest release. And how could she resist? Selene was sitting there like a moist, delicious fruit, begging to be tasted.

Heart pounding, Zelda leaned forward between Selene's thighs and buried her mouth gently in the soft pubic hair. As her nose was tickled by curly black hair, the salty scent of sweat rose against her nostrils, mixed with the scent of linen, and something musty and sweet that was all Selene's. The smell stirred something ravenous in Zelda, and she started sliding her tongue with abandon into the heat and moisture of Selene's sex.

Selene stirred in response, frowning against the pleasure. She whispered Zelda's name, and she sounded so helpless, Zelda paused to smile. Then she closed her eyes and sucked long and slow on Selene's clitoris. A shiver went through Selene, and as Zelda kept hungrily sucking, Selene trembled, muscular body straining against her ropes, until she gave a choked gasp and suddenly climaxed.

Down on her knees, Zelda watched with satisfaction as Selene's muscular belly trembled. She looked up to find Selene looking down at her, pink-cheeked and panting and in shock.

"My . . . My lady," panted Selene, who seemed too embarrassed to speak. She looked down at Zelda helplessly.

Zelda smiled up at her. "Welcome home, my knight," she said warmly and reached up, cupping Selene's cheek. "We have bound you here and are waiting until the enchantment wears off."

Selene frowned. "Enchantment?" she said and seemed on the verge of protesting.

"I suppose I could end it faster," Zelda said thoughtfully. She rose to her feet and gazed intently down at Selene, her golden hair suddenly whipping back on a hot breeze as she cast the Binding spell. Her eyes glowed, and she could feel it, Selene's heartbeat beside her own, growing louder and stronger. She could even distinguish it from Calain's. Calain's heart was beating calmly, while Selene's heart was racing a little, both from her recent pleasure and from the gripping power of Zelda's spell.

Zelda noticed that Calain could feel the spell being cast, but she did not stir from her slumber, only frowning deeply. Her cheeks were slightly pink, and Zelda knew she had likely climaxed with Selene as she was dreaming.

With the spell cast and the Binding done, Selene gaped up at Zelda in disbelief. She had likely never dreamed Zelda would Bind her.

"It may yet take some time for Wick's enchantment to fade," said Zelda soothingly as she tugged Selene's drawers back up. "We shall leave you bound here, but not for much longer." So saying, Zelda leaned down, kissed Selene on the lips, and left smiling.

Chapter 6

Selene sat there, her sex still throbbing slightly from the touch of Zelda's ravenous mouth, feeling foolish and sheepish. She had spent the last few weeks in silent anguish, believing she meant nothing to the group, that she had no place among them, that Calain despised her and Zelda did not love her, only for Zelda and Calain to storm Arlonhold – wild and panicking that she had been "captured" – and drag her back to Wolf Fortress with them.

And the most shocking thing: Zelda had Bound her! In doing so, she had broken Selene's Binding to Wick, officially claiming Selene as her knight and in her service. Perhaps they had loved her far more than she had dared suppose. She was so ashamed of her brooding dramatics that she didn't know how she would face any of them.

Selene thought of breaking her ropes so that she could dress and eat, but then the others would think she was attacking and in the thrall of Wick's power, and they would just restrain her again. And so, she sat there, feeling silly for all that had happened and wondering miserably if they had harmed Wick.

After some time, Calain finally awoke and stretched her arms above her head. She wasn't wearing her armor, so the toned shape of her muscular upper body was apparent though her tunic. Selene looked on Calain's masculine beauty with quiet envy. It was Calain's beauty and strength that made Zelda's sex throb with hunger, her pale lashes flutter, her cheeks flush pink. Selene knew she would never be as beautiful as Calain.

But was it truly lust alone that had drawn Zelda and Calain's hearts together? Zelda seemed to think Calain was noble and good, while Calain seemed to think Zelda sweet and innocent. Or at least, that was what both had believed in the beginning. Selene suspected the two quite disillusioned now in the wake of their recent argument. And yet, they loved each other still. And they both loved Selene, the most surprising thing of all.

Calain yawned, looked around at Selene, and grinned.

Selene glowered and was on the verge of a lecture, but she halted when Calain laughed fondly at her glowering, as if to say it was typical of her. Selene heaved a frustrated breath.

"What did become of fair Wick?" Selene asked, determined not to display any predictable behavior in order to avoid Calain's teasing.

"'Fair,' is she?" said Calain derisively. "I see the enchantment hasn't worn off. She seduced and enslaved you!"

Selene's lips tightened. "She did no such thing!" she retorted angrily. "I did go willingly to her when she invited, and 'twas I who did contact her first!"

"But why?" demanded Calain in amazement. She leaned forward, resting her elbows on her spread knees, and her brows were pinched together in guilt as she said, "Did you leave because of my jests about the necklace?"

"Partly," Selene admitted. "But I have never truly felt as if I held a place at Zelda's side. She will always love thee best, and I am fine with that—"

Calain snorted skeptically.

"—but I did not feel I had a place among you. You are her true love, and she and Cassandra bond through their magick – something I shall never possess nor understand – and even

Gweneth did grow close to Zelda as we did journey through Sirione. Zelda has no use for me. The babe, Aereth, did not care for me either."

Calain's eyes narrowed in disbelief. "Surely, you jest. Aereth adored you! She did favor Gweneth, but she imitated everything you did – your broody mannerisms, your seeming confidence, your constant whining—"

Selene glowered.

"The babe even styled her hair in the same ugly plait—"

Selene's glower deepened.

"—That you couldn't see it is beyond me," continued Calain. "I am the one the child loved the least, and I deserved that judgment after I did abandon my duty to her and her mother. It is because of my abandonment that she was lost to the fae."

Selene cast her eyes down. "When I didn't hear her laugh. . . or the sound of her voice . . . So it is as I feared. She is gone. The curse hath pulled her back."

"Aye," said Calain heavily. "And only the gods do know when she shall return. Cass thinks it could be decades."

"Shite," Selene muttered, staring at her boots. She hesitated and said, trying not to sound too pleased, "Aereth . . . imitated me? Truly?"

Calain rolled her eyes. "Truly. Only a fool would not have seen it," she said in irritation—which was how Selene knew she was being honest and not merely seeking to comfort her.

"And the rest of you," pressed Selene. "Did you not grow weary of my unwanted counsel? You are women grown, yet I commanded you always like babes."

"I won't pretend thou aren't sometimes most wearisome," said Calain, "but I admit we were a little lost without you. We had to call on Arryn the Dog Knight for aid, a circumstance I am none too eager to live again."

Selene smiled, amused by Calain's open hatred of the elven knight. "Why do you detest her so? She hath done nothing but aid us."

Calain hesitated and admitted darkly, "I fear she is better than I in every way. She is a better knight . . . And a better person. She would not have slain Ellanara and put sweet Zelda in peril."

Selene frowned. "Don't be a fool! Zelda loves you madly! It's why I'm tied to a chair and you are not."

To Selene's great amusement, Calain seemed to take comfort in her words.

Calain laughed, thinking back fondly. "Tis true you always knew what to do when the rest of us did not. We were frantic to find you, and Zelda was beside herself when you vanished. . ." She hesitated and admitted grudgingly, "As was I."

Selene smiled, her dark eyes amused to see Calain's discomfort.

Calain made a face, annoyed that she had been forced to share her feelings. "Now," she said, rising to her feet, "if you are done whingeing, I shall head upstairs and make sweet love to our lady Zelda, whilst you are forced to sit here and feel every second of it."

Selene scowled, watching as Calain strolled smugly to the door. "After everything you just said, you shall leave me bound here?" she demanded hotly. "Calain, the others think I am enchanted! You must tell them I am not!"

Calain smiled roguishly over her shoulder. "No, I don't think I will. Love thee as I do, we are still rivals, Selene. I shall leave thee to stew in thy angst. Thou dost seem to enjoy it." And she swaggered smugly from the solar.

Selene wanted to be angry but instead, she found herself gazing after Calain fondly and thinking she was very glad to have her for a friend.

Chapter 7

When Calain went upstairs to the old knight captain's bedchamber, Zelda was there alone, sitting in an armchair beside the fire. She looked sad. Her head was bowed as she gazed into the flames, her long golden hair falling in a curtain over one shoulder and down the side of her face. She was sitting very still and appeared so lost in thought, she didn't hear Calain moving through the room until the red knight was almost upon her.

Zelda started and looked up and smiled to see it was Calain. But the smile was sad and forced, and she looked forlornly at the fire again.

"What is the matter, my lady?" Calain asked, gently scooping Zelda into her arms.

Zelda clung to Calain as the knight settled in the armchair, pulling the sorceress down on her lap. Zelda rested her head against Calain, her golden hair brushing Calain's chin.

"Is it Aereth?" Calain asked.

"Only partly."

"Then it's Wick. "

Zelda sighed. "You don't know how lucky you are," she said heavily, "to have friends who love you so dearly. Cassandra, Gweneth, and Selene would all die for you, while I . . . I have always been alone. Wick hates me, and is she wrong to? I suspect she did not steal Selene – Selene went to her willingly, as we had earlier supposed – and you are keeping it from me to protect me."

Calain looked down at Zelda guiltily. "Tis true that Selene went willingly to Wick, the fool. I believe it is as we thought. But Wick did try to keep her there. Of that she is guilty."

"And I hurt her. I hurt her for feeling lonely and wanting what we have."

Calain frowned, stroking Zelda's hair to comfort her. "Then why do you not try reconciling with Wick?"

"Because even if she forgave me – and she hath no reason to—I know I would be a terrible friend!" Zelda admitted helplessly. "I am too self-centered, always focused on my own survival. . . I would just treat her awfully all over again. We both know it."

Calain kept stroking Zelda's hair to comfort her. "Zelda," she said gently, "you have always been focused on survival because your life has been so difficult. You had to survive your uncle and Perth. And you did tell me how you felt isolated at Vira'Toss because the other women did fear your attraction. When you are safe and well again, you will no longer need to obsess over your survival so, and then you shall have friends. I shall see to it."

Zelda smiled, looking up at Calain in the doting way she had come to love. "My knight is so sweet," said the sorceress warmly. "I wish it were as simple as that. We still need a home. We cannot linger here! Queen Cilia knows we were hiding here before. She sent her letter here to me."

"And I suppose you do not wish to return to Ellormest and continue our quest for Edhen," said Calain hopefully.

Zelda laughed softly. "Why do you hate Arryn so? She saved your life! She saved mine!"

"But she also made love to you," Calain said darkly. "It is a trespass I cannot forgive."

Zelda sighed. "Calain! *I* made love to *her*! She did not attempt anything with me. It was I who started it. I did it to bring you to me, if you recall."

"And because you wanted to, I suspect," said Calain at once. "I can feel how your heart doth beat faster when Arryn is near. You like her."

"Is that so terrible? She's my friend." Zelda blinked as she realized. She smiled. "Arryn is my friend."

Calain smiled as well, her heart warming to hear the happy little note in Zelda's voice. She stroked Zelda's hair again and kissed her head. "Well . . . I suppose if having Arryn for a friend doth make thee so happy, then I cannot object."

Zelda smiled up at Calain and kissed her on the cheek, which made Calain very happy.

"So where shall we go?" Calain said after a content pause. "We traveled all those weeks to Edhen only to wind up back where we started."

"Cassandra suggested traveling south, to Honione," said Zelda.

"Hmm. Tis not a bad idea," said Calain thoughtfully.

Zelda looked up. "Really? What's Honione like?"

"A lot of humans," said Calain. "So no more elves would try to kill us – or it wouldn't happen as often, at least. Honione grew out of the first human settlement. Knight Octava took us on a trip there when we were nearly graduates, to fight the monsters for practice and to test our bravery and skill."

Zelda stiffened. "Monsters?"

"Oh, aye," said Calain with a laugh. "And 'twas good practice. Minotaurs, fauns, centaurs, ogres, and bridge trolls—"

"I don't want to live among monsters!" Zelda cried.

Calain laughed again. "We would live in the city, my lady, not the Aelwith Wilds. I only wonder if Queen Cilia's wrath has cooled or if she will send more Rose Guard knights to slay us. If she truly believes we are working for Hidden Dragon, it is likely she shall."

Zelda didn't seem happy about that, and Calain looked down at her apologetically. It was because she had slain the queen that they were in this mess – still in this mess months after it had happened! Calain kept promising to help Zelda find a place to settle down and open a shop, some place where she could be safe and happy and stop running, but she had failed to deliver that promise again and again.

And if Calain was honest with herself, a large part of the reason she despised Yrsa and Melvalda and Arryn was the fact that they could provide Zelda with a life Calain could not. All three women had offered Zelda comfort and security: Yrsa would have taken care of Zelda the rest of her days, Melvalda would have kept Zelda safe at Ravenhold, and even Arryn would have allowed Zelda to live inside Edhen – assuming she was the Dragon of Edhen, as they all suspected.

But what did Calain have to give? Just months ago, Calain had complained that Zelda was a peasant with no last name, but Calain was a peasant as well. She had no home, no riches, no castle, no secret hidden forest . . . She had nothing except her sword arm and her love for Zelda, and both had failed the sorceress more than once.

Overwhelmed with shame and misery, Calain suddenly held Zelda tight and buried her face in her hair. Perplexed, Zelda reached up and touched Calain's face. "What is the matter, my knight?" Zelda whispered.

"I don't deserve you," Calain said heavily. She lifted her face and stared with wet eyes into the flames. "Selene ran away thinking she had no place here, but I am truly the unworthy one."

"That is not so!" Zelda said at once. She shook her head, dabbing at Calain's sudden tears with the wing of her long sleeve. "Calain, my love, do not weep. We shall figure things out . . . *together.*" She smiled into Calain's eyes, and Calain had to admit she felt better. Looking into Zelda's pretty blue eyes always had that effect.

"All right," said Calain hoarsely. "So we shall go to Honione and try to make a life for ourselves. And this time, I shall make life good for thee, Zelda, not difficult and full of strife."

Zelda smiled and shook her head. "Silly woman," she said in exasperation. "You have made my life a wonderful adventure! I have Aereth, I have traveled to other dimensions, I have seen half the realms!" She kissed Calain's lips, and they smiled at each other.

Zelda closed her eyes and happily nuzzled her head again under Calain's chin, and Calain held her tightly in her strong arms, and they sat beside the fire in content silence for a time, just listening to it crackle softly and feeling its warmth on their skin.

"Shall you Bind the others as you did Selene?" Calain asked eventually. She thought Zelda seemed amused that Calain had made peace with it.

"Yes, of course," said Zelda. "I want you all tied to me, so if we're ever separated again, we can find each other. I can feel Selene's heart right now. It's beating very slow and calm. But then . . . Her heart is always so. Like a steady drumbeat."

"What is my heart like?" asked Calain, amused.

Zelda blushed a little. "Yours is always strong and a little loud," she said fondly. She smiled. "And a little wild."

Calain grinned. "I shall be curious to know what Gweneth's heart feels like. And Cassandra's. Where are they anyway?"

"Gweneth went to water the horses," said Zelda. "And Cassandra insists on patrolling the battlements. She's convinced the Rose Guard is going to show up any minute, and I am afeared she is right. We should pack up and move as soon as Selene is well."

"She is well," Calain admitted sheepishly.

Zelda looked up at her quickly. "What do you mean?"

"I spoke with her before coming here," Calain said with a shrug. "She seems her old self, but I left her tied to the chair . . . just in case."

Zelda looked at Calain reprovingly but she also seemed amused. "Good," she said. "Then we should set out soon. One more night here, and then we leave for Honione in the morning."

"Hmm. One more night?" said Calain, her eyes on Zelda's cleavage as she peered over her shoulder.

Zelda smirked over her shoulder at Calain. "Yes, my love. One more night here, within warm walls, in a large, soft bed. Let us make good use of it." She touched Calain's chin with her slender fingertips and kissed her on the lips. Calain felt her heart skip a happy beat.

SELENE REALIZED THAT by Binding her, Zelda was starting to make decisions, to give instructions and commands. She was coming more comfortably into her role as their sorceress. Perhaps their recent mad adventures had given her confidence. She certainly had more knowledge about the world now.

Suddenly tired of sitting bound to the chair, Selene tensed her muscles, and they flexed as the ropes tore and fell away. She sat still again as the ropes piled the stone floor, listening intently for the sound of running boots. When no one came, she rose and left the solar, leaving the empty chair and the tattered ropes behind.

Out in the hall, the fortress was silent. Someone had lit the torches lining the stone corridor, and their orange flames glowed bright in the evening gloom.

Selene went from room to room, checking for the others. She went to the kitchen first but no one was there and the oven was cold, dark, and devoid of fire. She checked the old armory, thinking Gweneth would be there, as it was one of her haunts, but it was empty as well, full of nothing but weapon and armor stands and open trunks.

Finally, Selene went to the old barracks where the knights had slept during their last stay at Wolf Fortress. No one was sleeping there now, but there were traveling satchels strewn across the beds. When Selene recognized one as belonging to Gweneth, a sudden idea came to her.

She moved into the room and opened Gweneth's satchel and there it was: Gweneth's leather phallus and harness were nestled inside, tangled in bandages and wine-stained linen. Selene was taking the pleasure toy from the satchel when the sound of soft sobbing made her pause. It was Zelda, sobbing in ecstasy. Selene smiled at the leather phallus in her hand.

CALAIN LAY ON THE FOUR-poster in naught but her smallclothes and watched with one bulging arm behind her head as Zelda crawled on all fours to her. She had just fingered Zelda to a climax, making her sob and moan as she wiggled against Calain's fingers. The sorceress had paused to wash herself in the nearby basin, and now she was crawling to Calain again.

Calain reclined on her back, her eyes narrowed, her lips smiling as she watched Zelda crawling to her. Zelda's great breasts were swinging and trembling as they hung down, and her shapely thighs flexed as she came. She crawled up Calain's body and leaned down and kissed her, her eyes soft.

As they were kissing, Calain heard movement at the door and looked past Zelda to see Selene standing there. To Calain's surprise, Selene was wearing Gweneth's leather phallus and harness . . . and her dark eyes were narrowed with lust. Calain knew what things looked like from Selene's perspective: Zelda kneeling with her backside in the air, the fat lips of her sex poking between her thighs. Selene's eyes met Calain's and Calain's green eyes smiled. Selene smiled back.

Calain kept kissing Zelda, pretending she hadn't noticed Selene, so that Zelda was taken by surprise when Selene climbed up on the bed and – in seconds – had plunged the rigid leather phallus through the heat and moisture of her sex. Zelda gasped and her lashes fluttered as she was filled to the base. She glanced back and her cheeks flamed to see Selene behind her, looking at her with glittering hunger.

Selene knocked Zelda's knees wide apart with her own, then she leaned down over Zelda, so that the sorceress was sandwiched between them, and she began to thrust, hunching her back to get in deep, her panting mouth Zelda's ear. Zelda's eyes hooded and her sweet lips parted in a gasp as Selene rode her. Calain was beside herself, for Zelda's great breasts were jiggling against her with each thrust, she could see Zelda's backside jiggling as well, and watching as Zelda's thighs trembling to hold her up was maddening.

Green eyes hard with lust, Calain gripped the back of Zelda's neck and kissed her roughly. Zelda shivered and moaned against Calain's strong lips, for Selene was fingering her clitoris as she rode her. Selene's other hand fumbled for one of Zelda's heavy breasts, and she massaged it in a hard hand as she hunched her back and grunted again to get inside. This time she plunged the phallus so deep, Zelda's sex split wider and strained to clench it, and the sorceress screamed softly.

Calain groped Zelda's other heavy breast, thrusting her hungry tongue in Zelda's mouth. Zelda's tongue was just as hungry, sliding almost commandingly against hers, forcing its way deeper and harder – just as the leather phallus plunged deeper and harder through the dripping lips of her sex.

Rocking helplessly on her knees, Zelda's body trembled. Calain could feel her heartbeat accelerating and knew what was happening: Zelda was about to climax.

Sure enough, the sorceress tore her lips from Calain's and choked out a shrill cry as her body shuddered, large breasts shivering against Calain's chest. Selene stopped thrusting and carefully the slid the phallus out. Weak and content, Zelda sank down on top of Calain, who closed her arms around her.

Selene removed the leather harness and dropped on her back beside Calain, panting from her efforts, and watching Zelda with soft eyes. Zelda was lying on Calain's chest and her eyes were closed as she panted. She was smiling. Selene reached over and stroked her long golden hair, and she wiggled contently beneath Selene's touch.

With sudden possessiveness, Selene hooked a strong hand on Zelda's narrow waist and pulled her from Calain and onto her own chest. Zelda's lashes fluttered in surprise, but she nuzzled her body against Selene and closed her eyes contently. Selene closed her arms around Zelda and stared at the ceiling, still panting to catch her breath.

Calain laughed softly. About two months ago, if Selene had taken Zelda from her arms, Calain would have punched Selene in the face and they would have been brawling. Now it seemed like a natural thing to do, passing Zelda from chest to chest, taking turns holding her and making love to her.

As Zelda was lying on Selene's chest, Calain crawled up behind and spread Zelda's thighs, so that she was half-kneeling and her backside was in the air. Zelda gasped when Calain plunged her face in her sex. The sorceress was moist and hot, and the fat lips squirmed against Calain's face, the golden pubic hair tickling her. Zelda wiggled at the intensity and moaned, but she could not have squirmed away. Selene was still holding her tightly, and Calain was gripping her thighs to keep her still. And so she lay trapped between the two knights as Calain's sucked upon the lips of her sex and licked her throbbing clitoris, until she was panting and pink-cheeked.

"Her clit is so fat," Calain muttered, sucking the clitoris in her lips yet again, so that Zelda cried out.

"I wish I could see what thou were doing," said Selene breathlessly. She sounded beside herself with arousal, and Calain could understand why: Zelda's great breasts were crushed against her, and the sorceress was moaning and gasping in the maddening way that always drove Calain wild.

Calain heard someone enter the room behind her but did not stop, her face moving against Zelda's sex, which was so helplessly displayed to her.

"What the devil have you two done to Zelda?" said Gweneth's voice with a laugh. The swish of a wineskin.

Zelda colored up, slightly embarrassed that Gweneth – the one most likely to tease her later – had walked in to find her trapped between Selene and Calain as Calain went down on her from behind. She looked as if she was being held captive. . . She looked luscious, Calain thought: her massive breasts crushed against Selene, her narrow back and its deep line, her plump backside in the air . . .

Another swish of the wineskin as Gweneth took another drink. Then the mattress shifted as Gweneth crawled across. She drew near to Calain, and when Calain shifted aside, Gweneth slid her tongue between the fat lips of Zelda's sex, while Calain continued sucking on her clitoris and frowning with delight as she did. The intensity of this made Zelda gasp and squirm all the more, but now Calain and Gweneth combined were gripping her thighs, and she could hardly move.

Calain loved the little mole on the back of Zelda's right thigh. She licked it, saw Zelda tremble, and licked it again, trailing wet kisses up Zelda's thigh to her soft backside, which she kissed and spanked softly, pausing to watch as it jiggled from the soft blows.

Zelda twisted and moaned against the pleasure. "Oh gods . . ." she whispered, frowning in ecstasy when Calain and Gweneth switched: Calain plunged her tongue in Zelda's sex while Gweneth sucked her clitoris.

Selene, as if she could stand watching no longer, gripped the back of Zelda's neck and kissed her hard on the mouth, muffling her cries. Zelda kissed Selene back, moaning against her lips, as behind her, Calain and Gweneth continued sucking and licking.

More movement at the door told Calain that Cassandra had finally come. She laughed to herself: why did it always seem as if Cassandra were last? Calain looked up and sure enough, Cassandra was standing there, watching them with longing. She had leaned in the doorway and folded her arms, as if she had no intention of joining.

Gweneth looked over her shoulder and licked Zelda's moisture from her lips. "Come here, Cassie," she said. She smirked. "Zelda likes it best when it's all four of us banging her!"

Zelda blushed, darting a playful glare at Gweneth.

"We should change positions," said Calain. So saying, she lifted Zelda by the waist easily and muttered, "Spread your legs, fair Zelda." Zelda was gripping Calain's arms and blushed prettily but obeyed: she spread her thighs, revealing her pink sex and its fat lips, and Calain lowered her onto Selene's face.

"It is because I love thee that I give thee this honor," Calain said playfully to Selene, and Zelda blushed, giving Calain's arm a playful slap. But Zelda didn't have much time to be angry: Selene was soon licking between her thighs and she was staring in shock into the distance, her eyes wide and her lips apart.

Gweneth moved in at once and grabbed one of Zelda's heavy breasts in her fist. She watched with serious satisfaction as the nipple jutted out hard, and then she was sucking on it as Zelda's head fell back from the pleasure.

Calain sucked on the other heavy breast, rolling her tongue against the hard little nipple. Her kisses trailed hot up Zelda's neck to her mouth, and she thrust her tongue in Zelda's mouth in a hard kiss. A thrill of delight went through her when she felt Zelda's heart race from the sudden kiss.

Cassandra crawled across the bed, and then she was lying nearly on top of Selene as she closed her mouth on Zelda's clitoris and sucked it, even as Selene slid her tongue between the swollen lips of Zelda's sex. Zelda's thighs trembled from the combined pleasure of both their mouths.

The four knights closed around Zelda, sucking her, groping her, and kissing her, until she had trembled between them and climaxed yet again, her head falling back in a helpless cry. This time she looked so exhausted that they let her sleep, all of them lying on their backs in the bed, watching the fire and lost in their thoughts.

Calain held Zelda to her chest again and stroked the sorceress' hair as she dreamt. She stared at the fire and her chest was filled with a wonderful content. There she was, surrounded by her friends, with her true love sleeping in her arms, the most beautiful woman in Vallinwir. She didn't know what she had done that the gods would bless her so, but she was glad.

"So now you just take my things without asking? Are we that familiar? Are we lovers?" said Gweneth into the silence. She was speaking to Selene, who looked around at her in surprise. "My cock!" Gweneth snapped. "If I'd been wearing it and fucking Zelda's pussy, you probably would have taken it still."

Selene smiled at the ceiling. "Consider it payment for all the aggravation thou hast cost me."

Gweneth laughed quietly. "Fair enough." She glanced at Calain. "So where shall we go after this? You know we cannot stay in Wolf Fortress. Everyone and their mother doth know we have lingered here."

"And there are too many . . . dark memories," said Selene somberly, and everyone knew she meant Aereth, who had been tricked by Queen Anindel within these very walls.

Calain felt another sting of guilt, knowing she had not been there, that Aereth had been taken because Zelda had been out rescuing Calain.

"Cassie wanted to go to Honione," said Calain. "I told Zelda, and she agrees."

Gweneth lifted her brows. "Are the three of you mad, then? Honione is dangerous!"

"Gwen!" protested Calain with a laugh. "We wouldn't be living *in* the Wilds! We would take Zelda to a city—"

"As if cities were safe," dismissed Gweneth. She looked at Cassandra. "Why Honione?" she demanded. "Did you have a vision? You wouldn't suggest the place unless there were a reason."

Cassandra was slow to answer. She was lying near the edge of the bed furthest from Calain and it was difficult to see her around Gweneth, who was now sitting up on her elbow.

"Yes. I . . . had a vision," Cassandra admitted softly.

The atmosphere changed almost instantly. The knights lost their smiles and the drowsy content left them to be replaced by tense fear. Selene also sat up, and now she and Gweneth both were staring at Cassandra, who lay on her back, staring at the ceiling.

Anytime Cassandra had a vision, danger was near at hand. She never had visions about pleasant things, and if she did, she did not share those visions with the others. Calain lay there, holding Zelda in her arms and feeling the dread welling up inside her. Cassandra's last vision had been of Queen Ellanara and her death at the hands of Calain, an event which had changed their lives drastically.

Cassandra sat up, and now Calain could see her. Her pale blonde hair was loose and falling down one side of her face. She drew her knees up and hugged them, and she almost looked like a child as she said slowly, "A messenger raven shall come, summoning us to Honione. If we don't go, the Rose Guard will find us here . . . and slay us. They are sending a small army this time. I believe Calain's destruction of the Gold Keep did rattle them."

Gweneth's mouth fell open. "And you didn't think to tell us this?!"

"What was the point frightening you?" said Cassandra, looking calmly into Gweneth's eyes. "If we go to Honione, they will not find us and it will not matter. And if they do find us, why not spend our last day happy together," her eyes went to Zelda's sleeping face and softened, "whilst making love to sweet Zelda?"

Gweneth looked at Zelda as well and seemed unable to find an argument.

"But the enchantments here . . ." said Selene, sounding defeated.

"The Rose Guard shant come alone," Cassandra answered. "Cilia shall send her court mage, a very powerful sorceress, whose elven light could break the enchantments placed upon Ellondhold —"

"*Lythara*," sneered Calain. When everyone looked at her, she added, "She is the one who did banish Zelda and I to Menosea. But wait . . ." She gently laid Zelda aside and sat up, looking past the others at Cassandra. "Why were we summoned to Honione? We don't know anyone there!"

"I have a sister there," said Gweneth thoughtfully. "Though I can't imagine what Ase would want with me. She and I were never very close."

"I suppose we shall see when the letter comes," said Cassandra. "The vision did not tell me what was in the letter, only that it caused us to venture forth to Honione."

As if Cassandra's words had summoned it, a raven appeared in the window with a flutter of its wings. A scroll of parchment was tied to its leg. The knights exchanged grim glances, then Selene slid to the edge of the bed, walked to the window, and took the parchment from the raven. The bird screeched and took off again as she unscrolled it and silently read. She went still.

"Come *on*, Selene," complained Gweneth, rising from the bed and joining Selene. "What the devil does it say already?" She read the letter over Selene's shoulder, and she, too, froze.

Selene and Gweneth both looked at Calain.

Heart pounding, Calain rose from the bed, took the letter from Selene, and read the following,

My dearest daughter,

When I learned you were imprisoned in the Gold Keep in Eriallon, I did journey there from Honione to beg the queen for mercy. Half through the journey, however, I learned that you had escaped and were alive still, that you had been seen leaving your father's farm near Alleren.

I am almost afraid to hope thou lives still, but my terror hath made me realize how time is precious and how I must seek to make amends before it is too late. You deserve to know why I did leave you, for I am most certain your father hath not told thee, afeared as he is that you shall stop loving him.

I am living east of City Erhyrst, in a cottage due north of the Solden Stones. But if your anger is too great, my child, and you do not wish to come, I shall understand. Too long has it taken me to reach out to you, my daughter, who did deserve so much more from me. You deserved the world.

Your loving mother,

Lowri

Calain's hand was shaking when she finished reading the letter. She resisted the urge to crumple it, resisted the tears that rose. Selene touched a comforting hand to Calain's shoulder, but Calain jerked away with gritted teeth, turned, and walked to the door. As she left the room, she heard Zelda sit up and say sleepily, "What is happening?"

Chapter 8

The knights told Zelda about the letter, and Zelda listened sadly, caught somewhere between pity and surprise. She had never dreamed that Calain's mother, after so many years of silence, would reach out to her daughter. And now Zelda had another reason to feel guilty: the slaying of Queen Ellanara had not only touched the lives of Zelda and the knights but also the lives of their families.

Neserie had hated Zelda for "ruining Selene's life" and had told her so to her face several times, while Sune and Kare hadn't been too pleased that their daughter was a fugitive, though they had been sweet to her regardless (Sune mostly blamed Calain), and Cassandra's mother, while very kind to Zelda, likely worried for Cassandra daily, knowing that she was running from the law in the service of a rebel sorceress.

As Zelda and the knights dressed themselves, there was a heavy feeling on the air. Now they all knew they must leave Wolf Fortress immediately, or else be overcome by an army of Rose Guard knights. The knights donned their armor, as if in preparation of the onslaught, and packed their satchels and prepared to set out. Calain alone did not ready herself, as she had disappeared after the arrival of the letter.

"I have looked all over for her," Cassandra said, reporting to the kitchen after a thorough search. "She is nowhere to be found."

"Could it be that Calain has finally become somewhat clever?" joked Gweneth, who was sitting at the table and filling a wineskin from a bottle.

"Time is running out," said Selene grimly. "We need to find her and leave the fortress at once. There is no time for brooding."

Zelda laughed tonelessly. "Calain doesn't brood, Selene. She barely thinks on her actions at all."

Gweneth laughed at that. "Aye, sorceress. So you've come to know her after all! I wasn't aware a word passed between you aside from heavy breathing."

Zelda smiled at this teasing. "I shall follow Calain's heartbeat and find her," she said, rising from the kitchen table. She looked at Selene. "But it is Selene who will speak with her."

Selene had been pacing with her arms folded, but she stopped to regard Zelda in surprise.

Zelda smiled. "Come, Selene. I shall take you to Calain."

Zelda knew that, out of all of them, Selene was the one Calain would listen to most when it came to her mother. She knew because she remembered the memory she had seen in one of Edolel's books. In the memory, Calain's father had come to Falcon Isle and told Calain that her mother had left them. Calain had been quite young then, merely an adolescent, and had run from the fortress in misery, likely intent on not returning. It was Selene who had sought Calain out to comfort her, and whatever Selene had said must have worked, for Calain had returned to the fortress and become a knight.

It wasn't hard to follow Calain's heartbeat, for Calain's heart was beating hard with anger. Zelda followed it as it grew louder and stronger, nearer and nearer, until she realized they were leaving the fortress altogether. Before long, they were walking through the gate, and Zelda suddenly had a flashback of young Calain running out of Falcon Fortress and into the grass.

Selene must've recalled the same image, for she said half-irritably and half-sadly, "This is just like Calain."

When Calain's heartbeat had grown to a pulse in Zelda's ears, she finally spied the knight on the edge of Dark Bloom Forest, sitting upon a rock and staring at the grass. Her head was bowed, and tendrils of bright red hair hung in her face. She looked so forlorn that Zelda saw Selene's face softened in sympathy.

"I shall speak to her as you request, sorceress," Selene said heavily, "though I do not know what good it shall do her. In any other circumstance, I would simply grab her and tell her to move her arse."

Zelda laughed softly. "I am sure you shall think of something kind to say. I shall call the others down and we shall ready the horses." And with that, she walked away, the blue skirts of her gown trailing behind her, leaving Selene to approach Calain alone.

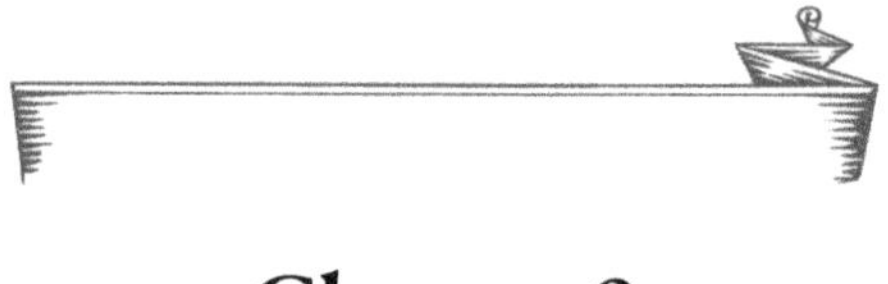

Chapter 9

Selene didn't know why Zelda was so confident she could comfort Calain, especially after all that had recently happened, but sometimes Zelda was like Cassandra in how she mysteriously knew things, so Selene didn't bother questioning it. Instead, she went to Calain, and after hesitating, she folded her arms and stood near her, wondering what to say.

"Calain, tis time to depart," Selene said at last. "The Rose Guard will soon be upon us. Surely, you can brood on horseback."

Calain laughed tonelessly. She glanced up at Selene and seemed amused by how awkward she was. "Zelda put you up to this?" she said, dropping her eyes again.

Selene sighed and sat on the grass beside Calain, staring ahead at Wolf Fortress. "What is the matter?" she said. "So thy mother contacted thee. We don't have to see her when we venture to Honione."

"But what if I don't go and I regret it?" said Calain unhappily. "I spent years angry with my mother, believing she had abandoned me because she was wicked. But I did abandon my sisters in arms and fair Zelda . . . and Aereth. Am I not wicked for that?"

"No," said Selene at once.

Calain looked at her skeptically. "You are saying that to soothe me, so that I'll shut up and don my armor."

"No," Selene said. "If I wanted you to shut up and move out, I'd have just grabbed you by now."

"Hmm," said Calain, considering. "That is true."

"And I did only recently abandon all of you, did I not?" added Selene pointedly. "What a hypocrite I would be if I did yell at thee now."

"But you've always been a hypocrite," Calain teased and laughed when she received a light elbow jab on the leg. She glanced sideways at Selene again. "So you truly don't think me wicked for leaving? Gweneth does. It was the reason she beat me at your grandmother's house. And Cassandra, she is disappointed in me as well, though she is too gentle and kind to say so. From you I expected a lecture, but you made no move to do so, even before you did leave us."

"Ha. Only because I have learned tis a waste of breath. You never listen," said Selene, shaking her head. "But what is it you fear, Calain? That your mother will reveal she had some grave reason for leaving? If you go to see her, all you shall learn is that you are just like her, something thou already knoweth."

"Hmm," said Calain, realizing. "I suppose you're right."

"And if thy mother despises thee and you have a falling out, you shall always have your sisters in arms. And fair Zelda."

Calain looked at Selene gratefully, her green eyes warm. "Remember when we were girls and my pa came and told me that Lowri had left us?"

"Yes, of course."

"I ran from the fortress. I didn't want to be a knight anymore. I just wanted to find my mother and ask her why, what I did that was so wrong that she should leave. At first, I thought she left because I was wicked. Then I grew older, and I thought she left because she was wicked."

"And now?"

"Now I think she left because she was a person." Calain gazed off thoughtfully a moment, then looked at Selene again. "Do you remember what thou did say to me that day?"

"That you were a fool and that I hated you?" guessed Selene, who did not remember.

Calain laughed and waved a hand. "After that. You said you would always be there for me. And then you broke that promise. So did I when I left and abandoned Zelda."

"Calain . . ." Selene began apologetically.

"Let us make a new pact," Calain went on. "From now on, we shall always be there for each other and for Zelda. Dost thou promise?"

"I promise," said Selene, smiling. She clapped Calain's knee. "Now come. You are sitting outside naked, you realize?"

Calain glanced down and realized she was indeed naked. Selene draped a blanket she had brought around Calain's shoulders, and they laughed together as they reentered the fortress.

Scrying them through a bowl of water as she sat in the kitchen, Zelda laughed as well.

Hearth and Home

Book 10

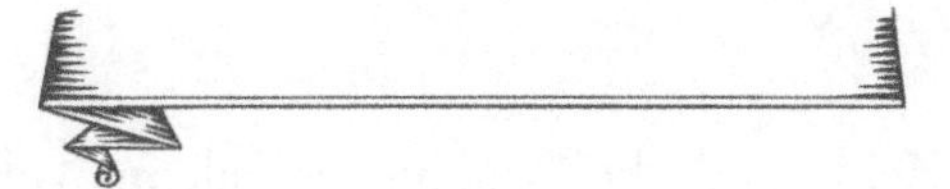

Chapter 1

Once Zelda and the Knights of Falcon had agreed on journeying to Honione, the next thing they needed to decide was how they were going to get there. Realm Honione was far south across the *Arinath Sea,* past Ellormest and Eriallon both, and thus, it could not be reached on foot. Their only option was to take a ship from Priine or coax their terrified horses through an ancient elven portal, which didn't seem likely to work.

It was as they were weighing their options that Zelda lamented the fact that she could not cast portal spells between the realms, only portals that opened other dimensions, but when Gweneth reminded her of Arryn's Summoning Stone, Zelda also admitted she did not wish to summon Arryn again. She did not want to find herself relying too much on the Wolf Knight's aid and did not want to seem as if she were taking advantage of her friendship.

"Arryn is the only friend I have now," Zelda said, and Calain knew she was thinking of Wick. "I do not wish to . . . befoul that in any way."

Calain was sitting beside Zelda and put a soothing hand on her shoulder.

They had left Wolf Fortress far behind, fearing that the Rose Guard would converge there upon them, and were camping in the forest of Dark Bloom. They sat around a low fire, finishing their morning meal, as the horses grazed nearby. Having learned from Cassandra that the Rose Guard was upon them, everyone was in low spirits. They had been traveling for days in relative silence, always moving in the direction of the ancient elven temple where the portal stood waiting. It was as if they already knew the portal was their only hope, even though they were apprehensive to approach after Calain had been overrun at one.

Calain was sitting between Zelda and Selene and trying not to think of the reason they were going to Honione in particular. Her mother's letter was still in her satchel, rolled up and slightly crumpled, and at night when no one was looking, she took it out and read it again and again. She had not seen her mother since she was eleven. Why now, after all this time, had she chosen to reach out? Because Calain was in danger? Did she truly think she could have saved her? Her mother was a peasant, she was no one! And yet, she had been willing to venture all the way to Alleren to speak for her, even if it meant her death! Calain didn't know what to think. If the letter were true, then her mother had loved her all this time, and she had hated her for nothing.

"Well, however we get to Honione, we have to figure out it quickly," said Gweneth, who was chucking small twigs in the fire. "The Rose Guard is still coming for us, or did you all forget? Queen Cilia's daft arse is mad enough to believe we're actually working with the elves! Would probably be best if we put as much distance between ourselves and Eriallon as possible."

"The Rose Guard will be waiting at every port for us in case we flee," said Selene seriously. "Let us not forget what happened in Arionol." She looked unhappily at Cassandra, and so did Zelda, Gweneth, and Calain: Cassandra had nearly been lost to them, having martyred herself so they could get away.

Calain did not want a repeat of last time. It seemed almost as if events were playing on a loop: Cassandra predicted the arrival of Rose Guard knights, they came, she sacrificed herself so that they might escape. If the Rose Guard were to show up in Priine again, there was no doubt in Calain's mind that Cassandra would volunteer to hold them off as they boarded a ship. But for all her visions and magickal powers, Cassandra was still just one woman. Eventually, there would come a time when she would not be so lucky as to survive her martyr complex.

"Selene is right. We cannot allow Cassie to fight off a horde of Rose Guard knights for us again," said Calain. "We have no choice but to make for the portal."

"Assuming we can even get the infernal horses to go through," said Gweneth, "if we take the portal to Honione, we'll turn up in the middle of the Aelwith Wilds. That's where the old elven ruins are. Popping up there in the middle of bloodthirsty minotaurs and centaurs would be foolhardy!"

"But we have little choice," Selene reminded her. "Either we stay here and perish or we go there and perish."

"You are so very certain of our perishing," said Cassandra, who had a small smile. She was the only one who seemed calm, relaxed, and even amused by the situation. Calain found that a little strange as it was Cassandra – having seen the vision of them murdered at the hands of the Rose Guard – who should have been taking the situation most gravely. She could only suppose that Cassandra – as ever – knew more than she was letting on.

"I can place a calming spell on the horses," Zelda said, staring at the fire. "They'll go through the portal like mindless sheep, but they'll never forgive me." She smiled sadly.

"The horses will understand," said Calain, remembering that Zelda could speak to them and had an odd sort of friendship with each one.

"Then it's settled," said Selene. "We shall make for the portal and take it to Honione. I shall scout ahead and see if any Rose Guard knights are waiting for us at the temple."

They stayed at camp all day, resting and discussing the journey ahead in soft, serious voices, and when night fell, they packed up, doused the fire, and set out for the ancient elven temple.

As they led the horses forward in a line, Calain glanced around at the silhouettes of the trees and thought Dark Bloom was so familiar now, it almost felt like home. Its beauty distracted her from anxious thoughts of her mother, at least. And Aereth.

Aside from the sobering effect of Cassandra's vision, Zelda and the Knights of Falcon were still mourning the loss of Aereth. When before they had traveled so jovially, singing and telling stories and teasing each other, now they were silent and somber. It was as if Aereth's loss had sucked the life from them. Even making love to Zelda the night before had been more about comfort than their lust.

Selene scouted ahead that afternoon, reporting back that the temple was clear. When they arrived that evening, as dusk fell orange across the sky, it was still so. Zelda cast her calming spell on the horses, and then they each passed through, guiding a steed forward by its reins.

Calain was the last to pass through the portal, and she glanced back once at Dark Bloom, saying a silent farewell to the forest.

As Calain understood it, the portals worked by sensing where a traveler wished to go. As Calain passed through leading Arthur, she focused on arriving at the elven temple in Honione.

The light swirled around Calain and made her stomach churn, as it always had. She knew it was scanning her mind, searching for her desired location. Then she had passed through and was on the other side. She caught a brief glimpse of spidery, naked tree branches against a gray sky before spots clouded her eyes, and as she leaned forward to gulp for air, she was vaguely aware of Gweneth screaming Zelda's name.

The ground was quaking, a beast was roaring, and beside Calain, Arthur reared up, bucking in horror. Still dizzy and gasping, Calain straightened up and grabbed the horse's reins.

"Arthur! What the devil is wrong with . . .!" Calain's voice trailed off: lying on the ground in a pool of blood . . . was Zelda.

Chapter 2

The ogre must've been twenty feet tall, a mountainous creature, with gray skin and small, watery eyes. Its hairless head was round like a boulder, and two sharp ears pointed from it either side, while tusks reached from its drooling bottom lip. It wore nothing except a dark brown loincloth made of fur, and in its meaty fist was a giant club.

The ogre was outside the temple, towering over a broken wall as it reached in to slam the club, and it was like a child throwing a tantrum. It roared when Cassandra threw a rock at its face, then slammed the club again and again with bright, vengeful glee, so that the already-broken walls of the old temple quaked and crumbled even further, raining debris on them and shaking the ground.

Cassandra and Gweneth were running back and forth, angrily hurling stones and yelling, trying to distract the monster as Selene ran forward to collect Zelda.

"Horsey!" the ogre bellowed, bringing the massive club down on the neighing horses. Calain yelled in fury and horror when the club – just missing Lucky—smashed Sunny, Cassandra's tawny horse. There was a horrible whinny of pain, and when the club came away again (dripping dark blood), the horse lay in an indistinguishable pile of golden fur, bones, and flesh.

Cassandra let out a scream of rage such as Calain had never heard from her. Then, as if attacking her horse was the last straw, the sorceress-knight lifted her hands, and a stream of fire blasted the ogre straight in the face.

The ogre dropped its club with a mighty bang – Cassandra, Gweneth, and the horses scattered – and with its face aflame, stomped away bellowing, the earth trembling in its wake.

As Cassandra and Gweneth chased down the horses, Selene came to Calain, carrying Zelda close. Calain could see that Zelda was bleeding from her head. Her golden hair was stained red, her expression was slack, and Calain could feel that her heartbeat was barely a patter. She was draped over Selene's arms like a broken doll.

Selene looked at Calain, her face covered in dust and tears. "Take her, Calain!"

Calain stood frozen, staring at Zelda through a sudden veil of tears.

"We must flee before the beast returns!" shouted Gweneth, running up and pulling her speckled stallion, Bron, along by the reins.

Cassandra had captured Lucky and Apple and was leading both horses by the reins as she drew near. "Calain is in shock," said Cassandra to Selene. "You must carry Zelda yourself."

Selene didn't argue. She sat Zelda in Apple's saddle (Zelda slumped forward, head lolling) and climbed up behind her.

Calain couldn't move, couldn't breathe, couldn't stop staring at Zelda. Cassandra drew close to her and said soothingly, "Good Calain, you must sit your saddle. You must ride."

Something in Cassandra's gentle voice stirred Calain from her horror. She blinked, nodded, and climbed shakily into the saddle, taking up Arthur's reins.

And then they rode, galloping hard through the marshland. They followed behind Selene, and all of them kept glancing at Zelda's slumped body, wondering how much time they had before she perished of her head injury. The Solden Stones were not far, and from there on they would head north in search of Lowri's cottage. If only the Aelwith Wilds would be merciful, Calain thought. Twice they were forced to stop and fighting off raids of goblins and a troll whose home they had galloped across unwittingly. Yet another ogre in the distance waved its club but appeared too lazy to cross the marsh water between them, and they hurried on.

"Gods be *damned* that your mother was mad enough to live on the edge of this place," Gweneth growled when they had been chased for an hour by a minotaur, whose hooves shattered the earth in their wake.

But eventually, they passed the Solden Stones, which were little more than an endless row of stone pillars that stood randomly from the earth like bones. The pillars were all that remained of an old elven colosseum. They formed a giant circle in a muddy clearing, and Calain knew they were so large that what they could see of the pillars above the mud was only the very tip of them.

Another hour, two, then darkness had fallen, and they had come at last to the edge of the Aelwith Wilds, having traveled directly north from the Solden Stones. In the fall of darkness, they were riding by Cassandra's wisp-light, still galloping, the horses foaming for water and heaving for breath. The yellow glowing lights of fireflies drifted from the grass, and here, the earth was less moist and much more solid, thumping firm beneath the trot of their horses' hooves. The trees were also sparser, there appeared to be no monsters or beasts, and in the distance, Calain could see the silhouette of City Erhyrst.

Just when it seemed they would not find the cabin—and just when Gweneth was swearing and complaining again – they saw it. The little cabin stood just beneath an immense tree, made of thatch and logs of wood. Smoke was rising from the chimney, and a candle lantern stood in the window, glowing with narrow yellow flames. The Knights of Falcon dismounted, climbed the wooden step, and approached the cottage door, which was round, like an elven door.

There was a woven grass mat before the door, and Calain stared at it as her muddy boots touched it. She was still in shock from Zelda's injury – not just from sorrow and fear but also because Zelda's head injury had affected her in some distant way – and she was tearstained and shaking and afraid . . . Afraid of facing her mother.

Gweneth glanced sympathetically at Calain, then lifted her hand and knocked on the door.

There was a moment's shuffling on the other side, the soft murmur of a voice, and then the door flew open. Calain looked down. There was her mother, only much older than Calain remembered her. Like Arthur, she had shriveled down into a little old person, with long gray hair and a wrinkled face. But her eyes . . . Her kind blue eyes were just the same as Calain remembered.

"Calain?" whispered Lowri, who was standing just as still with shock and emotion as Calain was. "You came!" she said happily and tears filled her eyes. Then she noticed the other knights, and her eyes went to Zelda, who was hanging limp in Selene's arms. She touched a concerned hand to her mouth. "Oh, but what happened here? Bring her in! Bring her in!" she cried, stepping back to admit them.

Selene went first, then Calain, Gweneth and Cassandra all filed in behind her, and the door shut quietly behind them – of its own accord, which was strange, Calain thought.

"Over here on the bed!" cried Lowri, hobbling quickly to a small pallet against the wall. The narrow pallet was piled with wool coverlets and pillows.

Selene followed the old woman and laid Zelda's limp body carefully on the low bed.

"I shall fix a potion for her at once," said Lowri, going to the fireplace and setting her cauldron over it. She started rummaging in cabinets and pulling out armfuls of herbs and jarred ingredients. She did a double take when she noticed them all standing there staring at Zelda and nodded her head at the nearby table and the chairs that surrounded it. "Sit, sit!"

Calain moved shakily to the wooden table and sat in a chair. So did the other knights. And then they fell to looking around the cottage and watching as Lowri stewed her potion over the fire. Selene was staring almost numbly at Zelda, and Cassandra reached over and touched her shoulder. Calain saw there were tears staining Cassandra's cheeks, Gweneth's as well. Their hair was also tousled and flying, and their armor was stained with blood from having tried to help Zelda. Calain knew she probably looked much the same and suddenly realized they probably all looked shocking to Lowri, who indeed kept glancing at them in concern.

Gweneth dropped her face in her hands and sat that way for a long time. Calain wanted to do the same. The heaviness of the fear of Zelda's death was weighing down on her. Instead, she distracted herself by looking around the cottage. It was a modest one-room home, with dried herbs hanging from the rafters, piles of books, baskets of fruits and dried roots. The room hardly had any furniture aside from a wooden bookshelf, the low bed Zelda lay on, and the small table with the four chairs.

Calain's wet eyes went back to Lowri. "You live here alone, Ma?"

Lowri smiled. "We shall come to that in a minute. First, I need to know what caused the young woman's injury." She lifted a bundle of herbs and squinted at it. "It will make healing her much easier."

"We were set upon by an ogre," said Selene tonelessly, her eyes still on Zelda. "It smashed the temple we were in, and a brick struck Zelda on the crown."

Lowri tisked. "The gods should damn me for asking you to come here! But I had no idea you would bring a lady."

"Zelda is a sorceress of great power," said Gweneth, finally lifting her tearstained face from her hands. She rested her elbows on her knees and sat forward as she said hoarsely, "We always did depend on her to heal our wounds, but now when she needs aid, we are helpless."

Lowri looked at Gweneth kindly. "That is not true! You brought her here to me! And in doing so, you may have saved her life!" She smiled. "She is your lady, is she not? You are all in service to her?" Her inquisitive eyes went to Calain.

"Aye, Mother," said Calain. "She's the one I killed Ellanara for."

Lowri nodded, tossing a handful of green herbs in the cauldron. She snapped a fat red root in halves and tossed it in next, then they watched as she stirred a ladle dramatically through the contents. "So she is Zelda, the one wanted by all of Eriallon. And these knights are your sisters in arms, who did help you escape Cilia's so-called justice." Her eyes went to Selene, Gweneth, and Cassandra. "Thank you for helping my babe! She hath my fiery temper and impulsiveness." She laughed. "I suppose I am partly to blame for Ellanara's death!"

The Knights of Falcon laughed as well, and Calain thought the atmosphere grew calmer. It was sinking in: Zelda was safe. Perhaps in only a few hours, she would be sitting up, talking and laughing with them.

When the potion was done, Lowri scooped a wooden cup through it and brought it to Zelda, tipping it against her lips. Zelda frowned and moaned as she feebly drank the contents.

"Can she hear us?" asked Selene, who was hovering over Lowri's shoulder. "Is she conscious?"

"Just barely," sighed Lowri. She glanced up at Selene with her kind eyes, took her arm, and patted her hand. "Come," she said, leading Selene back to the table, "the healing potion will take some time, and hovering and wringing your hands will not speed up the process!"

Selene – still looking anxious and numb – sat at the table again and stared into space.

Lowri took up a broom and started sweeping the mud crumbs they had tracked in toward the door. "Are any of you hungry? I could throw something together."

"Do not trouble yourself, fair lady," said Cassandra.

Lowri shrieked out a laugh. "A fair lady, am I? Ha! I haven't been fair nor a lady for quite some time, living out here in the bush!"

"You are not a sorceress, and yet, you survive this dangerous land alone," said Cassandra with interest.

Calain frowned as she watched her mother sweeping. "Aye. And since when do you know herblore, Ma?"

Lowri smiled. "I did learn a thing or two from my wife. She enchanted the cottage, you know. To keep the monsters away, to keep me safe."

Calain lifted her brows. "Wife?" She glanced around, looking for evidence that some other person lived there, but there was none. "Where is she then?"

Lowri smiled again, this time sadly. "She did leave five years before." She laughed tonelessly and kept sweeping. "I suppose once I sprouted gray hairs and lost my charms . . . As if I was so very young when first we met! Ha!"

"She *left*?" said Gweneth in loud disbelief. "After all that? After you gave up your family for—!" Selene shushed her.

"No," said Lowri with another laugh. She looked at Calain. "You friend is right: Eachna was a wicked woman," she said with a grin, "but it was why I loved her. I do believe she kept me around to help raise her children. She couldn't have been bothered to do it herself."

"Children?" said Calain darkly. "How the devil many did she have? And how *dare* she put the burden on you!"

Lowri smiled. "I must take responsibility for my part in it, Calain. I was in enamored of her, child." She glanced at Zelda, who was sleeping peacefully on the pallet nearby. "Much as you are enamored of your lady, I am certain. Eachna had two children, Brigid and Lyne, and I adored them." She looked with soft eyes at Calain. "Much as I adore you."

Calain almost scowled, thinking that if her mother had truly adored her, she would have found a way to take her from her father! But Calain had to remind herself that she was already at Falcon Isle when her mother left them. Lowri wouldn't have stood in the way of Calain's desire to become a knight.

"I am sorry you have been alone," Calain told her mother. "You should have written to me."

"And said what? 'The woman I abandoned you for has left me, come and keep me company?'" Lowri looked up, raising her brows pointedly, then went back to sweeping.

"So you did leave me for a woman," said Calain, realizing at last that she and her mother were more alike than she'd ever suspected. She knew her parents had had an arranged marriage. Such was the way in the little farming community outside Alleren. Her mother had been forced to wed Arthur, and they'd had Calain so late in life because she had refused for many years to lay with him. But then came a time when they realized they needed children to run the farm, and so Calain was born.

"Yes," said Lowri heavily, "and I am not . . . proud of that. But there is a little more to the story. It isn't as simple as my having running off. Nothing ever is when it comes to your father and I." She shook her head.

Calain stood. "Then tell me, Mother. I came all this way to know the truth." She brought her chair over to the fire and sat it there, beckoning Lowri to sit in it. Lowri seemed to have been avoiding that moment, but she set the broom aside and sat on the chair, as Calain had asked her. Calain sat at her feet near the fire, waiting.

"My girl," said Lowri, smiling down at Calain and touching her red hair. "Please don't judge your father and I too harshly."

"I shall listen without anger, Mother," Calain said, but her mother only laughed.

"You are *my* daughter," Lowri said, smiling. "That means you shall likely storm off when I have told you all. Thankfully, I have your sorceress held hostage here, so I know you shall return."

Calain smiled. Her mother had always been playful like this, but it was true she had a temper. There had been nights when she had yelled at Arthur for this or that, and Calain had hidden under her bed with Siobhan. Calain prayed her mother did not ask about Siobhan.

"Your father did lay with another woman," said Lowri, and Calain tensed.

"He betrayed your honor!" Calain growled.

Lowri held up a hand for silence. "Now . . . because I desired only women and the marriage had been arranged, I felt no jealousy. But I was angry that he had gone outside the marriage while I was not permitted to, even though I wasn't remotely attracted to him and suffered greatly for it. I did learn through tavern gossip that your father had lain with an elven lass out in Honione. A redhead like me! Your father was always such a lecher for the red. As you know, there aren't many elves in Honione, so it wasn't hard to find her."

Calain stared in surprise. "You came all the way here just to find the woman my father did lay with?"

"Well, I had relatives here, mind you. So it wasn't as if it was out of the way! It was how your father met the woman to begin with! We came here often to visit my sister, and Arthur snuck off and lay with her! Your father and I were married two decades before you were born, so this betrayal did last for years. And he didn't stop while I was pregnant with you! You were born in Honione. Did you know that? You aren't even an Eriallon native. This is your home." Her eyes softened and she touched Calain's hair again.

Calain impatiently gestured the affection away. "Mother! So you found the woman here while visiting with family? And what did you do?"

Lowri smiled. "I fell in love with her."

Calain stared again. "You what?"

"I fell in love with her," Lowri repeated. "And she did desire me as well. Eachna had put in the letter that she no longer wished to see Arthur, as she now favored me. That put a crimp in your ol' pa's swagger, I bet. I'd have given anything to have seen his face when his little friends read that letter aloud in the middle of the tavern."

Gweneth hooted with laughter, clearly enjoying the story.

Calain frowned. "All that I can forgive, but why didn't you come back for me? Didn't you want me? Or at least wish to see me? I would have left the academy for you—"

Lowri's eyes softened again. "Of *course*, I wanted to see you, sweeting. But your father had the neighbor write back that I had best not show my face on the farm again, or he'd shoot me. He didn't want me anywhere near Falcon Isle either. And I believed him. He was good with a bow."

Calain scowled. "So Pa ran you off and then lied to me!" She tensed, on the verge of springing up and perhaps running out the door, but remembering what her mother had said about her predictable temper, she kept her seat and clenched her fists instead.

"Don't be angry with your father," said Lowri gently. "He wanted to save face, so he told you a lie. What would you think of him if you knew the truth? I don't mean that I condone the vile thing he did, but I understand."

Calain cast her eyes down. She was beginning to realize her father wasn't the good, noble man she had always seen in him. Instead, he was just a man. He had cheated on his wife, run her off, and then married a young woman less than half his age! Every time Calain thought of Siobhan – who was *also* attracted to women alone, same as her mother – lying under her father and crying her way through sex she did not want . . . No! She would never tell her mother about that! She would never tell anyone. The betrayal was hard enough to bear on her own. Witnessing her mother's anger and disgust would only make it worse.

"So you just stayed here," said Calain, trying to breathe the anger from her voice, "and lived with the elven woman all this time?"

"We weren't alone. I helped raise her daughters, I told you . . . your sisters."

Calain went still.

Lowri smiled. "Your pa fathered two girls on Eachna: Lyne and Brigid. Your half-sisters."

Chapter 3

When Lowri had finished her story, she bid the knights remove their armor and rest, and they did so as she laid out blankets on the floor for them to sleep near the fire. But Calain couldn't sleep. She didn't know what to do with the information her mother had given her, so she caved to her impulses and left the cottage, taking water for the horses. Outside, as crickets chirruped and a cool fog rolled in from the marsh, she watered the horses and unsaddled them and groomed them, all the while trying to process everything that had been said. Her father was a liar and cheater – now she knew where she got it from, she realized – and now her father's advice that she should slay Zelda's lover made sense: Arthur had been willing to slay his own wife for straying!

And Calain had two sisters, half-sisters she had never met. The older one was a woman named Brigid. She was a sorceress of the Order of Vira'Toss, but because she was much older than Calain, she had graduated from the tower years ago and was off on her own adventures, working to uncover the secrets of the dragons. Brigid's work was apparently confidential, and so, she hadn't told Lowri much beyond the fact that it involved dragons, which seemed to make Lowri proud enough.

As for the woman named Lyne – the younger one—Lowri happily announced that she was an assassin for the Order of the Emerald! Calain wasn't supposed to tell anyone, of course, but Lowri was beaming with pride when she disclosed the information. Then she went on and on in ecstasy about how her daughters were powerful, strong women living lives of romance and adventure and submitting to no man's whims. Calain thought Lowri sounded a little envious. As her mother was gushing, she couldn't help looking at Zelda's still body and thinking that adventure wasn't fun or romantic. It was terrifying.

Calain was standing on the porch with her hands in the pockets of her trousers when she heard the door open and shut behind her. She recognized Gweneth's light step without having to turn. The shorter knight drew near and stood beside Calain, her eyes on the swamp. They stood in silence for a moment, and then Gweneth said,

"Your mother hath news of the happenings in Erhyrst."

"Shall I like this news?" asked Calain apprehensively.

Gweneth smiled. "Well, you know how Lythara accused Zelda of working with Hidden Dragon? Apparently, she had reason to think the elven uprising was on the move. The queen of Honione has been assassinated."

Calain lifted her brows. "Truly?"

Gweneth nodded. "Aye. Three nights ago. Was stabbed in her bed – *and* shot." She gave a low whistle. "Those elves sure hated her something fierce."

"I wonder if we shall take the blame," said Calain dully. "Once people know we fled to Honione . . ."

"But we're safe here, that's the thing," laughed Gweneth. "Almost as soon as the queen was slain, an army of elves just started bloodying the streets. I mean, they didn't even march inside the city! They just appeared – *poof* – out of nowhere and started killing people."

"By the gods . . ."

"Magick. Had to be. And they've already sat an elven queen's arse on the throne as well – *in three days*, while the cushion was still warm from Queen Ffion's farts. Can you believe it?"

"Aye. It's a strategic position," said Calain thoughtfully. "If humans wished to retaliate, they would have to come by sea or go through the Aelwith Wilds to reach the castle . . . gods help them."

"And the elves are guarding the portals now. Just going around and setting up posts at every one, trying to stop human armies advancing."

"I suppose with the elves guarding the portals and ruling Honione, the Rose Guard shant come here."

Gweneth grinned. "That's the thing, that's what I'm working up to – Queen Cilia is *terrified* she's next!"

Calain laughed. "I suppose she should be."

"She's locked herself away in the Gold Keep and has every Rose Guard in the army guarding it. She won't be sending any of them after us, looks like. News is traveling fast because the sorceress network is panicking."

"Oh?" said Calain, suddenly feeling overwhelmed and indifferent to it all.

Gweneth gave Calain an irritated side glance. "Calain, I can't tell if you've got troll dung in your ears or if you just don't care! There is going to be a full-on war! The Order of Vira is going to be summoned to fight! It's almost *convenient* that we're out here in the wilderness, away from it all. I wonder if Cassandra did know all along and brought us here for that very reason."

"So who is the new queen?" Calain asked. It was true that she didn't feel very enthusiastic about any of it. She just wanted Zelda to be well. But she had to admit, she was curious to know who was now ruling Honione.

"Her name is Nuala," Gweneth answered thoughtfully. "They say she's of the royal bloodline, of the elves who used to rule Vallinwir. The last living descendant. The elves want to raise her as the queen of Vallinwir and make all the realms bow to her."

Calain stared at the trees and couldn't say that she cared so long as she and Zelda were safe.

"Don't you get it?" said Gweneth impatiently. "This means we're free! The elves are in charge now, and *they* aren't going to arrest us for killing Ellanara! Hell, they're probably *glad* we did it."

They are, thought Calain as Imodel's sweet face surfaced in her mind.

"We didn't do it," Calain corrected Gweneth unhappily. "I did it with my foolishness and recklessness. That we have our lives back is a happy accident. My actions would have doomed us all to constant fleeing. How is fair Zelda? Hath she stirred as of yet?"

"She slumbers still," said Gweneth heavily. "But the wound is healed. She hath stopped bleeding and breathes more fully." She absently touched her heart, and Calain knew she was listening to Zelda's heartbeat: Zelda had bound Gweneth and Cassandra to her before leaving Wolf Fortress. Now all four knights were Bound, which meant any future group sex was going to be very intense for all of them.

"Your mother hath said we should live here," went on Gweneth.

Calain raised her brows. "Did she?"

"Aye. And is it really a bad idea? Who would be mad enough to wade through all the ogre shit in the Aelwith Wilds just to find us? No one will chase us out here. And the city is nearby. We could go there for supplies and be back here in days. Zelda would be safe. We all would."

"I suppose we could expand the cottage," Calain said thoughtfully. "As it is right now, it is far too small for the six of us." Her eyes brightened with inspiration. "We could build Zelda a tower with her own bedchamber and rooms for all of us and my mother."

"And a training yard in the front," said Gweneth, sounding as excited as Calain felt. "And a stable for the horses."

"And maybe get some chickens from town, so we can have eggs to break our fast."

"And a cow, if it wouldn't be too much trouble. . . No, on second thought, a cow would just attract goblins and ogres. We'd never get it through the wilds."

"Maybe Zelda could with magick," Calain suggested.

"And wine. We'd need a larder for wine," added Gweneth. She glanced at Calain. "But let's not get too attached to the idea. Perhaps Zelda wouldn't want to live here. Look what did happen to her today."

Calain smiled. "Zelda will love it. We shall build a fortress around her, and when she wakes, she will be overjoyed."

Gweneth shook her head. "Calain, you dunderhead," she said. "We couldn't possibly build a home for Zelda that fast!"

"I know," said Calain, "but you are forgetting my sister is a sorceress."

Chapter 4

When Lowri told Calain that one of her sisters was a sorceress, Calain had suspected that the old woman had some way of contacting Brigid immediately, much as Zelda could summon Arryn with a stone or contact Wick through a mirror. She hadn't been wrong. When she told her mother that she wished to build a home for a Zelda and required Brigid's aid, Lowri took a small seashell off the mantelpiece and smiled at it.

"This is how I call to Brigid," Lowri said, handing Calain the seashell. "I simply call her name into it, and she comes. Though be warned: she did take after Eachna. She is not... very warm."

Calain took the seashell outside, and standing alone in the yard, she called Brigid's name into it, thinking that magick was strange and beyond her. A second later, and the light of a portal split the air. Calain stepped back, her red hair whipping in face, as the light divided to reveal a stormy sea and cracks of lightning. Walking across the sea through the storm was a beautiful woman with long red hair. She was not dressed in a gown like most sorceresses but instead wore tight leather trousers and a leather bodice that was open over a tunic, showing a hint of cleavage. In her hand was a metal stave that closed at the end over a pale green stone that was round as an eye.

The woman's hood was down and her cape was flaring behind her as she walked across the sea toward the portal and passed through, stepping down on the grass to stand opposite

Calain. The portal closed behind her, causing their hair to fall limp around them, and for the first time, Calain stood facing her older sister. Brigid blinked calmly, and Calain saw her own green eyes looking back at her. Calain didn't think Brigid looked that old, even though she was supposed to be at least fifteen years older. She had to remind herself that sorceresses aged very slowly. So did elves, and her sister was also a half-elf.

Brigid was not very tall, however. Arthur had always been short, even before reaching old age, and it seemed as if Brigid had taken after their father. She was at least a head shorter than Calain, which made her entrance across the stormy sea a little less intimidating.

"So," said Brigid, who did not seem at all surprised to see Calain, "Mother finally got a hold of you, did she?"

"So you are Brigid, my sister. I am Calain. I seek your aid."

Brigid looked at Calain with interest, and Calain was glad. For though Brigid was her half-sister, they were still strangers, and the woman had no reason to help her with such a tremendous task. She had worried that Brigid would say no.

"You do understand that there shall be a price? I do not aid anyone without payment, not even blood," said Brigid.

Calain lifted her brows. "So you would not aid our mother if she were to ask?"

Brigid smiled. "When you have lived a little longer, dear sister, you will find that blood means very little in this world. Ask our sister, Lyne, if you ever meet her."

"So there shall be a price," Calain said, frowning. She hadn't expected that. "My sisters in arms are just inside. We would put together all our gold to—"

Brigid waved a hand. "No, I have enough gold and then some." She tilted her head, studying Calain. "But if ever I need your aid, I shall call you, and I expect you shall come willingly."

Calian lifted her chin. "Of course, I shall. I am a knight! A woman of . . . honor . . ." She drifted to silence. Was she a woman of honor after all she had done? She stared at her boots.

Brigid smiled sympathetically. "Do not feel shame, dear sister," she said gently. "What you did in slaying Ellanara aided the elven resistance immensely, more immensely than you can possibly understand. Or did you think the elves of Menosea let you walk free simply because you had lain with Imodel?"

Calain's head snapped up.

"Not that I blame you," said Brigid dreamily. "Imodel has tremendous tits. And elven pussy tastes quite sweet, doesn't it? Like berries."

Calain felt her cheeks getting hot. "How dost thou know of Imodel?"

Brigid smiled. "I have been following your progress since you did flee the Gold Keep—and a little bit before, I confess. Lowri insisted once I told her you had been captured. I may have even come to your rescue just to stop her going there herself, the hotheaded fool." She laughed, thinking fondly of Lowri. "But you escaped on your own anyway. Very impressive, by the way."

"My thanks," said Calain awkwardly. All that time, she had been watched by her sister, who probably knew everything about her, the Knights of Falcon, Zelda, and even Aereth. It made her uncomfortable. First Melvalda, then Arryn, now her sister. How many witches had spied upon her adventures with Zelda? How many witches had seen Calain and Selene making love to Zelda on the riverbed? Calain felt so . . . exposed.

Brigid stepped closer and her expression was now grim. "If you are to aid me at some point in the future, then I must tell you who it is that I serve, and you shall keep the secret to your grave." She stared intently into Calain's eyes, and Calain stared back, wondering what she was getting herself into. What price would she eventually pay for Zelda's happily ever after?

"I do promise," answered Calain. "I suspect that my life shall be forfeit otherwise."

"It may very well be, dear sister," Brigid answered, "though not by my hand."

Calain frowned. "What do you mean? Speak plainly."

"I am an agent of Hidden Dragon," said Brigid flatly. "I am probably one of the only half-elves they would ever trust, given who my mother is. Eachna is quite famous among the elven and has always remained loyal to the old empire, even if her desire for humans is considered . . . uncouth. And my passing as a human makes me a very valuable spy. The resistance would be furious to lose me.

"I tell you this because, should I become captured or find myself in desperate battle against enemy forces, you shall need to understand what is happening when I have called you to aid me." Brigid lifted her chin. "So what of it, dear sister? Do you have some judgement of my doings? Do you think it wrong that I should aid the elves in bringing about the end of human rule?"

"I can't say that I care either way," said Calain honestly and shrugged. "What I do care about is Zelda's happiness and safety. The rest is background noise."

Brigid laughed, delighted by that. "Then we shall get on rather well." She reached into her cloak and pulled out a small stone. "I shall bind you to this stone, and when I have turned it, it shall bring you to me. You are no mage, so the stone shall simply bring you forth, wherever you are, whatever you are doing."

"I shant be able to resist?" said Calain indignantly. "So what then? Shall I become your pet? Always at your beck and call?"

Brigid smiled, this time not kindly, as if to say, "Precisely."

"My pet? 'Minion' is a much more dignified word, don't you think? It implies that you chose this servitude, and you have."

Calain could feel the outrage boiling just beneath the surface. Lowri had warned her that Brigid was not the nicest person, but she had thought surely Brigid would be fair to her own sister! Calain was about ready to storm back inside the cottage, but then she thought of Zelda, homeless and always on the run, always dirty and tired and in danger, and her green eyes relented.

"And if I let you bind me to that stone," Calain said, "you shall give Zelda a beautiful home, safe here on the edge of the wilds, and build it just as I ask?"

"Your lady will have the most beautiful enchanted castle that ever there was," Brigid said immediately. She held out her hand for Calain to take it.

Calain looked at her sister's small hand . . . and took it into her own. Brigid's eyes glowed with power.

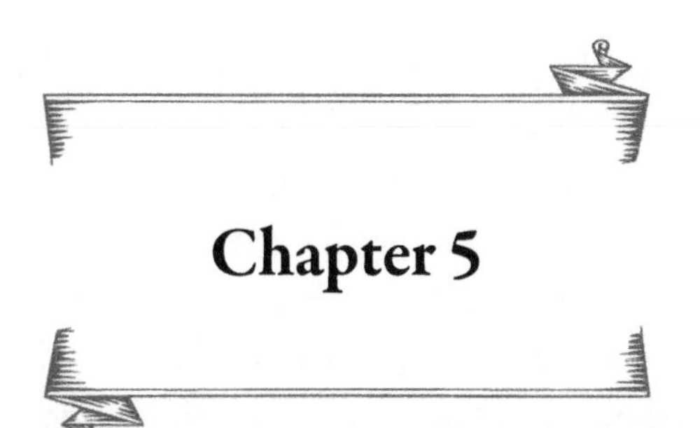

Chapter 5

When Zelda awoke, she thought she was still dreaming. She was wearing a long white nightgown and was lying on a beautiful four-poster bed, in a vast bedchamber, with a fire blazing on the hearth opposite the foot of the bed. The four-poster curtains were a pale green against the dark wooden bed posts, and they were partially drawn, so that Zelda could not see the entire room clearly. She could see silhouettes through the vaguely transparent curtain and realized she wasn't alone in the room.

"Where am I?" Zelda croaked and was met immediately with the sound of boots thumping. The curtain was ripped back to reveal the Knights of Falcon, all in boots and trousers, grinning down at her. She was touched to see the tears in their eyes. They practically converged on her from all sides, hugging her with trembling arms, kissing her cheeks and her lips. Zelda giggled girlishly when Calain and Selene kissed her cheeks playfully hard from either side, and her cheeks flamed red.

"All right! All right!" Zelda squealed. "Do release me before you break me with your mighty strength!"

The knights laughed and pulled their weight off Zelda. Calain sat on the bed and happily gathered Zelda in her lap, while Selene sat beside them, and Cassandra and Gweneth knelt before Zelda on the floor. Zelda reached out and touched Cassandra's cheek (Cassandra kissed her fingers) and smiled at

Gweneth when she playfully set her chin on Zelda's knee. Selene dropped her forehead against Zelda's hair in relief, and Zelda turned to her and kissed her on the lips to sooth her. Selene's dark eyes were warm when they looked at her.

Zelda's heart was racing so hard, it almost hurt, and she realized it was the combined strength of the knights. Their joy was overwhelming her. She couldn't pretend she wasn't touched.

Zelda glanced around, remembering she was some place strange. "But . . . where are we? The last thing I remember . . ." She hesitated. The ogre. The horrible, ugly ogre and its club. It had slammed the club on the temple, widening the hole in the ceiling and sending down a hail of broken stone. She remembered a sudden burst of pain on her crown and then . . . nothing.

"We are in your home," said Calain warmly. She was stroking Zelda's hair and looked down at her with soft green eyes. Zelda thought she looked as proud as if she had built the place herself.

"What do you mean 'my home'?" Zelda asked, baffled.

"We built it for you, sweet Zelda," said Calain. She hesitated. "Well, my sister did build it. She's a sorceress."

Zelda's brows went up.

"That's right," laughed Gweneth. "Calain's father was banging elves. She's got two half-sisters that hail from Honione, and the queen—"

Selene held up a hand. "Let us not overwhelm her."

Gweneth rolled her eyes but didn't continue.

"But I wished to show Zelda the castle," Calain complained, glaring at Selene.

Selene's lips tightened. "Zelda only did just wake from a head injury! She should not move about—"

"I can carry her!" Calain snapped.

Calain and Selene were glaring across Zelda at each other when Zelda suddenly burst out laughing, causing everyone to look at her. Zelda laughed on. It was so like Calain and Selene to start arguing that it had become something familiar and good that made her only laugh when before she would have screamed at them.

The knights watched Zelda laughing, their eyes soft with affection.

"I am fine, sweet Selene. I am certain Calain will look after me," said Zelda soothingly. She closed her arms around Calain's neck. "Come. Show me the castle, then, my love."

Calain lifted Zelda in her burly arms and actually stuck her tongue out at Selene as she carried her away, so that Zelda heard Gweneth and Cassandra laughing as Calain carried her from the room.

They descended a stair that was lit by torches in brackets on the walls, and Calain's arms were strong and yet gentle as they cradled Zelda carefully to her chest. At the bottom of the stair, they came to a long stone hall, also lit by torches, its floor lined with red carpet. Zelda stared in amazement. The hall was immense, and the doors lining the walls either side were huge, likely because they concealed immense chambers. Zelda wondered just how big the place was. It seemed endless.

Calain carried Zelda throughout the castle, showing her different rooms and even bringing her to the kitchen, where they paused to share cheese and wine and playfully peck each other on the lips. The larder was full to bursting with food, though Calain warned it was enchanted food summoned by her sister and was meant for temporary consumption, until Selene could head out to hunt again.

Zelda was amazed. The castle was beautifully designed with elven architecture, even the wooden furniture, which had been engraved with delicate flowers and leaves. Calain brought her at last to a room at the top of another tower, and nudging the door open with her boot, she said, "And this is your study!"

As the wooden door slowly swung wide, Zelda's mouth fell open in amazement. It was a vast study, with many bookshelves loaded with old tomes, a great wooden desk, several davenports with deep red cushions, armchairs beside a blazing hearth, and little tables loaded with empty glass vials waiting to be filled with potions. There were also utensils for making potions—little knives for cutting the herbs, a ladle for stirring, scissors – and stores of herbs were in bowls and bundles on the shelves. Sunlight was streaming in beams through the high arched windows and across the room, falling pure and pale over a world globe showing all of Vallinwir.

Zelda wanted down so that she could explore the room, and sensing this, Calain gently set her on her feet. Her hands hovered anxiously around Zelda, as if she thought Zelda might fall, but Zelda walked confidently forward, her long golden hair falling almost to her bare feet as she moved in her white nightgown. She went to the world globe and reached out and touched it with the tips of her fingers, spinning it on its stand. It rolled to a smooth stop on Honione.

"Do you like it?" asked Calain a little anxiously.

Zelda wondered how she could even ask! She looked up and smiled to find Calain watching her so hopefully. "Yes," she said happily. "It's wonderful! And you say your sister built it? She must be quite the sorceress."

"Well," said Calain, irritable as she came to Zelda across the room, "I designed it for you! I told her what to build!"

Zelda turned to Calain and looked up at her dotingly. "You had your sister build all of this? For me?"

"Of course, I did," said Calain softly. She frowned. "I love thee."

"Oh, Calain!" Zelda bounced up and pecked Calain on the cheeks and hugged her neck tight, and Calain laughed under the affection and closed her arms around Zelda.

"And now you have a home," said Calain, taking Zelda's hand and leading her to one of the davenports. They sat, still holding hands. "And it is enchanted. No one shall ever hurt you here, even if I abandon you, you shall be safe."

Zelda frowned and touched Calain's face. "Oh, Calain! I have forgiven thee! If only you would forgive thyself."

"I shall never forgive myself, I fear," said Calain heavily.

Zelda turned her eyes happily over the room again. "It's perfect," she said breathlessly. Her eyes darkened sadly. "It just needs Aereth. She is probably a woman now. I do miss when she was little. The sound of her small feet running through this place would have been so welcome each morn."

"She will visit, I am certain of it," said Calain soothingly.

Zelda held back tears. "Y-Yes, she will visit . . . one hundred years from now? Two hundred? A sorceress can only live three hundred years, but tis rare to exceed two hundred. Melvalda . . . she was ancient, but it was due only to the jewel she wore. It ceased her aging so that she could be with Talaedra." Zelda laughed sadly. "I should have asked her to make me such a necklace, so that I could wait for my babe to return." The tears finally came, and Zelda cast her pale lashes down as Calain frowned sadly and caught one with her kerchief.

Calain rubbed Zelda's hand. "Dear Zelda, do not weep! It breaks my heart so. What if I . . .gave thee children?" she asked tentatively.

Zelda looked up, staring at Calain intently. There were ways, of course, and she had wanted it, but she didn't think Calain had felt the same. And there was the fact that it was a complicated spell. Meddling with procreation had always been considered a

Dark Magick to the Order of Vira. They had not taught such spells at Vira'Toss. Zelda wouldn't even know where to begin.

"I was speaking with my mother," went on Calain. "She lived with a sorceress for years, they were lovers. And she learned that it was possible for a sorceress to have children with another woman, without the use of a potion. She wished to have children with Eachna, but she was too old at the time. Her thin blood hadn't the strength to bear forth."

"But you are sterile," said Zelda uncertainly.

Calain smiled and shook her head. "That won't matter. You would only need my hair and my blood. You wouldn't even have to give birth. You would . . . *grow* the child, in other words." She laughed. "I suppose like a carrot."

Zelda laughed as well but stared at Calain, intrigued. "I must hear more of this from your mother," she said. "It sounds like a complicated spell. I am not so great a sorceress as you like to boast."

"You are," said Calain, looking down at Zelda with a doting that made her blush and look down. "But you needn't ask my mother. She hath told me all that must be done . . ." Calain rolled her eyes to the ceiling and said irritably, "Me thinks she doth desire grandchildren."

Zelda laughed. "Hath she been pestering you, my knight?" she asked sympathetically.

"A little," said Calain, smiling. "But she never thought she would have grandchildren or that she would even see me again! No doubt she thought my anger was eternal, and that I would never come here." She frowned at the place on Zelda's head where the brick had hit her and reached out and cupped Zelda's face. "Perhaps we should not have."

Zelda tilted her head against Calain's warm touch. "We had to come here," she gently reminded Calain. "The Rose Guard would have slain us!"

"Yes," said Calain, sadly remembering. "Still, at least we are safe now. The queen of Honione has been slain."

Zelda's eyes grew round.

"There is war brewing now between human and elf, and Queen Cilia has forgotten about us for the moment."

"Mayhaps she'll be slain next, and then we can go on with our lives," said Zelda, remembering how greatly she had disliked the young queen, who had sent her into Eido Loth, likely with no intention of her return.

Calain laughed softly at Zelda's words.

Zelda looked up. "So what do we need to create this child?"

Calain's eyes brightened. "Then you are willing?"

Zelda nodded and squealed with laughter when Calain shouted and hugged her tight.

WHEN CALAIN AND ZELDA approached the others about having children, they were ecstatic. Calain was surprised. She had thought that – after the stress of raising Aereth, everything that had happened with Queen Anindel, and with the war between elves and humans looming on the horizon – the other knights would be firmly against bringing more children into the family. But Selene, Cassandra, and Gweneth were all enthusiastic about the prospect. Selene didn't just want one child, she wanted three, while Cassandra enthused about having a child to sing to again, and Gweneth brightly anticipated having a new audience for her rambling stories. And so, with the blessing of all four knights, Zelda began the process.

According to Lowri, creating a child would require blood, hair, and a Crystal of Indiris. The crystals often grew in wetlands and riverbeds, which meant they could be found there in Honione, in the Aelwith Wilds. Calain did not relish the thought of venturing out among minotaurs and ogres again, but she wished for Zelda's happiness to be complete, and while no child could replace Aereth, she thought more children could sooth the wound.

As Zelda prepared their blood and hair for the creation of the child (apparently, it had to be "fused"), Calain donned her armor and ventured into the swampland with Selene. Gweneth and Cassandra had volunteered to come as well, but Selene cautioned them to stay behind, reasoning that two knights on foot would draw less attention than four.

As much as Calain resented it, Selene was right about yet something else: because it was just the two of them traveling on foot, the creatures of the swamp largely let them be. Sleeping ogres stirred, stared at them a moment, and then lazily turned over, deciding they weren't worth the trouble, and minotaurs sat on rocks and picked their noses and also ignored them.

"I do believe these beasts were drawn to our horses," said Selene quietly as they passed two female ogres, who watched them grimly from the trees, their great breasts sagging in bras made of fur. "The horses would make a fine meal for any one of them, and they would likely wear the bones."

"And Zelda," said Calain darkly. "I do believe the minotaur did lust for her. She was the reason it chased us so."

"Yes, I had suspected that as well," agreed Selene, thinking angrily of the creature. "Here . . ." Selene pointed.

Calain looked and saw a cluster of crystals growing from a puddle just beneath a barren gray tree. She took a knee and pried them up carefully, then placed them in her satchel. Then she stood, and they continued walking, their eyes searching the damp earth for more.

"Do you think of having a child with Zelda?" Calain asked. "We could grow as many as we like."

Selene hesitated and admitted, "All the time. But she was your lady first, and so the two of you shall have the first children."

Calain looked at Selene fondly as they walked. "You know," she said, "I do believe she was both our lady first. This life we are living now was always meant to be. Or so it seems."

Selene laughed. "Aye. Who would have guessed journeying here would grant us a beautiful enchanted castle? The gods doth smile on us." She hesitated and frowned as she said, "Or perhaps tis too good to be true. Come clean, Calain . . ."

Calain tensed.

"Zelda did tell me that she sensed an odd magick about you, a magick that was not her own." Selene paused, and when Calain didn't speak, she went on, "What price did you pay for the life we now live?"

"I paid no price," lied Calain at once. "As ever, you worry too greatly, and your suspicion is for naught."

Selene was not convinced. "Whatever it was, you should not have made the decision alone. And yet, you would scold Zelda for doing the same –!"

Calain looked around.

"Yes, she told me. You scolded her for running off to Melvalda and sacrificing herself," Selene sounded angry now, "and yet you—!"

"Zelda gave herself to Melvalda because she loves me," said Calain calmly. "I know that now. And I did give myself to Brigid because I love Zelda."

Selene sighed. "You gave yourself how? Not that it matters, as I shall not be able to protect you from it!"

Calain paused. Selene was furious, and Calain was realizing with a happy little skip that it was because she cared.

"And you need not look so pleased with yourself!" Selene snapped when she noticed Calain smiling. "Here—there are more of them."

They knelt to collect more crystals.

Calain straightened up, carefully dropping the crystals in her satchel as she confessed with a deep breath, "I did pledge myself in service to Brigid—"

"Calain!"

"—and she may summon me as she pleases, when she pleases."

Selene grabbed Calain's arm. "Thou art a fool! An utter fool! Do you not think this sorceress will abuse this power over you?!"

Calain tensed. "It matters not! Zelda was nearly slain because my actions hath dragged her from danger to danger! She needed a home! She needed security! And I gave it to her the only way I knew how—"

Selene bitterly shook her head and kept walking – very fast now. Calain followed, annoyed – but not surprised—that Selene had not supported her decision.

"Brigid may be thy sister," Selene said darkly, "but thou art strangers, raised many miles apart, having never lain eyes on each other until mere days before—"

"She will not do anything to upset my mother!" Calain insisted, walking fast after Selene, who—.in her anger – was marching ever more rapidly.

Selene suddenly stopped, took a breath, and said gently, "Your mother will not live forever, Calain. Why did you not come to me? I am more thy sister than Brigid!"

And suddenly Calain understood: Selene wasn't just frightened for Calain, she was also jealous of Brigid.

"I acted alone to protect all of you," Calain said. "This way, none of you shall be hurt."

Selene sighed and wearily shook her head. "Calain, dost thou truly believe none of us would be hurt should you perish?" She didn't wait for an answer, instead turning to face the castle. "Come. If we linger, the others shall miss us and believe we are in peril."

Excitement leapt in Calain as she realized: it was time for the final step. She was going to be a parent.

Chapter 6

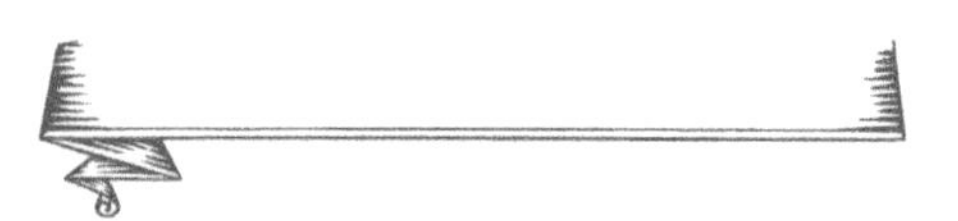

When Calain and Selene returned with the crystals, Zelda chose the largest, clearest one from the bunch and boiled it in her cauldron, inside the mixture of her and Calain's blood and hair. Then she took the crystal – which was about the length of her forearm—and plunged it in the soil of the courtyard garden. And every day, as if the crystal were some strange turnip, Zelda could be seen watering it and humming happily as she did so.

"This is the strangest magick that e'er I saw," laughed Gweneth, who watched Zelda in the courtyard from a window.

"Aye," said Calain, but she privately thought magick quite amazing. She had never thought in her wildest dreams that she would ever have a child, but magick had allowed her the experience. Twice now! She wondered if she would ever see Aereth again. She hoped daily that the girl would suddenly return and felt a sad longing in her heart each and every time she glanced at the castle gates from a window.

Gweneth also missed Aereth and was still drinking a little heavily, but the prospect of a new child seemed to lighten her mood. Calain was glad for that.

The crystal grew rapidly. On the fourth day, it was the height and width of a small child, and indeed, they could see a child standing inside it as if behind misty glass, eyes closed, as if the crystal were a bizarre sort of egg.

One morning, Calain went down to look more closely at the child and saw she possessed a wild wreath of strawberry-blonde hair. If only her little eyes would open, Calain would be able to see their color, but the eyes were closed in the sweet little face that so greatly resembled her own. The girl had Zelda's lips, though, and the almond shape of Zelda's eyes.

"She is a bit like a clone of us," said Zelda, who had appeared at Calain's shoulder. Her loving eyes were on the child in the crystal. "It is how she could be made without a man's part."

Calain put her arm around Zelda. "I shall protect her and love her all the days of my life," she swore softly. "I shall never leave again nor give myself over to fear and doubt."

Zelda smiled and rested her head on Calain's shoulder. "Good. Because if you stray again, I shall blast thee to smithereens. And then what shall I tell our daughter when she doth question me about the stain in the yard?"

Calain laughed, but her green eyes grew thoughtful as she said, "But what shall we name her?"

"How dost thou feel about the name Seren?"

"Seren," said Calain thoughtfully. "That is pretty. I like it." She hugged Zelda tight in her arm, and Zelda smiled.

As the child grew, the Knights of Falcon raced to sew clothes for her. Calain had never been good at sewing, but she sat up all night with the others, trying to learn for her child's sake. Zelda sometimes joined in, but she was mostly so busy fussing over the crystal-child that she hardly had time. She explained to them that the temper of the crystal had to be kept at a certain warmth. If the sunlight proved to faint, she would have to light a magick fire around the crystal to heat it. It would speed up the process – which none of them wanted, swamped as they were trying to make clothes – and so, Zelda struggled to keep the crystal warm with natural sunlight alone, experimentally moving the crystal around the courtyard and burying it in more sunny spots.

Lowri was more excited than any of them. She did her best to assist Zelda with caring for the crystal and went about the castle humming and singing jovially. Every time she saw Calain, she pinched her cheek and shrieked that she was going to be a grandmother, much to the amusement of the other Knights of Falcon, who laughed at Calain's irritated protests.

Brigid had raised Zelda's castle onto a cliff, so that it was high and overlooking the swamps of the Aelwith Wilds. If one were to look out a western window, Erhyrst City was visible from it, as well as Castle Eormed, which stood on a cliff overshadowing the sea.

They still hadn't decided on a name for their home. Over supper in the great dining hall, they sat at the long wooden table (close together at one end) and argued back and forth, joked and laughed, as they dined by candlelight on wine, roast pheasant, potatoes, greens, and bread. Calain and Selene bickered, Cassandra settled them down, Gweneth teased. Lowri tut-tutted when Calain swore and slapped her hand when she reached for an apple, telling her it was filthy and to wash it (this after banging a washbasin on the table, in which Calain wearily dipped her hands).

"We need a formidable name," said Gweneth, whose elbows were on the table as she chewed (Lowri prodded them off). "Something that will scare people, keep them away."

"The castle doth have enchantments for that," Selene reminded her.

Gweneth scoffed. "You put so much faith in magick! Why? Wolf Fortress also had enchantments! And yet, it did not protect Aereth! And we came all this way because it could not protect us!"

Zelda sadly cast her eyes down – as she always did when Aereth was mentioned – and Calain kicked Gweneth under the table. ("Ouch! Hey!")

"I think Cassandra should decide," said Zelda, looking at Cassandra fondly.

Cassandra swallowed a spoonful of hot stew and licked her lips, looking around at Zelda. "Shall I, my lady?"

Zelda smiled. "Well, you're the one who saved us with your vision! If you hadn't seen what was coming, we likely would have lingered at Wolf Fortress long enough to be slain!"

Everyone looked at Cassandra, who smiled – as if she knew this would happen, Calain thought – and said, "I fancy the name Velli'Ma."

"Velli'Ma," repeated Gweneth softly. "What does it mean?"

"In the old elven tongue," answered Cassandra, "it means . . . eternal joy."

Calain laughed with delight and so did Lowri. "I like that!" Calain said, gazing fondly at Cassandra across the table. She banged her fist on it. "We shall live in a castle of joy!"

The knights all cheered and lifted their goblets, and Zelda leaned over and kissed Cassandra on the cheek.

Chapter 7

The knights all had their own bedchambers in the great castle, just as Zelda had her own, but sometimes, they still crept from their beds and up the eastern tower to Zelda's. The knights even got together and discussed who would lay with Zelda each night, almost as if they were choosing who would take first watch. They cast lots whenever more than one of them desired her that evening, for as much as they enjoyed group sex with Zelda, each of them also enjoyed their alone time with her.

It was night and moonlight was streaming in through the window as Zelda lay in bed when there was a knock on the door. Zelda smiled to herself and called, "Come in!"

The heavy wooden door opened to reveal Cassandra, who was standing there in tunic and trousers, a wisp-light hovering white over her lifted hand. Her pale blonde hair was loose of its usual braid and the glow of the wisp-light lined the side of her face in white fire, so that she looked almost otherworldly as she stood there, a specter come calling.

Cassandra stepped into the room, letting the door close behind her. Her pale eyes were bright with hunger as she looked at Zelda, who had sat up, the coverlet still over her lap. Her breasts were heavy and full behind the white nightgown, her golden hair tumbling long around her. Cassandra absently let the wisp-light vanish and sat on the edge of the bed beside Zelda.

She stared at Zelda for a moment, then cupped her face, traced a thumb over her pink bottom lip.

"Thou art . . . so beautiful," Cassandra breathed, her eyes narrowing. Hooking a hard hand around Zelda's narrow waist, she leaned down and kissed her roughly on the mouth, thrusting her strong tongue hard against Zelda's.

Zelda trembled and eagerly submitted, as she always submitted to Cassandra's silent strength. Cassandra did not have to speak to make it clear she how desperately she desired Zelda. Her hard hands and the aggression of her kiss had always spoken for her. But there was something else now . . . There was something in Cassandra's eyes that was warmer, gentler . . .

"I do believe I love thee," Cassandra confessed when she noticed Zelda watching her curiously. "Perhaps I always have, to crave you like this." She smoothed her hand down Zelda's golden curls and her eyes danced over Zelda fondly. Then she kissed Zelda again, pressing her down to the green coverlet.

"You love me?" Zelda whispered happily when Cassandra was on top of her. She smiled at Cassandra from the golden nest of her long hair.

Cassandra's eyes were soft as she stroked Zelda's hair again. Then she kissed her on the lips – gently this time, her hand smoothing up Zelda's nightgown and over her bare thighs. She twitched aside the thin fabric of Zelda's panties as she was kissing her and slid two fingers deep inside.

Zelda's lashes fluttered and she arched her back, thrusting her breasts to the ceiling as Cassandra slowly fingered her. Cassandra pulled the laces on the front of her nightgown, so that it sagged open, revealing one of her large breasts and the rigid pink nipple. Cassandra's eyes burned when she saw Zelda's exposed breast. She kissed Zelda's lips again, kissed her neck, and then sucked gently on her nipple, pulling and releasing, then pulling again and burying her face in the soft mound.

Zelda gasped from the pleasure, her small fingers curling in Cassandra's hair as she was suckled, as she was fingered until her sex was moist and dripping.

Still sucking slowly at Zelda's nipple, Cassandra gently pulled her stroking fingers free of her sex and smoothed her hands over Zelda's thighs again, pushing up her nightgown. She leaned back, and Zelda watched breathlessly, peering down between her great breasts, as Cassandra lowered herself between Zelda's thighs and sucked with slow hunger on her clitoris.

"Oh gods . . ." Zelda whispered, staring wide-eyed at the ceiling as her clitoris pumped to life. Her thighs trembled as Cassandra's careful sucking and tasting continued. The knight smoothed gentle hands up her thighs to calm her, but they wouldn't stop shaking, to the point that Cassandra had to hold them in each hand as she buried her face between, sucking and licking with such passion now that Zelda squirmed breathlessly, thrusting her breasts and moaning with hooded eyes.

Cassandra reached up as she was sliding her tongue between the fat lips of Zelda's sex, and groped Zelda's breasts in fistfuls as she brought her to a breathless climax.

THE NEXT NIGHT, ZELDA was lying on her side in her bed when the mattress shifted and she felt a hard body against her back. She smiled: she knew it was Gweneth without even having to turn. Gweneth was spooning her under the coverlet, and Zelda blushed a little when she felt the brush of the leather phallus against the back of her thigh. Gweneth was wearing it harnessed to her hips. The harness was leather but the phallus itself was made from the member skin of a horse, so it was soft to the touch when it brushed Zelda's skin.

Gweneth groped one of Zelda's breasts through her nightgown and buried her kiss in her neck. Zelda moaned. She twisted around and kissed Gweneth over her shoulder, and as they moaned and frowned through the kiss, she felt Gweneth impatiently yank her gown up and plunge her hand down the front of Zelda's panties.

But Zelda's thighs were together. Fumbling and near frantic, Gweneth hooked her knee behind Zelda's leg, lifting Zelda's leg open with her own. And now with Zelda's legs spread, she slid her hand down Zelda's panties again and touched her sex. Her index finger and thumb found Zelda's clitoris and massaged it, rolling it back and forth until it swelled and throbbed, and Zelda moaned.

Gweneth's other hand tugged the laces of Zelda's nightgown, then pulled at the sleeves, so that the nightgown drooped around her bare shoulders, exposing both her breasts. "I did miss having thy fat tits to myself," muttered Gweneth, whose hungry eyes were looking at Zelda's plump and heavy breasts. She cupped one and massaged it, watching the hard nipple roll before thumbing it gently.

Caught in Gweneth's hard grasp, Zelda wriggled and sighed as she was groped and fingered. Gweneth's hands were relentless, roughly coaxing her to moist arousal, until the curly golden hair of her sex was glistening with the juices of her passion. Throbbing and blushing with arousal, she twisted around and caught Gweneth's mouth to hers again.

"Put it in me," Zelda whispered huskily.

"Thy pussy is dripping-moist," Gweneth whispered back, but her words were spoken almost absently as she gazed with soft eyes at Zelda's lips and breasts. She moved her hips, and Zelda felt the hard phallus plunge slowly through the swollen lips of her sex. Her sex clenched on it, and her eyes hooded as she leaned back against Gweneth and moaned.

Gweneth rolled onto her back, pulling Zelda on top of her, and caressing Zelda's fat little clitoris with one hand, she groped her breast with the other as she thrust the phallus up and in, grunting with arousal and with effort.

Zelda lay draped over Gweneth, gasping rhythmically as the phallus punched inside, stroking hard through the moisture of her strong walls. Gweneth was still relentlessly caressing her clitoris, so that it pumped wildly with arousal, but she let go, and taking Zelda's by the hips, she slammed her down on the phallus – over and over – and so fast that Zelda's big breasts were flapping as her rhythmic screams grew louder and louder until she climaxed.

BY THE TIME SELENE showed up, Zelda had expected that at least one of the knights would come for her each night, and she was a little thrilled by it, though she was casual and nonchalant during the day and seldom mentioned it.

Like Gweneth, Selene surprised Zelda by groping her as she was sleeping. But Selene, unlike the other Knights of Falcon, was gentle and submissive, and it wasn't long before Zelda was sitting up against the pillows, legs spread, as her small hand held Selene's face against her sex and commanded her tongue deeper, harder, suck there, kiss there.

Selene went down on Zelda with a sort of grunting desperation, and whatever Zelda told her to do, she did it immediately, her dark eyes blazing with lust and devotion as they gazed dotingly at Zelda above the nest of her curly pubic hair.

Zelda's head fell back and her thighs trembled as Selene's hungry mouth brought her to a climax. Panting, breasts heaving, golden curls tumbled half in her face as she whispered, "Oh, Selene . . . you always make me come so hard . . ."

"Do I, my lady?" said Selene hopefully. She rose up, and Zelda kissed her on the lips. As they moaned through the kiss, Zelda unraveled Selene's long , dark hair from its plait.

Selene was a gorgeous woman, but Zelda had always thought her dark hair one of the most beautiful things about her. It was long, straight, and silky, framing her serious eyes like a cloak of night. And it was so soft and sweet-smelling.

"Take off thy tunic," Zelda said softly, her eyes dancing fondly over Selene as she gazed up at her.

"As my lady commands," Selene said dutifully and pulled her tunic off with a toss of her dark hair.

Zelda drank in the toned muscles of Selene's shoulders and arms with warm blue eyes. Then she reached around and untied Selene's linen bra, letting it fall away to reveal her breasts. Zelda stared at them as they stood so perky and young. Out of all the knights, she had always thought Selene had the most luscious breasts. She cupped one and caressed it, and she smiled when Selene's cheeks flamed.

Zelda kissed Selene, pressing her down on the bed. She gently squeezed one of the knight's breasts and watched lustily as the pink nipple stood rigid. Then she sucked it carefully in her lips and closed her eyes, frowning in delight. She felt Selene's hard body tense with arousal beneath her. She unbuckled Selene's belt as she suckled her and roughly yanked her trousers and drawers down, and then Selene, cheeks bright and lips panting, was brought to a helpless climax as Zelda's golden head moved between her muscular thighs.

CALAIN DIDN'T EVEN restrict herself to Zelda's bed. Much like Yrsa, she wanted it all the time, during all hours of the day, and would sneak up suddenly behind Zelda in her study and rip the front of her dress open, groping her large breasts in fistfuls and kissing her hungrily on the mouth.

Another time, Zelda was sitting by the fire in one of the solars and enjoying a book when Calain came in, crawling playfully across the floor, and slipped her head up Zelda's skirt, going down on her. Zelda, cheeks flaming, had dropped the book as she slouched down with a soft scream, golden curls tumbling in her dazed face.

Of course, Zelda was equally as playful and mischievous, surprising Calain in her bedchamber as she was washing at her washbasin, groping Calain to stirring as she napped – suddenly ripping down Calain's trousers and going down on her in the middle of her study.

At one point, Zelda realized they had probably had sex in every room in the castle. A castle of joy, indeed.

Of course, Zelda and Calain did more than have sudden and wild sex. Sometimes they soaked in Zelda's bathing basin together, relaxing by candlelight, as Zelda rested back against Calain and enjoyed the occasional kissing and groping.

Other times, they went for long walks through the courtyard. The castle courtyard was immense, full of flowering trees, fountains, and stone benches, birdbaths and chirping birds. It was one of Zelda's favorite places in the castle, to the point that Calain insisted they take a walk through it every morning, simply because it pleased Zelda so. And of course, they couldn't resist stopping near Seren.

"How shall we know when Seren hath stopped growing?" Calain asked one morning as she and Zelda stood before the girl in the crystal. It had been a week.

"She will break out on her own," Zelda answered happily. "Like an egg."

"She already looks six years old!" said Calain, gazing anxiously at the child in the crystal shell.

Zelda laughed softly, taking Calain's hand. "Do not worry, my knight. She will emerge when it is right and far before she hath become an adolescent." She paused and asked quietly, "You are soon to be a parent. How does it feel?"

"Terrifying," Calain admitted blankly, and Zelda laughed. "Were you not afraid when you did wed Yrsa? You knew you would not grow the child in a crystal but birth her yourself. Many women have died in childbirth. You risked your very life for Yrsa."

Zelda stared at Seren but she was really thinking of Yrsa . . . and Aereth. It was the second time in days that she had thought of Yrsa, remembered all the deliciously rough sex, the ripping of her clothes. Not that any of it had resulted in Aereth's birth. It was the potion that had made Zelda pregnant, not the sex. She remembered Yrsa saying that she wished she could have put a baby in Zelda herself, and when Zelda blushed to her hairline, she had crammed two fingers into her sex and sucked hard on her clitoris, so that she gasped as her head fell back. A small part of her missed Yrsa, if she was honest.

"Tis true that I risked my life to bear Yrsa's child forth," said Zelda. She squeezed Calain's hand. "But it was about survival more than anything else. I had to do it to secure my place at Yrsa's side. This is different. I was not coerced into this by circumstance. I chose this of my own freewill, because I love thee and wish to have a family with thee."

Her response made Calain very happy, for the Falcon Knight suddenly hugged Zelda close in her arms, which trembled as she kissed her head.

Zelda looked up at Calain and laughed. "Why do you look so relieved, my knight?"

"Because you have told me that Yrsa's was a marriage of convenience," answered Calain. "I was afeared all this time that you truly loved her, that perhaps you might leave to find her and make a new child now that Aereth . . ." She trailed off unhappily.

Zelda shook her head. "Thou art such a silly woman," she said with a sigh, "that thou canst not see how greatly I do love thee. No matter. I suppose I have centuries to convince you."

They smiled at each other and kissed. As they were kissing, they heard a crack from the crystal. Zelda and Calain broke apart and looked around. Seren was punching through her crystal – and she was incredibly strong. Her little face was pinched in determination as her thin arms bent and straightened again and again. With each punch, the crystal cracked further, like a shattering mirror, until it finally burst open in a shower of fragments.

Calain hugged Zelda and spun her away to shield her from her blast, and when the crystal shards had settled on the stone path, she and Zelda slowly looked up to see Seren standing there, sleepy-eyed, rubbing a fist in her eye.

"I was sleeping for a long time," squeaked the child.

Calain's mouth dropped open. She went to the child, took off her cloak, and wrapped it about her to conceal her nudity. "Do you know who we are?" she asked, kneeling before the child.

Seren frowned. "Of course, I know you!" she said indignantly. She suddenly grinned. "You're my parents! You're Calain," her happy eyes went to Zelda, "and you're Zelda. And I'm your babe!"

"Well, not a babe any longer," laughed Calain, ruffling the child's red-blonde hair.

Seren glanced eagerly around. "Do I have siblings?"

"You have one," said Zelda, who was looking down at the girl with affectionate blue eyes. "Her name is Aereth, and she will come home . . . one day."

"Aereth," Seren repeated happily.

Just then, Selene, Cassandra, and Gweneth approached, having heard the noise of the crystal exploding open. Seren ran to them, shouting that she knew them, for they were all her aunts. She leapt on Selene, who caught her on her hip with a laugh, and started rambling about how she wanted to learn the bow, and Selene was the best hunter, so she simply *must* teach her! Selene looked very pleased by this as Gweneth and Cassandra stood by laughing.

"It would seem you have a fan, Selene," said Cassandra, a small smile on her lips as she stood with her hands in her pockets.

"Aye," said Gweneth. "Looks like Calain has competition. But what else is new?"

"And Auntie Cassandra shall teach me to sing," said Seren. She looked at Cassandra. "I heard you singing to me as I slept in my crystal. Will you teach me?"

"Of course," said Cassandra, and now it was her turn to look pleased.

Selene laughed. "Come," she said to Seren, "let us get you dressed and fed." She turned and carried Seren away into the castle. Gweneth and Cassandra followed, and as they went, Seren squeaked questions at them about the outside world – already, she was curious.

Calain turned to Zelda, baffled. "But . . . how doth she know so very much?"

Zelda was smiling as she watched the others leave the courtyard. She drew near Calain and snuggled into her arms, her golden hair under Calain's chin as she said, "She is our clone, Calain! We have given her our feelings and memories, passed them on through our blood. Because of that she knows many things, though not everything."

"She hath your eyes," said Calain happily. She was holding Zelda to her chest and asked in a softer tone, "Are you pleased, Zelda? Are you happy? Do you have everything you need?"

Zelda glanced up and was touched to see Calain watching her dutifully, as if she would run and fetch the moon if Zelda did but ask her for it. Her eyes softened as she looked up at Calain. "I have *you,*" she said warmly. "So, yes, sweet Calain, I am happy."

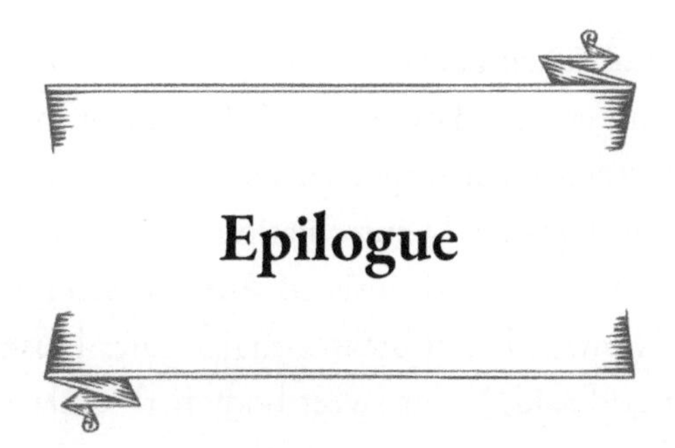

Epilogue

Aereth's heart was racing as she watched the portal open before her. In but a few moments, she would be back with Zelda and the Knights of Falcon. She had so much to tell them of her adventures in Elwenhal. She had slain giant monsters, explored the furthest reaches of the dimension, crossed the Shadow Plain – and she had wed Nimwe, who stood behind her even now, looking sullen that her wife was leaving.

They were at the top of a giant tree, where they had made a home in the cradle of branches. Gold fairy lights were bobbing around them, and birds were chirping in the eternal dusk.

"I shant be long, Nimwe," said Aereth, glancing back when she heard Nimwe's sigh.

Unlike her mother, Queen Anindel, Nimwe had never quite taken to wearing gowns. Instead, she was wild, wrapped only in a loincloth made of leaves. Her large breasts were bare, and there were leaves and flowers and acorns in her long white hair. She stood, her pointed ears drooping down a little, rubbing one arm and looking dejected. There were tears in her eyes.

Aereth frowned and turned away from the opening portal. "Do not weep, my wife," she said gently and took Nimwe in her arms. "I shall return to you! I must!"

"You shall forget me and find some other woman, I know it," said Nimwe bitterly. "Do you think I do not know about Enid? How you kissed her and lusted for her when you were a girl?"

Aereth was taken aback. In all her time in the fairy realm, Nimwe had never hinted nor remotely let on that she had known about Enid. Aereth half-suspected she had been waiting for the right moment to throw the information in her face.

"I *shall* return," Aereth insisted. She clapped a strong hand on one of Nimwe's heavy breasts, making her blush when she squeezed it and said, "Your sweet body hath enslaved me. You know that."

Nimwe looked up at Aereth with breathless longing, and looking down at her, Aereth realized that the beautiful woman who used to nurse her and had seemed so tall was now tiny beside her, a mere four feet in height.

Aereth had grown to nearly seven feet tall and was a muscular woman, wrapped in a dress made of animal hides and wearing sandals that wound up her bulging calves. On her back was a sword, which Queen Anindel had commanded the gnomes to smith for her, and upon her head was a crown of vines and red flowers, marking her as princess and wife of Nimwe.

"It has not enslaved you well enough," retorted Nimwe unhappily, "for you still must venture to that strange other land."

"The other land is my home," said Aereth gently. She took both of Nimwe's hands, gazing down at her and trying to make her understand. But Nimwe could never understand. She had never even left Elwenhal, and she seemed incapable of empathizing with Aereth, of understanding that she missed her mother and the knights. She was eternally selfish and wanted Aereth to stay in Elwenhal, never to return.

Queen Anindel was much the same way. When she learned that Aereth wished to visit her family, she became distant and cold. When Aereth came to her at court to say farewell, she didn't hug her or kiss her as she usually did but instead gestured impatiently as she said, "So go if it pleases you!" and took a bitter sip from her wine goblet as she sat at the head of the noisy feast table.

The surging energy from the portal suddenly grew stronger, so that licks of auburn hair danced around Aereth's eyes. Aereth narrowed her eyes against the wind and said to Nimwe, "Shall you kiss me before I depart?"

Nimwe hesitated, her slanted eyes momentarily as wicked as her mother's. Then her eyes relented and she said coyly, eyes down, "If it pleases you."

Aereth felt a little suspicious, but she knelt down anyway, resting on one knee, and gathered little Nimwe close in her bulging arms. They kissed, and Nimwe's lips trembled against hers. The fairy woman bowed her head, touching her forehead to Aereth's, and closed her eyes. She was so sad, Aereth rubbed her back and kissed her cheek.

"I shall return soon," Aereth promised.

Nimwe's small hands momentarily tightened possessively on Aereth's arms, as if to lament her own helplessness, then she cupped a hand under her own heavy breast and lifted it, offering it for Aereth to suck. Her eyes were warm with lust.

Without hesitation, Aereth clapped her strong hand yet again on Nimwe's heavy breast and squeezed it, so that the nipple hardened and beaded out a small drip of the same sweet milk she had grown so to love. She sucked tenderly on Nimwe's pink nipple, then suddenly hugged her tiny wife close and buried her face in it, with a sort of abandon she could not understand.

Nimwe laughed girlishly in delight at Aereth's aggression, then moaned and frowned as the sucking continued – growing stronger and more fervent and hungry. Aereth was sucking very hard now on Nimwe's nipple, turning her head as the soft mound rose against her face and trying almost desperately to pull as much sweet milk from it as she could.

Trapped in the wall of Aereth's hard arms, Nimwe's head fell all the way back, and she clutched blindly at Aereth's head, as the big woman buried her face in the swell of her great cleavage.

"A-Aereth!" Nimwe gasped. "Control yourself! You shall drain me!"

Aereth pulled her mouth away reluctantly, white milk on her lips, and looked at Nimwe in a daze. For years, she had sucked the sweet milk from Nimwe's breasts and was a little obsessed with its taste without fully understanding why. She saw the wicked glint in Nimwe's pretty eyes again when the small fairy lifted her head and looked at her. She extended her tongue and crammed it in Aereth's mouth. They kissed passionately, their heads turning as Aereth crushed her wife's soft hair in one hand.

When they pulled apart again, Nimwe was breathless and blushing. "F-Farewell thee well, my wife," she said, panting, smiling.

Eyes soft, Aereth kissed Nimwe a last time on the cheek, then rose and turned to the portal, which was now fully open upon a study filled with books. Giving Nimwe one last look, she stepped through the portal and heard it whooshing with wind as it sealed behind her.

Standing in the middle of the study, Aereth looked around and heard a scream: a little old woman with long white hair bounced up from an armchair beside the fire, tossing away her book and running fast to Aereth. Her great breasts crushed Aereth in a hug, and with wild happiness, she kissed Aereth again and again on both cheeks.

Overwhelmed, Aereth grabbed the old woman by the arms and held her at bay. "Who the devil . . .?" Aereth's voice trailed off as she looked into the old woman's eyes. They were Zelda's blue eyes.

"Mother . . ." Aereth said, her voice a dry crack. "You are so old . . . You are . . ."

Zelda's smile faltered a little. "Don't you know?" she said sympathetically.

Aereth mutely shook her head as the cold realization crept slowly over her.

Zelda looked up at Aereth sadly and touched her cheek as she said gently, "My little bear . . . It has been two hundred and fifty years."

Aereth's Return
Book 11

Aereth was in such a state of shock that she barely noticed what was happening when Zelda led her to an armchair beside the fire and sat her down. All the while, Zelda was speaking excitedly of the Knights of Falcon and their children and how everyone would be so happy to meet Aereth.

But Aereth could only think of Queen Anindel and Nimwe, and how the fae had deceived her. They had let her think only a small amount of time had passed, but it had been nearly three hundred years! Nimwe had known and had said nothing—absolutely nothing! Aereth felt sad, furious, and betrayed all at once, and it was several seconds before she realized Zelda had started to cry.

"I searched near and far for ways to b-break your curse," Zelda said, sobbing into her hands.

Aereth rose from her chair and knelt beside Zelda's chair. "Do not weep, Mother," she begged, stroking Zelda's long white hair. It was strange to her. She could remember Zelda's golden hair as if it had been yesterday. Now it was snowy white, and Zelda's young skin was lined, no longer smooth, but it was just as soft and warm.

Zelda shook her head and threw her arms around Aereth's neck and sobbed harder. Startled, Aereth hugged her weeping mother close and stroked her hair, and Zelda had been weeping for what seemed an eternity when Calain's voice preceded her into the room.

". . . is going on? Cassie said she felt a disturbance, something about vibrations—" Calain halted in the doorway, her mouth hanging open. "Aereth? Is that you?"

"It is I," said Aereth, grinning as she released Zelda and rose to her feet.

Calian practically lunged, taking Aereth in her arms, and she was just as strong as Aereth remembered. Aereth laughed girlishly as she was squeezed, and Calain pulled back, grinning at her. She had accidentally lifted Aereth clear off her feet and now she apologetically set her down again.

"But you're so big!" gasped Calain, who indeed was shorter than Aereth now.

Zelda drew near, taking Calain's arm and beaming up at Aereth. Her cheeks were still wet with tears, but she seemed to have forgotten them for the moment.

Aereth looked down at both of them, thinking the years had been quite kind. Two hundred and fifty years, and they had barely changed except for slight wrinkles and faded hair. Calain's once-red hair was a very pale gray but still as long and wild, pulled back in the messy ponytail Aereth so dearly remembered. Zelda was wearing a light blue gown with gold trim, and Calain a leather jerkin over a white tunic and brown trousers.

Quick footsteps in the hall, then a shout of "Goblin!" and Aereth grinned to see Gweneth in the doorway.

It wasn't long before all four Knights of Falcon, having been informed of the magickal disturbance by Cassandra, had poured into the room, all wrinkled and gray and crushing Aereth between them with the mighty strength of their bone-cracking hugs. Like Calain, the other three knights were wearing leather jerkins and trousers, and their hair had faded. Cassandra's messy, shoulder-length, yellow plait had turned completely white, as had Gweneth's undercut topknot, while Selene's long, immaculate braid was now a handsome dark gray, having faded from its former black.

But however much they had aged, the knights had not lost their stature nor their muscle tone. They were still hard-bodied, and all of them, including Zelda, looked like middle-aged women with fading hair. Aereth thought it remarkable but knew that sorceresses and their Bound knights always aged very slowly.

The fact that Gweneth, Selene, and Cassandra were still alive could only mean that Zelda had Bound them to her as she had Bound Calain.

Zelda and the four knights were just as amazed by Aereth's transformation and could not contain their astonishment. When Aereth left the knights in Ellormest more than two centuries ago, she had been a skinny teenage girl with barely any muscle, showing only the beginnings of womanhood. Now she was a woman, tall and muscular, wearing leaves and animal skins, with a great sword on her back, her long auburn hair falling in a messy, loose, red plait over one shoulder. She still had Yrsa's green eyes, they happily observed, as if Aereth could have changed them, and she still had Zelda's pretty smile.

After much hugging and laughter and exclamations that Aereth had grown so big and strong, they all went downstairs to the dining hall for supper, and Calain explained that her half-sister, a mighty sorceress, had built the castle for them. The castle was called Velli'Ma, and they were in the Aelwith Wilds, on the very edge of the swamp, not far from City Erhyrst in Realm Honione.

"I cannot believe it has been so long," said Aereth heavily. She poked her spoon idly in her stew and stared at it, not really seeing it. There was silence. When she looked up, the others were gazing at her in sympathy. Zelda, who was sitting beside her, reached over and touched her hair, her blue eyes wet with unshed tears.

"The important thing is that you're b-back now," said Zelda with emotion. Her pale lashes fluttered, trying to hold back tears.

"Oh, Mother," said Aereth miserably. "I am back in time to bury you, am I not?" She glanced around the table at their wrinkled faces, which had grown somber now with her mood.

"Anindel has stolen my entire life from me! You did not see me become a woman, and now I shall watch as you all slowly die."

There was silence. No one knew what to say. It had been that way when Aereth was a child as well: no one ever knew what to say whenever Aereth had an outburst – except Gweneth. Aereth was not surprised when Gweneth spoke up.

"Aye, Anindel stole a great deal of time from you," said Gweneth, "and we have missed many happy years together because of it. But do listen to your mother. We have right now, do we not? You can be with us right now!"

Aereth looked up again and saw Zelda and the knights smiling at her around the table. All of them had tears in their eyes.

"And though we may perish of age, we shall not leave you alone, Goblin," went on Gweneth. "You have sisters, four of them – though they are not here at the moment. All have flown the nest, as it were."

"And when we have passed on, you shall inherit the castle," said Zelda. "You and all your sisters. Isn't that wonderful?" She looked at Aereth imploringly.

Aereth stared at her soup. Nothing they had said had comforted her, not even Gweneth's words, true as they were. What cared she for sisters she had never met? They might as well have been strangers.

"How long do Wild Women live?" Aereth asked, looking from face to face. "Does Yrsa live still? She is my father. Anindel hath told me." She glanced almost accusatorily at Zelda (who had always refused to tell her of Yrsa) and immediately felt guilty when Zelda sighed and looked down at her plate with a trembling lip.

"You shall leave me to find Yrsa, shant you?" Zelda said. "When I finally have you back, you shall leave." She looked so forlorn that Calain – who was sitting opposite her – reached across the table and touched her hand. Zelda smiled sadly at the small gesture.

Aereth immediately felt guilty for her treatment of Zelda. Anindel told her how Cailan had disgraced Ysra, causing her to be cast from her tribe into the wilderness. It was to protect Cailan that Zelda had refused to tell Aereth who her father was. She did not wish for Aereth to hate Cailan, Aereth knew that now. Filled with shame, she leaned over and kissed her mother's cheek. Zelda smiled at that and seemed comforted.

"I shall come back," Aereth gently promised. "I just . . . need to find my place in this world."

Zelda frowned, lifting her indignant blue eyes. "Your place is here!"

"No," said Aereth unhappily. "My place here was forfeit when I did leave for Elwenhal. My sisters do not know me. I am a stranger to them, known only through your tales. And you are all at the end of your years, with only a small amount of time. It is not fair that I should cause you grief when you should be living your last days in peace."

"You are *our* child!" Gweneth said hotly, and Aereth thought she looked rather like her father in that moment. Aereth remembered the indignant old man. Sune had been tiny but quite short-tempered and outspoken, like Gweneth, who was the shortest of the knights. She realized with a pang that Sune would be dead by now. And Kare and Tai . . . and Enid.

Pushing away thoughts of Enid, Aereth's hand shook on her spoon as she poked again at her stew.

"You belong here!" Gweneth went on. "We have waited here all these years just to look into your eyes again. What can Yrsa do for you that we cannot?" She was becoming visibly upset. Beside her, Cassandra frowned sadly and touched her shoulder to sooth her. Gweneth ignored Cassandra, looking steadily at Aereth, tears behind her dark blue eyes.

Selene nodded seriously, her intense and rather hawklike eyes fixed upon Aereth. "This is your home. It has always been your home. It has stood waiting for you two hundred and fifty years!"

Calain nodded firmly in agreement with the others, and her hand was still over Zelda's in a silent attempt to comfort her. Zelda's head was bowed, and she was silently weeping. Selene and Gweneth were clearly distraught and struggling to hide it behind tight-faced masks. Cassandra alone looked at Aereth with calm interest and said, "What do you need, Aereth?"

Aereth looked around in surprise, though she didn't know why she was. Cassandra had always been the calmest, the most logical and reasonable, the least emotional. Much as Aereth loved Gweneth, she had always been the most argumentative and angry—even more so than Calain, who had just as short a temper—and Aereth could see it now, the protests welling up behind Gweneth's disapproving eyes as she stared at Aereth across the table. Gweneth was clearly struggling with the urge to order Aereth to stay at the castle, struggling with the reality that Aereth was no longer a child and she could no longer dictate what was best for her.

Everyone was looking at Aereth now. Zelda had lifted her head, tears still streaming from her eyes.

"Well, I need armor," said Aereth with a weak laugh, for she was wearing hides and leaves, which would not go over well with anyone she encountered during her travels, not even other Wilde Women, "and I need a horse and a satchel."

"You can acquire all of that in Erhyrst, nearby," Cassandra answered calmly. "I shall give you the gold."

"And I," sighed Gweneth, as if she had finally relented.

Aereth watched as Cassandra and Gweneth pulled out their coin purses and tipped gold coins out on the dark wooden table, and she felt a surge of affection for both of them. She also held back a laugh: same as always, Calain and Selene were low on gold and could only offer her their apologetic smiles.

"Where shall you go?" asked Zelda sadly and touched a small, wrinkled hand to Aereth's muscly arm. She seemed weary of arguing and was attentive now, ready to help Aereth in any way that she could.

"I wish to journey to Ellormest," Aereth said thoughtfully. When she saw their troubled expressions, she added, "I know I shall not find Enid and Tai there. They will have long since perished of old age. But I confess, I do miss the land. Maybe I shall find something else there."

"Hmm. If you wanted, we could accompany you to town for armor," said Cassandra thoughtfully. She smiled. "It would be like the day Zelda and I took you to buy shoes. Do you remember? We can recreate the entire day if you like. Zelda shall buy you sweets and I shall ride you on my shoulders."

Aereth's dark, thoughtful expression broke into laughter and smiles, and everyone at the table seemed to relax, even Gweneth, who had been looking both angry and forlorn.

Zelda laughed through her tears and lovingly stroked Aereth's hair, pushing it behind her ear. Her blue eyes were doting as she said, "But why Ellormest? I suppose it was the place where you grew up, now that I think on it." She sighed. "My precious little bear. I wish I could keep you here forever! I could, you know!"

Aereth laughed at this teasing and something in her softened, seeing how Zelda stared at her wistfully. She had missed Zelda's warm eyes and her small, soft hands, and the way she was always so frantic and doting. She had always been a gentle, loving parent, and yet fiercely protective – quite the opposite of Queen Anindel, who had been carefree and casual and had allowed Aereth to run wild, doing as she pleased in Elwenhal.

"Do not feel hurt," said Aereth gently, gazing around the table at her parents, "but I wish to venture forth alone. This is something I must do . . . alone, I think. But I shall return when I have made my peace with things." She smiled at Zelda and kissed her again on the cheek.

Zelda seemed pleased enough for the time being. She reached into a little pouch that she was wearing around her throat and brought out a small stone that was smooth and almost shaped like a chicken egg. Aereth recognized it at once as a Summoning Stone. She held out her hand and received it from Zelda. It was warm to the touch and glowing a gentle blue.

"If you ever find yourself in danger," said Zelda, practically begging, "turn the stone, and I shall feel it and come for you!"

"Oh, Mother," said Aereth, kissing Zelda's cheek again. "I shall be all right!"

Zelda didn't seem convinced, but she wouldn't know about all the beasts Aereth had slain in Elwenhal, the dangers she had braved, or the lands she had explored. In the fairy realm, Aereth was a mighty warrior princess of the fae court. In Vallinwir, in the eyes of her doting parents, she was that skinny little girl who squeaked silly questions at them and begged for sword training. And perhaps she would always be so.

When they had finished eating, Zelda and the knights showed Aereth to a room where she could change into proper clothes so that she could fit better among the people of Vallinwir. They also gave her food, a wineskin, and many pleas that she should return soon.

Gweneth was the last to bid Aereth farewell. She came to Aereth and stood with her ar the window. "It's like losing you all over again," she said, pulling back from a hug and gazing up at Aereth. Her blue eyes were wet with tears. "If you don't return in three days or else send word, I shall ride out and find you!"

"*Gwen*," scolded Calain behind her (she was standing in the room's doorway with her arm around Zelda), "Aereth is a woman now. She shall be fine. She seems a mightier warrior than any of we knights!"

Aereth swelled a little with pride to hear Calain's boasting. It was high praise coming from one of the most skilled warriors she had ever known.

"Just be careful," said Selene, placing a hand on Aereth's shoulder. "The Aelwith Wilds have taken even the greatest of knights."

Aereth looked down at Selene and held back a smile, knowing that Selene wouldn't have said that had she ever seen the wildest, darkest forests of Elwenhal. Instead, she assured Selene that she would be fine and kissed her on the cheek. Aereth kissed and hugged the other knights as well, then kissed and hugged Zelda, who held on the longest. Then Zelda and the knights left the room, leaving Aereth alone to change her clothing.

Still wearing her animal skins, Aereth sheathed her mighty sword in the harness on her back, and she was turning to gather her tunic and trousers from the bed when the tall mirror in the corner began to hum with power, its glass swirling with light.

Aereth halted, gazing with narrowed eyes at the mirror. The glass had begun to glow, as if some activity on the other side had stirred it to life. She had seen such mirrors before, for Queen Anindel had often used them to spy upon the mortal realm.

Suspicious that she was being spied upon now, Aereth slowly drew her great blade and approached the humming mirror, holding the weapon in both hands, ready for a fight. Many things had come out of Queen Anindel's mirrors – monstrous horrors, demons, howling spirits from the dark. What would emerge from Zelda's mirror?

Face grim and muscles tight with anticipation, Aereth drew level with the mirror at last – and absently lowered her sword at what she saw upon its glass. Within the ornate golden frame, a young and beautiful woman with wild golden hair was locked in fierce battle with a pack of howling goblins. The woman reminded Aereth of Zelda when she'd been young – beautiful, buxom, and with long golden hair—except she wasn't a sorceress but a mighty warrior, her hourglass body swathed in wild animal skins that lifted and flopped, briefly revealing her thighs as she turned about with a flash of her sword.

The woman was having fun, for her eyes were alight with the joy of battle – a feeling Aereth had reveled in many a time herself – but she was overwhelmed. There were just too many goblins!

Determined to help, Aereth lifted her blade again and leapt into the glass with a wild war cry.

Continued in Knights of Vallor

The Fairy Ring

Enid had been living with Tai for one year, but still, after all that time, she missed Aereth. Aereth was her first love and the one she truly desired. Years and years she had waited, heartbroken, hoping that someday Aereth might return from Elwenhal and marry her.

But five years passed, and Aereth never came, and the boys who pursued Enid in the caravan had become more aggressive and demanding, until one day, Tai broke a boy's arm in her defense, and they were both forced to leave the caravan.

Violence and fighting within the tribe simply wasn't allowed within the caravan. Many were sad to see Enid and Tai go, but it was the way of the sheep people. And so, the two young women were given three sheep, provisions, a sheep dog, and a covered wagon, and were sent on their way into Ellormest forest.

Enid was frightened in the beginning, but she soon found that life in the forest with Tai suited her. Tai was a strong woman and had gotten fairly good with a blade, her blonde hair – half plaited and half undercut in the style of the sheep people – tossing about her, long and wild, as she fought off attacking bandits with fire and blade.

Tai was also an incredible lover. Enid had never known such ecstasy as she had at night in the covered wagon, in Tai's strong arms. But the orgasms and the kisses and the passion only left her wondering what it would have been like with Aereth, the first to have kissed her, the first to have touched her.

Enid often laid awake at night, wanting Aereth. And it happened so often that eventually one night, as Enid lay awake in the sheepskins beside Tai, Tai rolled over and said, "It's Aereth, isn't it?"

Though it was early morning, they were lying near their low fire as the covered wagon stood nearby. The horse had been let loose with the sheep to graze, and the dog was guarding them.

Breakfast was already done, and the two of them, relishing in the warm morning sun, had decided to nap.

Enid had never drifted off to sleep, however, and apparently, neither had Tai.

Enid guiltily looked over to find Tai watching her sadly. Enid hated that – according to the traditions of their people – she and Tai were technically married, and yet, Enid was constantly thinking of some other woman. She wanted to be loyal in heart and mind, but her heart belonged to Aereth. Perhaps it always would.

Enid reached over with a shaking hand to take Tai's hand. She was so frightened of an argument. Things had been mostly pleasant between them. She hated when they argued.

"You don't have to say anything," said Tai. She sighed heavily. "I miss her, too – Not the way you do. I don't wanna fuck Aereth or anything," she added with a laugh, "but she was my friend."

Enid laughed as well and dropped her gaze. She could see her own red hair falling in twin rivers over her chest and down the sheepskin she lay beneath.

"There's an old story," said Tai slowly, staring at the sky, "about fairy rings. "They say if you dance in them, you dance with the fae. They say if you fuck inside a fairy ring... something similar happens."

Enid brightened with hope and squeezed Tai's hand.

AS IT TURNED OUT, FAIRY rings were all over Ellormest. Tai took Enid by the hand and led her to one not far from their camp. It was a perfect ring of mushrooms and flowers, growing in a small clearing of green grass. They stepped into the ring hand-in-hand, and the moment they did, Enid felt a current of magick so strong, her long hair rippled back and her lashes fluttered in surprise.

It wasn't the first time Enid had stepped into a fairy ring—as a child, she had run through them all the time – but this ring in particular was powerful. She had never felt a current of magick so strong.

"Whoa!" said Tai, eyes wide, for she was feeling it as well.

Enid's heart pounded. This was it: she was going to see Aereth! With a sort of fierce determination, she grabbed Tai by the collar (Tai cried "Whoa!" again in shock) and kissed her hard on the mouth.

The atmosphere changed at once. When they looked around again, they were standing in a beautiful forest whose trees were immense, as big as the trees of Ellormest but not covered in green sheets of moss. It was dusk, the sky pink and purple beyond the trees, and gold fairy lights bobbed along through the bushes and flowers. They were standing in small clearing that was full of flowers, and standing on the edge of it, staring at them in shock, was Aereth.

Enid couldn't believe it: Aereth was a woman now! She was practically seven feet tall. Like them, she had aged, but though it had been nearly seven years since last they'd seen her, she seemed younger than they were, as if she had only just entered adulthood while they were half-way to thirty years.

Aereth was beautiful, though. So beautiful, Enid couldn't move. She looked wild, standing there covered in animal hides and leaves. On her head was a wreath of flowers, her auburn hair a long, tangled mess beneath it. She was wearing a sword on her back and now had a few scars from her battles, cutting along her neck and arms. And she was bulging with muscles! She looked as if she could have kicked down one of the massive trees.

Aereth's green eyes lit with her smile. "Tai? Enid?" She lumbered toward them at a march, and with deep chuckles, locked them both in her arms and lifted them off their feet in a hug.

Enid and Tai's laughter echoed through the trees as Aereth turned about with them in her arms. She stopped spinning and set down Tai, though Enid she kept locked in her arm.

Enid trembled in Aereth's grasp, feeling small and soft, caught as she was in Aereth's hard arm. Aereth was still holding her up, so that she rested against Aereth's chest with her little sandals clear off the ground. Aereth was staring up at her and the green eyes were soft with admiration. They danced over Enid's face – Aereth pushed back Enid's hair to get a better look – and down her neck to her breasts. Enid realized with a blush that her breasts were sitting plump just under Aereth's face, and now Aereth's eyes were on them, burning with hunger.

"Her tits are like apples, aren't they?" Tai said happily.

Enid blushed brighter. "Tai!"

"They never got very big," went on Tai, "but they're firm, all right!"

"Tai!" Enid cried again, and Aereth and Tai laughed.

Aereth gently set Enid on her feet and gazed down at her with a soft affection that made Enid's heart flutter. Then Aereth looked at Tai and said with a frown, "But how did you get here? Humans aren't allowed."

"You're human," Tai pointed out.

"I'm enchanted, though," said Aereth. "I was bound to this place as a child." Her eyes echoed sadness. "You have to go before Queen Anindel—"

"No!" cried Enid, stepping forward. Her hands balled into determined fists at her sides. "I'm not afraid of any fairy queen! I w-want you!" she admitted, blushing brightly.

Aereth looked down at Enid sadly. "Enid . . . I knew you wouldn't understand."

"What is there to understand?" said Enid at once. Tears suddenly filled her eyes. "You should have been my wife, not some fairy woman's—"

"Hush! Keep your voice down!" Aereth begged, and for the first time, she looked frightened. She glanced over her shoulder, as if someone were coming.

But Enid refused to simply walk away. She had waited years, cried herself to sleep, dreamt of entering Elwenhal and tasting Aereth's lips, only to finally get here and be turned away? A hard, blazing look came to Enid's eyes as she stepped forward, hair whipping back, and yanking Aereth down to her, she kissed Aereth on the mouth. She was pleased when Aereth didn't pull away but kissed her back readily, as if she had been waiting for it, hoping for it.

Tai stood awkwardly nearby, casting her eyes around for an escape route, no doubt intent on slipping away unseen. But Enid grabbed Tai's hand. She took Aereth's hand as well, and she smiled as she walked backwards, pulling the two masculine women along. They were both staring at her now with quiet hunger.

"Is this really happening?" said Tai in amazement when Enid laid down in the flowers, pulling the two women down with her.

Tai leaned on her elbow as she lay beside Enid, and on the other side of Enid, Aereth did the same.

"Remember when we used to dream of this?" laughed Tai.

Aereth smiled. "I remember," she said, but her eyes were narrowed on Enid's breasts.

Lying between the two bigger women, Enid took a shaky breath. She didn't know why she was so nervous. Aereth and Tai were both staring at her. They took her hands and kissed them, kissed her neck. They were gentle, as if they feared hurting her, but they were fervent and hungry as well, kissing her skin and touching her body with such desire that it left her moaning.

Tai groped one of Enid's high breasts through her peasant's tunic and whispered huskily, "Like apples."

Aereth hesitated and groped the other one. Then, as if touching through the fabric weren't enough, Aereth smoothed her hand under Enid's shirt and over her warm, soft skin. Her hand slid under Enid's linen bra and pushed it and the tunic shirt back, so that both Enid's high, young breasts were standing bare from the crumpled fabric of her clothes.

Enid took another nervous breath, and when her breasts heaved from the motion, she saw Aereth's eyes blaze more than ever with hunger. Enid shivered, clitoris pumping hard to realize just how much Aereth craved her.

"You're beautiful," Aereth whispered and leaned down and took the hard pink nipple in her lips. Enid felt the pleasure flush through her as she was gently suckled. Then Tai leaned down over her other breast and suckled it just as gently, pausing to massage it and watch as the supple flesh gave in her hands.

Enid's clitoris was pumping harder now as they suckled her, burying their faces in the rising mounds of her breasts. She reached up and cupped their heads, curled her fingers in their hair. Aereth's hand pushed up her skirt, roamed hungrily over her thigh, and slid down the front of her panties. Enid's hand did the same, and then they were both fingering her as they sucked her nipples, Aereth's large fingers gliding inside her, Tai's smaller fingers thumbing her clitoris, which swelled fatter from her touch.

Enid moaned and sighed beneath them, squirming against the pleasure, arching her back and thrusting her breasts when Aereth's strong, insistent fingers stroked deep. She could feel them gliding in and out between her lips, deeper and yet so gentle. Her sex heaved and clenched, silently begging for more.

"Thy pussy is so wet and tight," Aereth whispered in Enid's ear, kissing feverishly at her neck. She trailed frantic kisses to Enid's mouth, kissed her lips and whispered, "Did your pussy grow moist the moment you did see me?"

Enid blushed prettily: it did. But how had Aereth known?

Aereth's fingering was growing rougher, faster, so that Enid's hips rocked and her breasts jiggled. As the pleasure mounted, she stared with wide, unseeing eyes at the canopy of leaves above, embarrassed by the shrill gasps that were coming from her lips.

Tai, breathless and beside herself with arousal, had stopped to watch as Aereth jerked her hand inside Enid's panties, bringing her to a rough, hard climax. Enid screamed softly as it happened, then sagged in the tousled mess of her red hair and clothes. She was vaguely aware of Aereth and Tai staring at her beautiful young body with glazed eyes.

"If we don't eat her pussy after that, I may just burst," said Aereth breathlessly.

Tai laughed.

Enid watched, heart pounding, as both women kissed her belly, then they lay between her legs and spread them wider, more fully exposing her pink sex (Enid blushed) and kissed her thighs. They looked at her, eyes intense with desire, as they trailed careful kisses up and down the inner curve of her trembling thighs. Enid, breathless and red-cheeked, watched with heaving breasts as they lowered their faces, and then their tongues were taking turns gliding wet and hot inside her, their lips were sucking on her clitoris, sucking on her lips.

Enid's eyes hooded and she melted, lifting her chin and thrusting her breasts as the pleasure swiftly mounted. As she was climaxing, she felt Aereth grip her thighs, crushing her sex to her mouth as she sucked hard on her clitoris – and she released her passion with a shudder and collapsed. She heard Aereth swallowing her moisture, felt Tai dotingly kissing her sex, and smiled, drowsy and content, as their adoring hands smoothed over her body.

Enid was in such a happy daze, she hardly noticed it when Aereth and Tai lay in the flowers either side of her. Their attention was on her, both their bodies turned toward her, their hands running over her curves. She snuggled close against Aereth and was glad when Aereth closed her bulging arms around her and kissed her head. Tai snuggled close against Enid's back, embracing her from behind, and Enid smiled happily crushed between them.

"I wish we could stay like this forever, the three of us," said Aereth after some time.

"Can't we?" Enid looked up at Aereth anxiously.

"Yeah," added Tai, frowning, "why can't we just stay here with you? The three of us would be immortal and go on adventures—"

"Because you're not really here," said Aereth, smiling sadly. "You're both dreaming."

"No!" Enid cried, the tears starting to her eyes. But she could already feel herself fading: back in the other world, she was waking. She clutched at Aereth's fur hides anyway, squeezed her eyes shut and bowed her head against her, as if clinging as hard as she could would prevent her from waking.

"Enid," Aereth said gently.

Enid looked up, sniffling with tears, to find Aereth gazing down at her warmly.

"I shall always love you," Aereth said and kissed Enid on the lips.

It was such a tender kiss that Enid bowed her head against Aereth and sobbed. Aereth held her close.

"Fare thee well, Tai," Enid heard Aereth say.

Tai laughed. "I had forgotten you spoke in that bizarre city fashion. Good journey, Aereth."

And then it happened, the thing Enid had been dreading: she awoke in Ellormest, lying in a ring of flowers and mushrooms beside Tai. She sat up immediately.

"Satisfied now, wife?" Tai asked playfully. "Aereth had a good tongue, I could tell. The way you gasped and shuddered—"

"Oh!" Enid cried miserably.

Tai sat up, looking baffled by Enid's sudden tears. Her sweet, oblivious Tai.

"Why are you crying?" Tai begged as Enid wept into her hands, shoulders shaking.

"You don't understand, Tai," Enid said wretchedly. "This wasn't about sex! I *love* Aereth! And thanks to her horrible curse, I shall never have her!" She wept into her hands again, and she was beginning to understand how devastated Aereth's mother, Zelda, had felt.

Tai watched miserably for a time, then closed her hand on Enid's shoulder and said seriously, "You have me. *I* love you, Enid. Or can't you see that?"

Sniffling quietly, Enid looked up and went still to see the look in Tai's eyes. Tai had never looked at her that way before. Enid had never suspected that Tai cared for her as anything more than a friend. Perhaps she had hidden her feelings, knowing Enid cared only for Aereth.

"Now come, wife," said Tai, standing. "We should fetch the sheep and move on."

Enid looked up at Tai, knowing that she was taking charge, trying to hold things together because seeing Aereth again – her best friend, the friend she had lost forever – had shaken her just as badly. She allowed Tai to help her stand, then Tai put an arm around her and guided her away, back toward their camp.

As they left the clearing, Enid glanced back a last time, saying a silent farewell to Aereth. Her first love.

The Main Course

That afternoon, the dining table in the castle's hall was laden with bowls of fresh fruit and bread, vegetables, wine, mutton, steak. But the main course, apparently, was Zelda. Zelda lay on the table in the nest of her golden curls, her large breasts standing plump from the open front of her soft gray gown. Calain had pushed up Zelda's skirts, and with each hand hooked behind Zelda's knees, was holding Zelda's bent legs aloft, thighs spread, as she went down on her.

Selene watched, feeling her clitoris pumping in her drawers. Gweneth and Cassandra were also seated at the table, watching. They had all been enjoying their noon meal when Calain had playfully grabbed Zelda and slammed her on the table, ripping her gown front open, so that her great breasts jiggled free.

Zelda's soft cries of delight were soon filling the room. Cassandra was seated beside Calain and watching with pink cheeks as Calain fed her tongue in and out of Zelda's pink lips, watched as Zelda's sex squirmed against Calain's eager mouth. Eventually, she took one of Zelda's thighs from Calain and kissed it up and down, frowning against her own arousal.

Gweneth was seated on the other side of Calain, also watching Calain's lips and tongue give Zelda pleasure. Selene thought she seemed a little intoxicated. She had a goblet of wine in one hand and like Cassandra, she was slightly pink-cheeked from arousal. But unlike Cassandra, she seemed content to watch as Zelda was pleasured on the table, her eyes glazed with lust.

Selene was sitting opposite the other knights, near Zelda's head, and had a full view of sorceress' gasping face and fat breasts as they stood from her torn gown. She kept squirming, arching her back and thrusting her breasts so that they jiggled. The little pink nipples were hard. Selene stared at them and heard her goblet crack and break in her fist.

Zelda was a delicious sight lying there on the table, back arched, legs spread, little toes pointed as she thrust her great breasts to the ceiling and cried out helplessly. Her shrill gasps became rhythmic and Calain's eager tongue plunged in and out, as Cassandra slid a finger in her sex and caressed her as CAlain licked and sucked.

Zelda was completely absorbed in what was happening, frowning and gasping, gazing baffled at the ceiling. But her blue eyes found Selene's and she smiled. It was a lusty little smirk that made Selene's heart skip. Zelda cupped her big breasts and offered them, and Selene's nostrils flared with want.

Gweneth laughed hoarsely. "Zelda knows you well, Selene. Suck tits was always your favorite."

Selene blushed. Looking across the table, she could see the lips of Zelda's sex swelling, the moisture that dripped from them and made Calain's lips glisten. Calain's face was buried between her thighs, her nose was moving against the little swath of gold hair, and the red knight was grunting as her mouth moved back and forth, thrusting in her tongue in hard.

Selene felt her sex throbbing and thought she would burst. Now that she was Bound to Zelda, Selene could feel it when Zelda was near climaxing. The pleasure was so intense that her hand was shaking on her broken goblet. Zelda was still looking at her, still hoping her have her breasts suckled. Selene set the goblet aside, and taking a grape from the nearby bowl, she pressed it in Zelda's mouth, letting her finger slide in deep. Zelda's eyes smiled at Selene, and she sucked her finger a little as she took the grape. Selene's sex throbbed with want.

But Zelda was climaxing now. She twisted her curvy body, thrusting her great, shivering breasts to the ceiling, and Selene watched, silently tormented by lust, as Zelda squirted with a soft, helpless cry in Calain's mouth.

Zelda collapsed again into the mass of her long hair, weary and content, her big breasts heaving, as Calain and Cassandra lazily kissed her thighs. Calain's kisses traveled up Zelda's body, over her belly. Leaning over the table, she paused to suck one of Zelda's hard pink nipples with frowning abandon, then kissed Zelda's neck, and finally, her lips. All of it Selene watched with her nostrils flaring, feeling the moisture as it lined her drawers.

Calain and Zelda went on kissing for some time that Selene noticed the others watching and becoming as tormented by arousal as she. Then Calain looked up, noticed Selene's suffering eyes, and said with a laugh, "Fair Zelda, spread your sweet thighs for Selene next, or she shall catch ablaze from her lust!"

"A true jest," said Selene irritably.

"No, I'm next," said Gweneth, setting aside her goblet. She dragged the bowl of grapes from across the table to herself, and as they watched, she slid two in Zelda's sex. Zelda's eyes grew round and she gasped in delight, arching her back and moaning as Gweneth hungry tongue sought to suck the grapes back out, now covered in Zelda's juices.

Cassandra, with soft-eyed interest, took another grape and gently pushed it between the fat lips of Zelda's pink sex, then watched with narrow-eyed lust as Gweneth ate it back out. As Gweneth and Cassandra were playing their grape game, Calain bowed her head over one of Zelda's great breasts and sucked, and with suddenly abandon, Selene finally bent forward and sucked the other one, until her face was crushed by the soft mound rising in her eyes.

Caught between the knights as they fingered and sucked her, Zelda squirmed on the table, gasping and blushing, arching her back and thrusting her breasts as if to escape the pleasure. Calain took her slender wrists and pinned them above her head to the table, as if to hold her still, and the gesture only pulled her breasts up higher, made them stand perkier and plump, so that Calain and Selene returned to suckling with renewed fervor.

By the gods, it was heaven. Selene could feel Zelda's heartbeat rising faster and faster, could feel her pleasure as if it were her own. Her sex throbbed, her lips fattened, her nipples were rigid beneath her tunic. She was so aroused, her thighs were trembling as she sucked long and slow on Zelda's nipple and released it, watching the fat breast wobble back into please.

Zelda's pink lips parted and she cried out, golden curls falling across her suffering blue eyes. Whatever Gweneth was doing with her tongue, it was making Zelda pinker, breathless, weak. Without even having to look, Selene could hear the smacking and slurping of Gweneth's mouth on Zelda's sex.

"Ah . . ." Zelda closed her eyes and frowned. It was coming. Selene could feel the pleasure building and then—"Ahhh!" Zelda thrust her breasts and climaxed helplessly yet again. She sagged, frowning, her eyes baffled as she stared at the ceiling, and Calain released her wrists, sitting at the table near her head and lovingly stroking her golden curls.

The four knights stared at Zelda's beautiful body as she lay there, trying to catch her breath. Finally, she looked up at them and laughed breathlessly as she said, "Shall we ever finish a meal without your ripping off my clothes, Calain?"

Selene noticed Zelda's panties were hanging off her ankle, half-torn, and nearly laughed.

Calain laughed softly, looking down at Zelda with great affection. "Not so long as I am young bodied and able, my lady."

Cassandra kissed Zelda's little foot, smoothed a hand over her thigh, and pulled the skirts of her gown back down for her.

Zelda sat up, and Selene took her by her narrow waist and pulled her gently down from the table, setting her on her lap. Zelda relaxed back against Selene, who carefully laced up the front of her gown for her, as the others watched, staring at Zelda's big breasts.

"By the *gods*, your tits are fine, though," said Gweneth into the silence, and everyone laughed.

They returned to their meal as if it hadn't been interrupted, talking merrily, teasing, exchanging jokes, and all was fine in the Castle of Joy.

About the Author

Ash Gray is a lesbian living in California. She writes lesfic (aka fiction for lesbians) in science fiction, fantasy, and paranormal settings.

Ingram Content Group UK Ltd.
Milton Keynes UK
UKHW042001200623
423745UK00001B/30